MW00779312

# PRAISE FOR SAMANTHA A. COLE

"No one does Alpha heroes like Samantha A. Cole!"

"Hot, sexy, and full of suspense . . . these words steam off the pages!"

"One of the most remarkable new voices in sexy, smart romantic suspense. You need to discover Samantha Cole right now!"

# TRIDENT SECURITY SERIES

A SPECIAL COLLECTION: VOLUME I

SAMANTHA A. COLE

SUSPENSEFUL SEDUCTION PUBLISHING

# SPECIAL COLLECTION VOLUME I
## INCLUDES:

*Leather & Lace: Trident Security Book 1*
*His Angel: Trident Security Book 2*
*Waiting For Him: Trident Security Book 3*

One of the most common questions I get about the Trident Security series and its multiple spinoff series is "What is the best reading order?"

Well, I've updated the boxed sets for the original series and added the books in the spinoff series so my readers don't have to go looking for the best reading order. Just get the boxed sets and you won't have to worry about missing books or coming across spoilers.

Enjoy!

◆Best reading order of the Trident Security series and its spinoff series

TS - original series
TSO - Trident Security Omega Team
DoTC - Doms of The Covenant
DMS - Deimos
BHS - Blackhawk Security
MKR - Master Key

★TS Book 1 - Leather & Lace (Devon & Kristen)
★TS Book 2 - His Angel (Ian & Angie)
★TS Book 3 - Waiting For Him (Boomer & Kat)
★TS Book 4 - Not Negotiable: A Novella (Parker & Shelby)
★TS Book 5 - Topping the Alpha (Jake & Nick)
★TS Book 6 - Watching From the Shadows (Marco & Harper)
★TS Book 7 - Whiskey Tribute: A Novella (Curt & Dana)
★TS Book 8 - Tickle His Fancy (Brody & Fancy)
★No Way In Hell: Books 1 & 2 - A crossover between the Trident Security and Steel Corps series (by J.B. Havens)
★TS Book 9 - Absolving His Sins (Carter & Jordyn)
★DoTC Book 1 - Double Down & Dirty (Gray, Remi, & Abbie)
★TS Book 10 - Option Number Three (Mitch, Tyler & Tori)|
★TSO Prequel - Mountain of Evil
★TSO Book 1 - A Dead Man's Pulse (Logan & Dakota)

★TSBook 11 - Salvaging His Soul (Jase & Brie)
★DMS Book 1 - Handling Haven (Frisco & Haven)
★DoTC Book 2 - Entertaining Distraction (Mike & Charlotte)
★DMS Book 2 - Cheating the Devil (Brad & Avery)
★BHS Book 1 - Tuff Enough (Tuff & Concetta)
★Trident Security Field Manual
★TSO Book 2 - Forty Days & One Knight (Darius & Tahira)
★TS Book 12 - Torn in Half
★DoTC Book 3 - Knot a Chance (Stefan & Cassandra)
★BHS Book 2 - Blood Bound (Chase & Rylie)
★MKR Book 1 - Master Key Resort (A prequel)

**The books of the Trident Security series and its spinoffs can be read as standalones, however, for optimum enjoyment they are best read in order.

# AUTHOR'S NOTE

The story within these pages is completely fictional but the concepts of BDSM are real. If you do choose to participate in the BDSM lifestyle, please research it carefully and take all precautions to protect yourself. Fiction is based on real life but real life is *not* based on fiction. Remember—Safe, Sane and Consensual!

Any information regarding persons or places has been used with creative literary license so there may be discrepancies between fiction and reality. The Navy SEALs missions and personal qualities within have been created to enhance the story and, again, may be exaggerated and not coincide with reality.

The author has full respect for the members of the United States military and the varied members of law enforcement and thanks them for their continuing service to making this country as safe and free as possible.

## WHO'S WHO AND THE HISTORY OF
## TRIDENT SECURITY & THE COVENANT

***While not every character is in every book, these are the ones with the most mentions throughout the series. This guide will help keep readers straight about who's who.

Trident Security (TS) is a private investigative and military agency, co-owned by Ian and Devon Sawyer. With governmental and civilian contracts, the company got its start when the brothers and a few of their teammates from SEAL Team Four retired to the private sector. The company is located on a guarded compound, which was a former import/export company cover for a drug trafficking operation in Tampa, Florida. Three warehouses on the property were converted into large apartments, the TS offices, gym, and bunk rooms.

In addition to the security business, there is a fourth warehouse that now houses an elite BDSM club, co-owned by Devon, Ian, and their cousin, Mitch Sawyer, who is the manager. A lot of time and money has gone into making The Covenant the most sought after membership in the Tampa/St. Petersburg area and beyond. Members are thoroughly vetted before being granted access to the elegant club.

There are currently over fifty Doms who have been appointed Dungeon Masters (DMs), and they rotate two or three shifts each throughout the month. At least four DMs are on duty at all times at various posts in the pit and playrooms, with an additional one roaming around. Their job is to ensure the safety of all the submissives in the club. They step in if a sub uses their safeword and the Dom in the scene doesn't hear or heed it, and make sure the equipment used in scenes isn't harming the subs.

The Covenant's security team takes care of everything else that isn't scene-related, and provides safety for all members and are essentially the bouncers. The current total membership is just over 350. The fire marshal had approved them for 500 when the warehouse-turned-kink club first opened, but the cousins had intentionally kept that number down to maintain an elite status.

Between Trident Security and The Covenant there's plenty of romance, suspense, and steamy encounters. Come meet the Sexy Six-Pack, their friends, family, and teammates.

### The Sexy Six-Pack (Alpha Team) and Their Significant Others

- Ian "Boss-man" Sawyer: Devon and Nick's brother; retired Navy SEAL; co-owner of Trident Security and The Covenant; Dom/fiancé of Angelina (Angel).
- Devon "Devil Dog" Sawyer: Ian and Nick's brother; retired Navy SEAL; co-owner of Trident Security and The Covenant; Dom/fiancé of Kristen.
- Ben "Boomer" Michaelson: retired Navy SEAL; explosives and ordnance specialist; son of Rick and Eileen.
- Jake "Reverend" Donovan: retired Navy SEAL; temporarily assigned to run the West Coast team; sniper; Dom and Whip Master at The Covenant.
- Brody "Egghead" Evans: retired Navy SEAL; computer specialist; Dom.
- Marco "Polo" DeAngelis: retired Navy SEAL; communications specialist and back up helicopter pilot; Dom.
- Nick Sawyer: Ian and Devon's brother; current Navy SEAL.

- Kristen "Ninja-girl" Sawyer: author of romance/suspense novels; fiancée/submissive of Devon.
- Angelina "Angie/Angel" Sawyer: graphic artist; fiancée/submissive of Ian.

### Extended Family, Friends, and Associates of the Sexy Six-Pack

- Mitch Sawyer: Cousin of Ian, Devon, and Nick; co-owner/manager of The Covenant, Dom.
- T. Carter: US spy and assassin; works for covert agency Deimos; Dom.
- Shelby Christiansen: stay-at-home mom; two-time cancer survivor; submissive.
- Curt Bannerman: retired Navy SEAL; owner of Halo Customs, a motorcycle repair and detail shop.
- Jenn "Baby-girl" Mullins: college student; goddaughter of Ian; "niece" of Devon, Brody, Jake, Boomer, and Marco; father was a Navy SEAL; parents murdered.
- Mike Donovan: owner of the Irish pub, Donovan's; brother of Jake.
- Charlotte "Mistress China" Roth: Parole officer; Domme and Whip Master at The Covenant.
- Travis "Tiny" Daultry: former professional football player; head of security at The Covenant and Trident compound; occasional bodyguard for TS.
- Rick and Eileen Michaelson: Boomer's parents. Rick is a retired Navy SEAL.
- Charles "Chuck" and Marie Sawyer: Ian, Devon, and Nick's parents. Charles is a self-made real estate billionaire. Marie is a plastic surgeon involved with Operation Smile.
- Will Anders: Assistant Curator of the Tampa Museum of Art Kristen Anders's cousin.
- Dr. Roxanne London: pediatrician; Domme/wife (Mistress Roxy) of Kayla.

- Kayla London: social worker; submissive/wife of Roxanne.
- Chase Dixon: retired Marine Raider; owner of Blackhawk Security; associate of TS.
- Doug Henderson: retired Marine; bodyguard.
- Reggie Helm: lawyer for TS and The Covenant; Dom/boyfriend of Colleen.
- Colleen McKinley-Helm: office manager of TS; girlfriend/submissive of Reggie.
- Carl Talbot: college professor; Dom and Whip Master at The Covenant.

### Members of Law Enforcement

- Larry Keon: Assistant Director of the FBI.
- Frank Stonewall: Special Agent in Charge of the Tampa FBI.
- Calvin Watts: Leader of the FBI HRT in Tampa.

### The K9s of Trident

- Beau: An orphaned Lab/Pit mix, rescued by Ian. Now a trained K9 who has more than earned his spot on the Alpha Team.

# LEATHER & LACE

Book 1

## SAMANTHA A. COLE

Suspenseful Seduction Publishing

*To my parents, who always encouraged me to follow my dreams.*

# CHAPTER 1

"*D*amn it!"

Kristen Anders slammed her laptop shut, took off her glasses, and shoved her fingers through her long brown hair in exasperation. Glancing at the digital clock on her cable box, she couldn't believe it was one in the afternoon. Three hours wasted. If she didn't come up with a workable story line soon, she would go insane. Now that her move to Tampa was complete, her things were unpacked in the rented two-bedroom apartment and the empty moving boxes were in the recycle bin, she had no more excuses not to get back to her latest novel. No excuse except her damn writer's block.

On the desk, her phone rang and she rolled her eyes when she spotted the name on the screen. Just what she needed . . . Jillian Tang. Her editor had given her three weeks to deal with everything involved in the move before she began demanding to see a new plot outline. And according to the *Playgirl* calendar her cousin had given her as a happy divorce present, those three weeks had come and gone four days ago and all Kristen had was a working title.

Hitting the answer button, she brought the phone to her ear. "Hey, Jillian."

"Don't 'hey, Jillian' me unless you have something more than a working title by now."

*Leather and Lace* would be the follow up to her first oh-so-non-vanilla romance novel *Satin and Sin*, which her readers had gone crazy for. "Not yet, and before you yell at me, do you want it fast or do you want it good?"

Jillian's laugh came over the line and Kristen had to smile. They spoke simultaneously, "Sounds like something my ex-husband would say."

Both knew what it was like to divorce a cheating husband.

After her laughter died away, Jillian jumped back on the original topic. "You know your readers are dying to get their hands on your next BDSM novel. I'm still floored you went that route after nine 'vanilla' romances, but with the way your sales soared, I'm not complaining."

Kristen's first two books had been self-published e-books. After they'd been downloaded in large numbers and received glowing reviews from her readers, Jillian had contacted her with a proposal to become a Red Rose Books endorsed author. She'd been thrilled since being sought out by the large publishing company, which specialized in the romance genre, was an honor most self-published writers could only dream of. The deal had benefited both parties. Red Rose Books signed a new and popular writer with an established fan base waiting on pins and needles for her next book and Kristen's books were now available in print as well as online. She no longer had to contend with editing, uploading, book cover designs, and promotions.

"I'm not complaining either, but I can't even decide which sub-character should become my new hero."

"Shit, I gotta run to a meeting." Kristen could hear the rustle of papers on Jillian's end. "Listen. Go into that fantasy world in your head and picture each one of those hunky guys. One of them will stand out. I'll call you tomorrow and you better have an answer for me. Love ya. Bye."

Dropping her cell next to her laptop, Kristen sighed. She got up and headed to the master bedroom, pulling her shirt off over her head as she went. She hoped a hot shower, followed by a change of scenery would help get her creative juices flowing. Plus she was hungry. Maybe it was time to check out the Irish pub a few blocks over. She'd passed by Donovan's several times over the past few weeks and noticed it was a popular place. Not too crowded at lunch time, it usually was packed by happy hour and stayed that way into the night.

Walking through her bedroom, she thought of calling Will to join her for a bite to eat, but the idea left her mind as fast as it came. As much as she loved her cousin's company, because he could always make her laugh and relax, Kristen knew she wouldn't get any work done with him around. Not long after her arrival in Florida, Will had taken it upon himself to show her around Tampa and introduce her to all his friends since he was the only person she knew in the area. Unfortunately for her, most of the people he hung out with were gay, not that there was anything wrong with being gay. She'd become comfortable with her cousin's homosexuality a long time ago, and even though she had a good time when she was with Will's crowd, she was tired of turning down date requests from his lesbian friends. Kristen had no sexual interest in women and none of the men in her cousin's circle were interested in her as anything more than a friend. They were a great bunch of people, but since her divorce was finalized, she found herself wanting to get back into the dating game. She wasn't looking for a steady relationship, her failed marriage had soured her on anything permanent, but maybe a friends-with-benefits thing would be something she could get into. Although the benefits portion of that might be a problem.

She wasn't very good at sex and, if she was honest, it bored her. She found she could finally admit it to herself even though her ex-husband, Tom, had used it as an excuse for cheating on her. Although she could orgasm while masturbating, she had never been able to come during sex. In the beginning of her marriage, Tom said it was because she didn't relax enough to enjoy it, which Kristen might agree with. She was so nervous in the beginning, wanting to please him, but not knowing how. But after more than six months of disappointing sex, her husband began to tell her she was frigid and unresponsive. Maybe she was. But having nothing else to compare it to, she wasn't sure if it was true or not. She'd been a twenty-four year old virgin on her wedding night and Tom was the only man she had ever slept with.

She stopped at her dresser and picked up the large envelope holding her divorce papers. It'd been a few weeks after their one year anniversary when she found out Tom had cheated on her with several women before and after their wedding. She'd kicked him out the same day, but she couldn't bring herself to even think about having sex with anyone else until the ink was dry on said papers. Whether her ex had or not, she took her marriage vows to heart and couldn't move on until everything was final. Although the papers in her hand were signed two weeks before her move to Tampa, she hadn't found an opportunity to spread her wings yet, or her legs, as Will had so eloquently put it.

Putting the envelope back where it was, she sat down on the edge of her bed and hugged one of her decorative pillows. When it came to sex Kristen believed she could take it or leave it, but what she missed was the intimacy which came with sex. She squeezed the pillow tighter and realized what she missed the most. It was the cuddling and pillow talk which occurred after sex. She could live without the act itself, but it felt like forever since she'd snuggled up to a warm body and felt content.

Content. *Huh?* What a boring word.

Her readers would be shocked to learn that the author of a best-selling BDSM book was only content with her sex life. Too bad life wasn't a steamy romance novel, with a hot and hunky hero knocking on her door, primed and ready to sweep her off her feet, throw her on the bed, tie her down, and do naughty, sensual things to her. *Right, like that would ever happen.* But that was what made great fiction. Fantasies. Fantasies of delicious and dirty sex.

Even though her own sex life was lacking, Kristen had read many erotic novels over the years and decided to spice up her last book by basing it around a private sex club for the rich and famous. To her shock and delight, it had become a bigger success than her first four out of nine vanilla books put together. Now she was supposed to write an even more exciting follow-up that her fans were clamoring for and she couldn't even decide which sub-character from the first book she wanted to write a story about.

Should she use Master Zach, the sexy movie star, who liked to flog his submissives to orgasm, as her new hero? Or Master Wayne, the blond billionaire who preferred to share his women with his best friend, Jonah. Or maybe she should pick Master Xavier who owned the sex club, Leathers, they all belonged to. He was the strong, brooding type women were always attracted to in romance books.

Kristen tossed the pillow back on the bed and stood to remove her sweatpants. She dropped them, along with her shirt, into the hamper as she walked into the bathroom. Reaching in, she turned on the shower and let it heat up, then peeled off her underwear. She stepped into the tub and the warm water surrounded her as she thought about Master Xavier. He hadn't been a main character in *Satin and Sin*, but somewhere during her writing sessions, the fictitious man had grown on her.

In her head, she brought up a picture of the strong alpha male as she had described him in her book—the same alpha male who had somehow ended up starring in a few of her own fantasies. Six-foot-two, jet black hair, startling blue eyes, a chiseled jaw with a hint of a five o'clock shadow, and a body that would make any heterosexual adult female drop her panties in an instant. She imagined his deep Dom voice resonating in her mind as he told her to touch herself while he stood there and watched. Grabbing a bottle of her favorite body soap, she squirted a small amount into her palms before putting it back on the shelf of the tub. She closed her eyes and roamed her hands over her heated skin with light sensual strokes.

"Touch your breasts," he'd say. "Play with your nipples. Pinch them and pull them."

Kristen did what her fantasy Dom told her to do, her hands caressing her heavy orbs. As she played with the sensitive peaks between her thumbs and forefingers, the growing sensations of pleasure shot straight to her clit, making it throb. Making her want to be touched there.

*"Spread your legs wider, my love. Let me see your bare pussy. It belongs to me and I want to see what's mine. I want to watch you finger yourself for me."*

Her breathing increased as she eased one hand down her torso. She wanted to move faster, but knew Master Xavier would never allow it. He would punish her if she sped things up without his permission. Maybe he'd spank her ass with his strong calloused hands, or perhaps bring her to the brink of an orgasm again and again, yet continue to deny her the ultimate ecstasy.

*"That's it, love, touch your pussy. Rub your pearly clit for me. Imagine it's my fingers touching you, loving you. Nice and slow. Such a good girl. Picture my tongue between your legs, licking your sweet cream."*

Kristen moaned as her fingers continued to follow her master's demands, as if they had a mind of their own.

*"You like that, don't you, love."* He wouldn't ask, but state it as fact and she wouldn't deny it. She couldn't.

*"You please me, love. You make me want to bend you over and take you from behind, fucking your wet pussy, slow at first. So very slow, until you're begging me to go faster. Harder. Beg me, love, beg me."*

"Please," Kristen whispered aloud as she felt the pressure build, threatening to send her over the edge into a vast abyss.

*"Faster, love. Faster. Come for me, love. Now!"*

And then she flew. Screaming her release, her body shook with the force of the orgasm which tore through her as she tried and failed to stay standing. Somehow she ended up on her knees on the floor of the tub without hurting herself. Gasping for air as if she had run a mile at top speed, she slowed the hand that was still between her legs as the last shudders quaking through her body faded away.

*Holy crap!* That had been the most explosive orgasm of her entire life and it'd been at her own hand while a fantasy man she'd dreamed up told her what to do. It was crazy—crazy, but amazing!

As she drifted back to reality, she noticed the water pelting her back had started to cool. Getting to her feet on shaky legs, she grabbed the shampoo, and rushed to wash and rinse her hair before it was too late. As she turned off the water and reached for a fresh towel, Kristen knew she had made her decision. Master Xavier was definitely going to be the hero of *Leather and Lace*.

# CHAPTER 2

*A* half hour later, carrying her laptop case, Kristen wandered into Donovan's Bar & Grill and fell in love with the place. The combination of the high tables and chairs in dark wood, along with the emerald green walls, gave the pub a comfortable atmosphere. Enlarged photos of Irish landscapes and points of interest hung in various groupings on three of the four walls. The fourth wall on her right was the setting for a beautiful cherry wood bar with brass accents. It ran the length of the long room with seating for at least twenty-five people with additional space between the bar and tables for those who preferred to stand. Behind the bartender and rows of liquor bottles was a large mirror framed with the same cherry wood. The Celtic carvings in the frame made it a work of art and Kristen wondered how long it had taken to make such a majestic piece of furniture. Above the mirror, several flat screen TV's hung from the ceiling and they were all tuned to sports channels, with the exception of one which was showing a news report. The TVs were muted while classic rock played through unseen speakers throughout the room, loud enough to be heard, but still low enough to allow patrons to talk without having to raise their voices.

After she took in the décor of the pub, she found herself

checking out its current occupants. A few tables were taken with groups of two to four people, and a couple of old-timers, arguing good-naturedly over some sporting event, had settled in for the afternoon at the near end of the bar. Taking a step further into the room, Kristen glanced down to the far end of the pub and almost stumbled, certain she had tripped over her own tongue. *Holy crap!* Standing and sitting at the other end of the bar, talking to the bartender, were six men who were almost as majestic as the bar itself. Talk about a *Playgirl* calendar fantasy come true.

"Who needs twelve hotties when these six are available?" she muttered to herself. Each one of them could take two months and Kristen would be more than happy.

"Hi, can I help you?"

Kristen's head whipped around to face the pretty young woman who had appeared next to her. She was dressed in a black polo shirt, with Donovan's Bar & Grill embroidered on the left side, and a pair of jeans. Her long strawberry blond hair was pulled up in a ponytail and her overall look was neat, yet complemented the laid-back feel of the pub.

"Oh, hi . . . I mean, yes," Kristen stammered, then paused, forgetting where she was and why she was there. Okay, get your girlie parts and brain cells under control, she told herself. It's not as if she had never seen a bunch of good looking men before, but damn, the testosterone rolling off the group had her almost melting on the spot.

Taking a deep breath she regained her composure and told the waitress she was there to get something to eat, and no, she wasn't waiting for anyone else. She was eating alone. Yup, she thought. *All alone. Table for one.* Oh well—at least between the eye candy at the bar and her earlier fantasy in the shower, she should have more than enough inspiration to start on Master Xavier's story.

The young woman grabbed a menu from the nearby hostess stand and gestured toward the rest of the room. "Would you like a table or a booth?"

"A booth, please." Kristen lifted her laptop case for the woman to see. "It'll be easier to get some work done."

"Gotcha. No problem. We have a few regulars who work through their lunch breaks. They tell me the booths are more comfortable than the pub tables."

Kristen followed the friendly waitress and realized she was being led closer and closer to the Sexy Six-Pack. The only unoccupied booths were at the back left side of the pub, directly across from them.

"Here you go," The woman placed the menu down at the booth she was giving her. It was the second to last one before the kitchen door. "Can I get you something to drink?"

Kristen put down her laptop and took the seat facing the front of the pub. "Do you have any iced tea?"

"Yes, we do. Sweetened or unsweetened?"

"Sweetened, please."

"Sure. I'll be back in a second. Oh, and the specials are on the back of the menu."

She smiled as the young woman walked over to the bar and placed her order. *Cheerful little thing.* Since it was a school day, it was obvious the waitress was out of high school, maybe by a year or two. And if Kristen had to guess, she was only eighteen or nineteen years old. As she stood at the bar waiting for Kristen's iced tea, one of the Sexy Six-Pack leaned over and said something to the girl, which made her giggle and blush. Kristen frowned. *Seriously?* The guy had to be in his mid-thirties, and here he was hitting on a girl who was just over the jail-bait age. Well, no one said perverts had to be ugly. Kristen had the sudden urge to say something, but she didn't know these people and the girl appeared to be enjoying the attention.

She was about to turn back to take her laptop out of its case when movement from the other end of the Sexy Six-Pack caught her attention. Her breath hitched as her gaze met a pair of ice blue eyes. *Master Xavier.*

*Oh. My. God!* Kristen couldn't believe it. If Master Xavier was a real, live person, this would be him. He had jet black hair, a little long at the neck, a firm jaw showing the start of a five o'clock shadow, and a body which almost had her glancing around to see if any of the few women in the pub had lost their panties. But it was those eyes, those amazing blue eyes looking right at her, as if they could see her soul, which had her spellbound. She was probably drooling, but, Lord have mercy, she couldn't look away. When the man's right eyebrow arched in obvious acknowledgement of her stare, her mouth went dry and she shifted her gaze to the floor before looking up again. Despite his intense look, she thought she noticed the corner of his mouth twitch as if he was holding back a smile. Oh God, how she would love to see him smile and wondered how it would transform his face. If it was anything like the rest of him, she knew his smile would be devastatingly gorgeous.

Neither of them moved, and her eyes worked their way back up to his, her pulse pounding in her veins. Just when Kristen thought she would drown without a drop of water in sight, those eyes disappeared as her waitress returned, her body blocking Kristen's view of the rear half of the bar.

"Here you go." The girl placed a glass of tea in front of her and took out a pad and pen from the small black apron tied at her waist. "Did you decide what you wanted?"

Shaking her head, Kristen tried to regain control of her senses and concentrate on the question. "Um . . . no. Can you . . ." She cleared her throat. "Can you give me a few minutes? I didn't look at the menu yet."

"Sure, take your time."

Anxious to see those eyes again, Kristen held her breath as the young woman moved away, only to see her Master Xavier look-alike was once again facing the bartender. Disappointment ran through her as she took a sip of iced tea to quench her parched throat and picked up the menu. Without a sound, she tried to will the man to turn around again as her gaze flicked back and forth from the menu to the bar area. This time she refused to be blatant in her observation of him and kept her head bent forward. Anyone watching her would assume she was scanning the menu, but her eyes kept shifting to view him out of the corner of her eye.

A few minutes later, her lunch order placed, Kristen resigned herself to the fact that the man was not going to turn back around. She pulled out her laptop, booted it up, and got to work.

---

DEVON "DEVIL DOG" Sawyer couldn't help himself. He was used to being a voyeur at the club, but here at his friend's brother's bar, he almost felt like a creepy stalker. Despite the feeling, he still spent the better part of the last hour staring at the brunette's reflection in the mirror. Well, it was only fair since she had stared at him first. And yes, now he'd gone from creepy stalker to a childish grade-schooler.

He and his teammates were taking advantage of a slow day to eat lunch and catch a Tampa Bay Rays baseball game when he first spotted her watching his friend, Brody, talk to Jennifer. For some reason she frowned at them and Devon wondered what she was thinking. The guys were always joking around with Jenn, otherwise known as Baby-girl, and there was nothing wrong with it. If it wasn't for them, Devon didn't think their niece would have adjusted to living in Tampa as fast as she had. The past six months had been rough on her, but it was obvious having her surrogate uncles around had helped her transition through the worst of it. Between them and the counselor Jenn was seeing, she was coming out of her depression and moving forward with her life. He was happy to notice she was smiling and joking more as time went by. She may have lost her parents without warning, and had her world turned upside down, but her uncles were determined to never let her forget they considered her family. She would always be loved and protected by them.

Devon studied the five men who were like brothers to him—although his older brother Ian, on his immediate left, was the only one who he was related to by blood. The others were brothers of his heart. They had gone through hell and back together and, by some miracle, survived with only a few battle scars. They always had each others' backs and it was rare if a day or two went by without seeing each other working at Trident, hanging out here at Donovan's, or playing at The Covenant—unless they were away on an assignment.

Brody "Egghead" Evans, standing at the end of the bar where Jenn picked up her bar orders, was the joker and flirt of the group as well as their resident tech-geek. The man could put most computer hackers to shame and, despite the FBI's best efforts over the years to recruit him, Brody preferred to stay with his team—first with the SEALs and now with Trident Security. Marco "Polo" DeAngelis, their helicopter pilot and communications specialist, was sitting next to Brody while talking trash about his buddy's beloved Dallas Cowboys. Marco had been born and raised in Staten Island, New York, and was a lifelong Giants fan. As he told it, no self-respecting Giants fan would pass on a chance to rank on a Cowboys fan. That was the only bad blood between the two men—otherwise, they were best friends, having known each other from basic training through SEAL training to being on the same team. Hell, they tended to be so joined at the hip, they'd even left the Navy at the same time to join Trident. So to their friends it came as no surprise when they shared their women on occasion. The duo was pretty popular with the submissives at the club.

He watched as Brody glanced over at the brunette and nudged Polo while tilting his head in her direction. The other man looked over his shoulder, then grinned at his ménage partner. "Sorry Egghead, but I've got plans with my sister tonight. Some other time."

Devon was surprised when his tense body relaxed. He hadn't realized his muscles had gone rigid at the thought of the two men hooking up with the woman he'd been eyeing for the last hour or so.

Next in line of his teammates was Tampa native Jake "Reverend" Donovan, their sniper and younger brother of Mike, the owner of Donovan's, who was tending bar for the afternoon. While Mike had learned the bar-restaurant business from their father and took over the pub upon the old man's death a few years ago, Jake had signed up for the Navy the afternoon he graduated from high school. From what Devon understood, the relationship between Jake and his father had been destroyed during the last semester of Jake's senior year following an argument. Foregoing the football scholarship to Rutgers everyone expected him to accept, Jake ended up going to basic training. Devon didn't know for sure what caused the deep rift between the two, but he had a feeling it was over Jake's sexual orientation. It didn't bother Devon or any of the other guys that Jake was gay, but with the "don't ask-don't tell" policy which had been in effect for years in the military, it wasn't something they had talked about while in the Navy. After the military, Jake was more comfortable keeping his personal life to himself, and the rest of them respected his decisions while still letting him know they supported him. Hell, Devon suspected his younger brother, Nick, was gay and it didn't bother him at all. Ian, Devon, and their friends all had their individual kinks and perversions, so who were they to judge anyone else.

Jake was talking to Boomer sitting on his other side and they seemed to be having an argument over something trivial. Boomer's head whipped around to stare at Ian with a look of disbelief on his face, and Devon smirked at his question. "You topped Savannah McCall? What the fuck? How come I didn't know this?"

Ian shrugged his shoulders, but the smile on his face told their explosives and demolition expert the rumor was true. The Boss-man had had a D/s relationship, brief as it was, with the thirty-year-old supermodel, who was still hot enough to grace the current cover of *Sports Illustrated's* annual swimsuit edition. "Before your time, Baby Boomer. She was still a struggling model when I met her many years ago."

"Holy shit and damn! As usual, I bow to your greatness."

Although they had all served on the same team for several years, Ben "Boomer" Michaelson ended up staying in the Navy for another two after the others retired. He'd only rejoined them a few months ago following a close call with an RPG, which almost cost him his left leg and landed him in the hospital for three months. Even though he now sported an artificial knee, the doctors had been fortunate to be able to save the limb, but it'd been touch and go there for a while. After recovering, he was ready to switch to a career which had a lower percentage of people trying to kill him with projectiles.

Boomer was the youngest of the group at thirty, so sometimes, to bust his ass, they called him "Baby Boomer." But they only resorted to that when they wanted to rile him up, since you didn't want to piss off the guy carrying the explosives too often. Boomer came from a long family line of military men and his father had been a SEAL before him.

Devon looked up as his brother stood from his stool. "Going somewhere, Boss-man?" Even though they co-owned their businesses fifty-fifty, Devon referred to his older brother as the head of the company since Ian had outranked him in the Navy and been their team leader.

Ian gave one of his usual grunts as he threw some money on the bar. "Yeah, I want to run back to the office and handle a few things before heading to the club. Are you going later?"

Devon glanced at the brunette's reflection in the mirror again before answering. "Not sure yet."

Ian took a quick look over his shoulder toward the booths behind him and then turned back to Devon with a knowing smirk on his face. "Uh-huh."

Devon chuckled as his brother clapped him on the shoulder. Telling the others he would see them later, Ian headed to the door, giving Jenn a peck on the cheek as he passed her. Through the mirror, Devon noticed the current object of his lust frowning again as she watched Ian kiss his niece on his way out. He groaned to himself as he realized she was most likely thinking they were a bunch of perverts, hitting on a pretty teenager who was young enough to have been fathered by any one of them. Well, maybe not Boomer since the guy would have been around ten or eleven at the time of conception, but without asking him, Devon couldn't be sure.

Yes, a lot of people would call him a deviant—*huh?* Devon the deviant . . . now that was pretty funny—if they knew about the kinks he and his friends enjoyed. And yes, in the past, Devon had been with a lot of nineteen year old girls, but he had been in his teens and early twenties back then. That pretty much ended when twenty-seven year old Ian introduced him to the BDSM lifestyle at the age of twenty-four.

For the first few years of Devon's Navy career he was stationed on the west coast, while Ian was based out of Virginia. They only ended up in the same place after Devon graduated Basic Underwater Demolition/SEAL training, otherwise known as

BUD/s, and was assigned to Ian's SEAL Team Four. A few weeks after their reunion, his brother brought him to a private sex club for the first time. The club was about thirty minutes from the base and a few of the guys were frequent visitors whenever the team was on U.S. soil and off duty. Ian had been in the lifestyle for a few years and recognized his brother could benefit from the control which came with being a Dom. Despite the five and a half years since their eighteen year old brother, John, had died, Devon had still been struggling with his grief.

He took to the lifestyle like a SEAL to water and spent his first few years learning from Ian and other Doms, as well as several experienced submissives who took pleasure in teaching a new Dom to be . . . well, a Dom. Ian always stressed it was the best way to become a good, responsible Dominant. In fact, the motto of the BDSM community was "safe, sane and consensual." An inexperienced Dom playing with an inexperienced submissive was a recipe for disaster and the chances of the submissive being hurt physically or psychologically increased dramatically. The last thing Devon or any respectable Dom wanted was to hurt an innocent submissive beyond what they needed.

As he got older, he continued to lean toward experienced subs, which meant he didn't often play with women under the age of twenty-five. It didn't mean there weren't older newbies, but it was more likely the submissives had done some experimenting by that age and were familiar with the dynamics of BDSM. The more experienced subs were aware not to confuse play-time with being something more than what it was. He had seen it happen over the years to other Doms with subs new to BDSM. No matter how many times it was explained to them that just because a Dom played with a sub a few times, it didn't mean they were in a traditional "boyfriend-girlfriend" relationship and he'd witnessed many a new, young, sub get their heart broken as a result.

That all said and done, it didn't mean Devon didn't like to educate a newer sub from time to time, but he made sure he observed the woman at the club over several weeks before approaching her to negotiate a scene. He could make sure she wasn't the type to cling and get too attached to him. Attachments were not his thing. One or two scenes were all he would do with a sub before moving on to the next one. He did have a few favorites, who he hooked up with more than others, but he was careful to wait several weeks or months between scenes with the same sub. Lucky for him there were plenty of unattached subs at The Covenant for him to choose from.

The Covenant was an elite and private BDSM club Devon owned with Ian and their cousin, Mitch. After Devon and his brother left the SEALs, a little over three years ago, they settled in Tampa and started their private security and protection business, Trident Security. When Mitch approached them about starting the club, they found a large piece of property with four warehouses. It had been seized by the government after they discovered it was being used to run an illegal drug operation disguised as an import-export company. It was on the outskirts of Tampa, far enough from any neighbors, and was perfect for their plans, so when the place went to auction, they bought it for a lot less than the property was worth.

The fenced-in property, complete with an armed guard at the gate, was surrounded by wooded areas and afforded them the privacy needed for the club as well as for Trident. With the government connections they'd made over the years, Devon and Ian's team did some contracted work for an assortment of alphabet agencies. They needed an office where no one would pay attention to their comings and goings, as well as the occasional visit from federal agents. The first building on the lot housed The Covenant. From the outside, it was a blue metal and cement warehouse. On the inside, however, it was a fetish lover's dream.

The other three buildings, identical to the first on the outside, were separated from the club by a second fence. The first contained the offices and war-room where Trident was run from. Toward the back of the building was a garage, along with weapon, ammunition, and equipment vaults. On the second floor, there were six spare bedrooms and bathrooms in addition to a rec room where the team could crash and watch the big screen TV or play darts and a game of pool. A small kitchenette completed the amenities.

The next structure contained storage areas on the second floor, and on the first, an indoor shooting range, a gym and training room, and a panic-security room in case of an emergency. The room was similar to an old nuclear bomb shelter except it was above ground with reinforced concrete and steel walls, and had been an unexpected find after they purchased the property. The last building housed Ian and Devon's apartments, although, like the other buildings, the outer façade gave no indication what was inside. When the renovations were completed, both had been more than pleased with the results.

Taking another sip of his cola, Devon went back to studying the brunette. Having been with many attractive women over the years —more than he dared to count—he wouldn't characterize her as a gorgeous woman, but more of a pretty girl-next-door. She was undeniably a woman who would get a second and third glance by most men. He wasn't a hundred percent sure due to the distance between them, but he thought her eyes were hazel. Her silky brown hair was pulled up in a ponytail, and he wondered what she would do if he walked over and removed the band holding it in place, allowing the soft strands to fall around her face. His fingers itched to find out.

She hadn't been wearing glasses when she'd first sat down but had put them on before she began typing away on her computer. The glasses gave her a naughty librarian look he loved to see on a woman, and he felt the semi-erection he had been sporting since he first noticed her swell a little more. Letting his eyes roam, he took in the heart shape of her face, her high cheekbones, and those plump pink lips which would look fantastic wrapped around his cock.

*Shit!* If he kept this up he would be hard as granite, and he hadn't even moved his gaze past her neck. Well, at least he hadn't in the last minute or two, and yup, now that the thought came to mind, he was staring at her chest. She was wearing a V-neck short sleeved T-shirt which gave him a tiny hint of her cleavage, and from his vast experience with the female body he would guess she was a

36-C cup. Not too large or too small, just the way he liked them. He wondered if her bra was the same fire-engine red color as her shirt and the thought made his mouth water. Swallowing hard, he watched as she leaned back and stretched her arms over her head in an obvious attempt to work out the knots which had to be in her back and shoulders after typing so long. The movement thrust her chest out a bit and . . . okay, it was official, he was now painfully erect. He shifted to ease the pressure and knew if he had any hope of walking out of here sometime this afternoon without his dick leading the way, he had to stop staring at her.

He may not have met her yet, but he'd bet his prized 1966 Mustang convertible she was a submissive. The question was, did she know it? He doubted it. After catching her eye earlier, he'd waited a few seconds before raising his eyebrow in a look which would've had most submissives questioning whether their words or actions were about to get them in trouble. He was delighted to see how fast her gaze had fallen to the floor before it crept back up to his face, as if she couldn't resist the urge to look at him. If Jenn hadn't interrupted his view of the woman, he would have given into the temptation to go over and introduce himself, something he hadn't done outside of the club in a long time.

Over the years, he learned most of the women he'd met outside of the BDSM community were either turned off by his kinks or only thought they understood what was involved with pleasure-pain before attempting to experience it for themselves. Devon had a few brief encounters in the past when the woman he was with began to panic when faced with his demands and attempts to push her out of her comfort zone. At that point, he would halt the scene without complaint and wait to see if she wanted to continue. If she didn't, he would make sure the woman was all right and back in the right frame of mind before he wished her well and walked out the door. He would never force his lifestyle on anyone—again, *safe, sane and consensual.* Most people didn't realize that a certain amount of pain could be morphed into intense pleasure with the right mix of trust and arousal. Without the proper mix though, any D/s encounter was doomed to fail. That was why he found it so much easier to leave his hook-ups to the submissives at the club. But damn, he wished he met his little librarian at the club because he could definitely get into her, no pun intended . . . or maybe it was.

"Oh my God! Really?"

Devon turned around at his niece's sudden loud exclamation. Jenn was standing next to the brunette and her voice lowered again, but it was still obvious she was enthusiastic about something. He strained to hear what she was saying, without success, and wondered what all the excitement was about. Whatever it was, both women were now smiling and chatting as Jenn took the empty seat in the booth.

Damn, he wished he was Jenn right now.

# CHAPTER 3

*A*n hour had passed before Kristen leaned back in the booth, happy with the rough draft of the first two chapters. Inspiration had struck and she managed to provide an interesting background for the story. By the end of chapter two, Master Xavier had just laid eyes on the future love of his life, Rebecca, for the first time. Kristen sighed as she stretched her arms over her head and looked around. Most of the tables were now empty and the waitress was wiping one of them down with a damp rag. Glancing over at the bar, she noticed the Sexy Six-Pack—she needed to stop calling them that—was now minus one, the man who kissed the waitress on his way out. The stool to the left of the man she had been drooling over earlier was empty and it appeared he had no intention of moving closer to his buddies, content to stay in his original spot.

"So you decided to come up for air."

Kristen turned her head to see the waitress now standing next to her and smiled. "Yeah, I guess I did. Sometimes I get so into my writing the rest of the world ceases to exist."

The young woman laughed. "I can see that. I came to check on you a few times and you were oblivious, so I kept refilling your iced tea."

Kristen looked down at the tall glass and saw it was indeed full again. Since there was a plate next to it with a few french-fries and some crumbs, it was a safe bet she had eaten her chicken salad sandwich, but didn't remember doing so. Yeah, she must've checked out of there for a while. "Thanks," she told the woman. "I appreciate it."

"No problem. What are you writing anyway? You were pretty much nonstop, but every once in a while you would look up at the ceiling for a few minutes, then say 'a-ha' and start typing again."

Kristen blushed in embarrassment. "Oh jeez, tell me I wasn't doing that too loud."

The waitress giggled and it made her appear even younger. "No, not at all. As a matter of fact, I think I was the only one who noticed."

"Thank God," she responded with an exaggerated sigh of relief. "I'm writing a book and sometimes I get carried away."

"Really? What kind of book? Fiction?"

"Yes." Kristen nodded. "A suspense romance. I've written a few which have been published and I'm starting a new one now."

"Oh wow, that's so cool. I have tons of romance books on my e-reader." She indicated the small tablet sticking out of the pocket of her apron. "I wonder if I've read any of yours."

"It's possible. I'm Kristen Anders."

The waitress let out a loud squeal. "Oh my God! Really?" Covering her mouth with her hand for a second, she continued at a lower decibel. "I'm reading one of yours now. I think it's your second one. I read so many books and I'm terrible at remembering the titles, but the characters are Jeb and Amy."

Kristen nodded. It always pleased her when she met one of her readers out of the blue. Her ex-husband had been condescending about her books, saying they were the result of her little hobby, and he was always shocked to hear people had bought them, read them, and indeed, loved them. "Yes, that's my second one, *Wildfire*. The first was *Hearts Ablaze* with Keith and Shannon."

"Yes! That's the first one I read. I loved it so much that I looked to see if you had written anything else and downloaded the next two in the series."

Kristen smiled when the woman took the booth seat across from her, probably not even realizing she was sitting down with a customer, but Kristen didn't mind. "I'm so glad you liked it. I love when I run into one of my readers and they tell me they enjoy my books."

"Oh, I do. I really do. You have a great mix of suspense and romance which makes me not want to put it down. When I was finishing *Hearts Ablaze*, I was up until about three a.m. because I couldn't wait to see how it ended. I mean, it's a romance, so there's always a happy ending, but I couldn't figure out who the murderer was. And I hate when I figure it out way before the author wants you to know who it is." The waitress extended her hand out over the table. "By the way, I'm Jennifer . . . Jennifer Mullins."

Kristen shook the proffered hand. "It's nice to meet you, Jennifer."

"Oh, it's so nice to meet you too. I've never met anyone famous before."

She couldn't help but chuckle at the girl's enthusiasm. "Well, I don't know if I'm exactly famous."

"Well, to me you are. Now I really can't wait to read the rest of your books."

"I'm glad, but don't buy them." She knew what it was like to work her way through college. Her parents had paid for her tuition and books, but Kristen had earned money for any extras and fun by working at a bagel shop near campus and then as a proofreader for anyone who wanted her services. She was sure the waitress needed her money for more important things than a few romance books, and if Kristen could save her a few dollars then that's what she would do. "I have a few print copies at my apartment you can have. I'll drop them off to you the next time I come in for lunch."

Jennifer squealed again, but not as loud as the first time, to Kristen's relief.

"Seriously? That's so nice of you, but you don't have to."

"I know I don't, but I want to. My publisher always gives me a bunch of hard copies to hand out to whomever I please, so it's no big deal," Kristen assured her.

"Jennifer."

At the sound of the male voice, both women looked over to the bar where the bartender was pointing to the front of the restaurant. Turning their heads, they saw a few people standing at the hostess station. Kristen was glad to see the bartender, who she assumed was the boss, wasn't mad Jennifer was chatting with a customer. Instead, he kindly let the girl know people were waiting. She didn't want the girl to get into trouble for being sociable, which made for repeat business from the customers, in Kristen's opinion.

Jennifer jumped up. "Oops, gotta get back to work. And thanks for offering to bring me the books. I'm here every afternoon, except Wednesdays when I have a class."

Nodding her head, Kristen confirmed, "Any day except Wednesday. Got it."

"I'll be back with your check in a second."

"Take your time." Kristen reassured her with a wave of her hand as the other woman turned to hurry toward the front.

What a sweet girl, Kristen thought to herself as she focused her attention on her laptop once again. Touching the mouse-pad, she brought it back out of sleep mode and her heart stopped. The screen was blank.

"Oh, no," she whispered as her stomach dropped. She couldn't remember if she'd hit the save button after she stopped typing, but the program was supposed to do an "auto-save" every few minutes. "Please, please tell me it's saved."

*Damn it!* She knew she should've gotten a new laptop before she started writing again. This one had been giving her trouble as of late, freezing and rebooting itself without warning, but this was the first time a manuscript had disappeared. She remembered creating a new file when she first started typing, but now she couldn't even get into the program to find it. She began hitting different keys as her panic began to rise. "No, no, no! This can't be happening."

"What's wrong?"

She looked up to see Jennifer had returned and was placing her check on the table with a look of concern on her face.

"I don't know." She continued to try and get the computer to respond. "It freaked out on me and I think I lost my first two chapters. Damn it—I hate friggin' computers!"

Jennifer put her hand on Kristen's forearm. "Wait, stop! Don't do anything else. My uncle is a computer genius. If it's there, he can find it."

"Your uncle?" she asked, but it was too late since Jennifer had turned around to face the bar and waved.

"Uncle Brody? Can you come here for a sec? We need your super-duper technical powers."

Kristen watched as the guy Jennifer had been laughing with earlier raised his eyebrow in a silent question and put his beer down before walking toward them. Well, he wasn't exactly walking, it was more like sauntering.

He smiled and chuckled as he approached. "No need to boost my ego with compliments, Baby-girl. You know I'll do anything for you." Putting his arm around the young woman's shoulders, he looked down at Kristen. "What seems to be the problem, darlin'?"

*Oh Lord, did he really just pour on the charm with a sexy drawl?* "Uncle Brody," as Jenn had called him, stood about six-two and didn't seem to have an ounce of fat on his chiseled body. His short blond hair was neat except for a small section which fell over his brow and his chocolate brown eyes twinkled as he flirted with her without shame. Wearing a tight black T-shirt with jeans, a silver belt buckle, and western boots, all he needed was a cowboy hat and she could picture him on a ranch, roping a few bulls. The man was sin on two legs, and knew it.

Kristen gave her mushy brain a mental shake and looked back at her laptop. "I don't know what happened. I was in the word processor and now, poof! It's gone. I think I lost the file I was working on."

"Poof, huh?" Brody teased and then gestured toward the empty booth seat across the table from her. "May I?"

Her head bounced like a bobble-head doll. "Oh, please. I'd appreciate your help. I know nothing about computers."

Sitting down, Jennifer's uncle turned the laptop to face him and started hitting keys. The difference between what she had been doing earlier and his actions was he appeared to have a clue what he was doing, while Kristen had none. Twisting her hands in her lap, she prayed he could find the file. She had been very happy with all she had written thus far and wasn't sure if she could remember the precise wording she'd used.

"Everything all right?"

She shivered at the sound of a deep male voice, which penetrated and reverberated throughout her body, making all her girlie parts stand up and take notice. Looking up she saw Jennifer had stepped away and the man with those beautiful blue eyes was now standing in her place, staring down at Kristen.

"Nothing I can't handle, Devil Dog."

Kristen was so glad the man named Brody answered his friend as he continued to type away on her keyboard, because her mind had become a complete blank except for the thought that she wanted to hear "Devil Dog" speak again. He was about the same height as Brody, but not as broad. Although his frame was a little leaner, he was just as sinewy, and her hands yearned to touch his chest and abs to see if they were as hard as they looked. Dressed in a navy blue T-shirt, jeans, and sneakers, he could be any guy walking down the street, but no, this was not any guy. This man made women forget their own names. This man was strong, virile, and commanded attention with his mere presence, yet she could imagine him being gentle when he needed to be. She continued to gawk at him until she noticed his mouth was turned up in an amused smile. He cocked his head toward Brody and it was at that moment she realized the other man had said something to her.

Swallowing her embarrassment, she looked across the table to see he also wore a grin.

"I'm sorry, what did you say?"

Brody chuckled at her. "I asked what the name of the file you were looking for was."

She felt her cheeks grow warmer and burn bright red. Seriously? He needed to know the name of the file? *Well, of course he did, you idiot . . . how else would he be able to find it?*

"Leather and lace," she mumbled, looking at the dark surface of the table and wishing it was a black hole she could fall into.

"What was that?"

Still looking downward, Kristen cleared her throat and repeated louder and clearer, "Leather and lace."

When neither man spoke, nor did she hear any typing, she glanced up and saw both were staring at her. Oh, Lord help her, this was so mortifying.

Brody's grin became even wider and when she looked into his eyes, she swore she saw the laughter he was trying to hold back. She didn't even want to know what she would see if she peered up into the blue eyes of the man still standing next to the table.

"Well, okay then." Brody gave her a flirty wink before he started typing again. "Here it is. Leather and lace."

Kristen eyes rolled at the way the man drew out those last three words with his sexy drawl before she realized what he said and sat up straighter in her seat. "Oh my God, you found it? Seriously?"

"Of course, darlin'. Piece of cake."

"Thank you so much," she gushed. "You saved my life."

He laughed at her exaggeration. "Well maybe not your life, but at least an hour's worth of work, right?"

"Right. Yes. I don't know how to thank you."

Her cheeks flamed again when he responded, "Well, now, I'm sure we can come up with some way you can thank me that we'll both enjoy."

Jeez, there was the adorable charm again and, *wait* . . . did "Devil Dog" growl?

"Did you find it?" Jennifer asked as she joined them again.

Brody stood and winked at her. "Was there any doubt?"

"Not at all, Uncle Brody," she said in a teasing manner. "I would never doubt your superior geek skills."

"Brat." Brody tweaked the young woman's nose in an obvious sign of affection before looking over at Kristen. "Check to see if everything you were working on was saved. If you give me a minute to grab my laptop from my truck, I can clean up your hard drive a bit so this doesn't happen again."

She nodded and spun the laptop back to face her. "That would be so great. I'd appreciate it."

As he strode toward the exit, Kristen felt the stare of the man next to her. Trying to swallow the sudden lump in her throat, she looked up and saw he was no longer smiling. The fact would've disappointed her if she hadn't seen the heat smoldering in his eyes as he studied her. Another shiver shot through her spine and her panties became soaked with a sudden rush of arousal.

"So." His voice had a low timber she felt from her head to her toes. "Leather and lace?"

"Is that the title of your new book?"

Kristen hadn't realized young waitress was still with them until she heard her question. Somehow she managed to pull her gaze away from those eyes which seemed determined to devour her and looked at Jennifer. "Um, yes . . . yes it is."

"You're writing a book called *Leather and Lace?*"

And there went her blush again at the sound of his deep, sexy voice, and her eyes flicked to his again. She was grateful Jennifer answered the question for her because Kristen couldn't think of a single response to save her life.

"Yup, Uncle Devon. She's a romance writer. I've even read one of her books and I started one of the others yesterday."

"Really?" he murmured, as if trying to figure out a complex puzzle. The man may have asked a question, but it didn't appear he expected an answer.

Wait . . . what? *Uncle* Devon?

"You're Jennifer's uncle, too?" she asked.

"Mm-hm. They're all my uncles." Jennifer gestured over to the remaining group of men, unaware the question had been directed at Devon. "We're not blood related, but I call them my uncles. I've known them all my life and, well . . . they're my family."

Devon broke eye contact with Kristen and beamed at Jennifer with love in his eyes for the girl he considered his niece. He put his arm around her and pulled her into a hug. "Damn right we're family, Baby-girl."

For a brief second Kristen was jealous of the younger woman

tucked up against his hard, yummy body as his strong arms enveloped her small frame. Jennifer hugged him back and gave him a quick kiss on the cheek before letting go and heading toward the kitchen door. "Gotta check on my orders."

After she disappeared, Kristen verbalized her earlier thought, "She's a sweet girl."

Devon nodded in agreement. "Yes, she is."

When he didn't say anything more, she opened her mouth to ask him a question, any question that would keep him there talking to her. But her words died in her mouth when Brody came back to the table and sat down again, oblivious to the mounting sexual tension between the other two. He pulled his laptop out of its protective case and set it next to hers. Taking a cable, he connected the two computers and glanced at her. "It will only take a few minutes to download the program, and then I'll show you how to run it when you get home. A full scan will take about an hour or two to clean up your hard drive depending on how many programs and files it has to search through."

"What's it searching for?" She didn't know much about computers beyond the bare basics.

He started to type as he answered her, "Excess files, temporary downloads, and malware among other things. Stuff like that can drag down your hard drive and cause problems like the one you had earlier. This program will also help protect you from any viruses."

"I already have an anti-virus program."

He winked at her. "That may be, darlin', but my program will stop those files from building up."

"Your program?" She smiled at his playfulness. When she was younger, if a man like Brody had flirted with her, she would've been too shy to respond. But since she began writing sexy dialogue for her characters, she'd gained confidence with talking to the opposite sex. She would never be a shameless flirt like some women were, but now she felt she could hold up her end of a conversation with a Casanova like him. His intense friend was a different story. Devon made her want to drop to her knees and let him do things to her.

Things she'd never experienced before. And she didn't know how the thought made her feel.

"Well, considering I wrote it, yup, it's my program," Brody responded to her question, sounding like a little boy who was showing off his project at a science fair.

Kristen let out a little laugh. The man was a charmer. "Wow, now I totally feel computer illiterate. I won't lose anything important, will I? My life is on it."

"Nope." His fingers were still typing away. "Your files will be safe. But if you don't have a flash drive to back up your files you may want to invest in one."

"I have one at home, but I don't like to bring it with me because it's so small, I'm afraid I'll lose it." She had a bad habit of misplacing things. If it was smaller than a bread basket, Kristen had lost it at one time or another.

"Go anywhere that sells them and you can find one which you can put on your keychain."

"That's a good idea as long as I don't lose my keys, which happens at least once a week."

While Brody continued to talk about her computer, once every few seconds Kristen's eyes drifted toward Devon who was still standing next to the table. He hadn't taken his speculative gaze off of her and she tried not to squirm. She gave him a small smile and wondered what he was thinking of.

---

Devon's mouth ticked upward when she flashed him a shy smile as he considered her with interest. Although she was engrossed in the conversation, he didn't get the feeling he was being ignored, since she kept glancing up at him as if confirming he was still there. Interesting. And what was even more interesting was the fact he wanted to rip Brody's head off every time the geek turned on his southern charm. It was obvious his buddy found her attractive—what heterosexual male past the age of puberty wouldn't—and it was only a matter of time before Egghead asked her out. The man didn't have the same reservations that Devon did about hooking up with a woman outside the club.

The more he observed her the more he wanted to learn about her. She smelled like wildflowers and fresh air, almost as if she had walked through a meadow on a spring day, subtle and enticing. He detected a northern accent in her speech—his first guess had been New York, but now he wasn't sure. And her laugh . . . damn, her laugh went straight to his groin. Thank God he had his shirt untucked to hide the semi-automatic which was sitting at the small of his back. The shirt was now doing a good job of hiding other things, like his erection, from her view.

What was it about this woman, whose name he didn't even know, who called to him like a mystic siren? Damned if he knew, but he was looking forward to finding out. He was about to extend his hand and introduce himself when he noticed Brody giving her a scrap of paper with his name and phone number on it. The bastard beat him to it. Well, Devon deserved it for dragging his feet for over an hour when he could have found some inane reason to approach her and strike up a conversation. As much as he wanted to pound his buddy to a pulp and claim the woman for himself, he would never cock-block a good friend.

Devon took a step back and pivoted toward the bar as the two climbed out of the booth. Through the reflection in the mirror he saw her thanking Brody and then his stomach sank as she wrapped her arms around the grinning geek and gave him a hug. There was nothing sexual about the contact, but it still sent bolts of jealousy through Devon. He could imagine his buddy's response if he knew Devon wanted to deck him. *You snooze, you lose, Devil Dog!* And yes, he was back in grade-school again.

Moments later he watched as his little librarian gathered her things, said goodbye to Brody and Jenn, then made her way to the exit. With a hesitant backward glance in his direction, she walked out the door.

It was times like this he almost regretted not drinking alcohol, because he could use the distraction.

# CHAPTER 4

*D*evon spent the rest of the week alternating between being in a shitty mood and dreaming about his little librarian. No, make that Brody's little librarian. The bastard.

He'd acted like a petulant child and avoided Brody, whenever possible, since that afternoon six days ago. He didn't want to hear how his buddy had hooked up with the brunette, whose name he now knew was Kristen Anders. She'd dropped off copies of her books for Jennifer at the pub and his niece was now reading the next paperback in an ongoing series of vanilla romances after finishing one on her e-reader. And yes, he knew the stories were vanilla because when no one was looking, he'd skimmed through Jenn's book, *Passions Uncaged*, after she left it on the bar for a few minutes while working.

Although he didn't read more than a few passages, the story was well written and Ms. Anders had evident talent. He was surprised to find her sex scenes were pretty hot—vanilla, but hot. It was also a little embarrassing knowing his niece was reading those same scenes. He thought back to when Ian and he had an awkward conversation with Jenn about what type of club The Covenant was. They had to tell her since she'd be driving past it and living three buildings down from it in Ian's apartment when she moved to Tampa. After much blushing and stuttering on their part, Jenn let them off the hook and told them she understood and it wasn't a big deal to her. It wasn't her thing and she wasn't one to judge. They were thankful she expressed no desire to see the inside of the club. She probably didn't want to think of her uncles having sex of any kind, just like they didn't want to think about her having sex with some horny little bastard someday. They'd both been a little shocked, and yet relieved, when she blew it off with a nonchalant explanation of how she'd read many books with similar clubs in them. Granted those clubs were fictional while theirs was a reality, but she got the gist of it.

Flipping through the book, he'd found Kristen was descriptive about what her characters were doing up in the barn loft, down by the creek, and of course, in the bedroom. And even though the writing was steamy and sexy, he doubted the author would be into his type of sex and play. But, unlike Devon, Brody Evans didn't mind the occasional vanilla sex. If he was attracted to a woman, Brody was willing to go with the flow for a few dates. The only problem for the women was, after those few dates and some romps in the sack, Brody became bored and they would be history. There was a long line of women with broken hearts trailing behind Evans. He didn't do long term relationships, either. And it had never been a concern for Devon, until now—the thought of Brody dumping Kristen after using her to scratch his current itch angered Devon almost as much as the thought of them dating in the first place.

Forcing the aggravating thoughts from his mind, Devon climbed out of his Mustang before shutting the door and locking it. He'd left the top up on the drive over to Donovan's due to passing rain showers forecasted throughout the day. The gray skies matched his mood as he strode toward the entrance to the pub where he was joining Jake for lunch. His teammate wanted to go over some observations he'd made on a runaway case he had been working on for the past week. The teenage girl's father hired them after she allegedly ran away when he grounded her for missing her curfew on a regular basis. Jake had yet to locate the teen, but was starting to suspect the reason she took off was more sinister than anyone realized. Since it was after twelve and Jake had mentioned he was hungry, the two men agreed to meet for a bite to eat.

Entering the familiar hangout, Devon looked around to find his buddy hadn't arrived yet. All but a few tables were taken, but they usually didn't sit at one, and he headed to the far end of the bar out of habit. He gave Jenn a quick wave as she hurried out of the kitchen with a tray of food. She gave him a huge smile as she passed him and successfully put one on his own face. Jenn could brighten up his foulest mood just by being herself. Her dad had been Devon's Lieutenant on SEAL Team Four for several years before taking a non-fieldwork promotion due to medical reasons. The man had also served with Ian for many years before that. Ian and Jeff Mullins grew to be close friends as eighteen year olds suffering through basic training together, and when Jeff's wife, Lisa, gave birth to a baby girl two years later, following a shotgun wedding, Ian became a godfather.

The Mullins had lived less than fifteen minutes from the Navy base and the team spent many a relaxing afternoon or evening being entertained and smitten with little Jenn. Over the years, team members came and went, but Jenn considered them all her uncles, Most of the men kept in contact with her through emails and phone calls after they'd left the team for whatever reason—retirement, transfer, or promotion. No matter what though, her uncles were always guaranteed a card from Jenn for their birthdays, Valentine's Day, Veterans Day, and Christmas. There wasn't a team member past or present who wouldn't drop everything and come running if Jennifer Mullins needed them. And with a great amount of pain, she discovered those words to be true in the worst way possible.

A little over six months ago, Ian received a phone call from a hysterical Jennifer. Before he could calm her down, a police detective took her phone and in a grave voice informed Ian that Jeff and Lisa Mullins had been murdered in their home during a suspected burglary gone wrong. The two were found shot to death in their living room by a neighbor who noticed the front door ajar while walking his dog at six in the morning. Knowing Jeff and thinking it odd, the neighbor went to knock on the door and was able to see the carnage from the foyer. The couple had both been shot several times sometime late the night before and detectives later found several rooms ransacked with jewelry, wallets, and computers missing from the home. It had been fortuitous Jennifer was spared from harm or finding her parents' bloody bodies because she'd slept at a friend's house, following a night out at the movies.

Within an hour of the phone call, Devon and Ian were on a plane heading to Virginia and never left Jenn's side over the ensuing ordeal. As soon as former team members were notified, they began arriving in droves. Jenn never had to do a thing except mourn her loss. Her "uncles" took care of everything from the funerals and burials, life insurance and veteran death notifications, to selling and packing up the house when Jenn moved to Tampa to live with Ian three months later. Jenn's sole remaining family members were on her dad's side, but they weren't close, and the Mullins had long ago named Ian as her guardian if anything ever happened to them.

After the funeral, while Devon returned to Florida to keep their businesses running, Ian had stayed in Virginia until Jenn completed high school. It'd been difficult for her to get through, but with her teachers, friends, and Ian's help and support, she was able to complete the requirements for her diploma. On a sunny day in June, over forty former and current Navy SEALs filled the stands of the local high school football field to watch their little girl graduate. Devon didn't think there was a dry eye among them.

Now settled into a dorm for her freshman year at the University of Tampa on the other side of the city, Jenn was doing well. Although she still had moments of depression and sudden bouts of tears, and who could blame her, she continued to see a trauma psychologist to deal with her loss. Devon believed, however, it was the love she received every day from her uncles which was the most helpful in healing her devastated heart.

"Hey, are you okay?"

Devon was startled out of his thoughts at the soft voice beside him and swiveled his stool to see Kristen looking at him with concern. He hadn't thought she could get any prettier, but today she was stunning. She wore a little bit of makeup, not that she needed it, and it was enough to highlight her eyes and lips. Her soft brown hair was down, framing her face and falling below her shoulders, the tips resting at the swells of her breasts. Today's cotton V-neck was a soft purple which complimented her pale skin tone and brought out the green of her hazel eyes. It was also a little deeper than the one she wore the other day, giving him a generous view of her cleavage. And just like that, his jeans became snug.

He didn't answer her right away and she seemed to get a little flustered. "Sorry, I didn't mean to bother you, but you seemed a little . . . well . . . I don't know, sad about something."

He shook his head. "No, no, I'm fine, and you're not bothering me at all. I was just thinking about . . . never mind, it was no big deal." There was no point dredging up the past to a stranger, no matter how much he wanted an excuse to talk to her. He forced his mouth into what he hoped was a convincing smile and it turned into a real one at her sigh of relief as the corners of her own mouth tilted upward.

"Good, I'm glad. I'm Kristen Anders, by the way."

He shook her outstretched hand, marveling at how soft it was and wondering if she felt the same jolt of awareness which rocked him to his core. "Devon Sawyer."

"It's nice to meet you." She paused, and he waited to see what she would say next, wanting to hear her lyrical voice again as much as he wanted his next breath. But a wave of disappointment hit him as she shook her head a little, pulled her hand from his and began to turn away. He opened his mouth to stop her from leaving when she spun back around and her words came out in a rush. "Look, I'm usually not this forward—actually I'm never this forward—but . . . but would you like to go out sometime?"

Devon couldn't have been more surprised if she had pulled out a gun and shot him between the eyes. *She* was asking *him* out? He must have hesitated too long because she held up her hand. "You know what, forget I asked. You don't have to answer the question."

He reached for her arm before she had a chance to run away. As much as he wanted to say, yes, he would love to go out with her, he found himself uttering, "I'm flattered, I am. But Brody's my friend and, well . . ." He left the sentence hanging, instead of telling her he would never poach his friend's woman.

Kristen frowned. "I don't understand. What does Brody have to do with anything?"

*Really? She had to ask?* Maybe he was wrong about her being sweet and innocent. Maybe she bounced from guy to guy. He gazed into her eyes. No, he didn't think he was wrong. Not about this. "Didn't he give you his phone number the other day?"

Kristen's smile returned along with a look of understanding. "He gave me his number in case I had any problems with the program he gave me."

Devon couldn't hide his shock. "You mean, he didn't ask you out?"

"Well, he did. But I didn't say yes."

Was she for real? He'd never heard a woman turn Brody down before. Egghead had women of all ages throwing themselves at him left and right. "Why?"

"Why didn't I say yes?"

He nodded.

"Well, he was nice and all, and don't get me wrong, he's good looking, but," she shrugged one shoulder, "I wasn't attracted to him."

His mouth curled up in a sexy smirk, and he lowered his voice. "*Huh.* So, does this mean you're attracted to me?"

Kristen blushed. "I wouldn't have asked you out if I wasn't. So, I guess the big question is . . . are you attracted to me?"

Devon knew he should deny it and send her on her way, a little embarrassed maybe, but with her gentle heart intact. And then she'd blushed. At that moment he knew there were a million and one reasons why he should say "no," but he couldn't remember what they were. His mind became a complete blank at her hopeful expression and he found himself saying, "Yes. Yes, I am very attracted to you."

God, he was a selfish ass. Here was a beautiful young woman and she was most likely looking for her Prince Charming and a "happily ever after," which she would never find in him. She would want a long term commitment and he was Mister One-Weekend-Only. Well, to be accurate, he was *Master* One-Weekend-Only. And there was another reason he should have said no. After reading the romantic scenes she'd written, he figured his vanilla librarian would run away screaming when he told her how he wanted to tie her up and flog her luscious ass until she begged him to fuck her into oblivion. He ached for her to kneel at his feet while he dragged his cock across her tongue. An image came to mind of what it would be like to pump in and out of her sweet mouth, until he came and she swallowed every drop. He wanted to own her, possess her, and then, when he had his fill, he would walk away as he always did.

Instead of doing what he knew was right, he found himself making plans with her for the following evening. By the time Jake arrived a few minutes later, Devon had a dinner date scheduled with her for seven o'clock at a little Italian restaurant around the corner from Donovan's. And she'd given him a sexy smile when she'd bid him goodbye.

A short time later, after Jake and he ordered a couple of burgers, his teammate let him know he'd caught at least part of Devon's conversation with Kristen. Keeping his eyes on one of the TV's over the bar, Jake let out an amused snort. "So, hell must have frozen over, huh?"

Devon frowned at the other man. "What the fuck does that mean?"

"It means, Devil Dog, in all the years I've known you, I can't recall you ever having a vanilla date with a woman, complete with dinner at a fancy little restaurant. The most effort I've seen you put into seducing a woman was buying her a drink while you negotiated a scene and found out her soft and hard limits."

"Fuck you, jackass," he retorted without any real heat, considering everything the man had said was true. Instead of admitting it though, he lied. "I've been on plenty of dates before."

Jake didn't respond, but gave Devon a look which said he knew his friend was blowing smoke out his ass.

"Besides, you're not one to talk, Reverend. When was the last time you went out on a date, huh?"

Devon was astonished as his buddy grinned and turned beet red at the same time.

"You're dating someone?" He couldn't believe it. His eyes went wide with shock. "How did I not know this? It's not anyone from the club, is it?" Jake Donovan didn't do relationships any more than the rest of them did, maybe even less.

Jake shrugged and then sighed. "Yes, I'm dating someone. No one knew until now because it's only been a few dates. And no, it's not anyone from the club, and before you ask, no you don't know him."

As curious as Devon was, he knew he wouldn't get anything more out of his buddy. He was surprised the man revealed as much as he did. So instead of asking more questions, he raised his soda glass in a gesture of good luck. "Well, here's to you my friend. I hope it works out for you. And if it does, there may be hope for the rest of us."

Jake touched his glass to Devon's and chuckled. "I wouldn't go that far, brother, because if that happened, hell *would* definitely freeze over."

# CHAPTER 5

Kristen couldn't believe she was there. She could imagine her ex-husband's expression if he knew she was standing outside a private BDSM club with the intention of going inside. She'd found out about The Covenant from one of her Beta-readers who helped proofread her novels. Although they had never met, she chatted with Shelby Whitman, a member of the club, through Facebook and email. When Kristen had mentioned wanting to see the inside of a sex club for research, the woman put her in touch with the owner, Master Mitch. After several phone conversations and a background check, the man had finally agreed to let Kristen tour the facility while it was closed.

When they'd scheduled the appointment, the Dom had been adamant that she come alone and leave her phone in her car. She'd balked at being in a strange place with a strange man with no way to call for help and he'd relented, but asked her to keep the phone off while in the club. His clientele valued the club's privacy and he would not put that at risk for anyone. Kristen was fine with his reasoning, but also told the man she would let her cousin know who she was meeting and where, for her own safety. She didn't want to be one of those women she saw on the news every once in a while, who disappeared without a trace. It was the same thing she would do for her date tonight with Devon.

She was still shocked she'd asked him out on a date. Ever since puberty she'd been shy around men, and the more attractive she found them, the shyer she became. But that was the "old Kristen." The "new Kristen" was starting over after a failed marriage. She was no longer a virgin, but she knew she was still inexperienced. The only position she'd ever had sex in was the missionary one. Maybe it hadn't been her fault she was cold in bed, maybe it'd been Tom's. She wanted to be a woman who wasn't afraid to try new things, a woman men found attractive, to have flirty conversations with them, filled with sexual innuendos. She wanted to find what she wrote about, what other women bragged about—a man who gave her incredible orgasms which made her scream and beg for more. Was Devon the right man? She wouldn't know unless she went to bed with him, and she didn't think she could have a one-night stand, so she had to get to know him better.

Glancing through her windshield again, she shook her head in disbelief. When she'd arrived a few minutes ago, she thought she'd gotten the directions wrong. After exiting the highway where Master Mitch told her to, she followed the side road past a small forest of trees. The area then opened up and she found herself looking at a large piece of property surrounded by a security fence topped with barbed wire. Behind the fence, there was a row of four warehouses reminding her of an industrial park. Another portion of fencing separated the first two buildings. Once Kristen pulled her car up to the security shack next to the gate to find out where she'd made a mistake in the directions, she had discovered she was indeed in the right place. The cordial, but armed guard had checked her driver's license and took a digital picture of her before he opened the gate and pointed to where she should park. He indicated she should take an awning covered staircase at the near end of the first building to the second-floor main entrance.

Parking next to the building, she'd stared at the blue metal and cement monstrosity and had a difficult time imagining this was the outside of an elite and private club catering to people's individual sexual fetishes. Now, Kristen climbed out of the car and locked the door before shutting it. She took one step then she froze at the sound of a dog barking. Looking around, ready to jump on the hood of her car if she had to, she spotted a large black lab-mix running back and forth and was thankful it was on the other side of the second fence. Despite his loud greeting, he appeared friendly, but she wasn't taking any chances by approaching the barrier between them.

"Hi, boy, good doggie. Stay on your side of the fence, okay? Good boy." she cooed in what she hoped was a soothing tone as she dashed to the stairs.

When she reached the doors, she found them locked, but located a doorbell and pressed it. As she waited, she took in her surroundings again and realized there was no signage indicating a place of business on any of the buildings and fences. She also couldn't remember seeing any signs at the highway exit or on the side road leading to the complex other than a street sign which read Fairwood Drive. Curious, she wondered what was in the other three buildings. There were a few cars parked next to the second one, but she didn't see anyone other than the one guard. She also noticed several security cameras, some on the buildings, including the one above the door she stood in front of, and others atop some of the nine-foot fence posts. It was a little overkill to her, but what did she know.

The door opened and she was greeted by a handsome man whom she guessed to be in his early thirties. "Hi, Ms. Anders? I'm Master Mitch. It's nice to meet you."

She would be embarrassed to admit he wasn't what she expected, which was an older, brooding, vampire-like looking man, dressed head to toe in leather. Instead, he reminded her of her high-school math teacher, who all the female students had crushes on. About six-foot-one, he had black/brown hair with gentle, blue eyes. His easy smile was framed by a trim goatee and mustache which might be adding a few years to his age. Instead of being dressed in black, he was wearing a navy blue golf shirt, blue jeans, and sneakers. It was obvious he kept himself in shape, maybe by running and playing sports, because he didn't have the bulked-up look weightlifters did. Despite his pleasant demeanor, she could imagine him transforming into a commanding Dom with submissives dropping to their knees to please him.

"It's nice to meet you, too."

He stepped aside so she could enter, and she was amazed how the outside of the building belied its interior. They were standing in a lobby which was decorated in a Victorian-era style. It was just large enough to contain a hotel-style check-in desk and a comfortable sitting area. The walls were painted a deep red while the carpet was a complementary gray. On several walls were paintings which some might call pornographic, but Kristen thought they were sensual and erotic. The space was separated from the main club by a set of large wooden doors which she swore once graced an old European castle somewhere. The dark wood was beautiful with intricate carvings and round wrought iron pulls.

Before Master Mitch allowed her through the doors, he took a moment to convince himself she was not taking any pictures or recordings of his business. He then gave her a privacy contract to sign, stating it protected his business and clients and it was legal and binding, having been drawn up by the club's lawyers. After she read and signed the paper, he took it from her and handed her several others.

"I thought these would help you with your research. The top two pages are general contracts which some members use when negotiating a temporary relationship between Dominant and submissive that's going to last more than one or two nights. Usually the contract indicates both parties agree to play for a certain amount of time, such as a week or a month, and what the play will consist of. At the end of the agreed upon time, both parties go their separate ways."

"Isn't a contract a little cold?" There was little she could do to hide the cynical tone in her voice or her shocked expression.

He tilted his head as if he was thinking about her question—a contract could seem cold to someone not familiar with the lifestyle. "You have to understand something. Although there are couples here who are married or in long-term relationships, there are many others who aren't looking for anything other than something temporary. This way there's an end date and there is no awkward quote-unquote breaking up at the end of the relationship."

Kristen nodded, writing a few notes in the notebook she brought with her. She understood what he was saying, but wasn't sure if she could ever sign a contract to have sex with a man that included a deadline stating when they would stop seeing each other.

"The other papers are the club's rules, a list of protocols which submissives are expected to follow, and a long list of BDSM activities. Submissives fill out the checklist with their hard and soft limits, or red and yellow limits as some people call them. Do you know what those are?"

Before she wrote *Satin and Sin*, she did a lot of Internet searches on every aspect of BDSM she could find. She was far from an expert on the subject, but she knew the basics. "If my research was correct, hard limits are something a submissive has no desire to try, things which are a total turn-off for them. Soft limits are things they're curious about and might be willing to try, but they've never done them before, or if they have, they haven't made up their mind on whether they want to do it again."

"Correct. And after they try one of their yellow soft limits, they tend to move it to the green, okay activity column, or the red, hard limit column. There are some activities which only appeal to a select few, while there are others that pretty much everyone is into. Submissives' hard and soft limit lists are available here at the front desk for the Doms to look at, so they know who would be receptive to a certain activity. On the checklist, the starred activities are not allowed in the club at all."

Kristen cocked her head. "Such as?"

"Such as fire-play and anything involving blood, urine, or feces, among a few other extreme activities."

"*Eewww.*" Kristen winced. She had read about body fluid play on the Internet and the thought of it still grossed her out.

He smiled and laughed at her reaction. If she had met him

anywhere else she would have a hard time believing he was a Dom. Despite his age, the man had a boyish charm to him.

"Exactly! I'm with you. Body fluid play does not appeal to me at all, but believe it or not, there are some people who get into it. Along the same subject line, every client must have a physical and blood work with one of our doctors every six months in order to keep their play privileges, and vaginal and anal sex without condoms is forbidden in the building, even between long-time partners.

"Let's see, what else can I tell you? Um . . . oh, we have a bar and alcohol is restricted to two drinks if members are planning to play. The bartenders have a computer program to track how many drinks have been served to a member. The same program is used to bill the members each month, so they don't need to carry any cash, just a key card. It's similar to what's used on cruise ships. The waitresses and security have handheld computers which track the same information and it's checked before a member is allowed to enter any play area, public or private. The same program is used to flag a member who is overdue for a physical."

Master Mitch continued to talk as Kristen scribbled in her notepad as fast as she could. "Every once in a while a client will ask to bring a guest. It's only allowed after a background check of the guest and they're not allowed to play at all while on the premises, unless they have been cleared by one of our staff doctors. It takes a few weeks before a guest is cleared, so it's not something which can be done on the spur of a moment. The client who invited the guest is held responsible for them and cannot leave them on their own. Guests are given a yellow wristband, so the Dungeon Masters and security know who they are. All clients have gone through extensive background checks and every few months their names are checked for any arrests or dealings with the police which may concern us, such as a domestic violence call at their house."

She looked up from her notes. "Wow. Isn't it a lot of work for you?"

"Well, we have a security company which does it for us, but it's necessary to keep our clients safe."

"Any other rules?" she inquired, finding the information he was giving her fascinating. There was plenty of data on the Internet, but sometimes it took a live person to help you understand a subject to the fullest.

"Well, it's obvious you've done some research on the topic, right? So you know what a safeword is, correct?"

She nodded. "If a submissive uses their safeword all play comes to an immediate halt."

"Right. We use color safewords here so there are no misunderstandings between our members, the Dungeon Masters, and security. If a sub uses a different safeword and a Dom doesn't heed it, a Dungeon Master may not know there's a problem. Red means stop, yellow means to slow down or pause to clarify an issue, green means they're good to go. Failure to heed a safeword is an automatic three month suspension of play privileges and a second offense results in termination of membership. But we've never had to terminate anyone for that reason."

Satisfied she would adhere to the privacy contract she signed, he finally opened the left wooden door and gestured for her to walk in ahead of him. Three steps past the threshold, she stopped short in complete awe of the fantasy land before her. The second floor where they stood consisted of an extra wide balcony in the shape of a horseshoe overlooking the main floor below. To her left, there was a large curved bar following the lines of the horseshoe bottom. The two long, opposite sides of the balcony contained many sitting areas similar to the one in the lobby. High above the sitting areas were horizontal tinted windows which let light in during the day and he told her the inside of the club couldn't be seen from outside at any time. Along the brass railings there were stools and pub tables where people could sit and observe what was happening below them. About twenty feet in front of the bar was a grand staircase with brass banisters leading downstairs, and reminding Kristen of the one her wedding party had taken pictures on at the hotel where her reception was held.

At the opposite end of the building, where the horseshoe ended was a wall with two doors, one glass and the other wood.

Master Mitch explained the glass door belonged to a small store where they sold a variety of sex toys and fetish wear. The other door was to a hallway leading to the business offices and an emergency exit. The locker rooms were located right below the bar. There was an entrance next to the double exit doors with a short hallway and two sets of stairs leading to the women's and men's locker rooms. Members could also enter the rooms from the first floor.

As they walked further into the club, his cell phone rang. Taking it from the holster at his hip, he looked at the screen. "I apologize, but I have to take this. Please have a seat at the bar, and I'll be with you in a moment." He placed the phone to his ear and stepped a few feet away from her. "Hey, Ian, what's up?"

She did as he asked and took a seat while skimming through the paperwork he gave her. She never realized how involved the lifestyle was—contracts, lists, protocols, and rules. It was a wonder anyone had time for sex. Although he'd said a negotiation between Dom and sub was a common part of BDSM, she couldn't help but think it was all so clinical, like going to her GYN for her annual physical.

She was disappointed it was the middle of the afternoon and the club was empty except for her and Master Mitch. She would love to take in the sights and sounds of the club when it was in full swing. It would have been a tremendous help with the descriptions she wrote of her fictional club "Leathers," but it hadn't been an option offered to her.

Several minutes later, Mitch hung up the phone and gestured for her to join him at the top of the grand staircase. She listened as he began to explain the different areas and pieces of equipment while he led her down the stairs to the "pit."

"The pit?" she had asked with curiosity.

He laughed and shook his head. "Yeah, in the beginning we called this the dungeon . . . a little cliché, but it's basically what it is. Somewhere along the line the observers upstairs began calling it the pit and it sort of stuck."

"I like it . . . it fits," she told him. "It makes me think of the coliseum in Rome."

"*Hmmm*, maybe we should schedule some gladiator games. The subs would love it."

Kristen chuckled, as she made a quick note on her pad. "I might steal that idea and put it in my book."

"Only if you give me partial creative credit," he teased.

Kristen laughed harder. "It's a deal."

When they reached the first floor, she took a few more steps, then rotated in a three hundred and sixty degree turn, taking in as much as she could. The red and gray color combination continued throughout this part of the club and was the perfect complement to the different pieces of equipment located in individual areas. Each was sectioned off by red velvet ropes hanging from brass hooks, while the wrought iron sconces and chandeliers completed the look.

"So, is it what you imagined it would be?"

Kristen turned back toward Master Mitch. "It's better than I ever imagined," she told him honestly. "I didn't think I would say this, but it's beautiful."

"Expected something more along the lines of a damp dark dungeon in some castle somewhere?" He laughed. People new to his lifestyle always seem amazed how elegant his club was.

"Sort of, I guess. I'm not sure what I expected, but I know it wasn't this."

He began to show her the different sections and stopped in the center of the huge oval room, next to a two-foot high stage. On it sat a seven-foot tall, wooden St. Andrew's Cross with black leather padding covering part of its surface, and it could be seen from every angle of the room. At the top and bottom ends of the cross were leather wrist and ankle restraints. Although it brought to mind medieval torture, Kristen knew it was common apparatus used in the lifestyle she was researching. An erotic shiver went through her as she imagined herself, naked and restrained on it, for everyone to see.

Shaking off the thought, she began to go through a list of questions she had written down before she came. She found his answers were valuable to her research as she took several more pages of notes. "How many members do you have?"

"Over three hundred and fifty, but some of them live in the area part time so they only come a few times a year. The waiting list is over two hundred people and that's only for this club. There are four other clubs in the Tampa area, but only two of those are private. The others are open to the public, which isn't safe in my opinion. They don't keep track of their members and anyone could walk in off the street and start to play. Anyway, The Covenant has an elite clientele and the reputation of being *the* club to belong to. And that's not my ego talking. We've worked hard to become the best in the area."

"Holy cow!" Over three hundred and fifty members, with more than half of that trying to get in? She had expected him to say less than a hundred members.

"Didn't think so many people were into kink, did you?"

Kristen shook her head in amazement as he continued. "We have a capacity for five hundred people in here as approved by the fire inspector, but I doubt we'll ever let the numbers get that high."

"Hey, Mitch, did you talk to Ian yet?" A male voice boomed and echoed in the empty club. As they both turned toward the grand staircase where someone was descending, Kristen heard, "What the hell are you doing here?"

She froze and searched her mind for an answer as a very sexy, and very pissed off, Devon strode up to her and stopped inches from her face. *Uh-oh.* This wasn't good. *Wait a minute . . . what the hell are you doing here?* What the hell was *he* doing here?

Mitch glanced from Devon to Kristen and back again. It was evident he was both amused and curious. "Um, last time I checked Dev, I run the place. That's what the hell I'm doing here."

Devon never took his eyes off her, and she suddenly wished she was anywhere but here when he growled. "Shove it, Mitch. I asked you a question, Kristen. Don't make me ask you again."

Kristen's back straightened. Who did he think he was? "Not that it's any business of yours, but Master Mitch was nice enough to give me a tour of his club for some research I'm doing for my book."

"Research?" His brows furrowed in confusion. "In case you hadn't noticed, this is a BDSM sex club, Kristen."

*Seriously?* "Of course I noticed, and it's obvious that little fact didn't get past you, now did it? Now, please leave and let me finish my tour."

Mitch's laughter was cut off by Devon's lethal glare, and he took a step back. He was clearly trying to hold back his amusement.

"What were you thinking, Mitch? A tour? What are we, fucking Disney World?"

"I had Marco do a background check on her. Brody was busy. After I confirmed she wrote fiction and wasn't some reporter trying to check the place out, I figured it was fine. She has no cameras or recorders."

"How the hell did you find out about the club in the first place?" He was back to questioning her again.

She raised her chin in defiance. There was no way she would let this man intimidate her no matter how much she was attracted to him—and damn it, was it getting hot in here? "One of my Beta-readers is a member, and she contacted Master Mitch for me."

Devon's eyes flicked toward his cousin with an unspoken question. "Shelby" was the response he received.

Kristen huffed. She'd answered his questions, but now she was becoming infuriated with him sticking his nose where it didn't belong. "This is really none of your business, Devon."

Devon stared back at her and growled again. "None of my business? See, that's where you're wrong, Pet, this *is* my business. I own this club."

Her mouth dropped open as she looked back and forth between the two men. "Y-You own the club? I thought Master Mitch owned it."

"He's my cousin. We're co-owners, along with my brother. So, allow me to re-introduce myself to you, Pet. I'm Master Devon."

Kristen's mouth went dry. *Shit!* There was no way this could be happening. Of all the things which could go wrong today, she hadn't expected this. He was a Dom? She knew she was in so much trouble, but didn't know why, or what to say, so she just stared at him, her chin almost hitting the floor.

"WHAT KIND of research are you doing? Your books are pretty vanilla when it comes to sex, so why the hell do you need to research a BDSM club?" Devon realized his mistake as soon as the words were out of his mouth, but there was no way to take them back.

"You read my books?"

She sounded as shocked as Mitch looked. *Great, just great.* It would be a long time before his cousin forgot this conversation. Devon crossed his arms, forcing her to back up a step. Since Marco had done her background check, the name hadn't been familiar to him. Brody, who usually did the checks, would have recognized it right away and mentioned it to him, saving him from this little surprise meeting. "I didn't read any of them. Jenn left one of the books you gave her on the bar. I was curious about you and flipped through it. Now stop dancing around my questions."

Mitch cleared his throat. "I have a question. How do you two know each other?"

Refusing to give his cousin any ammunition for future jokes, Devon rolled his eyes. "Shut it, Mitch."

But to his dismay, Kristen spoke at the same time. "We have a date tonight."

Mitch's eyes widened as if he hadn't have heard her right. Devon could almost guess what his cousin was thinking. *Devil Dog? On a date? Like a date-date? Damn, the end of the world must be near.* With flair for the dramatic, the asshole stuck his finger in his ear to clear any blockage. "I'm not sure I heard you right, can you repeat that? It sounded like you said you two had a date."

Before she could answer him, Devon growled—which he seemed to do a lot in her presence. "Mitch, if you know what's good for you, you'll go upstairs and do some inventory or something. I'll finish taking Ms. Anders on her . . . tour."

To Kristen's shock, Master Mitch sighed and headed toward the staircase. "Don't forget, she's not allowed to play."

"I know. I was there when we wrote the club rules."

The man didn't stop walking up the stairs, but raised his voice so she could still hear him. "Ms. Anders, don't worry. You're in good hands. Oh, don't forget, the club safeword is 'red.' I'll be at the bar if you need to use it."

Her eyes widened. There was no way he was leaving her alone with Devon, was there? The man looked like he wanted to spank her ass for the next three days straight and, good Lord, why did the thought make her wet?

Devon took a step toward her. Kristen's response was instantaneous and she took two steps back, looking for a way to get around him. He arched his brow and took another step. She tried not to react again, but before she knew it, he had backed her up to the wall and stopped right in front of her, blocking her escape. Without saying a word, he reached out and took her pad and papers, tossing them on a small table behind him before doing the same with her pen and purse.

He then took hold of her wrists and brought her arms above her head. There were only a few inches between their bodies and she could feel the heat of his. She wished he would take a half a step toward her and then she would know what it felt like to be in contact with his hard chest, sculpted abs and trim hips. Oh, and don't forget the massive erection he was sporting.

"Eyes up, Pet."

Heaven help her. She lifted her chin to find a perceptive grin on his face and she turned red, knowing she'd been caught staring at his crotch. He leaned forward, his mouth almost touching her ear and whispered, "You still haven't answered my question."

The words may have been simple, something you could hear in an everyday conversation, but somehow he made them sound erotic and the heated feel of his breath on her ear didn't help. She swallowed hard, her legs trembling. Not in fear—he wouldn't physically hurt her. She didn't know how she knew it, but she did. But no, it was the sexual electricity between them which had her unable to control her quivering muscles. "What . . . what was the question again?"

"Why are you researching BDSM when you write vanilla sex?"

*Couldn't he back up a little?* "Um . . . well, my first nine books are . . . are vanilla, but my last book was based on a BDSM club and . . . and now I'm writing the second one in a series."

"You gave my niece a kinky romance to read?" He didn't sound happy about it at all.

"Act . . . actually, I didn't give that one to her, only the others. It felt a little weird giving a nineteen year old a BDSM book."

She drew in a deep breath, relieved when he took a step backward. But her feeling of relief didn't last long when she realized her arms were stuck. Tilting her head up, she tugged on her arms to find he'd shackled her wrists with Velcro restraints dangling from the balcony overhang. How did she not know he was doing that? Oh God, she was trapped.

She gaped at him and was annoyed to see he was laughing at her with a sinister smirk, his arms crossed over his muscular chest again. Damn the man was gorgeous . . . and dangerous. Not in a bad way, but also not in a good one. And here she was with no way to escape. She wouldn't panic. Master Mitch was right upstairs. She was safe, wasn't she? "Let me go." She hoped the demand would sound confident, but instead, it sounded breathy.

He shook his head. "Not until your tour is complete."

Damn, how had she not noticed how arrogant the man was? "I didn't know class participation was part of the tour."

Devon let out a full-blown laugh. "Oh, how I love bratty submissives. They give me plenty of reasons to spank their asses beet red. And I'll tell you, at the moment, my hand is itching to get at your sweet ass."

"I'm not a submissive."

The look he gave her said he didn't believe her for a second before he turned around and took three steps to the table where he'd put her things. Turning a wooden chair around, he straddled it and sat down facing her. Without saying a word he picked up her pad and the papers Mitch had given her and began to look through them.

"Hey, that's my stuff. I didn't give you permission to look through my notes."

"Quiet."

He never looked up as he issued the deep-voiced command and it sent a shiver through her body. She began to glance around, trying to figure out how to get out of the restraints. She should be scared out of her wits, but for some reason, she wasn't. Instead she was turned on which freaked her out a little . . . well, actually, a lot. Yes, she had fantasized about this stuff and she wrote about it, but it didn't appeal to her in real life, did it? Apparently it did, because during her entire marriage, she had never once been this aroused and Devon had only touched her wrists. What would happen if he touched her in other places? Did she want him to? Her body screamed at her—hell, yeah!

She looked back at him and realized he was now reading the papers Mitch had given her. *Shit!* While Mitch had been talking on his phone, she skimmed through the soft and hard limit checklist. She didn't fill out the entire form, but had checked off what she considered to be hard limits for her. Everything else she skipped over, planning to go through the list again later to figure out what she thought she would like and what she wasn't sure about. "Hey, stop! That's private!"

Devon rolled his eyes and sighed, then got up from his seat. Without looking at her, he strode over to open a cabinet she hadn't noticed, which was built into the wall a few feet away from her. He grabbed something and then shut the door again before walking back to his seat. Pivoting to face her, he held up an object. "Do you know what this is, Pet?"

She had a feeling she did, but she bit her bottom lip and shook her head.

"It's a ball gag. Usually I only give an order once and expect it to be obeyed, but since this is new to you, here is your second and final warning. Stay quiet unless I ask you a question. Your only answers should be 'yes, Sir' or 'no, Sir' unless I ask you for a detailed answer.

Anything else out of your mouth will result in me using the ball gag. Understood?"

As her girlie parts began to throb, Kristen nodded her head and he frowned at her. "Y-yes, Sir."

"Do you wish to use your safeword? If you do, I'll let you loose and escort you out . . . without your research, of course."

*What?!* Crap, he was serious. "No, Sir."

---

DEVON PLACED the gag on the table where she was sure to see it every time she looked at him. He was pleased to see a shudder run through her body and a nervous, but heated look in her eyes. He loved to play the psychological games involved in BDSM and, damn it, he wanted to play the physical games with her too, but now was not the time. Instead he sat back down and looked over her checklist again. Having seen hundreds of them in the past, it didn't take long for him to read her partial list, but he pretended to take his time.

He waited . . . and waited. And yes, there it was. She began to squirm, her hips and feet moving ever so slightly, but enough for him to notice. She rubbed her thighs together and he knew without a doubt her pussy was wet. "I'm pleased to see most of your hard limits are similar to mine, but I'd love to see where you place the activities you haven't checked off yet. I'm also curious about why nipple clamps are a hard limit for you? I don't think I've ever seen that on a submissives hard limit list before."

Kristen swallowed hard, and her pink cheeks turned a deeper shade. "M-my nipples are too sensitive, Sir. The thought of clamps freaks me out."

Confused, he stared at her and tried to figure out what she wasn't telling him. Something about her statement felt off to him. "Out of all the hard limits you checked off, if you had to move one to a soft limit, which one would you choose?"

She paused in evident thought. "The bullwhip, Sir."

*What the hell?* "You would choose a whip over nipple clamps?"

"Yes, Sir."

With a surprised look on his face, Devon stood again and stalked toward her. "I think there's something more to it than just sensitive nipples, but I'll leave it alone for now. Have you ever been tied up or spanked before?"

"No!"

"But the thought of doing those things turns you on." He stopped in front of her. His words may not have come out as a question, but he still waited for an answer.

She opened her mouth with what he knew was a denial, but slammed it shut again when his eyes narrowed. "Don't lie to me, Pet." She was wise enough to remain silent, and he stared at her for a minute before speaking again. "I think I'm going to change our plans for this evening."

---

KRISTEN'S STOMACH DROPPED. "You're cancelling our date?"

Taking the index finger of his right hand, he reached up and set it on her left forearm. His touch was light as he trailed his finger down her arm toward her elbow, then further, touching her ear and neck. His eyes tracked the movement. From her collarbone, he followed the scoop-neck edge of her shirt, down to her chest, over the swells of her breasts, and back up to her right ear. Her breathing increased and her nipples had a mind of their own, pebbling into hard little nubs, begging for him to touch them.

"Oh no, Pet, not at all. I'm just going to add to it. We'll still go to dinner." He paused and her tongue shot out to moisten her dry lips. Heat flared in his eyes in response. "*Mmmm.* But afterward, we'll come here and I'll give you the full tour as my guest. Since Marco ran a security check on you, it won't be any problem. I do have a few requirements though, since our plans have changed. I want you to wear the sexiest dress or skirt you own and no underwear. And I mean no panties *or* bra, Pet. You will go to dinner like that. If you disobey me on this, I'll take you into the women's restroom and remove them myself. Understood?"

Kristen was salivating, her panties were soaked. Was it possible to come, while she was fully dressed, from a feather-light touch and his words alone? Her voice came out raspy. "Y-yes, Sir."

"And wear your hair down." He gave her pony tail a gentle tug. "I want you to read and understand the club protocols. You'll be expected to follow them, although I'll give you some leeway since this is new to you. If you have any questions, you may ask them at dinner. Last, but not least, I want you to finish filling out your limit list."

Her eyes widened because he couldn't be serious. "But I thought guests weren't allowed to play without a physical and . . . and stuff." At his raised eyebrow, she added, "Sir."

His finger retraced its earlier path, down her neck, across her breasts, and then back up again. "Correct. But by having you complete the list, I know what scenes I should let you observe. Now, before I let you go home to get ready for our . . . date, do you have any questions?"

She had more than she could count in the next hour or so, however, she found herself saying, "No, Sir."

"Do you want to cancel our date?"

Did she? Absolutely not! "No, Sir."

"Good." He reached up and removed the restraints from her wrists. "I'll walk you to your car."

# CHAPTER 6

"Try this one on. I think it will be perfect."

Kayla London took the little black dress from Kristen's closet and handed it to her as Will reclined on her bed, propped up on a few pillows. On the way home from the club, Kristen had called him in a semi-panic. He, in turn, had called Kayla. The woman was one of Will's closest friends, and Kristen had clicked with her the first time they'd met. Will introduced the two of them a few months earlier when Kristen had traveled to Tampa to find an apartment before moving. Kayla and her wife, Roxy, had become her fast friends, and although they teased her about it, they never tried to hook her up with one of their female friends.

After Kristen explained about her dinner date and where they were going after, the fashion-forward duo had come running to her rescue. She had no idea what to wear. It had to be something appropriate for dinner and hide the fact she was not allowed to wear underwear, yet sexy enough for the club.

She was so nervous. Her stomach still had butterflies fluttering around, which had started the moment she realized Devon had shackled her wrists. He'd worn such a wicked grin as he watched her struggle with the restraints for a few moments before giving up. She had a feeling if she had panicked, he would have released her without question, but she surprised herself by only asking him to let her go the one time. Then she'd become so focused on him and the tingling throughout her body, she'd pretty much forgotten she was being held hostage.

While he read through her notes, she'd studied him a little more. When she first met him, she'd thought he was walking perfection, but today, she'd noticed his nose was a tad crooked, as if it had been broken at one time. He also had a faint two-inch scar along his jawline, a little bit below his right ear and she wondered what had caused it. Those small imperfections only enhanced his good looks and made him seem even sexier, if it was at all possible.

As she walked into the bathroom and shut the door to change for the third time, Kayla told her, "I'm so jealous you're going to The Covenant tonight. Roxy and I put in a membership application six months ago, and from what I understand, the waiting list to get in is almost a year, unless a Dom sponsors you. And even then it takes a while."

Kristen pulled the cotton-spandex dress over her head and dragged it down her body, smoothing the fabric as she went. "I didn't know you two were . . . in the lifestyle."

"We don't advertis because most people don't understand BDSM and tend to be negative about it. Roxy got me into it when we first met years ago. She became a Domme in college, but didn't have much time to play when she hit med school. At the moment, we belong to another private club called Heat, but don't go as much as we would like. We would prefer the guarded privacy and exclusiveness The Covenant is known for. Some parents of Roxy's kids would flip if they found out she likes to flog my ass."

Kayla was a social worker and Dr. Roxanne London had a thriving pediatric practice. They were also the complete opposites of each other. Where Kayla was five-foot-two, a "size twelve on a good day and a fourteen on a bad one"—her words—and a blue-eyed blonde, Roxy was seven inches taller and a size six, with auburn hair and hazel eyes. Kayla was disorganized and loved sci-fi movies, while Roxy was a neat freak who went to at least one indie or foreign film a month, either alone or with a friend, because her wife had a tendency to fall asleep during them. But despite their differences, or maybe it was due to them, the two made the perfect couple.

"I can see why you would want to keep it private." She zippered the side of the dress and looked at her reflection from the waist up in the mirror above the sink. *Not bad.*

"Most members of the BDSM community do. If we run into other members in public, outside of the club, we either act like we know them from someplace else or don't know them at all."

Kristen opened the door and stepped out for them to see. She'd only worn the dress once before to a gala on New Year's Eve after she first got married. Her ex hadn't liked the revealing one-shoulder design, complaining she had too many men staring at her. But she loved how the ruching at the waist gave her size-twelve body an hourglass figure. The hem stopped mid-thigh, and she tugged it down a little, trying to hide the fact she had no underwear on.

"Bow-chicka-wow-wow." Leave it to Will to say something to make her laugh and forget how nervous she was.

Kayla whistled. "Damn girl, I'm going to have to borrow that someday. You look hot."

Kristen looked at her reflection in the mirror attached to her closet door, turning from side to side to see the dress from all possible angles. She may never be skinny by today's standards, but some of Will's friends had told her, with her generous curves, give her a blond wig and she would've given Marilyn Monroe some serious competition. "You sure I look okay? It's not too slutty looking?"

"Slutty? No. High class call-girl? Yes. And it's the way you want to look, trust me on this. Now, let's see what we can do with your hair and makeup. Will, can you find her a pair of shoes to wear?" Kayla led her back into the bathroom and Kristen tried to imagine Devon's reaction when he saw her. Would he like her dress or would he complain about it like her ex-husband had? She prayed it was the former.

DEVON GLANCED at his watch for the fourth time in under two minutes as he paced back and forth in front of Tuscany, the restaurant they were meeting at. She was ten minutes late. He had wanted to pick her up at her home, but decided not to suggest it, figuring she would be more comfortable this way, given the fact he was still a relative stranger to her. A fact he intended to rectify as soon as possible.

As much as he wanted to use her lateness as an excuse to spank her delicious backside, he was more worried she'd changed her mind and chickened out. He'd been shocked when he first saw her standing in the middle of the pit. However, the shock had morphed into anger and jealousy at the fact she was in his club with Mitch and not him. The two of them hadn't been doing anything other than talking, but, damn it, he wanted to be the one to introduce her to BDSM . . . especially since he now knew she was researching the lifestyle he loved.

Behind him, he heard the sound of heels clicking fast down the sidewalk. Turning, he froze as Kristen hurried toward him. She was beautiful. Her brown hair fell around her face in soft curls and he longed to run his fingers through them. Her styled hair and the subtle makeup, which lit up her face, made him realize she put in an extra effort while preparing for their date and the thought made his heart race. He watched as she approached him and he managed to get a peek of her black dress under the lightweight rain coat she wore. Although the temperature was cooler than normal for a late September evening, it wasn't cold or rainy out and he assumed the coat was for modesty. He hoped it meant her dress was a little out of her comfort zone.

"Sorry I'm late." She tried to catch her breath. "I couldn't find my car keys and then I couldn't find a parking spot." Unlike Donovan's, Tuscany didn't have a parking lot and customers had to find on-street parking.

"It's all right, Pet. I'll just take it out on your backside later."

Kristen gaped at him. "You want to spank me because I'm ten minutes late?"

"Yup." He looked at his watch. "And you're thirteen minutes late, so I think that calls for thirteen smacks. It's a decent amount for your first spanking."

Not giving her a chance to respond, he took her arm and escorted her into the restaurant. While they waited for the hostess, he helped her out of her coat and tried to keep from swallowing his tongue. Damn. When he told her to wear the sexiest dress she had, he didn't expect her to have one which made her look like a seductive siren. Between the dress, her mile long legs, and those three-inch black stilettos, the woman was going to give him a heart attack. He was going to have to fuck her in nothing but those heels sometime real soon.

He folded her coat over his arm, using it to hide the swelling in his pants, and leaned over to whisper in her ear. "You look gorgeous, Pet. I wish I could bend you over a table and fuck you right here in front of everyone. But since I can't, tell me, did you obey my orders? Did you leave your underwear at home? Because if you didn't, we're heading straight to the ladies room, and I don't care who sees us."

---

A PINK BLUSH rose to her cheeks and Kristen almost wished she'd disobeyed him because she could feel a rush of arousal coating her pussy. If he kept talking to her like that, it would be dripping down her legs soon.

"Yes." She whispered the word, afraid someone would overhear her and know how turned on she was.

"Prove it."

She gasped as her cheeks heated even more. They were in the front of a crowded restaurant and he wanted her to prove she wasn't wearing any underwear. How the heck was she supposed to do it without getting arrested for indecent exposure? "H-How?"

He must have read her mind because he chuckled. "Not the way you're thinking, Pet. Turn around, nice and slow, and let me feel if you have any panty lines."

He put his hand on her hip and she made a complete turn, his hand staying in contact with her body the entire rotation, across both hips, the top of her buttocks, and across her lower abdomen. When she was once again facing him, she glanced around and was relieved no one appeared to be paying them any attention.

"Very good, Pet. You saved yourself from additional punishment, although I'm sure I'll find something else which will add to the count before the night is over."

She was grateful to have his teasing interrupted when the hostess chose that moment to approach them and Devon gave his name which the reservations were under. It gave Kristen a chance to get her heated body back under control and inspect her date. He was wearing dark gray, dress slacks, black loafers, and a white button down shirt with the sleeves folded up to the middle of his forearms. His shirt wasn't tight, but it was the perfect cut to showcase his physique. He wore no jewelry other than a black dive watch on his left wrist. The look was simple, yet classic, and he could have graced this month's cover of GQ magazine and had millions of women drooling over him. And those thoughts gave her pause. The man could be dating a supermodel if he wanted, so what was he doing here with her? She glanced around and noticed, now that he was facing the other patrons, several women were gawking at him in obvious interest.

She tamped her jealousy down and when the hostess told them to follow her, Devon motioned for Kristen to walk in front of him. The whole way across the restaurant she got the feeling he was ogling her ass as they made their way to a table against the far wall. The thought made her smile and she put a little more sway in her hips. She could have sworn she heard a low growl and she giggled to herself.

When they reached their table, she was surprised he pulled out a chair for her to sit on before taking his own seat across from her. The gesture made her feel like a lady. She couldn't remember Tom ever holding out her chair for her. She watched as Devon draped her coat over the back of the empty chair next to him before the hostess handed them their menus and excused herself. Although there were only two place settings at the table, it could seat four people, which Kristen was happy about. She hated tables for two because there was never enough room and she always found herself knocking over a glass of wine or water. The last thing she wanted tonight was to look like a klutz.

A smartly dressed waiter approached their table and filled their water glasses. "Good evening, my name is Kevin, and I'll be your waiter. Can I get you anything from the bar while you look over your menus?"

Devon looked at Kristen and arched his brow in question. "Would you like a glass of wine or something else?"

"White wine, please—a Riesling if they have it."

He nodded then turned back to the young man who stood waiting. "A Riesling for the lady, and I'll have tonic water with lime. Thank you."

"You're not having any alcohol?" she asked, after the waiter left to get their order.

"No, I don't drink."

"Ever?" It sounded like it was the weirdest thing she ever heard, but she didn't know any men who didn't at least have the occasional beer or two.

"No."

The way he said the one word made it clear to her it would be best if she changed the subject. She opened her menu and began looking at the choices. Everything sounded so delicious.

"So, what's good on the menu, since this is my first time here? What are you getting?"

When he didn't answer right away, she glanced up and saw a sexy smile on his face. "Well, since what I want to eat isn't on the menu," he paused, and her face heated, "I'm having the steak pizzaiola. It's one of the chef's specialties. What do you prefer— beef, chicken, veal, seafood, or pasta?"

"I pretty much eat anything, but I'm leaning toward either the veal piccata or the mushroom-crusted salmon. Which do you recommend?"

"I've never had the salmon, but I can assure you, you won't be disappointed with the veal."

Kristen giggled. "You sound like a car salesman."

Devon laughed at her comparison. The waiter returned with their drinks and they placed their dinner orders. A few minutes later, they were enjoying Caesar salads and warm fresh Italian bread.

"So, Ms. Kristen Anders, tell me about yourself, other than what's in the short biography I read on the back of Jenn's book."

She took a sip of her wine. "What would you like to know?"

Shrugging his shoulder, he picked up a small pepper mill and added some black pepper to his salad. He held the mill up toward her and she shook her head. "I don't know—tell me about your family, where you grew up, what you did before becoming a romance writer. Things you've told other guys on a first date."

"Well, since I've only had a few first dates in my life, and my last first date was over four years ago, I'm not sure I remember what I talked about on them."

Devon stopped his salad fork halfway to his mouth and stared at her in surprise. "Okay, explain please, because I find it hard to believe you aren't beating men off with a stick."

Kristen blushed, which she did a lot around him, and stared at her own salad like it was the most interesting thing in the world. He put his fork down, reached across the table and placed two fingers under her chin, lifting it until she was looking at him again. His eyes were a deeper blue tonight in the low restaurant lighting. "Talk to me, Kristen. Believe it or not, I've never said this to a woman before, but you fascinate me, and I want to know everything about you."

She doubted it was true, but it did prompt her to start talking. "I was a bookworm through high school and college—kind of nerdy. I was shy around guys, I guess, and didn't date a lot. I had one serious boyfriend my sophomore year of college, but he got tired . . ." She paused, not wanting to finish the sentence.

"Tired of what, Pet?"

She didn't know what it was about that one word, but it made her heart pound faster and she liked the nickname. It felt intimate, though she doubted she was the only woman he used it on. "He got tired of me telling him no." She lowered her voice, so he was the only person who could hear her. She couldn't believe she was telling him this ten minutes into their first date, but she couldn't stop the words. "You see, I was a virgin on my wedding night two years ago. I met Tom my senior year, and although we fooled around, something in me wanted to wait. I know it sounds silly in this day and age, but it was important to me."

"It's not silly at all, Kristen. I think it shows what a strong woman you are. One who knows what she wants and what she doesn't. And you're willing to fight for what feels right to you. There's nothing wrong with waiting for the right guy, and I respect you for doing it." He paused when a look of disbelief appeared on her pretty face. "What?"

The corners of her mouth twitched as she held back a smirk. "I find it hard to believe you respect my long-term virginity when you own a sex club."

He let out a small snort. "Okay, I can see your point, but what I said was true. Guys have no trouble losing their virginity and having sex with any woman who is willing, but women are wired differently. Sex is more emotional for them . . . well, most of them. I hope my niece waits for the right guy, and don't even think of making me believe she is anything but a virgin."

"Yeah, well, in my case, the right guy didn't come along. My ex-husband had been cheating on me the whole time we were dating and while we were married. But I didn't find out until it was too late. The skanks he preferred wouldn't look like a good wife for a respected stockbroker, like the goody-two-shoes I was."

"What an asshole—excuse my language."

Kristen couldn't help snickering at him. "Let's see, you've told me you want to fuck me on a table and spank my ass, so I think calling my ex an asshole is rather tame."

He laughed along with her. "All right, enough about your ex-fudge pecker. Tell me about *you*."

"Little ol' me?"

Devon pointed his fork at her before digging into his salad again. "Yes, Pet. Little ol' you. Start talking or I'll start adding to the count of thirteen."

"You wouldn't," she gaped.

"Fourteen."

"All right, all right. Has anyone ever said you would make a good interrogator?"

"Fifteen."

"I was born in a log cabin . . ."

He rolled his eyes. She was pushing her luck. "Sixteen."

"No, it's true. I was born in a log cabin. My parents went to my dad's family's cabin in the Poconos a month before my mom's due date. They figured it would be the last chance they had to get away, you know, just the two of them. The next morning, mom woke up in full-blown labor. She didn't realize she'd been in labor for over twenty-four hours because the contractions weren't that strong, until all of a sudden she felt the need to push. Before my dad had a chance to get her to the car, I started crowning and, whoops, there I was. Dad was a cop, but he had never delivered a baby before. He did fine until the ambulance got there. After he let the EMTs in, though, he passed out, hit his head on a table and needed ten stitches. He always said that's why I was an only child."

They were both laughing as the waiter took their salad plates and replaced them with their dinners. Devon asked the young man for another round of drinks before turning his attention back to her. "I think I would've done and said the exact same thing. I've seen a lot in my life, things which would scare the hell out of most people, but delivering a kid would send me into a panic—and I never panic." He paused as a busboy stopped and refilled their water glasses. "So, okay, you're an only child. Are your folks still around?"

She nodded and picked up her knife and fork. "Yes. They divorced when I was ten. Mom, Elizabeth, was an elementary school teacher and never learned how to live with a cop who was always being called into work on days off and holidays. His rotating shifts didn't help matters. Although he's always been a good father, mom said dad wasn't even close to being a part-time husband.

Looking back, I'm surprised their marriage lasted as long as it did. As divorces go, it was friendly. No fighting over who gets what, or those sorts of things. Dad, his name is Bill, got remarried when I was fifteen to a nice lady, named Susan, who works in the courts. He retired from the Philadelphia police department two years later. He's now teaching criminal justice at the community college. Mom and my step-dad, Ed—he's an insurance adjuster—eloped to Vegas three months after my wedding and moved to the Jersey shore a few months later. I have two older step-brothers, but we barely know each other. They live near their mom about an hour from where we lived."

"So did you always live in Philadelphia? When did you move here?"

"Actually we lived a few miles outside Philly in New Hope, and then I lived in Ridgewood, New Jersey, after I got married. I only moved here a few weeks ago after my divorce was final."

"Why here?"

Kristen chewed and swallowed a piece of veal before answering him. "My cousin, Will, has lived in Tampa for the past six or seven years, and I loved the area the few times I came down to visit him. I wanted a new start, so here I am. What about you? Have you always lived in Tampa?"

"No. My brothers and I were born and raised in Charlotte, North Carolina. After the Navy, Ian and I decided to open our security business here. Mitch was raised here, and like you, we visited a lot and liked it. We were still getting our security firm on its feet when Mitch approached us about the club, and the rest, as they say, is history."

"It must've been difficult and expensive. I mean the club is beautiful, and I can't imagine what it took to transform the place while starting another business. And, oh my God, it sounds like I'm trying to find out how much money you have. Don't answer, I don't want to know. I'm just going to remove my foot from my mouth." She was babbling but couldn't stop. It was a bad habit which occurred when she was embarrassed.

Devon didn't look upset—instead, he seemed amused. He held

out a piece of steak and peppers on his fork. "Here, replace your foot with this."

When she reached for the fork, he pulled his hand back. "Uh-uh, Pet. Open your mouth and close your eyes. I want to feed you."

---

Kristen's eyes widened before she leaned forward and did as he requested. He eased the fork into her mouth taking care not to stab her with the tines. When she closed her lips around the fork and moaned as the flavors hit her tongue, he would have sold his soul at that moment to replace the fork with his throbbing cock. He eased the fork out of her mouth, allowing her to chew and swallow the food. "Mmmm, it's delicious."

Clearing his throat, he shifted in his seat. "Glad you like it. I'd offer you more, but I think if I did, I'd come in my pants."

Her eyes flew open again, and she had to see the desire in his eyes. Swallowing, she shifted her gaze back to her plate. "Um . . . so . . . um . . . what about you? You said you have a brother, Ian. Any others? Are your folks still in Charlotte?"

Devon paused for a moment. He always found it difficult to talk about his brothers. It was also one of the reasons he never dated outside the club. With a submissive, they didn't need to know him beyond the surface, beyond what he was willing to give. He rarely mentioned John to people who inquired about his family, since it always made the conversation depressive and awkward. "We have a younger brother, Nick. He's in the Navy stationed in San Diego. Ian's the oldest. Mom and Dad are still based out of Charlotte, but they travel a lot. My dad, Chuck, is in real estate and has done well for himself. He has a corporation now with a board which runs it for him when he's out of the country with mom. Mom, Marie, is a plastic surgeon, although now she only practices in Charlotte enough to maintain her hospital privileges. She has a small stake in a practice with four other doctors, but her main focus is working in third-world countries for Operation Smile."

"Isn't Operation Smile the organization which offers surgeries for kids with cleft lips or palates?"

He nodded and took a sip of tonic water. "Or other facial deformities, yes. When we were young, my brothers and I traveled all over the world with my folks, and by the time I went into the Navy, I was on my third passport. We spent every summer digging wells, building schools and huts, and everything else we could do to help."

"Wow, that's amazing!" She sounded impressed, and even though it hadn't been his intent, it pleased him. "I've never been out of the United States except for Jamaica on my honeymoon. And the most I ever did when I was younger was volunteer at the animal shelter five minutes from my house."

He could imagine a younger Kristen playing with, and caring for, a bunch of animals looking for forever homes. She probably cried after each one got adopted. "Yeah, well, it was fun when we were younger, but by the time we were in junior high, we wanted to stay home and hang out with our friends and girlfriends—typical teenage selfishness. When we hit high school and started working, my grandparents on my mom's side would spend the summer at our house so my folks could go do their thing. Nowadays though, Ian and I try to take a week or so a few times a year to meet up with my parents in whatever country they're in. We spend the time doing what we can to make some poor village a little less desperate for the people who live there."

---

KRISTEN COULD TELL how much he loved his family by listening to the affection in his voice. Although her parents and step-parents got along well and she loved them all, there were times she wished her folks were still together and had given her a brother or a sister.

"Kristen."

She looked up, realizing her mind had wandered and the waiter was clearing their plates while Devon stared at her.

"I'm sorry, what?"

"Did you want coffee or dessert?"

"Oh, no thanks. I'm full." *And I want to leave for The Covenant and jump your bones*—but she wouldn't say that out loud. Too bad they weren't allowed to play at the club.

"We'll take the check, thanks," Devon told the waiter, who nodded before taking their plates to the kitchen.

As he reached into his pocket for his wallet, Kristen jumped and grabbed her evening bag. "Let me split this with you."

She froze when he let out a low growl. "If you take anything other than a lipstick out of your purse, I will pull you across my lap right here and spank you until the cops show up."

Stunned by his fierce expression, she left her purse on the seat next to her. "I just thought since this was our first date, and I was the one to ask you out—"

He held up his hand. "Do not finish the sentence. Under no circumstances will I let you put a penny toward our dinner. You may have asked me out, but it was only because I thought you were seeing Brody. Otherwise, I would have done it. I've never allowed a woman to pay for dinner, and I'm not going to start now."

"Isn't that a little sexist?" She sat back and placed her hands in her lap, a little put off by his reaction.

He leaned forward, his arms resting on the table. "You may have written a book based on BDSM, but you still don't completely understand the lifestyle. Let me explain something about Doms to you, Pet. We like to . . . no . . . we demand to be in charge when it comes to certain things. Aside from the sexual aspect, we want to ensure our sub's safety and comfort. To treat them as if they are the most precious thing on this earth. I know a few Doms who will tell you their favorite part of a scene is the aftercare, because it's when their subs need them the most. It's when they connect the most.

"We care for our subs, giving them everything we can and wishing we could give them the moon if they asked for it—whether it's for one night only or a long-term relationship. We don't do it because we're sexist or think they can't take care of themselves. We do it because it pleases us in a way you can't imagine. It's something we crave beyond the basic human instinct and need to have sex.

The lifestyle is so much more than kinky sex and giving up or taking control. And all we Doms expect from our subs in return is respect and obedience . . . well, that and their orgasms. Now if you want to argue with me about money, I will be more than happy to continue the count. I believe we're at sixteen."

She'd tilted her head as she listened to all he said. This was what she'd been looking for when she'd gone to The Covenant for research. There was only so much she could find on the Internet, but what she hadn't been able to comprehend was the passion and need of a Dom to take control. Now she understood that part of BDSM, but she still had to discover why a submissive needed to give up the control. "No, it's fifteen. You said sixteen when you thought I was lying about the log cabin."

"Well, now it's back to sixteen for arguing with me about the count and the check."

"That's not fair," she huffed, crossing her arms across her chest like a petulant child.

Devon chuckled and, when the waiter returned with a small leather folder, he handed over his credit card. "Whoever said life is fair, Pet, wasn't a Dom."

# CHAPTER 7

$\mathcal{T}$he assassin took a swig of whiskey and watched as Eric Prichard rounded the corner onto County Road #32. The former Navy SEAL was starting the fourth mile of his evening run with four more miles to go. It wouldn't be dark for another forty minutes or so and the target would be turning around at a bank of mailboxes a little further up the road to backtrack toward his home. But if the coast was clear this time, he wasn't going to finish those last four miles. The assassin had been observing the man's habits for the past week, looking for his opportunity to strike.

After locating Prichard, he realized he would have to do the job away from the man's residence. The former SEAL and his wife had four children, and even though the assassin killed people for a profit without a second thought, he drew the line at murdering children. It was the only time his conscience wouldn't let him kill unless necessary, but oddly enough, the moment a kid turned eighteen they were considered expendable. Had his earlier target's eighteen-year-old daughter been home when he broke into their house and shot her parents six months ago, she would have been a third body the police found. A slumber party saved her from certain death.

It'd been three months since his last kill for the man paying him because the bastard didn't want to get his own hands dirty. The first kill on the list of seven men occurred six months ago. His temporary employer wanted them spaced out so no one would notice a pattern. Seven dead former Navy SEALs from the same team would raise a lot of questions, but by that time there would be no one left who could figure out the how's and why's. After he took out Prichard, the assassin would head to Tampa to track the last four names on his execution list—Ian Sawyer, his brother Devon Sawyer, Brody Evans, and Jake Donovan. He would have to find a way to take them out together while still making it look like an accident since, according to the files he had been given, they worked and hung out together along with two other former SEALs. He might be able to take out one or two before they realized they were targeted and went underground, making it much harder to kill the rest of them.

Stalking men who had been trained to do the stalking themselves was a delicate job. Over a week ago, he'd found a used car dealership two towns over from the bum-fuck town in Iowa where his target lived. The business lacked decent security so he picked the lock to the office in under a minute and helped himself to the keys to their available vehicles, some of which were kept in an overflow lot a few blocks away. Using a different car and different disguise each day, he was able to keep his target from spotting him, but there had been a few moments when the man seemed to sense he was being watched, so the assassin had to be smarter than his prey.

Finishing a count to three hundred, the killer-for-hire put the car in gear, took one last sip from his flask and pulled out from behind an abandoned laundromat. By now his target would be running back toward town on a straightaway while facing oncoming traffic. Although the man ran along the narrow shoulder, he didn't flinch when cars drove past. He'd passed Prichard twice this week on his run, but there had been cars with witnesses on the road.

Taking the turn Prichard had disappeared around minutes before, the assassin straightened the steering wheel and accelerated to the posted fifty miles per hour speed limit. His target was where he expected the man to be, unknowingly running at a decent clip toward his tragic death.

One hundred yards. He could see the target's black shirt, military green sweatpants, and white sneakers.

Fifty yards. He could read the yellow lettering spelling out "U.S. Navy" on the man's chest.

Twenty yards. The target looked at his watch and upped his pace.

Ten yards. The dead man running made eye contact with him a second before the assassin swerved.

A half hour later, he dropped off the used and now damaged car, wiped it clean of prints, and retrieved his own vehicle. He typed off a one word text on his burner cell—*Done*—then pulled out onto the road leading to the interstate where he would dismantle the phone and throw a part out the window every few miles.

# CHAPTER 8

*O*nce they were on their way to The Covenant, Kristen became nervous again. She had been twisting her hands together until Devon reached over and took hold of her left hand, intertwined their fingers, then rested them on her lap thigh. His thumb was now brushing her thigh, below her hemline, back and forth. With those soft, reassuring caresses, she tried to settle into the comfortable silence and let her mind wander.

She hadn't thought she would be interested in BDSM, but after her interaction with Devon earlier at the club, she wasn't sure now. She'd been so turned on she'd ended up masturbating in the shower before Kayla and Will got there. And instead of Master Xavier urging her on, this time it had been Master Devon.

"I meant to ask you earlier, but we got a little sidetracked. Did you bring your limit list with you?"

Kristen turned her head to examine his profile as he drove. "Yes, it's folded in my purse. I also reviewed the protocols."

He nodded and glanced over at her before returning his attention to the road. "Good. I'll look over your list when we get to the club. Do you have any questions about the protocols?"

She thought back to the papers she read. Most of the rules were pretty straight forward, but she still wanted to clarify a few of them.

"Yes, I do. Some rules were listed under the heading 'High Protocols' while others weren't. How do I know when I'm supposed to follow the 'High Protocol' rules?'"

---

DEVON HAD BEEN happy when she agreed to leave her car near the restaurant and ride to the club with him. He left the convertible top closed, not wanting the wind to ruin her styled hair. He wanted to save the pleasure for later when he got a chance to run his fingers through those soft brown curls. "Most of the members follow the relaxed protocols unless we are having an event which would require the more rigid ones, and everyone is notified of those in advance. There are a few Doms who insist their subs follow the stricter rules, but if one of them approaches you, I'll let you know. If it does happen, remember to keep your head bowed, do not make eye contact with the Dom or their sub, if they have one, and ask my permission to speak before saying anything to them. Never be rude to a Dom in any situation. You'll be next to me most of the time, but if for some reason I'm not there, and a Dom is bothering you, immediately look for a Dungeon Master who wears a gold vest or a security officer who wears a red, button-down shirt with a black bowtie and let them know. Just because you're a submissive does not give a Dom or another submissive permission to harass you for any reason. Most of our members are not a problem, but like every large group it has its jackasses and bitches."

"What's the difference between the Dungeon Masters and the security officers?"

He squeezed her hand before releasing it, needing both hands to navigate the sharp turn from the highway ramp to the road leading to the club. He missed the warmth and reclaimed her hand as soon as he was able. "The Dungeon Masters are experienced Doms who keep an eye on the scenes going on throughout the club. I think we have a total of thirty-two of them. They ensure all play at the club is safe and keep the subs from getting injured in case a Dom overlooks something such as a restraint too tight or a sub not using their safeword when they should. The security officers keep an eye on everything else and are the bouncers of the club."

A confused expression came over her face. "Why would a submissive not use their safeword when it's obvious to a monitor they should?"

Devon sighed as he stopped two cars back from the guard shack at the entrance to the club parking lot. The lead car must be either a newer member or guest who the guard didn't recognize because he was checking the driver's ID with a handheld computer. It was another one of Brody's toys the club used on a regular basis. "Sometimes what a sub thinks they want isn't what they need and not saying their safeword can be a destructive behavior. How can I explain it?" He paused. "Do you know what 'cutting' is?"

"I've heard of that. Isn't it when a person, sometimes teenagers, cut their arms with razor blades?"

The line of cars was now moving again and the guard waved at Devon as he passed. "People who cut themselves in order to feel whatever it is they are looking to feel, don't cut deep enough to bleed out, but it's still dangerous. They feel compelled to cut themselves, for whatever reason, causing damage to their bodies, and they usually can't stop without psychological help. It's what a sub who doesn't use their safeword when they should is doing— damaging themselves in order to feel whatever it is they are trying to feel. A good Dom needs to know how to find the fine line between what a sub needs to make them feel good and what is going too far and damaging the sub's psyche and body. If a DM thinks a sub is pushing his- or herself too far, to the point of severe injury via a Dom, the sub is referred to one of our contracted psychologists and can't play again unless they get an okay from the doctor. It doesn't happen often, but we're serious about our submissives' safety here— physically, psychologically, and emotionally."

He'd parked his car a few minutes earlier and sat there finishing his explanation before opening his car door. When she reached for the latch to open her own door, he stopped her. "Do not even think of opening your door. Stay there until I come around or I'll add to your spanking count."

She laughed out loud and he couldn't help but grin at her amusement. "Is this one of those things that brings you pleasure, Master Devon?"

God, how he loved how she combined his title with his name. He'd heard it from the mouths of hundreds of subs over the years, but never had a woman gotten him hard by saying those two words —until now. "Yes, my little subbie, it is. Now stay there."

He adjusted himself as he walked around the back of his car and then opened her door. Putting his hand out to help her up from the low seat, he couldn't tear his eyes away as the hemline of her dress crept further up her legs when she exited the car. He was almost tempted to push it up a little further so he could see if she was bare or not between her legs. Bare was his personal preference. "Didn't your ex ever open your door for you?"

"Now that you mention it, no he didn't."

"Well, there's another reason to hate the selfish prick-bastard."

Kristen laughed at him again as she tugged her skirt back down, which wouldn't go any further than the middle of her thighs. "You don't know him, how can you say you hate him?"

Reaching into his pocket he retrieved the item he had placed there earlier. "Easily, Pet. Any man who would cheat on, disrespect, and leave a beautiful woman like you deserves to be despised and degraded by the rest of his gender." He held up his hand and let the object dangle from it so she could see it. "This is a training collar, Pet. You'll wear it while you're here at the club with me. It'll let the other Doms know you're spoken for and they're not allowed to try and negotiate with you or demand you follow a certain protocol without my permission. I may order you to kneel, but another Dom would have to get my approval for them to tell you to do the same, except in extreme cases. Some Doms like to tease the subs and it's not considered rude here unless it's insulting, and I will not allow anyone to insult you. If I have to leave you for some reason, I'll ask a DM or security to keep an eye on you until I return. Understood?"

"Yes, Sir." She nodded and turned around, lifting her hair so he could fasten the collar around her neck. It was a simple black leather band and he regretted not having a nicer one to give her. He never had a sub wear one of his collars for more than a weekend, but this time he found himself not wanting to think about uncollaring her when they were done playing tonight.

When she turned back around, fingering the leather band, he found his hands reaching up to cup her face. Looking into her hazel eyes, he lowered his mouth to hers, a scant inch at a time, waiting for her to stop him, to let him know she didn't want this. But she didn't stop him and he sent up a silent thanks to whomever or whatever had brought this woman to him at this moment. The second his mouth touched hers, her eyes fluttered shut. The kiss was light, a soft brushing of his lips against hers, until she sighed and her lips parted, granting him entry. He deepened the kiss, darting his tongue into her mouth to tangle with hers, dying for a taste of her. He savored the sweetness of her wine, the tartness of the lemon from her dinner, and something delicious and unique to Kristen. And for tonight she belonged to him, he just didn't know how he would be able to let her go when they were done playing. *Mine.*

When her hands began to move up his arms toward his neck, he grabbed her wrists and put a reluctant end to the kiss. Her eyes reopened as if she was waking from a long slumber, and he smiled. "Sorry, Pet, but if I let you touch me, I'm going to go off like a rocket." He pressed his hips to hers in order to make his point. He gave her another quick kiss before releasing her wrists, turning her to his side and tucking her one hand under his arm. Thankfully, it was normal to see men walking around the club with hard-ons because his wasn't going down anytime soon.

Moments later, they were standing in the lobby at the front desk which was being attended by a slight, but toned man who was about Kristen's age. He was shirtless, but wore a pair of black dress pants and a red bow tie with gold trim. The man smiled and nodded at her before speaking to Devon. "Good evening, Master Devon, how are you tonight?"

"I'm good, Matthew. And you?"

"Very good, Sir, since I'm scheduled to scene with Mistress China later."

Devon winced knowing that meant the sub's cock and balls were going to be tortured before the night was over. It wasn't something Devon could imagine subjecting his man parts to, but the younger sub enjoyed it.

"Matthew, this is Ms. Kristen, my guest this evening. Kristen, Matthew is one of the club's long-time employees, and he's also a submissive. If you ever have any questions, he can answer them from a sub's point of view."

When she nodded, he took her arm and extending it outward over the desk so Matthew could place a yellow band around her wrist. When he was done, the sub patted her hand. "It's nice to meet you Kristen. This indicates you're a guest and not allowed to participate in any play. And Master Devon is right, if you have any questions, I'm an expert on club protocol. By the way, love your dress."

Kristen smiled at his friendly manner. "Thank you, and it's nice to meet you, too."

Devon took her hand and tucked it under his arm again before leading her over to a large man dressed in black slacks and a red button-down shirt standing next to the wooden doors leading into the club. "Kristen, this is Tiny, the head of security. Tiny, this is Kristen."

---

SHE TILTED HER HEAD UP . . . and up . . . and up. Good Lord, the man was tall . . . and broad. He was about six foot eight and two-hundred-seventy-five pounds of solid muscle. His neck was too thick to close the top button of his shirt so he was without a bowtie. Bald with a goatee, he reminded Kristen of a wrestler from the eighties who became an actor, Mr. G or something like that. The only thing he was missing was the gold chains. "Tiny?"

The man laughed and gave her a wink. "Yes ma'am. My real name is Travis, but I've gone by Tiny since I was born weighing thirteen pounds. It's a pleasure to meet you."

Before she could reply, Devon spoke again. "Tiny, would you be so kind as to keep an eye on my sub for a few minutes while I run and change? I'm afraid she'll cause a riot inside if I leave her unattended."

"Absolutely, Master Devon. I don't doubt she'd cause trouble in there. The Doms will be falling all over themselves the second they spot this cute little thing." Tiny took a step to the left and revealed a stool she hadn't known was behind him. "Have a seat up here, Ms. Kristen, and I'll keep the big, bad Doms from killing each other trying to get at you."

She doubted that would happen, but still smiled at his compliment. "Thank you, Master Tiny."

"Uh-uh, Ms. Kristen. It's just Tiny, since I'm not a Dom nor do I participate in the lifestyle. I only work here so I can check out pretty ladies such as yourself and pound on the occasional idiot who gets out of hand."

She laughed and relaxed again. "I get the feeling you're nothing but a big teddy bear."

"Hey, I like it. Tiny the teddy bear."

Devon helped her up on the stool before giving her a fast kiss on the lips. "Take out your list and hand me your purse. You won't need it inside so I'll put it in my locker for safe keeping." She did as he requested and handed him both. "I'll be right back, Pet. Stay here with Tiny, and you'll be fine."

"Yes, sir."

He grinned then disappeared through the big wooden doors leading into the club. The pounding music increased in volume before becoming a dull beat when the door closed again. She felt a little self-conscious sitting on the stool and turned toward the big man next to her after tugging at her dress to keep from flashing him. "So how long have you worked here?"

He opened the door to allow a couple to walk in, and waited until the music died down before answering her. "Ever since the club opened. Have you met Master Jake yet?"

Jake was the man who met Devon at the pub the day before while they were making their dinner plans. "Yes, I think so, but only briefly, and I didn't know he was a Dom then."

Tiny leaned against the wall, crossing his arm over his massive chest, and Kristen couldn't help but wonder what size shirt the man wore. "Jake and I go way back to our high school football days. After I got injured in the pros, I ended up doing bodyguard work in Hollywood. Then a few years ago, while I was down here visiting family, I ran into Jake, and he recommended me to Ian and Devon. When they offered me a job, I moved as fast as I could from L.A. I still do occasional bodyguard work for them when needed, but mostly I'm in charge of the club's security.

She found it odd he was working in a BDSM club, yet not participating in the lifestyle, and told him so.

The big man shrugged. "To each his own. Even though it's not for me personally, doesn't mean I find anything wrong with the lifestyle. Like I said earlier, at least I get to see a lot of pretty girls in hot outfits. And just when I thought I've seen it all, something happens that makes me laugh. It can be pretty entertaining working here."

"I'll bet. I'm glad you found a job you enjoy." Kristen watched as Tiny opened the doors to allow three women in various states of dress to enter the main club and found herself thinking she was a little overdressed. One woman was wearing a black leather mini-skirt and a matching bustier which left her midsection exposed. The shortest of the three had on a red satin and sheer teddy which stopped an inch above her knees, while the last one wore a sheer, black dress shirt over a bra and thong set. Two of them wore ballet-type slippers in place of shoes, but the blonde in the skirt had removed her slippers and held them in her hand, opting to go barefoot. Although two of the women were on the skinny side, the one wearing the teddy was a size or two larger than Kristen, and she wondered if she would be as confident looking as the other woman had she been wearing a similar outfit. After the door closed again, she looked back up at Tiny. "Do you miss playing football?"

He tilted his head as if thinking about his answer before verbalizing it. "Yeah, I do, sometimes. But unlike some guys who go pro, I knew I wasn't going to play forever. And when life hands you lemons . . ."

"You make lemonade," she finished the cliché for him.

"If you have a lemonade stand, little one, I'd be more than happy to stop by for a taste." A deep male voice startled her, and she tensed before turning to find a strange man standing a little too close for her comfort, although he wasn't touching her. "I'm sure anything you have to offer would be the sweetest of fruit."

She gaped at the man who was now devouring her with his gaze. This was what she had expected Master Mitch to look like when she met him. If she had to guess, the man was in his fifties, with a pointed nose, narrow eyes and mustache. His black hair was graying at the temples and upper lip. Slender, he stood about six-foot even and was dressed in a black dress shirt and leather pants with black boots. Never taking his leering stare off her, he addressed the large security guard. "Tell me, Tiny, who is this gorgeous creature? I see she has a collar. I may have to challenge her Dom to a duel to win her favor."

Was this guy for real? She looked up to see Tiny smiling down at her, and she relaxed only a fraction when he winked again at her. "Good evening, Master Carl. This is Ms. Kristen, a guest of Master Devon."

The older man sighed and frowned before he took a small step backward. "Such a pity since he can kill a man in a number of ways, I'm sure. Master Devon is a lucky man, but please come find me when he removes your collar, girl. I would love to play with you for an evening. I guarantee I'd make it most enjoyable for both of us."

An involuntary shudder passed through her body as she watched the man disappear through the club doors. She didn't like how he'd said "*when* he removes your collar" instead of *if,* and reached up to touch the thin band wrapped around her neck, not wanting to think this might be her only evening with Devon.

"Unless you're into a great deal of pain, you might want to avoid Master Carl. He's actually a nice guy, but a sadist."

Kristen's eyes widened, but before she could say anything in response to Tiny's comment, the doors next to him reopened and Devon stepped back out into the lobby. Her mouth watered at the sight of him. He'd changed out of his dinner clothes and was now wearing a tight black T-shirt which showed off his defined arms and torso. A pair of black leather pants hugged his lower body as if they had been painted on. Replacing a zipper, the crotch was laced up and showcased the large bulge behind it.

He grabbed her hips and helped her off the stool, pulling her close so their lower bodies made contact. "Ready?"

"I-I think so."

Tiny spoke up at the tremble in her voice. "She met Master Carl a minute ago."

Devon rolled his eyes. "Wonderful. He really needs to stop scaring the new subs." The sarcasm was evident in his voice, but then he became serious. "Relax, Pet. You're safe with me. No one will touch you in there except for me. If you have any questions, just ask. And if something makes you uncomfortable, tell me. I won't be upset if something bothers you, but I will be if you keep it from me. A major portion of this lifestyle depends on verbal communication between a Dom and sub."

The tension in her shoulders eased a little, but she was still worried. "What if I make a mistake?"

He brought his hand up to cup her chin. "You're bound to make a few mistakes, and it's expected. Everyone in there was new to the lifestyle at one point and mistakes happen. Okay?"

When she nodded, he frowned and raised his brow. It took her a second to figure out what was wrong. "I mean, yes, Sir."

Taking her hand, he nodded at Tiny and started for the doors. "Besides, mistakes lead to punishment, and punishment leads to pleasure for both of us . . . eventually."

Kristen's mouth dropped at his evil, yet amused tone of voice. What was she getting herself into?

---

DEVON STOOD next to Kristen at the balcony railing and watched her face as she took in the sights, sounds and smells of the club. Despite the early hour of nine-thirty, the club was close to being full, but due to the square footage of the building there was still plenty of room for members to walk around without having to fight their way through a crowd. Many of the activity stations in the pit were occupied and the sounds of spanking, flogging and ecstasy battled with the music filling the air. The beat of an instrumental version of the Rolling Stones' "Satisfaction" pulsed throughout the club. Ian had managed to find a company which made elevator music out of every possible genre. Wednesdays and Sundays, the music tended to be sensual jazz. Thursdays leaned more toward punk, techno and Goth, while Fridays and Saturdays usually had classic rock mixed with heavy metal pouring from the hidden speakers. The genre was subject to change if they were having a theme night which was about once every two months.

When they first walked into the bar area, several members had greeted them and he introduced the Doms and subs to Kristen. She'd been polite to everyone even though there were several times he knew she was trying hard not to stare at some of the states of undress. If they weren't used to it, people tended to have a difficult time talking to a naked or almost naked person's face while their private body parts were exposed. It was like being a virgin, who'd never seen a nude body, walking through a nudist colony—you didn't want to stare, but it was hard not to.

As he watched her try to look everywhere at once, he breathed in deep the aromas of leather, citrus, and sex, but it was the fresh, enticing scent of the woman next to him which held him captivated. He glanced around the upper floor and spotted several members of both sexes giving Kristen appreciative and interested looks. For the first time in his life, he found himself fighting the emotion of jealousy which was running through his veins. He wanted to strip her naked right where she stood and fuck her like a wild beast staking the claim of its mate for the entire world to see. The thought of another Dom collaring her, after he moved on to another sub, like he always did, made his stomach clench in pain. These feelings were new and strange to him and he didn't like or know how to deal with them. He didn't do relationships and he'd nothing to offer her beyond an introduction to his lifestyle and a weekend filled with intense pleasure and orgasms. The rules may state they weren't allowed to play at the club, but he had every intention of taking her back to his place at some point where there would be no restrictions other than her hard limits. But the notion of sending her away at the end of the weekend felt like a hot poker to his chest.

He watched as her eyes widened at the screaming of a female sub coming hard somewhere in the pit below them. Her nipples were distended, pushing at the fabric of her dress and he could sense her arousal. He wanted to dip his fingers under her dress and run them through what he knew would be her soaked folds. It appeared his little pet was a voyeur and he couldn't wait to let her observe a few scenes tonight. While in the locker room, he'd looked over her soft and hard limit list and been pleased with most of her choices, but he did have a few questions for her about them later.

Her tongue darted out to moisten her lips and he wished she was on her knees in front of him using that same tongue to taste and tease him. He was torturing himself with his fantasies of her and it took all his strength not to drag her off club property and fuck her silly. "Would you like something to drink? Since we won't be playing here, I can get you another glass of wine or would you prefer something else?"

"Water would be fine, please." The two glasses of wine she had with dinner were all she could tolerate and still be able to keep her wits about her. She wanted to be able to take in and remember everything she saw tonight so she could recall it all while writing tomorrow. She planned on letting Master Xavier and Rebecca have some wild monkey sex in the next chapter.

Devon stopped a bow-tied waitress walking by and grabbed two bottles of water from her tray. "Thank you, Cassandra," he said before sending the girl on her way again and handing one of the bottles to Kristen. "Bottles of water are the only beverages allowed in the pit. A lot of the subs walk around barefoot, and we don't want them to risk being cut by any broken glass."

She looked down at her shoes. "Should I take these off?"

Taking her hand and leading her to the grand staircase, he smiled. "Usually I prefer subs to be barefoot, but I love how sexy those killer heels make your legs look, so I want you to keep them on, unless, of course, they start to bother you." And yes, he was definitely going to fuck her at some point while she was wearing nothing but those shoes.

He nodded at one of the security guards at the top of the stairs and pointed to Kristen's yellow bracelet before walking past the man. As the owners, Devon, Ian, and Mitch were the only three people who didn't have key cards which needed to be checked before descending into the pit, and her wristband indicated she wasn't allowed to participate in a scene.

---

As THEY DESCENDED THE STAIRS, Kristen held on to his arm with one hand and the banister with the other. "I've always loved to wear high heels. I'm so used to them and can wear them for hours before I want to rip them off." She'd discovered designer Manolo Blahnik's shoes to be extremely comfortable, despite the height of the heels, and she owned a few pairs. They'd become her one major indulgence after the sales of her books had increased giving her a tidy savings account. It hadn't surprised her that Tom never asked how much she had in the account, which was in her name only. He couldn't imagine her books would ever be popular to the point she could live off the sales and still have money to splurge on a few indulgences. Boy, was he shocked during their divorce proceedings when he found out.

When they reached the bottom of the stairs, Kristen noticed a woman, a few years older than herself, hurrying toward them. She was wearing a hot pink bra and short pleated skirt that were only a few shades lighter than her bright pink straight hair which fell below her shoulders. The petite woman stopped right in front of them and opened her mouth to say something to Kristen, but then her eyes widened a fraction, and she closed her mouth again. Turning toward Devon, she lowered her gaze to the floor. "I'm sorry, Master Devon, forgive my impatience. May I please have permission to speak to your sub?"

He smiled at the sub. "Permission granted and, by the way,

happy birthday." He then looked at Kristen and nodded. She took it to mean she was also allowed to speak.

"Thank you, Sir." The pink-haired girl turned back to Kristen and began talking with exuberance. "Oh my gosh! You're her . . . you're you . . . you're Kristen Anders. I recognize you from your promo pictures."

Realization struck Kristen. "Are you Shelby?"

"Yes! I can't believe we're finally meeting. I mean we've been chatting online for so long I feel like we're already friends, but it's so awesome to meet you in person."

She always enjoyed the online conversations with the beta-reader, but now she found she liked the woman even more. She had such a bubbly personality which made Kristen think of rainbows and puppies. "It's so nice to meet you, and happy birthday. I can't thank you enough for putting me in touch with Master Mitch. He gave me a lot of information which will help me with my next book."

"I'm glad I could help. Did you start writing it yet? Who did you pick for the hero?"

Kristen laughed at her enthusiasm. Her beta-readers had been trying to get her to nail down the lead character for *Leather and Lace* for several weeks now, but she hadn't told them yet whom she chose. "The winner is Master Xavier."

Shelby squealed and clapped her hands like an excited child. "I knew it! I fell in love with him during the scene you had him do in the pool with Master Greg and Annette in *Satin and Sin*. He sounds like the ultimate dreamboat."

---

As the two subs chatted, Devon looked up to see Brody approaching with a broad smile on his face. The geek was wearing his usual dark T-shirt with snug blue jeans and brown cowboy boots. He preferred the well-worn jeans over leathers, saying they were more comfortable to him, having been born and raised in Texas ranching country. Stopping next to him, his friend clapped Devon on the shoulder.

"You're a lucky man, Devil Dog." He tilted his head toward Kristen. "She's hot, but there's got to be something wrong with her since she picked your sorry ass over mine. When she shot me down, I thought maybe she played for the other team. I must admit, though, I was a little surprised when Jake mentioned you were on a date tonight. I didn't think you knew what the word meant."

Devon smacked the man's shoulder with the back of his hand. "Knock it off, Egghead."

His buddy chuckled and changed the subject, but Devon knew once Kristen was out of hearing distance, Brody would continue to bust his chops. "Have you spoken to Marco today?"

Keeping an eye on the women next to him, still chatting about Kristen's books and her recent move, Devon shook his head. "No, I haven't. How's his sister doing?"

Brody's face became somber. "Not good at all. The doctors told them this morning to bring Hospice in as soon as they can. She's only got a few weeks left at the most." Marco's sister, Nina, had been battling inoperable brain cancer for over a year, but a month ago they discovered it had spread to most of her major organs. Now Devon knew they would need to give their friend a leave of absence so he could spend as much time as possible with her. "The only reason he's here tonight is for Shelby's birthday. She asked us last week if we would tag-team her tonight to celebrate, and you know how much I like that. The little girl right there has one of the most talented tongues I've ever had the pleasure of licking my dick."

Both men laughed, and then Brody interrupted the women's conversation. "Hey, birthday girl, your spanking bench is almost ready. Why don't you go over there and keep Master Marco company for a few minutes? Give him a little sass so he can look forward to your birthday whacks."

Shelby's grin lit up the room. "Yes, Master Brody." Before she headed to the station reserved for her scene, she gave Kristen a hug and turned toward Devon. "Thank you, Master Devon, for letting me talk to your sub. Besides Master Brody and Master Marco playing with me tonight, I think it was the best present I could get."

Devon reached out and gave the girl's pink hair a gentle tug. "It was my pleasure, little one. Enjoy your birthday."

As Shelby turned, Brody smacked the girl's backside, and she yelped, but walked away with a smile on her face. Brody then looked at Kristen and winked. "I'm a little offended you picked my boss here over me. I don't think it's ever happened before, but I'll get over it sooner or later. If you ask Master Devon, I'm sure he'll let you watch our scene with Shelby in a little bit. She'll be getting her birthday whacks along with a few birthday orgasms."

Kristen's eyes widened, and she bit her lower lip as her cheeks flamed red. Brody laughed at her expression. "Master Devon, I do believe your sub likes the idea. Bring her over in about ten minutes to the last bench, and I'll save a place for you up front."

Devon was focused on his sub as he agreed with his friend. "I think you're right. She does like the idea. We'll be there in a little bit." He continued to stare at her as Brody left them standing a few feet to the left of the staircase. When she licked her lips again, he sensed her need and took the bottle of water from her hand, unscrewing the cap before handing it back to her. "Drink up. You'll find it easy to get dehydrated in here."

She took a sip, and then must have realized how thirsty she was because she guzzled some more. After she drank half the bottle, he took it from her again and replaced the cap. "We'll walk around for a little bit on the way to their scene which is toward the back. But before we do, the locker rooms are right around the back of the stairs here. Would you like to use the restroom?"

Now that he mentioned it . . . "Yes, Sir. I think I will."

He lifted his hand to cup her cheek and used his thumb to brush her plump bottom lip. "I like hearing the word 'Sir' from your lips. I can't wait to hear you say it while begging me to let you come." Her mouth gaped open at his statement, and he took the opportunity to push his thumb between her lips and rub it along her bottom teeth. Her tongue poked forward and licked the tip of his finger and heat flared in his eyes. His dick hardened painfully, and he placed his other hand on her hip and pulled until she was flush against him from their chests to their thighs.

Bending forward, he replaced his thumb with his mouth and tongue. He didn't start the kiss as slow and gentle as he had in the parking lot. This time he plunged right in, taking her intense passion as he gave her his. Their tongues dueled, first in her mouth and then, to his surprise and delight, in his as she explored and tasted him. He took her arms, placed them on his shoulders and left them there as his hands traveled south. One hand stopped to cup the weight of one of her breasts while the other went to her ass, and he squeezed her lush flesh. It took everything in him not to lift the bottom of her dress, pick her up, and impale her on his rigid cock.

He was about to grind his throbbing erection into her clit when the sound of a single tail whip split the air, followed by a low moan. The loud crack startled Kristen, and she jumped back, her mouth tearing away from his, her breath coming in hard pants which matched his own. As much as he wanted to draw her to him again, he knew if he did he would be in danger of breaking his own club's rule of no playing with guests. Kissing was one thing, but he wanted to do so much more to her than just kiss. As they both recovered their breath, he took hold of her shoulders, turned her toward the door to the women's locker room, and gave her a gentle push. "Hurry back, Pet. I'll be waiting."

———————

KRISTEN GLANCED over her shoulder at Devon before walking on shaking legs to the locker room door. Holy lip-locks, the man knew how to kiss. With the taste of him still on her tongue, she entered the locker room, walked around a partition, which blocked the inside of the room from the doorway, and froze at the sight before her.

# CHAPTER 9

*A*s Kristen disappeared into the locker room, Devon heard his name being called by someone coming down the stairs. Looking up, he saw his brother and cousin approaching him with amused grins. Both wore similar leather vests without shirts and leather pants, but where Ian's leathers were black, Mitch's were dark brown. Devon rolled his eyes at their expressions, knowing what was coming and there was no way to avoid it.

"So, little brother, I hear you went on a date tonight. Do you even know what to do on one of those?"

Of course, Mitch had to add his two cents. "I don't think the boy does, Ian, considering his date appears to have abandoned him."

"She's in the bathroom, ass-hat." It was times like this he hated being so close to his family. They never missed an opportunity to give him or each other a pile of shit.

"So who's the lucky lady who managed to get you to pay for dinner before you screw her?"

"Fuck you, Ian."

"No thanks, I'm a pussy lover." Devon growled, and Ian relented. "All right, all right, I'll be good. Who is she?"

"You remember the girl who was typing away on her laptop last week when we were at the pub?"

"The cute brunette you were drooling over in the mirror?" Of course, Ian would have noticed since the man never missed much. Devon rolled his eyes again and nodded. "Very nice. Mitch told me how you ran into her here earlier. Just be careful you don't end up being written into a chick-lit book. Everyone will find out about your small Irish dick."

His brother and cousin laughed again, and Devon was about to tell them both to fuck off when the door to the women's room flew open. He expected Kristen to walk out, but, instead, a shy little sub named Colleen came running out, her eyes wide in panic.

"Master Mitch, Master Ian, hurry, please help!" She turned around and ran back into the locker room with Ian, Mitch, Devon, and one of the nearby bouncers following on her heels.

Ian and Mitch managed to get through the door first, and before he finished rounding the corner of the partition, Devon heard his brother bellow in his loudest Dom voice, "Stop!"

The female screeching and yelling in the room came to an abrupt halt. They hadn't been able to hear the commotion outside the locker room due to the pounding music.

Confused, Devon took in the incredulous scene before him and tried to figure out what the hell was going on. A sub named Heather was face down on the floor with Kristen sitting on her back. His date had the other girl's arm jacked up behind her back, and her hand was clenched around a mass of the redhead's hair. Another sub, Michelle, was sitting on the floor holding her stomach, trying to catch her breath, while Colleen was now standing in a corner to Devon's left, her eyes still wide and her hands covering her mouth as she stared at the other women. Although they were all quiet now, he could still hear the heavy breathing coming from the women on the ground.

While Mitch and the bouncer were as confused as Devon, Ian was downright pissed. Mitch managed The Covenant, but Ian was the head Dom, and Mitch often deferred to his cousin taking the lead in situations like this. The men watched as the three subs got to their feet, with Kristen taking two steps back to avoid Heather's swinging arms which were now loose again. "You bitch!"

"Enough!" Ian boomed, his anger evident. "Knees!"

Without faltering, Colleen, Heather, and Michelle dropped to the ground and presented themselves appropriately—on their knees, which were shoulder-width apart, their heads bowed, and their arms behind their backs, hands clasped around the opposite forearm. The only sub still standing was Kristen, who was looking at the other three in apparent shock.

Devon took a step forward, and her eyes swung up to meet his. In a low, controlled voice he told her, "I know this is new to you, Pet, but I suggest you drop to your knees as fast as you can." She hesitated. "Now."

---

*OH CRAP!* Kristen knew she'd screwed up big this time. She fell to her knees, mirroring the other sub's postures as best she could. Once she was in position, she heard Devon whisper, "Sorry Ian, this is new to her."

"Then she better learn fast or her ass is going to be red for a month."

*Is he serious? Yup, he probably is. Can this get any worse? Yup, it can.* She realized if it moved up another inch, the hem of her dress would give everyone a glimpse of her bare crotch. She was desperate to adjust it, but since she was in enough trouble she let it stay where it was and prayed it didn't move. She kept her gaze on the floor in front of her, yet she was dying to look up to see what was going on, but didn't dare. The door leading out to the club opened again, and she heard Tiny's voice.

"I got this in here, Anthony. Wait outside and keep everyone out. Kent is upstairs doing the same." The door closed, once again blocking the music blaring out in the main room.

The man, Ian—she recognized him as one of the Sexy Six-Pack from when she first noticed Devon—spoke in a deep tone she had begun to refer to as a Dom voice. "Does someone want to explain what the hell is going on here?"

Kristen and the girl in the corner, who was now crying quietly, didn't say anything, but the other two began talking over each other.

"We were just talking, and this bitch comes out of nowhere . . ."

"She attacked us for no reason . . ."

"She tried to break my arm . . ."

"Quiet!" Ian barked, obviously having reached the end of what little patience he had. "Michelle and Heather, go get your Masters and wait for me outside the office upstairs. I advise you to hurry because you do not want me to get there before you." Kristen didn't look, but one of the two must have tried to speak again as they got up because Ian added, "No. Upstairs with your Doms. I won't tell you again."

As the two women ran barefoot out the door another man walked in and looked around. Through her lashes, Kristen saw him drop to his knees and pull the crying girl into his arms to comfort her. The man appeared to be in his late thirties, while the girl was younger than Kristen's own twenty-six years, but she thought they made a cute couple.

"What the hell is going on, Ian? Why is my sub in here crying?"

"I'm about to find out, Reggie." Ian closed the distance between himself and Kristen, and she saw his feet stop a few inches in front of her. When he spoke, his voice wasn't as harsh as it had been, but she could tell he was still pissed. "Eyes up, sub."

She tilted her head back until she could see his face, but remained silent as his eyes bore into her.

"Do you want to tell me what this is all about?"

Kristen's gaze went from the man looming over her to the young girl sobbing in her Dom's arms and back again. "No, Sir, I don't. Not at the moment."

She waited for him to yell at her, but instead, Ian raised his brow at her words and then proved he was astute. "Tiny, would you take Colleen up to the office and wait with her inside away from the others, please?"

Tiny stepped toward the couple as they got to their feet. "Come with me, Ms. Colleen. I'll take care of you until Master Reggie can join you again."

Colleen looked at Kristen, then at each of the Doms, tears still falling from her pretty eyes. Her lips trembled. "Please, Master Ian. It wasn't her fault. She was helping me."

Ian looked over his shoulder at the sub, and his voice softened. "Go upstairs, little one. Everything will be all right. I promise."

The girl started to say something else, but Master Reggie gave her a quick kiss before handing her off to Tiny. "Go with Tiny, love. We'll get this all straightened out. I'll be upstairs in a few minutes."

After the young sub and head bouncer left, Ian took two small steps back, and his voice sounded weary. "Stand up, girl, and tell me what happened, although I have a feeling I already know."

Kristen stood, tugging the hem of her dress down as she did, and peered at the four Doms in the room staring back at her. She tried not to be intimidated, but it was no easy feat, with their stiff postures and stern faces. Ian, Mitch, and Devon stood in a similar manner, with their arms crossed and their feet shoulder-width apart, while Reggie had his hands on his hips. Kristen swallowed hard and took a deep breath. "I'm sorry, Sir. I didn't mean to cause any trouble, but when I came in to use the bathroom those two bit . . . I mean, those two women had the girl, Colleen, up against the lockers, and the redhead had her hand around Colleen's neck holding her there."

"Fuck!"

Kristen's eyes widened and shot toward Master Reggie who held up his hand in an apologetic gesture. It was obvious the man was keeping his anger in check for her benefit. "Forgive me, girl. Go on."

She nodded and kept her gaze on the man. "I didn't want to say this in front of her because she's upset enough as it is. They were in her face, and I didn't hear everything they said, but the gist of it was they thought she was too fat and ugly to keep her Dom happy, and if it wasn't for her daddy's money, she wouldn't have a Master."

She winced as Master Reggie exploded in rage. "They said what? Fucking cu . . ." He cut his vulgar insult short when he remembered there was a woman in the room. "God damn it, Ian! I've had all I can stand from those two bitches. I want their asses out of here tonight!"

Ian's stare never left her face. "Reggie, calm down. I don't need you having another asthma attack in my club. The last time we had to call the EMTs to the lobby, I think one of them creamed his pants when Shelby walked by, then cried when Mistress China threatened his manhood because she thought they weren't working on you fast enough." With those words, the tension rolling off the four men was released, and to her amazement, Mitch and Reggie began to laugh. Devon's posture eased a bit, and he leaned back against the wall, the corners of his mouth trembling as he held back his own laughter. She had a feeling he would be laughing out loud with the other men if he hadn't been so mad at her. Ian stayed where he was, looking at her. "Is that everything, little one?"

Kristen nodded. "That's when I stepped in and, well, you know the rest."

Ian's lips twitched, but he didn't smile. "Reggie, go upstairs to Colleen, and we'll be right behind you. After I mind-fuck those two for a bit, their memberships will be terminated."

Rather than heading toward the door, Master Reggie approached her and took her hand in his. "What's your name, girl? And whose collar are you wearing?"

"Kristen, Sir. And it's Master Devon's collar." She swallowed, and her eyes flashed to Devon before returning to the man in front of her. Well, she wouldn't be wearing it much longer, she guessed.

Master Reggie's brown eyes softened. "Thank you for sticking up for Colleen, Kristen. I'm grateful you were here and stepped in to protect her when I couldn't."

Her heart swelled at the gratitude in his eyes and voice, and she smiled at him. "I'm glad I was here at the right time. I hate bullies."

"So do I." He let go of her hand and walked toward the door, passing the other men on the way. "As a favor to me, Devon, please don't be too hard on your subbie's ass tonight."

Kristen bit her bottom lip when Devon didn't say anything and only nodded at the other Dom. He was no longer looking at her, instead his gaze was on the floor, and she knew she was in so much trouble.

"Little one." She looked back to Ian who no longer seemed to be pissed—at least not at her. His voice and his blue eyes, which were so similar to Devon's, had softened as he spoke to her. "I don't condone fighting in my club, but every once in a while—very, very rarely, I might add—I'll admit there's a good reason behind it. This is one of those times. However, next time, please try to alert security or a DM, and don't take on the bullies yourself. This time you had the upper hand, but it may not always be the case, and I'd hate to see you get hurt. Now if you'll excuse us, Master Mitch and I have some things we need to tend to, and I'm sure my brother is thinking up ways to punish you for putting yourself in harm's way."

Without waiting for a response from her, Ian turned and walked out of the room followed by Mitch, who winked and smiled at her before he left. She stood there waiting for Devon to say something to her. He still wasn't looking at her, and she began to fidget, knowing she had spoiled what was left of their date.

"If you'll give me back my purse, I'll call a cab to take me back to my car."

His eyes whipped toward hers, then narrowed as he studied her. With his head tilted to the side, he took slow and deliberate steps toward her. "Why do you want to leave?"

She twisted her hands and fingers together in front of her. "Well, I obviously ruined the rest of our evening. I know you must be furious with me for having a cat-fight in your club."

Devon stepped inside her personal space, but she managed to not take a step back, not that there was much room between her and the lockers. Grabbing her hands, he brought them up to his lips, kissing the back of one and then the other. She watched him, stunned he was being so gentle with her when he should be kicking her out the door. "Where did you learn to do that, Pet?"

She was confused, and her heart rate sped up at his closeness. "Do-Do what?"

"Kick subbie ass when it was two against one."

Really? Was he serious? "Um . . . I told you my dad was a cop. A few of the female officers he worked with ran a program for teenage girls on how to defend themselves, and I was a fast learner. Look, I'm sorry, Devon . . . I mean, Sir. I didn't mean to cause trouble and get them kicked out of the club. I saw what they were doing to her, and I snapped, I guess." She watched in amazement as his head fell back on his shoulders, and he began to laugh. And it wasn't a short, light laugh, but a full blown, belly laugh.

"Oh, Pet. How you fascinate me. You didn't start the trouble, but you ended it, and I'm proud of you. We've had a few complaints about those two harassing other subs, and they've been given fair warning their days here were numbered. The only reason they hadn't been kicked out before this was because their Doms are well liked. I would've loved to have been a fly on the wall to see Heather and Melissa's faces when you went all girlie-ninja on them."

"Girlie-ninja?"

"Uh-huh. My own personal ninja-girl. I kinda like it. That might be your new name for when we're not playing." His smile faltered a fraction, and he hoped she didn't notice. He had to stop saying things like that, things which sounded as if they'd be spending time together past the weekend. Before they took anything further, he would have to tell her this thing between them was only temporary. A few days of mutual pleasure, until he fucked her out his system, and then moved on. He wasn't going to have that conversation here in the club's women's room, but he had to explain it to her soon. "If we hurry, we can still catch the end of Shelby's birthday scene. I mean, if you want to stay."

Of course she wanted to stay. She wanted to shout, but tried to remain calm. "I'd like that."

He squeezed both her hands before dropping one and tugging on the other. "Great. Come on."

Kristen took two steps forward then came to an abrupt stop. Devon looked back at her with a questioning look. "Something wrong, Pet?"

"Um . . . I never got a chance to use the facilities."

Laughing, he let go of her hand and made a grand sweeping gesture toward the other room where the toilets and showers were located. "Be my guest. I'll wait for you outside. Try not to get into any trouble in the next three minutes, hmmm?"

# CHAPTER 10

*D*evon rushed his sub past several scenes. There would be time to come back to watch them at their leisure, but he wanted Kristen to see Shelby's scene. A ménage was on her list of soft limits and he wanted to see her reaction. The birthday girl's ass would have been spanked crimson by now, but there should still be enough time for his pet to catch the end of the scene, and he knew it would be a good one.

A Brody and Marco tag-team scene was pretty popular with the unattached subs, but because there were times one or both were working on an assignment it wasn't always a weekly occurrence. With Marco spending a lot of time tending to his sister lately, Devon didn't think the two had done a scene together in over two months. There were some ménage Dom duos who never did a solo scene, but Marco and Brody didn't need each other in order to enjoy a woman, which they did more often than not. It didn't mean they still didn't enjoy their threesomes when an opportunity arose.

Easing their way through the crowd which had gathered around the area the trio was using, Devon managed to find a spot where, if he placed Kristen in front of him, she would have an excellent view. He knew the moment she realized what she was watching, because he felt rather than heard her breath hitch as he held her back to his chest. He peered over her shoulder and saw her eyes were wide, in awe more than shock, he thought. The pulse at her neck quickened as her breathing also increased and her face flushed. He put his mouth next to her ear and whispered, "Like what you see, Pet?"

---

KRISTEN SHIVERED, but didn't answer because she couldn't find the words. In front of her was the most erotic thing she had ever seen. She'd never watched porn before, and even though she owned a *Playgirl* calendar thanks to Will, she'd never looked through the pictures in a sex magazine. The R-rated movies she watched never showed a sex scene like this. Shelby was bent at the waist, her upper torso resting on a red leather bench. Completely naked, her ass and upper thighs were as deep red as the bench. She was tied down, unable to move her arms or legs which were shackled to the bench. A wide strap across her lower back held her flush against the leather padding beneath her. The girl was sweating, moaning and writhing as much as the restraints allowed, which wasn't much. But it was the two men with her who had Kristen's attention, their bodies moving in tandem with each other, and the music pulsating overhead.

A man, she assumed was Marco, was standing behind Shelby, his leather pants unlaced and he was thrusting his condom-covered penis deep inside the girl's core. His feet were apart enough to keep his pants from falling down further. Their current position bared the upper half of his ass, which was hard as granite. In front, he was huge and Kristen couldn't help but wonder how he managed to fit without ripping the sub in two. Despite the din around her, Kristen was able to hear the slapping of Marco's exposed hips against Shelby's buttocks, and she was shocked to realize her own clit was throbbing in concert to the sound.

At Shelby's head stood Brody. While both men were tall and built, they were complete opposites when it came to hair and skin tone. Marco was dark Italian with hair almost as black as Devon's, while Brody looked like a combination surfer-Norse god with his blond hair and tan, yet fairer skin. Both men had removed their shirts and their upper bodies had the same sweaty sheen as the girl they were servicing. Rubbing the girl's bare upper back with his hand, Brody's jeans were un-zippered and hanging low on his hips as he plunged his cock into Shelby's welcoming mouth. He wasn't as thick as his counterpart, but was still well-endowed.

Shelby's moans got louder and Marco glanced at his friend. "She's about to come a fourth time, man. You better finish up soon if you don't want to visit the ER tonight."

Kristen watched as Brody nodded and increased the tempo of his hips. She turned her head a tad toward Devon, but didn't take her eyes off the threesome. His mouth was still near her ear and he must have anticipated her question. "Shelby tends to come hard and when she does she usually clamps her teeth together—it's an involuntary response for her. The Doms know this and back off on fucking her mouth when they sense she's about to come. Marco is going to slow down a little to keep her from going over the edge, and Brody's going to come before she does so he doesn't need his dick surgically reattached."

Brody grabbed a handful of pink hair. "Come on, Shelby, take it . . . take it all." The girl's cheek hollowed as she sucked him harder, and Brody threw his head back, tensing and roaring his release. Not a drop of semen fell from the sub's lips as he slowed his hips then pulled out of her mouth. Her lips were red and swollen while her eyes were half closed and glazed over. Not bothering to zipper his jeans after he tucked himself back in, Brody dropped to his knees next to the sub, petting her head and talking to her in a voice too low for others to hear. She gave a slight nod of her head, and Marco increased his own pace again while reaching around to finger Shelby's clit in a hurried motion. Her moans became louder, then turned into cries of jumbled words. Marco's hips and fingers never slowed, but it wasn't until he slapped her ass hard with his other hand that she screamed with such an intense orgasm it should have brought the roof down on top of them. As she went over, she took Marco with her, his body rigid as he came inside the latex barrier.

Around her, Kristen heard words of appreciation and praise for the trio. The scene had been watched by many, and she almost expected them to break out in applause. She felt Devon's hard erection as he pressed his hips against her bottom, and her empty vagina clenched with need. Her body was so aroused by what she'd seen it wouldn't take much to set her off. One, maybe two swipes of her clit and she would be flying. The thought surprised her. She could've never imagined she'd be so turned on watching other people have sex. But it hadn't just been sex she realized. It had been a sensual and erotic exchange between the three individuals involved and shared with the people who had been watching them. She couldn't think of the words to explain it. It hadn't been crass and dirty, but carnal and beautiful—a sensual dance as old as time.

The crowd started to disperse as Brody and Marco began to unshackle the limp and satisfied Shelby, rubbing her limbs to revive her slowed circulation. If she hadn't been mumbling in response to the questions the men were asking her, Kristen would have thought the sub was unconscious. There were "happy birthday" wishes called to Shelby as people walked away, but Kristen didn't think the girl heard them and she wondered if this was the subspace she'd read about during her research.

While Brody stayed with Shelby, Kristen watched as Marco stepped a few feet away from the bench and disposed of his used condom, tossing it in a nearby receptacle. He re-laced his pants then took a blanket someone handed him. With Brody's help, he eased Shelby up and wrapped the blanket around her naked body. He then picked the petite girl up in his arms without effort, turned and left the area with his charge. It was only after the sub was being cared for by his friend that Brody took a moment to zipper his jeans before he began to clean up the area. A female club employee who wore a red and gold bow tie with a black bra and miniskirt, the uniform of the club, stepped forward to help him. The employee took a towel and spray bottle and proceeded to wipe down the spanking bench. The scent of oranges, which had been faint earlier, now flooded Kristen's senses. She'd read somewhere the smell of citrus fruit could be an aphrodisiac, and now she understood why. It complemented the scents of leather and sex without being overbearing.

After Brody finished tidying up the area, he grabbed his black duffel bag, which was his personal "toy" kit, and walked over to where Marco was sitting on a nearby couch with Shelby on his lap. She was sipping from a bottle of water the dark-haired man held for her. Dropping the duffel bag at his feet, Brody sat down next to them, pulled the sub's legs across his lap and began massaging them. When she was done with the water, Shelby rested her head on Marco's shoulder and closed her eyes.

Kristen hadn't moved from where she stood and felt Devon shift his weight behind her a second before she felt two fingers drag against her soaked pussy lips. It had been so unexpected, she tensed for a moment before moaning at the delicious sensation, but the fingers left her body as quickly as they had appeared. Turning around, she watched him place the wet fingers in his mouth, sucking and licking them with earnest. His eyes flared with heat. The sight stunned and aroused her even more, and she hadn't thought it was possible.

After he had consumed every last drop of her cream, he removed his fingers and leaned toward her. "Just because we can't play doesn't mean I can't touch what belongs to me, and the collar you're wearing says you're mine tonight." He licked his lips, and all Kristen could do was stare at him. "You taste so sweet, Pet, like the purest of honey. I want to spread your legs and eat you for hours until I've had my fill. It pleases me so much that their scene turned you on." If his hands hadn't moved to hold her waist, she would've melted to the floor in a big pile of goo. Her eyes shifted downward and her flushed face became even redder. Devon took the two fingers, which a moment before had been in his mouth, and placed them under her chin. She could smell her scent on him. He applied gentle pressure so she was forced to look at him once again. "Don't be embarrassed, Pet. Your arousal is nothing to be ashamed of, just because it doesn't follow the norms of society. Here, in this world, it's normal. Here, there's no right or wrong way for Doms and subs to enjoy sex and all its possible facets, as long as they're safe, sane, and consensual. Understand?"

She nodded. "Yes . . . yes, Sir, but . . ."

"But what, Pet?"

Although she whispered, it was loud enough for him to hear standing so close to her. "Did she really come four times?"

———

OF ALL THE questions he expected her to ask, that hadn't been one of them. Devon let out a bark of laughter before answering her. "I'm sure she did and each one was probably as intense as the one we saw. Haven't you ever had multiple orgasms before?"

She shook her head, probably embarrassed, thinking she wasn't like most women. "No, Sir."

Her denial didn't faze him at all. He thought back to her limit list and the question mark she had placed next to "Coming on Command." "Okay, here's another question, and I'm not asking you these to make you uncomfortable. I'm learning what I need to know in order to take proper care of you when the time comes. And I guarantee the time *will* come and so will you." Her chin fell toward the floor, but she didn't say anything. "Have you ever had an orgasm during intercourse?" When she shook her head, he frowned. "I need verbal answers, Pet. I don't ever want to guess at what you mean or have any miscommunications between us. You have to tell me in plain English. Have you ever had an orgasm during intercourse?"

Kristen tried to look away from him, but he wouldn't allow it. "No, Sir. Not during intercourse. In fact, the only orgasms I've ever had are the ones I've given myself when I'm alone. My ex said it was because I was frigid and couldn't relax during sex."

Devon growled. "And yet another reason to despise the low-life pile of cow shit you were married to."

Her amusement was evident in her smile. "Do you realize every time you mention my ex, you call him something else?"

"No, I didn't," he chuckled. "But since I've developed a rather colorful language over the years, I'm sure I won't run out of new things to call him for a while. For now though, I don't want to talk about him anymore. I don't want him between us at all, tonight or any other time. So I want you to forget you were ever with him. I'm going to treat you like a virgin and start from scratch. I'm going to seduce you, arouse you, and by the time I'm done, you'll know exactly how non-frigid you are. You'll also know what it's like to have multiple orgasms because I won't stop until I'm completely satisfied you have nothing left to give me."

———

DEVON SPENT the next hour or so escorting Kristen around the pit. They'd been pulled into a few conversations and introductions were made, but after a few short words he was able to keep them moving while still being polite so she could see as many scenes as possible. He wanted to observe her while she watched the different scenes to get an idea of what interested her and compare it to her list of limits.

He found a flogging scene and another spanking which obviously turned her on. A wax scene had intrigued her despite the wariness on her face when she first saw the hot wax being dripped onto the female sub's large breasts and abdomen before it landed on the woman's clit causing her to scream as she came. When they watched Mistress China whip a sub tied to a St. Andrew's cross, Kristen had winced as the single tail left red lines up and down the man's nude back, ass and upper thighs. Devon sensed it was a little too much for her during her first visit so he didn't let her linger.

The most interesting reaction she had was when they stopped to watch a new scene start. The female sub was sitting naked on a bondage chair as her Dom plucked her nipples into stiff peaks, prepping them for the alligator clamps he had in his other hand. When the Dom placed the clamps on his sub, Kristen had paled and began to panic, her breathing becoming rapid. Devon was about to pull her away from the scene when he saw her hands move to her breasts as if she was trying to push away unseen clamps from her own nipples. He grabbed her shoulders and jerked her away from the scene. She hadn't gotten upset until she noticed the clamps and her negative response to a common piece of BDSM equipment bothered him. There was a story behind her reaction, and after he calmed her down, he was determined to get it out of her. Until then, the best he could do was hold her until her breathing slowed and the panic receded.

———————

KRISTEN TRIED to get her breathing under control as Devon held her tight against his body. He must think she's an inexperienced wimp. She thought she could handle watching the Dom put clamps on his sub's nipples, but as soon as the girl cried out in pain, something in Kristen flipped. It didn't matter that the girl was now moaning with pleasure. If Devon hadn't pulled her away from the scene, she was sure she would've vomited all over the place or at least passed out—which was so not the way to make a good impression.

She let him lead her to a sitting area closer to the middle of the room and was surprised when he sat in a winged back leather chair and pulled her down into his lap. The chair was situated so she couldn't see the scene which had upset her, and she knew he had chosen that one on purpose. He adjusted her hips until they were both comfortable before signaling a nearby waitress to bring him a bottle of water. Taking the bottle, he uncapped it and held it to her lips allowing her to take only a few small sips at a time. "Easy, Pet. Don't drink too fast or it'll make you sick."

She nodded before taking a few more sips as the bile which had risen to the back of her throat earlier, subsided. "I'm sorry. I don't know what came over me or why I reacted the way I did."

"I think you do."

Her eyes flashed up to his, then away again, but he wouldn't allow her to hide. With a tender touch, he cupped her chin and turned her head, so she had no choice but to look at him. She could tell he wasn't angry, but concerned.

"Tell me, Pet. Tell me what happened to you."

She tried to shake her head as her eyes filled with tears, but he was still holding her jaw. "I can't."

His concerned eyes softened in sympathy. His voice was deep—

demanding, yet kind. "You can, Pet. Trust me. There isn't anything you can say that I won't understand. Tell me, so I can help you heal."

Kristen blinked several times and took a deep breath. "I can't look at you when I say it. I've never told anyone, and it's embarrassing."

He caressed her cheek before pushing her head to rest on his shoulder. He turned his head, then kissed her forehead. "Don't be embarrassed. I've been in this lifestyle for over a decade, and I've pretty much heard everything. Not much surprises me anymore. Close your eyes and take your time. There's no rush, but you will tell me before we get up again. I don't care if your ass falls asleep, I'll just spank it awake again later."

She hiccupped, then giggled, as he'd intended, and the tension she was feeling eased. She closed her eyes and settled deeper into his embrace. Taking another deep breath, she began to speak. "I told you earlier I dated a guy in college before my ex. He was the one who got tired of me saying 'no' to actual intercourse, but we still fooled around a bit." Devon didn't say anything as he continued to caress her shoulders and back while nuzzling his cheek against her hair. "We dated for about three months and everything was great until one night we went to a party and Derek had a little too much to drink. Later we went back to his dorm room alone and we were making out and stuff. I had my shirt off, and he'd pulled my bra down so he could . . . God, this is so embarrassing." Devon remained quiet, letting her tell him at her own pace.

She took another deep breath. "Anyway, he was sucking and licking my breasts when he started to get a little rough. He kept trying to get my pants undone. I'd never been afraid of him before, but that night, I guess because of the alcohol, he got aggressive, and I was scared. I tried to push him away, and he bit my nipple, hard. I think if I hadn't screamed at the top of my lungs and hit him in the head, he would have bitten it off."

She didn't know when she began crying, but the tears were pouring down her cheeks and she paused to catch her breath. Devon's hands never stopped as they caressed her back, legs and arms, and the constant motions helped calm her. Despite being in a crowded club, she felt as if it was just the two of them, far away from anyone else. He was murmuring words of sympathy for her ordeal and praise for telling him about it as his lips brushed against her forehead. She felt the tension in his body with the obvious anger he had toward the man who'd hurt her, but he kept it in check.

"I grabbed my shirt and ran back to my dorm room. Thank God my roommate had gone home for the weekend. When I looked, his teeth marks were deep enough to make me bleed. It hurt so badly and I cried all night. I was in pain for almost a month. I couldn't stand to wear my bras because my nipple was super-sensitive. But it was worse without them because my shirts would constantly brush against it, so I wore my padded sports bras until it healed, but it still hurt. And to make everything worse, Derek came to see me the next day when I wouldn't answer his calls or texts. He didn't even remember doing it. He said I must've been cheating on him because he didn't do it, and he would tell everyone I was a cheating whore if I reported it."

"So you never told anyone? Never went to the doctor?" He spoke the words into her temple as he continued to pepper her with the sweetest touches of his lips.

She shook her head. "I know I should've, but I was so scared and mortified. Anyway, I broke up with him right then. I was glad we didn't have any classes together, but I still saw him on campus, and three days later, he had a new girlfriend. I never talked to him again. When Tom and I started dating and I wouldn't let him touch my breasts, he asked why. I told him they were overly-sensitive, and he didn't push me after that. I can touch them, and eventually I got to the point where I could let him touch them as long as he was gentle, but I would freeze up if his teeth made contact. I guess it's one of the reasons I'm lousy in bed. I don't think I'll ever be able to relax enough to make a man happy."

Without warning, Devon grabbed her hair and pulled her head back so he could look her in the face. He was frowning, his eyes flashing in anger, and this time it was aimed at her. He wasn't hurting her, but a sliver of fear raced through her. "Pet, I'm only going to say this once, and if I ever have to repeat myself, I'm going throw you over my knee and make sure you can't sit for a week. I will not tolerate you putting yourself down, *ever*, especially because you're experiencing a version of PTSD. Do you know what that is?"

She'd heard of Post-Traumatic Stress Disorder, but she thought it only happened to soldiers in combat or people who witnessed a murder or something just as bad. He was waiting for a response, so she nodded her head the best she could while he still had a firm grip on her hair. "What happened to you was not your fault. It was not safe, sane, nor consensual. No one, and I mean *no one*, should have to go through what you went through. You were violated by a man you should've been able to trust, and he took your trust and destroyed it. I never want to hear you say you're lousy in bed or you can't make a man happy. What you experienced between those two cocksuckers may have buried your passion and your trust in men, but I've seen glimpses of your passion, and I know it's there, waiting to come to the surface. That dick hurt you physically and mentally. And the fucking amoeba you were married to never took the time to learn about you—your body and mind. He didn't learn what pleases you and what frightens you like a lover should.

"When I'm with a woman, her pleasure, her desires, her needs, and her orgasms are what matter to me the most. My need for sexual release is at the bottom of a long list. It's almost an afterthought, and I will not allow it to happen until my sub is thoroughly and completely sated and she can't take anymore. My satisfaction comes after I've given her everything I can and I've taken everything she has in return. I want to be the man who can make you trust again. I want you to see and feel how good sexual play can be.

"Stay with me tonight . . . for the weekend. I want to be the man who gives you orgasms you never knew existed. I can't give you more than that. I can't offer you forever—it's not in me—but for this weekend, I can offer you the chance to learn what pleases you and how incredible sex can be with a man who places your needs, your pleasure, before his. I want to teach you what it means to feel cherished. If it's not what you want, tell me now, and I'll take you home. But don't deny yourself the chance to explore your sexuality. Don't ignore what I can see in your eyes and body language you crave. If it's not with me, find someone you can trust and make it happen."

Kristen stared at the man who held her captive, not only with his hands, but with his words. She knew he was right. She was a passionate woman, but it was buried deep within her and no other man had looked for it and put her before himself—until Devon. Did she want him? No question about it, she did. Did she trust him? She didn't know why, but the answer was yes—yes, she trusted him with her mind and with her body. She only hoped she didn't lose her heart to him because she couldn't go through the pain again. This is what she'd told herself she wanted last week—a friend with benefits, nothing long term. And if he was willing to teach her and let her explore, she would take whatever time he offered her. And when the time came, and they went their separate ways, she would thank him for everything he had given her.

DEVON COULD ALMOST HEAR her brain process everything he'd said. He wanted her more than he'd ever wanted a woman, but this was her decision and he would abide by it, even if it killed him. She was looking into his eyes and his cock stirred the moment he knew she'd made up her mind. He knew what her answer would be, but he needed to hear the words, and he refused to proceed without them.

"Teach me, Sir."

# CHAPTER 11

*D*evon stood and set Kristen on her feet, holding her hips until he was sure she was steady. Grabbing her hand, he almost dragged her up the grand staircase, across the bar area and out the double wooden doors. He didn't say a word to her, or anyone else on the way, and several people barely managed to step out of his path before he ran them down. He wanted to strip her naked and he couldn't do it here, not with the rules they had in place. As they crossed the lobby toward the front door, he heard her say from where she trailed behind him, "Devon wait, I need my purse. It's still in your locker."

He didn't slow down, but turned his head so she could hear him. "You won't need it. We'll get it tomorrow morning." He was too impatient to stop for anything. He wanted to spend hours proving his words to her. She would be satisfied many times over before he found his own release or he would die trying.

Throwing open the outside door he reduced his pace a little so she wouldn't lose her balance on the stairs while going down with her stilettos on. Instead of heading toward his car, he turned in the direction of the gate in the fence separating the club from the rest of the compound. As they approached, Beau, Ian's large lab-pit mix, came running to greet them, happy to see someone who would play with him. *Sorry buddy,* Devon thought, *I've got bigger plans tonight, and they don't include a rubber ball covered in dog slobber.*

---

"WHERE ARE WE GOING?" Kristen eyed the black canine who was now bouncing his big body off the other side of the fence. "Does he bite?"

Devon placed his hand on the security scanner which would unlock the pedestrian gate instead of the drive-thru one. "My apartment is in the last building and he only bites when we tell him to, or if one of us is being threatened." Before he pushed open the gate he addressed the excited mutt, "Beau, *pfui, fuss,*" the foreign words being pronounced as "fooey" and "fooss." The dog quieted and sat while the two humans walked into his territory and his favorite one closed the gate again. The dog's impatience was obvious, and his stubby, little tail twitched while the rest of his body remained still. As the two began walking across the compound, he fell in step almost attaching his furry body to his human's right leg.

Kristen was a dog lover and watched the animal in amazement as she kept pace with Devon. "What did you say to him?"

He slowed his pace a little when he realized she was almost running to keep up with his long stride. "Beau is his name. The other two words are 'no' and 'heel' in German. Ian found him as a pup and had him trained by a guy who specializes in protection and security dogs, and his commands are given in German so bad guys can't give him a command. He only knows a few words in English from being around us, and they're all harmless."

Kristen was impressed. "That's so cool. I might have to remember that for one of my books." Devon stopped short, and she almost stumbled past him before he grabbed her arm and steadied her. "What's wrong?"

His face was serious and borderline angry. "I want to make something perfectly clear. This thing between us, what we are about to do, is not research, Kristen, it's real. I don't want to be a story in one of your books. If that's why you're with me, tell me now, because if I find out later you're using me for that reason, I swear there'll be hell to pay."

Is that what he thought she was doing? Before she lost her temper, she took a moment and thought about it from his point of view. Yes, she had come to The Covenant for research, but she came back with him because she wanted to. Because she wanted him. She brought her hand up to his cheek, and she saw his stern face relax. "I can see how you might be worried, and I can't say I won't unconsciously recall how you've made me feel tonight while I'm writing, but I would never use you or anyone else that way, Devon. I swear to you, I'm here because I want you, and not for research for my books, but to discover the woman I hope . . . I believe is hidden deep inside me."

He leaned down and took possession of her mouth, hard and fast. Clutching her hips, he pulled her to him until there was no denying how much he wanted her. When she moaned into his mouth and began rubbing her body against his, he ripped his mouth from hers, grabbed her wrist and began pulling her along again. "Come on, woman, before I throw you to the ground and fuck you right here. I wouldn't mind, but I'm sure you'll be more comfortable in my bed."

Giggling at his impatience, she followed him into the last warehouse through a ground floor door which he also opened using a hand scanner. Again the exterior of the building belied the interior. There was a wooden apartment door a few steps in from the outside door. Brown carpeted steps to their left led to a second floor landing and another door. The sheet-rocked walls had been painted a soft beige.

Devon pointed to a much smaller door to the right of the first floor apartment door and spoke to the dog. "Beau, *geh rein,*" he instructed the canine pronouncing it "gay rine," the German words for "go inside." "Your boss will be home in a bit." The dog reluctantly, but obediently, approached the door, and a red light on a small black box at the top of the door turned green. Ducking his head, Beau pushed open the top-hinged door and disappeared while the door fell back in place and the green light returned to red. Taking Kristen's hand in his, Devon led her up the stairs.

He stopped at the second floor door and used yet another hand scanner to unlock it. She looked toward the floor and smiled when she noticed another doggie-door set in the sheet-rock. Devon opened his apartment door and gestured for her to go in first. Looking around his living room she couldn't believe they were in an old warehouse. The walls and ten foot ceiling had all been enclosed with sheet-rock and the spacious room was comfortably decorated. The walls were painted a pale moss-green while the furniture was made using dark-stained woods. A large, L-shaped, brown leather couch took up two of the living area walls with two recliners in a muted fabric completing the sitting area. The large framed pictures on the walls, a coffee table, end tables, lamps and throw pillows on the couch were well coordinated.

Two large horizontal windows were located high on the outer wall above the shorter end of the couch allowing plenty of light to come in, but prevented anyone on the outside from seeing in without a ladder. Window treatments in the same fabric as the throw pillows framed the glass. Across from the longer length of the couch was a huge entertainment center which contained a sixty-inch flat screen TV, a complicated-looking stereo, a gaming system and an assortment of photos of family and friends. Beyond the large sitting area was a six-seat bar, although there were no bottles of liquor on the shelf.

Attached to the living room, but still its own open space was a dining area with a teak wood table and chairs with seating for eight and a matching buffet table and china hutch. Two beautiful wrought iron chandeliers which looked similar to the ones in the club hung from the ceiling over the dining area and living room. Past the dining area was the entrance to a huge eat-in kitchen with stainless steel appliances, oak cabinets and black granite countertops. The walls in there were painted ivory. Opposite the front door and between the living and dining areas was a hallway which led toward the back of the apartment, where she assumed there were bedrooms and at least one bathroom. The entire apartment looked bigger than the three-bedroom cape she grew up in.

Turning, she saw Devon had been watching her. "Your place is beautiful."

His grin was sheepish. "Thanks, but I can't take any of the credit. I mean, come on, I'm a guy who spent most of his adult life living on Navy bases, and sleeping on the ground in places you couldn't imagine when we were on assignment. Can you see me picking out curtains or couch pillows? When my mom saw my card-slash-dining table and mismatched couch and folding chairs, she hired an interior decorator to come in and give it a major overhaul. The result is what you see, and it finally got Mom's approval. At least Ian's place wasn't much better than mine at the time, and he got the royal treatment, too." He took a few steps toward the hallway and added, "Make yourself comfortable, and I'll be right back."

As Devon disappeared into the back of the apartment, she continued to look around. Spotting the photos again, she approached the entertainment center to see them better. There were two pictures of the Sexy Six-Pack. In one they were all dressed in military camo fatigues and holding some huge weapons while in the other they were playing a three on three basketball game. The photo looked like it was taken outside in the compound. There was a picture of Mitch, Ian and Devon dressed in their club leathers in the lobby of The Covenant. They looked a few years younger, and she wondered if it was taken when they first opened the club. She moved to another group of pictures. The first one was of a much younger Devon in his Navy dress blues flanked by an older man and woman she assumed were his parents.

Behind her she heard him come back in the room and was about to turn toward him, but something stopped her. Looking at the picture again, she focused on the older man who looked so familiar. Devon stopped next to her and she realized he'd changed into a pair of sweatpants and his feet were now bare. "Those are my folks, Chuck and Marie."

The names didn't ring a bell, so she moved on to the next photo which was of four boys, three of whom were in their teens. Two of them looked like twins, and she thought one of them was Devon. She pointed to the boy on the left. "Is this one you?"

---

DEVON NODDED THEN TOOK her hand and led her to the couch where they both sat down. "Yeah, that's me. Right before Ian left for basic training."

"What about the other two? I take it they're your other brothers."

Turning toward her, he ran a finger up and down her bare arm while the fingers from his other hand played with her hair. "John's the one who looks like me, and Nick is the little guy."

He knew nervous tension was behind her questions, rather than her curiosity, but his family wasn't something he talked about often. If he didn't take command of the situation, her brain might override what her body obviously wanted. When it looked like she was about to ask another question, he plunged his fingers into her silky strands before grabbing hold and pulling her mouth to his. "I don't want to talk anymore."

Then he slammed his mouth down on hers and took what he did want—her.

# CHAPTER 12

*H*e was inhaling her, and Kristen loved every second of it, but when she tried to move her body closer to his, he drew away again. Without a word, he stood and pulled her up next to him before leading her down the hallway to his bedroom, which she barely noticed was decorated like the rest of his place. What she couldn't miss was the main focus of the room—a stained black oak, four-poster bed with a gray and maroon, patterned comforter on it.

Devon let go of her hand, leaving her standing next to the bed while he sat down on it and leaned to the side, resting his upper body on one elbow. "Undress for me, Pet. I want to see all of your luscious body and I want your eyes on mine the entire time. Unzip your dress and let it slide slowly down your body, revealing one delicious inch at a time. Don't think. Follow my orders and feel. Feel how beautiful you are to me. You have no idea how much I want you, but you will soon."

She swallowed and felt her pulse increase. His seductive voice was mesmerizing. She could do this. After all, it's what she told herself several times she wanted. Hesitating only a second or two, she reached up to the dress's side zipper and began to lower it. Slowly. Her eyes remained focused on his blue ones, and she realized his stayed on hers in return—he wasn't looking at her body, but into her mind. Her confidence went up a few notches. When the zipper stopped at her waist, her hand went back up to the thin strap holding the dress up, and she pulled it down her right arm, inch by torturous inch. His nostrils flared as if searching for her scent, and yet his gaze never left her face.

As the fabric of the dress dragged across her excited nipples, making them even harder, her breath caught and a rush of arousal moistened her inner thighs. By the time she got the dress down to her waist, she wanted to rip it the rest of the way off, shove her hand between her legs and relieve herself of the intense pressure which was peaking there. She used both hands to shimmy the dress over her voluptuous hips, and once it cleared them, the dress fell to a heap on the floor. Taking one step to the side, she toed the discarded fabric out of the way.

It was only then, when she stood completely naked in front of him, did Devon's eyes lower as he took in every inch of her. "Turn all the way around."

This was more disconcerting than when she had done it fully clothed in the restaurant. However, this time it wasn't his hand touching her, but his hungry stare. When she completed the rotation, Devon got up and held his hand out to her. Without hesitation, she placed her hand in his and let him help her climb onto the big bed. "Lay down on your back in the middle of the bed, Pet. Legs together, straight out. Put your hands above your head and grab the posts in the headboard, then keep them there. Your trust so far has me humbled, but I don't think you're ready for me to restrain you in this setting. However, if you remove your hands without permission, there will be consequences. Understand?"

After she'd positioned herself as he'd ordered, she licked her lips then nodded. "Yes, Sir, I understand."

"Good girl. You're absolutely beautiful, Pet."

She blushed as she watched him grab the hem of his shirt and lift it over his head, tossing the tee on top of her dress. Her eyes widened at the sight before her and she licked her lips again. She couldn't help it. His torso was sculpted perfection. If he'd lived in the time of Michelangelo, the statue would be called *Devon* instead of *David*. He and the rest of his friends might forever be the Sexy Six-Pack in her mind, but the man before her had a sexy eight-pack. It wasn't a body gained only in a gym, although he obviously spent time working out with weights, but there was a fluidity in his muscles when they moved, which came from swimming or other cardio activities. She'd bet he loved to mountain climb or some other extreme sport. When he saw her interest in the black script tattoo over his heart, he rubbed his hand over it, but didn't explain the letters and numbers.

Leaving his sweatpants on, even though they did nothing to hide his erection, he crawled onto the bed and stretched out on his side next to her so he was eye level with her chest. Placing the fingers of one hand on her stomach, he began to rub in small, sensual circles which gave her goose-bumps. Heat emanated from his fingers into her body as he gradually began to make the circles bigger and bigger until he was brushing the underside of her breast and the top of her shaven mound, never quite touching her where she wanted him to. Even though he was watching his hand and where he was touching her, he knew the instant she closed her eyes. "Eyes open, Pet. Follow my hand. Watch how your body responds to my touch."

She did as she was told and noticed the heaviness of her breasts and how the throbbing in her clit intensified. She tried to rub her thighs together to create some much needed friction between her legs, but his hand lifted from her abdomen and he gave her a sharp smack on one of her thighs. Her hips jolted in surprise. "Don't move, Pet. You don't give yourself pleasure here. That's my job, and I'll do it in my own good time."

The impact hadn't hurt beyond the initial sting, but it did startle her, and so did her increased arousal. Before she could process it, his hand dragged up her torso and cupped the weight of her breast closest to his face. Devon lifted the orb, massaged the flesh, and ran his fingers around its base before moving his hand over to do the same to her other one. While he was tending to her second breast, he pursed his lips and blew on the nipple of the first one from about two inches away. The sensation sent lightning bolts to her clit, and she involuntarily arched her back. He then took his index finger and began to draw lazy circles around her breasts, switching from one to the other, starting at their base all the way toward her nipples, yet stopping short of touching the hardened points. Kristen was almost panting, and for the first time since her horrible experience in college, she wanted to beg a man to touch her nipples.

Devon didn't stop what he was doing. "Take your left hand, and run your thumb and forefinger through what I know is your soaking wet pussy and coat them with your juices. Do not touch your clit or put them inside you. Just get them nice and wet."

She removed her hand from where it had been this entire time and did as he ordered. Moaning, she ran her fingers through her folds, gathering as much of her moisture as she could. When she held up her fingers for him to see, he gave her further instructions. "Now, take them and play with your left nipple. Roll it between your thumb and finger and pull on it."

Her mind flashed to a similar command she'd dreamed Master Xavier giving her, and her breathing increased along with the aching need in her pussy. And, oh, how she remembered how that scenario had ended. The second her wet digits closed around her left nipple, Devon's moist tongue swiped at her right one. The combined sensations had her crying out for more and all thoughts of the fictional Master X fled her mind.

Devon's tongue licked her nipple again and again, keeping pace with her fingers pleasuring her other one. If she sped up, he sped up . . . if she slowed down, he slowed down. He may have been the one issuing commands, but she was starting to understand the control she had too.

"Wet your fingers again. After you put them back on your nipple, I want you to do the same with your other hand and take over this one for me."

She did as she was told and after she was in control of both breasts, Devon slid further down the bed. "Don't stop playing with them, Pet, and spread your legs wide for me. Eyes on me and what I'm doing."

She separated her legs and he climbed over her right one before settling himself between them. He pushed her ankles toward her hips until her knees were bent to his liking with her feet flat on the bed. She was now so exposed there was nothing left for him to imagine. She watched as he ran his calloused hands up the insides of her thighs and stopped at her unprotected core framing it with both thumbs and forefingers. His mouth was only inches away from where she wanted it the most. Tom had only touched her there, he'd never given her oral sex, and she knew Devon was about to do something she had only experienced in her dreams. She waited, and waited . . . wanting to beg him to do something other than stare between her legs while her fingers continued to pluck and pinch her nipples. His eyes lifted to hers. "I love how your pussy is bare, Pet. It's so beautiful, my mouth is watering. Tell me, how long have you been doing this?"

"D-Doing what? Waxing down there?"

"Yes, how long have you been waxing your pussy? Did you do this for the donkey scum-sucker, or am I the first one to see you like this? I want an honest answer, Pet."

Her empty vagina clenched in desperation, searching for something, anything to fill it. "I tried it for the first time six months ago for research. I liked it and kept getting it done. So the answer to your question is—you're the only person who has seen it."

His grin was almost evil-looking. "I'm so pleased to hear that, Pet."

He closed the gap between them and stiffened his tongue to lick the length of her dripping slit. She screamed his name and her hips sprung from the bed, but he grabbed them and put them back where they belonged. "Stay still, Pet, or I won't let you come. And I didn't tell you to stop playing with those gorgeous tits of yours."

"Y-Yes, S-Sir," she panted. Her fingers began to move again, and this time when he licked her like she was an ice cream cone, she managed to keep her hips from moving—barely.

"Mmmm, straight from the source. This is so much better than licking your sweet nectar from my fingers, not that I didn't enjoy it immensely. You may come whenever you need to, Pet."

Devon continued to pleasure her with his tongue, alternating between impaling and swiping her with it, as his thumb began to rub the hood covering her clit she moaned. The first time he plunged his tongue inside her, her eyes rolled back into her head as her body began to climb. Oral sex was better than she'd ever imagined. He'd said earlier he wanted to eat her for hours and, right now, she'd let him.

He shifted his hands, resting one above her mound and using his fingers to expose her little jewel to his mouth while he took two fingers from his other hand and thrust them inside her hot, wet channel. His probing fingers searched and found the spot where it felt as if he was rubbing her clit from inside her womb. The three-pronged assault on her nipples, clit and G-spot proved to be too much for her to take and she screamed as she came apart at the seams. White lights flew before her closed eyes. Her body shook as her legs quivered. The muscles of her vagina clenched his fingers in a hard grip, refusing to let them go. Devon's tongue lapped at her faster to catch every drop of her release and moments later, she went over the edge again, screaming even louder this time.

As she began descending back to Earth, his mouth returned to her clit and his fingers began to work to send her airborne for a third time. She was shocked to feel her body begin to climb once more. She didn't think she could handle another orgasm if it was as intense as the first two. Her hands had left her breasts sometime during her first release, and now both fists were clutching the comforter as she pleaded with him. "N-Nooo, not again, please!"

"Yes, Pet," he growled into her mound. "Again!"

His mouth and fingers were relentless and whether she wanted to or not, she was soon coming again. Her third orgasm was the strongest one yet, and she would be surprised if it didn't kill her. If it did, it would be a helluva way to go.

Ten minutes or so later, Kristen's fuzzy mind began to clear as she lay cuddled in Devon's arms. In less than one hour the man had proved her asshole ex wrong. She was far from frigid. In fact, she was a raging volcano in the hands of a man who knew how to please a woman. From where her head rested on his chest, she looked down the length of Devon's body and saw he still had his sweatpants on with his hard-on bulging inside them. She realized despite her three powerful orgasms, he had yet to come. "Devon . . . I mean, Sir?"

He kissed the top of her head. "Yes, Pet?"

"You didn't . . . I mean . . . don't you want to . . . um?"

He let out a low chuckle. "Don't worry about me—the night is still young. Have you come back to Earth?"

Picking her head up, she smiled down on him. "Yes, and I have a request."

"Anything, sweetheart."

Suddenly she felt shy and blushed. "Teach me how to please you?"

***

ALTHOUGH DEVON WAS SMILING at her vague request, he wasn't going to let her off the hook. "Please me how? You've been pleasing me all night."

She rolled her eyes, and his hand on her ass pinched her flesh. "Ow! That hurt!" Her eyes flashed in annoyance.

"Then don't roll your eyes at your Dom." He tried to sound stern, but she was so cute when she was irritated with him. "Now, what is it you want, Pet? In plain, simple, and dirty English."

"Fine," she huffed. "I want you to teach me how to give you a blowjob. Is that plain and dirty enough for you?"

It was all he could do not to laugh at her petulance. "Plain enough, yes. Dirty enough, no. But we'll work on expanding your naughty vocabulary later. For now, before we go any further, you have a punishment coming to you."

She squealed as she sat up. "Now?"

Pushing himself into a seated position, he placed a pillow between his back and the headboard, making himself comfortable. "Yes, Pet, now. I waited because I wanted your first few orgasms to be only the result of pleasure. Since I've proven you're not unresponsive as you've been told in the past, it's time for your spanking. Come lay across my lap."

She hesitated and he gave her a moment to come to terms with what she was about to let him do. He knew she would comply with his order, but she was new to BDSM. This was her first punishment in the world of sexual play and it had to be her decision whether or not she wanted to take the final step forward. When she finally accepted this was what she wanted, she crawled over and lay across his thighs with her ass in the air.

He rubbed the pale flesh of her ass and squeezed her cheeks to warm them up. "The count is sixteen, Pet. I'm going to let you choose this one time. After the first eight, you can choose for me to give you the remainder now, or your second option is to receive the other eight when we wake up in the morning, because you will be staying in my bed for the rest of the night. Is that clear?"

He could hear the nervousness in her voice when she responded, "Y-yes, Sir."

As soon as the words were out of her mouth, he lifted his hand and slapped it back down on one cheek. *Smack.* He was pleased when she yelped, but didn't move. Her ivory skin turned pink and he held his hand to it for a moment to keep the heat in. *Smack.* This one landed on her other cheek. Again, she let out a little cry, but remained in place. He knew after the sting registered it would begin to morph into something she wouldn't be able to explain at this point.

*Smack. Smack. Smack.* These were a little harder, and she squealed and began to squirm. His hand on the middle of her back kept her from going anywhere. He aimed the next three along the creases where her ass and thighs met. *Smack. Smack. Smack.* He paused as she began to sob and he smoothed his hand over her red buttocks, giving her a chance to get her breathing under control. Despite her cries, she'd managed to keep her hands in front of her with a tight grip on the comforter. It pleased him she resisted what would've been a natural response for a new sub to reach around and try to protect her flesh from his punishment. He dipped his fingers between her legs, and she moaned when he found what he'd expected—she was very aroused. "That was eight, Pet. Should I continue or save them for the morning?"

KRISTEN WAS SO CONFUSED. Her ass was on fire, and all she could think about was how much she wanted him to thrust his cock deep inside her and fuck her. She was soaked. Even though tears were falling from her eyes, she wanted to get this over with and move on to the point when he would let her come again. Waiting to receive the other eight until morning would only make her anxious all night. "I-I'll take them now, Sir, please."

"Very well, I'll make them quick."

The next ones were harder than before and although she was crying from the pain, she was also panting and getting wetter by the second from the heat which followed. When the last spank had been delivered, she breathed a sigh of relief. He let her rest as he caressed her tender skin. After her breathing was back under control and her tears were no longer falling, he helped her up and she knelt next to him on the bed, not wanting to sit yet.

Devon brushed her damp hair from her face. "I'm proud of you, Pet. You did very well for your first spanking. Now the reasons for your punishment have been erased, and we can move on to more enjoyable activities. I believe you asked me to teach you something."

Her tear-stained cheeks creased when she smiled at him. "I did, Sir. I asked you to teach me how to give you a blowjob."

DEVON SHIFTED HIS HIPS, so he was reclining a little bit, and shoved the elastic waistband of his sweatpants down over his aching cock. "I'll be more than happy to, Pet. Scoot down on the bed and pull my pants off the rest of the way." After she removed his clothes, he spread his legs to give her room. "On your knees between my legs, Pet. I want to see your red ass up in the air while you pleasure me. Get comfortable."

When she was in position, he fisted his cock hard and pointed it toward the ceiling. A drop of pre-cum oozed from its slit. "Lick it." He watched as she leaned forward and extended her tongue out to swipe the head. She savored his taste before licking him again, and then again. Her inexperience was obvious, but rather than turning him off, it made him harder. "Take your hand and wrap it around me." He removed his own hand as hers took its place. "Tighter, Pet. Aaaahh, yeah. Like that. Now take the head between your lips while pumping your hand up and down, slowly."

*Shit!* Her innocence would be the death of him. "That's it. Now take me into your mouth as far as you can. Watch your teeth." She dragged him in and out of her mouth, a little further in each time, her confidence growing with each pass. "Use your tongue on the way out. Fuck! You're a natural at this, babe. I'm not sure I'll last long."

Without being told, she increased her pace and his eyes rolled back into his head. "Take your other hand and roll my balls in it, gently." He fisted his hand in her hair and thrust his hips up sending his dick to the back of her throat. She gagged, and then instinctively began to breathe through her nose. Without a doubt the woman was going to kill him with bliss.

"Pet, I'm not going to last much longer. No matter what, I promise I'll get my cock in your sweet pussy tonight, but if you don't want me to come down your throat, you better tell me now."

Refusing to stop, she tightened her grip on his shaft and balls and sucked him harder and faster. It was all the encouragement he needed and he roared as he came deep in her mouth. He felt her swallow several times, and the movement of her throat extended his orgasm, forcing a long groan from his mouth. Despite his release, he was still hard. Reaching down, he surprised her by grabbing her under her arms and pulling her up until she was straddling his hips. He leaned over and grabbed one of the condoms he'd placed on the nightstand when he changed his pants earlier. She lifted up on her knees, and he rolled it on before lining his cock up with her opening. As soon as his head was inside her, she lowered herself all the way down on him. She was so tight, but her wetness eased his entry. He grabbed her hips and began to rock them up and down in time to his own. "Oh God, sweetheart. You feel so fucking good."

KRISTEN COULDN'T BELIEVE another orgasm was building up inside her. Never in her life had she known sex could be so incredible. This was what women bragged about and what she wrote in her books. She clenched around him, and he groaned, so she did it again. His finger found her clit and, when he pressed down, she screamed as waves of ecstasy flowed through her. Before she knew what was happening, Devon flipped them so he was now on top of her, and he began to pump his hips feverishly. *Holy crap!* There was no way she could come again. But he proved her wrong, and this time she took him with her, and as one they flew over the edge.

# CHAPTER 13

*D*evon sat in his office waiting for Boomer to join him. The youngest member of the team had sent him a text telling him he was running about ten minutes late due to a flat tire on his jeep. There were files and paperwork on Devon's desk which needed attention, but his mind was on the brunette he woke up next to this morning. He couldn't remember the last time he spent an entire night in bed with a woman, but it had been many years. Thinking back, it must've been while he'd been in the Navy, and not in his own bed, but one in a hotel. No other woman, aside from Jenn, his mother, Aunt Marsha, and the interior decorator, had ever been in his apartment here in the complex. All his sexual encounters occurred at the club—until last night.

He'd awoken to Kristen's seductive hand grazing across his chest and abdomen before she began to explore lower. Instead of letting her know he was awake, he kept his eyes shut for a few moments enjoying her touch. She'd been about to wrap her soft hand around his hard dick when he surprised her by flipping her over to her stomach, grabbing a condom, and sliding into her from behind. It had been quick and carnal, and somehow not satisfying enough because he took her again a few minutes later in the shower. But not before taking his time to soap up and touch every inch of her luscious body and making her scream at the top of her lungs as she came for him again. He wondered if Ian had heard her in his own apartment below, despite the soundproofing they'd installed in the walls and ceilings of the units. In one night and early morning he'd given her eight or nine orgasms—he'd lost count at some point—and found his own release four times. And yet he wished she was here in his office so he could fuck her silly on his desk. Kristen may be a lot of things, but frigid was not one of them.

He couldn't get enough of his Ninja-girl librarian. The woman had so many different layers to her and he didn't think he would ever discover them all if he tried for the rest of his life. For some strange reason he couldn't explain, he hadn't removed her submissive collar after he'd dropped her off at her car this morning. He noticed she touched it often, as if it grounded her, and the thought pleased him more than it should.

She'd been so eager and responsive last night, it blew his mind. He couldn't remember a time when a woman's innocence had turned him on the way Kristen's did. He also couldn't recall ever being so at ease with a woman he had sex with. After she left The Covenant yesterday afternoon, he'd looked through her background check Marco had done several days earlier. He'd been surprised to see she hadn't sought alimony during her divorce even though her ass-monkey ex, Tom Rydell, made a good living as a stock broker and the goat-fucker would've deserved it if she had. Most women would've taken their revenge against a cheating husband out on his bank account. Kristen hadn't. In addition to being a Beta-reader herself for other authors, her own books earned her decent money and it's what she was able to live off of in comfort. She was making her own way in the world and was proud of it.

Devon had never found a woman to be so enticing beyond a basic sexual attraction and despite his thoughts, or maybe because of them, he couldn't wait to see her again tonight. They'd made plans for a late dinner at his place and even later dessert since he would be working until around seven. He would have to retrieve his toy bag from his locker at the club because he knew what her next lesson was going to involve.

He heard a knock on his door and lifted his head to see Boomer walk in and sit down in one of the leather chairs on the other side of his desk. "Hey Devil Dog, sorry I'm late. I must've run over a nail last night. Damn tire was flatter than a piece of road-kill this morning."

Glancing at the small clock inside a brass anchor which sat on his desk, Devon noted the time. "No problem, man. Shit happens. We still have a few minutes before we have to leave for the airport to meet up with King Rajeemh and his lovely offspring."

He said the last three words with sarcasm and an eye roll. King Rajeemh was the ruler of the small North African country of Timasur, near Mali. The man owned several homes around the world, but the nearby gulf-front Clearwater Beach mansion was one of his favorites. He and his family visited several times a year and used Trident Security to assist his personal bodyguards while they were there. For royalty, the king was a laid-back man and kind to anyone in his employ as long as they didn't insult or betray him. His son, Prince Raji, the heir to the throne, was exactly like him. But his daughter, Princess Tahira, was a completely different story.

The exotically beautiful twenty-three-year-old was a spoiled brat, plain and simple. She treated her minions as if they were bugs on the bottom of her shoe—unless she wanted something from them. She also had a thing for American men and had unsuccessfully propositioned every man at Trident along with the contract employees the company used when they needed extra man-power. And damn, could she pout and get revenge when she didn't get what she wanted.

Last time she was in Florida, it was Brody who she'd blatantly hit on when her father's back was turned. After the geek shot her down for the third time one morning, she proceeded to drag him and the rest of her security detail to every shoe store within a fifty mile radius. She then spent five hours trying on every single pair she liked—not once, not twice, but three times, asking the former SEAL his opinion on each pair, as if Brody knew the difference between a pump and kitten heel. Devon didn't know the difference either, but later the same night, Brody had gone on a half hour rampage, bitching about the little princess and her fetish, so they'd all gotten an unwanted lesson on women's shoes. They'd finally begged Shelby to scene with him to shut him up, not that the sub minded.

"Why am I stuck on this assignment again?" Boomer had been complaining for the past two days since they found out the royal party was making a last minute change in their itinerary after a visit to New York where King Rajeemh had been attending a conference at the U.N.

"Because it's your turn in the princess rotation."

"And why is it you and Ian are not in the rotation, again?"

Devon smirked. "Because we sign your paychecks, ass-hat."

The younger man frowned. "I knew there was some fucked-up, bullshit reason. Can you just shoot me now and put me out of my impending misery? You know how much I hate shopping unless it's for a new gun or toy for the club." Devon chuckled before Boomer's frown turned into an evil grin as if a thought had suddenly occurred to him.

"So, speaking of the club . . ."

*Uh-oh.*

"Tell me about this . . ." He snapped his fingers a few times. "Um, what did Egghead call it? Oh yeah . . . a date. That's it. Tell me about this date you went on last night. I heard she was smokin' and kicked some serious ass in the locker room." Boomer had apparently shown up at The Covenant after Devon had dragged Kristen out of there.

"You went on a date?"

Both men's eyes whipped toward the open office door and saw Paula Leighton standing there. Boomer turned back around so the woman couldn't see him and mouthed the word 'sorry'. The thirty-year-old office manager had been working for them for the last three months after Mrs. Kemple retired to be closer to her newborn triplet grandchildren in Miami. The older woman had worked for them since the beginning of Trident and was a surrogate mother of sorts to all of them. She'd been a godsend when Jenn first came to live with Ian, giving the younger girl an understanding and sympathetic female shoulder to lean on and taking her shopping for things she would need for her college dorm room. They'd thrown her a big party at a local restaurant and given her a handsome severance check when she left them after training Paula, and the gray-haired woman was deeply missed.

Efficiency wasn't Paula's problem. The problem was she was overly nosy about their personal lives and tried to insert herself into them. She also made it not-so-subtly-known she wouldn't mind going out with any of the men she saw every day in the office, but it appeared her hopes hung on Marco. In a way, Devon felt sorry for her because she tried too hard to fit in, and as a result it made it much more apparent that she didn't. The men tried to be subtle, yet let her know they weren't interested in her other than as the woman who ran their office. Even if any of them were attracted to her, none of them were stupid enough to get involved with a company employee. If things didn't change, Devon would have to have a talk with Ian about letting her go and looking for a replacement. At the moment, he didn't want to answer her prying question and posed one of his own. "Paula, what are you doing here on a Saturday?" It was a testament to where his mind had been earlier when he realized he never heard the alert on his phone, which sounded when the interior gate was opened, not only when Boomer drove up, but also when Paula had arrived.

The woman waved her hand as if her unexpected presence was no big deal. "Oh, I forgot my wallet in my desk yesterday after I paid some bills during lunch, so I swung by to pick it up. I was going to use the restroom before I left. So, who did you go out with last night?"

Standing, Devon picked up his shoulder holster and put it on before placing his SIG Sauer 9mm semi-automatic in it.

"No one you would know." His response was vague on purpose. He grabbed his keys and cell phone off his desk before retrieving the light-weight sports coat, which would conceal his weapon in public, from where it was lying over the arm of his couch a short distance away. They didn't need to leave for another ten minutes or so, but he didn't want to give Paula a chance to ask any more questions. "Come on, Boomer. Don't want to keep the princess waiting." Passing the woman on his way out he added, "Have a nice weekend, Paula."

---

"OKAY, sweet cheeks, lunch orders are in, mimosas are at hand. Start dishing the dirt."

Kristen rolled her eyes at Will and realized she was playing with the leather collar which was still around her neck. She forgot to take it off this morning and didn't want to now. Devon hadn't told her to take it off and it didn't feel right to do so without his permission. "I have no idea what you're talking about."

"Don't be coy, Kristen, or I'll have Roxy spank your ass."

They all snorted and giggled at Kayla's comment, and Roxy added, "I don't know, honey, I think she might like it too much." The four of them laughed even harder, drawing a few stares from the Saturday brunch crowd at The Gallery. The place was a combination art gallery/restaurant the others had introduced her to. The place served great food and displayed paintings from local artists which were for sale. Some of the painters showed a lot of talent and every time they'd gone there to eat, sold paintings had been replaced by new ones. There was one painting which caught Kristen's eye when they'd first sat down and, after taking a better look, she realized it was similar to the art in the lobby of The Covenant. She wondered if they'd been done by the same artist and decided she'd have to ask Devon about it tonight over dinner.

Kristen looked at her friends and cousin and was once again grateful for her new life in Florida. Two months after they got married, Tom had transferred to the New York City office of his company so they'd moved to New Jersey, across the Hudson River from Manhattan. At first, she'd been happy to follow her new husband anywhere, but it wasn't long before she became lonely. Her best friend from high school, who'd also been her maid of honor, had made a permanent move to Arizona after graduating from ASU. Kristen's other friends from high school and college were scattered all over the states with new careers and new families. Her parents and step-parents had their own jobs and lives to keep them busy. Most of their neighbors in Ridgewood, New Jersey had been two-income families who worked Monday to Friday, nine-to-five or later, so she hadn't bonded with any of them past the point of generic conversations. She'd thrown herself into her writing and her human contact soon consisted of only her husband, when he was home, her family and best friend over the phone, and her editor and Beta-readers online, with a few get-togethers with Tom's associates thrown in for good measure.

Now she had face-to-face friends again and it felt wonderful. "Okay, what do you want to hear about first? Dinner, the club, or after?"

Roxy called out "the club" while the other two demanded she tell them about "after."

She giggled and took another sip. "I'll tell you what—it's easier to go through everything in order." Her table-mates groaned before she lowered her voice so as not to be overheard by other patrons. "Okay, I'll do this part quick. I was thirteen minutes late meeting him, and he promised to spank me for each minute I was late. Dinner was great. I had the veal piccata and he had the steak pizzaiola. Good conversation, no turn-offs, lots of turn-ons, one minor faux pas on my part where it sounded like I was asking him his financial status. He didn't seem to mind. Lots of flirting, and he fed me a bite of his dinner. I let him drive me over to the club in his car. Nervous chit-chat, and we arrived safely."

Her companions laughed at her rushed, stunted recap of the first part of her date. She took a dramatic breath and then a sip of her champagne with orange juice. "Okay, moving on to the good stuff. When we got to the club, he opened my car door for me like a perfect gentleman and then kissed me senseless. And yes, the man can kiss."

She paused as the waitress dropped off their bruschetta

appetizer. "The club was absolutely amazing. It looks so different at night with the mood lighting and all."

Roxy spoke up. "And I'm sure having a bunch of nearly naked people walking around had something to do with the different atmosphere."

Kristen winced, then nodded, because that part had been awkward. "Yeah, it freaked me out at first. I was being introduced to all these people, some with all their private parts showing, and I didn't know where to look."

"It does take a while to get used to. When I first started taking Kay to clubs, it flustered her more than the actual scenes. Casual conversation is hard when you're trying not to stare at a chick's who-ha and jugs, or a guy's junk."

They all burst out laughing again, drawing even more attention to themselves, but they couldn't help it. Will was almost crying. "Who-ha and junk? Are those actual medical terms, Doctor? Yes, Mrs. Smith, your son playing with his junk is normal, and your teenage daughter's who-ha hasn't been popped yet, but she needs to get a bra for those jugs."

Kristen almost fell out of her chair because she was laughing so hard her cheeks and stomach ached. The others were just as bad. It took several minutes to get themselves back under control because they couldn't look at each without losing it again. She waved her hands in front of her tear-filled eyes. "Oh my God, Will, you did not just say that."

"Of course I did, sweet cheeks. It's what I'm here for . . . to look good for the men, and to be a comic relief and fashion stylist for my girls. Now get back to the juicy details, like why you're still wearing his collar. I may not be into kink," he pointed to her neck, "but I do know what one of those means."

"You fucking bitch!"

Startled, Kristen and her friends looked up to see a very pissed off woman standing over her. She was shocked when she realized it was the redhead whose butt she'd kicked last night. Heather or Melissa—she wasn't sure who was who. Either way, Kristen wasn't going to stay in a vulnerable position so she stood, as did Roxy and

Will, who were sitting on either side of her, while Kayla looked on from her seat tucked away in a corner.

"Because of you I lost my membership to the club, you bitch."

There was pure venom in her words and rage in her eyes, but Kristen refused to back down even though they were making a public scene. She'd bested the woman the night before and she would do it again today. She kept her voice calm, which was sure to piss the red-head off even more. "No, *you* lost your membership because *you* and your cohort were bullying a sweet, innocent girl who was too afraid of you to stand up for herself. It's what bully-bitches like you do. But I told you last night, and I'll tell you again . . . I'm not afraid of you, so if you want to try to take me on, I'll be more than happy to drop you on your fugly face again."

She took a step forward, but Roxy was quicker and moved in front of her, facing the woman who had interrupted their brunch with her rudeness. If she hadn't learned Roxy was a BDSM top, Kristen may not have noticed the authority in her voice. But now she clearly recognized the low don't-fuck-with-me-or-you'll-regret-it tone of a Dom/Domme, and she knew she'd never want to be on the good doctor's bad side. "Heather, I don't know if you remember me, but your friend, Scott, is an associate of mine from the hospital. And I doubt you want me to have a conversation with him over your behavior today, because from the sound of things, I'm sure he's already angry with you. Now, I suggest you leave or I'll be calling Scott faster than you can say 'yes, Ma'am.' Do I make myself clear?"

Kristen watched as Heather paled more and more with every word Roxy spoke. The Domme doctor was a healthy size ten and five-eleven in her low heels so she could be daunting when she wanted to be. She towered over the now-very-intimidated sub who Kristen expected to either pass out or pee in her pants. Without saying anything more, the woman spun around and tore out of the restaurant, leaving two very confused other women to take off after her. Roxy turned and looked at Kristen, her eyes gleaming with mischief. "Oh, girl, I can tell you haven't gotten to the good parts yet, and I can't wait to hear them."

As the three of them sat back down, Kayla batted her eyes at her wife and crooned, "I love when you go into your protective Wonder Woman persona. It's such a turn on." She then looked at Kristen while flagging down their waitress at the same time. "Start dishing, girl, this is going to be good. Waitress, another pitcher of mimosas, please."

# CHAPTER 14

*A*t a quarter after seven that night, Kristen was slicing tomatoes in Devon's kitchen for a salad she was throwing together. Across the island from where she worked, the man's broad back was turned to her as he sautéed a skillet filled with penne ala vodka. He was handsome, a good conversationalist, an even better Dom, incredible at sex, and now, he cooked! What more could a girl want?

She hadn't eaten anything since noon and now her stomach was growling. The rest of brunch had been uneventful as she recapped for her friends the remaining details of her date. She told them enough to satisfy their curiosity, but still kept many of the details to herself.

She felt so at ease with Devon as they prepared, then ate their dinner, and it felt like they'd known each other a lot longer than they actually had. He talked about his day taking care of the security for a king and some spoiled princess from a small country in Africa, and she told him about her brunch at The Gallery, complete with the run-in with Heather. At first he reacted as if he wanted to commit murder, but calmed after she explained how Mistress Roxanne had taken over. "Roxy's wife, Kayla, told me they applied for membership at The Covenant a few months ago. They currently go to another club, I think she called it 'Heat,' but since Roxy is a pediatrician, Kayla said they wanted the increased privacy your club provides."

"What's their last name? I'll tell Mitch to put their application at the top of the list. As long as there are no red flags, we'll have it approved within the next few weeks. It's the least I can do for the way she protected my sub."

Her heart did a little flutter when he said "my sub." She knew he didn't mean it as possessive as she thought it sounded, but she still liked it. "It's London, and thanks. That would be so great. They're a really nice couple, and I know they'd appreciate the gesture."

"There's nothing to appreciate. It's my way of thanking them."

They sat down at the dinner table with Devon at one end and Kristen in the seat catty-corner to him. She picked up her fork and pointed it at him before digging into her meal. "So tell me more about your family since I told you about mine last night. You said your parents are Marie and Chuck Sawyer. Can I assume your dad's real name is Charles or Charlie?" Out of the blue, the name clicked in her brain. Her eyes grew wide and the fork slipped from her fingers and clattered against her plate. "Oh. My. God. Your dad is Charles Sawyer? *The* Charles Sawyer? I thought he looked familiar. I read an article about him in *People* magazine. He's like the Trump of the Carolinas and Virginias."

He laughed and shook his head in amusement. "Don't tell him that, dad doesn't get along with Trump. He thinks he's too egotistical."

She couldn't believe he was joking how his *billionaire* father—yes, that was with a *B*—didn't care for another *billionaire* like they were two neighborhood guys who didn't get along. The man in front of her was the heir to a fortune which ninety-nine-point-nine percent of the population could only dream of. *Holy crap!* She picked up her fork again. "Didn't I . . . didn't I read how he and your mom were raised in middle-class families, and he started with a small real estate agency?"

He took a bite of pasta, chewed, then swallowed. "Yup, it's true. Two years before Ian was born, dad managed to buy his first apartment building out of a foreclosure. The man is shrewd, a quick study, and some would say, extremely lucky. By the time I was three or four, he'd made some wise investments and owned a bunch of buildings and strip malls in both North and South Carolina and built his empire from there. He's the CEO of Sawyer-O'Toole, which is Mom's maiden name, but his staff and the board handle the day-to-day operations when he's traveling with my mom.

"Is that how you had the money to start your businesses? Oh, wait! There I go again, don't answer that." She had to stop putting her foot in her mouth because she didn't seem to have a filter around him.

"No, don't worry about it. We grew up comfortable, more comfortable than my parents did when they were young. But mom and dad always made sure we weren't spoiled. We did chores for our allowances and went to public schools. I told you how we worked in the poor countries my parents took us to. At fourteen, when we were old enough to get our working papers, we had to either get jobs or volunteer an average teenage work week at a non-profit organization. When we graduated from high school, we had to choose between a four-year college degree, holding at least a 3.6 GPA, or four years in the military. Dad had served a four-year stint in the Army before marrying my mom and always said that's when he grew up and became a man.

"Dad set us all up with trust funds, but we couldn't access them until we were thirty. At eighteen, we started receiving a small monthly stipend which was only enough for bare-bones living expenses. If we wanted anything more, it had to come from an earned paycheck. Nick hasn't even gotten access to his full trust yet, since he's only twenty-five. Anyway, Ian and I used part of our trust money to purchase this compound, start our security business, Trident Security, and the club. My father might have given us the seed money, but he made sure we earned it over the years and knew what it was like to work hard for what we wanted. In the Sawyer family, life was not handed to you on a silver platter. My folks are the greatest and kindest people I know, and they taught us what it meant to have pride in ourselves, our work, and the world around us."

Kristen was impressed with his parents' dedication to raising their sons the right way. "Wow, I went to school with a bunch of spoiled kids who could've learned so much from your parents. Most of the kids nowadays expect everything to be handed to them with no work involved. So, you and your brothers all chose the Navy over college?"

Sadness clouded his handsome features and he swallowed hard. He was clearly struggling with how to answer her. Not wanting him to be uncomfortable, she was about to change the subject when he stood, walked over to the entertainment unit, and picked up the photo of the four brothers she'd been looking at the night before. "Ian went into the Navy right after high school, but I chose college. The University of North Carolina at Chapel Hill with a business major, in fact. Ian's two years older than me. He was off saving the world while I was partying after class. I still managed a 3.8 GPA my first semester, although, it might have been higher if my statistics class hadn't been so early in the morning."

He sat back down next to her and handed her the framed picture. He seemed to forget he'd told her who was who last night and pointed to each of the four young boys in the photo. "This is Ian, right before he left for basic training. That's me, and the little guy is Nick, who was about six back then. And this here is my other brother, John."

The odd tone of his voice when he mentioned John had Kristen studying the photo a little bit more. Devon and John each had one of their arms around their older brother's shoulders while Ian held Nick under his armpits so the boy's feet were hanging in mid-air. All four of them were mugging for the camera. "He looks exactly like you. Are you twins?"

"A lot of people got us confused, but no we weren't. We were Irish twins though, since he was eleven months younger than me." She noticed the past tense he was now using. "And Nick was a surprise. Anyway, John and I hung out with a lot of the same people since we were so close in age, but he was a year younger in school.

During high school, we partied like most kids, finding ways to get beer and liquor without getting caught. I knew he was drinking a lot on the weekends, but hell, we all were. For the most part, we managed to keep our parents from finding out, but there were a few times we weren't as careful as we thought which resulted in getting grounded. When that happened, Mom would give the housekeeper a few days off with pay, and we had to clean the house for her, while completely hung over. I didn't know which was worse, the sound of the vacuum on a pounding head or cleaning the bathrooms which five guys used." He let out wry chuckle and shook his head at the memory. His meal forgotten, he took a deep breath and continued. "Anyway, John got hooked on alcohol, and I never knew it. None of us did. I didn't think a seventeen year old kid could be an alcoholic, but I was wrong."

He sighed, but continued, and Kristen got the feeling he didn't talk about this often. Her heart clenched by how he was trusting her with his past and emotions. "I'd returned to college for my second semester. Christmas and New Year's had been great. Ian couldn't make it, but was able to call home from somewhere overseas, I forget where, on Christmas morning which, of course, made my mom and Nick's day. I was back at school, getting settled into my new classes, hanging out with my friends again. I'd hooked up with this girl right before vacation, and we picked right up where we left off. We were making out in my room one Friday night after a few hours at a local bar. There was a knock at my door. I had her half-undressed, and we were laughing and having fun like normal nineteen-year-olds, so I yelled at whoever it was to fuck off. The knocking turned into pounding, and I got up to open the door and tell whoever it was to take a hike. It was my dad and my Uncle Dan, Mitch's dad. The look on their faces . . . I assumed it was Ian, but it wasn't. It was John.

"He'd ditched school that morning after mom, dad, and Nick left for work and school. I don't recall why, but the housekeeper was off that day too. Dad forgot something in his home office and swung by to pick it up at lunchtime. He found John on the kitchen floor with one and a half empty bottles of vodka. He drank so much he'd passed out, then vomited and aspirated. There was nothing the EMT's could do. We found out later his blood alcohol level was four times the legal limit. Here I was having a great time, partying at school, and making out with some girl, trying to get into her pants, while my kid brother was on a medical examiner's table." His hand rubbed the left side of his chest. "That's what my tattoo over my heart is—his initials, and dates of birth and death."

Sometime during his story Kristen had moved her chair closer, and now had his other hand in hers. "It wasn't your fault. Alcoholics are usually pretty good at hiding their problem. John obviously hid it well so you can't blame yourself."

"Part of me knows that now, but part of me will always carry the guilt of knowing my brother was spiraling out of control and I didn't stop it. I saw he'd been drinking a lot over the winter recess, but I refused to admit he had a problem. Anyway, it took three days to get Ian home from the middle of nowhere, and then we went through the whole Irish wakes and funeral. The night of the funeral, a few family members came back to the house after the service and restaurant get-together.

"I don't know why, but I hadn't cried at all the entire week, I guess I was numb. I was sitting on the patio with Mitch's older brother, DJ—Dan, Jr.—and Ian came out with a couple of beers for us. I took one sip, maybe two, and threw up all over the place. Once there was nothing left in my stomach, I dry-heaved for almost an hour, and then I broke down and cried. Ian sat on the grass with me and didn't let go of me until I got myself back under control. I haven't touched a sip of alcohol since." Devon took a deep breath as a lone tear was falling down his left cheek. Kristen took her hand off his arm and wiped it away with her fingers. "I can't believe I told you all of that. My team knows the basics of what happened, but I've never told anyone the whole story."

She leaned forward and brushed her lips against his before sitting back again. "I'm honored you told me. I'm sorry you had to go through that. I don't have any brothers or sisters, but if I did, I don't think I would've survived the same kind of loss without having a complete breakdown."

Obviously embarrassed about crying in front of her, he stood and began to clean up from their meal. "Well, for a while there I didn't think I would survive, either. I didn't go back to school after the funeral. John had wanted to follow Ian into the Navy. Since he couldn't, I guess I thought I should go in his place. Whatever the reason, it was the best decision I ever made, and I've never regretted it. The Navy gave me a purpose and a way to control the guilt I felt."

Following him into the kitchen, she began to put away the leftovers in a container he handed her while he tackled the dirty dishes and pots. "Is that why you started playing in the lifestyle? For the control?"

He nodded. "Ian thought it would help me get past it, and in some ways it did. At least it gave me an outlet to release the grief which had built up over time."

They finished cleaning up in silence, and the domesticity of their actions had her suddenly longing for something more. Something she swore she didn't want, and Devon told her he couldn't give her. Something which would last a lifetime. But she wouldn't have a lifetime with him. She would only have this weekend.

# CHAPTER 15

*S*haking herself from her wayward thoughts, Kristen found him watching her from a relaxed position, leaning against the kitchen counter, his arms overlapping across his gray T-shirt covered chest and his legs crossed at the ankles. "Where did you go, Pet? I lost you there for a minute."

Not wanting him to know what she'd been thinking, she tried to brush his question off. "It wasn't anything important. Do you want some coffee?"

The Dom in him must not have liked her answer because he frowned and his eyes narrowed. "Strip."

"Wh-what?"

He didn't move from his position, but his posture no longer appeared relaxed. "I won't repeat myself, Kristen. You heard me loud and clear. Either say your safeword or do as you're told."

Hesitating only a split-second longer, she pulled her sleeveless, emerald green shirt over her head and placed it on the counter next to her. His eyes roamed over her body as she continued, and they were the only part of him that moved. She felt his disconcerting gaze as if it was a caress across her skin, giving her goose-bumps and increasing her pulse. After removing her sandals and white capris, she stood there in her flower print bra and thong underwear. But it wasn't enough to satisfy him. "All of it, Pet. You've already earned a count of five. Hesitating earned you five more. If you hesitate again, I'll keep adding more."

*Crap!* Ten wasn't *too* bad, but since he was obviously upset about something, she didn't want to add to it. Her ass had barely recovered from last night's spanking. She got rid of the last of her garments then stood there waiting for him to say or do something. It was weird to be standing buck naked in his kitchen while he remained dressed. A minute went by . . . then another . . . and he just stared at her in silence. She began to fidget. When she opened her mouth to ask him if she was supposed to be doing something, he abruptly pushed off from the counter, causing her to flinch. "Face the island. Put your chest and stomach on the countertop. Rest your head on the backs of your hands and spread your feet as wide apart as you can."

Following his instructions, she laid her upper body across the island and the coolness of the granite was a shock to her system. A moment of panic hit her when he left the room and came back with a black duffel bag, setting it on the other countertop behind her. Taking slow deep breaths to keep from hyperventilating, she heard him rummage around in the bag and tried to see what he was doing, but from her current position she couldn't.

"Do you know why I'm angry, Pet?"

He wasn't yelling at her, but the flat, low tone of his voice was louder to her than any shout she'd ever heard. A shiver of fear mixed with arousal confused her. "N-No, Sir."

"When I asked you where you had gone in your complex brain, what was the answer you gave me, word for word?"

Her mind raced—what had she said? "Um, I think I said it wasn't anything important, Sir."

She tensed when he approached and stood behind her widespread legs. She waited for him to touch her, spank her, do something to her, but he made no contact with any part of her body. The longer he stood there and didn't touch her, the more she wanted him to, in any way he wanted. The suspense of the unknown was killing her. After a minute or so, he spoke again.

"I'm not your ex lump of cow-turd, Pet. When I ask you a question, I expect an answer worthy of your intelligence. 'It wasn't anything important' was not an intelligent answer. If I wanted you to give me a non-answer, I wouldn't have bothered to ask the question in the first place. For your little lie, you've earned a count of five. Would you like to revise your answer now, or would you prefer I give you your five, then tie your hands behind you? Then I'll leave you standing here for the next hour with one vibrator in your pussy, another in this sweet ass of yours and a ball gag in your mouth, while I go sit on the couch and find a ballgame to watch."

Seriously? "I-I'd l-like . . ." She cleared her throat and tried again. "I'd like to revise my answer, Sir."

"Very well, but I suggest you think about your answer carefully. You only have one chance to impress me."

She was so nervous, it took her a few moments to remember what she'd been thinking about before his big, bad Dom-ness showed up for a visit. What had they been doing? She remembered they'd been cleaning the kitchen and putting away the dishes. *That's it!* She took a deep breath. "It'd occurred to me, Sir, I've never shared a meal with a man where we cooked and cleaned up together, aside from my dad when I was little. That I was enjoying something so incredibly simple surprised me and I wanted to do it again sometime. I-I know you . . . I mean . . . we said this was temporary and I didn't want you to think I was reading into things and wishing things could be different, so it was easier to brush off your question. I'm sorry, Sir."

He placed his hands on her bare back and began to caress her skin from her shoulders to her bottom and back up again. "Now, that wasn't so hard, was it? I may not always like or agree with your answers, but I will not allow you to lie to me. Understood?"

"Yes, Sir. I'm sorry I disrespected you with my first answer."

She couldn't see his face, but she heard the smile in his voice. "Thank you, Pet. And by the way, I also enjoyed cooking and cleaning with you, and it surprised me too. I don't think I've ever done that with a woman who wasn't my mother. You never did it with your fucktard ex?"

A little giggle came out of her mouth. "Please, the douche-bag couldn't boil water without a ten page instruction booklet."

He let out a bark of laughter. "Douche-bag? Very good, Pet, you're learning. Now, let's forget about the ass-nugget, and get back to you and me. Let me get you prepped, and then I'll give you your punishment. When it's over, all will be forgiven and forgotten, and then we can move on to some fun for the rest of the evening."

*Prepped?* What the heck did he mean by that?

"Relax, Pet." She didn't realize she'd tensed up again. "I would never do anything to harm you, you know that, right?"

"Yes, Sir." And she did, although she noticed he used the word "harm" instead of "hurt." Had it been on purpose? When he spanked her the night before, it hurt at first, but then it transitioned into intense pleasure. She'd been dripping with need by the time he finished.

His hands were now stroking her legs, arms and hips, in addition to her back and buttocks, in a soothing circular motion. She began to relax at his ministration and finally let out a deep sigh. She didn't notice when he removed one of his hands until she heard a pop and felt a cold liquid land a little bit above her ass before oozing down between her cheeks. It was cold and her body jerked a little, but she remained in place. The hand rubbing her back eased lower and his fingers parted her, working the lubricant into the hidden valley and over the sensitive hole within. Her leg and butt muscles tensed and he slapped her right ass cheek with his other hand. "Don't clench. This will be a lot easier on you if you relax."

Kristen took a deep breath and tried to do as he instructed. He didn't say what "this" was, but she didn't need him to. This morning in the shower, he'd told her he would soon take her in the ass, but he had to prepare her for it first. However, she hadn't expected her preparation to begin tonight. This was one of her soft limits and he seemed determined to test it sooner rather than later.

As he added more lubricant, one of his fingers stopped right at her untried entrance. Part of her wanted to stop him, but the other part of her wanted to push past her fears and self-imposed sexual restrictions. This man was giving her a chance to explore her deepest, darkest fantasies. Fantasies she would've denied having before meeting him.

"Don't tense up, Pet. I'm going to start putting my finger in. You'll feel some pressure and discomfort, but if it hurts to the point you can't take it, say the word 'yellow' and I'll ease up and start over. Remember to breathe and bear down. It may take a while, but I promise, you will have a plug in this virgin hole of yours before we go any further tonight."

Oh God, she knew he meant it and his words made her clit throb while her mind raced. She'd never been touched by a man there before and the feel of him at her anus scared and thrilled her at the same time. This was what she told herself she wanted. Her Dom telling her what he was going to do to her, and her only choices were to let him or say her safeword and end everything. Swallowing her fear, she forced her muscles to relax. "Yes, Sir."

"Good girl." His finger rimmed her puckered opening, working in the gel which would ease his entry. He began to push in and her body naturally fought the invasion. His hand landed on her left cheek this time. "Don't fight it. You will let me in."

She moaned, not knowing if it was because of the heat spreading from where he spanked her or the feeling of him easing his finger into her ass. Whenever she started to tighten her muscles surrounding her anus, he retreated for more lubricant and inched back in, a little further each time. He got to a point where she wasn't sure if she could handle the burning sensation flaring through her when he reached around with his other hand and found her clit, pinching it once, hard. The new sensation caught her off guard and switched her mind away from his finger in her ass.

As soon as it relaxed, he pushed his knuckle past her sphincter and lit up the nerves inside her. A flash of pain came and went before it was replaced with a feeling of being filled and wanting . . . no . . . needing more.

She groaned and shifted her hips, looking for something, anything which would give her the relief she desperately sought.

The movement earned her another smack. "Stay still," he growled. "You'll take what I give you, when I give it to you, and not a second sooner."

His finger felt huge as he stroked it in then out again, never coming all of the way out of her. He'd rotated his knuckle on each outward drag, stretching her a little more. She was panting and sweating, wanting to pull away from him, wanting to push back for more. "Please, Sir."

"Please what, Pet?"

"More. Sir. Please. More." She was reduced to one word sentences. Anything beyond that would require thought and she couldn't think, only feel.

"I think you're trying to top from the bottom, sweetheart, but I'm feeling a little generous." She didn't know what she expected, but it hadn't been for him to remove his finger completely. She cried out at the abrupt loss and her breath hitched when she felt something larger than his finger at her entrance. He squirted a little more lube on her ass and began to work what she knew was an anal plug into her. It felt huge and she didn't think he would ever be able to get it inside her. Reaching around her hip, he pinched her clit again and the plug slid home. The sensations proved to be too much and she screamed as an intense orgasm washed over her. White and black spots flashed before her closed eyes and her body trembled as wave after wave of pleasure pulsated through her while Devon rotated the plug which was now seated to its hilt, deep in her anal cavity. Her breathing was heavy as she floated back down.

"Tsk, tsk, tsk. Such a naughty sub, coming without permission. You should know better and it brings your count up to fifteen, Pet. Now stand there and take them like the good girl I know you can be. But I feel I must warn you, clenching will make it more . . . intense, but if you relax too much you risk losing the plug. And trust me Pet, you don't want lose it. You won't like the punishment for that offense."

"Yes, Sir," she gulped.

She felt him step away from her and anticipated the first smack, but it didn't come. Instead, she once again heard him retrieve something from his duffel bag. Her mind ran through the possibilities of what he was getting and none of them boded well for her. She'd been so worried she hadn't heard him approach again until she felt a sharp sting as something struck her ass cheeks. She couldn't help the sudden shriek which escaped her mouth, but somehow she didn't move. Her breathing increased again in short pants. Whatever he'd hit her with, he was currently dragging it up the inside of one of her legs and down the other. "In case you're wondering, Pet, it's a riding crop."

Before she could answer him she felt the torture device strike her ass just above her thighs and she went up on her toes and clenched her leg muscles. Unfortunately, that reminded her of the plug in her ass. Sensations of pain and pleasure warred inside her and she couldn't tell which one was winning the battle. The sound of the crop connecting with her bare skin was more of a thud than a slap, but it didn't mean the damn thing didn't hurt. But as the initial sting eased she felt the increase throbbing in her clit and she worried she wasn't going to be able to hold back another impending orgasm. By the time he reached fifteen she was one touch away from falling into the great beyond. She heard him toss the crop on the counter behind them before his fingers dipped between her legs and he discovered how embarrassingly wet she was. He stroked her folds. "You liked that, didn't you, Pet? Would you like me to give you permission to come this time?"

"Oh, God, yes! Yes, Sir. Please, Sir, let me come!"

"Since you asked so nicely . . ." One of his fingers moved further and tapped on her clit, which was all it took to send her over while screaming her throat raw. She'd never thought she could pass out from intense pleasure, but that's exactly what happened next.

---

DEVON LAY ON HIS SIDE, his head in his hand as he leaned on his elbow. It was four o'clock in the morning, and he couldn't sleep. So instead, he was watching Kristen as she slept next to him. She was still naked, her long hair spread out on the pillow under her head, and he fought the urge to touch her because she deserved the rest after what he'd put her through the night before. But he needed a connection to her so he reached out and rubbed a few strands of her brown locks with his fingers.

Reveling in the feel of her silky strands, he thought about all he'd told her last night and was surprised how comfortable he'd felt about admitting who his dad was. While his SEAL teammates had known about his dad, few others in the Navy, beyond a couple of his superiors, had ever been told. And no one at the club, with the exception of their teammates, Mitch and Tiny, had any idea that Ian and Devon's father was *the* Charles Sawyer. Their family and friends called him Chuck—even Jenn called him Grandpa Chuck, to the older man's delight, since she was the closest thing to a grandchild he had at the moment—but to the rest of the world he was Charles.

He'd further surprised himself when the horrible events surrounding John's death had poured out of him until all his guilt and grief were laid out in the open for her to see. He'd never told anyone the entire story and he was still having a hard time wrapping his brain around the fact he'd told Kristen after knowing her only a few hours—their brief encounters before their date notwithstanding. And for Christ's sake, he'd cried in front of her . . . how screwed up was that?

Looking down at her angelic face, he felt how perfect it was having her here in his bed, and the feeling terrified him. He'd told her before they started this . . . this thing . . . that he couldn't give her long term, but as he listened to her slow, shallow breathing, he couldn't imagine letting her go. The more he thought about it, the more he realized there was no reason why he had to. Maybe he'd never had a real relationship because none of the other women had been right for him past a few hours of mutual pleasure. Everything about Kristen called to him on levels he never knew existed. Maybe he'd been biding his time until she came into his life. For the first time, he was enjoying being with a woman on a level other than D/s. The sex was incredible, but beside that, he liked all the talking and snuggling he did with her. Normal everyday activities were fun with her by his side.

He decided right then and there, he wanted to see where they went from here and try to have a relationship with her. If, in the end, it didn't work out, he'd still be a better man for having known her. But if it did work out, he was looking at a future filled with happiness . . . happiness he never knew existed before now . . . happiness he now craved.

After she'd passed out for a few moments on his kitchen island, he'd picked her up and carried her to his bedroom then explored her body while he waited for her to recover. He took her first while she was on her back, sending another orgasm through her before he flipped her over with her knees tucked under her, and entered her from behind. In that position, he could see the red marks he'd left on her butt cheeks and the royal blue plug sitting snugly between them. The marks would fade by the next afternoon, but she would certainly be feeling them in the morning. Between his dick and the plug up her ass, she'd been so tight, and it hadn't been long before both of them found their release.

In the master bath, he'd filled his huge Jacuzzi tub with hot water and sat them both in it after removing her plug. At first, she'd been a little embarrassed as he took the soap and a loofah and began to bathe her from her neck to her toes, but she got over it after a minute or two. Four mind-blowing orgasms had rendered her brain and limbs useless so she relaxed and closed her eyes as he'd taken care of her. He chuckled when he thought back to the night before at the club. She'd been shocked when Shelby had experienced four intense orgasms within a fifteen to twenty minute time frame. His pet wasn't shocked anymore.

She began to stir next to him and her eyes fluttered open. "*Mmmm*, what time is it?"

Devon's cock came to attention at the sound of her sexy, sleepy voice and to the way she stretched her body like a lazy kitten before she cuddled up to him. He kissed her nose. "A little after four."

She closed her eyes again and mumbled, "What? Why are you awake so early?"

"Just thinking."

"Anything good?"

Devon tightened the arm wrapped around her and gave her a quick squeeze. "It's always good when I'm thinking of you."

Lifting her head, she peered at him. "Really? And what was so good about your thoughts of me, *hmmm?*"

He reached up and tucked a few strands of hair behind her ear before he inhaled deeply and took a leap of faith. "I was thinking how I didn't want this weekend to end." Shifting onto his side so he was face to face with her, he continued, "The last time I spent more than a weekend with a woman, was the girl in college. Since then, I've never had time for a relationship or, if I did, I never wanted to put the effort into one. Any woman I hooked up with knew it was a temporary D/s connection and come Sunday night, it was over. Monday morning would arrive and I'd move on without a single regret."

She placed her hand on his bare chest. It was over his tattooed heart, and he didn't want to read into it, but he liked it there. It felt like her hand belonged there.

---

"Do I hear a 'but' in there somewhere?" Kristen whispered, not daring to let hope rise within her without hearing his words.

He covered her hand with his own. "Yes, you do. It's Sunday morning and I have no desire to take the collar off your neck and let you walk out my door for good tonight. You have no idea how much it scares the hell out of me, but it's not as scary as the thought of this being our last day together. Kristen, I know I said this was temporary, and I honestly don't know if it still is, but all I know is, I want to see where this thing between us goes. Come tomorrow morning, I want to see you again. Please say yes."

Kristen swallowed the lump in her throat. She realized this was a big step for him since he'd used her name as opposed to the nickname she'd come to expect. As for his wanting to explore whatever this was between them, she'd been thinking the same thing. She didn't want to walk out his door and never see him again.

"Yes, Devon. Yes, I want to see you again after today, to see where we go from here."

He breathed a sigh of relief before claiming her mouth with his.

# CHAPTER 16

*L*ate Wednesday morning, Devon sat at his desk finishing the last of the paperwork which had been piling up since the week before. It'd been three whole days since he'd seen Kristen and his frustration was starting to get to him.

They'd spent a few hours at the beach on Sunday afternoon after he made his early morning confession. While wading in the calm waters they'd talked some more. He answered her questions about his adventures traveling with his folks to foreign places and his SEAL training. She told him how she majored in English in college and found she could make some extra money to supplement her bagel shop paycheck by becoming a Beta-reader for other writers.

"I love to read and I found out I was a good proofreader. I would proof everything from magazine articles to college term papers to complete novels. I even did a seven hundred page history text book for a professor who was self-publishing it. It was a great way to take something I enjoyed to do and get paid for it, and the extra money helped while I was in college."

She drifted on her back along the surface of the water while he stood on the sandy floor and held her ankles so she wouldn't float away. "So, my little Ninja-girl, how'd you go from Beta-reader to writer?"

"One day I was reading a manuscript from a new client. It was so bad, I was ready to rip my hair out by chapter two. It amazes me how some people graduate high school and have no concept of proper grammar, punctuation, and spelling. I was on the phone bitching about it to Will and said an off-hand remark of how I could write a story better than some half-assed author-impersonator and he said, 'Well, why don't you.' And the rest, as they say, is history. With help from one of my clients, I self-published my first two books before I was contacted by my current editor and things took off for me from there."

Tugging her feet, he pulled her further into deeper water, away from prying eyes. He wanted to touch her, but there was a group of children playing in the shallow waters and he didn't want to contribute to the delinquency of minors. "So what did the dick-whacker think of your writing?"

She giggled. "The whacker thought it was a stupid hobby and there was no way I was going to be the author of the next great American novel. What he didn't understand was I wasn't doing it to be great. I was doing it because I enjoyed it and if what I wrote brought enjoyment to my readers, then I was happy. After we got engaged, he told me he didn't want his wife to work because he made enough to support us. I refused to give up my proof-reading because I had connected with several of my authors and I loved helping others develop their stories. He didn't think I could make any money as an author myself, and it kept me busy, so my little hobby was okay with him."

"Prick-meister. He said that because he was jealous of you. Instead of being proud of you and showing you off to anyone who would listen, he belittled you out of jealousy."

"I never thought of it that way. I just thought . . . Oh, God, Devon, what are you doing?" She moaned as her eyes rolled back in her head.

He smiled. While they'd been talking he'd pulled her toward him, and her knees were now straddling his hips and his back was to the shoreline blocking her body from everyone's view. One hand was supporting her lower back as she floated while the fingers of his other hand were under the crotch of her bathing suit teasing her hard little clit.

"I'm playing with my toy, little subbie. This belongs to me, remember? I can play with it whenever and wherever I like, and right now, I like. Now be a good girl and stay nice and quiet. I don't think the parents of those kids by the shore want them to get an impromptu sex education lesson."

Her long hair drifted around her head while he played with her, bringing her to the edge several times and easing off right before she flew over. She'd begged him and moaned as quietly as she could until he relented and gave her what she needed. He'd watched in amusement as she managed to keep her head above water and covered her mouth with both hands to keep her screams to a minimum as she bucked against his fingers. After she recovered and he managed to get his straining erection back under control, they'd headed back to the beach and basked in the sun for a few hours.

It had been a wonderful day, but on their way to get something to eat, Devon received a call from an old teammate who informed him of the death of another former SEAL they'd served with several years earlier. Eric Prichard had been struck and killed by a hit-and-run driver while on his evening run, leaving behind his devastated wife and four children.

Devon apologized for needing to cut their day short and dropped Kristen off at her apartment, promising her he'd call her later. He then met Ian at the office to clear their schedules for the next several days and run through their current cases and details, including King Rajeemh's, ensuring everything could be covered by their contractors for a few days. Boomer had been thrilled he was being yanked from his princess babysitting duties until he heard the reason why.

Early Monday morning, the six former SEALs and their niece boarded a plane bound for Iowa to bury one of their own and assist his family with anything they needed. Devon's heart broke when he saw Jennifer with Prichard's kids. He knew the sorrow surrounding her must've brought back the nightmare events she lived through months earlier with startling clarity. But somehow, Jenn managed to tamp down her own grief and focused on helping out with the four little ones, all of whom were under twelve. Her parents would have been proud of the adult their daughter had become.

The next two days were long and emotional. After *Taps* had been played at the grave site and the former SEALs pounded their trident pins into the wood of their colleague's coffin, they all gathered to celebrate the man's life with friends and family. Later that night, they coordinated with former teammates to ensure Dana Prichard would have all the support she needed to get through the next few months as a new widow, and then headed back to Tampa. Everyone, except Ian who continued on to Miami for an early meeting the next morning, headed straight home, completely exhausted. It'd been after ten p.m. when Devon pulled into the compound after dropping Jenn at her dorm, and it was too late to call Kristen. He hadn't wanted to disturb her since she, herself, had been busy the entire day at a "Meet and Greet" luncheon followed by a book signing event for her fans.

He'd been looking forward to seeing her later today, but now thoughts of her were making him hard. This morning he was the only one in the office besides Paula, and Ian wasn't due back until tonight from Miami where he was meeting with a new client. Devon made plans for dinner with Kristen over the phone right after he woke up this morning, but right now he wanted to see her in the worst way. He was about to pick up his cell to call her when the thing lit up, displaying Ian's name. "What's up, Boss-man?"

"Hey Dev, I'm on my way back early. Larry Keon called. He wants to meet with the team about something. I didn't get the details yet because he called as he was boarding a flight from D.C., but he sounded worried about something. Carter's coming too."

Devon sat up straighter with those last three words. T. Carter was black-ops. Even though the team had known him for the past ten years or so, having worked with him in numerous situations around the world, they still didn't know which alphabet agency he belonged to. Hell, they didn't even know his first name. The man had contacts in the CIA, FBI, NSA and Pentagon to name a few— and those were only the domestic agencies. He also had plenty of other contacts around the globe. Devon wasn't sure, but he wouldn't be surprised if POTUS had Carter on the White House speed dial. If he was coming to them for a meeting in their office there was something to worry about. It was bad enough the FBI's Deputy Director, the number two man in the agency, who was one of Trident's highest government contacts, was flying in rather than calling, but if Carter would be there, something serious had or was about to happen. "Shit, that isn't good. What do you need me to do?"

"Call the team and tell them to get their asses in for a two o'clock rendezvous. Keon's landing ten minutes after me so I'll wait for him. Oh, and give Paula the rest of the day off. I don't want her anywhere near the place while we chat with our friends."

"Got it. Anything else?"

"No, that's it. I'm walking into the airport now. See you at two."

Ten minutes later, Devon had alerted the team and sent Paula on her way after assuring her several times they could run the office without her for a few hours. He also stressed they didn't need her to take notes at the meeting and she would still be paid for a full work day. After the annoying woman left, he then took a moment to call Kristen and say hello. She picked up on the second ring. "Hello, Master Devon." He smiled because the woman practically purred.

"Master Devon, hmm? My pet sounds horny."

She laughed. "I'm definitely horny. You spoiled me for three days then I go for three days without. Yup, I'm horny. Can you meet me for lunch? I can't wait 'til dinner."

Devon's phone beeped with an incoming call and he reluctantly removed it from his ear and looked at the screen. *Carter*. "Pet, hang on a second for me, please. I have another call I have to answer." When she acknowledged him, he hit the button to switch the call. "Hey, my friend, I hear you're coming for a visit. Want to tell me what's going on?"

"Not over the phone, Devil Dog. I'm about an hour out. How about meeting me for a bite to eat beforehand? It's been a long morning."

The wheels in Devon's head began to spin and a thought came

to him. Glancing at the clock, he saw he had plenty of time. "I got a better idea, if you're up for it. How does a subbie sandwich sound to you?"

There was a pause, and then Carter's deep voice rumbled over the phone. "It sounds tasty, my friend. Where should I meet you, the club?"

"No, we'll be in my office waiting for you. Can you make it thirteen hundred sharp?"

"Absolutely. See you in a few."

After Carter disconnected the call, Devon switched back to Kristen. "Pet?"

"I'm here," she responded.

"Do you remember my librarian fantasy I told you about?"

She giggled. "You want me to do it now, Sir?"

"Uh-huh. I want you to put on a professional, but sexy skirt, a white button down shirt, those stilettos of yours I love, and your glasses, and drive to my office. The guard will buzz you past the second gate. Park at the first building, ring the doorbell and I'll let you in."

"Whatever you say, Master Devon. Are you going to let me spank you for not returning your library books on time?"

Devon laughed out loud as his dick hardened at her playfulness. "You'll pay for your sass, little girl. Now, I also want you to put your hair up and no underwear, Pet. No one else is here. You have exactly forty five minutes to ring the bell and if you're a minute late, you'll end up over my knee. Do you understand?" It would give him fifteen minutes before Carter arrived.

He could hear the excitement and arousal in her voice. "Yes, Sir."

"Good, I'll see you then and not a minute later."

Disconnecting the call, Devon sat back and smiled for a moment before getting up and heading to his apartment for supplies.

A SHORT TIME LATER, Devon's phone alerted him to the gate being opened outside his office and he brought the compound's security camera images up on his computer to watch Kristen pull in next to the building. He glanced at the clock and saw she was two minutes early, but as he watched the video feed, he wondered what she was doing—she hadn't gotten out of her Nissan Altima yet.

He watched as she removed a strapless bra she apparently wore to prevent anyone else from seeing her dark nipples through her thin white blouse before she tucked the lacy garment into her purse. She then checked her makeup and hair in the mirror under the car visor, but still made no effort to open the door and get out. He zoomed the camera in toward her face and saw her glance several times at the middle of the dashboard where the clock radio would be. Well, well, well . . . his sassy little girl didn't want to be early or on time even. It seemed she wanted to ensure she was a tad late, guaranteeing herself a punishment. He barked out a laugh at her antics. He'd created a subbie monster.

When she finally got out of the car and said hello to Beau, who'd been waiting to greet her, Devon's breath caught and his cock lengthened. She was sexy as sin, his fantasy come true, in a snug, gray pencil skirt which landed an inch below her knees, the white blouse with the top few buttons almost obscenely undone, and those kick-ass heels of hers. She'd followed his orders and her hair was twisted up in a tidy little bun. He watched as she put her reading glasses atop her pert little nose and walked toward the main entrance. Standing, he didn't wait for the bell to sound before heading out to greet her.

The doorbell rang seconds before he opened the door to let her in. "You're late, Ms. Anders."

"No later than your library books, Sir," she sassed as she walked past him into the reception area, apparently not too worried he was in Dom-mode.

His mouth and hands twitched, and he couldn't wait to get both on her. "Come with me, Ms. Anders, and we'll discuss the penalties in my office." He turned and walked away, knowing she would be right on his heels.

After they entered his office, he shut the door, but didn't lock it. Carter would need to get in. Kristen stood in the middle of the room and he walked around her slowly, looking her up and down, building her anticipation. He would've liked to have drawn out the suspense a little longer, but he was on the clock to get her where he wanted before his friend showed up. Circling his desk, he sat down in the comfortable leather chair. "Come here, Ms. Anders. It's time for you to pay for your tardiness."

He watched her eyes and nostrils flare before she made her way over to him in silence and stopped at his side. "Pull your skirt up to your waist and place yourself across my lap." Without argument, she did as he ordered, presenting her bare cheeks for her punishment. He shifted her on his legs until she was off-balance. With her feet in mid-air, she touched the floor with her fingertips to steady herself. The woman had the type of ass most men loved to bounce off of as they fucked their lovers from behind, enjoying the soft cushion of flesh. He rubbed his hand over her enticing globes as he spoke. "It'll be ten, my little librarian, and you'll count out loud and thank me after each one. Understand?"

"Yes, Sir."

He loved the breathy, nervous hitch in her voice. After squeezing her butt cheeks several times to get the blood flowing, he lifted his hand and smacked it back down.

"Ow! One, Sir. Thank you."

*Smack.*

"Two, Sir. Thank you."

He continued to the count of ten, increasing the intensity with each smack, and then looked at the work of art he'd created. Her ass and upper thighs were bright red and he could make out several of his overlapping hand prints. He caressed her abused flesh before dipping his fingers between her legs to check her level of arousal. She was dripping. *Perfect.*

He helped her stand before swiveling the chair so he was facing her. "Kneel, my little librarian. Take my cock out and stroke me."

Without lowering her skirt, she dropped to her knees and greedily reached for his zipper, licking her lips as she did so. The gate alarm sounded on his phone and he glanced at the time, then at his computer where the security feeds were still up for him to see. Carter was only a few minutes early, but he knew the man wouldn't come in until his appointed time. Devon's hips jolted as Kristen's hands made contact with his stiff cock, and his eyes zipped back to her face. Her stare remained on his as she dragged her clenched fist up and down his shaft, and he grabbed the opaque scarf he'd placed on his desk. Leaning forward he rendered her temporarily blind and secured the ends of the material behind her head. "Suck me, Pet. Slowly, and don't stop until I tell you to."

Using her hand as a guide she lowered her mouth to his groin and his eyes rolled back in his head when her wet lips and tongue surrounded his thick flesh. *Fuck!* The woman hadn't been lying when she said she was a fast learner. She licked and sucked him like an expert instead of a woman giving her second blowjob ever. Three minutes of sexual torture later, the door to his office opened and the black-ops warrior walked in. Kristen was so into what she was doing she didn't hear him enter and shut the door, but she definitely heard him when he spoke. From where his friend stood, he couldn't see her or Devon's lap behind the desk. "What's up, Devil Dog?"

Kristen froze as he'd expected her to, and he grabbed the bun in her hair and growled. "I didn't tell you to stop, Pet." He felt her hesitation before her head began to bob again.

Across the room, Carter's eyes widened and an amused grin spread across on his face as he took several steps toward the desk and peered over the top of it. "New secretary?"

His friend was joking because he knew Devon would never get involved with an employee, even if it was a quick one-time fuck, which this wasn't. "Nope. This is my naughty librarian, who better start sucking harder before she earns another punishment. Her ass is already sore from her first one of the day."

They both almost laughed out loud when she immediately increased her efforts.

Carter walked around the side of the desk and got a view of Kristen's red backside. "Very nice." He raised his eyebrow at Devon in a silent question—what was he allowed to do?

For Kristen's benefit, he responded. "One of my pet's soft limits is a ménage. She was able to see Brody and Marco in action the other night with Shelby, and my little subbie's pussy was sopping wet by the time they were through. Pet, the voice you hear belongs to my good friend Carter, and I do believe he's happy to see your red ass and dripping pussy."

The other man looked down at the blindfolded woman and in a deep commanding voice asked, "Is this what you want, sub? Me, a perfect stranger to you, who you won't be able to see, fucking your sweet pussy from behind while your Master comes down your throat? If it isn't, stop sucking his cock and say your safeword. If you don't want this, I'll turn around and leave. It will be the only consequence of your safeword, and your Master will continue as if I'd never been here. If you don't want me to leave, you have to verbalize what will happen if I stay."

Carter was an experienced Dom and in high demand with the subs at The Covenant whenever he was in town and had time to stop by. He always made sure a sub knew what she was getting herself into and there were two options available to her—continue down the road they were going without any detours or stop altogether with no penalties. The submissive held all the control in the scene.

Devon held his breath as Kristen's head slowed and then she let go of him. He knew she'd taken a moment to digest the unknown man's words and evaluate her thoughts and feelings. "I understand, Sir, and I do *not* want to use my safeword. Please fuck my pussy while I suck my Master's cock until he comes."

Carter grinned at his friend. "How can I refuse such a polite and pretty sub?"

Instinctively knowing he would keep her safe from harm, Kristen took Devon back into her mouth as he watched his friend kneel down behind her. Carter began to gently rub his hands over her ass cheeks, hips and thighs, letting her get used to his touch before going any further. After a brief moment when she tensed at the feeling of unfamiliar hands on her body, she began to relax and renew her enthusiasm in giving Devon his blowjob. As she lapped and slurped his shaft, her hand reached up to cup his balls causing him to moan. "Just like that, Pet. Don't stop . . . nice and easy while Carter gets you ready."

Devon opened the drawer next to him and retrieved the condoms and lube he'd put there earlier. He placed them on his desk where the other Dom could reach them and then held up one index finger, bending it a few times to let Carter know she wasn't ready for anything other than a finger in her tight ass. Carter acknowledged him as he lowered one hand to her folds between her legs and grabbed the tube of lubricant with the other. He dripped a fair amount of gel into the crack of her ass then began to work it into the rim of her puckered hole while he plunged two fingers into her soaking wet pussy and fucked her with them.

Kristen moaned around Devon's cock and the vibrations took him higher. Not wanting to come too soon, he grabbed a handful of her loosening hair and forced her to slow her pace while his other hand caressed her cheek, neck and shoulder. He worked his way down into her shirt where her lush unrestrained tits were swaying in time with her movements. Her nipples hardened with a brush of his thumb and he gently rolled and tugged on them. Every time he'd played with her breasts, he distracted her in some other way. He didn't think she was aware of him pinching them with more pressure each time because she was so aroused when he did it, the pain instantly changed to pleasure which shot straight to her womb and aroused her even more. He could now lick, suck and pinch them without her tensing at all, but it would be a while before he tried to graze them with his teeth and he didn't know if she'd ever be able to take the nipple clamps. If she never got over her fear of them he would accept it, but for now he wanted to try and erase every bad memory she had of her previous sexual encounters until only he existed in the far reaches of her mind.

---

KRISTEN'S HEAD was in a wild spin. If someone had told her a week earlier she would be on her knees, blindfolded, sucking Devon's huge erection in his office, in the middle of the afternoon, while a complete stranger finger fucked her pussy and ass, she would've said they were crazy. Now, she was the crazy one—crazy with the intense pleasure and sensations running through her body and loving every minute of it. She knew if she'd said "no" then Carter would've left and Devon wouldn't be mad or disappointed. However, if she did say it, then she would be the one disappointed for not trying something she'd fantasized about.

She could distinguish the difference between the two men's touch, but she wasn't sure how because it didn't feel as if a stranger was touching her. It felt like the other man's hands were an extension of Devon's. In her mind, Devon was the only one touching her, with four hands, not two. Carter's fingers were pretty much the same size as Devon's. In fact, they both had the hands of men who were accustomed to hard work, yet they were gentle and talented enough to bring a woman extreme gratification. A brief thought of how the two of them must've done this before with other women popped into her head. But it disappeared just as quickly when the fingers in her vagina moved to rub her fluids over her clit sending bolts of electricity through her and rendering her mind useless to anything, but her four-out-of-five senses. With her eyes covered, her senses of touch, taste, smell, and hearing were heightened. She felt Carter's hands and fingers on her. She savored Devon's taste on the buds of her tongue. She inhaled his musky and masculine scent. And finally, their dueling groans and encouraging words filled her ears along with the crinkle of a condom wrapper.

Carter pulled his lower hand from her body, and she heard the hum of a zipper. She then felt him align his cock with the entrance to her core as his finger continued to play in her ass. She whimpered as he eased himself into her wetness, his hips rocking back and forth as he progressed a little at a time, giving her body a moment to accommodate his thickness. "Fuck, she's tight." He groaned in ecstasy once he buried himself deep inside her. "Damn, her pussy feels like heaven, man."

"I KNOW THE FEELING. Pet, you have permission to come whenever you need to." Devon let his head fall back against the leather chair and was tempted to close his eyes and just feel, but the desire to watch her take everything they gave her was even stronger. His dick disappearing behind her red, swollen, wet lips was a sight he didn't think he'd ever tire of seeing. She was a pretty woman to begin with, but in the throes of pleasure she was stunning.

As she sucked him in and out of her mouth, she swiped her tongue across his purple head on each upstroke, licking drops of pre-cum from his slit. She remembered everything he'd taught her the first time, and her desire to please him brought him more pleasure in return. Her moaning and breathing increased as Carter drove her higher and higher until her orgasm grabbed her and sent her tumbling. She screamed around his dick, and he began to fuck her mouth in earnest. Tightening his grip on her scalp, he held her where he wanted her as he increased the pace of his thrusting hips, plunging into the deep cavern of her mouth and making contact with the back of her throat. When she gagged a bit, he shortened his strokes. "Breath through your nose, Pet. I'm going to come and you're going to swallow every drop."

He felt and heard her acknowledge him with a muffled, "um-hmm" and let himself go. Her mouth and throat moved greedily as she swallowed his seed. "That's it, baby. Fuck, you're such a good girl." As the last drops left him, Carter did something which sent her over the edge again with the man following her right after, roaring his own release.

For a few moments the only sound in the room was from the three of them breathing hard. Then Kristen moaned as Carter slid out of her, murmuring words of praise. He looked at Devon as he got up from his knees. "If you've got her, I'm going to run upstairs to one of the rooms and take a quick shower." When Devon nodded, his friend leaned over Kristen's torso and kissed the back of her head while she rested her forehead on her Master's knee, her blindfold still in place. "Thank you, love. That was wonderful. Thank you for letting me share you with Master Devon. You're a beautiful woman, and he's a lucky man." When he looked back up at him, Devon knew Carter understood this woman was important to him. She wasn't just another sub, and it'd been the operative's honor to participate in her first ménage.

After Carter disposed of his condom in the trash and left the room, closing the door behind him, Devon tucked himself back into his pants and pulled the zipper up. Standing, he leaned down, picked Kristen up in his arms and placed her exhausted body on his couch. He covered her with a knitted blanket which was draped over the back of the couch, a decorative touch courtesy of Mrs. Kemple. Retrieving a wet washcloth from his office's half-bath, he proceeded to clean Kristen as she fell into a subspace induced sleep.

He took off her shoes and blindfold to make her comfortable, and then took care of himself in the bathroom. Sitting on the edge of the couch next to her, he spent the next twenty minutes or so caressing her from head to toe as she slept. When he heard the gate alert sound from his phone, he sighed and gently roused her. "Pet, are you okay?"

"Um-hmm. Wonderful."

He chuckled at her sleepy, sated voice. "I need to go to a meeting down the hall. I want you to stay here and sleep awhile. The door will be shut and no one'll disturb you. I'm leaving a bottle of water and your purse here next to you. If you need me for anything, text me, and I'll come right back, okay? When I'm finished, we'll get something to eat."

"Mmm-hmm, 'kay. Love you."

# CHAPTER 17

$\mathcal{D}$evon froze at her murmured words, but she'd slipped back into slumber. Did she realize what she'd said? Had she fallen in love with a man who'd never said those words to anyone besides those he considered family? And why was he not running for the hills as soon as he heard them?

A soft knock interrupted his thoughts and he left her sleeping, grabbed his cell phone and locked the door, shutting it behind him as he exited. Ian was waiting for him in the hallway. "Just waiting on Carter, Brody, and Marco. Boomer and Jake pulled in right behind me."

"Carter's upstairs—he'll be back down in a minute."

Ian nodded, his face became grim. "Keon didn't come alone. Two NCIS agents are with him."

Devon's eyes widened. "Fuck. What the hell is going on?"

His brother turned on his foot and began to walk toward the conference room with Devon on his heels. "It's not good. I only heard the basics on the way here. I'll let Keon tell everyone at once."

A few minutes later, Trident Security's six main personnel sat around the large conference table, along with Deputy Director Larry Keon of the FBI, black-ops agent T. Carter, and NCIS Investigators Nathan Dobrowski and Barbara Chan.

Brody was booting up his laptop while Keon stood and began to hand out identical folders to everyone, but Dobrowski and Chan who had their own copies with them. Chan also had a laptop open and it was hooked up to the large Hi-Def monitor hanging on the wall at the one unoccupied end of the table. Beau had joined them and was snoring loudly from somewhere under the long table. Keon remained standing as he spoke.

"Information has come to our attention that several recent deaths of former Navy personnel may be part of a larger plot." Pictures of retired SEALs Eric Prichard, Quincy Dale, and Jeff Mullins popped up on the monitor, along with their dates of death, or in Quincy Dale's case, an estimated date. A round of surprised curses from the teammates followed.

"Are you fucking kidding me?" The rhetorical question came from Boomer. "What the fuck is going on? Did anyone know Dale was dead?"

The others shook their heads as the youngest team member looked at their stunned faces. This was news to all of them. Their former teammate lived in Alaska and had little contact with his buddies since his last tour ended about two-and-a-half years ago. Facial scarring from burns he'd received in an RPG attack had the man living like a hermit.

Keon raised his hand to calm the room down before he continued. "We only found out about Dale on Monday. It's what raised a red flag. Dale's brother hadn't heard from him in four months or so and, from what I understand, it wasn't unusual these last few years. Robert Dale finally decided to take a three hour drive out to Quincy's place this past Saturday and found his brother's decomposing corpse in his cabin. The medical examiner estimated he'd been dead about three months. A 9mm Smith and Wesson was found with the body and his prints were on the gun. At first the troopers figured suicide. With Dale's recent history, it wouldn't have been too difficult to believe."

"Except Dale didn't own an S&W nine." Boomer spoke with the certainty of a man who'd known his friend's habits well. "He hated them. Said they never felt right to him, the grip and weight were all wrong. I remember him arguing with some grunt about it on his last tour. He would've bought a thousand other guns before he bought an S&W nine."

Keon nodded. "Exactly what his brother said. And someone filed off the gun's serial number which raised a few more doubts. Robert said Quincy would've never bought a gun with the number gone and he wouldn't have done it himself. Nothing else was out of place—no prints or trace evidence. The state troopers asked the M.E. to scrutinize the entry wound to be on the safe side. The M.E. states the shot to the head was close too, but not quite possible for Dale to have done it himself. The doc said it was an awkward angle which didn't make sense. It wouldn't have been comfortable for a person to hold the gun so far back behind the ear. Suicides by a bullet to the head seem to be a common way to go in desolate areas of Alaska. The doc knows his stuff and ruled it a probable homicide."

Barbara Chan took over. "A homicide death notification of a SEAL following so closely to a hit-and-run death of another from the same team made me curious. I ran a list of the team's current and retired members through the VA computer and Jeff Mullins' name popped up, along with his wife. The burglary-homicide set my internal panic alarm off. Three members of the same team dead within six-months and all of them are unsolved."

"Someone's hunting SEALs." Devon hated to state what they were all thinking, but it needed to be said.

"And not just SEALs, but Team Four specifically. Prichard knew something was off," Keon said. "Early this morning, I had a local agent go interview Prichard's wife. According to the police report, he was wearing a concealed pistol in an ankle holster when his body was found. The wife said it wouldn't have been unusual when he'd been active with the team, but since they moved to Iowa after his retirement, she didn't think he wore it much anymore. Quiet little town and such.

"After a few more questions, she remembered something from a few days before he was killed. Prichard asked her if she'd noticed anything odd or if she'd seen anyone in the area she didn't recognize. She hadn't, and asked him why. He shrugged it off and said it was probably nothing. It was the last time he mentioned anything to her. I guess in her shock and grief she forgot about it. Her eleven-year-old son overheard her talking to the agent and said that the day before his dad's death, the two of them were driving home from the kid's football practice, and Prichard kept looking in the mirrors. He took a long route home, making some turns he didn't need to. He was also slowing down and accelerating for no reason. The kid thought it was weird, and Prichard said he was just checking something out. Nothing happened, and they got home without any trouble, but I think it's a good assumption he knew he was in someone's cross-hairs. The questions are—did he know who or why, and why didn't he say something to the sheriff or call someone from the team for backup?"

"I think he was trying to before he was killed." All eyes turned to Marco. "Curt Bannerman mentioned something to me at the funeral. He'd gotten a voice mail about two hours before Eric was killed. All Eric said was he needed to talk to Curt about something, and he should call him back as soon as possible. Curt couldn't return the call until twenty hundred hours and by then it was too late."

Keon sat down and sighed. "You need to talk to Jennifer Mullins and see if anything unusual happened in the days leading up to her parents' murders."

"I agree." Ian shot off a quick text to Jenn asking her to come to the office in a little while. "I'll have her stop by later so we can talk."

"The good news is—as if there could be good news in this mess —if the reason these men were killed is linked to a specific mission, and it wasn't only because they were SEALs or more specifically SEAL Team Four, then we're able to narrow it down to a nine month period six years ago. So at least we have a starting point."

Jake's eyes narrowed. "How do you figure?"

"Because," Ian explained, "it was the only time frame when Jeff and Dale were on the team together. Dale joined us nine months before Jeff retired. Unfortunately, according to Dobrowski here, we were active during most of those months, and there's a list of over thirty individual missions. Some lasted only a day or a week, but a few were longer and spanned five countries. Two in the Middle East, one each in Africa, Colombia and Brazil, and as a team, we're responsible for over seventy confirmed deaths while on those missions."

Chan chimed in again. "We know it's a lot, and we have other investigators getting in touch with, and interviewing, all SEALs who were active in Team Four at the time. You six are all on the list and the only ones working together in a large group with the security clearances you have, so we came here to pick your minds and review the mission reports with you."

The teammates groaned. Thirty missions with seventy plus kills could produce an astronomical amount of intelligence, evidence, paperwork, and photos.

"The Pentagon has been working since Monday night to get us copies of everything. I received a call when we got off the plane, and the files will be here first thing in the morning from D.C. I don't think I need to state the obvious, gentlemen, but I will. This involves highly classified mission reports. Despite your level of clearance, you're all considered civilians now, which means we had to get permission from far up the food chain to get you access to them, even though each of you wrote some, if not all of them. These reports will not be censored and redacted. As of their arrival at around nine a.m. tomorrow morning, this room will be in lock down. Nathan or I must be present whenever any of you are in this room with the reports, and nothing leaves this room without our approval. Six MPs will be posted outside in rotating shifts of two. No one, other than the ten people currently in this room, is allowed in here. That pertains to any support staff you have."

Brody laughed out loud. "Paula's gonna go nuts! Ian, can I be there when you tell her?"

With a few chuckles, the tension in the room eased at the thought of their nosy office manager being left out of the loop and banned from the room. If the woman had been a cat, her curiosity would've killed her a long time ago.

Devon glanced at the individuals around the table and his gaze fell on one man. "Hey, Carter, how do you figure in to this whole frigging mess?"

The big man's face showed no emotion as he shrugged his shoulders. "I'm just here for the food."

Devon snorted as the rest of the team let out barks of laughter. Years ago, Devon had been undercover for a mission in Rio de Janeiro when he unexpectedly ran into Carter, also undercover, at a swanky gala with over five hundred people. A Colombian drug lord the team had under surveillance was in attendance, and Devon drew the short straw for getting into a black-tie monkey suit. When he'd gotten a brief minute alone with his buddy, he asked a similar question and had gotten the same answer. Every once in a while the stale joke reared its ugly head when their friend didn't want to lie to them and couldn't tell them the truth. In other words, if he told them, he'd have to kill them.

Keon stood and the NCIS agents followed suit. "Ian, I don't need to tell you and your team to watch your backs. If you need anything, let me know. I have to head to the Jacksonville office tomorrow for some unrelated business. My time for the next week or so will be split between here, there, D.C. and New York, but I'll be available by cell if something comes up. In addition to NCIS, you have the complete support of the FBI. We're involved because the murders occurred in three different states and they may be the result of any one of the jobs you've done for Uncle Sam, including some sanctioned by the FBI. I didn't know Mullins as well as you all did, but he was a good man. He and his wife and the others didn't deserve what they got, and I'll be damned if Team Four loses anyone else on my watch."

After Keon and the two investigators left for a local hotel, Carter stayed long enough to offer his input. "What Larry said, goes for me too. A few of my informants are keeping their ears to the ground and listening for any traffic about the team. I'm going to go beat a few bushes and check out a couple of things. If anything pans out, I'll let you know. I've gotten used to your ugly mugs so stay safe and say hi to Jenn for me. Tell her I'm sorry I missed her and I'll see her soon." As he passed Devon on the way to the door, he lowered his voice so no one else could hear and added, "Say goodbye and thanks to your little librarian, too. I'm looking forward to actually meeting her next time."

The room was silent for a few minutes after Carter left. Ian's phone chimed with a text and he looked at the screen, then at his team. "Jenn's on her way over. Any ideas of what started this shit storm?"

Jake answered first. "Not off the top of my head, but I have to admit I'm worried about Jenn. Not only do we have to question her about the worst night of her life, but is she in danger here with us? Is this going to be easier or harder for her to know it wasn't a random crime and her folks were murdered because of something from her dad's service? The man was a hero to her."

Ian nodded. "I was thinking the same thing. But I think she's mature enough to know there was no way her dad could have foreseen this five years ago. If he had, he would've taken steps to protect his family. And she's safer here with us since we now know there's a threat. I'll assign her a protection detail for school, and she'll stay here with us for now. Jake, talk to your brother and ask him to take her off the schedule for a few days, at least until we have a better idea of what is going on." At the other man's nod he continued. "As for questioning her, it'll be a little tough. I'll call Nelson and see if he can squeeze her in for a session tonight or tomorrow morning." Dr. Brett Nelson was the trauma psychologist Jenn had been seeing since coming to Florida.

Everyone looked at Devon when he stood. "Kristen's napping on my couch. I'm just going to go check on her before Jenn gets here. Someone want to order a bunch of pizzas since we're going to be here a while?" If any of his team was surprised at his first statement they didn't show it. They couldn't have missed Kristen's Altima parked outside and knew someone else was in the building.

Boomer grabbed his phone. "On it."

There was an immediate chorus of "no anchovies" from the rest of them as Devon walked out the door.

# CHAPTER 18

K risten was just waking up when Devon entered his office. Her eyes blinked several times before she stretched and smiled seductively at him. "Good afternoon."

He crossed the room and sat on the edge of the couch next to her. "How are you feeling? Did you sleep well?"

"Mmm-hmm. How long was I out?"

He glanced at his watch. "About an hour and a half. You earned it." He chuckled as her cheeks flamed.

"Is he still here?"

"No, Pet. Carter had to leave. But next time he stops by, I'll give you two a formal introduction." His grin faded. "I have to cancel dinner tonight. Something's come up, but I still want you to spend the night in my bed. I don't know what time I'll be back in my apartment, maybe around nine or ten, but you can go over anytime you want. If you come with me now, I'll have Brody scan your handprint into the system. It won't get you in every secure area, but it'll open the gate and my apartment for you."

Her eyes and smile widened. "Wow. Is this your version of giving me the key to your place?"

Laughing, Devon stood. "Yeah, I guess it is. And I want you naked as the day you were born when I get there. Now, come on, let's go see Brody. We have pizza being delivered in a little bit, so I'll feed you before you go."

A half hour later with her skirt straightened, bra back on and hair down from its bun, Kristen sat in the conference room with Beau at her feet. She ate her pizza and listened as the Sexy Six-Pack and Jenn talked about everyday subjects. It was obvious how close they all were, and their easy banter and teasing was fun to listen to. "I have a question. Why do you call Devon, Devil Dog? I mean, it's obviously a play on his name, but is there something more to it?"

Everyone laughed as Devon rolled his eyes and sighed. "It goes back to a parachuting practice/demonstration we were doing right after I joined Team Four. We were doing high-altitude jumping. After I jumped, I decided to see how many somersaults I could do before I had to pull my cord. Normally, it wouldn't have been an issue, but what no one told us was Admiral Richardson, a real stickler for protocol and stuff, was watching with a bunch of other big-wigs on the ground. After I land, the admiral gets in my face, reaming me a new asshole. He was beet red, yelling at me, and some of his words were getting jumbled. I guess instead of asking me if I thought I was a daredevil, he asked me if I was a devil dog. The next day someone had emptied my locker at the base and filled it to the top with Drakes' Devil Dogs, those little chocolate cakes." Staring at his way-too-innocent-looking teammates he added, "I still don't know who did it, but I was eating Devil Dogs for months."

"Yup, and the bastard didn't share either," Brody piped up. "And he wasn't happy with his new nickname for a long time since 'Devil Dog' is a standard in the Marines. Of course, when someone doesn't like their nickname, it pretty much becomes permanent."

Kristen smiled. "I guess he didn't like it because of the rivalry between the Navy and Marines, right?" Devon nodded around a bite of pizza and rolled his eyes again. "So does everyone else have a call sign?" She thought that was the military slang for it as she looked at Brody. "Yours is egg-something, right?"

"First off, darlin', they're not call signs . . . they're nicknames— plain and simple. Call signs are for missions. And yes, mine's

Egghead, a bow to my superior computer hacking skills. By the way, we've already approved yours. I'm diggin' the Ninja-girl tag."

She gaped at Devon. "Seriously? You told them?"

He just grinned and shrugged his shoulders as everyone else laughed. From there, the men went around the table.

"I'm the explosives and demolition man, so I ended up Boomer," Ben told her. "Nothing embarrassing about it."

"Except when we call him Baby Boomer," Jake quipped, making the younger guy groan and flip his buddy the middle finger. "Mine's Reverend. I'm a sniper, and when I first joined Team Four, one of the guys said I was sending my targets to meet their maker."

"Yup, and because everyone feels the need to confess their sins to you, Father Donovan." The room filled with laughter again. "Anyway, I'm Polo."

When Marco didn't explain further, Kristen asked, "Why Polo?"

The room got quiet, and she was confused as everyone, including Jenn, stared at her. Brody deadpanned, "Wait for it."

*Wait for what? What's the big deal about calling Marco, Polo?* The second her eyes lit up, Boomer chuckled. "Ding, ding, ding . . . she gets it, just under the wire."

She giggled. "Okay, so I was a little slow on that one. I get it now. From *The Travels of Marco Polo* and the game. We used to play it in the pool when I was a kid." She looked over at the man who'd yet to answer. "So, Ian, what's your call sign, I mean, nickname?"

Before he could respond, Brody jumped in. "He doesn't have one, at least not any we can say in front of two pretty ladies. We tried a few names for him over the years, but nothing ever stuck. Now he's the Boss-man."

Ian smiled, but it didn't reach his eyes. "And don't you forget it, ass-hat."

---

AFTER THEY FINISHED EATING, Devon walked Kristen to her car and kissed her sweetly before he opened her door for her. "I'll see you later, Ninja-girl. And don't forget, you better be naked when I get there."

He watched as she drove away with a wide grin on her face. His own smile faded when her car disappeared through the outside perimeter gate as his thoughts returned to what they now had to put Jenn through. Making her relive the events leading up to her parent's murders was going to be hard on her, but Doc Nelson agreed to meet with her and Ian first thing in the morning to help her deal with the repercussions. By the time Devon walked back into the conference room, the rest of them had cleaned up their meal and Ian had moved to sit next to Jenn, ready to offer his god-daughter the support she was sure to need. Even Beau seemed to sense she would need him because he was now sitting on her other side with his big head resting on her thigh as she stroked his silky-soft ears. The dog's eyes were closed in what had to be canine ecstasy.

They all remained quiet as Ian took Jenn's hand and spoke to her. "Baby-girl, we have to ask you some questions, and I wish we didn't, but it's important."

The young woman's eyes widened at Ian's serious, yet gentle tone. "What's wrong, Uncle Ian?"

"We need you to think back to the days and weeks leading up to your parents' murders. Did anything happen that you thought was weird at the time? Was your dad nervous or upset or worried about something? Did he ask you or your mom anything odd? Did you see anyone near your house who was a stranger to you, or if you knew them, was it unusual for them to be there?"

They watched as Jenn's eyes filled up, but to her credit, her tears didn't fall. She took a deep breath. "Something else happened, didn't it? Something happened to make you think my parents weren't killed because some burglar didn't expect anyone to be home when he broke in, right?"

Ian sighed, clearly hating what he had to tell her. "We received some information this afternoon which possibly links your parents' deaths to Eric's hit and run accident, which we now believe was no accident." He paused, and Devon knew this was killing him.

"Sweetheart, Quincy Dale was found shot to death in his cabin. He'd been killed about three months ago. His brother went to check on him after he hadn't heard from him."

Jenn's hand covered her mouth in shock. They'd known she was going to take Dale's death hard. The man had been a big American history buff and always captured Jenn's attention with stories from Christopher Columbus' discovery all the way through to the twenty-first century. Though Dale had withdrawn from pretty much everyone else, he stayed in contact with Jenn through emails and the occasional phone call. She was the only one who could bring a smile to his scarred face these past few years. He even left his lonely mountain twice for her—to attend her parents' funeral, and then to watch her graduate from high school three months later. Devon realized Dale had probably returned from Jenn's graduation right before he was murdered.

Jenn could no longer hold her tears back. "Oh, no! Not Quincy! I sent him a couple of emails over the summer, but with the move, school, and work, I just realized he hadn't answered me. He would do that sometimes when he got into one of his funks, and then send me a whole bunch of emails at once. Uncle Ian, what's happening? Quincy was the nicest man in the world. Why would someone kill all of them?" Her questions may've been addressed to Ian, but she turned her head to survey all of them, hoping someone had an answer for her.

Devon spoke to her softly. "We don't know, Baby-girl, but we'll find out, I promise. And you know I don't make promises I can't keep."

"I know, Uncle Devon," she whispered before clearing her throat and speaking up again. "Okay, so let me think. You know I was at my friend's house the night . . . the night it happened. I'd also spent most of the day shopping with Dana and so I only saw my parents that morning. I remember they were talking in the kitchen when I went down for breakfast. Dad said . . . he said something like, if he needed to, he would call you, Uncle Ian, but he wanted to look into something first. They changed the subject when I walked in, and I didn't think anything of it since you two were always on the phone with each other and Dad had done some research and work for you before. The week before, Dad was also out more than usual, and in his home office on the computer a lot. I remember a few nights when he didn't come home until after dinner. When I asked him where he'd been, he said he'd been working on something for you, and it was no big deal."

"For me?" Ian asked with a confused expression on his face. When Jenn nodded, he looked at Devon. "I didn't ask him to look into anything for me. Did you?"

"No." Devon shook his head as the other men all denied having asked Jeff to look into anything.

Jenn sighed. "I'm sorry I don't remember more, but nothing else stands out. I mean it was six months ago, and I was such a mess after."

Ian lifted her hand and kissed her knuckles. "It's okay, Baby-girl. If you think of anything else, let one of us know. For now though, I want you to stay in your room here. I don't think you're in any danger, but I'd rather not take any chances. Tomorrow morning there'll be a few men assigned to protect you when you're not with us. I know you can't miss any classes if it can be avoided, but Mike is giving you the next few days off until we get a better idea of what's going on."

Her bottom lip trembled and six Navy SEAL hearts were breaking for her. "Are you . . . are you all in danger?"

Ian stood and pulled their niece to her feet and hugged her tight. "Nothing's going to happen to us, Baby-girl. You're going to be stuck with us for a long time."

---

THE ASSASSIN ANSWERED his vibrating phone from his current perch in a tree a fair distance away from the fenced-in compound. "What?"

"How long do you expect this to take?"

The man funding his current excursion sounded anxious after

having been calm the past six months. "Why, has the time frame been changed?"

"The party wants to make an announcement in two weeks. I want this dead and buried, literally, before it happens. If any of them are still alive, certain things may come to light and I refuse to accept the possibility."

"It'll be done by then. After the rest of my money is deposited into my account, you'll never hear from me again and this number will no longer be available."

He hung up, not caring if the other man had anything else to say. Picking up his binoculars, he went back to watching the increased activity at the compound. On Monday, the four men he'd been hired to kill had boarded a plane to Iowa to attend the funeral of their fallen teammate, along with the other two and the Mullins girl. He'd been a little surprised to see her. After her parents' death, he'd assumed she would go live with her father's family, but it made no difference to him either way. She cheated death once, but if she, or anyone else, ended up being collateral damage this time around, it didn't matter to him.

Until today, the compound had been quiet with only one security guard at the front gate which gave him the opportunity to check out the security systems. He'd been pissed to find Trident Security was closely monitored by multiple cameras and sensors stationed inside and outside the fences. Whoever designed their system was good—almost too good. He had yet to find a way past their defenses. There was also a big dog which appeared to be well-trained in addition to being a pet.

If it hadn't been difficult before, with the amount of people going in and out of the compound today, it was damn near impossible to penetrate. Devon Sawyer and the woman who he'd learned was their secretary had been the only ones in there during the morning. Then around noon, the secretary left in a huff and about an hour later an unknown woman arrived. He'd wondered if Sawyer was banging them both, but then an unexpected person showed up.

*Carter.* He didn't know if it was a first or last name. He only knew the man was so dark in the world of black-ops that many informants and contacts whispered the guy's name in awe and fear. While he'd never met or dealt with the agent, or whatever his title was, from the stories he'd heard, anyone who'd ever underestimated the man was either dead or missing and presumed dead.

A few minutes before two p.m. was when it started getting crowded in the compound. The rest of the former SEALs showed up along with three people who carried themselves like feds. Then all was quiet and mundane again for a while. The feds and Carter left, pizza and the Mullins girl showed up, and about a half hour later, the unknown woman drove away. He watched as Devon Sawyer kissed her and knew he had the answer to one of his questions.

The assassin's gut started to twitch again around five p.m. Six more unknown men arrived. Seeing them armed and alert, he recognized that these men were highly trained and intelligent— definitely former military. The Sawyer brothers and Brody Evans joined them outside and it was obvious they were talking about the compound and its security system. Jennifer Mullins was even escorted by two of them from the second to the fourth building. Something was wrong. They were increasing their ranks. The question was, why?

DEVON LOOKED at his watch as he climbed the stairs to his apartment after checking on Jenn who was going through some boxes of things from her life in Virginia. She was looking for some family photos of her grandparents and great-grandparents her mom had scanned onto CDs several years earlier. "Some of them were my aunt's photos, but she lent them to mom to make copies for me to have. I need them for an assignment. We have to do a family tree as far back as we can for my *Sociology and The American Family* class."

He'd leaned against the front door frame as she sat on the floor of Ian's living room with the boxes in front of her and Beau at her side. "Are you okay with doing that, with everything going on?"

Jenn sighed. "I think so. My professor and I had a conversation the first week of school. I had a question about something and stayed after class. We talked for a bit, and she asked me about my family. Dr. Nelson convinced me it was okay to talk about, you know, everything if I'm comfortable with someone, so I ended up telling Professor Palmer what happened. I was glad I did because she really understood. Her brother-in-law killed her sister a few years ago after they got into an argument. He's in prison now. Anyway, Professor Palmer told me if this assignment was too hard for me to deal with, she would understand and I could do something else instead. But, Uncle Devon, I want to do it . . . I don't know, I feel like I have to do it. I feel if I don't, I'll be letting my parents down. Is that weird?"

Devon smiled at her. "I don't think it's weird at all, Baby-girl. I think it's your heart's way of letting you know it's healing and you're getting better every day. You'll always live with what happened. I mean, how can you not? But the point is you *will* live, not just exist like some people do—people who aren't as strong as you. I know your parents are proud of you, as we all are. I knew someday we were going to have to start seeing you as a grown-up woman and not a little girl anymore, and I think the day has come. I'll still call you Baby-girl out of habit though."

After getting up off the floor, she stepped over Beau's bulky body and gave Devon a hug. "I wouldn't want it any other way."

Returning the embrace, he squeezed her tight. "Me neither, Baby-girl, me neither."

It was now a little after nine as he opened the door to his own apartment, and his body and mind were suffering from a combination of fatigue and anticipation. The last few days were catching up to him, but all he could think about now was climbing on top of Kristen's sumptuous body and sinking into her hot wet core as deep and for as long as he possibly could.

She wasn't in the living room or kitchen, so he walked toward his bedroom in search of her. He knew she'd only gotten there about ten minutes before he did because, like the interior gate, his apartment door also sounded a short, one-note alert on his phone when the door was opened. Walking into his bedroom, he found it empty except for an enticing trail of discarded clothes and underwear leading to the bathroom. From where he stood, he could hear his shower running and smiled. She must have been in a rush when she got here.

He entered the bathroom and could see her naked silhouette as she shampooed and rinsed her hair behind the thick glass block wall which separated the open shower stall from the rest of the room. With a silence which had been embedded into him by the military, he stripped, then skirted the wall and grabbed her around the waist from behind. He held tight as she jumped and shrieked. "Oh my God, Devon, you gave me a freaking heart attack!"

He chuckled as he moved the length of her long wet hair over her left shoulder giving him access to the right side of her neck. He lowered his mouth to the area below her ear and began licking and nibbling on her skin. She moaned and tilted her head, inviting him to do more and he was happy to oblige her. His hands moved as if they had a mind of their own. One lifted to the swell of her breasts while the other inched lower to the treasure between her legs. His cock was erect and hard against her ass and he mentally cursed himself because he'd forgotten to grab a condom. Oh well, he'd have to enjoy her with his mouth and hands for now and after he got her into his bed he would find his own release.

He grabbed the bar of soap from its shelf and began lathering up her body. It wasn't the flowery stuff she used, which he loved on her, but he liked knowing he was covering her with the ocean-fresh scent of the soap he used daily. He was marking her body in more ways than one—staking his claim. "Reach up and put your arms around my neck and keep them there." After she did as she was told, he asked, "I don't mind finding you naked in my shower, Pet, but why were you so late in getting here? Had I gotten here a few minutes earlier, you would've earned a very thorough spanking, because you obviously would've been still dressed, violating my direct order."

Kristen moaned as his hands continued to clean every inch of her. "Mmm. Sorry, Sir. I'd been struggling to get one of the chapters in my book just right. I'd rewritten it several times, but still wasn't happy with it. On my way back home this afternoon, I came up with the perfect way to write it." She paused and widened her stance as he began to wash her bare pussy with the suds in his hand. "Mmm, that feels so good."

"So, that's why you were running late?" He lessened the length of his stroke while increasing the pace and pressure right atop her clit which was peeking out from its hood and begging for the attention. If the rocking of her hips was any indication, he had her so focused on what the fingers at her mound were doing that she didn't seem to notice the ones playing with her soapy breasts were pinching and rolling her nipples with more pressure than usual.

Soon she was panting hard, grinding her ass into his groin. "Oh, S-Sir, please. I-I'm going to come."

"But you don't have permission to come yet, Pet." He smiled at her groan of frustration. "You still haven't answered my question and you know I don't like repeating myself."

As he increased the speed and intensity of his actions, she screamed his name while trying to move away from the insistent fingers on her clit. He then eased back off, not wanting her to come until she answered him, yet still keeping her on the edge. "Yes! That's w-why I was . . . I was late. I was s-so into what I was writing, I . . . Oh, God, Devon, pleeeease . . . I-I lost track of time."

He pinched her clit and nipple at the same time. "come now, Pet."

And she did. She came harder and longer than she'd ever come in her life. If it hadn't been for Devon's strong arms holding her up, she might've melted down the drain with the water. As the last of the shudders left her body, he rinsed the soap from her skin before helping her sit on the shower's built-in tiled seat. He quickly washed and rinsed his own hair and body before turning off the water and retrieving three towels from the tall cabinet outside the shower. He hung one on a hook on the side of the cabinet and took the other two to tend to Kristen. He held her arm to steady her as she stood, then ran the first towel over her arms and legs before wrapping and securing it around her upper torso. Then he told her to bend forward and flip her hair over her head so he could towel dry it for her.

After he was done taking care of Kristen, Devon grabbed the last towel and took care of himself. *As it should be,* he thought—she deserved to always come first. She was his sub, his woman, his . . . love. His mind seized onto the sudden thought while his body followed her into the bedroom where they dropped their towels and climbed into his bed. Was this love he was feeling? He couldn't be sure since he'd never been in love before, but there was no other word which seemed to fit.

His dad would be laughing his head off his shoulders if he knew what was going on in his son's mind. The man had always said "when you meet the right woman, she's going to have you wrapped around her finger so fast, you won't know what hit you." His dad was right. In their short time together, Devon had fallen for her hard. He couldn't imagine going back to being the man he'd been a little over a week ago—a man who'd never met her, never talked to her, never touched her . . . never loved her. Yes, it had to be love—there was no other way to describe the fact that she was the other half of his soul. Wow, go figure—Devon Sawyer, a self-proclaimed bachelor for life, was in love. But he wasn't ready to tell Kristen or anyone else that. He wasn't ready to put his heart and his soul on the line. She might not even be ready to hear it since the ink on her divorce papers was barely dry. She'd said she loved him as she fell asleep earlier, but he was certain she didn't realize it, and had no clue if she meant it. Neither one of them had spoken about it. But for now, he might not be able to say the words aloud, but he could show her with his body. He lay down beside her and pulled her body beneath his, then proceeded to do something he'd never done in his life. He made love to a woman—his woman.

# CHAPTER 19

*D*evon sighed as one of the two Navy MP's standing sentry unlocked the conference room door. He followed Brody, Jake, NCIS agents Chan and Dobrwski, and finally Beau, into the room before the door was shut behind them again. The others would be there soon to continue the daunting task in front of them. They'd spent over twelve hours yesterday going through boxes and boxes of reports and photos and had barely made a dent in them. Close to one hundred file boxes were piled up around the perimeter of the room.

Paired off into three groups, each pair took a different mission and reviewed every minuscule piece of data. Then to make sure nothing was missed, each mission was handed off to another pair until the entire team had reviewed every file. It was a tedious process and today they were picking up where they'd left off. As they took seats around the large table, Jake began to hand out the food he'd picked up for everyone at a deli on his way in.

"How many questions do you think Paula will have today?" Brody quipped as he unwrapped one of his two huge bacon, double-egg and cheese sandwiches. It was one of the other reasons he'd earned his nickname—the big man was addicted to eggs. He could eat them, prepared any way possible, for each meal of the day as long as they were accompanied by some form of meat and his favorite hot sauce.

"Shit, I hope not many. Otherwise I'm going to fire her ass by the end of the day," Devon responded, taking a seat with a coffee and egg sandwich of his own.

Yesterday, Paula had proven Brody's prediction to be correct. She'd been obviously annoyed over not being allowed in the conference room and not being privy to what they were doing in there, especially with armed guards at the door. Of course, she hadn't voiced her displeasure, but throughout the day, she'd knocked on the door, asking the most inane questions over stuff she already knew, just to get a peek over someone's shoulder when they opened the door.

Barbara Chan swallowed a bite of her bagel with cream cheese. "If she pulls that shit again today, I may have one of the MPs shoot her on principle."

The door had opened again, and Ian walked in, catching part of the conversation. "Please don't. The carpets were redone a few weeks ago, and I don't want blood on them," he remarked as he shut the door and grabbed a coffee, sandwich, and seat in that order. "I'll talk with Paula, again. I don't want to fire her if I don't have to because none of us have the time or desire to teach someone new how to run the office. Unless anyone wants to volunteer." His team shook their heads emphatically. "I didn't think so. If things continue, I'll call Mrs. Kemple to see if she can come back up from Miami for a week or two to train someone else. In the meantime, we've got a killer to catch." He started handing out the bulky files. It was going to be another long day.

Two hours later, Devon's eyes began watering after reading close to a million typed pages. Okay, it wasn't a million, but it sure as hell felt like it. His phone rang and he looked at the screen, pleased to see it was Kristen. Answering it, he asked her to hold on while he exited the conference room and walked down to his office, closing the door for some privacy.

"Hi, babe."

"Hi. How's everything going? Did you find anything?"

He'd told her a censored version of what was going on yesterday morning as they shared breakfast in his kitchen before they both left for the day. He might have a bull's-eye on his back and the team agreed that if she was with him, she had a right to know. They doubted she was in any danger, but he was still concerned about her safety and had two of their contracted security men keeping an eye on her. The men excelled at their jobs and he'd told them he didn't want her to know they were there because he didn't want her to be worried. Jenn also had two bodyguards taking her back and forth to her college classes. With her parents' murders, there was a stronger possibility she could be a target. In addition to those four and their regular guard at the front gate, there were five other highly-trained and armed men patrolling the compound at all times. They also had people watching Brody's, Jake's, Marco's and Boomer's places when the men weren't there. "No, not yet. What are you up to?"

"Trying to get my word count in for the day, and I'm almost there. If you don't mind, you were my inspiration for the shower scene I just wrote."

Her voice was low and seductive and his brain replayed their own shower scene this morning in his head. It had been extremely satisfying for both of them and he chuckled. "No, Pet, I don't mind. In fact, I look forward to inspiring you more tonight. I'll have to give it some thought on how I can be your carnal muse. But for now, an idea occurred to me. I want you to bring your laptop with you tonight."

Curious, she asked, "Why?"

"I want you to read me the shower scene you wrote."

"What?! Devon, I can't read it to you!" It was one thing if he wanted to read it himself, but something altogether different to read it to him. The scene was so hot, she'd blushed when she wrote it and knew how red her cheeks would be when she said the words aloud to him.

He laughed at her shock and obvious embarrassment. "Sure you can, and you'll do it naked. As your Dom, I'm ordering you to, and you know what happens when you don't obey my orders."

Her aggravated sigh sounded heavy in his ear, and his grin

widened. "Fine. Yes, Sir." But she instantly brightened again. "Okay, change of subject. I was calling to ask if you wanted to go to Clearwater Beach tonight. One of my classmates from high school is touring with an improv troupe, and they're doing a show at a hotel over there at nine. I messaged her on Facebook, and she said she'd hold a table for eight for me if I wanted it. Will, Kayla, and Roxy said they would love to go, and I was wondering if you and three of the guys or maybe Jenn wanted to come with us. I understand if you don't with everything going on, but I figured it was something different to do. You guys could probably use some comedy relief after the past few days."

He had to agree with her. It'd been a long and stress-filled week, and a much needed humor break would ease some tension. "It sounds great. I'm in and I'll see who else wants to go. Why don't you come here at eight and we'll all drive over together."

"Awesome. I'll message Sara to hold the table, and the girls and Will to meet us there. It'll be easier for them instead of backtracking to your place."

"Perfect." He glanced at his desk clock and saw he still had hours of tedium left to go. "Let me get back to work, and I'll see you later. Oh, and don't forget your laptop, Pet."

He smiled as she groaned and could imagine her eyes rolling at his reminder. "Yes, Sir."

A LITTLE AFTER 8:00 p.m., Devon, Kristen and Jenn climbed into rear seat of Brody's Ford F-150 while Jake took the front passenger seat. Brody put the vehicle in drive as did the driver of the Cadillac Escalade which pulled out behind them. Two guards who were assigned to Jenn would follow them to and from Clearwater Beach as a precaution. Jenn and Kristen chatted along the way while the men stayed alert for anything out of place. Devon was aggravated they hadn't found any clues to why four of their friends were murdered and his mind continued to search for an answer. It would take at least three more days to go through the files and he hoped the solution was in them somewhere. If it wasn't, he didn't know where they would go from there.

Fifteen minutes into their excursion, they were heading down a two-lane highway and began to cross a bridge which ran over a large lake. Behind them, a gray Hummer changed lanes behind the Escalade and accelerated to pass both vehicles on the left. Devon watched as the truck with tinted windows came along the driver's side next to him and his internal alert system flared up. Before he had a chance to warn Brody, the big truck swerved to the right, smashed into them and forced the Ford into the metal guardrail which was no match for the forty-five hundred pound pickup. As the women screamed and the men cursed, their vehicle went airborne, falling toward the lake thirty feet below them. The impact of the truck hitting the water hurt like hell, and the driver and passenger airbags deployed when the front bumper struck first due to the weight of the engine.

After the vehicle settled, the interior of the cab began to fill with water at an alarming rate. Devon shook his head to clear it and swiftly evaluated the situation. He released his seatbelt before reaching over and doing the same for a stunned Jenn and Kristen.

Jenn screamed, "Uncle Brody!"

Devon glanced toward the front seat and saw Jake trying to free their unconscious friend. Knowing Jake could handle Brody, Devon turned himself around, lifted his feet into the air, and kicked out the back window. If he didn't get them out of the sinking truck soon, they would be going under the water with it. He grasped Kristen first, since she was sitting next to him, and shoved her out the opening before reaching for Jenn. After both women were safely out of the cab and in the murky water, he turned to help Jake get the still unconscious Brody into the back seat and then out the window as gently as they could. They didn't know what injuries the big man may have, but any further damage they might do by moving him was better than him drowning.

Devon looked and saw it was about a fifty yard swim to the shoreline. He grabbed the two women and pushed them toward it. While he helped them, Jake began to swim with his arm around

Brody's chest, dragging the man's body in a rescue hold. As they neared the shallower water, Devon heard shouts from above and also from the land ahead of them. Glancing up, he froze when he saw one of their two bodyguards, standing at the water's edge, aiming his semi-automatic pistol at them.

*Fuck!* One of their contractors was a traitor? They were sitting ducks, and he surged forward to put himself between the women and danger just as the man fired his weapon three times in rapid succession. Devon yelled, while trying to pull his own waterlogged weapon from its holster at his lower back, and quickly looked to see who was hit because it hadn't been him. It was then he saw what appeared to be a large log floating in the water about ten feet away over his left shoulder. But it wasn't a log—it was an alligator . . . a very large, very dead alligator. He looked back at the bodyguard who had since lowered his weapon and was now wading into the water to render assistance while staying alert for more gators. Devon breathed a deep sigh of relief and gave their savior a grateful wave.

———————

DEVON SAW Ian and Boomer running toward them as the first ambulance pulled away from the hectic crash scene carrying a now semi-conscious Brody and one of the bodyguards for his protection. He'd used a borrowed cell phone to contact them, since he and everyone else who'd been in Brody's totaled truck now needed new ones if they couldn't dry theirs out. Ian reached the group one step ahead of the younger man and immediately checked on Jenn and then Kristen, both of whose cuts and bruises were being treated by EMTs and paramedics. After he was convinced they were going to be okay, as well as the bruised and battered Jake and Devon standing protective watch over them, Ian turned his worried eyes to meet his brother's and barked, "Sit-rep."

Devon shifted his stance and grimaced. Wet jeans sucked big time. "Guy came out of nowhere. If he was tailing us, then he's good because none of us realized he was a problem until it was too late. The security detail didn't seem to faze him. Gray Hummer, two or three years old, and the plates were covered with dirt so they were unreadable. Tinted windows so we couldn't make out any features, but the driver was definitely male and he was alone. Police have put out an APB, but I'm not optimistic since it was most likely stolen."

Right after their vehicle went airborne, the guard driving the Escalade slammed on his brakes and let his partner out to help the victims, then took off after the Hummer, alerting 9-1-1 in the process. But the brief pause had given the suspect the chance he needed make a clean getaway.

"How's Brody?"

"Got his bell rung, but he was coming around when they left for the hospital. I sent Henderson with him." Henderson was the bodyguard and former Marine sharpshooter who'd prevented them from becoming dinner for the eight-foot alligator. Devon planned on giving the man a bonus for making the difficult and deadly shot into the gator's puny brain.

"Ow!"

Devon's eyes whipped back to Kristen at her pain-filled cry and he growled at the female EMT who'd obviously done something to hurt her. The woman ignored him as if people growled at her all day long. "I don't think it's fractured, but you're going to have a nice size bruise on your shin."

Kristen glanced at Devon after she was lifted onto a gurney for transport to the hospital. "I can deal with a bruise considering we were nearly killed."

She didn't look or sound angry, as if she blamed him for putting her in danger, but Devon couldn't help but think she should. If it hadn't been for him and his hazardous past, she wouldn't have gotten injured. A cut on her forehead would need several stitches and she most likely had a concussion. Like the rest of them, she also had multiple smaller cuts and bruises all over her. He cringed as he thought she could be dead thanks to him. As her Dom and lover, he was supposed to protect her and he'd failed. His gut clenched. If she stayed with him, there would always be a chance someone from his past would come to seek revenge on him for whatever reason. And putting her life at risk, because he was selfish enough to love her, wasn't something he was willing to do. He needed to let her go, before she got hurt again or, even worse, killed.

Next to him, Ian grabbed his shoulder in a firm, yet gentle grip. When he tore his eyes away from Kristen and looked at his brother, Devon saw the sympathy and understanding in the older man's eyes. Ian leaned toward him and kept his voice low.

"I know what you're thinking, and you need to stop. This wasn't your fault, just like John's death wasn't your fault. Kristen's alive, and you'll do your best to keep her that way. But brother, she could be hurt walking across a street one day whether she's with you or not. Shit happens. You love her. I can see it, and so can everyone else. And for some unknown cosmic reason, she loves you too. None of us are going to live forever, Dev, so do you want to be happy or miserable for the rest of your life? I think it's a no-brainer, but, then again, you don't have much of a brain. It must go with your small Irish dick."

Devon snorted at Ian's last comments, but didn't answer him. He had to give this some thought. His brother had made a point, but it still didn't make Devon feel better as his woman was placed into the back of an ambulance. After they had her loaded, he climbed in and took a seat on the bench next to her, clutching her hand because he needed to touch her. He may not have made a final decision about their relationship yet, but no matter what, he would continue to protect her with his life.

# CHAPTER 20

*F*ive long hours later, Devon was helping Kristen climb into his bed after he'd gotten them both undressed, and showered the last of the murky lake water off their bodies. Her body was marred with cuts and bruises, and it was all he could do to tamp down the anger of what had happened and the fear of what could have happened to her. He tenderly washed her hair and skin before toweling the excess moisture away. The laceration on her forehead had taken twelve small stitches to close, but the plastic surgeon did his best to prevent any visible scarring after it healed. While she did have a minor concussion, as he earlier suspected, the emergency room physician assured them she could go home as long as Devon stayed close and monitored her for any related symptoms.

Brody hadn't been so lucky and, after much bitching on his part, the big geek was admitted to the hospital overnight for observation with a moderate concussion. Devon knew the only reason they'd been able to convince Brody to stay, despite the double vision and nausea he was having, was Ian's threat to retrieve a spare set of wrist restraints from his SUV. The boss then told Brody he'd call Mistress China to have her come torture the injured man. Their teammate was now in the capable hands of four rotating bodyguards and one very pretty nurse he'd been hitting on as the others left the emergency room.

Ian was taking care of Jenn in his apartment downstairs. Their niece had suffered a fractured wrist, which was now in a cast, along with her own set of cuts and contusions. When they'd all arrived home, an anxious Beau hadn't been able to figure out which one of his favorite female humans needed him more, but in the end the dog had followed the younger woman to her bedroom. Somehow Jake and Devon had fared better than the others, walking away with moderate bumps and bruises which would most likely make them stiff and hurt like hell in the morning. In fact, Devon was shocked they'd all walked away from the crash with minor injuries. The airbags and seatbelts had done an unbelievable job.

Boomer and Jake were taking refuge in the spare bedrooms above the Trident offices inside the secure compound. Ian had increased the personnel guarding all of them and sent two additional guards to Marco's place. He wasn't taking any chances with his team's lives. As much as Ian and Devon wanted to bring Marco and his sister to the compound, moving Nina, who was now confined to a hospice bed, wasn't feasible. Devon had spoken to their teammate after he'd first called Ian and Boomer to the crash scene, but told him to stay with his sister. The only reason he'd called was he wanted to make sure Marco and the men watching his house stayed alert. The poor guy was torn between staying with Nina, or leaving and having her friend take over for him. He didn't want to lose the time he had left with her, nor did he want her harmed by whoever was after the team.

Devon had also contacted Will from the hospital and assured him Kristen was okay, but banged up a bit. She'd be fine and there was no need for him and her friends to come to the ER because they would only add to the chaos around them. He hadn't wanted to tell the man in great detail what had happened, but a news crew had shown up as Kristen's ambulance pulled away from the scene and the story was on the eleven p.m. broadcast. What they had managed to keep under wraps was the fact the crash hadn't been an accident. They were able to convince the Tampa detectives who'd arrived to investigate that the other driver must've been a drunk who lost control of his car. The last thing they wanted was for whoever was gunning for them to realize they knew someone was targeting Team Four. Despite leaving Tampa's finest in the dark, Ian let the NCIS agents and Keon know what happened, with full disclosure.

After Kristen was settled under the covers, Devon went and retrieved a bottle of water and some acetaminophen, which the doctor said she could take every four hours, and set it on the night table next to her. The doctor didn't want her taking anything stronger with her head injury. Devon made sure she didn't need anything else before he climbed into the bed next to her and pulled her to cuddle against him.

"Are you sure you're okay, baby? I know I've asked you the same question every five minutes since we swam out of the lake, but I need to keep hearing the answer."

She turned her head from its resting spot on his shoulder and placed a soft kiss on his bare chest before getting comfortable again. Her hand rested over his heart and tattoo. "I'm fine Devon, I swear. I was terrified when it was happening, but it's over now, and everyone is okay. I'm relieved and a little sore, nothing else. It could have been so much worse, but we're alive and I just want you to hold me."

He picked up her hand and brought it to his lips. "I'm so sorry, Pet. It's all my fault you were hurt. God, when I think about how you and Jenn could've been killed it makes me want to tear someone apart."

Kristen winced as she shifted and propped her upper body on her elbow, so she was glaring down at him in anger. "How dare you! This was not your fault, Devon. You didn't run us off the road! Some maniac did, and he's probably the only one who knows the reason why. I will not let you blame yourself for another person's evil acts. He may have killed your friends, are you saying you feel responsible for that, too? Are you saying you could've somehow predicted the future and stopped him before Jenn's parents or the other two SEALs were murdered? Because if you feel you're responsible for everything that's happened, I'm going to do what Ian threatened Brody with and call Mistress China."

The tension in his body eased, and he chuckled at her annoyed rant. "Oh Pet, did you just threaten your Dom?"

Returning her head to his shoulder, she huffed. "Yes, I did, Sir. Because my big, bad Dom was blaming himself for something he has no control over. It seems to be a bad habit of his. And if you think you're going to un-collar me and let me go over this—yes, I heard what Ian said to you—then you've got another think coming."

"Thing."

She looked at him in confusion. "What?"

"You said 'another *think* coming.' It's another *thing* coming."

Scowling at his arrogance, she huffed again. "Really Devon? You're going to argue with an English major? Google it sometime. It's another *think* coming. And why are we even arguing about this? The point is, you'd have to come up with a far better reason to make me walk away from you."

Devon's mouth gaped open. The woman never failed to surprise him, and then, she did it again. "So, is it true what Ian said? Do you love me?"

Her question shocked him, causing his breathing to hitch before he lifted her chin and looked into her eyes. They were filled with unshed tears, but, more importantly, they were filled with hope and love—for him. "Yes, Ms. Kristen Anders, I do. I love you. I've never thought I'd find a woman who could steal my heart as you have, but I'm so glad I did. I love you, Pet."

"Good, because Ian was also right about something else. I love you, too. After my marriage fell apart, I never thought I would say those words to a man ever again. But I'm glad I did, and I'm glad it's you."

Devon leaned down and kissed her as tenderly as he could. And then he held her close to his side long after they both fell asleep.

———

AFTER THE LATE news broadcast ended, the assassin used the remote to change the TV channel from his motel room bed before downing the last of his bottle of whiskey. He was pissed at himself. He'd taken a big chance, something he rarely did, and it didn't pay off. After watching the compound for several days, he hadn't been able to figure out how to get all four targets together. The security had increased and there was no way in, so he needed an opportunity to get them outside the compound.

He'd set up his own surveillance camera in a tree as close to the monitored fence as he dared. While parked a half mile away from the place, he'd watched on his laptop as three out of his four targets, along with the two women, climbed into a Ford pickup and he tailed them looking for an opportunity. How they'd all walked away from the crash was beyond him, but they did, and as a result his job would be much harder. If his employer hadn't been calling every day demanding immediate results, he wouldn't have taken the chance he did. The bastard had shortened the time frame and given him five days to complete the job or he wouldn't be paid the remainder of his money.

*Fuck!*

# CHAPTER 21

$S$aturday came and went with no new information on the driver of the Hummer who tried to kill them, and no leads were found in the boxes of files in the conference room. They were only about halfway through them and everyone was on edge.

Kristen had only brought one change of clothes with her on Friday night, since she'd planned to sleep at Devon's. Instead of allowing her leave the compound again, he sent one of the bodyguards to her apartment to pick up a few more clothes and a short list of items she requested. He wasn't letting her out of his guarded home until this nightmare was over. He liked knowing she was in his apartment and he could walk over at any time to see her. The thought of asking her to move in with him had crossed his mind several times this morning, but he didn't think either one of them was ready for that big step.

While Devon was with his team, minus Brody, poring over pages and pages of mission reports, Jenn and Beau hung out with Kristen in his apartment. The two women were sore and stiff, so he'd propped them up on opposite ends of his "L" shaped couch with pillows and blankets. He left water, acetaminophen, snacks, the house phone, computers, books, and the TV remote within reach, and told Beau to guard them with his furry life before finally heading over to the office.

Despite a pounding headache and some lingering nausea, Brody managed to get himself discharged from the hospital and was brought back to the compound by his bodyguards late in the afternoon. He immediately crashed in the bedroom next to the one Boomer was using.

Devon had retrieved Kristen's laptop when he grabbed her duffel bag from her car, and she'd worked on her daily word count, managing to write more than she'd expected to. Jenn had several assignments for college which kept her busy during the day as well. Will had called and insisted on seeing his cousin was okay for himself, so Devon invited him, as well as Kayla and Roxy, over to his apartment for a simple Chinese takeout dinner. Since he wasn't willing to risk leaving the compound with Kristen, it'd been the only other option. Jenn, Ian, and Beau joined them, while Jake and Boomer tended to a woozy and grouchy Brody as they hung out in the rec room above the offices, eating pizza and watching a ballgame.

The two groups of family and friends sitting at Devon's dinner table immediately liked each other and the conversation flowed. Once Jenn learned Kayla was a social worker, she'd latched onto the woman, asking her all sorts of questions which the older woman was happy to answer. Jenn was still trying to find her future niche in the world and was considering social work as her major. Roxy and Ian discovered they had mutual acquaintances, and between them and The Covenant, the two had plenty to talk about. Despite the man's effeminate mannerism, Devon found Kristen's cousin funny and easy to talk to. He was surprised to learn Will was an assistant curator at the Tampa Museum of Art, because the stuffy sounding position didn't fit with the man's loud and bubbly personality. He'd laughed when Will told him how Kristen referred to Devon and his teammates as the Sexy Six-Pack, which elicited a groan and eye roll from his Ninja-girl.

The evening was enjoyable and relaxing despite their brush with death a day earlier, however, Devon and Kristen were relieved and exhausted when everyone left a little after nine o'clock. Kristen was grateful Devon had eased her cousin's concerns over her safety and promised to keep him posted. After being there for her when her marriage collapsed, she knew it was difficult for Will to leave her safety in Devon's hands, but her cousin finally decided the man was trustworthy and would guard her with his own life. Will even joked that if anything else happened to her, he would find a way to sneak in and redecorate her Dom's apartment in purple and florescent green with farm animal themed fabrics.

Less than ten minutes after closing the door behind their guests, Devon had Kristen naked in his bed. Neither one of them were up for anything strenuous, so instead, he made slow, passionate love to her. He skimmed his soft lips over every cut and bruise from her head to her toes. When she insisted she wanted to do the same to him, he made her stay reclined on her back with her head on her pillow, and by moving and twisting his body, he brought each one of his bruises to her mouth. After she was satisfied she had kissed every one, he settled himself between her legs and leisurely pleasured her. They were both so aroused by the time he put on a condom and eased himself between her wet folds, it was only a minute or two before she found her release with him following a few moments later. It hadn't been the explosive ending they usually reached, but a gentle free-fall over the edge, and what it lacked in physical intensity, it more than made up for in emotional strength. It was a confirmation they were alive . . . and in love.

THE NEXT MORNING began as a repeat of the day before, with pages and pages of boredom making Devon's eyes cross. They were getting nowhere fast despite the fact all six of them were back to reading the reports, along with the two NCIS agents. Brody's double vision and nausea were pretty much gone this morning, and he was sitting at the conference table with the rest of them, his chair tilted back and his sneakered feet upon the table. After the first hour, Ian finally stopped harping at him to keep his size thirteens on the floor.

They were about to break for lunch when there was a knock on the closed door. No one groaned, since it couldn't be Paula who was off for the weekend. From his seat, Ian yelled, "Come in."

One of the MPs swung the door open and they all froze at the sight of a pale and shaking Jenn with a wide-eyed Kristen holding the girl's arm to steady her. Jenn's eyes were filled with tears, her chin trembling. "U-Uncle Ian."

Everyone jumped up from their seats as Ian raced to their niece's side. Somehow he managed to hide the brief flash of panic which shot through him and everyone else in the room. "What's wrong, Jenn? What happened?"

She lifted her non-casted arm toward him and it was then they saw she was holding a thin CD case. It was a blank one which was used to copy files. "I found this in the storage box with my CDs."

When she didn't say anything further, Ian looked back at his teammates and saw the same confusion he was feeling on their faces. He took the case from her and opened the cover. "What the . . ."

Devon watched as his brother's face paled a few shades. "What is it?"

Ian read the words on the surface of the disc aloud. *"Ian—if something happens to me, this is my last will and testament—Jeff."*

"What the hell?" Brody stepped over and took the computer disc from Ian, then brought his laptop out of sleep mode. "Why the heck would this be in Baby-girl's things? Shouldn't this be with his lawyer? I mean, his lawyer had his will, right?"

Ian nodded as he pulled Jenn into his arms and hugged her tight. "I'm sure it's nothing, sweetheart. Your dad's lawyer probably gave him a copy of the will and somehow the disc ended up with your stuff when we packed everything up." He looked intently at Kristen over Jenn's shoulder.

"Why don't you go back to Dev's with Kristen, and we'll check it out. If it's anything you need to know about, I promise I'll tell you, okay? Kristen, would you mind calling for some pizza for everyone. Order enough pies for the MPs and guards, too. Lunch came around fast, and we're all getting hungry."

Devon was proud of Kristen. She realized Ian was worried

about what was on the disc and took command of Jenn by wrapping her arm around the young woman's shoulders. With a reassuring smile and false bravado she turned to lead the girl back down the hallway. "Sure, no problem. And no anchovies, right?" Before the door shut again, he heard her say, "See, I told you it was probably a copy. Come on, Beau, we'll get you some kibble, too."

As he sat down and inserted the disc into his laptop, Brody grumbled, "You know, I never thought I'd say this, but I'm getting really sick of pizza." His teammates and Dobrowski all crowded around him as the file was scanned. "It's only one file. A Word doc." The document came up on the screen. "Three pages long."

"Print it," Ian ordered.

The nearby printer started spitting out pages and Ian went to grab them. The rest of them began to read over Brody's shoulder. The computer geek was the first to comment. "Is Jeff fucking kidding me?"

Barbara Chan had remained seated, since she wouldn't be able to see anything with six big men surrounding, and reading, the fifteen-inch screen. "What's it say?"

"It's a list of SEALs he worked with over the years and what he bequeathed them upon his death."

The agent looked puzzled and shrugged. "So? What's wrong with that?"

"Well, he left me his snow-blower and a pair of snowshoes. When was the last time it snowed in Tampa? He left Ian his collection of shot glasses from around the world—I didn't know he had one—and a paperback copy of *Uncle John's Bathroom Reader*. Prichard was supposed to get a surfboard and one of those singing mounted fish, which is ridiculous since the man lived in fucking Iowa."

Boomer chuckled, reading over his friend's shoulder. "It's not as bad as what I got. A dancing reindeer and his old combat boots. My feet are two sizes bigger than his. What the hell am I going to do with those?'

Pointing to a name on the list, Jake started laughing. "Oh man, Urkel must have pissed him off at some point. He left the guy a collection of used jockstraps and a deflated basketball." Steve "Urkel" Romanelli had been their Heavy Weapons Operator, and the man to beat on the basketball court when they were playing one-on-one.

"The whole list is like this—it's fucking nuts," Brody added. "Did Jeff have a fucking screw loose, and we didn't know about it?"

Ian had taken a seat across the table and was shuffling through the pages in front of him. "No, it's a coded message. Do you see how the names aren't indented, but the rest of the entry is?"

"Yeah."

"It looks like the names are in random order. They're not alphabetical or in order of service dates, or even how he was closer to some more than others. Devon doesn't show up on the list until the bottom of the second page, and he's listed as *Sawyer, Devon*. Marco is two above him, and he's down as *Marco DeAngelis*. By the way, Reverend, he left you his ugly Christmas sweater and a yellow rubber ducky. Sometime you're going to have to tell us what that's all about." Jake rolled his eyes as Ian flipped one of the pages over and grabbed a pen. "He's using some first names, some last, and some nicknames. Start reading off the names, Brody, exactly as he has them."

"Okay, You're first. 'I.' Next is *Archer, Pete . . . Neil Radovsky . . . Boomer . . . Urkel . . .*" Brody continued down the entire list, then eyeballed Ian, along with everyone else.

"*Ian, bury me in the place I hate the most—Jeff Mullins.*" While the rest of them watched in total confusion, Ian jumped up from his chair and started searching the content papers taped to the front of each box they hadn't gone through yet.

Dobrowski hurried over to help. "Which one?" he asked.

"Colombia. Ernesto Diaz."

"It's over here, I think." The agent sidestepped to several stacks of boxes under the large video screen on the wall. "Yeah, here it is. Four boxes."

Ian rushed over and grabbed the top cardboard box with Dobrowski picking up the second. Devon scratched his head in confusion. "Um, Boss-man, you going to clue the rest of us in?"

Dropping the box on the table, Ian threw the lid off and started removing the large files, tossing one at each member of his team. "Don't you remember how much Jeff was complaining about being in the jungles down there? Said he'd rather be any place else on earth. He hated it there. It was his last mission with us, and he was bitching because it had to be with all those damn mosquitoes and creepy crawlers." Ian kept a file for himself and took his seat again. "Jeff figured something out. Something which had to do with this mission, and for whatever fucking reason he had, he was investigating it himself. He needed to give us a starting point, but couldn't risk the hint being found if something happened to him. Anyone looking at the list would think the guy was joking around or, like Egghead said, just plain nuts. Whatever evidence or notes he had were probably stolen with the rest of the stuff taken to make it look like a burglary gone wrong. The answer we're looking for is somewhere in these four boxes."

"Son of a fucking bitch." Like the rest of the team, Devon grabbed the file which had landed in front of him, sat down, and started poring over every little detail of the month-long mission.

# CHAPTER 22

*T*he assassin was back in his tree for the second day in a row, watching the compound. He'd been there since dawn, covered in camouflage to escape detection. He took a sip of warm, brown liquid from the flask he'd brought with him, annoyed to find it only had a few drops left. Adjusting the sniper rifle which was resting on his legs, he went back to scanning the area a few degrees downhill from his position with his high-tech binoculars.

The first thing he'd done was calculate the distance between his roost and the door to the building where his targets had all gathered again. Even though he had two days left to eliminate them, he was getting nervous and wanted to get the job over with, so he could head to the tropics and lose himself in his four Ws—whiskey and a warm, willing woman.

The hair on the back of his neck had been standing up for the past hour, but he couldn't figure out why. He didn't see anything in the compound or the surrounding wooded area which would trigger his unease, yet the feeling wouldn't leave him.

He saw the two Navy MPs leave the building after their replacements arrived, and glanced at his watch as they drove from the compound. Nineteen thirty hours. It shouldn't be long now. As soon as his targets were out in the open, four quick shots would end their lives. He was out of options. Short of dropping a bomb on the compound or bringing in some help, this was his last resort. After his failed attempt two days ago, the men were now alert, and would do everything they could to thwart further efforts to eliminate them. He had a stolen motorcycle stashed on a bike trail about a third of a mile behind him. With the panic and confusion, along with no gate in the fence on this side, he would have enough of a head start to get away without any problems. Putting away his binoculars, he readied his rifle. As he peered through the high-powered scope, he took a deep breath and waited.

---

EIGHT HOURS, eight pizzas and a lot of coffee and bottles of water later, there were two points they all agreed on and neither identified who wanted them dead. One, Polo and Boomer were probably not targets, and two, Prichard's name was on the killer's hit list out of pure circumstance. The first two hadn't been on that particular mission. Boomer had been sidelined with a broken ankle, while Marco's grandmother, the woman who'd raised him and his sister, had passed away in New York a few days before they left on the mission. He'd taken a hardship leave to help his sister with the funeral and aftermath of settling the crotchety old woman's meager, yet messy estate. Unfortunately for Eric Prichard, he'd taken Marco's vacated spot for the mission—a spot which wound up getting him killed. A fact that was getting to Marco more and more as they pored through the files.

Only a team of seven had been sent to Colombia for a month to gather intelligence on drug lord Ernesto Diaz. The man had his hands in a few pots other than the one which contained his cocaine empire. Among them were a sex-slavery ring and arms trade. He was killed in a raid of one of his warehouses while making a high-grade weapons sale with members of Al Qaeda. Team Four had been a part of the raid six months after their original mission. Due to a diagnosis of rheumatoid arthritis with increasing symptoms, Lt. Jeff Mullins accepted a promotion to a base position in Little Creek,

VA, and ended his time in the field after the mission they were now reviewing. He hadn't been on the raid, so that file wasn't with the ones they needed to search.

Although sitting there reading wasn't a strenuous activity, they were all exhausted and bug-eyed when Ian finally called it a day. "We'll pick up again first thing in the morning. I know it's here, we just haven't found it yet. Keon sent me a text earlier. He'll be here around ten a.m."

As the team cleaned up the pizza boxes and coffee cups, the two NCIS agents gathered their things with a promise to bring breakfast in for everyone around eight. Sometime within the past hour the MPs had changed shifts and two new men stood in the hallway. After everyone else exited the conference room, the door was locked again behind them.

It was still light outside as they poured out into the parking area, stretching and inhaling the fresh air. Devon was anxious to see Kristen and check on Jenn. He and Ian had gone up to Devon's apartment earlier with one of the pizzas for the two women, and to tell their niece what they found on the disc. Of course, they'd down-played it as a comical last will and testament of things her dad wanted to leave to the men he'd worked with and loved like brothers. She accepted their explanation, but they could tell she was still bothered by her find.

After exchanging a few fist bumps with his team and verbal goodbyes with the agents, Devon turned in the direction of his apartment when a single shot from a high-powered rifle rang out, echoing through the air around them. Almost as one, with adrenaline surging through them, the team, agents, and men guarding the compound dropped to the ground, un-holstering their weapons and looking for a target as they did. Whoever was after the team was getting desperate if he was firing on the heavily armed compound.

Time seemed to stand still as they all tried to assess the situation. No other shots were fired as everyone scrambled for cover. As the echoed report faded and silence ensued, Ian called out with more calm then any of them felt, "Anyone hit? Sit-rep!"

As everyone responded they were all okay, nobody was hit, and the shot had come from the north-west, outside the fence-line, Devon's cell phone rang. Thinking it was Kristen or Jenn scared out of their minds, he answered the call without looking at the screen, but it wasn't one of the two frightened female voices he expected to hear. An unruffled and familiar deep rumble came over the line. "Tango eliminated. Half a klick from your eleven. I'll be in after I'm sure he was alone. Call Keon for clean-up."

The call was disconnected, and a stunned Devon stared at the phone in his hand for a moment or two. Translated, the brief, one-sided conversation meant their enemy was dead about a third of a mile almost straight ahead of Devon's position, and the deputy director was needed to cover up what'd happened. The only problem was, Devon had no clue what *had* happened. He yelled out for all to hear, "Stand down, but stay alert. Tango's been taken out by one of ours. He's clearing the area before he comes in." Looking at the confused faces of the NCIS agents and his teammates, in a much lower voice he simply said one name, "Carter."

---

THREE HOURS LATER, the FBI's Deputy Director walked into the conference room of Trident Security and sat down with a heavy sigh. Larry Keon had gotten the next available flight from Jacksonville after receiving Ian's call and had a local agent pick him up at the airport instead of waiting around for a rental. Personnel from the FBI's Tampa field office were swarming the woods behind the compound and processing the scene which included a corpse missing a good portion of its skull and brain. The dead body was thanks to Carter and his trusty MK11 sniper rifle which was now hidden in the trunk of Devon's classic Mustang. The man wasn't taking any chances the local feds would try to confiscate his baby, and his own vehicle was too far away at the moment. Two other crime scenes, one where a stolen motorcycle was parked and at a local motel, were also being combed over. The dead man's motel room was located after a key was discovered on the body.

Because the compound was considered a crime scene for the time being, the club had to be closed for the night. Thankfully, it was a Sunday and early enough in the evening when they alerted their members via a mass text, another one of Brody's ideas which came in handy every once in a while. There hadn't been any members in the parking lot when the shot was fired, and the handful of staff and members already in the club never heard it over the music. Ian called Mitch, after they got the all clear from Carter, and told him to shut it down and send everyone home. The compound was now in lock-down with only the necessary personnel.

Devon moved Kristen and Jenn, along with their furry bodyguard, from his apartment to the rec room above the conference room because he needed them as close to him as he could get them. He'd been terrified when he and Boomer, only seconds after Carter's call, sprinted across the compound, up the stairs and into his living room, only to find the women weren't there. His heart started beating again when he found them in his walk-in closet with Beau in battle-mode, a bunch of kitchen knives, and one of his 9 mm handguns which Jenn knew how to shoot, if necessary. Devon wouldn't admit it, but he'd almost cried with relief when he saw both women were safe and unharmed. And now, because the two had no federal security clearance to be with the team while they met with the investigators, upstairs was the closest comfortable place for them to be.

The conference room was now close to being filled to capacity with the six men of Trident, Carter, Dobrowski, Chan, Keon, and three FBI agents from the local office. The lead investigating agent had been brought up to speed, although some information was intentionally omitted by Keon after the incident on the bridge two nights earlier. Special Agent in Charge Frank Stonewall wasn't happy with Carter, who refused to say a word to him, including his name and who he worked for, until the deputy director joined them. It didn't help when Ian, his team, and the two NCIS agents weren't forthcoming with tons of information, but at least they'd given him a few limited answers.

Stonewall had been firing questions at Carter every few minutes for the past two hours to no avail. The red-faced fed even threatened him with arrest which only brought a bark of wry laughter and a shake of the undercover agent's head. After Jake heated up the last three pieces of leftover pizza for him, their friend ate in silence, then reclined back in his chair and closed his eyes. No one in the room was fooled though—the spy was one hundred percent alert. Now, he was still relaxing in his chair, with his eyes open again, and his feet resting on the table mirroring Brody's own laid-back position. It drove Ian crazy when anybody put their feet up, but the boss was letting the infractions go for now.

Once the door was shut again, SAC Frank Stonewall glared at the man, who was still wearing his camos, and all but snarled, "Okay, Keon is here. Now start talking."

Carter didn't move and his blank face never changed as he glanced at the two men with Stonewall and then to Keon. The latter understood what the operative never said. "Frank, why don't you have your agents here go check on the status of the scenes."

Stonewall was ready to blow his cork, but conceded he was outranked, and with a brief nod of his head, dismissed his equally pissed-off subordinates. He was your typical fed from a bad movie —short, balding, overweight with a rumpled, ill-fitting suit, and an arrogance you wanted to beat out of him. After the others left, he crossed his arms and lifted an eyebrow at the black-ops agent and waited.

Slowly pulling his feet down, Carter leaned forward with a stern, don't-fuck-with-me expression which most men feared, and rested his elbows on the table. Devon almost chuckled when Stonewall flinched. If he hadn't been looking directly at the SAC, he would've missed it, but it was there nonetheless. The team knew what Carter was going to say, since he'd filled them in before anyone else got there, but first he would lay down some ground rules with the overconfident Stonewall.

Staring at the man, he addressed him in what his friends knew was his best Dom and super-spy voice. "The name's Carter . . . one word . . . and it's all you need to know about me. Don't write it down, and forget it after you leave this room. Don't ask who I work for because you won't get any answers you like. For this instance, you can say I report to Keon. Call it a temporary assignment or whatever you want, I don't give a crap. Don't ever threaten me with arrest or anything else again. I don't answer to you and can have your cocky ass demoted and working in some bum-fuck weigh-station you've never even heard of before midnight. I have more federal security clearance than you could ever dream of, so sit your pompous ass down and stop acting like I'm one of your minions, or worse, a criminal, because that shit only pisses me off. And since someone is gunning for my friends here, and almost succeeded in taking at least one of them out tonight, you don't want to piss me off any more than I already am."

A few mouths around the table twitched and some bottom lips were bitten, but no one dared crack a smile. After a glance at Keon, who gave him a single nod, and then a pause to let them all know he still wasn't happy, a noticeably paler SAC Stonewall did what he was told and took a seat. He then indicated for Carter to continue with a polite flash of his upturned palm, although it probably almost killed him to do so. The fed was finally getting a little smarter.

Leaning back in his chair again, yet keeping his feet on the ground this time, Carter relaxed and related the information he had, and the events leading up to when he killed the hired assassin. "Keon, as you know, I've been pounding the pavement trying to find out why these guys have a bull's-eye on their backs. Aside from a few vague and unsubstantiated rumors, no one's come forward with a who or a why. After the quote-unquote drunk driving accident which totaled Brody's truck and sent everyone swimming the other night, I decided to head back here to keep a closer eye on things.

"I got back in the area around eighteen hundred hours and did a little scouting outside the line of detection of Egghead's security system to see if I could figure out who was targeting them. I knew the team was sequestered inside the compound, so it was a good bet the tango would be trying to find another way to get to them. The geek's system is one of the best I've ever come across so . . ."

"Wait a minute. *One* of the best, my friend? Oh, no . . . it is *the* best." Brody always became indignant whenever his almost-unbeatable-system was questioned. Everyone in the room who knew it groaned, except Carter who rolled his eyes.

"Or so you keep telling everyone. Anyway, I took a defensive position beyond that point and was scouting the area through my scope. It was damn lucky I spotted the guy when I did because he was preparing to take his shot." He gave his shoulders a dispassionate shrug. "I took mine before he took his. My shot was justified. I had no chance to warn the team or anyone else and there was no opportunity to take him alive. After I eliminated the threat, I went over to see if I could figure out who he was. Unfortunately his face is pretty much gone, and his fingerprints were removed a long time ago with acid." His gaze shifted back to Keon. "That's all I got. Write it up, and as usual, Larry, leave my name out of it and then shred it."

Even though it wasn't all Carter had to say, and the redacted report wouldn't actually get shredded, Keon acknowledged him with a single nod. He would get the rest of the info from the man after the local SAC was out of earshot.

# CHAPTER 23

*A*fter Carter finished talking, he sat back and crossed his arms. SAC Stonewall eyed his superior with a stunned expression and began to turn red again. "That's it? That's all I get? What the fuck am I supposed to do with that? I've got three crime scenes and a dead John Doe out there, for fuck's sake."

Keon sighed with what felt like the weight of the world on his shoulders. He took his glasses off and rubbed his eyes. Damn, he was exhausted and at fifty-five, he was getting way too old for this crap. "You'll do exactly as the man said and forget you ever laid eyes on him. From this moment on, this entire incident is classified. I'll have some people in your office first thing in the morning. They'll take possession of everything—photos, SIM cards, evidence, reports . . . everything. If I find out there are copies of anything or something accidentally gets left behind or lost, shit's going to come down on the head, which is you, Frank. Understand? There's already someone responding to pick up the body. Now, why don't you go check on your agents? I have a few more things to discuss with these people."

The irate federal agent stood and stormed out of the room, not bothering to shut the door behind him. After one of the MPs in the hall did the honors, Brody performed his best James Bond impersonation, even though their spy-friend didn't have a British accent. "'The name's Carter . . . one word . . . and it's all you need to know about me. Don't write it down, and forget it after you leave this room' . . . damn, I wish I could remember the rest." Smiles and snorts of laughter filled the room, while the man being teased only gave them a small smirk and remained quiet. "Shit. I love you, man. Every time I see you, I almost end up peeing my pants."

Boomer snickered harder. "I think Stonewall was close to it for a moment there and not 'cause he thought Carter was funny. You, dude, are the one person I never want to be on the wrong side of."

"Amen," Devon added when everyone else nodded in agreement.

Wanting to get the conversation back on track so he could leave for his hotel and get some much needed sleep, Keon glanced at Ian. "No luck on the Colombia files yet?" The last he'd heard, they got the coded message from their former lieutenant and narrowed down their search to one mission.

Ian shook his head with mild exasperation. "No. We almost finished going through the paperwork between waiting for you to get here and Stonewall's questions. We'll finish up tomorrow then there's a ton of photos we took which need to go through. Whatever Jeff found or thought he found has got to be in there somewhere. I'm not wrong about this."

The deputy director nodded. If Ian said the information they needed was there, then it was. "Like I said, I'll deal with Stonewall and get him off your backs. Do you need anything else for now?"

Ian scanned the faces of his team and they all shook their heads. "No, we're good. Just need some down time and a few hours of sleep."

Keon turned his head back toward the black-ops agent and sighed. "Okay, tell me the rest."

While remaining in his comfortable position, the man filled in the gaps of information for everyone. "I recognized our corpse out there right before I blew his head off. Name's Rueben Vega, mercenary for hire out of Colombia . . . the question still being, who hired him? Unfortunately, my contacts haven't been able to come up with any possible answers for me yet, but they're working on it. Vega had deep connections to Ernesto Diaz and his brother Emmanuel. He used to be one of the best, but rumor has it he's been hitting the booze too much over the past year and getting sloppy. I was a little surprised to find him here. It's been a while since I've heard he was associated with a job in the states, but that's not to say he didn't visit for other reasons. He didn't work exclusively for Diaz, but a majority of his jobs were contracted through their empire. His cell phone was a throw-away and had the history bleached . . . new technology to wipe it clean and there's no way to recover it.

"You all know Emmanuel has been rebuilding what the U.S. of A. destroyed when they took out Ernesto. He's not at the point of operating on the scale his brother had been, but he's getting there. I thought the hit on the SEALs might be some sort of payback for Ernesto, but according to my sources down there, it didn't come from the Diaz family. However, I firmly believe whoever hired him used the connection to do so. Whoever it is, he also has a connection somewhere within Uncle Sam because how else would they've known which men were on that mission. I've got a lot of ears to the ground, and hopefully one of my contacts comes up with something soon, but for now, that's all I've got. Wish it was more." Carter looked at Ian and raised an eyebrow. "Mind if I grab a shower and bed upstairs for a few hours?"

Ian jerked his chin up once. "*Mi casa es tu casa*. You know you can crash here anytime. And thanks again for having our sixes. As usual, we owe you."

The black-ops spy stood and smiled a real smile for the first time since he walked into the compound over three and a half hours earlier. "Anytime, and by the way, this time . . . I wasn't just here for the food."

*Thank God for that.*

A FEW MINUTES LATER, the team stood out in the compound, checking in with the guards, making sure the perimeter was secure and seeing Keon, Chan, and Dobrowski off. After the feds finished up at the scene outside the fence line, Ian arranged to have four snipers take position beyond Brody's system's limitations as a precaution. It was highly unlikely whoever hired Vega would hear about the man's demise anytime tonight, but the team wasn't taking any chances.

As she climbed into the passenger seat of the rental car her partner was driving, Barbara Chan looked at them. "Let's try this again, gentlemen, shall we? This time without the gunfire. We'll see you at oh-eight-hundred with breakfast."

Devon and the others nodded at the woman, then he turned around, headed back inside and took the stairs to the second floor. He found Jenn and Kristen sleeping on the two couches in the rec room. Tucking a blanket around his niece, he was careful not to wake her. She'd be fine there until morning with the rest of the team in the rooms down the hall and Beau sleeping on the floor next to her. He gently woke Kristen who, although a little heavy-eyed, willingly stood and let him lead her back to his apartment. He knew he was being selfish by waking her, but he needed her in his bed with him. They'd survived another close brush with death, but thanks to Carter, the only person needing a rush order on a new coffin was the enemy. The team hadn't told the two women how close they'd come to a different conclusion of events, since they'd been freaked out enough by the rifle shot.

By the time they walked up the stairs to his place, Kristen was once again wide awake and Devon could see his own desire mirrored in her eyes. The moment he shut his apartment door, he had her flattened against it, his hands delving into her hair, and his hips grinding hers. He kissed her with an intensity he couldn't rein in and she gave it back to him in spades. The only sounds were their heavy breathing, moans, and wet mouths and tongues dueling with each other.

He ripped her clothes from her body as fast as he could without hurting her, then removed his own as well. Grabbing her below her ass, he lifted her up so she could wrap her legs around his hips, and ground his steel erection into her mound. The change of position brought her breasts up, so he easily dipped his head to lick and suck them until she was begging him for more. Her fingers were clutching his hair, her body writhing in his arms.

"Please fuck me," she panted as her head fell back against the door with a thud and her eyes fluttered closed. Her moans of pleasure and desire were almost his undoing.

She shifted her hips, trying desperately to position his cock at her entrance when he tightened his grip and lifted his head. "Easy, Pet. Slow down. I don't have a condom with me."

"Don't care."

Devon froze at her words and she opened her eyes again. "I was tested after I found out my ex was cheating on me, and you're the only man I've been with since then. I've been on the pill for several years to regulate my periods. Please. I want to feel you, all of you."

Staring at her beautiful face, he knew he couldn't say no to her, nor did he want to. The thought of taking her with nothing between them thrilled him. "I'm tested every six months for the club and had my latest physical right before we met. I've never had sex without a condom. Baby, are you sure about this? This is a big step for us and I need you to be certain."

A frustrated moan escaped her. "Yes, I'm positive. Please fuck me now."

When she again tried to impale herself on him, he wouldn't allow it. "My way," was all he growled as he lifted her away from the door. Shifting his hands to her ass, he carried her down the hall and into his bedroom.

Setting her on his bed, he ordered her to lay down in the center of it and put her head on the pillows. While she hurried to do as she was told, he worked his way around the bed, pulling out the leather straps he'd attached to the four posters earlier in the week. He'd kept them tucked under the mattress, waiting until he found the right opportunity to surprise her, and it appeared that now was the perfect time. At the end of the straps were wrist and ankle restraints. She was still bruised from the accident, and he was glad he'd chosen ones with a thick faux-fur lining.

At her wide eyed expression, Devon smirked. "I've wanted to do this to you since the afternoon I shackled your wrists at the club. Stretch your arms up and out toward the corners and spread your legs wide. Do you trust me, Pet?"

There was no hesitation in her verbal and physical responses to his commands and question. "Yes, Sir."

He could see her pulse had increased by the rapid throbbing of the artery in her neck. The sight caused his own heart rate to surge. He grabbed her right arm and brought the leather restraint to her wrist. Before he attached it he asked, "What's your safeword?"

"Red, Sir."

His cock jumped at her husky answer. He swiftly worked to restrain her wrists, taking a moment after each strap was secured to check he could place two fingers between the fur lining and her skin. He needed them tight enough so she couldn't get out of them, yet loose enough so they didn't hinder her circulation or further bruise her tender skin. When he was confident she was comfortable, yet at his mercy, he turned to his nightstand and took several items out of the drawer. An evil grin crossed his face when he heard her breath hitch at the sight of his chosen torture devices—a small leather flogger, a clit clamp, and the largest anal plug from the set of four he'd been using on her. He'd been increasing the size of the plugs he had her wear for several hours at a time during the past week. This would be the last one he would need to prepare her for when he fucked her tight ass for the first time.

He placed the flogger and the jeweled clamp on the edge of the bed next to her where she could see them from her confined position. Although he'd told her he wouldn't clamp her nipples due to her fear, tormenting her clit was on her soft limit list and therefore fair game. He'd picked out the green and amber stone decorated clamp at the club store the other day with her hard little nub in mind. Taking the plug and a tube of lubricant, he walked around to stand at the far end of the bed and took a moment to study her.

Damn, she was stunning. Her mouth was red and swollen from their make-out session in the other room and her hair was messed from him running his fingers through it. Her cheeks were flushed and her nipples had stiffened, shamelessly begging for more attention. And her pussy . . . fuck, her pussy was drenched with her need for him. He wrapped a tight fist around his cock, dragging his hand up and down the shaft several times as he watched her tongue shoot out and moisten her dry lips. As much as he loved to fuck her sweet, hot mouth, he had other ideas for her body at the moment.

Dropping the plug and lube within reach, he climbed up on the bed between her widespread legs, ran his fingers through her wet folds and brought them to his mouth. He couldn't resist taking a quick taste of her. She moaned at his actions and he watched as more of her juices flowed from her core. After licking his fingers clean, he grasped the back of her knees and bent them upwards toward her chest. He then moved forward on his knees, spreading them out before resting the back of her thighs on the front of his. The position she was now in was perfect for what he intended to do. Reaching back he grabbed the tube and applied a generous amount of lubricant on her exposed asshole. Being gentle, he breached her entrance and eased one, then two fingers into her, working to get her ready for the larger object. Kristen was panting hard, but she concentrated on keeping her ass muscles and sphincter as relaxed as she could. "Oh God, Sir. It feels so good. Please . . . more, please."

How he loved to hear her beg—it was music to his Dom ears. He alternated between plunging his fingers in and out of her hole and scissoring them open to stretch her further. "Oh, you'll be definitely getting more, Pet. Trust me, you'll be getting a lot more."

While he kept up the rhythm he'd established, he grabbed the anal plug with his other hand and covered it in more lube. When he was sure she was ready, he pulled his fingers from her tight cavity and replaced them with the plug. Her sphincter tightened for a moment as he worked the larger item into her and suddenly he was able to get past her body's natural defenses and the plug slid home.

Her rim closed around the notched end, greedily holding it in place. More liquid flowed from her pussy lips and she groaned.

"Don't forget, Pet. You're not to come without permission."

"Y-Yes, Sir. Oh God!"

Her thighs quivered and her hips jerked upward when he flicked her still hidden clit. But that was about to change. He lowered her legs as he climbed back off the bed. Grabbing one ankle and then the other, he restrained them until she was spread wide open, her pussy exposed for what he planned for her next. Stepping into his bathroom, he hastily washed his hands before returning to her side and grabbing his next torture implement.

The flogger was made of soft black leather with a knot tied at the end of each of the dozen strands extending out from its handle. Starting at her right foot, he dragged the ends up to her shoulders then back down again on her opposite side, her eyes tracking them every inch of the way. He repeated the entire process, once then twice, teasing her until her breathing was short and heavy and her hips began to shift in impatience. "Don't lose the plug, Pet."

His mouth turned up at the corners when he saw her clench the muscles in her butt, which in turn sent tiny shock waves through the nerves being affected by the foreign object. The sensations caused her to groan, and she, once again, begged him for relief. "Beg all you want, sweetheart, but I'll continue at my own pace. You won't get what you want until I'm good and ready to give it to you."

Returning to her right foot, he began to lift the strands off her skin and then let them fall back down softly. After another full rotation around her body, he would start over and make the contact a little harder each time. When the thudding increased to the point her skin began to turn a pale red, he concentrated on her thighs, hips and breasts only. He'd near her crotch, but not close enough for the contact she didn't even know she was pleading for. Finally, he flicked his wrist hard and the knotted strands connected with her clit and pussy lips. She shrieked as the pleasure-pain shot through her and her empty vagina clenched in search of something to hold on to. Devon repeated the strike again and again, until she was alternating her screams between his name, curses and pleas for mercy. Her wrists were straining against their leather and fur manacles to no avail. When he finally tossed the flogger to the floor, she was so close to her orgasm it would've crashed over her if he struck her clit one more time, and he gave her a few moments to come back from the brink of ecstasy.

Grabbing the clamp, he positioned himself between her legs once more. Her little pearl was no longer in hiding and he was able to attach the clamp without any further coaxing. Kristen was so far into all the different sensations running rampant through her body, he didn't think her brain even registered the clamp. The small weighted stones were attached by a thin piece of fishing line to the rubber coated ends. It was designed so they would hang down, pulling on the little nub. For now though, they would be in the way, so he rested them along the crease of her hip.

Reaching down, he undid the restraints around her ankles and once again, bent her knees up toward her chest. Kneeling at her sopping wet entrance, he lined up his uncovered cock and plunged into her with one smooth thrust, burying himself to the hilt without pause, despite the huge plug in her ass. Her walls cinched around him and he saw stars. "Oh fuck, sweetheart. You feel so good, like silk." She jerked her hips trying to get him to move, but he stilled her with his hands. "No, Pet. Give me a second or it'll all be over too soon. Fuck, I've never felt anything like this before. You're my heaven and hell all wrapped into one incredibly tight, hot package."

"Oh, please, Sir. Oh God, Sir, please . . . I need . . . I need . . ." Devon loved how the word "Sir" was so natural to her now. It flowed from her mouth without thought whenever he had her aroused to the point of mindless pleading.

When he thought he could move without exploding, he dragged his dick from her passage only to stroke right back inside again. He punctuated his words in time with his tortuously short, slow thrusts. "I know exactly what you need, my love, and I'm going to give it to you right now."

He sped up and found a rhythm which had her hurtling toward the most powerful release she'd ever experienced. When she reached the edge, he abruptly released the clamp from her clit, allowing the blood to rush back in, and she screamed her throat raw as she plummeted into a vast chasm. Wave after wave of pleasure-pain crashed over her as she pulsated around him. It was only two thrusts later when he followed her, shooting his seed deep into her womb and extending her orgasm, convinced he would never recover from the impact.

# CHAPTER 24

*A*fter removing her wrist restraints, it'd taken Devon longer than ever to recuperate from their explosive lovemaking the night before. When he could get off the bed and stand without falling, he'd stumbled to the bathroom and retrieved a wet cloth to clean Kristen with. His sweet Ninja-girl had fallen asleep immediately after he removed her plug and settled her on her side so he could spoon her from behind and hold her in his arms for the rest of the night.

Now, the sun was up and it was seven forty-five. He had fifteen minutes before he needed to meet everyone down at the conference room to find the name of the person who wanted some of them dead. He had showered, put on a comfortable pair of his tan military DSUs, otherwise known as tactical pants, a navy blue T-shirt and his light-weight black combat boots, and was now sitting on the edge of the bed next to a still sleeping Kristen. She deserved the rest after he'd wakened her around three a.m. to take first her mouth and then her pussy once again. As much as he wanted to take her sweet ass, he'd refrained from doing so last night because they both would've been too exhausted for the bath she would need right afterward to prevent extreme soreness this morning.

With a light touch, he was playing with her hair and staring at her face when his eyes dropped to the simple black leather band still around her neck. It wasn't good enough for her, and in his mind he began designing a permanent collar he wanted her to wear. Permanent? Holy crap! Yeah, it was pretty much official. Devon Sawyer's confirmed bachelor days were over . . . permanently. He'd found his true love, his perfect submissive, and yet his equal. She was the woman he'd never known existed and now wanted to spend the rest of his life with. First, he would collar her in a ceremony at the club and then, when she was ready, he would also put a ring on her finger. In all honesty, while the ring would make their union legal, it was the collar which would mean the most to Devon. It would be a symbol of Kristen's ultimate trust in her Dom to cherish her in every possible way—mind, body and soul. To keep her safe from harm, to pamper her silly and most of all, to love her every day of their, hopefully, very long lives.

But for now, his team needed to find the person responsible for the murders of four members of Team Four's family, and as soon as possible, before anyone else was hurt or, God-forbid, killed. Placing a kiss on her forehead, he left her sleeping and headed out to the office.

As promised, the NCIS agents brought bagels and egg sandwiches for everyone. As they ate their handheld breakfasts and coffee, they dove back into the daunting task before them. Thankfully, Paula was heeding the orders and advice Ian had given her in private on Friday, and was back to being an efficient office manager with minimum interruptions.

It was a few minutes after ten a.m. when Devon was looking through a stack of about one-hundred and twenty 8 by 10 photos he'd taken the night of the gala in Rio de Janeiro when he was keeping an eye on Ernesto Diaz. There had been over five hundred people in attendance at the biggest hotel in the city, so Devon tried to get a photo of everyone Diaz had made contact with. At one point the drug lord had disappeared into a small sitting room down the hall from the main ballroom. Devon had waited a few moments before following, pretending he was looking for his lost date for the evening.

He'd barely managed to get three quick, yet hazy photographs of Diaz in the room using a hidden camera in a pair of false eyeglasses—a little James Bond-like, but quite effective. The pictures he took were from the hallway looking past the partially open door into the room before Diaz's bodyguards interfered and ordered him to return to the ballroom or risk bodily harm. With no other choice, he was escorted back down the hallway and was pissed he couldn't get pictures of the person or persons Diaz was meeting without jeopardizing his cover. And it was unlikely their spy-friend would know who Diaz met since the Colombian hadn't been Carter's target while he was there.

Devon finished inspecting the clearest picture out of the three and was about to move on to another photo when he realized there was a reflection in a medium-sized mirror on the wall behind Diaz. "Hey, Egghead, can you do something with this?" He held up the photo with his finger pointing to the mirror for Brody to see.

The geek squinted at what his teammate was referring to, then jumped up out of his chair and headed for the door. "Yeah, I should be able to enlarge it and clean it up some. Let me grab my scanner from the war-room."

The war-room was the extra-large office Brody used which housed his many computers, multiple HD screens, servers and assorted gadgets. The team was convinced, if he needed to, Egghead could launch a space shuttle from the room. It was also one of the places in the office which Paula didn't have access to, and the man took great pleasure in knowing it drove the office manager crazy with curiosity.

A few minutes later, Brody had the picture scanned into his laptop and the photo appeared on the big screen on the wall of the conference room. He was playing around with an image enhancing program and the person in the mirror became larger and clearer, yet he still seemed a little fuzzy to everyone . . . well, everyone except for Brody. "Son of a fucking bitch! You've got to be kidding me!"

Everyone stared at the stunned and irate man as if he had two heads. Ian asked, "You know who it is?"

The geek stared back at everyone. "You don't?"

When they all shook their heads, Brody opened his mouth to say something, but then quickly shut it again and took the photo off of the big screen before looking at Ian with obvious worry in his eyes. Having trained and worked with him for a long time, his boss understood the man's hesitation. Turning to the two NCIS agents, he said, "I know you two have a certain level of security clearance, but I get the feeling we've stumbled across something which could possibly jeopardize your careers or lives and those of your families if it becomes known you have this information. You have two options —take the risk or step outside for a moment. I swear to you, no evidence will be removed or erased from this room."

The two agents eyeballed each other, and it was obvious after a moment they'd made their decision. As they both stood, Barbara Chan hinted to her partner, "I think I left my cell phone in the car, do you mind helping me look for it?"

Dobrowski nodded and turned toward the conference room door. "Sure, it'll probably take five minutes to find it."

The moment the door shut behind them, Brody brought the image back up on the large monitor and began typing away at his computer again. The large screen split in two and a photo, courtesy of CNN, appeared to the right of the enhanced photo Devon had taken. The rest of the team stared at the two images in utter disbelief. The man was a little younger and leaner in the five-year old photo and had a trim mustache and goatee, but, without a doubt, he was the same man in the news photo—Senator Luis Beltram from Brody's hometown of Dallas, Texas. And if the rumors were true, the next Democratic candidate for President of the United States. *Holy fucking shit!*

Hailed as the first ever Hispanic-American candidate for the Oval Office, Beltram had been elected to the Senate seat for his state a little over two years ago and fast-tracked through the Democratic Party. The lawyer turned politician had been born and raised in Texas, lost his working-class single mother to cancer as a teenager and somehow managed to finish high school and put himself first through college and then business law school. He'd chosen his battles and political platforms with care and was well-liked by his constituents, fellow democrats and even a few republicans. An announcement of his candidacy was expected by the press within the next week or so, but the evidence currently in the Trident Security conference room would end the man's political career faster than a jackrabbit on amphetamines.

The knowledge of the senator having a private meeting with a Colombian drug lord who not only ran one of the largest drug cartels in South America, but also a sex-slave business, would not go over well with the American public. The fact Diaz also supplied weapons to terrorists who were determined to undermine the American way of life would be the final nail in Beltram's coffin. The team was sitting on political dynamite.

Using the room's speaker phone, Ian contacted Keon to give the man one of the biggest shocks of his life. "We've got him, and it's not good."

There was a short pause on the other end of the line. "I'll be there in fifteen minutes."

---

BY THE TIME Keon walked into the room eighteen minutes later, the two agents had returned and the large monitor was once again blank. No one said the senator's name in front of the agents because for the rest of the investigation, the less they knew, the better off they were. Brody hacked into numerous systems and managed to locate the tenuous connection between Beltram and Diaz who'd also been born in Texas before his family moved back to Colombia when he was six. Beltram's illegitimate father had been a cousin of Ernesto Diaz's mother making the two men second cousins. Luciano Esperanza had been a longtime associate of the Diaz cartel and was a name the team had recognized. He'd died of cancer about seven months after his cousin.

When the future lawyer was in college, Beltram had the paternal information on his birth certificate, which was on file with the Texas State Department of Health, changed from his sperm donor's name to "no information available." Unfortunately for the senator, he didn't know, or forgot, the original copy stayed on file with the new certificate, which is how Brody located the information.

Keon sat down and sighed. "Tell me."

Ian nodded at Dobrowski and Chan, who once again left the room. This time, with the Deputy Director of the FBI present to keep an eye on the boxes of classified information, there was no need for subterfuge. Ian then glanced at Brody who hit a button on his laptop, bringing up the two photos again.

Usually a passive man, the team had never seen Keon pale in obvious disbelief before, but it's exactly what they saw now. However, it only took him a few seconds to recover from his shock. "Holy shit," he mumbled before clearing his throat. "Is Carter still here?"

Ian shook his head. "No, he was gone when everyone got up this morning. One of the guards said he pulled out around oh-five-hundred."

THREE NIGHTS LATER, the man known by one name picked the lock to the back door of the comfortable bi-level home on the outskirts of Dallas. He was inside within twenty seconds, and, with his gloved hands, pulled out his weapon. The two men from the target's private protective detail had been eliminated by a drug-induced slumber and were hidden behind some shrubbery on the four-acre property. The burglar alarm and back-up systems had been interrupted with a quick flick of a Swiss army knife, rendering it useless. The target's wife and college-age children were not at home, and it was amazing how easy it was to get close to someone who thought he was invincible.

Having thought he was safely ensconced inside his house with the alarm set, Senator Luis Beltram was relaxing in his home office, sipping a glass of amber liquid from an eight-hundred dollar bottle of Macallan scotch. His gray suit jacket and tie were laid over the back of one of the two guest chairs opposite the desk at which he sat. His white shirt sleeves were rolled up to his elbows. This was the last night he'd be alone before the Secret Service took over his protective detail when his presidential nomination was announced tomorrow afternoon. The press would then start camping out at the end of his driveway. He smiled to himself, enjoying the silence which permeated the five-bedroom ranch. At least he did until the door to his office swung open without a sound and he found himself staring down the barrel of a SIG Sauer P226, complete with silencer. Beltram froze at the sight before putting his drink down and easing his hand toward his desk drawer.

"Come on, now. I know you don't have any morals, but you're not exactly stupid. After all, you've come this close to being the next American president." Carter took three careful steps into the room, knowing full well the senator had a handgun in the drawer he was reaching for. The spy wasn't worried though, because the arrogant bastard would be dead before his fingers ever touched the brass pull-handle.

Without any abrupt movements, Beltram brought his hand back and placed it next to his other one on the wood surface of his desk in full view of his unwelcome visitor. Sweat was forming on his brow and upper lip and his skin was paler than it had been a few minutes ago, yet those were the only signs of the man's fear. His eyes barely blinked. "Who are you and what do you want?"

Carter's mouth ticked up into a smirk. "Who I am is not important. What I want, however, is something altogether different. I want to save this great nation I live in from having a traitorous scumbag like you as its president. I want to avenge the deaths of three Navy SEALs and one very nice lady who didn't deserve to die when and how they did. But first, I'm curious. Why were they killed in the first place? Payback for killing Ernesto Diaz? How did you find out Team Four was responsible for your cousin's death?"

If the man was shocked to hear Carter knew of his familial connection to the Colombian drug lord, he didn't show it. In fact, the smug fucker snorted, picked up his glass of scotch again and eased back into his black leather chair. In the process, he pressed his knee to the inside panel of his desk and hit the silent panic button there. The movement didn't go unnoticed by the man with the gun.

He now had less than ten minutes to finish the job and escape without being discovered at the scene of an assassination. The senator was crazy if he thought he had a way out of this.

"Please. Whoever fired the shot into Ernesto's heart did me a favor. I was going to have to have him eliminated at some point anyway. If someone found out about my relationship to him, my career would have been over."

His weapon still aimed at Beltram's head, Carter took several more steps forward, stopping between the two guest chairs on his side of the large desk. "Then why? What did Jeff Mullins have on you?"

Before answering, the senator took a sip of his expensive scotch, savoring the taste on his tongue and the burn down his throat. The man was cockier than a rooster in a hen house. "I was at a political function for one of my constituents in Virginia and was introduced to Mullins by Admiral Richardson. I didn't know who Mullins was, but I got the feeling he knew me and wasn't happy about it. I had a friend do a little discreet checking and found out Mullins was a retired SEAL, specifically one who had been on a fact-finding mission in Colombia and Rio de Janeiro looking into Ernesto. I remembered meeting my cousin in Rio at some big shin-dig down there at the time and put two and two together. Mullins must've recognized me from there and if he made the connection, there was a good chance the rest of his team would, too. It was a risk I couldn't take." He shrugged as if ordering the deaths of seven highly-decorated SEALs was no big deal.

"Did you always know Diaz was related to you or is it something that came as a surprise?"

"After my mother passed away, God rest her poor soul, I found a copy of my birth certificate and decided to find my bastard father. The search led me to family I didn't know I had. Ernesto and I became . . . associates, I guess you can call it. He funded my education and lifestyle, and I, in return, became a valuable asset in Dallas for him."

He paused. The backup guards for his missing protective detail should be here at any moment, so he just had to keep talking. It didn't matter what he said since the intruder wouldn't be alive in a half hour. "Now, I've answered your questions, so how much is it going to cost me to get you to walk out of here and leave me alive?"

Carter fired one barely audible bullet into Senator Luis Beltram's head and another into his chest, then turned around and strode out the door before the dead man's forehead hit the desk in front of him.

"Not a damn penny."

# EPILOGUE

*Ten Weeks Later . . .*

Devon peered at Kristen sitting next to him in their first class seats on their flight to Nepal. He normally didn't flaunt his money with expensive purchases, but he flew first class whenever he could, especially if they were spending sixteen hours in the air. She was staring out the window and he could tell she was nervous by the way she fingered the diamond and platinum collar around her neck. It was stunning on her, yet simple enough so she could wear it every day. For when she got dressed up, there was a large blue sapphire pendant which could be added with a small hidden latch and hook. The sapphire was her birthstone and he loved how the color complimented her ivory skin. She said she loved it because it matched his eyes. He'd removed her black leather collar and replaced it with the one he and a jeweler with BDSM experience had designed for her during a surprise collaring ceremony at the club seven weeks ago. What she didn't know was he had also purchased a matching engagement ring for her at the same time. The ring was sitting safely in its little blue box in his carry-on luggage. He planned on them being an engaged couple before they returned to the states in two weeks, in time for Christmas.

They were on their way to meet up with his parents at a medical clinic located about an hour away from the airport they'd be landing at soon. It was the first time she would be meeting his folks and, although he tried to assure her Chuck and Marie Sawyer were down to earth, and would love her at once, she was still anxious to get the introductions over with.

He'd met her parents and step-parents at Thanksgiving. Her step-mother had invited her mother and Ed to join them for the holiday after Kristen let them know she was bringing home someone special. Devon had liked her parents almost immediately and he'd won them over by the end of their first day together. Before they left for Tampa again two days later, he'd taken Kristen's dad aside to ask permission to one day put a ring on his daughter's hand and Bill Anders had granted it along with a handshake and back slap. Her father told Devon Kristen's limp-dicked ex had never asked for his blessing and, if he had, Bill would've told him no. He thought the guy wasn't good enough for his daughter, but, at the time, she'd seemed happy and he didn't want to disappoint her by voicing his disapproval.

A lot had happened over the past ten weeks. After they'd returned from Pennsylvania, Kristen had moved in with him permanently. It wasn't as if she didn't spend every night and almost every day there anyway, but she wanted her parents to meet Devon before making the final step. She'd been packing her things since he'd first asked her to move in with him several weeks earlier, so the actual process of moving her things had been easy a few days after Thanksgiving. With the help of the team and a few of the club's employees, they'd made fast work of the job, and within one afternoon they were officially living together. He loved how Kristen's personal items were now mixed in with his, and whatever furniture didn't make the move into Devon's place was donated to a local women's shelter.

Nina DeAngelis had succumbed to her cancer five weeks ago. Marco and his sister's friend, Harper, were both devastated over their mutual loss. The team was pleased to see a large turnout of Trident associates and club members at the funeral. It had been a beautiful, yet tearful moment when about twenty-five of Nina's former students stood at the front of the church and sang "Amazing Grace" in honor of their beloved teacher.

Brody bought a three-bedroom house, which was closer to the compound than his one-bedroom apartment had been, and would be closing on it after the first of the year. He'd told Devon, although he didn't need all the extra space, the property was a good investment and a write-off on his taxes, which he needed. He also replaced his totaled truck with a brand new model thanks to his insurance money.

Jake had confided in Devon when he'd broken up with the guy he'd been seeing shortly after the whole drama of being the target of a hired assassin. His now ex-boyfriend was a cop in nearby Clearwater and had been pretty pissed because Jake never told him about the attempts on his life. He'd found out about them a few days later after coming across a newspaper picture. It was taken after the accident on the bridge and showed a soaking wet Jake and Devon standing watch over Jenn and Kristen while they were being tended to by the EMTs. Jake said he didn't tell the guy because he didn't want to worry him, but Devon got the impression there was more to it.

Jenn was almost done with her first semester, but was having a hard time with the coming holidays. This would be her first Christmas without her parents and they were all doing what they could to make it a little less depressing for her. At least they'd been able to tell her that, although the person responsible for killing her parents would never serve a day in jail, justice had been served. As for Carter, no one at Trident had seen him since the night he'd saved their lives with one bullet.

Kristen was also an official full-time member of the club now, along with her friends, Kayla and Roxy London. The wife and wife couple had brought Will Anders as their guest for Devon and Kristen's ceremony, and Will was considering the lifestyle after meeting Shelby and Matthew, the submissive who worked the front desk at the club. Will clicked with the other two and become fast friends with them. The subs had been answering a lot of Will's questions about the lifestyle and although Will hadn't submitted a membership request yet, Devon expected one soon. There was a Dom who Will was interested in and his curiosity about BDSM appeared to grow as each week passed.

Devon glanced back down at the folded copy of the Tampa Tribune sitting on the tray in front of him. The article it was turned to was a follow-up story on the assassination of Senator Luis Beltram two and a half months ago, on the eve of his anticipated Democratic presidential nomination. Yesterday in a press release, the Deputy Director of the FBI, Larry Keon, reported how the man who'd murdered Beltram in his home was in turn killed by U.S. Navy SEALs in an attempt to capture him in the jungles of Colombia where he'd fled. It was still unclear why Rueben Vega killed the senator and the investigation was at a standstill. The Trident Security team knew a motive would never be found and it wouldn't be long before Beltram was old and forgotten news.

Devon didn't realize Kristen had said something until she took his hand in one of hers and used her other one to touch his chin and turn his head toward her. "I'm sorry, honey, what did you say?"

She smiled because she'd caught him daydreaming. "The pilot said we're getting ready to land. You need to put your seat and tray up."

He was surprised he hadn't heard the pilot's announcement.

"What were you thinking about just now?" she asked as they prepared for descent.

With a seductive grin, he leaned forward and put his mouth against her ear. "I was thinking that I can't wait for you to read me the last chapter you wrote a few hours ago. While you were typing away your breathing and heart rate sped up a few times, and I know I'm going to like it." He turned her hand in his so he could put his fingers on the pulse at her wrist and was pleased to feel it accelerate again as her face turned pink. He loved how he could still make her blush so easily and knew if he put his hand between her legs he could get her off before they landed. However, the stern-faced stewardess, who was now sitting in her jump seat less than ten feet in front of them, would have a fit.

Over the course of writing her book, he had Kristen read many of the steamy passages to him and the sex they had afterward was always off the charts. Several nights ago he had her play with herself while she read aloud and he forced himself to sit across the living room from her while her fingers delved in and out of her drenched pussy. He ended up flipping her over the end of the couch and fucking her into oblivion before she even finished the chapter.

"I know you will since yesterday morning was my inspiration," she whispered.

His face lit up and his dick hardened as he remembered interrupting their morning coffee to bend her over the kitchen island and spread her ass cheeks. Before he'd rammed his cock in her tight hole, he first knelt behind her and tongued her rimmed opening, driving her higher and higher until she begged him to fuck her hard and fast, which he was more than happy to do after he made her come twice. Thankfully, he'd made sure there was a tube of lubricant in every room of their apartment, and in both of their vehicles, because it turned out his little pet loved to have her ass fucked whenever he wanted. But although he loved taking her ass and mouth, he would never get enough of her hot, wet pussy. And it's where he planned to shove his cock the first chance he had after they got off the stifling plane. He shifted his hips to give his hard-on a little breathing room.

"Are you sure they're going to like me?"

It took him a second to follow her change of subject. "Sweetheart, they're going to love you. Even Ian and Jenn told you they would before we left. I can guarantee my mom is going to be spoiling you rotten before the day is over. She's been bugging Ian and me to settle down for the past ten years. I'm just glad I'm no longer on her nag list."

She giggled at him. "At least until she wants grandchildren."

Devon's thumb which had been rubbing her wrist abruptly stopped and his brain seized. "Um, wow. We . . . uh . . . we never discussed kids, did we?"

Her pretty eyes filled with worry. "You don't want children?"

He thought about it for a moment. How could he have ever

thought of being a father when he hadn't been able to imagine being a husband before meeting Kristen? There was no doubt he could be a good one, having been raised by one of the best. An image of a little girl or boy with soft brown hair and striking hazel eyes came to mind and he knew what to say. "As long as they take after the most beautiful woman in the world, I want as many as we can possibly have." He brought her hand to his mouth and kissed her knuckles. "I love you, Ninja-girl."

"I love you, too, Master Devil Dog."

# HIS ANGEL

Book 2

## SAMANTHA A. COLE

Suspenseful Seduction Publishing

*To my parents, who always encouraged me to follow my dreams.*

# CHAPTER 1

"Come on, Beau," Ian Sawyer called to his lab-pit bull mix as he walked up the driveway to Brody Evans' new house. The large, black dog finished a quick call to nature on Brody's curbside mailbox before running to his owner's side. Ian often wondered if the mutt had some Great Dane in its pedigree because he was tall enough that Ian, at six-foot-three, could almost pat the dog's head without bending over. It hadn't always been the case. When Ian had first found the six-week-old pup shivering and crying next to its dying mother outside his front door, Beau couldn't have weighed more than seven or eight pounds at the time.

Ian thought back to the night he'd heard the intruder alert go off on his phone, a little over a year and a half ago. He'd been in his apartment watching the eleven o'clock news. The residence was located within his business compound which was surrounded by a security fence to keep out unexpected visitors. At least it did until the furry duo broke in.

When the alert had gone off, he'd switched the TV channel to bring up the compound's multiple CCTV camera angles. Expecting to see a guard, his brother, or one of his team members walking around, he'd been surprised to see an animal limp its way toward his front door. Zooming in, he saw it was a badly injured dog carrying a small puppy in its mouth. By the time he'd gotten outside, the mother had expended the last of her energy and collapsed a few feet away. The pup was dirty, a little malnourished, and covered in fleas, but overall in good health. The mother, though, had been torn to shreds by another dog or some other animal. When Ian approached the pair with caution, she'd nudged her baby closer to the human she was entrusting him to and then passed away without a sound.

After rushing the puppy to a nearby veterinary clinic which was open at all hours, Ian returned, followed the path the mother dog had taken and found she'd dug under the fence line to get to his door. On the other side of the fence, he'd followed drag marks leading into the woods. A little ways into the brush was where he'd discovered two additional puppies which had both died several hours earlier. Ian retrieved a shovel and the mother dog's body, then buried the three of them under a tree at one o'clock in the morning before heading back to the compound to fill in the hole under the fence.

The pup had been bathed, neutered, chipped, and received his shots, then Ian took him home. The six men who made up the primary core team of Trident Security were all retired Navy SEALs, and for the first few weeks the poor dog had gone by the name "FNG" for "'fucking new guy." But that changed as soon as Ian's goddaughter met the little guy for the first time and had given him a new name. Jenn had been reading *Beau Geste* in school and dubbed the pit bull mix with the same moniker.

When Beau was three-months old, Ian had an old Navy friend begin training the dog in the same fashion as military working dogs at a nearby facility. The dog had taken to the training as if he'd been bred for it. And although he now was a full-fledged protection and tracking dog, when he wasn't on-duty the big guy was an even bigger goof-ball who just wanted to get belly rubs or play fetch until he dropped. The dog was a well-loved addition to Trident Security and had full access to the business facilities as well as the residential apartments within the compound.

Ian and his brother, Devon, lived at the company compound, which they owned. As for the other four men of the Trident Security team, they all resided within ten minutes of the facilities. Brody was one of their teammates and had purchased his place about two months earlier. Tonight, Ian had brought the dog along to a last-minute barbecue since the house had a fenced-in backyard. Beau would have plenty of green grass to roll around in, something he didn't have at the paved compound.

The door was unlocked, so Ian let himself in, with Beau making a beeline to the kitchen to greet the rest of his favorite humans. Brody was the first person to reach down and pet him. The tall, broad man, also known as "Egghead," was the team's computer geek and master hacker. He'd designed and/or programmed all the security and tracking systems, computers, and gadgets the team used. He was also the team flirt and joker, and was rarely without his signature smile and quick wit.

The rest of the crew in attendance were Jake "Reverend" Donovan, team sniper, Marco "Polo" DeAngelis, communication specialist, and Ben "Boomer" Michaelson, demolition and explosives expert. Last, but not least, was Ian's younger brother, Devon "Devil Dog" Sawyer, who was their breacher and lead climber. Ian was their team leader and interrogator, the same position he'd held in SEAL Team Four. While each man had their individual specialties, they could take over each other's positions if the need arose. They worked so well together there were times they could almost read each other's minds.

When Ian entered the kitchen, everyone paused long enough to greet him before resuming their conversations again. He leaned down and gave Kristen a quick peck on the cheek as she smiled at him.

Kristen Anders was the only non-team member in Brody's house at the moment. She was Ian's future sister-in-law, an author of erotic romance novels, and the love of Devon's life. The guy had popped the question three months ago between Thanksgiving and Christmas and, after crying for several minutes, she'd said yes. They'd been in Nepal at the time, visiting Ian and Devon's parents while their mother was performing surgery at a clinic there for Operation Smile. The two had spent about ten days helping Chuck Sawyer, the brothers' father, and many other volunteers build a school in a nearby village.

The proposal hadn't been a surprise to anyone but their parents since Devon had collared his submissive eight weeks earlier in a ceremony at The Covenant. It was the BDSM club which the brothers' also owned along with their cousin and club manager, Mitch Sawyer.

While Brody was preparing boneless chicken breasts for the grill, Kristen was patting ground beef into hamburger patties. When Beau plopped down on the floor next to her, she slid off a flip-flop and raised her foot to scratch his underbelly, much to the dog's delight. She glanced back at Ian. "Where's Jenn? Didn't she come with you?"

Ian leaned against the counter next to her, crossing his arms over his sculpted chest, and grumbled, "Nope. She went shopping with some friends from college this afternoon. Apparently, she has a date tonight."

Her eyes lit up with the opposite reaction he'd had after learning his goddaughter was going on a date. With a guy. Who probably wasn't any good for her. Who probably only wanted to get into the pretty girl's pants. He'd kill the bastard if he knew who he was.

Before Kristen could respond, Brody's eyes narrowed from where he stood a few feet away in front of the opened refrigerator door. "Jenn's going on a date?" His loud voice was filled with shocked annoyance. "With whom?"

The hush which fell over the room was interrupted by a short squeal of delight, as five pairs of curious, angry eyes and one pair of elated ones stared at Ian. He let out a loud sigh. "I have no idea. She refused to tell me because she knew I'd have you investigate him."

The big, protective men all scowled, but it was Brody who responded. "If she won't give you his name, tell Baby-girl she can't go. It's as simple as that."

A loud groan sounded and everyone turned toward Kristen who was rolling her eyes as if she was in the presence of six idiots. "Guys, come on. Your niece is nineteen years old and will be twenty in three months. She's an adult whether you like it or not. She's smart and can hold her own if she needs to. You can't ground her for refusing to let you harass some poor kid who wants to take her out."

The men were all Jennifer Mullins' surrogate uncles. Her father had been their lieutenant in the SEALs, and the team spent many off hours at the man's family home near their base. The once little girl had grown up with over forty "uncles" who she still kept in touch with through emails and phone calls. But she'd always been closest to these six men. When she was born, her parents had asked Jeff's best friend, Ian, to be her godfather and legal guardian if anything ever happened to them. Ian had been happy to do it, but never thought he would need to take their place so early in her life. Later this month would be the one-year anniversary of her parents' murders.

The team had found out this past September their deaths weren't the result of a burglary gone wrong, but instead, was part of a larger plot to kill several former members of SEAL Team Four. A Texas senator with bigger aspirations had hired a hit-man to take out Jeff Mullins, Ian, Devon, Jake, Brody, and two others. He'd realized they had been on a fact-finding mission years earlier and may have recognized him as a man who'd met with their target. The senator's distant cousin was a Colombian drug lord, who he'd developed a clandestine relationship with in exchange for the financial backing to climb out of poverty into college and then law school. In return, the senator became Ernesto Diaz's asset in Dallas. Besides being the head of a lucrative drug cartel, Diaz had been involved in sex-trade and arms-dealing. The FBI and Navy investigators had made the connection between the deaths of Jeff and Lisa Mullins, Eric Prichard, and Quincy Dale. The men of Trident security had been tapped to sort through boxes and boxes of classified missions they'd been on in order to figure out why Team Four had been targeted. It was only after two attempts on the lives of the remaining four men on the hit list did they found out who wanted them dead and why. Since then, both the senator and hit-man had met with their own untimely demises. During all the chaos, Devon and Kristen had met and fallen in love.

Devon pinched his fiancée's ass hard, and she jumped and

squealed, almost dropping the raw hamburger in her hands. "Who says we can't? And don't roll your eyes at a roomful of Doms, Pet."

The others all chuckled knowing the sweet submissive wanted to glare at them and say something snarky before she thought better of it. Her ass would be spanked red if she did. "Fine, but come on guys. This is the first date I've heard of her go on since she moved down here. You should be happy she's doing something fun, especially with the anniversary of her parents' deaths coming up. I'm sure if there's a second or third date, she'll introduce you to the guy."

Ian had stayed with Jenn for three months in Virginia following the murders so she could finish up her high school education. She'd moved to Tampa and into Ian's apartment before moving again into a dorm room at the University of Tampa where she was now enrolled. It'd taken her a while to deal with the loss of her parents, which everyone understood. But between counseling, her new school and friends, and her beloved uncles, Jenn was coming out of her shell and returning to the bubbly, out-going woman they all knew and loved. The men mumbled their reluctant assents and changed the subject.

"Hey Boss-man." Brody handed Ian a bottle of Bud Light. "It seems you're shit-out-of-luck with my new neighbor."

Ian's eyes narrowed and grew cold. "What're you talking about?"

Brody shrugged his wide shoulders. "Some guy's been hanging out with Angie all day and they seem kinda chummy. His car was in her driveway all through last night. A little scruffy-looking, which I wouldn't think was her type, but it's obvious they know each other pretty well. *Too* well to be a relative."

Ian had met Brody's next-door-neighbor, Angelina Beckett, once while helping his buddy move into his new house. She was a pretty woman, about thirty-three years old, with a killer body which made Ian's cock react like a snappy salute to an Admiral—fast and stiff. With long blond hair down to her shoulder blades, soft green eyes, lush breasts, and an ass he would love to get his hands on, she'd starred in several of his dreams over the last two months. More than once he'd gotten off in the shower imagining her on her knees in front of him, giving him the blow job of a lifetime. Since their introduction, he'd only had a few glimpses of her, but his teammate must have noticed his interest in her.

Without saying another word, he uncapped his beer and took a swig before making his way out to the patio with Beau on his heels. While the dog ran straight to the grass and began to sniff everything in sight, Ian sat at the outdoor table facing Ms. Beckett's backyard. She was also sitting at her patio table with her back toward him, although her chair was turned at a slight angle so she was facing her guest. The strands of her long hair were twined together in a braid which lay down the center of her back, atop her teal blue shirt. He preferred her hair down and wished he had the right to walk over there and undo the confined tresses. Shifting his gaze to the strange man who sat at a ninety-degree angle next to her, Ian studied him.

Brody was right. The man was a little on the disheveled side with a scraggly beard and mustache, and shoulder length hair. But otherwise, he appeared clean, wearing a black T-shirt, blue jeans, and white sneakers. He seemed to be around the same age as her. What pissed Ian off, though, was how the guy had Angie's bare feet in his lap, massaging them, as the two spoke. He watched as Angie's boyfriend's eyes flashed to his, then back again to hers. Ian wasn't fooled. In that split second the stranger had noticed, evaluated, and determined Ian wasn't an immediate threat. It was obvious the man had training. To Ian, his body and its language screamed former military, yet he was almost able to disguise it. In fact, if Ian hadn't been just like him, he may have underestimated the man.

As the rest of Ian's team filtered out to the patio and took seats around the table, the man's gaze flashed over to them before settling again on Angie. Ian watched as she stood with the grace of a prima ballerina, her long legs and heart-shaped ass encased in faded capri jeans making his mouth water. When she turned toward her back door, he heard her say to her boyfriend, "Give me a few minutes to freshen up and we'll go grab something to eat. I hope you're in the mood for Mexican."

The moment she disappeared into the house, without hesitation, her boyfriend turned his attention to the six men beyond the chain-link property fence. Standing, he approached them like a lion taking interest in an intruder to his domain. He was about six-one, two hundred and ten lean pounds, with brown hair and eyes. Several tattoos were peeking out from under the arms of his short-sleeved T-shirt. He was also smart enough to stop two feet away from the chest high divider when he noticed Beau run over and place his big body between his humans and the stranger. Ian took it as a good sign the dog, while in protective mode, wasn't growling a warning.

Wary, Brody stood and walked over to the fence to greet the man. "Hi, I'm Brody Evans, Angie's new neighbor."

Crossing his arms over his muscular chest, the other man nodded at Brody before turning his intense gaze toward Ian and Devon. "I'm aware of whom you are, Evans. I was wondering if I could meet with you and your employers, the Sawyer brothers over there, sometime tomorrow morning at the Trident Security offices."

Ian's eyes narrowed as his stunned teammates looked back and forth between him and the stranger who knew quite a few things about them while they knew nothing about him, including his name. None of them were happy with the fact either. Staying in his seat, he leaned forward, put his beer bottle down and pinned the bearded man with a warning look. "Who are you?"

He made a quick glance over his shoulder, and Ian wondered why he didn't want Angie to hear the confrontation. "My name's James Athos, and I'll explain the rest tomorrow, but for now, let's just say we have a mutual friend and I need your help."

Ian raised one eyebrow, his icy stare never wavering. "Friend? And who would this friend be?"

"A man named Carter."

If any of them were further surprised at the guy's revelation of knowing their longtime friend, associate, and U.S. government spy, T. Carter, they didn't show it. Carter was so deep into the world of black ops to the point where Ian's team had no idea who the man actually worked for. He seemed to have very high connections in every alphabet agency in Washington D.C.—FBI, CIA, NSA, et cetera—as well as in the Pentagon, 1600 Pennsylvania Avenue, and several foreign countries. He was also the man who'd killed the hit-man targeting the team several months ago, and most likely the senator who'd hired the guy, although none of them would ever know for sure. Ian's eyes flashed to the backdoor beyond Athos before returning to the man's face. "Tell me one thing . . . is she in danger?"

Athos shook his head. "No, and I'd like to keep it that way. I also don't want her to know anything about our conversation. Angie means the world to me and I'll do whatever I can to protect her. What time can I meet you?"

Ian did a mental check of tomorrow's schedule. "Oh-eight-hundred?"

As Athos nodded his agreement, the woman in question chose that moment to come back outside and lock the door behind her. Now wearing white canvas slip-on shoes and carrying a small white purse she strolled over to where her boyfriend stood. With automatic reflexes, the men relaxed their tense expressions, giving her no indication anything was wrong. When she stopped next to Athos, she looked at Brody, then the rest of the men with a friendly smile on her pretty face. "Hi Brody, hi guys. I see you've met Jimmy."

Ian felt a jealous punch to his gut as the other man put his arm around her shoulders and gave her a tender kiss to her temple. "I introduced myself, babe. I'm glad your new neighbor seems like a nice guy. I was worried you were going to get someone like the last asshole who couldn't seem to keep his hands to himself. That was until I had a little conversation with him and threatened to tell his wife after I beat the crap out of him." There was a not-so-subtle warning in there to the other men.

Angie rolled her eyes and smacked the guy in the stomach with the back of her hand. "I told you I had it under control. And you didn't threaten to beat him. If I recall, you threatened to cut off George's manhood and shove it down his throat, followed by his individual fingers. Now come on, I'm starving. Take me to dinner."

"Your wish is my command, babe."

She looked back over the fence and gave the men a cute little girlie-wave. "Have a nice night everyone." As they turned toward the path leading to her driveway, Ian could have sworn she looked straight at him with a flash of heat in her eyes. But it was gone so fast he must have been mistaken. Whether it was real or imagined didn't matter to his dick which twitched inside his khakis at the sight of her retreating buttocks. Fuck, how he wanted to take a bite out of those ass cheeks.

"What the fuck?" Boomer asked. "Who the hell is he?"

Ian was still staring at the spot where the two of them had disappeared around the side of her house. "I don't know, but you can be sure I'm going to find out. You know how much I hate surprises."

No one said anything more about the mystery man as Kristen came outside with a plate of hamburgers and chicken cutlets ready for Brody to grill. A few minutes later the conversation returned to the normal banter which always occurred when they were all together, however, Ian was no longer in a relaxed and talkative mood.

## CHAPTER 2

*A*ngie sat across from her best friend, Jimmy, as they ate at a new Mexican restaurant she'd been dying to try. They continued to catch up with each other, and she wished his visit didn't have to be so short. While they'd both been raised in upstate New York, after high school graduation, she'd attended college in Florida, while he had gone into the Marines. Six years later, he'd been recruited by the DEA and had to change his last name for safety reasons. He now worked in their Atlanta office. At least she didn't have to worry about his job as much as she used to since he was no longer working deep undercover assignments. Those had kept them from seeing or talking over the phone to each other for months at a time. Now he worked with a team who backed up the undercover guys, but he still had his beard and long hair which she hated, but knew was necessary. He was a good-looking guy when his facial hair was trimmed close, but without it, the man was an absolute hunk and had been since she first met him their freshman year of high school. They'd tried dating once in their sophomore year, but it didn't last long because both of them were afraid to ruin the strong friendship which had developed between them. He did, however, take her to their senior prom, after she broke up with the guy she'd been seeing a month earlier. Now the two friends tended to bust chops about each other's dates, yet remained protective of each other. That was why she hadn't been surprised when Jimmy had made the veiled threat to Brody and his friends . . . talk about hunks.

While her best friend excused himself to use the restroom, Angie's mind drifted back to her new neighbor and his friends . . . to be more specific, one friend . . . Ian Sawyer. With his black hair, blue eyes, handsome face, and a sculpted body which made her panties wet, the man could be a movie star if he wanted to. Brody had told her Ian was retired from the Navy and owned the security consulting company Brody and the others worked for. Lately, she'd been thinking of having them upgrade her burglar alarm system. Jimmy always bugged her about how easy it was to bypass the one which had come with the home she'd purchased three years ago. She doubted the owner of the company would do it himself, but she often found herself fantasizing about him coming over and installing a new alarm. In her fantasies, he had on the tight faded jeans and snug, royal-blue T-shirt he'd been wearing the first day she met him while he was helping his friend move in. The color of his shirt had made his eyes stand out to the point she was certain she could drown in them. And, holy crap, his deep voice had sent shivers up and down her spine before settling between her legs. When Brody introduced her to his teammates, she thought Ian had held her hand a moment longer than the others, but it was probably wishful thinking on her part.

"And I was thinking of dying my hair purple and getting a heart tattoo that says 'bite-me' on my forehead."

Angie shook the wayward thoughts from her brain and stared at Jimmy, who was laughing at her shocked expression. "Huh? What're you talking about?"

"I was wondering where you were. I sat back down and asked you a question, but you were on another planet. I wanted to see how long I could talk gibberish before you noticed."

She threw a piece of tortilla chip at him. "Jerk. What was the question?"

Tossing the wayward chip in his mouth, he chewed and swallowed before answering her. "How's work going? Any new clients?"

Angie was a graphic designer who worked from home. She had several corporate clients who sent her a large amount of work, as well as many individual clients, needing one-time-only or occasional projects. "I do have a new client, and I'm so excited about them. I've been contracted to be one of the designers of romance novel covers for a publishing company called Red Rose Books."

"Really? That's awesome, Ang. How'd you hook up with them?"

Grabbing her smartphone, she brought up a photo and showed it to him. "This was one I did for a former advertising client who's now writing romance books. She thought of me when she was self-publishing her first book and asked if I would design the cover for her. Someone from Red Rose saw it, thought it was edgy and something they'd be interested in, so they tracked me down. It's a great contract with a decent payout for each one I do. I'll be doing about one or two a week so I can still concentrate on my other customers."

Jimmy smiled at her. He was always her biggest supporter when it came to her art. "Great. Mr. Abraham would be proud you've come this far."

Mr. Clark Abraham had been her high school art teacher and the first one to recognize the artistic talent even Angie hadn't known she had. He'd introduced her to the many different mediums of art and encouraged her to try them all until she found what fit her best. In addition to graphite pencil drawings and computerized graphic arts, she also dabbled in oil painting and had sold several pieces at a local art gallery over the years. Thinking of the gray-haired man who'd become her friend and mentor was always bittersweet. He'd suffered a heart attack in his empty classroom during lunch period one afternoon the year after she graduated and by the time someone found him it'd been too late. "Yeah, I know he would have." Lowering her voice a few octaves, she imitated the old man, "Reds, Angie, why are you so obsessed with the reds? Throw some blue and green in there, maybe a little yellow. Surprise me sometimes, will ya!"

The two of them laughed as they finished their meal and talked about everything under the sun. Angie was going to miss her friend when he headed back to Atlanta tomorrow morning, but for now she'd make the most of their time together.

IAN THREW the pen down when he realized he'd been chewing on it and looked at the small brass anchor clock on the right side of his desk. His brother had an identical one and both had been gifts from their mother when they finally had desks to put them on. He heaved a sigh in frustration because it was only oh-seven-thirty. He had another half hour before Angie's boyfriend showed up and started answering the many questions Ian had for him. Before he left Brody's last night, he'd told the geek to find out everything he could about James Athos and call him as soon as he had it. In the meantime, Ian left a message with Carter to contact him ASAP, which knowing his friend, it could be a while. He didn't have a direct line to get a hold of the guy, no one did, and had to leave a voice mail at the number he'd memorized years ago. Carter would check his messages only when it was safe for him to do so, which meant it could be hours or days before he got a chance, depending on what he was working on.

The quiet in the empty office he usually enjoyed was getting to him this morning. Standing, he headed outside for some fresh air with Beau following on his heels. He'd tossed and turned all night with thoughts of Angie doing erotic things to him, alternating with speculation of what her boyfriend wanted with Trident Security. Brody had called him a little before midnight with an update, brief as it was. He was able to get a copy of the thirty-three-year-old's Georgia driver's license and found out he had some minor drug and assault arrests on file with no jail time served. All which could be part of an undercover persona, as Ian had a feeling it was. The interesting part was, prior to nine years ago, James Athos didn't exist, and Ian wondered how well Angie knew her boyfriend.

Pushing on the office entrance door, he stepped outside, inhaled deeply and looked around. From the outside, the complex looked like what it had formerly been—an abandoned warehouse facility on the outskirts of Tampa. Over three years earlier, when he first saw the property, Ian knew it would be perfect compound for Trident Security. The company he co-owned with his brother specialized in personal security, investigations, and the more-than-occasional black-op for Uncle Sam. The complex was once used by an import-export company until the authorities had discovered the main product being processed through there had been cocaine. After the business shut down, Ian was able to purchase the ten-acre lot of land at a government auction for a fraction of its estimated value.

The property contained four identical two-story warehouses lined in a row, and was pretty much isolated from everyday traffic, sitting a good mile away from the main thoroughfare. With a mini forest of trees between the buildings and highway, it was afforded a great deal of privacy. After extensive renovations, the smallest and last of the warehouses on the property had become the living quarters for both Sawyer brothers. Ian's three thousand square foot three-bedroom 'apartment' was on the first floor, while stairs led up to Devon and Kristen's place, which had an identical floor plan. The remaining six thousand square feet of the warehouse behind the two apartments was being used as storage, but that was going to change when they added two new apartments. One would belong to Ian's goddaughter, and the other was for Nick, the youngest of the Sawyer clan and current Navy SEAL based in California. It would be his for when he visited and eventually retired from the military.

Glancing over at the main gate, Ian waved hello to the morning guard while Beau sniffed along the compound's fence-line. When a person entered the compound through a manned security gate, the first warehouse they came to was home to The Covenant, a club which catered to those who enjoyed some kink in their lives. This was another reason why the property had been ideal for them. A few years earlier their cousin, Mitch, approached the brothers with the idea around the same time they were trying to get Trident Security off the ground. The exclusive club they all belonged to prior to that had closed down after the owner was indicted for tax evasion. The closing had left the members searching for a new place where they could practice their individual sexual fetishes without them becoming public knowledge. Since Ian and Devon were focused on Trident, Mitch, with his MBA, was the obvious choice to manage the club. There were times, however, his cousin deferred to Ian on some issues since he was the more experienced Dom.

To get from the first warehouse to the remaining three in the compound, visitors had to pass through another security gate which was unmanned. To get through that one, a person had to be either buzzed in or scan their hand print on the sophisticated identification system. The first of those buildings, which Ian was now standing in front of, was separated into two areas with the main offices of Trident security at the front. At the back end was a large vehicle garage along with the equipment, weapon, and ammunition vaults. The next structure contained an indoor shooting range, a gym and training room, and a panic-security room in case of an emergency. Some might call the Sawyer brothers paranoid, but one never knew when one's enemies might come calling, so it was always better to be prepared. In fact, several months ago, the team had almost been picked off by a sniper who'd set up in a tree just past the security system's line of detection. As a result, Ian and Devon were working on acquiring several undeveloped properties surrounding theirs so they could extend their lines of defense outward.

Ian picked up the hard rubber ball Beau had dropped at his feet and played fetch for about ten minutes until Devon strolled over to greet him, a cup of coffee in his hand. "Morning. Brody find out anything?"

He filled his brother in as he threw Beau's ball one more time before turning around and walking back inside to his office. Stopping along the way in their break room, he grabbed his third cup of coffee of the morning and a blueberry muffin from a Tupperware container. The leftover muffins from yesterday were courtesy of Mrs. Kemple, their office manager since the inception of Trident Security. She'd resigned and moved to Miami to help her daughter with newborn triplets last summer after training a new manager. Unfortunately, her replacement, Paula Leighton, had become too nosy for her own good and was fired three weeks ago after Brody found her one morning looking through files in the team's war-room. It was one of the few places which she knew damn well she wasn't supposed to have access to. He'd run over to the club to help Mitch with a computer glitch and left his office door open, thinking he would be right back. After he was gone longer than expected, Paula's curiosity must have gotten the best of her because when Brody returned, she was standing in his war-room with her nose in one of his files. Ian had fired her that day. Marco had been the most relieved about the woman's termination since she'd seemed to have her eye on him for a relationship which went beyond co-workers, and the man had not been interested at all.

Mrs. Kemple had come back for a short time to train Colleen McKinley, a submissive from the club. When Ian had been talking to Colleen's Dom, Master Reggie Helm, a few hours after firing Paula, the Dom mentioned his sub wasn't happy with her current job and was looking for a change. Ian brought her in for an interview the next day and hired her on the spot.

The only problem they faced with Colleen so far was getting her to call them all by their first names and not Master or Sir while at the office. It also took the guys a little getting used to seeing her in something other than the lingerie her Dom liked her to wear at the club. Her clothes tended to be quite conservative and professional looking at work. At least they didn't have to hide from Colleen the fact that Trident Security was run by, and employed, a group of Dominants, like they had with Paula. Mrs. Kemple had known about the club since it opened and never batted an eye over it.

Five minutes before eight, Ian's phone rang. It was the guard at the front gate advising him he was buzzing one James Athos through the second gate. Brody, who'd come in a few minutes ago, stood and went to the front door to escort the man in, while Ian and Devon remained in the conference room. Ian would've preferred to have this meeting after he spoke with Carter, but the spy hadn't gotten back to him yet.

Brody walked back in with Athos right behind him and both men took seats at the table. Ian wasn't in the mood to offer Athos coffee, or anything else, and apparently neither was his brother, who also remained silent.

"I'm sure you investigated me last night and are frustrated with what you found and, more importantly, what you didn't find. Did

Carter return your call yet? Because I know that's the first thing you did after I left." Athos leaned back in his chair and rested one ankle on the opposite knee as if he didn't have a care in the world, but Ian knew it wasn't the case. The man had something on his mind and was worried about it.

Ian tapped his hand on the table. "No, he didn't. Now instead of me asking you the hundred and one questions I have, why don't you start from the beginning and tell us what you want."

"As I'm sure you've figured out, Athos isn't my last name. There are only two people in this world who can conclusively connect me to the man I was nine years ago. One is Angie and the other is my handler at the DEA in Atlanta." Ian raised his eyebrow, but said nothing. Neither did Devon nor Brody, but the geek jumped onto his laptop, presumably getting the number to the Atlanta office. "I was recruited from the Marines after a six-year stint, four of which were spent in Special Forces. I was given a new identity and my military record was expunged. Spent my first three years undercover with a biker gang, out in Arizona and New Mexico, who were running a lucrative cocaine business from over the border. It took me a while to work my way up the ladder, but, after a long investigation, we were able to shut down the pipeline. But as you know, you shut down one of those fuckers, three more pop up. From there, I've worked my way around the states until I got tired of living under rocks with the scum of the earth. My handler, who was also my recruiter, pulled me in and I've been working with a support team out of the Atlanta office for the past two years. Again, it was under a new identity—as far as anyone at the DEA knows, my last name is Austin. One of the advantages of coming in was I'm able to see and talk to Angie almost anytime I want to, but I still keep my connection to her a secret from my co-workers."

Ian held up his hand to interrupt. Athos's statement from yesterday was still eating away at his gut. *Angie means the world to me . .* "Who is she to you?"

The man's hard face softened. "I told you yesterday, she's my world—she is and always will be. We met our freshman year of high school and clicked right away. She's been my best friend ever since.

If it wasn't for her, I would've fallen apart years ago after my mother and baby sister were murdered by a drug dealer whom I didn't know my sister got herself mixed up with. It was while I was still in the Marines and overseas. I would've hunted the bastard down and killed him myself if the cops hadn't already done it before I could get home. Angie was my rock, my savior, and she's the only family I have now and I'm all she has. Her folks were older when they had her and both of them died several months apart of natural causes in their late fifties. She had a much older brother who was killed in a car accident when she was nine, and I think that's what eventually killed her folks because neither one of them ever got over it. Anyway, we've always been there for each other over the years, and it would destroy me if anything ever happened to her because of me."

"You went into the DEA as a way to avenge your sister and mother's deaths." Ian didn't ask it as a question, and Athos didn't deny it. "So where do we fit in?"

"Before Angie closed on her house three years ago, I did what I always do when it comes to her and ran a check on all her neighbors." He shrugged. Even though some of the inquiries he'd made were technically illegal, he didn't seem ashamed to admit it in front of men who most likely would've done the exact same thing. "When she mentioned Evans moved in next door, I checked him out too. I saw his connection to Trident Security and remembered Carter mentioning the name one night a few years ago. He'd said if I ever need help with anything in Tampa or the rest of Florida, I should contact Trident, and you guys would get it done. Just to make sure things hadn't changed, I got in touch with him again and he told me he trusted you guys with his life. I've known the man for over seven years, he's saved my sorry ass twice, and so it was a good enough endorsement for me.

His voice became hard again and filled with venom. Ian could see the barely contained rage in his eyes. "Two weeks ago, an undercover agent, Aaron Reinhardt, working in New Orleans, was tortured and killed. We have no idea how he was made, and if they broke him or not. I saw the crime scene photos and wouldn't be surprised if the poor guy did crack—most agents would've. The worst part was his parents and brother were found dead with him. Their bodies were discovered before anyone ever reported them missing, dumped next to a garbage bin behind a strip mall near their family home in Illinois. Small consolation, his family wasn't tortured, but each was shot once in the back of the head. Like most undercover agents, Aaron's next of kin was only available to his handler. We both have the same handler, Artie Giles, and both trusted him with the information—I still do. Whoever found out about his family, it didn't come from Artie.

"Aaron was a friend of mine." It was obvious Athos had respected the dead man. "I worked with him on and off for years. He was one of the good guys and this was supposed to be his last undercover because he'd gotten to the point where he wanted to meet a nice girl and settle down. When we found out what happened, I told Artie I wanted the job. I maintained and updated my cover, which I cultivated over the years, in case I ever needed it again. I'm heading to New Orleans after I leave here today to start working my way under. I told Angie last night after dinner, and right now she's really pissed at me, although I can't blame her. I'd sworn to her I was done with undercover work, but this is something I need to do. I can't let the bastards win."

He leaned forward and set his elbows on the conference table. "So, this is where you all come in. I need you to keep an eye on her for me without her knowing it. If she finds out, she'll be pissed off enough to fight any attempts to protect her and end up getting herself hurt or killed. She's smart, but stubborn at times, and I'm worried if my cover gets blown, someone could come after her to get to me. Like I said though, it's highly unlikely because Artie is the only one who can make the connection between the two of us. His files are kept in a safe at his home office and the name Athos and my birth surname don't appear anywhere in my file and neither does Angie's name. There's only her cell phone listed along with the pass-phrase he has to say to verify it's him who's calling her. They're also on two separate papers so if someone gets into his safe somehow, the two don't appear related. Neither of them have ever met nor spoken on the phone. If anyone claiming to be from the DEA contacts her without that phrase, she has instructions on how to disappear without a trace until I can catch up with her. No one else in the agency knows she exists in my life."

"As far as you know. Nothing is ever one hundred percent hidden," Ian said wryly.

"True." The agent nodded his head in reluctant agreement. "But I've been as careful as possible over the years. Hell, I've spent a small fortune on burner phones because I destroyed each one after I called her. I still do, even though I'm no longer under. I don't want something or someone from one of my past gigs to come back and bite me on the ass."

Athos was about to say something more, but Ian's cell phone rang. He glanced at the screen and then at Angie's friend before hitting the speaker button to connect the call. A deep voice rumbled over the line. "Ian, you rang? Sorry I couldn't get back to you sooner. What's up?"

He leaned forward so he could be heard without raising his voice. "No problem, Carter. It seems I have an acquaintance of yours sitting in my office with Devon and Brody."

The sounds of traffic in the background came through the speaker. "Really? Who?"

Ian arched his eyebrow at the DEA agent indicating he should announce himself.

"Hey, man, its Athos."

There was a two second pause. "Confirm."

"Tinkerbell gives good head."

While the other three men smirked and shook their heads at the inane pass-phrase, Carter barked out a laugh. "Long time, no hear, dude. How's it hangin'? Have you shaved the bush yet?"

An amused snort escaped Athos. "A little low lately, and no I haven't."

"Ian, all is good. I trust this scruffy-faced jackass as much as I trust you, and you know that's a lot. He loves his alphabet soup at oh-four-hundred, and whatever he says is on the level."

Alphabet soup was a reference to the multiple abbreviated

government agencies in the US, and "at oh-four-hundred" signified the fourth letter of the alphabet which was "D." It was as close to saying "DEA" as the spy would get over the phone. As Athos said earlier, Carter's endorsement was all Ian needed.

"Do you need anything else? I've only got a minute." In a reflexive reaction, Ian shook his head and said "no" at the same time. "All right, cool. A-man, you take care of yourself. If you need anything, ring me up. It's been a long time since you and I raised hell together. Devil Dog, tell your pretty fiancée I'll be in Tampa in a few weeks, and I'm looking forward to being re-introduced to the little librarian."

While Brody and Ian gave him curious looks, Devon chuckled. There was a story there they weren't privy to, but they had a good idea what it might be. Master Carter was known to take the third spot in an occasional ménage when visiting The Covenant. "I'll tell her, and I'm sure she'll be looking forward to it too. Hey, how'd you know we got engaged? You haven't been here in months."

"The almighty Carter knows all. I gotta go. Catch ya all later."

The connection dropped and Ian looked at Devon and Brody, who both nodded their silent approval, and then at Athos. "Give us the details."

# CHAPTER 3

*A*ngie paced back and forth across her living room, wondering what the hell she was doing. One of her friends insisted on hooking her up with a blind date, and it was something she swore she'd never do again after the last disastrous one. However, here she was all dressed up with nothing to do but wait another fifteen minutes before she left for the restaurant where she planned to meet Melvin Fromm, an accountant.

*Really? Melvin?* When her friend had told Angie about him, she'd called him Mel not Melvin, which is how he'd introduced himself when he first called her. It was all Angie could do not to imagine him showing up with a pocket protector and glasses held together with a piece of tape. She was going to kill Mandy if this didn't work out—not that she expected it would. Which brought her back to her original question—what the hell was she doing?

It'd been over three weeks since Jimmy dropped the bomb he was going back undercover for one more case, and she was still pissed at him. She'd no idea why after two years he decided to go back and, as always, he couldn't give her details because it was classified. At least, that's what he always told her. But she figured it was more of a cross between he couldn't give her any details and he didn't want to worry her with them. Either way, she was in the dark, and she would be apprehensive until he contacted her again. And from experience, she knew it could be a week or six months from now. *Damn him.*

She'd always understood why he'd gone to work undercover for the DEA. It was his way of getting some sort of revenge for the deaths of his family. Mrs. Andrews had been a very nice, single mother whose husband walked out on her two months after their daughter, Ruthie, was born, for another woman with no kids. The only time she had ever gotten child support from her ex was when his paycheck was finally garnered by the court when Ruthie was three. That had lasted two months before he moved out of state and disappeared for good. As a result, the woman worked hard at two jobs for the next eighteen years to support Jimmy and his younger sister. Some mothers may have grown to resent their kids in a similar situation, but Dorothy Andrews' children were her world and she let them know she loved them every chance she got. She'd also loved Angie as much as her son's best friend had loved her right back.

Little Ruthie had been a sweet girl who'd gotten mixed up with the wrong crowd in high school. It had ultimately led to her and her mother being shot to death over what the police described as a case of mistaken identity. One of her girlfriends swiped some drugs from a dealer they both knew, and the dealer blamed the missing drugs on Ruthie. It wasn't until after the police killed the suspect that the other girl came forward and admitted her role in the incident. The same girl died of an overdose two years later.

Jimmy Andrews, now Jimmy Athos, was determined to rid the world of as many drug dealers as he could. Angie wished it wasn't at the expense of his life, though. Not only was he in danger of being killed on the job, she also worried about him in other ways. He rarely dated, as far as she knew, and when he did, the dates never resulted in any relationship which lasted past the two- or three-week mark. She was afraid he would never find someone to love and grow old with, not that she'd found her soulmate yet either. There were times she wished they'd tried a romantic relationship between them, but the fear of losing everything had always stopped them. For some reason, Angie had been positive that's what would've happened, so instead, they were more like brother and sister. A shrink might say they were using each other to replace the siblings they'd both lost, but neither of them had ever felt that way, having discussed the subject a few times over the years. In the end, she wanted him to be happy with no regrets when he looked back on his life while on his deathbed. However, she didn't think it was possible for him, at least not at this point in his life.

Sighing, Angie looked at the time on her cable box again and was about to grab her purse when her cell phone rang. Glancing at the screen she saw it was Melvin calling her ten minutes before their date. She groaned, knowing what the man was going to say with the last-minute call. Connecting the call, she walked to her back door and stepped out on the lanai because she had a feeling she was going to need some fresh air.

———

Ian took two steps across Brody's living room toward the sliding glass door which led out to the patio and stopped. What the fuck was he doing? He was only supposed to swing by and pick up a file his employee had to leave at his house after getting a frantic call from a corporate client very early that morning. The geek had hopped into his truck and headed straight to Orlando after alerting Ian to the problem. One of the company's own computer geeks had figured out a way to embezzle $800,000 from a corporate account. They needed Brody's help to figure out how the guy did it, and how they could prevent it from happening again. So, Egghead was now near Disney World for at least another day or two, and Ian was standing in the guy's living room. And he was trying to talk himself out of going out the back door to see if Angie was in her own backyard.

After Athos had told them what he wanted them to do, they got to work doing what they could to keep his best friend safe. They'd gotten lucky when she agreed to have her security system upgraded. Brody brought up the subject as subtly as he could while talking to her over their shared fence, and the woman took the bait. The next day, her new neighbor and Boomer installed their best system while telling her it was a normal setup for normal people who led normal lives and were probably not in any danger. Athos told them to spare no expense and gave them a credit card number to cover any cost differences from a basic unit. He had to let her pay something for the new installation, otherwise she'd be suspicious.

The teammates installed the whole system in one day. Then while Brody took Angie around the house and showed her all the neat features of it, Boomer took the time to install the last few things they didn't want her to know about. He'd placed a few strategic audio bugs and remote cameras, then installed a tracking device on her phone, wallet, and car. He'd also managed to get a few of them inside several of her shoes which he'd found in her closet. Looking at how worn the soles were, he was able to pick the ones she seemed to wear the most. The flat discs were very small and he tried to put them where she or anyone else wouldn't notice them. If she did find one, chances were slim she would know what it was.

Brody had also gotten friendlier with his new neighbor, not too friendly or Ian would've killed him, but enough so he found ways to check on her before and after work. Two days ago, he even invited her to join him for dinner on his patio and threw a couple of steaks on the grill for them. They wanted her comfortable enough with the geek in case anything ever went wrong. Athos had given them his handler's number, and a backup pass-phrase Angie was aware of in the event they had to bypass the DEA altogether.

If Brody knew that for the past three weeks Ian had been watching the live footage of Angie walking around her house, he would have laughed at what a stalker his boss was being. The feed was being recorded on equipment in Trident's war-room for security purposes, in case they needed to review it for any reason. But Ian hadn't been able to help himself from bringing up the feeds on his computer a few times a day just to see her. None of the cameras were in her bathroom, and the cameras in her bedroom only faced the windows and door, thus giving her a small amount of privacy so he didn't consider himself a stalker. He was a voyeur—what the difference was he wasn't sure, but if someone asked, he was certain he could think of something.

With the file he needed in his hand, he was about to turn around and leave when movement outside one of the windows caught his eye, and he realized it was Angie on her own patio.

Sighing and calling himself ten kinds of an idiot, he continued toward the sliding glass door, opened it, and stepped outside. He took one look toward her backyard and almost swallowed his tongue.

"Fuck," he muttered to himself. She was standing with her head down, dressed in a navy, wrap-around cotton dress which stopped an inch above her knees. The V-neck, while conservative, showed some of her ample cleavage, which made him want to beg to see more. Her legs looked amazing and a pair of navy and white, polka-dot heels brought her height up three inches to about five-foot-eleven. He could imagine where the top of her head would come to if she was standing next to his own six-foot-three frame. Her blonde hair was down the way he liked it, and he longed to run his fingers through the gentle waves which gave the strands some volume. Her makeup was subtle, and her jewelry, understated. All combined, it was one tempting, little package making his mouth water.

It took him a moment to notice she was on her cell phone, and he heard her say, "No, really. It's all right. These things happen." She paused to listen to whoever was on the other end of the call. "Yes. That's fine. Call me if you want to reschedule, and I'll think about it. Bye."

Ian realized she hadn't known he was there until her pretty, green eyes met his and widened a bit before she gave him a shy smile and a little wave. "Hi, Ian." He was surprised she remembered his name since, as far as he knew, she'd only heard it the first time they'd met, and he craved to hear her say it again. He'd never thought hearing his name being verbalized could be a turn-on, but that was before he heard it fall from her plump, red lips.

"Hey, Angie." He took a few steps toward the fence and was pleased when she did the same. "You look very nice tonight. Going somewhere?" He figured from her conversation that her plans had been canceled, but he was curious as to what they had been in the first place.

She shrugged, although she didn't look too disappointed her

plans had changed. "I was supposed to go on a date, but he canceled at the last minute."

"Must have been a blind date."

Giving him a curious look, Angie tilted her head. "It was, but how did you know?"

His blue eyes grew darker as his gaze covered her from head to toe and back up again. "Because if he knew how exquisite you look right now, he never would've canceled. He'd be thinking of how he could end the night with you in his bed."

A blush stained her cheeks, and after a moment, she tore her eyes away from his, gesturing with her head toward her backdoor. "Well, his loss, I guess. I'll just go change into a pair of sweats, pig out on a container of Ben & Jerry's, and find some old movie to watch."

"Or, you could let me take you out to dinner." What the hell had made him say that? Oh, yeah, the little head in his pants did. Glancing down, he was happy to see his khakis were loose enough to cover his semi-hard-on. He was also dressed nice enough, with his black polo shirt and loafers, to take her to dinner—if she said yes, of course.

She was still blushing and the pinkness was not only on her cheeks, but her upper chest as well. He wondered if it was the same color as her nipples, and the thought made his dick twitch.

"You don't have to do that. I'm sure you have other plans," she told him.

"One thing you should know about me, Angie, I never say things I don't mean, and I don't do anything I don't want to do. I just order one of my employees to do it for me." She smiled as he'd intended. "I'd like to take you to dinner, if you'd let me." He tried to keep the desire he knew was in his eyes to a minimum. If she knew how much he wanted to strip her naked, tie her to his bed, and do nasty, erotic things to every inch of her body, she'd run from the yard, screaming.

Her expression was more eager than shy, and he liked the combination. "Well, since I'm already dressed, and I think I'm running a little low on the Ben & Jerry's . . . yes, I'd like to go out to dinner with you. But this isn't a date." At his raised eyebrow, she added, "I mean, it's not like this was planned, so we'll go Dutch."

Shaking his head, he smiled at her. "Uh-uh. I asked you to dinner, and it's my treat. I'm not expecting anything in return, Angie, just the pleasure of your company for the evening. And maybe a goodnight kiss, if you decide you had a good time."

Now why did he tack on that last sentence? He was about to give himself a mental ass-kicking when she beamed at him. "We'll see." She turned toward her door as his heart beat a little faster. "Let me grab my purse and I'll meet you out front."

FIVE MINUTES LATER, Angie was sitting in the passenger seat of Ian's Ford Expedition, wondering how she ended up there. Did he ask her to dinner out of pity for her having been stood up at the last minute? Or did he truly want to spend some time with her? When he'd said she looked exquisite, her girly-parts had stood up and taken notice. Could he really be interested in her? And what about his comment about a goodnight kiss? Was he planning on kissing her later? Would she let him? The way her body had tingled when he'd taken her hand and helped her into the high seat of the SUV, she knew if asked to kiss her right now, she would let him.

She thought about what little she knew about him from talking to Brody. Of course, when she'd asked her neighbor a bunch of questions the other night over their steak dinner, she'd made them sound as if she were curious about the whole team and not one member in particular. She knew Ian was single, never married, and thirty-eight years old. He had a nineteen-year-old goddaughter, Jennifer, who lived with him when she wasn't at college at the nearby University of Tampa. Ian had taken the girl in after her parents were murdered a year ago in a brutal home invasion in Virginia. His brother and business partner was Devon, who was engaged to a woman named Kristen. Angie had gotten a glimpse of the other woman in passing when they'd visited Brody, but she hadn't been introduced to her yet.

The other men were all single as well. They'd served together on the Navy's SEAL Team Four, which she'd been impressed to learn. She'd heard what SEALs had to go through physically and mentally to achieve the well-respected position. Ian had held the highest rank in the group as Lieutenant, but only for the two years before he retired. There had been a three-year period when all six had been together before they started retiring, one or two at a time. Ian and Devon had started up Trident Security and hired their former teammates as trusted employees as soon as each one left the Navy. Trident performed numerous security jobs for their clients including bodyguard work, home and business security systems, investigations, corporate security, and recovery of kidnap victims or stolen merchandise. The company also did the occasional job for the government which Brody said he couldn't elaborate on. They contracted several agents from another agency who supplied man-power to companies like theirs, and they were talking about hiring six more people to create a second team.

Angie suddenly realized Ian had parked the car after their brief ride and was shutting the engine off. She looked through the windshield and saw the quiet steakhouse they'd agreed upon. Without saying a word, Ian got out of the car, closed his door, and walked around to open hers while she waited. Somehow, she knew he would do that, and she liked the gesture. It'd been a while since someone other than Jimmy had opened a door for her.

As they walked across the parking lot, Ian took her hand and hooked it under his elbow. He skillfully avoided puddles left over from the late afternoon shower which had passed through the area, and held the restaurant door open for her. She got the feeling he wasn't doing all those things to impress her, but he did them naturally for any woman he was out with. The thought made her feel like this evening was somewhere between routine and special to him, but she hoped it was leaning toward special.

After they were seated and ordered their drinks, instead of picking up his menu, Ian rested his forearms on the table and studied her for a moment. "So, tell me about this blind date you were going on, so I can get this jealousy I'm feeling out of my system."

She laughed, figuring he was kidding, but played along. "Well, there's not much to tell. My friend hooked me up with Melvin Fromm, a thirty-five year old CPA with rude manners since he canceled on me ten minutes before I was supposed to meet him. And the best excuse he could think of was 'something came up.'"

The corners of Ian's mouth twitched twice before he could no longer hide his grin and a quiet snort. "Melvin, huh?" She nodded with her own amused smile. "Okay, I don't think I have to worry about him sweeping you off your feet anytime in the future, so I'll tamp my jealousy back down. I'll just be grateful the idiot canceled on you because it gave me the opportunity to spend the evening with an incredibly beautiful woman."

Oh, Lord, why couldn't she stop blushing around this man? It wasn't as if she'd never had a good-looking guy compliment her and flirt with her before. She dated often, but for some reason, Ian took it to a whole new level for her. Their drinks were delivered, a draft beer for him and a cosmopolitan for her, and they fell into an easy conversation about normal, everyday subjects. It wasn't until their waitress checked on them for a third time, did they pick up their menus to order something.

"So," Ian said, after the waitress left to place their orders, "tell me what you do as a graphic designer because I've never met one before. Wait . . . first tell me how you became one. Is it something you always wanted to do?"

Angie took a sip of her drink then shook her head. "Actually, I never realized I had any artistic ability, beyond doodling, until my sophomore year at high school when I had to take a mandatory art class. My teacher, Mr. Abraham, was the first person to see I had talent and pushed and inspired me to learn more about every artistic medium out there. He became my mentor, took me to art shows and museums, and helped me cultivate my own style. I ended up with pencil drawings, oil painting, and computer graphics as my main interests, although I dabble in some watercolors and sculpting when inspiration hits.

"I earned a partial scholarship to the School of Visual Arts in New York and earned my Masters of Fine Arts. I spent the next six years working for a large graphic design company in New York City before I couldn't take the bitter winters anymore. The last straw was when a taxi hit a slush puddle near me and covered me from head to toe in cold, nasty water while I was on my way to work." Ian gave her a sympathetic laugh at the image of her looking like an irate, drowned rat. "Anyway, I'd visited a few friends who live in Tampa before and knew I liked it. So, I packed up, moved south five years ago and never looked back. I'd been doing some side work for a few internet clients while still in New York, so I branched out and built my own business from there. I design websites, printed brochures, graphics for magazines, books, and company logos—basically whatever a client wants." She took out her cell phone and flipped to the e-book cover she'd shown Jimmy a few weeks earlier. "This is a book cover I designed for a client last month, and it ended up getting me a new contract with a publishing company."

He took the phone from her and studied the picture. It was a photo of a man's bare muscular back and shoulders stopping just above his neck down to his black leather covered ass. A bullwhip was between his two hands and stretched taut across his back from shoulder to hip. Female hands came from around his front, clutching both of his butt cheeks, and were the only parts of her body which were visible. Her long fingernails were painted a deep red which almost looked like blood. From how the woman's hands were situated, anyone looking at the picture would know her face was in the guy's crotch, and it made one wonder if she was giving him a blowjob yet or not. The book's title *Lydia's Desire* and the author's name were done in the same red as the woman's nails. Ian looked up at Angie and smiled. "A guy's ass and naked back aren't my thing, but I know a lot of women who would be drooling over this cover. It's erotic-looking with the whip."

"Well, it was an erotic romance with BDSM and all, so I had to spice it up some. It was actually a good book."

Handing her phone back to her, he raised one eyebrow. "You read books with erotica?"

Putting her phone back in her purse, she shrugged her shoulders, a little embarrassed she'd admitted that. "There's so much of it out there nowadays, it's hard to avoid, even if you aren't into it. You can't always tell by the title and cover of a book, but some of it is fun to read and fantasize about."

---

IAN TOOK a casual sip of his beer. She'd answered his question loud and clear, even if her response was a bit vague. He knew she was submissive by her mannerism, but being a submissive and knowing you were one and wanted to participate in the lifestyle were two different things. Not just apples and oranges, it was more like mice and elephants—they were two different species, and one could crush the other if not careful. He intentionally lowered his voice to his Dominant tone. "Does the BDSM lifestyle interest you?"

Her blush was back again, and her eyes shifted down to the table. His heart rate picked up, and his cock began to harden. Whether she admitted it to him verbally or not, the subject interested her, and he wondered if she'd experimented with sex before. At thirty-three, he doubted she was a virgin, but what had her past sexual encounters consisted of? Had they been pure vanilla, or had she let any of her lovers tie her up, spank her, or flog her? Had any of them pushed her limits, fucked her heart-shaped ass? Given her orgasms which took forever to come down from? Had anyone ever fucked those moist, red lips of hers and come down her throat? In some ways, he wanted her to tell him she practiced the lifestyle, and in other ways, he didn't want to think of any man doing any of those things to her. He wanted to be the one to introduce her to his world of kink. Thinking she would appreciate it, he decided to let her off the hook . . . for now.

He cleared his throat to let her know he was changing the subject. "My soon-to-be-sister-in-law's cousin . . . huh, how's that for a-round-about way for saying I know a guy . . . who's the assistant curator for the Tampa Museum of Art. They're opening a new exhibit tomorrow night at some big gala for their staff and benefactors. Since my brother and I recently made a donation, we received invites. I was going to go stag, stay for a half hour and then beat it, but now I have a better idea. Would you please put me out of my misery by attending it with me so I don't have to talk to a whole bunch of stuffy, boring people? Kristen and her cousin, Will, would kill me if I bail, so I have to make an appearance."

Her face became animated with excitement. "Is that the exhibit that's on loan from the Louvre?" When he nodded, she gushed, "Oh my God, I would love to go. I was planning on taking a whole day off next week to go see it."

"Well, you can see it tomorrow night, as long as you don't mind me not knowing a bloody thing about art. I can look at something and say 'yes, I like it,' or 'no, I hate it,' but that's about it."

Her smile was flirtatious and infectious. "I'd be happy to teach you a bit about what I know."

"Only if you let me teach you a bit about something I know some time." Ian was going to hell. He knew it the moment the word "deal" came out of her pretty red lips and he couldn't help but think, what a way to go.

The waitress brought their meals, and Ian waited until she walked away again after making sure they didn't need anything else. "The gala starts at seven, so I'll pick you up about twenty of, since we'll be dealing with Friday night traffic. Oh, and it's black tie."

Angie picked up her knife and fork and started to cut into her chicken cordon bleu. "I have the perfect dress then. A friend of mine got married at the Guggenheim last year, and it was black tie, also. I only wore the dress once, and I always hoped I could wear it again because I love it."

"Well, in that case, I can't wait to see you in it." And hopefully, he thought, peel it off you at the end of the night.

# CHAPTER 4

*A*ngie checked her hair and makeup for the fourth time in five minutes. She had to stop fussing or she would ruin what her hairdresser and a makeup artist at the salon had worked so hard to do. Her hair was pulled up in a romantic up-do with one ringlet falling down around her face from the top of each cheekbone. She had so many bobby-pins and so much hairspray on that it felt like a helmet, but there was no way she could mess it up, as long as she stopped fooling with it. The makeup was more than she usually wore, yet it was still understated. The shadow, liner and mascara around her eyes made the green color pop and she loved the effect. She wore simple jewelry, a pair of diamond stud earrings which had belonged to her mother and a gold bangle bracelet Jimmy had given her when she'd graduated from art school.

She looked at her reflection in the wardrobe mirror on the back of her closet door and checked her dress again too. Thank goodness she kept up her workouts three times a week or the thing might not have fit. She'd gained about five or six pounds, mostly in her hips and thighs, since she'd been at her friend's wedding, but the spandex lining in the black size-ten dress had enough give so it still looked great. The top was a halter style which looped around her neck with a gold chain and the front had a built-in bra support so her girls were fine. The chiffon material stopped under her arms, leaving her shoulders and most of her back bare before starting again at her waist line and falling straight down to her feet. There was a slit up her left leg which went to the middle of her thigh, and she completed the look with a pair of shimmering gold Michael Kors shoes with four-and-a-half-inch stiletto heels. She was glad Ian was so much taller than some of the guys she had dated because she was able to wear the really high heels she loved so much.

Her mind drifted back to when Ian had dropped her off after dinner last night. He'd escorted her to the door, taken the keys from her hand and opened the lock for her. He didn't turn the doorknob because she would've only had thirty seconds to get inside, close the door and enter the alarm code before the cops were sent. When he'd stood near enough for her to feel his body heat, but not touch, she'd wanted to pull him closer.

Handing her back her keys, his voice became low and sexy. "So, did you have a good time?"

A shiver had assaulted her body. She'd known what he was asking. He'd said earlier if she had a good time, he wanted a goodnight kiss. And she'd definitely had a good time, in fact, she had a great time. "Yes, I did. Does this mean you're going to kiss me?"

She had frozen in place, unable to believe she'd said the words aloud. She'd never been shy about dating, foreplay and sex before, however, she wasn't normally too forward either, taking her cues from the man she was with most of the time.

Ian's mouth had ticked up in an amused grin before he lifted his hand to cup her chin and pulled her toward him. With their lips a scant inch from touching, he'd whispered, "It does."

And then sparks flew.

Holy shit could the man kiss! He'd been gentle at first, using only his lips as they moved seductively over hers, giving her the opportunity to pull away if she wanted to. When she didn't, his tongue began probing the seam of her lips, encouraging her to open them and grant him access to her mouth. She hadn't been able to refuse, and the instant her lips parted, his tongue was inside her, tasting and exploring every inch of her mouth. He hadn't been sloppy as some men could be with their tongues—no, his actions were a cross between tender and insistent as if he was savoring and devouring her at the same time. He didn't do anything else but hold her chin and kiss her. No other parts of their bodies touched. When he'd all-too-soon ended the kiss, easing away from her, she'd groaned and almost begged him to take her right there outside her front door where anyone could see them.

He'd paused a minute to let them both catch their breaths before telling her to go inside, turn off the alarm, lock the door and reset the alarm. She noticed through the long narrow window beside her front door he'd waited until he saw her re-arm the control panel before he smiled and walked back to his car. She had been rooted to the spot for a long time after he'd pulled away, remembering every second of the incredible kiss. After she'd shed her clothes and gone to bed nude, which was normal, her mind was still focused on how her body had come alive the moment it had made contact with his. While her brain wandered, her hand had moved to the juncture between her legs almost on its own volition. It hadn't taken her long to stroke herself to an orgasm so strong that, afterward, she'd drifted asleep with her hand still between her legs and dreams of Ian in her head.

The doorbell rang, and she was startled out of her reminiscing. Grabbing her evening purse and shawl from the bed, she practically ran to the front door and swung it open. Good Lord, he was gorgeous standing on her doorstep in what she believed was an Armani tuxedo which had to have been made for him because the fit was perfect. The five o'clock shadow which had graced his jaw the night before was gone, and she wanted to rub her hand across the soft, recently shaven skin. There wasn't a thing out of place from the top of his dark-haired head to the tips of his shiny, formal black shoes, and the man exuded power, authority, and, most of all, sex. She was sure she'd be fighting the women away from him tonight. When she took a deep breath, his cologne hit her nose, and she almost swooned. It was her favorite—Oud Wood by Tom Ford— and knowing he wore it with her in mind made her lightheaded.

It took a moment for her to realize they were both silently

staring at each other when he cleared his throat. "I'm going to be the envy of every man at the gala tonight. Angel, you look stunning."

As she blushed from his compliment, her eyes almost filled up. No one had called her "Angel" since her older brother, Sam. He'd been killed in a car accident along with three other members of his senior high school football team in a tragedy which had shocked their home town. Nine years older than Angie, her brother had adored and doted on her and he'd been her hero. She realized how much she missed hearing someone call her the pet name, as if she was the most precious thing in the world. Swallowing hard, she opened her mouth to tell Ian how good he looked too, when the alarm control panel next to her started beeping rapidly, warning her to enter the code before the police were alerted.

"Crap!" She scrambled to enter the six-digit number, fumbling once and needing to start over while Ian remained where he was, chuckling at her dilemma. When the alarm was silenced and the light turned green, she turned to him with a sheepish smile. "Sorry. What I was about to say was, you look wonderful too."

He reached out to take her wrap and held it up for her, placing it over her shoulders when she turned around for him. Pivoting back to face him, she took in his heated gaze and thought if they didn't leave now they'd be heading straight to her bedroom. As if he had the same thought, he took a step backward and held out his arm for her to take. "Shall we?"

Angie reset the alarm, locked the door before pulling it shut behind her and tucked her hand under his proffered arm.

With the evening traffic being heavier than usual, the ride took closer to thirty-five minutes. As Ian drove his dark gray Audi RS 5 coupe, instead of his SUV, through the streets of Tampa she told him what she knew about the exhibit they were going to see when he asked her about it. The large collection on loan from France consisted of 18th century art worth about two-hundred-million dollars. While it centered on most forms of paintings, there were also numerous sculptures in many different mediums included. It'd taken the Tampa Museum of Art almost eight years to negotiate and plan for the exhibition which would remain in Florida for six months before returning to its home in the Louvre once again. Angie had spent a two-week class trip in Paris during the break before her final semester at art school and had seen the exhibit there. However, she always wanted a chance to see the beautiful works of art again to study them at her leisure and she was so excited she now had the chance. But, she thought, being on the arm of her handsome date was going to make the experience unforgettable.

---

WHEN THEY PULLED up to the front entrance to the museum the place was all decked out with lights, a red carpet and red-vested valets. Several photographers waited for a chance to get a picture of Tampa's own and visiting elite. The mayor, governor, and several celebrities who lived in the area were expected to attend, as well as prominent business owners and other local, well-known residents. Ian got out of his car, leaving his door open for the young man waiting to move it to a parking area, took his claim ticket, and rounded the car. Another valet had helped Angie from the vehicle, so Ian took her hand and pulled her into his side. A few photographers called his name, and he paused for half a second for them to take his and Angie's picture for the society pages. Although he hated the attention, he'd learned early on if he gave the vultures what they wanted for a brief moment they didn't hound him later. His brother and he had a very successful and reputable business in Trident Security and an even more successful club in The Covenant. As a result, they'd earned frequent invitations to elite functions, although very few people outside of the private sex club knew the Sawyer brothers and their cousin owned it.

Even less people knew about their relationship with Charles "Chuck" Sawyer, a billionaire from Charlotte, North Carolina. Their dad had worked his way from a small real estate business to a corporate empire, owning hotels, resorts, malls, apartment complexes, et cetera, throughout the Carolinas and Virginias. Chuck and his wife Marie, a plastic surgeon, had taken pains to make sure their children were raised with morals and strong work ethics. They tried their best to keep them out of the public spotlight which came with their father's money and the boys had to earn everything they were ever given. When they reached their teens, they all had to either get a job or volunteer at a non-profit organization of their choice. Chuck Sawyer had set up trust funds for each of his sons provided they either go into the military for four years or get a four-year college degree. Full access to their funds didn't kick in until they reached the age of thirty.

Ian had chosen the Navy long before his senior year, as had their brother Nick, who at twenty-five was thirteen years younger than Ian. Devon, two years Ian's junior, originally chose college, but left after one semester when their other brother, John, died of alcohol poisoning. He'd skipped a day of school his senior year of high school and went on a morning bender in their home. When their father found him at noon, he was cold and blue having aspirated on his own vomit. No one had suspected the teen had spiraled downward into the void of alcoholism.

Devon never returned to school and joined Ian in the Navy in some sort of subconscious effort to take over John's career plans. Although Ian hadn't agreed with the reasoning behind Devon's enlistment, in the end, it'd turned out to be the best thing for him.

Escorting Angie up the carpeted outdoor steps and into the museum, Ian couldn't help the mixture of pride and jealousy striking him when he noticed other men and some women admiring and lusting after her. He held on to her hand a little tighter, unwilling to allow one of the sharks to move in and steal her away from him. Looking down at the beautiful woman next to him, he knew he hadn't exaggerated earlier—she was stunning. The black and gold dress fit her like a glove. When she'd turned around earlier to let him put her wrap over her shoulders, he'd taken one look at her toned, bare back and shoulders and had felt his cock jerk with desire. With the open back of the dress, it was obvious she wasn't wearing a bra. He'd been seconds away from canceling their plans and dragging her into her bedroom, when she'd turned back around to look at him again. Somehow, he found the strength to give her his arm instead of falling victim to his lust.

His thoughts ventured back to the night before when he'd walked her to her door. With Angie's wide-eyed and O-shaped mouth expression, he'd known she hadn't meant to voice her question about him kissing her aloud, but he was glad she did. When it came to women, Ian didn't like having to guess what they were thinking, feeling or wanting. His former fiancée, Kaliope Levine, walked out on him ten years ago after telling him she was tired of him not being romantic, able to read her moods and anticipate what she wanted, among other things. Now he wanted everything spelled out between him and any woman he dated. He was never letting another woman get that close to him again, but while he was dating someone, he wanted no misunderstandings between them. He wasn't a mind-reader. It was one of the reasons he loved the lifestyle he was in. Openness and honesty were a big part of it and it suited him just fine.

After Ian took Angie's wrap and gave it to the coat check, he added the claim stub to the valet one inside his coat pocket. He placed a possessive hand on the skin of her lower back above the edge of her dress and steered her in the right direction. He let the warmth of his hand sink into her body and was thrilled to feel a shiver go through her. As he led her toward the wing where the exhibit and gala were taking place, he stopped at a tuxedoed waiter holding a tray of champagne. Taking one glass, he handed it to Angie before acquiring one for himself, never removing his other hand from her back. They began walking again and as they approached the entrance to the north wing, he heard a male voice call his name. Scanning the people around him, he spotted Will striding toward them. The man extended his hand, forcing Ian to remove the one on Angie's back before returning it to its original spot after greeting his friend. Will looked curiously at Angie, and Ian introduced them. "Will, this is my date and Egghead's new neighbor, Angelina Beckett. Angie, this is Will Anders."

The two shook hands as Will gave Angie a quick head to toe inspection. "I always knew you had good taste, Boss-man. Angie, it's a pleasure to meet you, love. Too bad I don't swing your way, because you are absolutely gorgeous. I do have some lez friends who would be interested though. Just say the word."

If Ian didn't know Will was gay and joking with her, he might have ripped the guy's throat out. As it was, he was leaning toward removing the man's tongue from his mouth. Angie grinned at Will, obviously charmed and not at all embarrassed by what the man had implied. "It's nice to meet you too, and thanks for the offer, but dating women isn't my thing." She changed the subject with ease. "Ian tells me you're the assistant curator here. I envy you."

"Angie's an artist," Ian explained. "Although, I haven't seen her work yet, except for a digital piece, I'm hoping she'll show it to me someday."

He watched the other man's face light up even more. "Really, love? What's your medium?"

"Mostly oils and graphite," Angie replied, "but I fool around with clay and watercolors sometimes. I've sold a few paintings over the years, through venues which feature amateur artists like me, but if it wasn't for my graphic design business, I would definitely be a starving artist."

A man with a rosebud pinned to the lapel of his black tuxedo rushed up and informed Will he was needed at the front door. Before he hurried away, Will said, "I would love to see your work, and if you ever want a personal tour of the museum, let me know. Ian—my cousin, Dev, Roxy, and Kayla are waiting for you near the bar to your left when you walk into the great room. They didn't want to start looking around without you. I'll see you both in a bit. Ciao."

While the assistant curator took off in one direction, Ian guided Angie toward the main room of the exhibit and spotted the foursome right away. Since he wasn't sure if she remembered his brother's name, he introduced her again to Devon, and then to his fiancée, Kristen, followed by Dr. Roxanne and Kayla London who were good friends of Kristen and Will's. They were also new members of The Covenant which, of course, he didn't add. The three women looked radiant in their evening wear and his brother had donned his Hugo Boss tuxedo for the occasion. Kristen was wearing a blue dress with a high waist and her brunette hair was up, similar to Angie's. Her jewelry included the matching blue sapphire and diamond submissive collar and engagement ring which Dev had a jeweler design for her. Roxy's thick auburn hair was down past her shoulders in soft waves and she had forgone her usual Domme black for a beautiful red evening gown. It had more than one man in the room lusting for the sexy siren, but Roxy only had eyes for her submissive and wife. A blue-eyed blonde, Kayla was the complete opposite of her spouse, with her shorter hourglass frame decked out in a dark gray gown with cap sleeves.

After everyone greeted them, Angie's eyebrows furrowed in thought. "Kristen Anders. Why do I know that name?"

Before the woman could say anything, Kayla piped up first. "Kristen doesn't like to brag, so I'll do it for her. She's a popular author of romance novels. Maybe you've read one of them."

Ian wasn't prepared for the response the statement got from Angie. She gasped, her eyes going wide in surprise. "Oh my gosh!"

Kayla grinned and elbowed Kristen's arm. "See, I keep telling you you're famous."

"No, yes, no, I mean, yes," Angie stuttered before laughing and holding her hand in the air like a crossing guard stopping traffic. She took a deep breath before attempting to speak again. "Okay, let me start all over. I swear, I'm not normally a blithering idiot, and I do have social skills." The others chuckled with amused expressions. "Yes, I've read all your books, but it's not why I recognize your name. I just got a contract yesterday from Red Rose Books to design the cover of your new one."

It was Kristen's turn to be flabbergasted. "Oh my God! What're the odds of that happening? My editor told me they were giving *Leather and Lace* to someone new because the woman in Seattle, who did *Satin and Sin*, was taking a hiatus due to health problems. This is so cool. Talk about a small world."

"I'm so excited to design it now. We'll have to chat later so I can get your input before I start playing around with ideas." Ian could only imagine what Angie would come up with after seeing the other book cover she'd done.

"Great! I haven't had much input in my covers since I signed on with Red Rose. Now they narrow it down to three similar covers and my editor and I chose one."

As the two women continued to talk about the publishing business with Roxy and Kayla giving their occasional input, Ian and Devon both took a half step to the side and looked at each other while rolling their eyes. As much as they were proud of Kristen's success and popularity, chic-lit was not their thing. What Ian had latched onto, though, was when Angie said she'd read all Kristen's books. He assumed they included the last one, *Satin and Sin*, a book which had surprised Devon when the couple first met, since it was a best-selling erotica romance involving a BDSM club. The follow up, *Leather and Lace*, which the women were now discussing, was a story about one of the previous book's sub-characters, Master Xavier. Ian glanced at Angie with his brain spinning. It was the second time she'd admitted she read erotica and the thoughts currently flying through his mind might shock her. But then again, maybe not.

---

THEY SPENT an hour or so roaming through the crowded north wing of the museum, looking at the exhibits and talking about a gamut of subjects, including art, literature and local news. Angie found herself growing more comfortable with Ian and his family and friends as the evening progressed. Will had popped over to visit a few times before rushing off to avert another crisis or two, and numerous people greeted the group while further introductions were made. She found it interesting how every time Ian introduced her to one of the many women drooling over him, he barely glanced at them before his gaze returned to her. And when it was a man who was being introduced, Ian would tuck her closer into his side in what appeared to be a possessive gesture. She liked his responses and hoped she wasn't misreading them and his interest in her. She also liked how his hand was in contact with a part of her body—her back, neck, hand or arm—as much as possible. The rough callouses on his palm and fingers felt seductive against her soft skin. As they walked from painting to painting, she found he understood art more than he admitted to her, and probably to himself. He listened to her, not with half an ear as some of her past boyfriends or dates had, and held his own as they discussed what they did or did not like about each piece.

When a new round of champagne flutes, along with a tonic water and lime for Devon, arrived for them via another sharp-dressed waiter, Angie looked about and spotted a ladies' room a short distance away. She excused herself to the group and Kristen chimed in she wanted to go with her.

Devon groaned. "What is with women that they must go to the restrooms together?"

Everyone laughed when his fiancée deadpanned, "It's in the women's rule book of socialization, sweetheart. Why don't you look it up some time?"

Growling softly, he grabbed Kristen around the waist and whispered something into her ear which made her blush and bite her bottom lip. Angie could have sworn she heard the woman mumble, "yes, Sir," before joining her on the walk across the room, while the other four members of their group stayed and chuckled behind them.

The elegant ladies' room was almost empty and after quick stops at the toilets followed by the sinks, Kristen met Angie at the mirrored vanity located near a sitting area. After two other women exited the facilities, they found themselves alone. Angie finished reapplying her lipstick and looked at the other woman's dress and shoes. She'd been admiring the blue, empire waist creation and silver Manolo Blahnik heels all evening and told her so.

Kristen grinned with freshly painted lips. "Thanks. I had the shoes, but Will and Kayla took me shopping the other day for the dress. I'm fine when it comes to picking out every day clothes but I get flustered if I have to play dress-up. I can never tell if I look drab, slutty, or sexy."

"My vote is drab and slutty, you bitch."

Angie gasped at the sudden insult as Kristen whirled around with rage in her eyes and faced the woman who'd said it. Neither one of them had noticed her come in. Crossing her arms over her chest, Angie's new friend stood taller as she stared at the skinny redhead in a white strapless gown. "Seriously, Heather? Who let your skanky ass in here? You wouldn't know art if it slapped you. Oh, wait a minute, it looks like you already took an oil painting to the face or is that your makeup? I can't quite tell."

If Angie hadn't been so shocked she would've laughed at Kristen's retort because it was a good one considering the building they were in.

"Honestly, you cow, I have no idea what Master Devon sees in your fat ass." The redhead's hatred-filled gaze zeroed in on Angie next. "And let me guess, you're Master Ian's new fuck. Don't get too comfortable, whore, everyone knows he goes through subs like a pig goes through slop."

*What? Wait a minute . . . Master Ian? New fuck? Whore? Subs? Pig?* Shock and pure anger at this stranger who came in hurling insults at them took over Angie's mind and body. She stepped forward to confront the nasty woman when a hand on her forearm stopped her. Looking at Kristen, she was surprised to see a satisfied smirk on her face. But Kristen wasn't staring at Heather. Her eyes were focused on the person who'd come through the door and was now standing behind the bitch . . . Roxanne London, and *holy crap*! The good doctor looked furious and intimidating.

Heather must have realized there was someone behind her because she glanced back over her shoulder, and Angie was amazed to see the redhead's face lose all color . . . at least what wasn't painted on. Roxy's pleasant demeanor from before had disappeared, and in its place was an angry, commanding, take-no-prisoners attitude. "Apparently, you don't learn, Heather. You know better than to blurt out private business in a public venue. You also know I told you last time you started harassing Kristen that I wouldn't stand for it. And now you've insulted another friend of mine who, I assume, has no idea who you are and doesn't deserve your malice. I suggest you run out and explain yourself to Scott because I'll be a minute behind you, and he and I are going to have a serious talk about your continued behavior. Now as much as I would love to see how Kristen put you flat on your face in an arm-hold the first time you two met, this is neither the time nor the place."

She stepped to the side and gave Heather a path to the restroom door. "Out. Now."

As the redhead rushed out the door, they heard her mumble under her breath, but the words were unintelligible. After the door closed behind the awful woman, the three new friends looked at each other and burst out laughing. When they finally got themselves under control, Angie opened up her mouth to ask one of the many questions on the tip of her tongue. Before she could say anything though, Roxy held up her hand and looked behind them to where the toilets and sinks were.

Kristen caught the other woman's concern and told her they were alone in the facilities. Roxy gestured to the sitting area before taking a seat on the small couch and crossing her long legs, leaving the two low-backed upholstered chairs for the other women. "In case you're wondering, I saw Heather walk in here and knew she was going to be her usual rude self, so I came in as backup. Although I'm sure you all would've had things under control."

After they joined her around a small cocktail table, Roxy looked at Angie with a mix of sympathy, concern and understanding. "I can tell you're shocked and confused by the look on your face. I'm sure this isn't the way Ian wanted you to hear he was a Dominant, and I really think you should take most of your questions to him. Seeing the way he looks at you, I think his interest in you is obvious. I don't know where you two are in your relationship and it's none of my business about when, and if, he was planning on asking you to go down that road with him. He's a good man who, in the short time I've gotten to know him, I've come to respect one hundred and ten percent, and he would never force his lifestyle on anyone. That being said, if you want to take a moment and let the shock wear off and ask us a question or two, we'll answer them the best we can."

Angie turned toward Kristen, who nodded her agreement, then took a deep breath and said the first thing which came to mind. "Holy shit, who was that crazy bitch?" When the other two women laughed and relaxed, she continued. "Okay, that wasn't a serious question—actually it is, but we'll get back to it later. So, are you all into . . . it . . . I mean the BDSM lifestyle too?"

Kristen nodded again. "Yup. I'm a newbie of only six or seven months now. I met Devon at his friend's pub and ended up asking him out on a date, not knowing he was a Dom." She let out an unladylike snort. "Hell, I didn't even know I was a sub. Anyway, if you read *Satin and Sin*, you know it involves BDSM, and when I went to the club Devon and Ian own, with their cousin, Mitch, for research . . . oops."

Angie was sure her eyes were wider than Kristen's. "Th-they own a sex club?"

Roxy leaned forward and took command of the conversation again. "Yes, and despite what some people . . . what most people might think, it's a very private, very elite club. It's where like-minded people who enjoy a range of kink in their lives can practice safe, sane and consensual activities which may or may not include sex. Kayla and I joined The Covenant after a long application process where our lives were examined with a fine-tooth comb. This is not a place where anyone off the street can walk in and start flogging someone. And unlike Heather, most people in the lifestyle don't announce their participation, or anyone else's for that matter, when out in public. There's several other people in attendance here tonight who I know from the clubs, but they either pretend they know me from somewhere else or not at all. I've been a Domme since college and Kayla became my submissive, and then my wife, when we met a few months after I finished med school. I was the one who recognized she was a submissive and introduced her to the lifestyle I'd come to enjoy."

Trying to take everything they said in, Angie took another deep breath. "Okay, I'm not completely naïve. I've read lots of fictional books on the subject and I've even browsed the internet when my curiosity was piqued a few times while reading those books. And I'll admit, if I'm being honest, some things did turn me on. But I never knew anyone in the lifestyle, so I just shoved the thoughts and questions I had to the back of my brain and left them there. I figured there weren't real places like that and everything I heard or read was part of a fantasy world."

The restroom door opened up, startling them, and four chatty women walked in and headed toward the toilet stalls. Roxy stood, placed her hand on Angie's shoulder and lowered her voice so she wouldn't be overheard. "You need to talk to Ian. Like I said, he's a good man. If you are interested in exploring, he's one of the men I would recommend you do it with. If not, he'll understand and no harm done."

"I agree," Kristen concurred, while nodding her head. "He's one of the nicest guys I know, and I'm not saying that because he's going to be my brother-in-law. Oh, and by the way, what Heather said about Ian being a pig . . . nothing I've seen or heard has ever given me the impression he's a total man-whore." She giggled. "I'm not saying he's a saint, but what man is?"

Angie grinned at Kristen and then at Roxy, feeling a little bit more at ease. "Okay, I'll talk to him, but not here."

"Good." The doctor took a few steps toward the door and glanced back over her shoulder. "Can you tell my beautiful wife I'll be back in a few minutes? I need to have a conversation with a colleague of mine."

As the other woman stormed out the door on a mission, Angie looked at Kristen to clarify the statement. "Heather's Mast . . . um, boyfriend . . . is a doctor on staff at the same hospital Roxy is. Look, I know this is a shock—it was for me too. But I've never regretted any part of my relationship with Devon. In fact, I can't imagine how I ever lived without the . . . um . . . things he does to me and with me. My ex-husband had me convinced I was a cold fish in bed. Turns out, he was the problem because my sex life now is incredibly hot, and I wouldn't trade Devon for any other man in the world. He cherishes me like I'm the most important person in the universe."

She leaned forward and dropped her voice into a dramatic whisper. "And showed me what it was like to have multiple orgasms." Kristen laughed at Angie's astonished expression and twined their arms together, tugging her new friend in the direction of the door. "Now, let's get back to our handsome dates before they send out a search party."

## CHAPTER 5

*I*an got an uneasy feeling in his gut when he saw Angie and Kristen walk back toward Devon, Kayla and him. There must've been the usual long line in ladies' room because they were gone an awful long time. Although they were chatting with each other as they approached, there was a pensive air about them. "Everything okay?"

As Angie stopped by his side, Kristen sidled up to Devon and put her arm around his waist. He watched both women glance at each other before Angie seemed to find something interesting to stare at on the floor, and his concern grew. What his brother's fiancée said next made his stomach drop and he felt the blood drain from his face. "We . . . um . . . had a run-in with Heather in the ladies' room, and I'm sorry Ian, but she sort of ran her mouth off and said some things she shouldn't have about you and the club." Her eyes flashed to Angie, who was now blushing, and back to him with an optimistic expression on her face. "I think it's okay though, but you two need to talk about a few things."

*Shit!* Ian dragged his hand down his face in anger and frustration. Damn, Heather was a spiteful bitch. This was not the way he wanted this to happen. He'd planned on talking his way into Angie's place tonight for a nightcap. After telling her being a Dominant was a major part of his life, he'd pray she was still interested in him and didn't kick him to the curb. Although his ears were buzzing, he heard Kristen report how Mistress Roxanne made a brief appearance and handled things.

Upon hearing that, Kayla responded with a pout. "Damn. I hate when she goes into her Wonder Woman persona and I'm not there to see it. She knows how much it turns me on."

Ian ignored the women's giggles and took hold of Angie's elbow, leading her toward an unoccupied corner of the great room, behind a sculpture worth about seventy-five thousand dollars. When he was certain they were out of earshot, he looked at her with a pang of regret. "I'm sorry, Angel. It's not how I wanted you to learn about me and my lifestyle. I was waiting for the right opportunity to tell you."

"So, you *were* going to tell me?"

Okay, she wasn't running for the hills yet. Her face seemed to be filled with curiosity and something else he couldn't quite put his finger on. It didn't mean he was in the clear, but it did give him hope. "Yes, of course. I'm . . . it's a part of me I can't ignore or change. I'm not ashamed of who I am. I was going to tell you later tonight when we were alone, but now that it's out, I'll understand if you want me to take you home." And he would. It would kill him, but if she wanted nothing to do with him after this, he'd walk away and try to scrub the memory of their kiss from his brain.

She seemed to think things over for a moment before responding, "If you want to leave now, it's fine with me. But I'm having a good time, so I'd prefer to stay a little while longer and finish looking at the exhibit. That is, if you don't mind. It'll give me time to recover from my initial shock and think for a bit. This way, when we talk later, I'll be better prepared to ask you some questions, and boy, do I have questions." He chuckled at her wry grin. "I'll admit, Ian, I'm curious, but this came from left field and it's something I've only read about before. That doesn't mean I'm willing to jump into things completely blindfolded . . . *er*, so to speak . . . but I am willing to talk later if you want."

Ian's heart soared and his cock twitched in his pants. He still had a shot with her, and from what she said, it might not even be a long shot. He stroked his fingers along her jawline, pleased when a flash of desire appeared in her eyes. "I'd like that very much, Angel."

"Just tell me one thing."

He took a deep breath. "Anything."

"Please tell me that nasty bitch, Heather, and you never . . ." She wasn't sure what words she wanted to use so she left the sentence hanging there, hoping he would fill in the blanks.

"Oh, hell no!" Ian barked. "Please give me some credit. She was a member of the club with her Master a while back, but had a bad habit of harassing other submissives, and her membership was revoked as a result. She's obviously still holding a grudge. You'll have to ask Kristen about the night she got the name Ninja-girl. My future sister-in-law knows how to kick some bitchy ass."

Leading her back toward their little group, Ian was thrilled to know he still had a chance with his beautiful angel.

---

ANGIE PACED BACK and forth across her living room trying to gather her thoughts and Ian wasn't making it any easier for her. During the rest of the evening, he'd relaxed back into the person he'd been before Kristen told him what happened in the restroom. Now, he was sitting on her couch having shed his tuxedo jacket and tie. One ankle was propped up against the opposite knee and one arm was on the armrest of couch while the other was lying across the back of it. He was patient as he observed her walk, pivot, walk, and pivot again, without interrupting her. She didn't know what to say. She had so many thoughts running through her head it was a jumbled mess. Before they left the museum, Kayla, Roxy, and Kristen had all given her their cell numbers in case she had any questions Ian didn't answer or she was too embarrassed to ask him.

Angie wasn't ashamed to admit she was one of those women who loved sex. Most of her past boyfriends, and a few temporary hook-ups which she would qualify as being somewhere between one-night-stands and actual relationships, had been enjoyable in bed. Sex had rarely been the reason for breaking up with those men. In fact, a few of them had taken control in the bedroom—not to the point of what the BDSM stories she read described, but enough she was aroused even more than usual. Her problem with those men had been outside the bedroom. Some became boring to her after a while, and others had only been interested in the sex and their dates revolved around it. The longest relationship she ever had was a little over six months and it should have been over way before then, but the guy had been sweet and kept saying he loved her. And although she liked him, she hadn't wanted to hurt him because she didn't feel the same way as he did. But in the end she had to. Her main problem was she couldn't find a man who could hold her interest in and out of the bedroom, and she refused to settle.

Coming to an abrupt halt in front of Ian, she tossed her arms out to the side in exasperation. "Okay, I'll admit I have no idea how to start this conversation, so can you do it, please?"

Smiling a devastatingly sexy smile, he held out his hand to her. "That's what the Dom in me was waiting for. Come here, Angel, and sit next to me."

She hesitated only a brief moment before placing her hand in his and taking a seat. He didn't release her hand, and she found it comforting despite her unexpected nervousness. "Easy, sweetheart, you're shaking." She didn't realize she was until he said it. "I'm not going to throw you down and ravage you like some pirate sailing the seven seas . . . well, unless you ask me to." She giggled and relaxed a little. "How about I tell you about how I started in the lifestyle, why I like it, and stuff like that, *hmmm*?" She nodded, and he kissed her knuckles before resting both their hands on his thigh. "Okay. I was introduced to BDSM when I was twenty-two, almost twenty-three, by one of my chiefs in the Navy. He told me he watched me one night when a bunch of us were out at this bar with some Navy groupies. Said he saw something in me which made him believe I would be interested in the lifestyle. Apparently, I acted like a Dom before I even knew what one was.

"So, one night, he and two other guys we knew took me to my first club and, shit . . . talk about a culture shock. Here I was, not a clue what I was doing there, and all these men and women from ages twenty to seventy were walking around in everything from normal clothing to leather, lingerie, or their birthday suits. Sounds of spankings, whippings, moaning and groaning, sex and intense orgasms were coming from different scenes, and I didn't know where to look first. Hell, I was embarrassed and intrigued at the same time.

"I didn't play my first night or during my next few visits either. Instead, I just walked around and observed. I talked to everyone who was willing to talk to me and explain what they got out of their individual kinks and what made them a Dom or a submissive. It didn't take long for me to learn a submissive has all the control in every D/s relationship."

Angie's eyes narrowed in confusion. "How's that possible? Don't they have to follow their Dom's orders?"

"Every true D/s relationship—and I'm not talking about people who claim to be in the lifestyle to justify hurting someone, like a domestic abuser, or people who dabble in a little slap and tickle in the bedroom. I'm talking about a true power-exchange relationship between a Dominant and submissive. In every relationship or one-time encounter, it's the submissive who willingly allows his or her Dom to give them what they want and need. Submissives maintain all the control of a scene from their negotiations with a Dom, to their hard and soft limits, and their safewords. They can end a scene anytime they want if something doesn't feel right to them. In my club, we use the universal color system so there's no confusion over a sub's safeword. Green is good, yellow is to slow down or clarify something, and red means stop. And I mean everything stops, and the scene is over. The Dom immediately starts aftercare, if needed, and they talk about what went wrong, why the sub felt it necessary to stop, and how to avoid the situation in the future."

Ian paused, and she took a moment to take all it in. She heard his breath catch when she stood, so she smiled to reassure him. Taking off her shoes, she went into the kitchen and retrieved two bottles of water from her refrigerator, then handed him one. They both opened their bottles and took a drink. She could feel the wheels spinning inside her head. "Okay, I think I understand what you're saying. Like I told you, I've read books based on BDSM before so it's not a completely foreign concept. But it's hard taking what I thought was a fantasy world and bringing it into the real world." When she sat back down next to him, he took her hand again and placed it back on his thigh with his own, as if needing the direct contact with her. "You said you'd tell me what you get out of being a Dom."

"My submissive's pleasure and trust, pure and simple." It wasn't the answer she expected, but then she didn't know what she expected. "Nothing gives me greater pleasure than knowing I've given her everything she needs to achieve her own pleasure and/or emotional release, and she trusted me to give it to her."

"Emotional release?"

Leaning forward, he placed his water bottle on a coaster sitting on her cocktail table and sat back again. "*Mm-hm*. BDSM is not all about sex—far from it. Although that's usually an enjoyable end result of everything else. It's about getting one's individual needs met and sometimes it means pain is involved, whether the final result is pleasure or something else. Let me give you an example. There was this female submissive I met when I first started apprenticing under a few skilled Doms. And before you ask, no, I never played with her since I was far too inexperienced for what she needed. Ava was a very nice, but reserved woman, around thirty-five years old at the time, and her kink was to be whipped until she finally broke down crying. But there was never any sex involved with her scenes. One night, I got the courage to approach her, and I explained my confusion about the fact she wasn't getting pleasure from her scenes. She told me she was very young when her mother married her step-father, a verbally cruel man. Little things always seemed to set the guy off, and if Ava cried, he'd get angrier. He'd start throwing things and breaking her toys or throwing her clothes and possessions out. So, to save the things she loved, this little six-year-old girl managed to shove her emotions so far back into herself to the point she couldn't cry for any reason."

Angie gasped. "How awful. The poor girl."

"Exactly. That little girl who stopped crying turned in to an adult woman who couldn't cry unless a Dom broke through her subconscious barriers to the point she could find her emotional release and let her tears fall. That's why she was in the lifestyle. It was a cleansing therapy of sorts for her." He paused. "I've seem to have gotten sidetracked because I'm supposed to be telling you why I'm in the lifestyle."

"My fault, sorry."

Ian brought her hand to his mouth for a quick kiss. "Don't apologize for asking questions, Angel. It's what tonight is all about. Anyway, I prefer to be in charge in the bedroom and sometimes out of it too. When I scene or play with a sub, I like pushing her limits, teaching her things which can make her pleasure and inner-self better than they were before. I like being responsible for my sub's pleasure and emotional or physical health and giving her what she needs, which may not always coincide with what she wants. A sub's safety and well-being are important to me. As the Dom-in-Residence, or head Dominant at the club, all the subs' safety and well-being ultimately fall under my protection. I know every sub and slave's name at The Covenant, and I'm aware of their hard limits and what they're looking to get out of the lifestyle. If I see a sub not getting what they need or pushing themselves to where it could be detrimental to their physical or psychological well-being, then I step in and do what I can to get them back on track. We have several doctors and psychologists as members who are willing to talk to any other member, whether it's a sub or a Dom, who could benefit from their expertise. Doms aren't perfect, and anyone who claims to be is a fool. We make mistakes and learn from them and grow right along with our subs."

At some point, Ian's thumb had begun rubbing over the back of her hand and the sensations it was evoking had a direct connection to Angie's clit. She was finding it difficult to think, but one thing he said did confuse her. "You said sub or slave. Aren't they the same thing?"

He shook his head. "No, not at all. A slave tends to be in a 24/7 relationship with their Master, giving entire control of their lives over to them. From what they wear and eat, to what they do each day, and of course the sexual aspect of it. It's not for everybody, it isn't for me, and can be quite an undertaking for some Doms. It's a lot of responsibility for them and after a while, some find it's not what they really want. A Dom/submissive relationship is not as extreme and usually consists of control of a sub's safety and pleasure, although every relationship is unique."

"Wow. This is a lot more involved than I realized. I thought it was just about tying a woman up and spanking her."

When she paused, he let the silence drag on for a few minutes while she digested all he'd told her, her teeth nibbling on her bottom lip. When he brought his thumb up to rescue her tender flesh, she was tempted to nibble on that instead. "I take it some parts of all this interest you since I'm still sitting here and you haven't tossed me out on my ass yet."

Angie smiled nervously. "Yes, I'll admit, I'm intrigued, but I'm also a little scared."

"I'd be worried if you weren't. This is something new and out of your comfort zone. But, if you're willing to test your limits . . . I'd be more than happy to help you explore. If you want, we can sign an open-ended contract which outlines our D/s relationship and lists what parts of the lifestyle you're interested in, or not, and what I expect from you."

Her smile turned into a small frown. That sounded so formal and business-like. "A contract?"

"It's not as cold as it sounds, sweetheart. More often than not, Doms and submissives sign an agreement which defines their relationship so there's no confusion or false expectations. There are general contracts we have available at the club, but each Dom and sub can change it to suit their needs. The negotiations they do prior to signing a contract forces them to talk about everything so there is no guessing between them. Think back on some of your past relationships. Were there times you wondered what your boyfriend was thinking about, or you wanted something you weren't getting from him, but weren't sure how to bring up the subject?"

She nodded, understanding how much communication there was between a Dom and sub. "Yes, there were. Sometimes I'd go nuts trying to get one of them to tell me what was on their mind."

"Exactly." Ian smiled. "See you're learning already. Is a D/s relationship something you want to try, Angel? With me?"

Her gaze met his for the first time since she sat back down and when she swallowed hard, his eyes fell to the movement in her throat. The pulse in her neck picked up speed, as well as her breathing, and it seemed that was all the encouragement he needed. His other hand, which had been resting on the back of the couch, wrapped around the nape of her neck before he closed the gap between them. Pausing with their lips not quite touching, he waited. When her breath hitched, he brought his mouth down on hers. A heartbeat or two later, her lips parted, and he changed the angle of his mouth so he could plunge his tongue inside her depths.

*Heaven.* Like the night before, his mouth was pure heaven with a bit of hell mixed in. Just enough to make her want to let him take her over to the dark side of sex. His hand skimmed down her bare back, stopping at her waist before working its way back up again. Her shivers made her nipples harder than they already were, and he pulled her into his lap, never letting her mouth go. They stayed that way for a few minutes, devouring each other. Her hands moved up around his neck, and she shoved her fingers into the hair at the back of his head. When he pulled away and looked at her with lust-filled eyes, she knew her green ones revealed her own desire. They were both panting, and as much as she wanted him to take possession of her mouth again, he apparently had other things he wanted to do to her. "Let me give you a little taste of my world tonight, Angel. No pain, just pleasure. And no intercourse. I want to make you come for me. I want you to shatter under my touch. Will you let me please you?"

His whiskey-smooth tone of voice had moisture pooling between her legs, and she didn't hesitate to answer him. "Oh, God, Ian. Yes, please."

Cupping her chin, he waited until he had her complete attention. "Say it, Angel. I want to hear you say it. I need to know you understand what you're agreeing to. And if we are going to play, I want you to call me 'Sir.'"

Angie hesitated this time. Was this really what she wanted? Her mind and body were screaming at her to tell him anything which would make him kiss her, touch her, and do anything he wanted to her.

"It's one thing to say 'yes' to me, but I need for you to say the words yourself. I won't go any further until you tell me exactly what you want. I need to know we're on the same page here."

This was a big step she was taking, but she knew if she didn't take it, she would regret it for a very long time. "Yes, Sir. Please make me come. Please give me a taste, and show me what it's like to be your submissive.

He ran his thumb along her jawline, leaving a tingling in its wake. "It will be my pleasure, Angel, and all yours, too. Now, I want you to go into your bedroom, undress completely, and lie down naked in the middle of your bed on your back. You have three minutes to do that for me before I follow you." When she hesitated again, he lowered his voice and added, "The clock is ticking, sweetheart."

She jumped off his lap and hurried to her bedroom before she could change her mind. Fumbling with the catch which was holding her dress in place at the back of her neck, she was ready to rip it apart before it suddenly released under her trembling hands. Letting the entire garment fall from her body to the floor, she kicked it out of the way and added her thong and stockings to the pile. She climbed atop her queen-size bed and situated herself as he'd ordered, propping her head on her pillow. And then she waited.

---

ATHOS PACED BACK and forth in the one-room studio apartment he'd rented in New Orleans. He took another gulp of water from a bottle and willed the last of the cocaine out of his system. Why anyone would freely put this junk in their body was still beyond him. The only reason it was pumping through his veins and cells at the moment was because his other choice was a bullet in his brain. If it wasn't for Angie, he would've preferred the bullet.

He'd gotten lucky and ran into a guy who knew him back in the day when he was U/C in the southwest. After spending the night pretending to get drunk with the asshole, he had his in to the underground drug business of the city. After a few minor-league, illegal activities he got the chance to meet Manny Melendez, one of the local cartel leaders, and the guy probably responsible for the deaths of Aaron and his family.

It was obvious the scumbag was nervous about anyone new walking into his operation. But between some recent arrests and gang-related deaths of his minions, he was in need of new hands willing to get a little dirty. So, Athos had a choice at their meeting—powdered crap or a hollow-nosed bullet up his nose.

After Melendez was satisfied with his recruit, the two of them and five other pieces of shit went to release a little of their temporary superman energy brought on by the drugs. Melendez wanted to send a message to an up-and-coming gang and took it out on a few wanna-be bangers they'd found a few blocks into Melendez's territory. If Athos had to beat the crap out of someone to maintain his cover, at least the mouthy little punks deserved it.

Now, as he was coming down off his high, the few cuts and bruises he'd received in the brawl were making themselves known. But with the coke in his system, he didn't want to add anything else, whether it be OTC drugs or alcohol. He flopped down on the bed and fumbled with the TV remote until he found a ballgame to watch. Who was playing, he didn't know or care, as long as there was a familiar noise in the background.

He closed his eyes and thought of Angie. He knew it was the right thing to have someone watching her, and Carter swore the men at Trident were the best. He wasn't thrilled with their extra-curricular activities in the club the Sawyer brothers owned, but as long as she didn't need to go there for any reason, it wouldn't be a problem.

Toeing off his boots, he let his mind wander and exhaustion began to pull him under a veil of sleep. Maybe it was time to break away from the DEA. He'd put hundreds of dealers in jail or six-feet under over the years. Maybe it was time for him to find a life outside his quest for vengeance. He could move to Tampa to be near Angie. Maybe get a job with Trident. *Maybe. Maybe. Maybe.*

# CHAPTER 6

*I*an counted off the one-hundred and eighty seconds in his head. In the meantime, he removed the diamond cuff links from his wrists, placed them in his jacket pocket, and rolled up his sleeves to his elbows. He took another drink from his bottled water then put it back on its coaster. His erection was aching in his pants, and he tried to ignore it. He would take care of it later on his own. When he told her there would be no intercourse tonight, he'd meant it. Tonight wasn't about his own release. It was about introducing his angel to the power exchange between a Dom and a submissive.

*One-seventy-eight. One-seventy-nine. One-eighty. Ready or not, Angel, here I come.*

She had left the bedroom door ajar, so it only took a slight nudge to open it all the way. His breath caught and the aching in his groin increased ten-fold. He hadn't thought she could look more beautiful than when she'd answered his knock at her front door earlier in the evening. He was wrong.

Striding to the end of her bed, he took in the sensual sight before him. Her hair was still up in its bun, or whatever the hell women called it, and her head and upper shoulders rested against two plush pillows. Ivory-colored skin covered every inch of her, and she had no tan lines, which didn't surprise him since it'd been a colder-than-usual February and March. He wondered if she would wear a one-piece or bikini bathing suit when the warmer weather returned and couldn't wait to find out. Most Doms preferred their subs to be naked under their clothing, but not Ian. He liked a woman in sexy clothing and even sexier underwear. He had a fetish for lacy bras, panties, and lingerie, finding women tended to feel more beautiful when wearing them—and naughtier.

Her modesty had kicked in at some point while she was waiting for him. Her hands each covered a large breast and one knee was bent, leaning over the opposite thigh so her pussy was hidden from his view. The uncertain pose turned him on more than if she was completely exposed to him, but he was dying to see all of her. Glancing above her head, he was happy to see the headboard was wrought iron with intricate scroll work and gaps large enough for her hands to go through. It would give her something to hold on to. His gaze ran from her head to her toes and back up to her anxious, but heated eyes. From the light coming in through the open doorway, he watched her pupils dilate with desire. Her tongue sneaked out of her mouth, wetting her lips, now devoid of lipstick, and he groaned. His little angel was going to be the death of him before the night was over.

"You're the most beautiful woman I've ever seen." He loved how her blush deepened with his words. "But I'm going to show you how to feel that beauty. If at any time you get scared or unsure I want you to say the word 'yellow.' If you absolutely can't take something, say the word 'red'. But be warned, sweetheart—if you say the word red, everything stops for the night. We'll discuss your fears, then I'll go home, and we'll try something else next time. Understand?"

She silently nodded her head, and he frowned at her. Realizing her mistake, she corrected it. "Yes, I understand. 'Yellow' for scared, 'red' for stop everything."

"Good girl. When we are playing, you are to refer to me as 'Sir.' Now, we're not at the trust level where I could restrain you so I'm going to have you restrain yourself. Move slowly and bring your hands above your head. Grab hold of the headboard and make sure you're comfortable because you're going to keep them there for me." He held his breath as her hands left her luscious breasts and inched upward, skimming over her collarbones and shoulders, past her head before they grasped two thin pieces of iron. He'd been right about her nipples—they were pink and aroused and made his mouth water.

Walking around to the side of the bed, he toed off his dress shoes before sitting down on the mattress next to her in the area between her chest and hips. He placed one hand on the comforter on the opposite side of her, using it to support some of his weight, and studied her from the breasts up, touching her only with his gaze. "Tell me, Angel, when you're alone in this big bed, how do you pleasure yourself?"

She stared at him wide-eyed, biting her bottom lip again, but didn't answer. He let the Dom in him take over. He tweaked one of her nipples before releasing it, and she squeaked. "I asked you a question and I expect an answer, or you can expect an appropriate punishment. Now, I'll make it a little easier on you since this is new. Do you use your hand to pluck these gorgeous nipples while your other hand plays with your clit and wet pussy lips? Do you finger fuck yourself to an orgasm or do you use a vibrator or dildo? There's no right or wrong answer here, but I want an honest one. And there better be a 'Sir' in there."

"I . . . I . . ." Angie cleared her suddenly dry throat and tried again. "I do all that, S-Sir. Sometimes together or sometimes without my vibrator and just my hand."

"Where do you keep your toys, sweetheart?"

———

*WHAT?* He wanted to see her vibrators? *Oh crap.* If she told him where they were, he might see the small anal plug she sometimes used when she was feeling especially naughty. Maybe he wouldn't notice it in the darkened room. She closed her eyes, counted to three, and blurted out, "In the bottom drawer of my nightstand next to you, Sir."

She watched as he sat back up and leaned over to open the drawer. He took out her favorite nine-inch, silicon vibrator and held it up for her to see, his eyebrows raised in amusement. "I've never seen a florescent-green one before. Interesting."

He put the vibrator on the bed and leaned toward the drawer again after turning on the bedside lamp so he could see better. *Oh mighty Zeus, please strike me dead with a lightning bolt so I don't have to die of embarrassment.* Next thing she knew he was holding up her pink anal plug and her mind brought up an image of him fucking her ass with it, causing her to groan and clench her thighs together.

"Well, this is an unexpected, but delightful surprise." She looked at him through her lowered lashes and saw a satisfied smirk on his face. "But we'll save this for next time, even though it's on the small side. We'll have to work you up to something larger."

He chuckled as her eyes widened. *Larger?* Why did the thought terrify and excite her all at the same time? After placing the plug back into the drawer, he pulled out her bottle of K-Y lubricant and a small paperback. She groaned again when she saw the book in his hand. Sometimes, when she wanted to arouse herself faster, she'd read a short erotic story out of it and imagine she was the naughty woman getting spanked, eaten, and fucked by the hunky guy. The dirty words turned her on, and it wouldn't take long for her to come.

"*Spank Me.* Catchy title. You know my brother mentioned he sometimes has Kristen read him the sex parts of her books after she writes them. Says it's a real turn on. We'll have to try that another time too, but for now, I have other plans for you."

He tossed the book back into the drawer and closed it again. She noticed her green vibrator and K-Y were still out and wondered what those plans of his were. "Straighten your knee and spread your legs apart, Angel, and keep them that way. If you close them or take your hands off the headboard, I'm going to stop what I'm doing and let your impending orgasm fade away before I start all over. That's called orgasm deprivation, and it's quite frustrating, as you can imagine. Understand?"

She could barely get her breathy response out of her dry mouth. "Yes." Frowning, he raised his eyebrow, and she quickly added, "Sir."

"Good girl." Ian waited until she moved her legs, then nudged the inside of her knees until she spread them even wider. "Just like that. Keep them there."

She was surprised when he dropped the lube and vibrator on the comforter between her legs and left them there before turning back to face her. She was further shocked when he didn't touch her body with his hands. Instead, he leaned forward and brushed his lips across her forehead. "Close your eyes, my sweet angel."

When she did, light kisses peppered her eyelids, nose, cheeks, ears, and jaw. He avoided her mouth and took his time exploring her face before moving downward. Her neck, shoulders ,and collarbones were next and by this point she was breathing heavier. Every kiss seemed to send bolts of electricity through her body to her throbbing core, boosting her arousal further and further. Each time his lips touched her skin she felt the tip of his tongue dart out for a brief taste before moving on to the next spot. Her body was covered in goose-bumps, and she was more turned-on than she'd ever been in her entire life, and he hadn't even gotten to her breasts or pussy yet. Lord help her when he did, because she was sure she'd go off like a ton of fireworks. She was desperate to close her legs so she could try to create a little friction and give herself some relief, but his warning of what would happen if she did blared in her head. There was no way she wanted him to stop and start all over.

---

Ian trailed his mouth further down her delicious body, bypassing her nipples, but giving the upper and lower swells of her breasts little licks and nibbles. He shifted onto his hands and knees and crawled between her legs while he explored her abdomen, still only using his mouth and tongue. As he inhaled deeply, the scent of her body lotion mixed with the aroma of her arousal, and the combination made him light-headed and harder, which he hadn't thought was possible. He felt the shivers which coursed through her body when he kissed and licked the creases of her hips. Again, he bypassed where he knew she wanted him the most, and tasted her from her hip down to her left foot. After nibbling on each individual toe, he licked her arch, making her foot and leg twitch. When she giggled and moaned at the same time, he moved over to her other foot and did the same. He loved how, even though she was ticklish there, she still managed to keep her legs spread wide for him.

She was a natural submissive, eager to please him, and didn't even realize it. On his way back up her right leg, he stared at her pussy, letting it draw him nearer with an invisible string. She was almost bare, but kept a small trim patch of blonde hair on her mound above her clit, proving the hair on her head was its natural color. He liked his women waxed or shaven since it increased their sensitivity and pleasure. As he kissed and suckled on the inside of her knee, he watched as her ass cheeks and vagina clenched at the same time. Her hips levitated off the bed a bit and juices flowed from her folds, soaking her even more. She was drenched for him, and he forced himself not to dive in for a taste. He wanted her to the point she was begging him to feast on her.

Crawling back up her body, he latched onto one nipple, sucking it hard into his mouth before laving it with short swipes of his tongue. He began to alternate between sucking, licking, and grazing his teeth on the hard nub, encouraged by her hedonistic moans and cries, increased breathing, and mumbled words of surrender. When her hips bucked off the bed again, seeking fulfillment in her core, he moved over to her other breast and gave it the same treatment. Her reactions amplified, becoming almost frantic, yet she still held her ordered position. Releasing her breast from his mouth with a pop, he looked up at her face. "Tell me what you want, Angel. What part of your body do you want me to eat next?"

She was rocking her head back and forth, her hips bucking as she pleaded with him. "Please, Sir! Eat my pussy, please! Make me come! I need to come!"

Ian moved back down between her legs, shoved his hands under her ass, and lifted her to his waiting mouth. "Then come for me, sweetheart." He ate her like a man starved—licking and sucking on her labia before spearing his tongue into her slit as deep as it could go. She shattered around him, screaming her release to the heavens above, but he didn't let up, drawing her orgasm out as long as possible.

When she finally started floating back to Earth, he slowed his ministrations while making sure he drank every drop of her sweet cream. She was panting, but somehow managed to get out a few words. "Oh, oh, my God, t-that was incredible. Holy crap!"

Smirking up at her, he stayed right were his was and reached for her vibrator and the bottle of lube. "But I'm not finished yet, my little angel. As a matter of fact, I'm not even halfway done with you yet. You still have a few more orgasms I want to claim as mine tonight."

Lifting her head so she could see him better, she stared as if he were crazy. "Wh-what? You can't be serious. There's no way I can do that again so soon."

With a devilish grin, he snickered. "Oh yes, you can, and you will."

Not waiting for her to respond, since it wasn't going to make a difference unless she said her safeword, Ian flipped the top of the bottle up and poured some lubricant on the index and middle finger of one hand. When he was sure there was enough, he recapped the bottle and tossed it to the side. "Keep your legs spread, but bend your knees up and place your feet flat on the bed." When she did as she was told, the new position allowed him to see the puckered rosette further back from her pussy. He began to rub his lubricated fingers up and down the crevice of her ass in short strokes over her little hole, loving how she moaned as the sensations assailed her. "Relax, sweetheart. This is just like when you use that little plug on yourself." His middle finger circled her rim, then pushed in. It slid in easier than he'd expected, and it pleased him to know her use of the plug made her body willingly accept his invasion. Slowly, he fucked her ass with the one finger, twisting it as he pushed it further and further into the forbidden recess of her body with each pass. As she moaned and begged, her anus and vagina clenched at the same time, and the pressure almost crushed his finger.

He continued finger fucking her hole and picked up her vibrator with his other hand. Flicking the "on" button with his thumb, he grinned when her head flew forward at the sounds coming from her toy. Her eyes grew wide. "Oh, no! Ian, Sir! Please don't!"

Chuckling, he touched the quivering toy to her inner thigh and dragged it upward, drawing out the anticipation. "Six little words, and not one of them was a color."

She didn't use either safeword, and he knew she wasn't going to because she was enjoying this way too much. Her clit had long since uncovered itself from its hood, and the moment he touched the vibrator to the hard, little bud, Angie went off like a rocket again, screaming louder than before. She bucked wildly, and the finger in her ass almost dislodged. He lifted the vibrator off her clit until she began to float back down before he reapplied the humming toy, sending her right back up again . . . and again . . . until she had nothing more to give him. She was half unconscious when he pulled his finger from her tight little hole. He'd never gotten the opportunity to put his second finger in, and his tongue was the only thing to penetrate her sweet pussy. He gazed at her in amazement. She was the most responsive, sensuous woman he'd ever met, and he knew when he eventually got his cock inside her she might very well kill him.

Rising from the bed, Ian walked into her bathroom and turned on the light. He soaped and rinsed his hands before retrieving two washcloths from a stack in the wicker tower next to the tub. Soaking them, he added soap to one of them before wringing out the excess water from both. He returned to the bed and, with a gentle hand, cleaned her up. When he was done, he reached down and lifted her into his arms so he could work the comforter and sheet down to the bottom of the bed. Once she was back on one side of the bed with the covers pulled up to her waist, he closed the bedroom door to block out the lights which were still on in her living room. Rounding the other side of her bed, he climbed in next to her, still fully dressed. If he took his clothes off, he wouldn't be able to stop himself from taking her. He pulled her close into his embrace and as she drifted off to sleep, he heard her mumble, "Thank you, Sir."

EIGHT O'CLOCK THE next morning Angie woke up alone and completely rested. She knew Ian hadn't left before four a.m. because that was the last time she'd roused in his arms before cuddling closer and falling back asleep again. Stretching, she looked around and noticed a piece of paper on her nightstand. Unfolding the note, she read the words on it and smiled.

*Hope you slept well. I'd like to see you today for lunch. Will call around ten. Wear something sexy. I left out the underwear I want you to put on. Ian.*

He'd gone through her underwear drawer? While it should have sounded stalker-ish, it didn't. Instead, it turned her on, and she scanned the room again, spotting her sheer, white, lace bra and thong set he'd left on top of her dresser. It was one of her favorites with its pink trim and tiny bows. The cut of the bra gave the girls a lift up and in, with one bow nestling between them. The other one was at the "y" junction of the thong, and would sit right at the top of her ass.

She was excited he wanted to see her again so soon and hopped into the shower with a cheeky grin on her face. While the water warmed up, she removed all the bobby pins which were still in her now ruined up-do. Her body still tingled from all the attention it'd received from Ian's hands, mouth, and tongue. Never in her life had she had multiple orgasms and, honestly, she'd thought they were a myth. But he had proven her wrong over and over. It wasn't until halfway through her shower routine when she realized that, although she had come several times, he hadn't at all. In fact, he'd kept his clothes on the entire night. The thought stunned her. Not one of her ex-lovers had ever gotten her off without doing the same.

A few minutes later, she finished her shower, dried off, and wrapped her wet hair in a towel before applying her favorite body lotion. She walked back into her bedroom and retrieved the bra and thong Ian had picked out for her. As she put them on, she could almost feel his hands and fingers on her, caressing her. She wondered which other sets of her undergarments he'd touched and if she would feel the same sensations when she wore them.

Now in her underwear, she went to her closet to find something sexy to wear, as per his instructions. She settled on a tight gray mini-skirt and a snug short-sleeve sweater. The deep V-neck was low enough to be sexy, yet not too revealing to be considered slutty. Before she went out she would finish off the outfit with her knee-high, black leather boots—the ones with the three-inch heels. For now though, she laid the clothes on her bed. Throwing on her short silk robe, which she always felt sensual in, she headed to the kitchen for a cup of coffee and granola cereal for breakfast.

Five minutes after ten, her cell phone rang from across the room. Hoping it was Ian, she hit the save icon on her laptop, so she didn't lose what she'd been working on, and dove for the phone. "H-hello. Crap!" She fumbled the phone, and it fell to the floor. "Wait! Hold on!" Snatching it up again, she looked quick to make sure she hadn't dropped the call and saw it was still connected. "Hello?"

His low chuckle came over the line, and it aroused her instantly. "Hi, Angel. Everything okay?"

Giggling, she plopped down on the couch. "It is now. Sorry about that, I dropped the phone."

"I figured as much. Did you sleep well?"

*Holy cow.* How did he make a simple question sound so loaded with sex? "I did. You tuckered me out, and I slept later than I usually do."

"Glad I could be of service." He paused, then his voice became deeper, silkier. "What are you wearing right now?"

A delicious shiver went through her body. "What you left out for me, and my robe."

"Take your robe off."

Looking around her living room, she realized the vertical blinds on her sliding glass door were drawn open as usual. Not that anyone was in her backyard to see her, but Brody had gotten into the habit of popping over during the day to say hi. "Um, just a second. Let me go into my bedroom."

"No," he growled into the phone. "That's not what I told you to do, Angel. Where are you? And don't say your bedroom."

*Really? Is he serious?*

"Answer the question, Angel. You don't want me to ask it again because your bottom will pay for it later."

*Holy shit!* "Um, I'm in my living room, but the blinds are open on my doors and windows. What if Brody comes over to say hi?" He was the only person who knocked on her back door.

Several miles away, Ian knew that wasn't going to happen since his employee was right down the hall in the war-room, remotely finishing some work from Orlando. But he wasn't about to fill Angie in on the fact. He had a feeling she would like the idea of possibly getting caught while being wicked and wild. "That's not my concern. If he does, he's going to get an eyeful and probably jack-off. Now, do as you're told and take off your robe. Let it slide down your incredible body until it pools at your feet. Let me know when you're standing there in your underwear."

His voice was pure velvet, and Angie let it wrap around her as the silky material slid off her shoulders and dropped to the ground. She was certain he could hear her increased breathing. Her heart was pounding as well, in anticipation of his next command. "Okay, it's off. I'm in my panties and bra."

"Good girl. Now go into your kitchen and open your freezer." Frowning in confusion, Angie did as she was told and opened the door. *Oh, no!* He had to be kidding her! Sitting front and center, so she couldn't miss them, were her florescent green vibrator and bottle of K-Y.

As soon as he heard her gasp, Ian snickered. "Your toy and lube should be nicely chilled by now. Put the phone on speaker and set it down." When she did, he gave her further instructions. "Take out your jolly green giant and put the batteries back in, they're sitting on the counter."

She groaned at his pun. "Really, Ian? The 'jolly green giant' is a name for my peas and carrots, not my vibrator." Her hand shook a little as she grabbed the adult toy and her anxiety went up a few notches as well as her excitement when she felt the freezing plastic. She knew exactly what he was going to make her do with it.

"I'll call it whatever I want, sweetheart, and since we're playing, you should be calling me 'Sir.' Are the batteries in it yet?"

"Yes, Sir."

Back in his office, Ian got up and locked his office door before grabbing a hand towel from the room's attached half-bath. He sat again at his desk and released his throbbing erection. The fist-fuck he'd given himself this morning, followed by a cold shower, had done nothing to relieve the aching in his groin. He opened the bottom drawer of his desk and toward the back found a tube of lubricant he hadn't used in a long while. He wished he could have seen her face when she first saw her vibrator in the icebox. Before he'd called her, he told Brody to let her hidden kitchen cameras and audio bugs to go dark for a while. He would love to watch the scene which was about to take place, but it would be a breach of trust without her knowledge. At least he would hear her over the phone. "Grab the K-Y and hop up on the kitchen island, Angel. You're going to fuck yourself with that ice-cold cock and make me come in my hand while I listen to you."

*Holy shit!* It'd been a long time since Angie had indulged in phone sex with a man, but this was already hotter than anything she'd ever experienced. She moved the phone to the island and set the lube and vibrator beside it. Using her hands and arms, she jumped up and twisted, gasping as the cold granite registered on her bare ass cheeks. "O-okay, I'm on the island. What next?" Her heart was pounding and her pussy was quivering.

"Take off your thong, but leave the sexy bra on. Put some lube on your pussy lips and get them all nice and wet."

"I think I'm wet enough." She ripped her thong down her legs and threw it on the floor. "I don't need the K-Y, Sir."

His voice became stricter. "I didn't ask your opinion, Angel. When I tell you to do something, you do it without questioning me unless it jeopardizes your safety or frightens you. Do you understand?"

She grabbed the cold bottle and immediately realized why he

wanted her to use it. The chilled liquid on her hot sex was going to be torture. "Yes, Sir."

"Good girl. Now talk to me, nice and dirty, while you finger fuck yourself."

That she could do. She always enjoyed dirty talk during sex. "I have the cold lube on my fingers, a lot of it. I'm spreading my legs wide and my bare pussy is open for you to see. I'm drenched. Have been since I first heard your voice on the phone." Angie gasped as she touched her nether lips, the chilled lube sending shivers and goosebumps throughout her body. "Oh, God! It's s-so cold, but it's heating up fast. I'm spreading it all over. One finger is going into my slit, ooohhhhhh, now two. I'm rubbing my clit with my other hand and fucking myself with my fingers. You're kneeling in front of me, staring at my pussy. Oh, Sir, it feels so good. I'm soaked and I wish you were here to lick my juices up with your tongue. Oh yes, eat me and fuck me with your fingers, Sir . . . Faster."

"Slow down, Angel." Ian's groan sounded tortured. "You're killing me here. I've got my fist around my cock. It's so fucking hard, and all for you. Get the vibrator, sweetheart. Turn it on and touch it to your nipples through your lacy bra, but keep finger fucking yourself. Whatever you do, don't come until I tell you to, sweetheart. You won't like the spanking you'll get."

Whimpering at the appealing thought of him smacking her bare ass with his hand, she grabbed the cold, plastic toy and flipped the switch on the end of it. "Okay it's on and . . . oh crap! It's so cold and my nipples are so hard. Oh lick them, Sir. Please, suck them into your mouth and heat them up again. Oh fuck, I can feel it going from my tits to my pussy."

"Baby, you're so fucking hot. I wish I was there to see you. I don't think I'd be able to watch you more than a minute though, before I rammed my cock into your hot pussy and fucked you until neither one of us could walk. Put the vibrator on your clit, Angel, and keep those fucking fingers moving in and out."

"I'm still pumping them. I'm so tight and wet, and you feel so good. I'm about to . . . *ooohhhhhh*! Shit! Oh, it's so fucking cold and its making my clit throb harder. Please Sir, touch my clit again . . .

*Aaahhhh*! Oh, fuck yeah . . . Oh please, Sir, let me fuck myself with your hard cock. Let me put your shaft deep into my pussy."

"Shit, baby, do it. Put that frozen cock in your hot little pussy and fuck it hard." Back in his office, Ian's own breathing was keeping pace with Angie's panting. He was going to explode the moment he let her come. How long had it been since he had phone sex with a woman? And had it ever been this good? He doubted it.

Angie shrieked. "*Aaahhh*, fuuuuccckkk!!! Oh sh-shit, it's still ice cold, but my tight hot walls are melting it fast. Oh fuck me, Sir! Hard and fast."

Ian's hand tightened around his cock and sped up. He grunted and groaned as the sounds of her fucking herself for him rushed over the phone. "Yeah baby. Damn, I can feel your hot, wet sex around my dick. It feels so fucking good. Rub your clit. Get there, Angel, get ready to come."

"I'm ready, Sir, please hurry!"

"come now!"

On opposite ends of the phone lines the sounds of ecstasy reached each other's ears as they both exploded, squirting their individual come together, as wave after wave of intense gratification hit them. Angie screamed her release, but Ian didn't want his secretary or anyone else to overhear him masturbating in his office. It was hard to keep his cries of completion to mere growls and murmurs, but somehow, he succeeded. For the first time since he saw her dressed for her blind date two nights ago, his dick was finally sated and flaccid, and he still hadn't gotten inside her . . . yet.

## CHAPTER 7

*A*t twelve noon, Angie pulled her Toyota Camry up to the security shack at the gate leading into the fenced-in compound. Thank goodness Ian had told her there were four blue metal warehouses in the complex, otherwise she would have thought she made a wrong turn somewhere, although she'd only made one turn off the main highway. The compound was in the middle of nowhere, but he'd said both his businesses and home were located on the property. She wondered where his home was because she didn't see any houses. The guard at the gate approached her car, and she rolled down the driver's window. "Hi, my name is Angie and I'm here to see Ian. He said you would know I was coming."

The burly, mustached man with a gun on his hip, tipped his navy-blue baseball cap at her and smiled. "Good afternoon, Ms. Beckett. I'm Murray, and Ian did indeed tell me you were coming, but I still need to see some ID."

She grabbed her purse. "Oh right, I'm sorry, he told me that. And you're going to take my picture for future reference?"

"Yes ma'am. You won't need your ID again, but until the other guards get to know you, they'll scan your registration sticker and bring up your photo on the computer before letting you in. Due to the nature of Ian's businesses, security and privacy are a high priority here." He took her license, ran it through a scanner he held in his hand. When the machine beeped, he handed it back to her and then scanned her vehicle registration sticker on her windshield. "Thank you, ma'am. Almost done. Let me grab the camera."

A few moments later, her picture taken, the gate slid open and Angie drove through it. It closed behind her as she parked next to the first building like Ian told her. There was another gate and fence separating this warehouse from the others, but that one was unmanned. As she climbed out of her Toyota Camry, she saw Ian bounding down a flight of stairs on the outside of the building with a large, black Labrador mix heeling tight at his left leg. Smiling as he reached her, his hands cupped her face and his mouth came down hard on hers. His kiss was insistent and the moment her lips parted, his tongue plunged inside—licking, tasting, consuming. As quickly as the kiss started though, it ended when he pulled his lips away and groaned, touching his forehead to hers. "That phone sex was one of the hottest experiences of my life, Angel. If I don't stop kissing you, I'm going to bend you over the hood of your car and fuck you like crazy, and I won't care if Murray or anyone else is watching."

Angie couldn't help the shudder which went through her, nor the moan which escaped her mouth. Ian lifted his head and stared at her for a moment before his face lit up with a seductively evil expression. "You like the sound of that, don't you? It seems as if my little angel is a bit of an exhibitionist." She blushed and tried to look away, but his hands still held her jaw and he wouldn't let her. "I think we'll have to explore that theory, but in the meantime, come with me and I'll show you the club. Like I told you on the phone, we have strict rules which apply to everyone from the owners down. No play takes place between a member and a guest anywhere in the club until a full background check and health exam are completed. And if Devon, Mitch, and I skimp on rules, then members are going to start asking for favors and it will just cause problems. So unfortunately . . . this will be a no-touch tour when we get inside because if I *do* touch you, I'm going to throw the rule-book out the window."

She laughed despite the fact she felt the same way. Turning her attention to the dog sitting anxiously at their feet, she admired its patience. He appeared to be waiting for the okay to jump on her and lick her to death. "Who's this sweet boy? I saw him at Brody's one day, right? What breed is he?" Extending her hand, she tried to allow the pup to sniff her, but instead he looked up at Ian. His stubby little tail was wriggling madly, but he remained sitting next to his owner.

Ian looked at his charge with pride. "This is Beau. I found him as a pup, and all we know is he's a lab-pit mix. When he's not being a goofball or a pest with his rubber ball, he's a trained guard dog and tracker. Beau, this is Angie. *In Ordnung.*"

Given permission, Beau stuck his nose in her hand and sniffed with gusto. Angie's confusion was evident. "*In Ordnung?* What does that mean?"

"It means 'okay' in German. He only knows a few words of English. Most military, police, and security dogs are trained in German because it's not a common language in the states."

Angie leaned down to pet the dog's head and scratch his soft, velvety ears. She laughed when he did a canine version of a happy dance. "I've heard that before, or read it somewhere. That way, unless the bad guys know German, they can't give the dog commands."

"Exactly." Taking her other hand, Ian pointed toward the fence between the buildings and Beau's head swiveled in the same direction. "*Geh rein.*"

The dog bounded for the fence, his big tongue hanging out the side of his mouth, and Angie saw a swinging doggie door had been cut into a portion of the chain link. There was a small black box above it, under a clear plastic hood. As Beau approached it, the light on the device turned from red to green and back to red again after the dog passed through the door to the other side. He ran toward the next building and disappeared through another doggie door.

Tugging on Angie's hand, Ian led her toward the stairs he'd come down earlier. "He has a microchip under his skin which unlocks the dog doors for him. That's the headquarters for Trident, and he'll find someone in there to bug for a game of fetch."

Ian placed his palm on a scanner next to the door and she heard a click as the door unlocked. Looking around for a sign, she didn't see one. "This is the club?" It couldn't be. The building was blue metal and tan concrete, a basic run-of-the-mill warehouse.

He let her enter first and she gasped at the interior. "Yup, this is my club, although you can't tell from the exterior."

The enclosed area she'd stepped into was similar to the small lobby of a five-star hotel with a reception desk and sitting area consisting of a couch, chairs, tables, and lamps. Adding in the gray carpeting, dark red walls, stylish furniture, artwork and accessories, the first word which came to her mind was opulent. There were a set of antique, carved wooden doors with wrought iron pulls which blended with the décor and she assumed they opened into the rest of the club. A painting on one wall caught her eye, and she stepped forward to take a closer look. The scene was erotic, yet beautiful and elegant, with two naked women at the feet of what appeared to be an equally nude, bearded Greek god. Handfuls of the women's hair were wrapped around his palms and wrists as he pulled their heads back, demanding their surrender. And, *holy crap*, the god was hung like a horse! Tearing her eyes away from the huge erection, she looked at the signature of the artist and was surprised she recognized it. "I know her. I mean, I don't know her personally, but she's local, and I've seen her paintings in some galleries around Tampa. She's very good."

She hadn't realized Ian was standing so close behind her until she felt his warm breath on her ear, and she almost jumped at the low rumble of his voice. "Yes, she is. We have several more pieces of her work inside. She's a member of the club, but a bit eccentric and doesn't stop in often. It seems when she does make an appearance, she's looking for creative inspiration more than kink."

Angie snorted and giggled. "I can see if your style is erotica, then coming to a kinky sex club for inspiration makes sense."

Stepping away, he laughed along with her as he crossed the room to the reception desk. He picked up a stack of papers and handed them to her, sans two. "Put these in your purse and read them over later. It includes the rules and protocols of the club and a submissive limit list. Learn the rules and protocols, appropriate punishment is administered for infractions. First rule for you to learn is, when we're in the club you will address me and any other Dom as Master or Mistress and their name if you know it. But if you don't, use Sir or Ma'am. The second rule is, rude or insulting comments are frowned upon and will usually result in a form of discipline for a sub. Innocent teasing from other Doms is normal, but if a Dom is rude to you, let me know, and I'll take care of it. But I doubt it will happen. When you're here, you will wear a simple collar I will provide you with later. It shows other Doms you are spoken for, and they must speak to me before interacting with you beyond pleasantries. It also means no one is allowed to touch you or discipline you without my consent, and since it's something I rarely give, you won't have to worry. Other submissives will ask my permission to speak with you if we are standing together. If I give my consent to them, it's implied you may speak to them as well unless I tell you otherwise. I know this is a lot to take in at once, but most of this is in the protocols I gave you. Understood?"

*Holy shit.* This was way more than she expected, but in no way did it dissuade her. The more she learned, the more she wanted to experience it. "Yes, Sir. I understand so far."

"There's a submissive limit list in there which I want you to complete later and return to me. Check off which activities you enjoy, which ones you want to try, and which are hard limits which you have no desire to try. The starred activities at the end are extreme ones which are not permitted in the club." He paused. "Now, if learning to play in BDSM with me is what you truly want, then there are a few more requirements we need to go over so we can scene in the club."

If last night and this morning were indications of the "play" he was referring to, then she was all for it. "Yes, Sir, that's what I want."

Obviously pleased with her answer as well as her easy use of the word 'Sir,' he continued. "You'll need to have a complete physical, including blood work, with your gynecologist or one of our staff doctors and have them complete the form at the back of the rules. Are you on birth control?"

She nodded, not the least bit embarrassed about the important question. "Yes, I get the shot every three months because I find it easier than the pill. I also had my annual physical with my GYN a few weeks ago so it won't be a problem to have her fill out the form."

"Good. Members need to have a physical every six months to maintain play privileges. Condoms are mandatory here at the club, but I always use them. My health clearance is on file here if you'd like to see it." She shook her head. "Okay, the next thing is, every potential member and guest has to go through a background check to make sure they're not a threat to the safety and privacy of others. Is that going to be a problem for you?"

Angie bit her lip and her eyes widened in alarm, causing Ian's smile to disappear. "Um, well, let's see, you already know about my addiction to Ben & Jerry's, but there is one incident I was involved in that might be a problem."

She couldn't hold back her grin and it became obvious she was teasing him. He let out a breath and shook his finger at her. "And what would that be, my little brat?"

"When my friend and I were twelve, we got kicked out of Girl Scout camp for sneaking over to the Boy Scout camp so we could spy on them while they were changing out of their bathing suits."

He threw his head back and let out a hearty laugh. "Oh, you naughty little trollop."

She tried to look innocent, but didn't think she was convincing him. "What? We were curious after we heard two of the older girls talking about what boys' wee-wees looked like. They were thirteen and more experienced than us. Unfortunately, we were caught before we could see anything good. When I got home at the end of the week, my mom took me for my first GYN appointment and my dad grounded me for a month."

"I get the feeling it wasn't the first or last time you were grounded." He laughed again and shook his head when she shot him a saucy grin. "You're absolutely adorable. You obviously kept your parents on their toes." Giving her one of the two papers he still had in his hand, he also handed her a pen. "Okay, these are the last things we need to go over. The first one is a privacy contract stating no cameras or recording equipment are allowed in the club. Cell phones must be placed on vibrate and carried in a pocket or purse.

If anyone gets a call or text, they're not allowed to take out their phones unless they're here in the lobby or outside and that includes the locker rooms. You cannot repeat to anyone who or what you see here in the club. Privacy and anonymity in BDSM is valued and expected. If you run into someone from the club in public somewhere, either pretend you know them from somewhere else or don't acknowledge them at all. It's not considered rude to pretend you don't know them and you shouldn't be offended if they do the same. Read this over and sign at the bottom. It's a binding contract with legal consequences if it's violated."

Angie read over the paper and it was pretty much what he'd told her. Turning around, she leaned over the coffee table in the seating area for something hard to write on while she signed it and heard Ian groan. Looking over her shoulder, she saw he was staring at her ass. Knowing the hem of her skirt was a scant inch away from showing what she was hiding underneath, she gave a seductive wiggle of her hips, making him growl this time. He gave her a quick and stinging slap to her ass which made her yelp and him chuckle.

"You're killing me, Angel. Keep it up and I'm going to be spanking your sweet ass real soon. I love bratty submissives as much as I love disciplining them." An idea seemed to come to him, and she gave him a wary look as he grabbed his phone, sending out a quick text before putting it back into the pocket of his cargo pants.

"What was that about?"

Grinning, he shook his head. "Nothing for you to be worried about . . . yet." He took the pen and contract she handed back to him, placing them on the reception desk. "One of the submissives who works the desk will file this later. This last page is a general contract. We'll go through it and sign it later. For now, let's get on with the tour, shall we?"

He opened one of the double doors and gestured for her to precede him. Angie's jaw dropped in astonishment two steps over the threshold. The currently empty club was gorgeous and the décor from the lobby extended into the great space before them. The huge 'U' shaped upper floor they were on overlooked the floor below. There was a curved, dark wood bar along the base of the 'U', or horseshoe, and at the other end, there was a small store and offices. Down the sides of the balcony were numerous sitting areas against the walls and pub-style tables and chairs at the brass railing so people could observe what was happening on the first floor. Across from the bar was an elegant grand staircase leading downward. In the center, hanging from the ceiling above the first floor were three large wrought iron chandeliers which matched the sconces on the walls. "Wow, Ian this is beautiful. It's something out of an old French castle or something. I don't know what I expected, but this wasn't it."

"Thanks, I'm glad you like it." He was obviously proud of the place. "A lot of hard work went into making The Covenant the premier place to practice BDSM in the Tampa area. Devon and I toured a few elite clubs in the U.S. with Mitch, and some in Europe, before deciding on the final plans. We found and consulted with designers who had experience in the lifestyle before we settled on this look. New members and guests tend to have the same reaction you did. The door next to the bar over there leads to staircases into the locker rooms below, and there are entrances downstairs too. Some people come straight from work or some other place, and this way they can change into their club wear here. Come on, let me show you the pit."

"The pit?'" she asked curiously.

He chuckled. "It's what we call downstairs."

"I would think you'd call it a dungeon."

Looking at his watch, he picked up his pace and led her down the grand staircase. She was wondering what the hurry was.

"It was called the dungeon in the beginning, but members who like to watch from up above dubbed it the 'pit' not long after we opened and the name stuck." They reached the bottom of the stairs, and he watched her face as she took in the large playing area with a mixture of awe, curiosity, and even a touch of eagerness.

All along the walls were individual scene stations, each blocked off with velvet red ropes and brass stands normally used at a theater. Because of the square footage, they were able to put ten large roped off areas on each side under the straightaways of the upstairs horseshoe. The locker rooms were located under the stairs and bar. Down two separate hallways on the far end of the pit, under the store, offices, and storage areas, were twelve suites and theme rooms for private play. Inside the downstairs 'U' were numerous sitting areas. Some of them had couches, wing-back chairs, and chaise lounges, while others consisted of small tables with matching chairs where conversations and/or sexual play could take place. All the furniture was either leather or wood, which was easy to clean.

But the pièce de résistance of the club was the large St. Andrew's cross atop a small two-foot-high stage in the center of the pit. The seven-foot-tall medieval torture device was covered in black leather and had wrist and ankle restraints at the ends. And it was where Ian was leading her to now. "We use this for demos and commitment or collaring ceremonies like the one Kristen and Devon had a few months back. Step up on the stage, sweetheart."

His voice dropped to that whiskey-laced tone she was starting to recognize as his Dom voice and her eyes widened. She only hesitated a brief moment before taking the two steps up and saw his gaze trail up and down her body. "I love the knee-high leather boots. Those you can keep on. As for the sweater and skirt . . . undress to your bra and panties, Angel."

"I-I thought we couldn't play?" She was nervous and excited at the same time, and the statement came out as a question. Ian's mouth turned up into the evil grin he liked to give her—the one which made her body shudder and her pussy lips quiver with anticipation.

He crossed his arms over his chest and spread his legs shoulder width apart. "Just because we won't be playing or touching, doesn't mean I don't get to see the pretty lingerie you have on. I've been fantasizing about it all day. Now, either undress or say your safeword."

Angie gulped, but she grabbed the bottom of her sweater and pulled it over her head, tossing it to the floor next to her. Her nipples tightened under the sheer lace of her bra at his heated stare, and she felt a gush of her juices flood from her pussy, soaking her little thong. Her eyes latched on to his as she reached behind her, releasing the catch at the top of her skirt and pulling down the zipper, feeling each tooth release from its mate. When the garment fell to her feet in a puddle, she stepped out of it and kicked it over to join her top on the floor of the stage.

"You're beautiful, sweetheart. Absolutely exquisite. Turn around slowly for me, all the way . . . holy fuck! I should fall to my knees to thank the Lord above for bestowing such beauty on your backside, Angel. I want to bite down on that little pink bow and rip those off you with my teeth." His words made her heart beat faster. She wasn't used to a man being so vocal about her body. When she completed the rotation, he pointed the cross behind her. "Step back against the cross. Lift your arms up and grab hold of the wrist restraints then stay like that."

She'd just taken hold of the second Velcro cuff when they both heard the upstairs double doors open and the sounds of men's voices. Angie was about to bring her hands down to either cover herself or dive for her clothes when he stopped her. "Uh-uh, Angel. Unless you want to use your safeword, stay the way you were. I've decided to push your limits a little more today. The team and I need to have a meeting, and afterward I'll show you the rest of the compound. Of course, I'll let you get dressed again before we go outside." Turning his head, he raised his voice so the others could hear him. "Stay upstairs for a count of thirty."

The voices went quiet, and he looked at her again. "You have twenty of those seconds to use your safeword. If you do, then you can get dressed and have a seat on the couch over there for a few minutes until we're done. I won't be mad or disappointed at all. If you don't use your safeword, then my men and I will have our meeting while you give us something beautiful to look at. No one will touch you or say anything which will make you uncomfortable. They'll just admire your lovely body like I'm doing."

As Ian checked his watch, Angie's mind raced. She'd never been undressed in front of more than one man before. While the thought of it made her nervous, it aroused her even more. She swallowed and made her decision known. "I'll stay where I am, Sir."

He smiled and her heart squeezed knowing she pleased him.

"Damn, she makes a pretty ornament. We should have all our meetings this way."

Angie gasped and her cheeks burned red, but she stayed where she was and didn't utter a word. She hadn't realized how fast thirty seconds would be. The five other members of his team, including her next-door neighbor, had come down the stairs and approached the two of them. She wasn't sure who made the comment since they were all staring at her—not lewdly, but appreciatively—and it made her feel beautiful, sexy, and downright naughty. Here she was in her underwear, looking like a dancer in a strip joint, and she wasn't embarrassed. *Crap!* She was an exhibitionist. How come she never knew that?

She saw Jake break away first, smiling and shaking his head, before taking a seat in a winged-back chair. The rest all smiled or winked at her before also sitting down until Ian was the only one still standing in front of her. "You please me, Angel, very much." She glowed under his praise. "I'd like you to keep your arms up for now, but when it gets uncomfortable, just let me know. Understand?"

When she nodded, he shook his head with a frown. *Oh yeah!* "Yes, Sir. I understand."

"Good girl. This will take about fifteen or twenty minutes, but I suspect you'll tire way before we're done. Don't worry about interrupting since you're already a delicious distraction."

He turned and took the last seat facing her. From how they were all situated, they could look up and see her easily, except for Jake whose back was to her. She thought it odd he wasn't looking at her like the others were, but it didn't bother her. In fact, she was getting wetter by the second and clenched her thighs together. Devon had started whatever meeting they were having, but her eyes remained on Ian's face. When he saw her squirm, he pointed at her feet and indicated with his hands that he wanted her to spread her legs wide. *Shit.* The thong gave her limited coverage in her crotch, and they'd all be able to see most of her glistening pussy. She closed her eyes and took a deep breath before spreading her legs then looking at Ian again to see his approving nod. She then stood there, in her underwear, while the men had their meeting, all but ignoring her except for the occasional glance, grin, or wink.

Devon opened a file in his hand. "We've narrowed the new team of six down to fourteen candidates. Eleven men and three women, all highly recommended by their superiors, or in some cases, their subordinates or protected assets. Four are with the FBI with military background. Seven are recently retired or about to be retired from various Special Forces, one of whom was a P.O.W. for a week in Afghanistan. Two are from SWAT teams—one in L.A. and the other from Chicago. The last one is from the Secret Service and has experience with high level targets. He was the one who personally, and single-handedly I might add, prevented the kidnapping of the House Speaker's young daughter on a family vacation to Jamaica last year. I'm sure everyone remembers the incident." Three low-level and over-zealous members of Al Qaeda tried to take the twelve-year-old girl from the hotel her family was staying at. Two other Secret Service agents were shot to death, and if it wasn't for Cain Foster, the child might have been beheaded at some point for a videotaped jihad.

Ian took over, his gaze flicking to her every few moments to make sure she was okay. "We'd like to try and get at least one of the three women on the team if we can, but not at the expense of passing over a better qualified asset. Having a woman on-call for an op, if one is needed, keeps us from having to track one down through our contractors. We are considering hiring one of the women for reasons other than the Omega team, which is what the second team will be called."

Boomer snorted. "As long as they know they're not the Alpha team, which is what I just decided our team is going to be called." The group of men chuckled at the pun since they were all alpha-male Doms at the club and, prior to adding a new team, they'd never needed a team name for themselves.

"What's the extra position?" Jake asked.

Devon grinned like a guy with a new toy. "Chopper pilot."

"Holy shit, we're getting a helicopter?" It was Boomer's turn to sound like a kid in a toy store . . . or a Dom in a sex toy store, because he looked like he was ready to blow a load, and it wasn't because there was a woman in sexy lingerie standing less than ten feet away from him.

Ian nodded. "Yup, I've got a line on one and I'm hoping we can work out a deal by the end of the month. As you know, we purchased the ten acres north of the compound last month and that's where the helipad will be built. Polo, I know you have plenty of flight time, and we'll use you as backup, but I don't want an empty spot on the team if you have to stay behind with the bird on an op."

Marco nodded his head. "Fine with me. I'll take it up and do some training with the new pilot in case I need to take over in an emergency."

"Good idea." Ian paused when he glanced over at Angie. "Excuse me a second," he said to his team as he stood and approached the stage. "Are your arms tired, Angel?"

Her arms were a little uncomfortable, but she was doing her best to keep them up. She shook her head, not wanting to disappoint him. "No, Sir, not really."

His eyes narrowed, his expression stern. "You're squirming, and I can tell by looking at your face you're not comfortable. Now, would you like to try answering the question again, this time honestly, and not with what you think I want to hear?"

Damn, she should have told him the truth the first time he asked. "Um, sorry Sir, but yes my arms are tired."

"The apology better be for not telling me the truth, and not because you're sorry your arms got tired in that position. You lasted longer than I expected. You may bring your arms down." He walked a few feet away and returned with a wooden, straight-back chair, spun it around, and placed it on the stage so if she sat on it properly she'd be facing the cross behind her. "Straddle the chair, Angel, and rest your hands on your thighs."

Angie didn't know what shocked her more, the position he wanted her in so they'd all have a view of her crotch through the narrow slats of the chair, or the fact she obeyed him without hesitation. After she'd done as instructed, he told her to spread her knees wider. When he was satisfied, he went back to his own chair and continued with his meeting while she sat there, her juices dripping from her slit. She didn't want to look down, but she was certain she was making a puddle on the seat under her pussy. Her walls clenched with need for a cock to fill her. And not just any cock, her sex wanted only one . . . Ian's. She was so high on lust, she was tempted to interrupt their meeting and beg him to fuck her right there in front of everyone and, of course, that thought inflamed her desire even further.

Less than ten minutes later, Ian got to his feet and addressed his men. "Read the candidates' files, and give Devon or I any recommendations or concerns. We'll be starting the interviews next week, and I want you each to meet as many of them as your caseloads allow. If there are no questions . . . get lost and enjoy the rest of your Sunday. I'm taking the rest of the afternoon off to spend time with my beautiful sub."

Grins and winks were sent her way again as the men all said goodbye to her, and then she was alone with Ian. Sexually frustrated beyond anything she'd ever known, she groaned when he picked up her clothes, shook them out, and handed them to her. She'd forgotten they couldn't have sex or anything close to it while they were in the club. As she scrambled to get dressed, she hoped his house was nearby. If it wasn't, she was going to force him to do what he said earlier, and have him fuck her over the hood of her car while Murray, and anybody else who was around, watched.

# CHAPTER 8

"Where are we going?"

Ian was leading her on foot across the parking lot and through the pedestrian gate in the fence to the larger section of the compound. As they walked past the building housing the Trident offices, Beau came running out from behind it and heeled at Ian's side without being told. "My place. We converted the last building into large apartments. Mine's on the first floor, and Devon and Kristen live on the second."

They continued across the paved lot with their canine escort. Harder than granite, Ian not-so-discreetly adjusted himself for the third time since they climbed back up the grand staircase and Angie smirked knowingly when she caught him in the act. He was just as aroused as she was, if not more so, and he couldn't wait for them to be alone. When they reached the outside door, he placed his palm on a scanner like the one outside the club. Opening the door for her, he let her enter before him. There was an interior door to his apartment and next to it was a smaller dog door for Beau. Although the dog came in the same outside door they did, he didn't wait for Ian to open the second door, opting to use his own entrance. He disappeared inside as Ian stepped forward to scan his palm once again. To their left was a staircase which led to the second apartment.

When the door in front of them opened, he yanked her inside impatiently. The door slammed shut at the same time he shoved her against the wall next to it and crushed his mouth to hers. There was nothing gentle about the kiss, and he was grateful she didn't object. In fact, she was just as rough in return. Taking control, one of his hands plunged into her hair, and he made a fist. He pulled the strands only enough to sting and loved how it made her react even more frantic against him. He maneuvered her head to where he wanted it so he had better access to her mouth which he was devouring. Her hands wrapped around his neck and held him just as possessively. From their chests to their groins they were fused to each other. Her nipples were hard, but not as hard as the erection he was grinding against her mound. They fit together like the pieces of a jigsaw puzzle. His other hand dragged down her side to her hip and under her skirt to her ass. He squeezed, and she moaned into his mouth. Bending her knee, she brought it up to his hip, wrapping her leg around his thigh, desperately trying to get closer to him even though it was physically impossible to do so.

The door next to them popped opened, and Ian ripped his lips from hers at the same time they heard a female shriek. "Oh my God, Uncle Ian! I'm so sorry. Oh, crap. Never mind, I'll go upstairs to Uncle Devon's."

"No." The word came out hoarsely, and Ian cleared his throat. "No, don't, Baby-girl. They went out to meet Will and some friends for lunch. Just go into the kitchen and give us a minute, okay."

They were still joined at the hip and, although he knew how it looked, there was no way Ian was pulling away from her in front of his niece with the throbbing erection he had. His forehead was resting on Angie's as they both tried to slow down their breathing.

"It's all right, I'll go someplace else."

He glanced over at the pretty young blonde as she was about to close the door again. He took one look at her swollen eyes and tear-stained face and grabbed her arm. "Baby-girl? What's wrong?"

The moment he said it, he knew what she was going to say. Tomorrow night was the anniversary of her parents' murders. *Damn it.* He should have made sure she was okay today, but she'd been fine last night when he talked to her, and he'd figured she wouldn't feel the full impact until tomorrow. He'd been wrong.

"I'm so sorry, but I-I was thinking too much and didn't want to be alone today. My roommate's gone until tomorrow, and I didn't want to explain what was wrong to anyone else. But I'll go find Brody or Jake."

Although he was still leaning against Angie, he pulled Jenn into the room and turned her toward the kitchen. "Go in the kitchen. Pull out the fixings for sandwiches, and we'll be there in a minute. We haven't had lunch yet." She looked like she was going to argue, but he wouldn't let her and the concern in his voice was evident. "That's an order, Jenn."

After she did as she was told, with Beau on her heels, he shut the door and turned his head back toward Angie who'd stood there in silence as he dealt with his niece. He cupped her jaw in his hands and kissed her softly on the lips. Keeping his voice low, he told her, "I'm so sorry, Angel. I wasn't expecting this to happen, but tomorrow is a bad day for her. She's my goddaughter."

"It's fine, Ian. Don't apologize. Tomorrow's the anniversary of her parents' deaths, isn't it?" She was whispering and when his brow furrowed in confusion, she added, "Brody told me what happened and why she lived with you now."

He nodded and finally stepped away from her body. Glancing over his shoulder to make sure the coast was clear, he adjusted himself, groaning as he did. "When she's not at her dorm at U. of T., she's here." He watched as she straightened her clothes. "I'd like for you to stay and meet her, but I'll understand if you don't want to at the moment."

"I'd like to meet her, but wouldn't she feel better if I left?"

He ran his hands down her arms to her hands and held them, loving how her delicate fingers looked entwined with his larger, rougher ones. Her skin was so soft, he didn't want to stop touching it. "No, I think she could use the distraction. Besides if you leave, she's going to ask me twenty million questions and feel guilty, believing you left because of her. Typical teenage thinking, I know, and when she puts her mind to it, she's better than most military interrogators. She'll go a lot easier on you than me since she doesn't know you yet."

She laughed and looked downward at his bulging crotch. "Fine.

I'll tell you what—you go get your wee-wee under control, and I'll go introduce myself to your niece."

His raised eyebrow made her laugh harder. He reached around and pinched her ass, and she swallowed her surprised yelp. "Brat. And stop laughing because you'll be formally introduced to my 'wee-wee' later, and I promise you that's the last time you'll call it that."

Pushing off the wall, she let her hand brush against his groin as she sashayed toward the kitchen. Sexually frustrated beyond anything he'd ever known, he dramatically thumped his head against the wall and heard her laugh at him. Grinning, he watched her walk into his kitchen and greet his goddaughter. "Hi, I'm Angie."

---

FOUR HOURS later Angie was tucked under Ian's arm on the couch while Jenn was curled up in her favorite extra-wide chair with Beau snoring on the floor next to her. After Ian had gotten his body back down to a slow simmer, he'd joined them in the kitchen. Jenn had made her own sandwich and been putting the final touches on his usual choice as Angie was finishing her own creation. They'd also hauled out some coleslaw and Jenn's beloved sour cream and onion potato chips.

The two women had taken to each other instantly. It didn't take long to convince Jenn there was no need to apologize for her interruption, and Angie soon had his niece talking about school and her job as a waitress at Jake's brother's pub. While they'd taken the sandwiches and chips into the living room and gotten comfortable, Ian grabbed three bottles of water from the fridge and followed them. Now they were watching *The Princess Bride* which had followed *Robin Hood: Men in Tights*. Thankfully, both women were in the mood for some comedy instead of tear-jerking chick flicks.

Although he was enjoying it, Ian was having a hard time accepting how comfortable the domestic scene felt. It was a rare occasion if he brought a woman back to his place, and this was the first woman in a very long time he'd introduced to his goddaughter. Since his engagement had ended ten years ago, he'd dated numerous women. Some of the relationships even lasted for a few months, but every time a woman pushed him for more, he broke it off. He didn't go into a relationship intending to end it at a certain point, however, it's what always eventually happened. As long as the woman kept things light and uncomplicated, Ian was fine, but he refused to let a woman get too close to him again. Despite his best efforts to move on, it always came down to one thing—he didn't want to go through what he'd experienced when Kaliope broke his heart.

There had been a time when he'd believed in soulmates and thought he'd found his. He'd never been the most romantic man in the world. He didn't spout out poetry or think to bring a woman flowers just because he felt like it. She'd known how he was from the beginning of their relationship, but Kaliope thought she could change him. He'd tried to show her he loved her in his own unique way—he made sure her car was always in tip-top shape so it wouldn't break down on her; he shared the household chores with her, making sure he did the heavier stuff and never let her take out the dirty garbage; he praised and supported her in everything she did whether it was a success or failure. She'd been a local newscaster in Virginia while he was stationed nearby, and fantasized about landing an anchor position on a national news program. Unfortunately, so did every other TV reporter in the United States. The competition could be harsh and even though Ian had been proud of her no matter what she did, it hadn't been enough for her. If he tried to comfort her after an audition with a larger network fell through, she'd get mad, yelling he was only patronizing her. The worst had been when she'd told him he was holding her back from her dreams. He had cherished Kaliope and, in the end, it hadn't been good enough for her. Now Ian kept his relationships simple, refusing to have his heart ripped out ever again.

When the end credits began to scroll up the sixty-inch flat screen TV, Jenn got up and gathered the crumb-filled plates left over from their earlier meal. "I'm going to my room to work on my term paper. Don't worry about me for dinner. I'll nuke something later." She leaned down and kissed his cheek. "Thanks for everything, Uncle Ian. You too, Angie, and it was so nice to meet you. Again, I'm really sorry I interrupted your afternoon."

They both smiled at her, telling her it was fine and she had to stop apologizing for needing company. After she and Beau left them alone, Ian grabbed the last of their lunch residue and an empty bowl of popcorn, carrying it all into the kitchen while Angie looked around the apartment again. If she could call it an apartment since it looked more like a huge penthouse suite in an upscale hotel. The living room had couches and chairs with seating for at least ten people, along with a massive entertainment center. Behind the couch was another conversation area where a four-seat wood and mirrored bar stood. A dart board hung between the bar and corner of the room, with a section of cork protecting the wall from misthrows. The attached dining area contained an eight-seat formal table, chairs, and china hutch with two extra chairs which could be used when the leaf was in use. An eat-in gourmet kitchen was on the other side of the dining area complete with stainless steel appliances. It was a party hostess's dream.

Earlier in the afternoon, Angie had taken off her boots and tried to get comfortable on the couch next to Ian without her crotch showing under her short skirt. Noticing she was uneasy, Jenn had offered her a pair of yoga pants and a University of Tampa T-shirt to change into. Grateful, Angie had accepted the offer and used the master bedroom suite to make the quick change. There were also two additional bedrooms, the furthest one away from Ian's room was obviously Jenn's, and a guest bath off the hallway. The two smaller bedrooms were bigger than Angie's own living room. The only thing odd about the apartment were the horizontal windows in every room were elevated about eight-feet up the ten-foot walls, allowing plenty of light in without anyone being able to see in from outside. She figured it was a security feature due to his line of work. With the exception of the young woman's pink and purple chic bedroom, the rest of the house was beautifully decorated in earth-tones. Ian had explained his mother had taken over after the apartments became livable and hired an interior decorator for both her sons. Otherwise, they would have looked like typical bachelor pads with mismatched furniture and nothing on the walls, but the dart board. As it was, he had to convince the decorator to include it in the décor.

She was looking at an older photo on one of the end tables when Ian came back into the room. The picture was of him and his brothers about twenty years ago. Ian was in the center with two slightly younger boys on either side of him and he was holding another boy, around the age of six, up by the armpits. "This is you, the oldest, but which one of these two is Devon? Are they twins?"

He pointed to the teenager on his left. "This one's Dev. The little guy in front is our brother Nick, and this is John, and no, Devon's eleven months older, but a lot of people had trouble telling them apart."

"Do Nick and John live in Florida too?"

Taking her hand, he tugged her up from the couch and pulled her close. "Nick is twenty-five now and in the Navy in San Diego." A sad expression took over his face. "And John died when he was seventeen."

Feeling awful for his loss, she realized they had more in common then she originally thought. "I'm sorry. I lost my brother when he was seventeen and I was nine. He was killed in a car crash with three of his friends."

Ian cupped her cheek, his thumb caressing her jawline. "I'm sorry for your loss, too. Unbeknownst to us, John had become an alcoholic and got drunk one day after cutting school. He died after he passed out and threw up. Aspirated. My dad found him." He swallowed hard at the memory. "We all took it hard, but Devon took it really bad. He was torturing himself over some misplaced guilt that he could've stopped John from spiraling down. The problem was, the kid hid his addiction well and none of us knew about it. And we're a close-knit family. Anyway, Dev thought he should've been able to see the problem and take control over the situation. The fact that he didn't became an issue for him. His hurt and anger were starting to get the best of him, so after we ended up on the same SEAL team, I introduced him to the lifestyle to help him deal with it. Taking control of other aspects of his life gave Dev the ability to deal with John's death."

Bringing her hands from around his waist and up his chest, she explored his physique as she spoke. "Is that why Devon doesn't drink? I saw him only drinking tonic last night." Had the gala only been last night? It seemed like so much had happened between Ian and her since then.

"Yeah." He pulled her hips into his, rubbing his erection against her. "But I really don't want to talk about Devon or anyone else but you right now. We have some unfinished business to take care of, little one."

Feeling wicked, she licked her lips, slow and seductive, and he groaned at the sight as she walked her fingers up his chest. "What about Jenn?"

Bending forward, he nuzzled her neck. "She'll be busy with her term paper, and my bedroom is far enough away she won't hear a thing, as long as we keep our voices and your screams down to a whisper."

"Sorry," she mumbled as she blushed.

He took her hand and led her down the hallway past Jenn's closed door. "Don't be. I love how vocal you are. I just don't want my niece to know it, and I'm sure she doesn't either. And don't worry because she always uses her headphones and listens to her IPod while doing schoolwork." After closing and locking his bedroom door behind them, he pulled her back into his embrace and kissed her. It didn't start off as explosive as their earlier one did, but it wasn't long until they were back up to that level. They spent several minutes consuming each other before Ian eased back and released her. He walked over to a small sitting area next to a gas fireplace on the far side of his bed and sat on a blue and green, striped upholstered chair. He picked up a remote and soft jazz music filled the air. "Strip for me, Angel. Nice and slow. Tease me. Do you remember what your safeword is?"

Damn, he made her hotter than lava when he spoke to her in that deep, commanding voice. "My safeword is red, Sir."

She loved to dance and swinging her hips to the music came naturally. She proceeded to give Ian the best strip-tease and lap dance of his life. It didn't take long for her to shed her tee and yoga pants, but then she slowed down. Trailing her hands up and down her body sensually, she played with her breasts and clit through the fabric of her underwear until Ian had to undo his pants to get some much needed room for his straining erection. She was shocked and thrilled to see he'd gone commando, and she moaned, knowing his hard shaft had been one zip away from her touch most of the day. The dark purple head was weeping, and she looked forward to tasting him, but not yet. She wasn't done teasing him.

Turning around, she bent over and reached back to spread her ass cheeks, smiling and wriggling her hips when he growled. "Fuck, Angel. Someday soon I'm going to take your sweet ass and fuck it hard and fast. And I promise you, you'll love every minute of it."

Her pussy quivered at the thought of him fucking her there, a place where no other man had been. Standing back up, she remained facing away from him as she reached back and unhooked her bra. Holding the front in place, she lowered the straps, inch by inch, until her arms were free. She took the lacy piece and threw it over her head in his direction. When she saw he caught it, she began to shimmy her hips and lowered her thong, drawing out the process as long as she could. She then stepped out of them, turned around and threw them at him as well. This time when he snatched the garment, he brought it to his face, inhaling deeply. His blue eyes flared and darkened with heated desire. "Damn, sweetheart. I wish I could bottle your scent and carry it with me everywhere. Run your fingers through your pussy and taste yourself. I want you to taste what I do when I eat you."

*Holy crap!* She'd never tasted herself before, but even though she blushed, the demand didn't turn her off. In fact, she felt her reaction to it gush from between her legs as if her body was giving her plenty to sample. Leisurely, she ran her flattened hand down her abdomen while her fingers stretched downward, leading the way. They brushed over her clit and into her saturated folds. After gathering her moisture, she brought her fingers to her mouth and licked each finger one by one, moaning at the spiciness when it hit her tongue.

Ian crooked a finger at her. "Come here, baby, and do it again. It's my turn for a taste."

She sashayed several steps forward and stopped with her legs straddling his knees. Repeating the process of collecting her cream, she brought her hand up and held it a few inches from his mouth, making him reach for her. Grabbing her wrist, he parted his lips, took two of her fingers and sucked them clean before moving to the next two and, at last, her thumb, which he nibbled on. The sounds of his slurping and satisfied humming made her want to put other things in his mouth, mainly her tits and clit.

"On your knees, Angel. I want you to suck me."

*Oh, thank fuck!* She loved giving head and was dying to taste his pre-cum which was seeping from the tip. She knelt before him and crawled forward between his knees when he spread them apart. He still had his cargo pants and shirt on, and this time she felt wicked that he was dressed and she was naked. When she reached for his cock, he stopped her. "Your mouth only, sweetheart. Hands behind your back, like when you were a kid, bobbing for apples."

Smirking, she licked her lips and did as she was told. Using his thumb and forefinger, he positioned his dick so it was pointing at the ceiling. With his other hand, he grabbed a handful of her hair and guided her mouth to take in his tip. She swiped her tongue across the head and tasted him. He was delicious, and she did it again before he slowly began to impale her mouth with his shaft. Shifting his hips forward so she could take more of him in, he set the slow pace he wanted her to use as her head bobbed up and down. He eased the grip of his hand in her hair then pushed away the loose strands which had fallen around her face and tucked them behind her ears so he could see her mouth better.

Reaching down, he played with her nipples as she worked him in and out of her mouth. He pinched, pulled, and rolled her stiff little peaks, and when she purred, she knew he felt it down the length of his cock and into his balls. Using her tongue, she licked him like an ice cream cone on every up stroke, teasing the v-shaped notch on the underside of his cock, and it was his turn to hum with satisfaction.

Ian's eyes rolled back into his head. "Fuck, Angel. The only thing better than how this feels is how you look taking my cock between your plump, red lips. Suck me, baby, as hard as you . . . *aaahhhh*, fuck! Shit! Do it again." He began to breathe heavily, his hips jerking upwards, and she took him so far back into her mouth that he hit her throat. *Fuck!* She either had no gag reflex or had exceptional control.

When she swallowed, her throat closed around him, and he saw stars while moaning in ecstasy. He was going to have to stop her soon because he wanted to be in her pussy when he came inside her body for the first time, but it felt too good to stop her yet. "Holy shit, baby. I want to thank, then kill the bastard who taught you how to give a blow job, 'cause you're so fucking good at it. But I don't want to imagine you doing this to anyone else but me."

He couldn't take it anymore. Grabbing her hair again, he pulled her off him, but she managed to take one last swipe of his head with her tongue, the little brat. Giving her a hand, he helped her stand. As she licked her swollen lips, he told her, "Climb up on my bed and get on your hands and knees so I can take you from behind. You were teasing me with your hot little ass earlier in the lobby, and now I'm going to spank it before I fuck you. There are consequences for teasing a Dom when you haven't been told to do so."

Angie all but dove onto the bed. She needed him inside her and wasn't ashamed to admit she longed for the roughness he was offering her. She'd always wanted to be spanked, but the one boyfriend who'd agree to do it hadn't been too into it and the experience left her wanting much more than she had gotten. Two of her other boyfriends had looked at her as if she were crazy when she told them what she wanted so she stopped asking for it. But she had a feeling Ian was going to give her, not only what she wanted, but what she craved.

After she was in position, she looked over her shoulder at him. He was standing beside the bed looking at her ass while he removed his clothes. "Eyes forward."

She snapped her head back around and heard him open a drawer of the nightstand then the sound of condom wrapper being opened. The bed dipped as he climbed up behind her, and she was startled when he began caressing and squeezing the globes of her ass instead of spanking her right away. "Beautiful, Angel. You've got the prettiest ass I've ever seen. And it's going to look even prettier when I turn it a nice shade of pink."

She wasn't prepared for the first smack, and even though he hadn't hit her too hard, she still let out a yelp and instinctively tried to move forward. Ian grabbed her hips and held her in place. "Going somewhere, sweetheart?"

*Damn him.* He sounded amused, and she rolled her eyes, grateful he couldn't see her face. "No, Sir. I just didn't expect it."

"Well, now you will. Remember, Jenn is down the hall, so no yelling."

She was glad he reminded her about his niece because Angie had forgotten about the younger woman. It must've been why he'd raised the volume of the music a little before he'd joined her on the bed because it would muffle the sound of his hand hitting her bare flesh. His other hand lifted and smacked her other cheek. This one was a little harder than the first, but she stayed in position and bit back her squeal. By the time he gave her the third, fourth, and fifth spanks, her ass was starting to feel like it was on fire. He hadn't struck the same spot twice, spreading them out across her cheeks and upper thighs. And instead of trying to get away, she was bowing her back and pushing her hips higher, giving him better access. Was it wrong to enjoy the pain to the point she was soaking wet and ready to beg him to fuck her? He stopped after the eighth one and held his hand atop the flesh he'd just smacked, keeping the heat in, and she moaned. "Are you okay, Angel? Give me a color—green, yellow, or red?"

"Green . . . Sir." Her breathing had increased after the third or fourth spank and now she was outright panting. "Oh, God . . . so green."

"Really?" She could hear the smile in his voice. "Why don't I feel for myself, *hmm?*" Before she could respond, his hand slid down between her legs. "*Mmmm.* So nice and wet. But no coming without permission."

He removed his exploring fingers, and she heard him clean them with his mouth. She felt him move closer to her and rub the head of his cock through her drenched folds before shoving it deep into her pussy in one swift motion, groaning as he did so.

*Holy crap, he's so big!* She felt so full as he held himself inside her, waiting for her body to adjust to his size. She had to hold back the urge to beg him to move and prayed he wouldn't make her wait too long before giving her permission to come because she was on the edge of the precipice.

He dragged his shaft back out as her greedy pussy clenched, attempting to keep him in. He stopped with the head just inside her, and she pushed her hips back trying to get him to go deep again. His hand smacked her right butt cheek, and she gasped. "You don't set the pace, sweetheart. I do. And right now, I'm savoring the feel of you around me, so stay still."

"Y-Yes, Sir. S-Sorry, but you feel so good."

---

IAN EASED BACK inside her until he was buried to the hilt and repeated the cycle, complete with a hard spank on her ass, several more times. "Damn, Angel. You feel incredible. So hot and tight. I don't think I'm going to last very long."

It might end up being quicker than he wanted, but he'd make sure it was good for her before he found his own release. The drag of her walls against his cock felt so good, it was absolutely sinful. Grabbing her hips, he couldn't help speeding up, setting an almost frantic rhythm as he pounded into her from behind. The sounds of flesh slapping on flesh filled the room as his hips bounced off her luscious backside.

"Oh God, I'm going to come. Please Ian!" Although her words were pleading whispers, he could still hear her desperation.

"Not yet, Angel. Almost." After a few more thrusts, when he felt the tingling in his spine shoot into his balls, he knew he had to send her over. Reaching around her hip, he located her clit and pinched it. "Now!"

That one word and pinch were all she needed as she shattered around him. Her cries of release were muffled as she yelled into the comforter and milked the seed from his body. She tightened around him, and he saw black spots before his eyes. He kept pumping his hips, trying to extend both of their orgasms for as long as possible, until her entire body finally sagged to the bed. He fell forward onto his forearms with one on either side of her head. With his chest to her back, he managed to keep some of his weight off her. They were both gasping for air, their bodies covered in sweat, and as much as it killed him to do so, Ian eased out of her.

When he was sure he could stand without collapsing, he caressed her back and ass as he crawled off the bed. "Stay there, sweetheart. I'll be right back."

He smiled at her mumbled reply as she straightened her knees and laid flat on her stomach. Discarding his condom in the bathroom, he reached into the shower and turned on the water to let it warm up. He moved back to the bedside and looked down at her satiated body, not surprised when he started getting hard again at the sight of her. He couldn't get enough of his little angel. After grabbing another condom, he wrapped his hands around her ankles and hauled her toward him. When she grumbled a weak protest, he smacked her pink ass and got her attention.

Flipping over, she glared at him. "What was that for?"

He gave her an evil grin. "The Dom in me felt like it."

"Well, tell the Dom in you to have a little sympathy for the half-unconscious. You wore me out."

Chuckling, he picked her up in his arms, carrying her into the bathroom and straight into his extra-large walk-in shower. "I hope I didn't wear you out too much, because I'm ready for more."

Her expression was one of shock as she looked at his groin after he let go of her legs, allowing her to stand. Grinning, he walked her backward under the spray of hot water coming from both sides of the shower as well as above. She reached down and made a fist around his still growing erection. "I think I might have some energy left since you're obviously up for it."

He let her slowly pump his shaft as he tossed the condom on a shelf and grabbed a bottle of body soap, squirting some out into his hand. Lathering it up, he started with her neck and shoulders and cleaned every inch of her body, spending extra attention to her breasts, ass, and crotch. When he was done, he allowed her to do the same to him, letting her explore to her obvious delight. She admired his two tattoos—the tribal band around his left upper arm and the American flag and anchor above his right shoulder blade. Her hands traced his various scars, asking how he'd gotten each one. He couldn't recall how he got some of them, but there were three he received in combat which he would never forget. The three-inch scar on his left upper arm and another five-inch one on his abdomen were knife wounds which had caused little damage. But a gunshot wound pucker on his left chest above his heart was a constant reminder of how dangerous some of his Navy tours had been. The doctors had told him if he'd been hit a little lower he would've left Iraq in a body bag.

He hadn't been wearing his bullet-proof vest as he left the mess hall when an Iraqi policeman, who'd been allowed on their base for training, decided he wanted to switch his allegiance. While two marines had been killed, he and another SEAL had been wounded in the three-second attack before the traitor was taken out by Marco who'd been a few steps behind Ian. Luckily, one of his ribs stopped the low caliber bullet, and after only two days in the hospital, he was able to return to the states until cleared for duty again. His Purple Heart was stored with the rest of his medals in a valet box on his dresser.

After he told her about the scars he could remember getting, she kissed each one, and he was touched by her tender actions. But he soon shook those thoughts from his brain, not wanting to let her close to his heart where he was most vulnerable because he was never letting history repeat itself. Grabbing her hips, he spun her around so she was facing a built-in tiled bench. He reached for the condom he'd tossed earlier. "Bend over, sweetheart, and put your hands on the bench. You can come whenever you need to this time." Ian sheathed himself, then squirted a little more soap into his hands. Running his fingers down the crack of her ass, he worked his slick fingers into her back hole. First one, followed by two. He soon had her moaning and writhing as he thrust them in and out, scissoring them to stretch her further. As much as he wanted to take her there, she wasn't ready for the size of him. He'd have to pick up a set of progressive anal plugs to prepare her properly. For now though, he'd use his fingers. As he continued to fuck her ass, he lined his latex covered cock up with her core and plunged into her. She came instantly, but he had more control this time and set a steady pace, determined to get one or two more orgasms from her.

ANGIE'S LEGS shook as one orgasm ebbed and another built behind it like waves in the ocean. Was it possible to die from too much incredible sex? She hoped not because she wanted to experience as much of it as she could before she died. Ian was a skilled lover who was able to make her body sing in ways it never had before. He shifted his hips and with the new angle found her hidden G-spot and sent her over the edge again. The combination of his cock and fingers taking her at the same time made her come hard, and if it wasn't for him holding her around the waist with his free hand, she would've sank to the tiled floor. The third time she exploded, she took him with her, and he grunted his release.

Several hours later, Angie awoke to Ian's mouth and tongue between her legs. The man was insatiable and, apparently, so was she as she came twice before he took her pussy again. With reluctance, he'd agreed to let her go home after she told him she didn't want to spend the whole night with his niece sleeping down the hallway. After making her promise to text him when she got home safe, he allowed her to get dressed in the clothes and flip-flops Jenn had loaned her. In the meantime, he threw on a pair of his own sweatpants and a tee. She grabbed her other clothes, and he walked her to her car, which was still parked down by the club, with

Beau as an escort. The lot was empty since the club had closed about an hour earlier, and the guard had secured the exterior gate after everyone had left before heading home himself. Before Angie got into her car, Ian kissed her with a vow to call her in the afternoon and then walked over to open the gate for her. She drove home with a very satisfied smile on her face and delicious aches throughout her body.

# CHAPTER 9

*A*ngie stood naked in her bathroom as she aimed the hairdryer at her wet locks. It was Friday evening, and Ian was taking her to his club tonight. They'd seen each other twice during the week, but Trident meetings, interviews, and cases prevented them from having more than one full night together alone. She hadn't seen him since very early Wednesday morning. Although they'd had some more phone sex, which was so hot she was surprised her local cell tower didn't explode, she was dying to see him again.

Monday, Ian had invited her to join everyone at Devon and Kristen's as the team got together for Jenn to help her through the first anniversary of her parent's death. Pizza, beer, and soda served as a simple dinner while they played poker and watched a video of pictures of the young woman and her parents from before she was born through her late teens. The final photos of her folks were taken during their last Christmas together. Many of the photos included some or all of the Trident team members, in addition to other former SEALs who made up Jenn's extended family. The men and their niece entertained Kristen and Angie with countless funny stories of the team's antics over the years. Angie had left the group a little after midnight when Ian and Brody ended up needing to have a late-night video conference with a client who'd called them with an urgent request for their assistance on some matter.

She'd spent Tuesday night in Ian's arms as they finally had his apartment all to themselves. They'd also gone through the contract and discussed her limits and his expectations. She was surprised none of his requests bothered her in any way. He would have control over her in the bedroom and push her boundaries, all within her green and yellow limits. He also had control over her well-being and safety, but instead of disliking it, she felt pampered and valued because he cared enough to make sure no harm came to her. While the contract was not legally binding, it took out a lot of the guess work of the relationship. But most of all, it stressed she had the ultimate control of their relationship through her safeword and limit list.

He'd been in Miami since Wednesday, but spoke to her by phone last night and asked her if she wanted to go to The Covenant with him. Waiving the club's monthly membership fee, he'd expedited her required background check. She, in turn, had her medical release completed for him so they were free to play at the club, and she jumped at the chance to go.

She'd been shocked when Brody had stopped by earlier in the day and gave her a small black shopping bag with red trim on it. He told her Ian had picked out two outfits for her from the club store and to choose one to wear to the club for her first time. Winking and grinning before he turned to walk away, Brody had informed her, "My personal favorite is the pink and white one."

He'd left her standing there with her mouth open. When she had recovered, he was long gone, and she raced into her bedroom to see what was in the bag. The first outfit—actually they weren't "outfits," they were lingerie sets—was a dark green, silk bra with matching short-shorts. But it was the pale, pink baby-doll top and thong with white trim which she chose to wear without a second thought. The material was sheer except for two small triangles—one over each breast.

Now, as she got dressed, she realized the hem stopped right at the bottom of her butt cheeks and if she bent over, everyone would see her bare ass even though it was already exposed through the thin material. The top's silk triangles covered the nipples of her 38Ds, but left little else to the imagination. She admired herself in the mirror, and instead of feeling slutty, she felt beautiful, sexy, and very,

very naughty. Technically it showed a little more than her bikini did during the summer, but she'd never worn a bathing suit with a thong. After she threw on a little makeup and a pair of white sandals, which Brody had recommended since at the club she would be barefoot, she pulled on a knee-length black cotton dress. Tank-styled, it was light-weight and she sometimes wore it as a cover-up for her bathing suit. Grabbing a thin wrap for the cooler evening air and her overnight bag, she left her apartment and drove over to the compound, excited for Ian to see her in the outfit he'd picked out for her.

He had told her to park outside his apartment, and as she pulled up, Ian stepped out of the building, and she almost drooled at the sight of him. Damn, the man was gorgeous. Tight, black leather pants covered his long, powerful legs and an open black leather vest showcased his sculpted chest, abdomen, and arms. Add in his black leather boots and he looked like he walked off the set of a biker movie. If the rest of the cast looked like him, she'd be front row center at the theater on opening night.

He opened her car door and extended his hand to help her out. His gaze raked possessively and seductively over her body, and that's all it took for her to become aroused. After giving her a long, leisurely kiss hello, he took her keys, purse, and overnight bag, and placed them inside his apartment door before returning to her. He removed a white and black braided band from his pocket and clasped the leather collar around her neck, telling her she was to wear it at all times whenever they were at the club. "I also don't want you at the club unless you're with me, at least until you become more comfortable and familiar with the protocols." He paused. "Scratch that. I don't ever want you in the club without me."

She didn't mind because she wasn't sure she wanted to go there without him. For some reason, it seemed like she would be cheating on him if she did. "Yes, Sir."

They chatted as they walked across the compound and up into the club lobby. He introduced her to Matthew, the submissive on duty at the front desk, and Tiny, the massive, bald, black bouncer at the door. Despite his intimidating size, Tiny was a very sweet man and called all the women "Miss" along with their first names, which Angie found endearing. Ian told her the man was the head of security at the club and also did the occasional bodyguard job for Trident.

After Tiny opened one of the double doors letting them step into the club, Ian instructed her to go through the other door which led to the locker rooms and leave her wrap, dress, and shoes in a locker. He handed her a simple lock to use and told her to return to him at the bar, pointing to where he intended to wait for her a few feet away. She went through the door and down the closest set of stairs which had a sign indicating the ladies' locker room. In addition to the lockers, there were the bathroom and shower areas, as well as a little lounge and vanity area. A few women were already there and two of them said a polite hello to her as they walked out the door leading to the pit. One of them was wearing a black vinyl cat-suit while the other one was dressed in only a thong with pasties on her nipples, and Angie couldn't help her gaping stare at their retreating backs. Another woman about her age smiled at her and held out her hand in greeting. "Hi, I'm Shelby. You must be new here."

Angie grinned at the woman's bubbly personality and her electric-blue straight hair which matched her bra and short skirt set. She shook Shelby's hand. "Hi, I'm Angie and, yes, tonight is my first night. I've never been in a club like this before, so I'm a little nervous."

Shelby's eyes widened a little and she laughed. "A newbie-newbie? Wow, are you in for a culture shock. I remember my first time about twelve years ago, and sometimes I'm still surprised I went back a second time after some of the things I saw. Who's your master?" At Angie's confused look, she added, "Your collar means you're someone's sub."

She was so nervous and excited, Angie had forgotten she had it on. Fingering the soft leather, she said, "Oh, right. I'm here with Ian . . . I mean, Master Ian."

The other submissive got a starry-eyed look on her face. "Master

Ian is such a dreamboat. In fact, his brother and the rest of the guys at Trident are too. I think it's some sort of a requirement they have over there."

Even though Angie agreed, she had a sudden pang of jealousy wondering if Ian and Shelby had ever hooked up together. Shaking it off, she told herself she had no right to inquire about his past lovers, even though she'd asked about the bitch, Heather, the night of the gala. He hadn't asked her about her past relationships so she assumed they were both leaving their own personal baggage behind them. The point was, he was here with her, and he'd told her earlier in the week that while they were dating, he insisted they be exclusive. Ian didn't like to share, which worked out well because neither did Angie.

"Just remember," Shelby was telling her, "don't be rude or snarky to a Dom or Domme and stay out of trouble. Those are the easiest ways to get a punishment." She giggled. "Unless it's what you're in the mood for. Remember your safeword, and if you're unsure of anything, tell Master Ian immediately. The Doms aren't mind readers, so you have to speak up if there's a problem or you're scared about something. And if Master Ian isn't next to you for some reason, and there's a problem, grab any of the Dungeon Masters—they're in gold vests—or a security officer in a red shirt and bow tie."

When Shelby left her alone, saying she would see her later, Angie picked out an empty locker. She felt a little better after talking to the friendly woman, but the butterflies in her stomach were still fluttering around. Before she lost her nerve, she threw her wrap and shoes into the small metal space and lifted her dress over her head, hanging it on the hook provided. Closing the locker, she put the small three-digit lock on it, then went over to a full-length mirror to make sure her hair and makeup were still okay. Satisfied, she took a deep breath and headed for the stairs again, convincing herself she was ready for anything.

Ian was right where he said he'd be, talking to Devon, Kristen, and another man Angie didn't recognize. She was happy to see Kristen again and felt less nervous when she saw the other woman in a red, lace teddy and panties. The others greeted her as she approached, but her gaze was on the appreciation she saw in Ian's face. It was obvious he was delighted with her choice of lingerie for the evening. He pulled her to his side and gave her a kiss which would've knocked her socks off if she'd been wearing any. When he finally let her up for air, he introduced her to the other man standing next to him. "Angie, this is Master Carl. Carl, be nice to my submissive, Angie. This is her first time in a club."

The older man appeared to be in his fifties and was slim and a little shorter than Ian. His graying black hair, goatee, black dress shirt, and leather pants almost gave him the look of a vampire, minus the fangs, but his smile put her at ease. "Ian, I do love the Sawyer brothers' taste in women. Angie, my dear, Master Ian knows how much I enjoy teasing new subs, but since he asked me not to, I will graciously welcome you to The Covenant. But if you're ever in the mood for a whipping, please come and see me."

Angie's eyes widened in astonishment, but she relaxed again when Ian growled while Devon and Kristen laughed. "That's what you call being nice?" He turned his head back to her. "Master Carl is a sadist, Angel, in addition to being a tease. He likes to make the subs nervous, but you have nothing to worry about because underneath, he's really a big softie."

Carl scoffed. "Oh thanks, Ian. If you give away all my secrets, I won't have any fun."

The others laughed and Angie heard another male voice whisper into her ear from behind, "I'm glad to see you chose the white one, darlin'."

Brody. He looked sexy in a tight, black T-shirt, snug worn jeans, and cowboy boots. The submissives of the club must fight over him all the time. For a computer geek, he was far from nerdy looking, with his broad shoulders and chiseled torso. And for some reason, he was the only one she felt a little embarrassed about standing in front of in her current state of undress. Maybe because, aside from the day she stood in their team meeting in her underwear, he'd seen her almost every day fully clothed. As her cheeks turned tomato-red, Brody winked and gave her a quick peck on the cheek and did the same to Kristen. "Hey there, Ninja-girl. You're looking as sexy as ever."

Angie was grateful Ian ordered her a glass of wine and took a beer for himself. She knew there was a drink limit if they were planning on playing, which he'd told her they were. He was carrying her membership card for her, and it was how the bartenders and security staff kept track of everyone's alcohol consumption. Access to the pit was denied if a member had more than two drinks.

The six of them chatted for a few minutes, and Angie began to relax even more, despite Ian's possessive hand resting on her right butt cheek under her baby-doll top, squeezing her bare flesh every once in a while. She looked around the bar and balcony areas, eyeing people in every shape, size, age, and ethnicity. They were also all in varying states of dress, and she found it pretty easy to figure out whether a person was a dominant or submissive by looking at what they were wearing. It was very odd seeing a few naked subs walking around without a care, but she imagined it was less of a distraction than being at a nudist beach where everyone would be undressed.

A waitress, dressed in a short, black skirt, red bra, and black bow-tie, approached the group and stopped next to Brody. She waited for him to stop talking, the whole time keeping her eyes cast downward. Brody finished what he was saying to Master Carl and turned to the patient submissive. "Yes, Cassandra. What can I do for you?"

"Good evening, Master Brody." The pretty brunette kept her gaze averted from the Dom's face. "Master Marco is a DM tonight by station four and requests you go see him when you have a moment."

He smiled and using two fingers, tilted the woman's face up so she had to look at him. "Thank you, sweetheart. If you're interested in doing a scene when your shift is over, come find me. Okay?"

Cassandra's face lit up. "Yes, Master Brody. I will. Thank you, Sir."

The submissive walked away, smiling, and Brody excused himself before heading toward the grand staircase. Master Carl left them a minute later, and Ian looked at Angie. "Ready to go downstairs?"

She took a deep breath and nodded. She'd made it this far, so what the hell. "Yes, Sir. I am."

"Good, because so am I." He had the smile on his face which always got her nervous and wet at the same time and her heart rate increased. He took her almost empty glass and left it on the bar with his own, explaining that only bottled water was allowed in the pit so the submissives walking around barefoot didn't have to worry about broken glass. Taking her hand, he led her to the stairs and gave her membership card to the security guard standing at the top. The man scanned it and then Kristen's before handing them back to the two Doms. Ian escorted her down the stairs followed by Devon and Kristen. They were about to break away from the other couple, when a much younger Dom approached them requesting to talk to Ian and Devon in private for a moment. Ian had mentioned earlier his cousin, Mitch, who managed the club, was home with the flu for a few days, so Ian or Devon might need to take care of a few things in his place. "Kristen, would you mind showing Angie the submissive waiting area? This will take a few minutes."

Kristen looked at her Dom for permission and he nodded. "Yes, Sir. Come on, Angie. I'll introduce you to some of the other subs."

Before Kristen had a chance to lead her away, Ian gave Angie a quick kiss. "Stay there until I come for you. There's a DM standing nearby if there are any problems which there shouldn't be. Okay?"

"Yes, Sir."

She was glad he took the time to make sure she was comfortable with leaving him because it made her feel safe. Kristen brought her to a sitting area halfway between the stairs and the stage where several other submissives were sitting and talking. One of them was Shelby, who jumped up and gave Kristen a hug. Her friend explained that Shelby was one of her Beta-readers and had arranged for her to tour the club with Master Mitch. It was during the fateful tour the author found out her date for that night, Devon, was part owner of the place.

The two women introduced her to four other submissives, two

males and two females. They all took seats on the couches, ottomans, and winged-back chairs and began to fill in the newest member of the club on all the gossip. All of a sudden, one of the male subs, who was also a newer member, gasped. "Who is *that* talking to Masters Devon and Ian? He's absolutely scrumptious."

Everyone turned to look back toward the stairs to see the younger Dom had stepped away from the two men, and they now stood talking to an older Chris Hemsworth look-a-like. Even from where the subs sat, they could see his stunning blue eyes, and with his shoulder length, dark blonde hair and chiseled face, the man was an utter hunk. If any submissive met the six-foot-four man outside of a club, they would immediately recognize his status as a Dom. He carried himself in a commanding, mysterious manner, and Angie guessed the man was popular with the subs, unless he had one of his own. Dressed in brown leather pants, boots, and a tan T-shirt, which hugged his muscular torso and arms, the man was swoon-worthy.

It was Shelby who clued everyone in after letting out a dramatic sigh. "*That* is Master Carter. He's such a dreamboat."

Angie almost chuckled because it seemed as if Shelby thought most good-looking men were "dreamboats," but Kristen's sharp inhalation caught her attention. She looked at her new friend to see the woman had her mouth open and was staring wide-eyed at the three men. "*That's* Master Carter? Holy crap!"

Shelby looked incredulous. "Haven't you met him yet, Kristen? Oh that's right—I don't think he's been here for about six months, so I guess it makes sense."

"I've, uh, met him, sort of, but I didn't know what he looked like." Kristen didn't look away from the men, and her answer had the other submissives eyeing her curiously.

Looking back at the male trio, Angie was about to ask her what she was talking about when she noticed Masters Devon and Carter were smiling broadly while staring at Kristen. She thought there might be a story behind the men's gazes, but Angie wasn't sure what it was. Master Carter suddenly winked at Kristen as Master Devon crooked his finger at his fiancée in a command for her to come to him. Kristen stood, but seemed to remember she was watching Angie for Ian and paused. Shelby eased her obvious concern. "I'll take care of Angie. Go before you earn a spanking, although I'll trade places with you if you want."

Shelby giggled when Kristen didn't answer her and rushed to her Dom's side, blushing furiously when Master Carter took her hand and kissed it. Angie now knew there was definitely a story between the three and vowed to ask her friend about it if she saw her later. She was so wrapped up in what was going on with the trio, she didn't realize Ian had approached her until he stood in front of her blocking the view of the rest of the huge room. He greeted the other subs by name as he held out his hand for her to take and helped her stand. "Come along, Angel. We'll walk around for a bit and you can observe some of the scenes then maybe we can have one of our own."

Angie felt warm, wet heat between her legs as she wondered what Ian was going to do for her first public scene. Although they'd gone over her limit list, he hadn't decided what would happen tonight, telling her he wanted to see her reactions first.

Ian started her tour at a spanking bench since she'd already gotten a taste of it earlier in the week. In addition to bare handed spanking, she was able to see a flogging, paddling, and cropping. Moving on to other areas, there was a male submissive shackled to the wall wearing nipple clamps, a very large vibrating anal plug, and a cock ring. His Domme was sucking on her sub's cock, yet denying the man an orgasm as punishment for an unknown infraction, and Angie almost felt sorry for the guy.

A scene involving a violet wand caught Angie's attention, and after seeing it to the end she asked Ian if she could modify her limit list. She hadn't known what electric play entailed and so she'd placed it in her hard-limit column, but now she wanted to try it sometime. He told her he was pleased she was keeping an open mind and was willing to grow with her new knowledge.

They stopped at a station which was larger than the others because it was used for bullwhip scenes, and it gave the Doms the room they needed for the longer whip. Currently, Master Jake was whipping a female sub, while a male knelt nearby on the floor, awaiting his turn. Ian explained that Jake had mastered the bullwhip over many years and was often asked by unattached subs to perform whipping scenes with them. Other Doms would also request for Jake to service their subs when they didn't have the expertise to do it themselves. Mistress China and Master Carl were also in high demand as Whip Masters, and the three tended to alternate Thursday, Friday, and Saturday nights between them to give the others a chance to have nights off. Each session with a sub was on average about fifteen minutes, and with several sessions scheduled per night, swinging a bullwhip for almost two hours straight was a strain on the upper arms and back.

The naked sub strapped to the St. Andrew's cross was slipping into subspace, and Jake slowed his strikes, but the crack of the whip still could be heard over the club music. Her back, buttocks, and upper thighs were covered in red slash marks, but not one of the strikes had broken her skin. Without warning, the moaning woman's knees gave out, and Jake dropped the whip, rushing over to help her Dom release the woman from her restraints. Her Master wrapped her in a blanket, picked her up in his arms, and carried her to a nearby chaise lounge, followed by the Whip Master. Laying her down gently on her stomach, the Dom pushed her hair away from her face and said something in her ear which made her nod her head although her eyes never opened. Jake monitored the exchange from beside them until he was satisfied the submissive was okay. Leaving her to her Dom's aftercare, he strode back to the station where the waiting sub was wiping down the cross with citrus scented cleanser so he could take his turn.

Angie watched as Jake ran a towel across his sweaty face and wondered why he didn't take off his soaking wet T-shirt since she was sure he would be more comfortable. He had a muscular body, and she didn't doubt he would make the subs drool if he went shirtless.

"He has some scars on his back which he doesn't let most people see," Ian explained. "They aren't as bad as he seems to think they are, but he's still self-conscious about them."

She didn't realize she'd voiced her thought aloud. "Did he get them in combat like you did?"

Ian shook his head as another Dom and his male submissive approached to speak with him. "No, sweetheart, he got them when he was younger, and it's his tale to tell you if he chooses to. Excuse me for a minute." He turned and began to talk to the other two men, while Angie watched Jake restrain the male submissive who'd stripped his clothes off and stood there naked.

While the Dom started with a light flogging as a warm-up, Angie scanned the areas around her. Nearby, she saw a man talking to Shelby, but it was obvious the woman didn't want anything to do with him. The blue-haired sub was about to walk away from him when the man reared back and, much to Angie's horror, backhanded her across the face.

# CHAPTER 10

*I*an was talking to a D/s couple when several things happened almost at once behind him. First, he heard a female cry out in pain, but it wasn't a normal cry he heard throughout the club on a regular basis. A second later he heard Angie scream his name and other people shout. In the mere seconds it took for him to turn around and locate the problem, Angie was gone from his side.

Panic seized him as he ran over to where a crowd had quickly gathered near the submissive waiting area. Pushing his way through, he took in the sight before him. Marco, in his Dungeon Master gold vest, had some guy face down into the floor, his eyes glaring with anger. One arm was yanked up the man's back in a hold he couldn't get out of, even though he was yelling and trying his best to shake the DM loose. Angie and Mistress China were kneeling on the floor, comforting Shelby who had tears coming from her shocked eyes and was holding a trembling hand to her face. From the look on Mistress China's face, the guy being detained was lucky Marco had gotten to him first. The diminutive Asian-American woman took great pleasure in giving pain to submissives and, at the moment, she looked ready to unleash her fury. Ian didn't recognize the man, but spotted the yellow band on the guy's wrist, indicating he was the guest of a member, just as Master Parker pushed through the crowd.

Parker Christiansen was a longtime member, whose construction company had done a majority of the renovations throughout the compound, and was a well-liked and respected Dom. At the moment though, he looked confused and pissed as he addressed the guy Marco had pinned. "What the fuck, Dave? What the hell did you do?"

"I didn't do anything. Now get this fucking gorilla off me. I'm going to sue if he doesn't get off me." Whoever Dave was, he was the complete opposite of Parker. Whereas Parker was a confident Dom, this guy came off as a whiny jackass.

Marco growled, but wouldn't let the man up. Instead he glowered at Parker and Ian. "This asshole backhanded Shelby. I had people in my way and couldn't get here fast enough to stop him."

Ian was pissed, but Parker was beyond livid. He looked at the crying submissive and it appeared he was going to explode. His jaw clenched. "He's my brother. Let him up, Marco."

Marco looked at Parker and then at Ian. Tiny and several other security guards had pushed the crowd back to give the Doms some room. Ian stood with his arms crossed and studied Parker's face. What he saw had him nodding once to Marco who released Dave and got to his feet after giving the guy a final shove in the back. As Dave stood, he was stupid enough to say, "What's the big deal? Everyone is slapping women around here, and I get in trouble for what you all are doing."

Dave brushed himself off, and Parker took a step closer to him, his voice low and barely controlled. "You okay?"

Not seeing the fury on Parker's face, the guy grinned. "Yeah, Park, I'm fine."

"Good." The Dom nodded his head once, then punched his brother in the face, knocking the bastard out. Without giving the prone man another glance, Parker hurried over to Shelby and crouched down in front of her. "I'm so sorry, Shelby. It's my fault. I shouldn't have left him alone."

He helped her stand, but Mistress China and Angie stayed by her side for support. Parker gently pulled Shelby's hand from her cheek and growled, "I'm going to kill him," when he saw the red and swollen area which was starting to bruise.

She grabbed his forearm, her eyes wide. "No, don't, Sir. I should have grabbed Master Marco or one of the other DMs. He was trying to negotiate with me. I saw his guest wristband and knew he wasn't allowed to play, but he wouldn't take no for an answer. When I tried to walk away, he hit me."

Parker drew the sub into his arms and held her for a moment while everyone else looked on. Ian cocked his head at Tiny who began breaking up the crowd with the other guards. The Head Dom then spoke to Parker. "Let's take this to the office. What do you want us to do with him?"

Parker didn't answer Ian right away, obviously too worried about Shelby. "Go to the ladies' lounge and put some ice on your cheek. When I'm done with Ian and my asshole brother, I'll take you home."

The man's lack of using Ian's Master title in front of a sub told the Head Dom how shaken the other man was.

"You . . . you don't have to do that, I can drive myself." Shelby's face flushed, and she wouldn't look at Parker. She seemed almost shy about being in the Dom's arms, and Ian found it interesting since the pretty sub was such an outgoing person.

"I need to do this, Shelby, please. I need to make sure you're okay and get home safe. This is not negotiable." He tipped her chin up with his fingers and made her look at him. "Please."

She bit her lip, but nodded her consent. Mistress China wrapped her arm around the sub's shoulder and eased her from Parker's arms. Despite being a bit of a sadist, the Domme tended to be a mother hen to the submissives. "I'll take care of her. We'll be in the lounge when you're ready."

Parker nodded his thanks to her while Ian spoke to Angie. "I'm sorry, but I have to take care of this. Please go with them and wait for me in the lounge. I'll be a few minutes."

"Yes, Sir."

He was surprised at the fierce look she threw at the still unconscious Dave. He almost expected her to kick the guy as she followed the other two women. Marco also went with them after asking another DM to cover his station. Ian could see his teammate was upset for not being able to stop the assault before it happened. He could be a big marshmallow when it came to the submissives and was the one they tended to go to if they needed someone to talk to, or some comfort.

Ian asked one of the nearby waitresses to bring an ice-pack to Shelby before turning to Parker who still seemed like he wanted to commit familial homicide. The other Dom handed his keys to Tiny and asked him to not-so-gently throw his brother in the back seat of his truck so he could drive him back to the guy's motel. He then turned to Ian, his face filled with regret. "Let's get this over with."

A few minutes later, Parker was pacing behind the closed door of Mitch's office as Ian sat against the front of the desk and watched him. "Fuck! I'm so sorry, Ian. I was only gone two minutes to take a fucking piss. I told him not to move from where we were sitting. He fucking knew he wasn't allowed to play or approach any subs. The only reason I even brought him here is he called me a few weeks ago and said he wanted to see the place while he was in town on business. Said he and his wife were thinking about joining a club in Boston. I knew I shouldn't have brought him here. He doesn't understand the lifestyle the way I do. I know he's cheated on his wife before, but I didn't think he was stupid enough to try something here. Fuck! I'm going to kill him."

Ian let him rant for another minute before the irate man at last took a deep breath and glanced at him. "I broke the rules. Do what you have to do." He plopped down into one of the chairs and hung his head in defeat.

Ian felt bad for the Dom. On top of being a nice guy, he was also one of the club's Dungeon Masters, and the last thing he would want was for someone to be hurt because of his actions, especially a submissive. But the rules had to be enforced. "I'm sorry I have to do this, but you know you're not supposed to leave a guest alone for this exact reason. You should have asked a DM or guard to watch him for the time you needed to leave him alone." The other man nodded, but didn't say anything. "I have to suspend your play privileges for the next twelve weeks. During that time, you'll take three DM shifts per week. I'll check the schedule and coordinate the dates and times with you tomorrow. Your guest privileges will also be suspended for two years."

Parker snorted. "Don't worry. I think this is the last time I'll bring anyone here whether they're in the lifestyle or not." He ran his hand down his face as he stood again. "I'll be back for Shelby in a few minutes. Dave's motel is about five minutes from here. I'll dump him into his room and come back. If I thought a cab would pick up the unconscious asshole, I'd call one. But since Shelby's being taken care of by China and Marco, I'll get rid of him first."

Ian nodded and followed him out of the office. At the main double doors, Parker continued out to the lobby while Ian took the door and stairs leading into the women's locker room. He found the three women and Marco sitting in the lounging area with Shelby sitting on the Dom's lap as he cradled her, talking softly. When she spotted Ian, she jumped up and latched onto his arm with a pleading expression on her face. "Master Ian! Please don't discipline Master Parker. It wasn't his fault. I don't want him to get into trouble. Please don't kick him out of the club. It's all my fault. I should've walked away sooner."

Marco and Mistress China both growled at her inappropriate guilt, and Ian grabbed the near hysterical submissive by her shoulders and guided her to sit down in an empty chair. This wasn't like her—Ian had never seen the bubbly submissive upset before. "Calm down, Shelby." His order was given in a commanding tone which instantly quieted the woman as he intended. "Master Parker knows he broke the rules and there are consequences for what happened. None of which were your fault, and I don't want to hear those words out of your mouth again. Understand?"

"Yes, Sir. But—"

"No buts, Shelby." He didn't make a habit of discussing a member's discipline with others, but he needed to reassure the worried sub. "I didn't revoke Master Parker's membership, but he did receive a suspension for his irresponsible actions. He accepted full blame for what happened and agreed with the punishment. Now, he'll be back in a few minutes to take you home so why don't you grab your things from your locker and change. Okay?"

Still crying softly, she stood and mumbled, "Yes, Sir."

Ian pulled her into his arms and hugged her. "It'll be okay, little one. I promise. I think the best thing you can do is dry your eyes, and when Master Parker comes back, give him some of your sass we all love so much and let him take care of you. I think it'll make both of you feel better, *hmm*?"

She pulled back and gave him a watery smile. "Yes, Sir. Thank you."

Marco took her arm and gave her a quick hug also, kissing her on the top of her blue-haired head. "Sweetheart, I'm sorry I wasn't there when you needed me."

"It's okay, Master Marco. You got there as fast as you could."

He gave her another squeeze and let her go to her locker before turning to Angie who'd been sitting quietly on the couch next to Mistress China. His steel gray eyes bore into her. "And you, little subbie, have some explaining to do to your Master."

*What?* As Ian's expression became stern, Angie's brow furrowed in confusion. "What did you do, Angel?"

"I-I didn't do anything."

She looked back and forth between the two Doms, as if not quite sure what Marco was referring to. Mistress China, in her black, full-length bodysuit and over-the-thigh boots, grinned and sat back to enjoy the show.

Marco shook his head and told Ian, "Your little sub tried to get to the jackass before I did. She was ready to jump on his back and start pounding on him. I almost tackled her by accident trying to take him down."

Ian's eyes narrowed at her as the Domme next to her sing-songed, "Somebody's in trouble."

Ignoring the other woman, he took a step forward to his very worried looking submissive. "Is that true, Angel?"

"I-I just reacted. I saw him hit Shelby and I . . ." Her words trail off. Ian knew the moment she figured out there was nothing she could say which would get her out of the mess she found herself in. She swung her gaze to the floor. "I'm sorry, Sir."

His hands on his hips, Ian tilted his head back and talked to the ceiling for a moment. "Lord, save me from subs who want to beat up people in my club and put themselves in danger." Marco snorted, knowing Ian was referring to his future sister-in-law's own fight in the locker room several months earlier which earned her the call sign "Ninja-girl" from the rest of the team. The big difference between the two incidents was Kristen had been taller and about twenty pounds heavier than Heather and another sub Michelle, and had taken self-defense classes. Parker's brother outweighed Angie by a good eighty pounds and had already hit another woman. Ian's gaze returned to Angie's face. "You may be sorry now, but you'll be extremely sorry after I spank your pretty ass for putting yourself in danger." He ignored her surprised gasp. "We have DM's and guards for a reason in the club, Angel. We do not need little subs disregarding their own safety. You didn't know him, he's a hell of a lot bigger than you, and he could have hurt you before anyone had a chance to do anything."

"You're right, Sir." She let out a heavy sigh and nodded. "I don't know what I was thinking. I just couldn't believe he'd hit Shelby, and my first instinct was to attack him before he struck her again."

Her agreement didn't change Ian's mind about her punishment as he turned to Marco. "Would you find a free spanking station and ask someone to grab my bag from behind the bar, please?"

The other Dom nodded and said to Angie before he left the room, "I'm sorry, little one, but you earned it."

She watched him walk away with her mouth wide open, then looked up at Ian with her apprehension evident on her face. "I-I'm sorry. I didn't mean . . ."

When she paused, Ian's expression tempered, and he let out a deep, slow breath. He squatted in front of her and took her hands in his. "I'm not angry, sweetheart. I heard you yell and turned around and didn't see you. I panicked. My stomach dropped, and I was terrified something happened to you. And because you acted with no regard for your own safety, you've earned your first public spanking." His stare never wavered as he let her process what he'd said.

Mistress China stood, and Ian had almost forgotten the other woman was in the room. She patted his shoulder and smirked. "I'm going to go and get a front row seat. It's been a long time since I've witnessed a sub's first punishment."

He kept his eyes on Angie as the Domme left the room. He could tell she had a myriad of emotions running through her mind from shock, embarrassment and worry, to anticipation, excitement and need. The thought of a public spanking was turning her on, despite it being a punishment, and she wasn't sure what to make of the fact. He let her think about her upcoming ass-whooping as Shelby returned to the sitting area in sweats, a tee and high-top sneakers. She'd removed her blue wig and her short spiked blonde hair looked like she'd run her hands through it. He got up from his crouched position and handed her the ice-pack as the door reopened. Parker strode into the lounge, his eyes seeking out the injured submissive. The men rarely came into the ladies' locker room, but it didn't faze anyone when they did. It wasn't as if they hadn't seen most of the women naked at one time or another.

After telling Ian he would call tomorrow to get the DM schedule, Parker tucked Shelby under one arm and escorted her out of the club. Ian knew the sub was in good hands and wondered if there might be a budding romance between the two. The way they'd looked at each other when Parker first walked into the room, he wouldn't be surprised. Turning his attention to his own submissive, he took her by the hand and led her back into the pit, finding the spanking bench Marco had reserved for him. If he still hadn't been shaking off the fear he'd felt when he'd heard her screech his name earlier, he might have enjoyed her nervousness. But this punishment was for his own need to reinforce his rule that her safety and well-being came before anything else, as well as be a reminder for her not to jump into a dangerous situation in the future.

The word had spread a submissive was receiving her first-ever BDSM punishment and the area around the spanking bench was surrounded by Doms and subs. It was a rite of passage for every new sub, and he knew it would set the tone for her future involvement in the lifestyle. After her spanking, he intended to reward her for pushing her own limits and accepting the consequences for her reckless actions. The crowd was making her more nervous so he turned her until she was facing the bench and her back was to the still growing throng of people. He gripped her chin and made sure she was focused on him. "I want you to say your safeword nice and loud so everyone hears it and knows what it is."

It wasn't necessary for the crowd's sake, but she needed to remember she had all the control despite the fact her ass was about to get a pounding.

She swallowed hard. "My . . ." She cleared her throat and tried again. "My safeword is red, Sir."

"Your punishment will be fifteen spanks with a paddle on your bare ass, Angel. Do you wish to use your safeword or are you willing to accept your punishment?"

Her eyes went from his to the bench and back several times before it finally settled on him again. She took a deep, but trembling breath. "I will take my punishment, Sir."

"And what are you being punished for?"

"F-for putting myself in danger, Sir."

He smiled and his gaze softened. "Good girl." He took Angie's hand again and led her to the kneeling side of the bench. It looked like a modified sawhorse with padding for her knees, torso and arms. He helped her get on it, with her knees bent and her waist lying over the center. The position angled her head down and brought her ass up so it was the prime target. She handled having her wrists and ankles shackled very well, but began to hyperventilate when he brought the Velcro strap across her lower back which would hold her in place. Her response was normal for an inexperienced sub, and Marco, who'd been standing inside the roped off area in case he was needed, crouched down in front of her. He ran his hand over her head in an attempt to calm her. "Easy, little one. Take deep, slow breaths with me. Keep your eyes on mine."

While Ian's hands moved in a soothing caress over her back, hips, and buttocks, his teammate continued to calm her down with words of praise and encouragement. Ian let the man do what he did best—comfort a sub. It was one of Marco's greatest pleasures about the lifestyle. He liked being needed and was damn good at it.

Angie's breathing slowed to a more normal pace, but her heart rate was still pounding, which was to be expected. When Marco asked her to repeat her safeword, she responded, "R-red, Sir."

"And what punishment will your Master be giving you, little one?"

She swallowed hard again, but her fear seemed to ease as her arousal grew. "Fifteen spanks with a paddle, Sir."

Marco smiled and continued to caress her head and cheek. "Good girl. Are you ready now? Do you want me to step back, or stay here with you?"

Ian saw Angie was surprised by his friend's offer and was pleased with her answer. "Please stay, Sir. I'm ready."

Apparently also satisfied with her response, Marco went down to his knees in front of her and gave Ian a nod to continue. Her Dom began to rub and squeeze her ass cheeks a little harder. Bringing the blood to the skin's surface would make impacts easier on her. He had no intention of bruising her, but her ass would be a nice shade of red by the time he was done. Her discomfort would be completely gone within twenty-four hours, but before it was, she'd definitely feel and remember it.

He eased her thong down from her hips to the middle of her thighs and left it there. It hadn't been in his way, but it would make her feel more exposed. He was thrilled to feel the fabric of the crotch was drenched with her juices. As anxious as she was, she wanted this more than she feared it, even though she knew this would be different than the simple bare-handed spanking he'd given her the other night. That had been a play spanking, and this most certainly was not.

Stepping over to where Marco had placed his toy bag, Ian retrieved the wooden paddle he'd planned to use for her first punishment spanking. It resembled one from a ping-pong set, yet was a little larger and not covered in rubber. The size would allow him to spread out the strikes on her buttocks instead of hitting the same spot over and over, which is what would happen if he used a larger implement. He also grabbed an anal plug, lube, and a small flogger which he would start with. The plug would give her something else to focus on, something he usually didn't use for a discipline spanking. If this had been a pleasure spanking only, he would also consider placing a vibrating bullet inside her pussy, but he didn't want her too distracted, after all it was a punishment. The purpose of a light flogging prior to a spanking was to help the submissive relax a little more and release the body's endorphins. Sometimes a Dom would bypass a warm-up if the spanking was for punishment, but for Angie's first time, he wanted to make it bearable so she wouldn't fear future spankings. If everything went as he expected, by the time Ian finished meting out her discipline, she would be moments away from an intense orgasm despite her flaming backside.

He walked back over to where Marco knelt in front of her and he waited for her to raise her eyes to his. "I'm going to put an anal plug in you, Angel. It's a little bigger than what you've used in the past, but not by much. Next, I'll start off with a light flogging. It won't be painful, more like a hard caress. After I've warmed your sweet ass up, I'll move to the punishment phase. If you need me to slow down at any point, say the word 'yellow' and if you cannot take the paddle, say your safeword 'red.' And remember, sweetheart, you as the submissive, have the ultimate power here."

Her cheeks heated as he spoke. He knew part of her wanted to take the easy out he was offering her. But another part of her wanted to satisfy the cravings and need which had probably been churning through her body since he told her of the spanking he was about to give her. Showing that she trusted him with her body, she went with the latter. "I remember, Sir. I'm ready."

Ian kissed the top of her head and moved to stand behind her, trailing his hand lightly down her back to her ass as he went. A strong shiver went through her body and into his, shooting straight to his groin. He placed the flogger and paddle on the bench between her knees which were spread wide. Her bare pussy was glistening and he couldn't wait to see it dripping.

Opening the bottle, he poured lubricant into the crevice of her ass and on the plug. Her little rosette clenched then relaxed as he began to rub the tip of the toy up and down between her butt cheeks. As he pressed downward on her puckered hole, it gave way to the invasion and he heard her groan and beg for more. More than happy to give it to her, he eased the plug in and out of her, a little deeper each time, until the flared portion spread her the widest. Ian paused for a brief moment before giving it the final push it needed, and watched as her rim closed around the notch, holding it in place. His cock hardened painfully as he imagined replacing the plug with it and fucking her tight hole until neither of them could walk. *Soon.*

Grabbing the flogger, he took a step backward and got into the proper stance before flicking it toward her. The first gentle strike of the soft, supple leather strands landed on her outer thigh. Although she flinched from the sudden impact, he knew it hadn't hurt. He aimed more strikes to her other outer thigh and several down her back and ass cheeks. As he watched the tension ease from her body, he sped up, giving a little more oomph to the strikes. The next two landed on her inner thighs and he saw her strain to bring her body closer to him, not further away. She was surrendering to him and begging for more. He placed two more again on her inner thighs and then flicked his wrist, watching as the small knots at the end of each strand struck her on her pussy. Angie gasped, then moaned even louder. It was music to a Dom's ears. He began another cycle, starting with her outer thighs and then ending with a singular assault to her pussy and clit. This time a pleading cry escaped her lips and he stepped toward her. Caressing her ass, he leaned forward. "Are you okay, Angel? Give me a color."

Angie was panting, and he knew she was ready to beg for the orgasm which was just beyond her reach. Knowing there was a crowd of people staring at her exposed ass and pussy was turning her on even more. "Green, Sir. I'm good."

Ian smiled and gave her ass cheek a squeeze. "Yes, you are, Angel. Very good. I'm going to move to the paddle now. Try to stay relaxed."

*RELAXED? Was he serious?* How the hell was she supposed to relax? Taking a deep breath and exhaling, Angie focused on the beat of the pulsating music, on Marco's tender words and touches, on Ian's caresses of her lower back, ass and thighs, and on the plug in her back hole.

By the time she heard the crack of wood against flesh followed by the sudden sting, she'd been taken off guard. The first strike landed on her right ass cheek. Expecting one right behind it on her other cheek, she was surprised to feel Ian's hand rub the spot he'd hit. Just as she began to ease into the caress, a strike landed on her left cheek. Again, he rubbed the spot and despite the pain, she couldn't help think it wasn't so bad. She was wrong.

Ian began to spank her with the paddle repeatedly, with only a momentary pause between them. Each hit landed on a different place on her cheeks and sit spots above where her thighs and ass met. And each was harder than the last. She lost count as her ass began to burn. *Oh God, how many was he giving her?* Fifteen hadn't seemed so bad when he'd said the number, but she was so lost in the mixed sensations of pain, pleasure, want and need, it felt like he'd given her dozens of them. She was panting and straining against the straps which held her in place. Marco was still with her, watching her responses carefully and murmuring words of reassurance. Despite the onslaught of pain, never once did she want to say either of her safewords. Her ass was on fire, the heat spreading throughout her body, and all she wanted to do was beg Ian to fuck her. She hadn't known she was crying until she noticed the spanks had stopped and Marco thumbed away the tears on her cheeks. Ian's face appeared next to the other Dom's. "That's eleven, Angel. The last four will be the hardest and then I'm going to let you come if you want. Give me a color."

"Green! Please, Sir! Don't stop! Please let me come!" She screamed the words so loudly, the members up in the bar area had to have heard her over the music and distance. She was so wrapped up in her arousal and need, she didn't hear most of the crowd chuckle appreciatively at her response. They also praised the new sub's commitment to seeing her punishment through to the end.

Ian smiled at his angel. "It'll be my pleasure, sweetheart."

---

Returning to his former position, he took the correct stance to paddle right atop the crack of her ass, where the end of the anal plug sat flush between her cheeks. Rearing back, he hit the same spot four times, the sound of wood against flesh resonating through the air. *Smack. Smack. Smack. Smack.* Ian dropped the paddle and thrust two fingers straight into her soaking wet pussy. That was all it took to send her screaming over the edge of release. Rubbing her clit with his thumb, he prolonged her orgasm for as long as he could until her entire body sagged with relief.

As Ian withdrew his hand from between her trembling legs, the crowd broke out in applause for the exhausted sub. Her ass was bright red and her juices coated her thighs. The two Doms worked quickly to release her restraints and rubbed each limb to make sure her blood was circulating properly. Marco stood, grabbed a red blanket from a nearby shelf and handed it to Ian. "I'll take care of your stuff for you."

Ian nodded before wrapping his sub in the blanket and carrying her over to a large leather winged-back chair. He sat with her on his lap and let her ass hang over the side of his thigh so she wasn't too uncomfortable. After she took a few sips of water from the bottle someone had handed him, she cuddled into his chest as his strong arms held her. His heart squeezed when she looked up at him through swollen wet eyes and sighed. "Thank you, Master."

# CHAPTER 11

*F*our days later, Angie was at home and working on the cover for a new novel from Red Rose Books. The publishers had received the final drafts for Kristen's novel and her editor, Jillian, called Angie with high praise from her employers. They loved it and asked her to design the cover of another anticipated book from a different author. While she worked, she talked on her cell phone with her friend Mandy who had called her all excited about a new guy she'd met. Angie had just finished centering the title where she wanted it when her doorbell rang, a little before two in the afternoon. Figuring it was her UPS man dropping off some new work for her, she clicked the save icon on her laptop and ended her call with Mandy.

Leaving her phone next to her computer, she got up to answer the door. When she looked out the oblong side window, she frowned when she saw two men dressed in off-the-rack suits. One man spotted her and held up a wallet sized folder which contained a badge and an ID which said, "United States Drug Enforcement Administration" in gold letters.

Panic assailed her. The only reason for someone from the DEA to be ringing her doorbell was if something happened to Jimmy. She punched the security code into the alarm panel, unlocked the doorknob and deadbolt before throwing open the door. "What happened? Where's Jimmy? Is he hurt?"

The shorter of the two men, who'd shown her his ID through

the window, spoke in a calm, but commanding voice. "Are you Ms. Angelina Beckett? May we come in to talk to you for a minute?"

"Yes, yes, please." She stepped back to allow them to walk into her home even though a warning bell began sounding in her brain. Ignoring it, she shut the door before spinning around to face them. "Please tell me what happened."

The two agents walked into her living room while looking around. They seemed satisfied with what they did or did not see and again the shorter one spoke. "Ms. Beckett, I'm Agent Jackson and this is Agent Holstein with the Atlanta office of the DEA." The taller man with the stern face gave her a curt nod, but remained mute. "We've been instructed to take you into protective custody."

"Protective custody? Why? Who told you to do that?" The alarms in her brain were getting louder by the second.

"Agent Athos, otherwise known as Agent Austin, is worried about your safety. He thinks his cover has been blown and, like I said, he wants us to take you into protective custody and bring you to one of the DEA's safe-houses."

The warnings were now screaming at her. "Is that all he said?"

Both agents' eyes narrowed in confusion. The taller one seemed to be getting impatient, but it was still the shorter one who spoke. "Isn't that enough?"

*Shit!* She never should have let them in the house. Now she had to think of a way to get out of there in one piece. "Um, yes. I mean I thought maybe there was a specific threat or something." Angie jumped at the sound of a loud knock at her sliding glass door and glanced over to see who it was.

*Oh, thank God.* Brody stood on her patio, curiosity and a bit of concern in his eyes as he looked at the two men in her living room and back to her. He motioned for her to unlock the door and she dashed toward it as Agent Jackson spat out, "Who the hell is that?"

She saw the man reach for his holstered gun out of the corner of her eye, but was relieved when he didn't draw the weapon. Somehow, she had to warn Brody something was terribly wrong. As she opened the slider, she responded, hoping he would catch on fast to her dilemma. "Oh, this is my boyfriend, Brody. We've only been dating a few weeks. Brody, these men are from the DEA. This is Agent Jackson, and I'm sorry I forgot your name."

The taller man spoke for the first time. "Agent Holstein, and I'm sorry Ms. Beckett, but we really have to get going. The sooner we get you to the safe-house the better."

Brody had obviously caught on because his arm went around her waist and pulled her closer into his side. Although he acted calm and convincingly confused, she felt the tension rolling off him. She prayed he was good at the bodyguard thing he did for a living. When he spoke, he thickened his southern, Texas drawl. "DEA agents? Safe-house? Darlin', what're these men all talkin' about?"

She played along, hoping they would get out of here alive. "I'm sorry, honey. I know we had plans for this weekend, but do you remember my best friend, Jimmy, who I told you about?" He was still looking at the other men, but nodded, so she continued. "Well, what I didn't tell you was Jimmy is with the DEA and does undercover work for them. Apparently, they think his cover may be blown and I might be a target so they need to take me into protective custody."

"Really? Like in the movies?" Good Lord, the man could act "aw-shucks'" dumb when he needed to. And she was positive it was an act. "Well, if y'all have to keep my baby safe . . . can I go with her?"

It was Jackson who answered while his partner glowered at the new arrival. "I'm afraid not, sir. I promise we'll take good care of her for you. She'll only be gone a few days, a week at the most, until we can ascertain she's in no danger."

Brody shrugged his shoulders as if this entire scenario was no big deal. "All right, if you think it's best. Darlin', why don't I help you throw a few clothes in a bag and I'll say goodbye to you in private."

"We don't have time for that. We can get you some clothes and anything else you need once we have you safe."

Plastering on a fake pleading smile, Angie jumped at the opportunity to distance them from the two agents, if that was even who they were. All she did know was Jimmy hadn't sent them, and neither did his handler. "Oh, please. It'll only take a few moments to throw a few things into my duffel bag. I'd feel more comfortable with my own stuff. And I really want a minute to say goodbye to Brody. We'll be quick." She was halfway to her bedroom door with her boyfriend-for-the-minute in tow, but stopped and grabbed her cell phone and laptop from her make-shift office desk against the wall in her dining area. "I'll just throw these in with my clothes so I can work while you guys are keeping me safe."

Both men looked beyond annoyed, but Agent Jackson reluctantly nodded when she and Brody reached the entrance to her bedroom. The instant they were over the threshold, Brody grabbed her around the waist as he closed the door behind them and said loud enough to be overheard, "Com'ere, baby-doll, and give me some sugar. I love you so much. I'm gonna miss you."

As soon as the door was shut, he quietly locked it and dragged her toward her bedroom sliding door which also led out to the lanai. She kept her voice to a whisper "I'm sorry, Brody, but I'm in big trouble. Jimmy didn't send them."

He glanced back at the alarm control panel next to the door leading to the living room, making sure he wasn't going to set off the alarm when he opened the slider. His Texas twang had faded, along with the volume of his voice, although there was still a hint of the drawl. "I kind of already understood that, darlin'."

He looked down and a bit of relief came over his face when he saw she had sneakers on. "As soon as I open the door, we're going to run through the backyards away from my place. I wish we could go get one of my guns, but we'd have to pass by your living room. Head for the wooded area two houses down. From there, we'll cut through to the next street over. Ready?" She nodded anxiously, but remained silent. "Here goes nothing."

He silently slid the door open, and they took off across her other next-door neighbor's yard, running as fast as they could . . . well, as fast as Angie could. They were almost at the second yard when they heard the agents kick in her bedroom door and as they reached the woods she heard one of them yell, "Hey! Fuck!"

Brody glanced over his shoulder, but Angie kept running

forward. Thankfully, a short distance in, the denser foliage provided them with more coverage. He weaved them through the vegetation and as they reached the clearing of another back yard, she heard someone crashing through the brush behind them, followed by more cursing. Even though Brody was moving faster than she was, she urged him on. "Hurry, I hear them."

"This way." He tugged her arm, and she almost lost her phone and laptop she was still clutching. They rounded the house and ran diagonally across the street past another dwelling, into a backyard which had a wooden four-foot fence separating it from the rear parking lot of a small strip mall. As they approached the fence, Brody grabbed her by the waist and just about threw her over it, vaulting the barrier himself a second later. Angie was shocked she'd landed on her feet and still had her electronics in her hands. Thank goodness she ran three miles four times a week, otherwise she would've passed out by now. As it was, her panic was making it hard for her to catch her breath.

Brody clasped his hand around her upper arm and took off running again. As they came around the side of the building, she stumbled, but his grip kept her from falling. When they reached the sidewalk, he turned right and kept sprinting as he hauled her past stores and businesses. She had no idea if they were still being followed and didn't dare look. He, on the other hand, glanced back several times, but didn't slow them down. One block over, he pivoted and hustled them across the street into the parking lot of another strip mall. She realized he had a plan in mind and her thoughts were confirmed when he ran up to the door of a restaurant named Donovan's. Vaguely she remembered Jenn worked here and Jake's brother owned it. Throwing the door open, Brody dragged her inside, slowing, but not stopping as he hurried her down the length of the bar and barked at the startled bartender. "Mike, call Ian. Tell him 'code red.' If you can't get him, call Jake or Devon. If two guys in suits come in claiming to be feds, call 911."

Mike, whoever he was, apparently knew what Brody was talking about because he threw down the rag he'd been using to wipe down the bar and snatched up the phone behind him. Brody still didn't stop moving, leading her down a hallway, past the bar's restrooms, and into a room marked "Private." He pulled her into the office, shut the door, and locked it. Finally, they came to a complete stop, and she was gasping for air. She was a little pissed he wasn't even breathing heavy, as if running four or five blocks on a zig-zag course while someone was chasing them was an everyday occurrence.

"What . . . what if . . . they come in here?" She got the words out in between gulps of air. Her heart was pounding in her brain, her lungs on fire, and if they were found, she didn't think she could run another step.

Brody took her phone from her hand, opened the back of it and ripped out the battery and SIM card, putting everything into the pocket of his sweatpants. He walked over to two safes which were bolted to the floor underneath the paper-laden desk. Placing his middle finger on a scanner on the face of one of them, he waited three seconds and the door clicked open. Reaching in, he pulled out a holstered Sig Sauer 9mm pistol, checked to see the magazine was filled to capacity with brass tipped bullets, then shut the safe door. He clipped the re-holstered weapon to the back of his sweatpants which ended up pulling them further down on his hips with the heavy weight of it.

Angie wasn't afraid of the weapon, in fact, she was glad he now had one. "You've obviously planned for situations like this, huh?"

"When we first started Trident, the team came up with a bunch of emergency plans. Never had to use one from my own place before, but I'm happy to know they work." He saw her glance nervously at the office door. "We lost them a while back so we're safe until Ian gets here. When he does, we'll go out the back and get in his car."

She looked where he pointed and saw another door she assumed led to an alley or lot behind them. "Why did you come over, anyway?" It wasn't unusual for him to stop by in the morning or evening, but not in the middle of the afternoon. "I'm not complaining, mind you."

There was a sharp single knock on the door they'd come in through, and Angie jumped, but Brody held up his hand to calm her. The door didn't open, but she heard a male voice say, "Ian's six minutes out. He'll honk twice. Seems to be all clear out front."

Brody responded with a single knock of his own on the wooden door before turning around to face her again. "I was working late last night so I took today off. I was heading out for a run when I saw the strange car in your driveway with government plates. I went around back to check on you, not wanting to interrupt if you didn't need me. But when I saw your face, I knew something wasn't right. By the way, you did phenomenal. You stayed calm, helped me figure out something was wrong and acted like a pro. You ever think about becoming an actress?"

She didn't answer him. Something about what he'd said made her think he wasn't being one-hundred percent truthful with her, but at this point it didn't matter. She needed his and Ian's help to get to the storage unit where her emergency vehicle, money, fake IDs, and two bags full of clothes and other necessities were kept. After that, she could get out of town and follow the orders Jimmy had drilled into her over the years.

On the first of every month, she drove around Tampa on lesser used roads with no set pattern. Once she was sure she wasn't being followed, she'd head to the storage unit rented under a fictitious name and check on everything. With the outside unit's door open, she'd start up the old Chevy Nova's souped up engine and let it run for a few minutes to ensure the batteries stayed charged. Then she'd turn it off again and lock the unit back up until the first of the next month, when she did the whole routine again. Every six months she drove the car out and took it for an oil change and a tune up. She'd always thought the whole process was a little too much James Bond-ish, but now she was grateful she'd followed Jimmy's instructions to the letter.

"How did you know they weren't who they said they were and your friend didn't send them?"

"They didn't know the pass-phrase." When he didn't say anything, she explained, "Jimmy set up an escape plan for me years ago in case his cover was ever blown. If he sent them, they would've said a certain pass-phrase which only the two of us and his handler know. They didn't say it, so neither Jimmy nor his handler sent them. Now I have to get to my emergency stash and get out of town until he contacts me."

Brody nodded, but didn't say anything and she wondered what he was thinking about all of this. He had to be regretting checking on her, but if he hadn't, she had no idea how she would've gotten away from the men. Suddenly she remembered something he said. "You said the plates on the car were government plates? Does that mean they really were from the DEA?"

He nodded again. "Yeah, the plates were government issued, but I won't know which agency and from what city until I run them through my computer. If they are real agents, then your friend has even bigger problems. He's got traitors inside his department."

Angie gasped, her eyes became huge and she started to tremble. "Oh shit, I didn't think of that. What if something's happened to him? What if he can't get in touch with me?" It would kill her if anything happened to Jimmy.

Pulling her into his arms, her neighbor hugged her. "Easy, honey. One thing at a time. First we'll get you someplace safe and then we'll track him down."

# CHAPTER 12

*I*an drove like a madman on cocaine. He'd raced to his car
and just started the engine when Mike called him, telling
him they had an emergency—Brody was in the restaurant's office
with a blonde woman Mike didn't know. But Ian knew instantly who
it was and thanked the stars above for his teammate. He didn't know
how Egghead knew Angie was in danger, but he was thankful the
geek had her in hiding.

Less than two minutes earlier than Mike's call, another call had
come in. The screen read 'Unknown' which was common in his
business with all his contacts who preferred to remain anonymous.
Throwing down the pen he'd been using to do some monthly
accounting, he'd picked up his cell and answered it. "Sawyer."

"Daisy Duck is fucked. Get her out of there."

The line went dead, and he'd shot out of his chair, grabbed his
gun, and took off running. Athos was the caller and the stupid pass-
phrase meant Angie was in danger. Ian's heart was pounding out of
his chest as he jumped into his car. Then Mike called and Ian
almost didn't answer his phone. Thank fuck he did.

He pulled up behind Donovan's and laid on the horn twice,
desperate to see his angel and make sure she was unharmed. The
back door to the bar opened as he hit the lock release on the door
handle next to him. Brody rushed Angie toward the SUV and
almost threw her onto the rear seat before diving in after her.

"Stay down." He didn't need to say the words because his
teammate knew the routine and soon had Angie lying across the

entire back seat covered with his own body. Without looking back, Ian hit the gas, getting them out of there as fast as he could.

Fifteen minutes later, Brody had filled him in about what happened, and they were almost at the private airstrip where Trident's small jet was kept. When he finally felt it was safe, he told the two they could get up then looked into the rear-view mirror to prove to himself Angie was alive and okay.

Her confusion was evident as she whipped her head around while looking for any familiar landmarks. "Where are we? I need you to take me to my emergency storage unit so I can get out of town."

Pulling into the tiny unmanned airport, he didn't answer her until after he drove into a hanger and the rolling door came down behind them thanks to Jake, who he'd called on his way to Donovan's. Jake in turn contacted their pilot, a retired Air Force captain, who they had on retainer, as well as a contact who'd be waiting at their destination with a vehicle for them. He threw the car in park, leapt out, opened the rear passenger door, and hauled Angie out into his arms. He hadn't realized he was crushing her until she told him she couldn't breathe and he reluctantly released her.

"Ian, what's going on? Why are we here? I need to get my stuff and get out of Tampa."

"I know, Angel, but your plans have changed." He didn't need to look to know Brody was getting the plane set so they could take off as soon as their pilot, Conrad Chapman, known as CC, got there and did the last minute pre-flight checklist. Jake was outside making sure no one sneaked up on them. Ian was positive they weren't followed, but he had to check and make sure the men at her house hadn't tagged her with a tracking device somehow. He popped his trunk, retrieved a scanner and ran it over her entire body until he was satisfied she was clean. The scanner had beeped when it had gotten to her sneaker, but a specific frequency code showed it was one of the Trident trackers Boomer had hidden in her shoes. He'd have Brody check her laptop before they left, but her phone, if she had it, would be left in the vehicle.

She was baffled and began to panic. "What are you talking about? What are you doing? I have to get out of here!"

Taking a deep breath, he blurted out, "Goofy has a crush on Minnie Mouse." Shit, he felt fucking ridiculous saying that. What was with Athos and his bizarre Disney pass-phrases?

"What did you say?"

Her fingers covered her mouth, as she stared at him in shock and took a step backward. Away from him, damn it. It was obvious she'd heard him so he didn't bother repeating it. "Athos was afraid something might go wrong on his mission so he asked us to watch over you and get you someplace safe if something happened."

The betrayal he saw in her eyes was more than he could take. "He what?" Her voice was shrill, hurting his ears, but he knew he deserved it. "You've been . . . what? Babysitting me? I don't know who I'm more pissed at, Jimmy or you. Is that why you asked me out and why you've been spending so much time with me? Jimmy asked you to? Oh God! Is that why Brody was so interested in my life and was checking on me all the time? Why he wanted to be friends?"

"Yes, he was checking on you to make sure you were safe, but being your friend was Brody being Brody." He ignored her gasp of outraged disbelief as the side door to the hanger flew open and CC barreled past them on his way to the plane, not bothering with pleasantries. The man knew this was urgent and acted accordingly. Ian kept his eyes on Angie's horrified ones and waited until the pilot was out of earshot again. "And no, it's not why I asked you out. I asked you because I couldn't fight my attraction to you anymore, and I very much wanted to get to know you better. If you believe anything, Angel, believe this. What's happened between us has been one hundred percent real."

She shook her head in suspicion and took another step back. He gritted his teeth because they didn't have time for this. "I'll explain everything on the plane, but we need to get in the air and away from the people after you."

"Why should I trust you?"

The question hit him square in the chest and almost knocked

the air out of his lungs. It was hard to regain his composure, but somehow, he managed it. "Three reasons. One—Athos trusted me to take care of you. Two—I knew the pass-phrase and there's only one person who could've told me that stupid thing . . . a person you trust more than anyone else in the world." Fuck, it killed him to say that, but it was true. They hadn't reached the point in their relationship where she trusted him one hundred percent and he'd just taken three giant steps backward on that journey. "And three— because I care about you. You're my submissive and it's my responsibility to keep you safe."

He reached for her arm, but she pulled away from him and snarled, "Don't touch me. I swear, Ian, if you touch me right now, I'm going to scratch your eyes out. And I'm not your submissive. Not anymore."

*Fuck!* As much as he wanted to prove her wrong, now was not the time. Biting his tongue, he gestured toward the jet. "Okay, fine. If you don't want me to touch you then get on the damn plane. The longer we stay here, the greater chance whoever is after you tracks us down."

He counted to three, and she still hadn't moved beyond crossing her arms over her breasts while giving him a dirty look. Athos had been right—she was stubborn when she was angry. Taking a step forward, he gave her one last warning, in his deepest, firmest Dom voice. "Angel, if you don't get on the fucking plane, I'm going to throw you over my shoulder, carry you on, and tie you to a fucking seat. And once we're safely in the air, I'm going to spank your ass until my hand falls off and you won't be able to sit for a week."

As pissed as she was, she obviously recognized the very real threat as well as worry in his voice. Despite the fact he'd lied to her —they had all lied to her—she had to know he would keep her safe until they could locate Jimmy. After she was reassured her best friend was okay, she would probably kick both of their asses . . . and maybe Brody's too. She threw her hands in the air. "Fine! I'll go with you, but don't touch me and don't talk to me unless it's absolutely necessary. And I want to know everything that's going on.

No more keeping me in the dark like some shrinking violet who can't take care of herself because I won't stand for it."

Not giving him a chance to respond, she spun around, grabbed her laptop from where it sat on the back seat and stormed over to the stairs leading to the interior cabin of the small jet. She glared at Brody, who was waiting at the bottom of the stairs, when he took her computer. She didn't respond to him when he told her he needed to check it for tracking devices. Instead, she crossed her arms again and waited while he scanned it then nodded to Ian that all was good for the moment. The geek wouldn't turn it on until they reached the safe-house where he could scramble any signal the computer might send out which could be used to find their location. Ian would've preferred to leave it behind, but he knew all her work was on it so he made the small concession.

Without a word to anyone, Angie took her laptop and stomped loudly up the stairs, disappearing into the cabin. Jake heard the plane's engines start up and approached Ian who was still standing next to his SUV, trying to get his emotions under control. Devon and Ian had filled the rest of the team in after Athos had left the office that day. "Dev, Boomer, and Marco are headed to Angie's to see if they can find any prints or anything the agents may have left. They'll review the surveillance footage to get stills for Brody to send through his facial recognition software. Dev is also calling in reinforcements for the compound and to keep an eye on Jenn and Kristen. He'll assign someone to sit on Angie and Brody's houses. If the agents aren't stupid they'll be able to connect Egghead to Trident without much effort. Once we know what's going on with Athos, and the compound is secure, Boomer and Marco will be ready for whatever we need them for. Dev will stay and hold down the fort."

Ian nodded. His team knew what needed to be done and he trusted them to do it. Brody walked over to join them and handed Angie's disassembled phone to Ian, who tossed it through the open back door of his vehicle before slamming it shut. Wisely, neither man said anything more to their boss who was beyond pissed and terrified Angie's life was in danger. He should've never agreed to keep the protective measures from her. It was too late now, so the best he could do was guard her with his own life and try to win back her trust. He'd worry about everything else later. Whether she wanted to admit it or not, he was still her Dom and she was still his submissive. They had a signed contract and he was going to hold her to it as long as he could. He just prayed she wouldn't decide to walk out on him because of this. He wasn't ready to let her go yet, and God help him, he wasn't sure he ever would be.

Brody boarded the plane with Ian following, and pulled up the stairs as Jake raised the hanger bay door. After the jet taxied out into the open, the overhead door was shut and Brody let the stairs down again for his teammate. Less than five minutes later, they were airborne and Ian let out a sigh of relief. For now, his angel was safe and he planned on keeping her that way.

# CHAPTER 13

*T*hey'd been in the air for more than a half hour, but Angie's anger was still at a near boil, and she hadn't spoken to Ian or his teammates yet. Sitting in one of the luxury seats in the first of two rows of four seats across, she'd placed her laptop on the one seat between her and the aisle in a blatant act which told the others not to attempt to sit with her. As much as she wanted answers, she didn't think she could face them just yet without wanting to throw something at one of them, especially Ian. The three of them were behind her somewhere and she'd been so pissed when she'd boarded, the rest of the interior of the small jet was a blur to her. Now as she stared out the window at nothing, but clouds, she replayed the past few weeks over and over in her head. One of the things which stood out most in her mind was, she'd been so wrapped up in her work and time with Ian, she'd barely thought about Jimmy. For the first time since they were teenagers her thoughts of, and worry for, her best friend had taken a back seat to someone else. That'd never happened with any of the other men she'd dated over the years. And damn it to hell, the two jackasses had kept her in the dark about something which concerned her; something she should have known about from the start. She knew over the years Jimmy had sheltered her as best he could from the world he was determined to clean up, one scumbag drug runner at a time, but it still yanked her chain.

She peeked over when she saw someone out of the corner of her eye take a seat across the aisle from her. It was Jake, looking comfortable in a pair of jeans, navy blue shirt and black rubber soled boots. Brody and Ian were wisely staying away from her for now. Out of all Ian's teammates, Jake was the one she knew the least about. He was the quietest of the six men, yet he still had that commanding presence of a dominant male. She studied his profile. His chiseled jaw, high cheek bones and long eyelashes made her yearn for her sketch pad. She'd drawn several pencil sketches of Ian over the past few weeks, and a few of Jenn and Beau, but she itched to capture the hardness and sadness she saw in Jake's face.

He glanced over, caught her staring, and gave her a small smile. "Something on your mind?"

She let out an unladylike snort. "You have no idea."

Shrugging his shoulders, he said, "Try me. I may not be as talkative as Marco is when comforting a submissive, but I'm a good listener."

"I'm not a submissive," she spat out. "Not anymore. And I don't need comfort, thank you."

His left eyebrow rose as he gave her a "yeah, right—think again" look which irritated her because she could guess what he was about to say. "You can't turn it on and off like a switch, Angie. You can try, but you'll just end up making yourself miserable. Just because you're pissed off, doesn't mean your body stops craving what you've experienced over the past few weeks. It was a part of you that you didn't know existed, and now that you do, you'll never go back to the way you were before without regretting it."

Knowing he was right, but still unwilling to admit it, she turned and stared out the window again. Jake may work for Trident, but he hadn't done anything to be the recipient of her anger, and she didn't want to take it out on him. But Ian, Brody, and even Boomer were a different story, along with her pain-in-the-ass best friend. She heard Jake stand and expected him to go back to where he'd been sitting before, but he picked up her laptop, set it on the seat he'd just vacated, and sat down beside her.

"Talk to me. It doesn't have to be about D/s stuff or anything to do with Boss-man since he's a sore subject with you at the moment.

You must have a thousand questions about what happened today and, while I don't have all the facts yet, I'll answer what I can."

Angie shifted in her seat, putting her back to the window and studied the man. In his eyes, she saw the same compassion and understanding she'd seen in Marco's when he stayed with her during her public spanking. The thought of that night and how she'd screamed her release for all to hear made her cheeks warm. She forced herself to think of something else, not wanting him to know where her mind went and how those thoughts still made her body tingle. "Where are we going? Let's start there."

"Fair enough. We'll be landing in Spartanburg, South Carolina in a little over an hour. From there it's about another hour and a half drive to the safe-house in Maggie Valley, North Carolina."

"Safe-house? Whose?" *Did everyone have a safe-house nowadays?*

Jake nodded and settled into a more comfortable position since she was asking questions. "It belongs to Ian and Devon, but it would take a long time for it to be traced to them since the ownership is buried under a bunch of unrelated businesses and false names. Ian and his dad found the place when he first joined the SEALs. One of the older guys told him if he had the opportunity, he should find a place where no one could track him down. With all the terrorists, drug cartels, and scum of the earth we've dealt with over the years, it's not paranoia to think we all have prices on our heads for one reason or another. But we're lucky most of them have better things to do instead of hunting down our identities and homes. And it's why Ian and Dev put so much money into the security at the compound. As for the safe-house, we've used it several times over the years, but not always for emergencies. It's up in the mountains and a great place to get away sometimes. But we always take precautions if we go there and our flight plan states we're going to Myrtle Beach in South Carolina. There are closer airports to Maggie Valley, but this way it's harder for someone to track our movements."

Angie was a little stunned. She knew what the men at Trident did could be dangerous sometimes, but to have a bounty on their heads was something she only thought happened in the old Wild

West, or to criminals on the FBI's Most Wanted list. "How long do I have to stay there?"

"Until we hear from your friend and figure out how to put an end to the threat against you. I don't want to scare you, but you said you wanted to be kept in the loop. I don't know if the men at your house were real agents, but we'll find out when we get to the safehouse. From what we can gather, they were going to kidnap you and use you against Athos to get information out of him." He grimaced and added, "And probably as revenge for his infiltrating the drug cartel he was undercover in."

The look he gave her said the rest—there was a very good chance neither Jimmy nor she would survive if the cartel got a hold of them. Despite her fear, a kernel of hope she hadn't known was missing began to fill her. "So, does that mean Jimmy is still alive? If they want me, that must mean they don't have him."

The tilt of Jake's head wasn't completely reassuring. "As of a little while ago, he was alive and we assume not captured because he contacted Ian to let us know something was wrong and told us to get you out of Tampa. Boss-man got the call right before my brother called him from the pub. If he can, Athos will be on his way to meet us in North Carolina."

"That was your brother—the guy, Mike?" She had only gotten a glimpse of the man and hadn't noticed any resemblance, but Jake nodded. "So, what happens next?"

"We wait until your friend contacts us and help him when he does. In the meantime, we'll keep you safe and try to figure out who's after you. Then we end it."

Her stomach dropped at how deadly those last four words sounded. "End it? How?"

Jake's eyes hardened and bore into hers. "We eliminate the threats, and make sure they'll never come after you again."

"Y-you'd kill someone for me?" There was a combination of disbelief and wonder in her voice, and she was sure the expression on her face matched it. "Why?"

"In a heartbeat, Angie. Because it's the way men like us are wired. Innocent lives are protected at all costs. It's not as if we have a death wish or anything, but if we're killed protecting or saving someone else, we'll make sure we fight to the bitter end to give them the best chance for survival. Whether you like it or not, if it comes down to my saving you or myself, just remember I want a traditional Irish wake, complete with bagpipes."

Angie swallowed hard. He'd said the last part with a teasing grin, but she knew he was serious. She saw the conviction in his eyes and knew he wasn't blowing smoke by saying he'd give his life for hers. He would do it without a moment's hesitation. She realized what had her longing to draw his face earlier. Jake Donovan reminded her so much of Jimmy Andrews after he became Jimmy Athos. She wondered what had happened to Ian's friend to put the same hardness and sense of loss in the man's beautiful, yet haunted green eyes.

She'd known what he meant by "eliminate," before he confirmed it, and she wasn't sure how she felt about it. The team might have to kill people to keep her safe, and she hated the fact they would have blood on their hands because of her. She wasn't naïve to think Ian, Jake, and the others had never killed anyone before. They were former Navy SEALs in an era where terrorists from around the world were more than threatening the American way of life, as well as the lives of those same Americans. They'd been in combat, seeing and doing things most people had never imagined, but now, they wouldn't be killing anyone for all America. Instead, they'd be killing someone for the sake of one person—her, Angelina Beckett, a graphic designer from Tampa, Florida, who wouldn't know a terrorist or drug cartel member if she tripped over him. With that knowledge, she was done asking questions for the moment and turned back toward the window. After a few moments, she sensed Jake stand and move back to the area behind her, leaving her alone in her thoughts.

---

IAN WAS ready to spit nails as he watched his teammate talk to Angie. A few minutes earlier, he'd been about to storm up to the front of the plane and force her to listen to him, but Jake had stopped him. She didn't need his frustration at the moment and it would only push her further away from him. He needed to get his emotions under control before he talked to her. So instead of doing it himself and screwing things up even more, he very reluctantly allowed his friend to talk to the stubborn, pissed-off woman and soothe her ruffled feathers.

If Athos was still alive, he should be on his way to South Carolina to a pre-arranged location. When he reached it, he would contact Ian, who would then send his teammates to retrieve the agent and bring him across the state border to the safe-house after making sure they weren't followed or tracked. Once they got the low-down on who, what, where, when and how, they would help Athos any way they could while keeping Angie safe.

While Jake talked to Angie, Ian sat in the middle area of the plane which was set up like a living room, complete with couches, recliners and tables, all bolted to the floor. Gazing out the window at nothing, he thought about how fast the beautiful submissive had gotten under his skin, a fact he was wary about.

They had fallen into a comfortable routine since their first public scene at the club last Friday. He'd taken her back to his place after she recovered from the sub-space she'd achieved from her orgasm and he fucked her several times until dawn, leaving them both happy and sated. Each morning she went home, only to return to him each evening and spend the night. They'd gone back to the club on Saturday night, and again on Sunday night, participating in one other public scene, as well as a private one in the office themed room, where she pretended to be his naughty secretary. He'd fucked her every way he could think of using the desk and chair to position her how he wanted, and even sat her atop a tall filing cabinet so he could eat her sweet pussy while standing up. He loved how she embraced her naughty side and often found his mind wandering during the daytime, thinking of different scenarios for them to play out.

The club was closed on Mondays and Tuesdays, so those two nights they'd cooked dinner in his kitchen, cuddled on the couch, and ended up pleasuring each other in a variety of ways. The woman was as insatiable as he was and more adventurous than he'd expected. He'd given her several pieces of lingerie he'd picked out from the club store, instructing her she was to wear them and nothing else while they were alone together in his home. Angie rocked lingerie in a way which rivaled any Victoria's Secrets model. If he had his way, she wouldn't wear anything, but the sexy scraps of material twenty-four hours a day. He'd even gotten into the habit of locking the deadbolt to his front door to ensure Jenn didn't walk in on them again by accident.

He watched as Jake rose, walked back toward the sitting area, and took his earlier seat on the couch between the two recliners Ian and Brody had occupied the entire flight. Egghead was catching a brief nap since there was nothing much to do while in the air and he hadn't had time to grab one of his own laptops. When they got to the safe-house he would have a smaller, but similar setup to the war-room back at Trident. From there, he would do what he did best and get them as much information about who was after Angie.

Ian glanced at Jake. "Does she still want my dick in a cock cage?"

"If I were you, I'd keep it out of her reach for a while. Your balls too." He chuckled when his boss winced and crossed his legs in an automatic response most men had at the thought of their reproductive organs being tortured. "Don't worry. I gave her some things to think about. She's worried about Athos, but I think she's also worried about you and the rest of us."

Confused, Ian tilted his head. "Me? Us? Why?"

Jake leaned forward and rested his elbows on his knees. "She may be submissive, Ian, but she's far from naïve. Angie knows there's a chance she, Athos, or any of us may end up six feet under by the time this whole thing plays out. Even though her friend is the one who brought this to her doorstep, no matter how unintentional and how much he tried to prevent it, she knows we'll do anything we have to in order to protect her. If any of us have to kill someone, which is a near one-hundred percent possibility, I think she's going to have a hard time with it. And God forbid one of us is caught in the crossfire . . . she's going to feel responsible no matter what."

Taking a moment to think about things from Angie's point of view, Ian knew his teammate was right. She wasn't a part of his world where killing someone, while not ever taken lightly, was something he wouldn't hesitate to do, if needed, to protect his teammates, his family, innocent people, and the woman he loved. *Oh, fuck!* He did not just think that. His stomach bottomed out, and he couldn't blame it on turbulence since there wasn't any. He couldn't be in love with Angie . . . he wouldn't let himself be. Falling in love with a woman only led to heartache, and Ian refused to go through it again. *Fuck!* He dragged his hand down his face in frustration and forced the thoughts of unwanted love to the back of his mind. He'd deal with that later.

# CHAPTER 14

*A*ngie still hadn't said a word to anyone, but Jake beyond necessary "yes" or "no" answers to questions. They had landed in Spartanburg and waiting for them was a black SUV with tinted windows, and license plates which couldn't be traced to any of them. Their pilot, CC, was instructed to grab a nearby motel room and get some rest until they figured out where they would need him to fly later on. He most likely would be heading back to Tampa to pick up, and return with, Marco and Boomer, but for now Ian wanted him available in case their plans changed.

On the way to Maggie Valley, they stopped off at a WalMart to pick up some food and supplies, along with clothing for Angie. While the team had spare clothes, among other things, at the safe-house, she only had what she was wearing. While Brody waited in the vehicle, Jake and Ian went into the store with Angie between them. They hit the women's section first and, at Ian's insistence, she grabbed two pairs of sweatpants, jeans, and some T-shirts. She found another pair of sneakers which were more appropriate for running than the simple Keds she had on. In the intimate aisles, she quickly picked out some socks, a package of plain, white Hanes underwear, and two sports bras. She gaped and put her hands on her hips when Ian threw the six-pack of bikini briefs back on the rack and picked out several pairs of lacy thongs and boy-shorts with matching bras. While Jake turned away to hide his grin, Ian crossed his arms, smirked, and stared at Angie, daring her to defy him. Thankfully, she didn't argue with him in the middle of the superstore. When she spun around and stormed toward the health and beauty section for toiletries, he and Jake followed with the cart.

Despite the fact they were on the run from bad guys, Ian decided to push his angel's buttons a little more. He couldn't help it —it was the Dom in him. As she passed the sexual wellness shelves on the way to get a toothbrush in the next aisle, he picked up a box of condoms and threw it into the cart. As he expected, she snarled and snatched the box, intent on putting it back on the shelf. Before she had a chance, he took a gentle but firm hold of her wrist, plucked the package from her hand, and placed it purposely back in the cart. Then to rattle her some more, he grabbed a second box and tossed it in with the first. Her green eyes flared with anger. She opened and closed her mouth twice before turning in an exasperated huff to continue her shopping.

After they finished up in the food aisles, they checked out with Ian paying cash for their purchases. In his panicked rush out of his office to get to her, he'd failed to grab one of his fake identities with accompanying credit cards. While the team all had backup alias IDs and credit cards at the safe-house, for now he would use cash so they couldn't be tracked through purchases.

Less than a half hour after they entered the store, they were walking back out with a cart full of bags. Brody was waiting for them in the fire lane, and after securing Angie in the rear passenger seat, Ian and Jake quickly filled the rear storage area with their supplies. In the deli section, they'd picked out several pre-made sandwiches, then added some chips and sodas from the choices available at the registers. It wasn't the greatest meal in the world, but everyone was hungry and far from being picky at the moment. They ate in silence as Brody drove them to their final destination.

For the rest of the ride, Ian sat next to Angie in the rear seat and tried to ignore the fact she was ignoring him. He couldn't wait to get to the house so they could have a conversation which wouldn't be overheard by his teammates. Although, he knew she wasn't going to talk to him without yelling, and hoped someone had left a ball gag and restraints at the house during a past weekend excursion. Ian had never brought a woman to the house before, but some of his team had, mainly Boomer, Brody, and Marco.

Before they'd left Tampa, the three men left their cell phones in Ian's vehicle. Ian had a throwaway phone in his trunk along with other gear. Athos knew if Ian didn't answer his cell, he was to contact Devon to get the number to the throwaway. This way they couldn't be tracked and Athos could still contact him. Ian shot a message off to his brother when they hit Maggie Valley's town border, telling him they'd arrived safely.

A few minutes later, Brody turned up the mountain road which lead to their safe-house, and two miles further he pulled into the gravel driveway. Ian looked at Angie as she gawked at the structure. He wasn't sure what she expected, but as far as safe-houses went, this one was top of the line. It was a beautiful mountain retreat which his dad had found for him over thirteen years ago. Having a billionaire, real estate investor as a father sure came in handy sometimes. The house had been owned by some Arab sheikh who bought and sold homes all over the world as often as most people up-graded their cell phones. It was built into the mountain so there was no backyard, but the front of the house overlooked a lake about a quarter of a mile below them. It was easily defended between the landscaping, bullet proof windows, and Brody's security set-up. Their nearest neighbor was a vacation house about two miles to the west. If a vehicle turned up the road leading to the house, an alarm would sound inside. There were also cameras and sensors in the woods surrounding the three open sides of the house. Most of the time, an alert would be the result of a large animal such as a deer or bear, but they'd rather get the alerts and have it be nothing instead of missing a human predator.

The house itself had eight bedrooms, each with its own bath. Six of them were on the second floor with the remaining ones on the first, along with a gourmet kitchen and a large living room with vaulted ceilings. A gym, game room and hidden panic room were located in the basement.

The house also had an open den area on the second floor, overlooking the living room, and it'd been converted into the mini war-room for Brody. While it didn't have everything the geek had in his Trident office, it had what was necessary to maintain security along with a sufficient computer system. A retired Navy officer, who'd been one of Ian's superiors when he first got out of basic training, lived about a half hour away and maintained the property and house for them. Devon would be contacting the former lieutenant to let him know the place was going to be occupied and to stay away until told otherwise.

Brody and Jake grabbed the bags from the rear of the vehicle while Ian escorted Angie to the front door and unlocked it with a scan of his palm, just like their system at the compound. He left the door open for his teammates who were a few steps behind them as he and Angie entered into the house. While she continued to take in her new surroundings, Jake began to unpack their groceries and Ian took the bags with Angie's supplies in them from Egghead. The geek headed up to the den to boot up the computers and arm the rest of the security systems which weren't up and running on a regular basis. As Angie followed him, Ian brought her bags into his bedroom and placed them on the king-sized bed. Without a word, he left her alone in there and wasn't too surprised when she came back into the living room several minutes later with the bags in her hands. He raised an eyebrow at her. "Going somewhere, Angel?"

She stopped in front of where he stood while glaring at him. "Obviously, that's your bedroom with all your clothes and stuff, and I'm not staying in there. I assume in a house this size there's an unoccupied room where I can stay."

Crossing his arms over his chest, he gave her a look which dared her to argue with him. "Of course, there are several unoccupied rooms, but you're not staying in any of them. You're staying in mine."

"Then where are you sleeping, because it's not with me?"

This time, instead of answering her, Ian took her by the upper arm and led her back into his bedroom, clothes and all, and shut the door behind them. He stood in front of her escape route so she had no choice but to listen to him. Or so he thought, as she threw the bags on the bed then stormed into the attached bath and slammed the door. He rolled his eyes when he heard the lock click. Did she really believe a puny lock was going to keep him out?

Instead of picking it, he retrieved one of those universal keys which opened most interior doors nowadays and let himself into the bathroom. He found her sitting on the closed toilet lid with her arms crossed like a pouting child. "Can't I have some privacy?"

"If you're going to act like a brat, then no. Now, are we going to have this conversation in here or the bedroom, where I'm sure you'll be more comfortable? Whether you like it or not Angel, we are going to talk. It's just your decision whether I spank your ass or not before we do. And you better believe I won't think twice about setting your backside on fire. Now what's it going to be?"

She'd gaped at him in disbelief when he called her a 'brat', and then his threat of a spanking resulted in a scowl. Without saying a word, she stood and stormed back out into the bedroom after he stepped aside to let her past. Before he could say anything, she spun around and pointed her finger at him. "So, was everything a ploy to spy on me, or were you spying on me, and getting me in your bed was just a fringe benefit?"

Ian growled and his eyes narrowed. "I was keeping you safe, not spying on you. And I never considered you a fringe benefit to a job." As soon as the last three words were out of his mouth, he knew they'd been a mistake. A horrified expression fell over her face and he wanted to kick his own ass.

"So, I was just a job to you? Is that how you do all your jobs, Ian, from under the bed sheets?" He recognized when a thought occurred to her, and he could guess what it was. "What about when you weren't around, huh? Brody wasn't home all day, so how were you keeping me safe then?" She watched as a guilty expression he couldn't stop came over his face, and he knew he was in deeper shit with her. "There are cameras in my house, right? Brody and Boomer put cameras in my house when they were setting up the security system, didn't they? Whose idea was it—yours or Jimmy's?" She didn't wait for an answer, and her voice was getting louder with every question until she was yelling. "You fucking bastard! Was everyone at Trident enjoying the show while I showered and got dressed every day? What about the night of the gala? Did you get a porn movie out of it? Out of what you had me do in the kitchen the next day? What's the going rate for amateur porn these days, Ian?"

He couldn't take it anymore. She was borderline hysterical, thinking the absolute worst of him, and wasn't letting him get a single word in. He tried to put his hands on her shoulders and barely shifted his hips in time when she tried to knee him in the groin. Furious she missed, Angie began to pound his chest with her fists. He grabbed her wrists and forced her onto her back on the bed after pushing her bags out of the way. He didn't want to hurt her, but he needed her to calm down before she hurt herself, so he straddled her hips and held her arms above her head. Squirming around and bucking her hips, trying to unseat him tired her out pretty quick and he relaxed a little when she slowed and then stopped fighting him altogether. Unfortunately for Ian, at this point, she started yelling at him again, calling him every name in the book, and a few she must've made up on her own. For the first time ever, he wished he'd brought another woman up to this house before, because he could use a set of restraints and a gag at the moment. Brody might have some in his room, but Ian wasn't about to bring one of his teammates into Angie's line of fire, and she was pissed off enough at Egghead. This was Ian's doing and he'd take full responsibility for it.

Improvising, he unbuckled his belt with one hand and pulled the leather from the loops around his waist. With quick, practiced motions, he flipped her onto her stomach, pulled her arms behind her back and had her wrists restrained before she realized what he was doing. Still cursing him out, she started to buck her hips again, trying to get him off her thighs. "Angel," he leaned forward and growled in her ear, "all you're doing is wearing yourself out and making me harder than I already am. All your hip action is making my dick remember what it's like to be inside your sweet body while I fuck you hard and fast. Now, calm down and listen to me, or my hand and your ass are going to get real intimate with each other and last Friday's paddling is going to seem like love taps when I'm done with you."

"You wouldn't dare!" She turned her head to glare over her shoulder at him. Her beautiful eyes were blazing with anger and her hair was in complete disarray.

He shifted to the side to give himself access to her ass cheeks and landed one hard smack atop the right one. She screeched and tried to move away from him, but with her hands tied behind her and his right leg still over her thighs, she couldn't go very far. His hand came down on her left cheek as she shrieked his name in a full-fledged fury. More followed. *Smack. Smack. Smack.*

He continued until her rage finally broke and she began to sob. Ian immediately rolled her to her side and pulled her to his chest, murmuring words of comfort. The last few hours of fear, anger, confusion, and hurt came pouring out of Angie with the buckets of tears she was crying. "It's all right, Angel. *Shhh.* It's all right. Please let me explain everything, and if you still want to stay mad at me, then I'll back off. But until then, you're going to listen to me, and no matter what, you're going to do what I say when it comes to your safety. Okay?"

It was several more minutes before Angie got her emotions and tears under control again. "L—Let me go."

"Not happening, sweetheart. Not until you hear me out."

She rubbed her tear stained face against his T-shirt covered chest. It was obvious she was still angry and hurt, but the fight had drained from her body and exhaustion had taken over. "Please, Ian. I promise I'll listen to you, but no more lies. I want the truth—all of it. J—just let my hands go and give me a moment alone in the bathroom. Please."

He eased her back so he could study her face. Her eyes were red and swollen, and his chest squeezed knowing he was the cause of her heartache. Even upset and bawling, the woman was beautiful. She blinked and looked into his eyes, and he knew she was telling him the truth about listening to him—and wasn't that fucking ironic? Reaching behind her, he undid the belt restraining her wrists as fast as he'd tied it on her. As she brought her arms back to her front, he rubbed them from her wrists to her shoulders, making sure there was no stiffness and her circulation was good. Before he let her sit up, he placed a single lingering kiss to her forehead and murmured, "I'm sorry, Angel."

He didn't explain further because he was sorry for more than he wanted to admit. He'd never meant to hurt her in any way, but he had, and now he had to live with the consequences, praying she would forgive him.

With a weary sigh, Angie pushed off the bed and walked into the bathroom without saying a word. This time she didn't bother locking the door after she eased it shut. Ian turned down the covers on the bed, picked her bags up from the floor, and unpacked her new things. He folded the clothes, neatly lining everything up on his dresser so she could find whatever she needed. From the attached bath, the toilet flush and water began to flow into the sink before shutting off again a few minutes later. Just as he was placing a winged-back chair next to the bed for their conversation, the bathroom door opened and Angie emerged, calmer, yet drained. Her hair wasn't as wild and her tears were gone, but her eyes were still red and swollen. She stood there, unsure of what to do next, eyeing the bed and chair. When he handed her one of his T-shirts, she looked at it in confusion. Turning her around to face the bathroom door again, he gave her a small push. "As much as I like how you sleep naked, I'd rather you wear this to bed in case we need to leave in a hurry. Jenn has a few things in the bedroom she uses, and I'll see if there's a pair of her running shorts for you after we talk."

Two minutes later, Angie walked out of the bathroom for the third time since they'd arrived at the house forty-five minutes earlier. She was wearing the T-shirt which came down to the middle of her thighs. He wondered if she'd removed her panties as well and gave himself a mental kick for even thinking it. When her bare legs drew his gaze, he tried to ignore the twitching of his cock and gestured for her to climb into bed. She frowned then looked out the window and he knew she was surprised to see the sun had set. It was after seven p.m. and six hours ago, her life had been normal.

After she climbed into the bed, Ian drew the covers up to her chest then pulled the chair closer to the top of the bed and sat down. For the first time in years, he was unsure of himself in front of a submissive. But Angie wasn't just any submissive . . . no, she was more than that, and he had no idea what to do about it. She watched as he dragged both his hands down his face in frustration before he spoke. "Let me tell you everything I know and then you can ask questions. Okay?" He waited for a response and when she nodded, he continued on a sigh. "Athos approached Trident after we met the night he was at your place. Apparently, he investigates all your new neighbors, which I would also do if I were him." He shrugged, unashamed. "I want to investigate any guy who Jenn goes out with, but she won't tell me their names because she knows I'll do it. Anyway, Athos told us he was going back undercover and there was a slim chance you might be in danger if his cover was blown."

Angie's brow furrowed in confusion. "Why would it be a problem all of a sudden? He always took precautions so no one could ever connect the two of us."

So much for saving her questions until the end. He hated what he was about to tell her. "Angel, the agent he was replacing was murdered along with his family after the cartel discovered he was a plant." He watched as the words took effect in her brain, and her eyes widened in horror. "It's why Athos asked us to protect you. It's also why he insisted on the security upgrades at your house. And yes, it's why we placed cameras there, as well as audio bugs and tracking devices in your car, phone, purse, and some of your shoes."

He could see she was about to start yelling again, so he held up his hand to stop her. "Let me finish. You wanted to hear all of this, so I'm telling you everything. You can holler at me all you want when I'm done." She crossed her arms, her anger still evident, but he was grateful when she remained quiet. "There were no cameras facing your bed or in your bathroom. The ones in your bedroom only faced the door to the hallway and the slider. I erased the audio from the night of the gala as soon as I got back to the compound, and the audio and video were both turned off while you and I were on the phone that morning. As long as there wasn't a reason, no one listened to or watched any of the recordings. Well, no one but me."

Her eyes narrowed and he glanced away for a moment before

taking a deep breath and forging ahead. "From the moment I met you, the day we moved Egghead into his house, I've wanted you. For some unknown reason, I was fighting my attraction to you, but every time I had a chance to go to Brody's, I took it, hoping to see you. The day Athos was over, I'll admit I was jealous as hell watching him massage your bare feet and seeing how familiar he was with you. I assumed you two had an intimate relationship, but Athos filled us in on everything the next morning. He told us how you met and became best friends, how you were there for each other after you both lost your families, and how much he tried to protect you over the years. Then he explained about his case and what he wanted us to do to keep you safe. At no time was my getting close to you part of the plan.

"Yes, Brody was keeping an eye on you and checking on you whenever he was home, but like I said before, he could have done that from a distance. Egghead is one of those guys who easily forms friendships, and I'm sure you two would've become friends even without this whole mess. It's just the way he is."

Biting his bottom lip, Ian paused, trying to gather his thoughts. "The night of your blind date, I was there to pick up a file I needed. I stood in the living room arguing with myself about going out the backdoor to see if you were there. Obviously, I lost that fight. I asked you out as a man wanting to spend time with a woman he was fascinated with, and for no other reason. I found myself checking your video feeds during the day like some crazy stalker and I'm not proud of it, but without even trying, you got under my skin. And once I had a taste of you, I knew it wasn't enough. I don't do long relationships, Angel. Not since my fiancée walked out on me ten years ago. She wanted someone more romantic, someone who could read her mind and anticipate her every whim. She wanted someone who would buy her flowers just because it was Wednesday or some other wacky reason. She wanted corny love songs, and sky-writing proclaiming how much I loved her." He snorted and shook his head. "And that's not me. I tried to show her I cared for her in my own way, but it wasn't enough. And I swore I would never go through that again. I would never again let a woman get close enough to me to the point where, when she left me, she took my shredded heart with her. And until I met you, it was never a problem for me." A bewildered expression came over his handsome face. "But you, sweetheart, you make me wish I never took that vow."

He closed his eyes, inhaled deeply, then slowly opened them again, afraid of what he would see in her face . . . in her eyes. Would she hate him, be disgusted with him? Would she never want to see him again, never let him kiss her again? God, he hoped not. His gaze focused on hers and he was surprised to see sadness instead of anger. Swallowing hard, he waited for her to say something and prayed it wouldn't be "get out."

"What was her name?" Angie whispered.

Of all the things he expected her to say, that wasn't one of them. "Um, Kaliope. Kaliope Levine. She was a . . um . . a news reporter in Virginia near the Navy base."

"Was she your submissive too?"

Ian nodded and his eyes left hers as he looked downward. "Yes, she was. I met her at a club up there. We were together for almost three years."

She reached over for his hand and gave it a squeeze before letting go again. The gesture shocked him, but not as much as her next words did. "I'm sorry for what she put you through, but I'm not her, Ian, and when this is all over, I think I'd like the chance to prove it to you. But for now, I'm still mad, and hurt, and scared out of my mind—for me, you, Jimmy, and your team." She heaved a sigh. "I want to try to sleep and maybe tomorrow I'll be more tolerant of everything you've done up to this point. I can't guarantee I won't yell some more, but I'll try to refrain from kneeing you in the balls."

Snorting, he gave her a wry grin. "My balls appreciate it, sweetheart." His face became serious again. "Look, I'm not sorry for protecting you, your safety was always a priority, but I will apologize for the way we all went about it. We should have . . . *I* should have told you from the beginning and I'm sorry I didn't. I stressed how trust is a large portion of BDSM, yet it should also be a major part of the rest of our relationship too. And I know I have to work at earning yours again." He hesitated a moment, uncertain how she would react to his next question. "Would it be all right if I sleep next to you tonight? I promise I won't push for anything more. I just want to hold you and keep you safe."

His stomach dropped and a wave of nausea hit him when she shook her head. "Not right now, Ian." Knowing he deserved it, he tilted his head in understanding and stood, ready to find another bed for the night. He'd said he wouldn't push her further tonight, and he meant it. "But if you happen to come back while I'm asleep, I won't exactly have a choice, will I?"

His heart soared. Smiling, he leaned down and gave her a gentle kiss on her forehead. "No, you won't, Angel." He kissed her again. "Good night, sweetheart."

Angie buried herself under the blankets and shut her eyes as Ian turned off the lamp and left the room, closing the door behind him. Within minutes, she was asleep.

# CHAPTER 15

*T*he sun had been up for only a few minutes when Angie awakened the next morning, wrapped up in Ian's arms as he spooned her from behind. Despite his morning hard-on, his shallow breathing and heavy arm around her waist told her he was still sound asleep. She'd been so exhausted last night and fallen asleep so fast she had no idea what time he'd joined her in the big, comfortable bed. She lay there for a few moments, soaking up his warmth, as everything from the prior day came rushing back to her. Less than twenty-four hours ago, she'd been doing a job she loved, dating a guy she liked a lot, learning more about herself each day and been truly happy for the first time in what felt like forever. Now, she was on the run from people who wanted to kidnap and use her against her best friend who was incommunicado while a drug cartel was after him. Her happy normal life was falling to pieces and she didn't know how to stop it.

She was also still wrestling with the fact Ian had lied to her, although she was working past it. Yes, the anger and hurt were still there, but so was the understanding of why he and Jimmy had done what they did. Jake had been right—men like her lover and her best friend were wired a different way. They needed to feel needed and protect the people they cared about at all costs, even if she didn't agree with how they went about it.

Her bladder began insisting she get up and relieve the building pressure so she eased away from Ian and climbed out of the bed. After she finished, she took a quick shower while avoiding getting her hair wet. Instead of washing it, she opted to put it up in an easy twist with a clip she'd picked up at the beauty section of the store. She threw on a pair of her new sweatpants and a T-shirt over one of her sports bras thinking maybe she'd take a run later when someone could go with her. Turning toward the bed, she examined Ian as he continued to sleep, now on his stomach with his hands under his pillow. His jaw and upper lip had the morning stubble which she loved having rubbed against her inner thighs when he went down on her. A lock of his hair had fallen onto his forehead and she fought the urge to put it back in its place. She didn't want to wake him, knowing he probably needed the sleep. The sheet had been pushed down, exposing his muscular back and upper buttocks. Damn, the man had granite buns she wanted to take a bite out of.

If she stared at him much longer she was going to jump his bones, so instead, she searched for her new toothbrush among her toiletries on his dresser. It was then she noticed he'd found a pair of cotton shorts, which she assumed were Jenn's, and left them out for her. No matter what, she had to admit he did show he cared in his own little ways, like making sure she was comfortable and safe, and always putting her first. When they had sex, he made sure she was satisfied before he took his own pleasure. He opened doors and held out her chair for her without a second thought. At dinner at his place, he'd fill her plate before taking his own meal. Her wants and needs always seemed to come before his. And above all, he was putting his life, and the lives of his team, in jeopardy because hers was in danger. She thought back to what Kristen had said in the ladies' room at the gala about how Devon made her feel cherished, and Angie realized it was exactly how Ian made her feel. So, what if he wasn't a flowers and poetry kind of guy. He may not be a romantic by definition, but she would take being cherished over romance any day.

After brushing her teeth, she grabbed the art pad and sketching pencils she'd found in the craft section of Walmart. Tip-toeing out of the room, she closed the door behind her. In the kitchen, she found a Keurig coffee machine and brewed herself a single cup of the Brazilian blend she selected from the carousel next to the machine. The house was quiet except for the sounds of her coffee cup being filled. Not wanting to cook so early and wake anybody else up, she picked out a bran muffin from the assorted box of sixteen Jake had left on the counter. Taking it, along with her coffee and art supplies, she went out to the front porch. It was chilly, but she wanted the fresh air so she placed her things on a small table and went back inside to retrieve a blanket from the back of the living room couch. After making herself warm and comfortable in a lounge chair, which gave her a beautiful view of the lake below, she had her simple breakfast and tried not to think about the danger they were all in.

When her muffin was gone, Angie picked up the sketch pad and pulled a pencil out of the package of six. Opening the pad to the first blank page, she let her mind wander as she began to sketch. A little while later, she was startled when she heard a voice behind her. "Wow, that's me."

She looked up over her shoulder and saw Jake standing behind her chair, appearing rumpled in a University of Tampa T-shirt and a pair of gray sweatpants. He must've just rolled out of bed, and she hadn't heard him come out the door. In his hand, he held a steaming cup of coffee as he studied the picture of his face she'd drawn from memory. She didn't need to confirm his statement since the sketch was close to what a photograph of him might look like.

"Why do I seem so sad? Is that what I look like to you?"

She nodded as he sat in a chair catty-cornered to her and crossed his sneaker-covered feet at the ankles, resting them on the bottom slats of her lounge. "Sometimes. When you think no one is watching, or your mind seems to be somewhere else, you get this sad, faraway look on your face."

"Huh," he grunted before taking a sip of his coffee, not contradicting her observations of him. "So, are you feeling better this morning? Not so stressed out and angry?" He narrowed his eyes and teased her. "You didn't murder Ian in his sleep last night, or cut off his most prized possession, did you?"

Laughing, she shook her head. "No, he's breathing and still has all his man-parts, but don't think I wasn't tempted a time or two."

He smiled and remained quiet as she considered his face then made a few small changes to the sketch she was still fiddling with. Without thinking, she blurted out, "Do you have a girlfriend?"

"*Ha*! Uh, no I don't, sweetheart." His amused expression confused her until he added, "I think the more appropriate question would be 'do I have a boyfriend?' and the answer would still be no." Her mouth gaped and her cheeks turned red, but he didn't seem fazed by her shock. "Yes, Angie, I'm gay. And yes, most people know."

"Wow." She shook her head, but smiled at the same time, not wanting him to think she thought there was anything wrong with being gay. "Um, sorry. It's just the gay guy friends I have aren't as macho and hunky as you are." She winced. "That sounded stereotypical, didn't it?"

He snorted and took another sip from his cup. "Macho and hunky, huh? Yeah, well that's the thing about being gay, it doesn't discriminate. We come in all shapes and sizes." She opened her mouth to ask him something, but changed her mind and glanced down at her sketch. "Go ahead and ask your question, sweetheart. I'm not ashamed of who I am."

Glancing back up at him, she shrugged her right shoulder. "I didn't think you were since you came right out and told me, and you're not embarrassed about it, which you shouldn't be. I just can't help but think about how you can work with Ian and the rest of them without being attracted to any of them. I mean, you're all good-looking men."

Jake nodded his head in understanding and didn't give the impression he was put off by her question. "I'll admit I fought a lot of attractions to straight guys throughout my whole career in the Navy—hell, pretty much my whole life—but when it comes to the team, we've been together so long that they've become my brothers. I have no more attraction to any of them than I do to my own blood brother, Mike."

"When did you realize you were gay?" Her eyes widened at her unintentional bluntness. Her brain-to-mouth filter wasn't working this morning. "Sorry, that's way too personal. Don't answer that."

"No, it's fine." He tilted his head and held her stare. "I like you, Angie, and I'm not like Brody who makes friends easily wherever he goes, so I hold onto the friends I do have. In the short time I've known you, I'd like to think we've become friends."

She gave him a shy smile. "I think we've become friends, too."

"Good." He raised his cup of coffee in a silent toast to their new friendship, then drank what little remained. "So, in answer to your question, I guess I've known since puberty, maybe a little earlier. Like most gay people, I struggled with it in the beginning because it was out of the norm from how I was raised, especially since my father was a homophobic jackass."

Wincing, she asked, "How did he take it when you came out, or haven't you ever told him?"

"Oh, he found out, somehow, when I was a senior in high school. Beat the ever-living shit out of me, too, thinking it would convince me to go straight. As if I had a choice. All my life, up to that point, he'd been living his life vicariously through me. He'd been a mediocre football player in high school, and here was his youngest son, the star quarterback on the football team with a full-ride to Rutgers. After he beat me near unconscious with his belt three months before graduation, I couldn't go to school for almost two weeks. My mother called me in sick with the flu or something, and nursed me back to health. My father wouldn't let her take me to the hospital or even a doctor—God forbid someone found out he'd beaten his son, the faggot."

He shrugged off the fucked-up memory. "Anyway, after I recovered, I was done with him. I threw my scholarship in his face and enlisted the afternoon I graduated from high school, which also happened to be my eighteenth birthday. If it wasn't for my mom and brother, I would never have seen my father again. As it was, we may have said less than a dozen words to each other for the rest of his life. He died four years ago and the only reason I ever regretted our estrangement was for how much it hurt my mother and brother."

Despite what he said earlier about them being friends, Jake suddenly seemed shocked by how much he'd told her and stopped talking. A look of surprise came over his handsome face when she stood with tears in her eyes and pulled on his hand until he was standing also, then hugged the stuffing out of him.

With only the sounds of nature around them, they held each other for a minute. Angie's heart broke for the teenager he'd been, and how his father had assaulted and disowned him for something which was beyond Jake's control. "Is that how you got the scars on your back?" He pulled away and looked at her with confusion in his eyes, probably trying to remember when she would've seen his bare back. "Ian told me it's why you didn't take your shirt off in the club the night you were Whip Master. You were soaked in sweat, but kept it on."

Letting go of her completely, he nodded. "Yeah, that's why. There's quite a few scars where the belt buckle did some permanent damage. I try not to show them to anyone if it can be avoided."

Not knowing what else to say, Angie grabbed her pad and carefully ripped Jake's sketch out before handing it to him. "I hope someday I can draw you when you're truly happy and find someone you love to share your life with. You deserve it."

He gave her a wry smile and kissed her on the cheek. "I don't know if that'll ever happen, sweetheart, but if it does, I hope he's the male version of you—kick-ass and tender, all wrapped up in one beautiful package." He paused and winked at her. "And not afraid of his kinky side."

The two of them laughed and Angie was about to say something snarky when the front door opened and Brody stuck his head out. "Athos is on the phone."

All thoughts of what she and Jake had been talking about took a backseat to her best friend's welfare. She was desperate to hear his voice and ran past Brody as he held the door open for her, then he and Jake followed her back inside. Ian was standing in the living room, talking on his cell phone. He looked like he'd just woken up, too, and as soon as he saw her, he told Athos he was putting him on speaker. Pushing a button, he held out the phone so she could hear and talk to her friend. "Jimmy? Where are you? Are you okay?"

"I'm okay, baby. I'm so sorry about this. Having you involved in this was the last thing I ever wanted. I'm on my way to meet you and we'll talk when I get there, okay? Just do what Ian tells you to do, and stay safe."

A little more at ease after hearing his familiar, comforting voice, she looked up at Ian and said into the phone's mic, "I will. You stay safe, yourself, and get your sorry ass here as soon as possible so I can kick it from here to the moon."

A chuckle came over the line. "That's my girl. I'll see you soon."


IAN GAVE Athos the location where Jake and Brody would meet him in Spartanburg, South Carolina, not far from the airport they flew in to. After they were certain they weren't being followed, the three men would return to the safe-house where they would all sit down and figure out how to get Angie out of this mess. After he hung up the phone, Ian sent a text to CC, telling the pilot to fly back to Tampa and pick up Marco, Boomer and Tiny. He'd bring them up to Spartanburg where another SUV would be waiting for them so they could drive to the safe-house. Ian then called his brother and filled him in, making sure all was safe and sound back at the compound.

Twenty minutes later, Jake and Brody were on their way back to South Carolina. They would reach their destination around the same time as Athos, who'd been taking the back roads since yesterday. In the meantime, Ian and Angie had about three hours to kill. She was staring out the front window looking at the lake when he came up behind her and wrapped his arms around her waist pulling her rear flush against his front. He knew he wasn't out of trouble with her yet, but was pleased to feel her relax into his embrace. Nuzzling his chin to her neck, he placed soft gentle kisses on the skin covering her pulse, loving how a shiver went through her. When she tilted her head to give him better access, he began to nibble and lick the tender area. She moaned and reacted by pushing her ass into his groin which made his dick happy and hard. He smiled against her skin when she said in a husky voice, "Just so you know, I'm still mad at you."

Ian slid a hand up to play with one of her breasts while the other hand slid down and cupped her mound. "I know. But how about we try a little make up sex, *hmm?*" The hand at her breast squeezed her lush flesh while his fingers down below began to rub her clit through her clothes. Her hips began to undulate as she reached back with both hands and grabbed hold of his ass, trying to keep him still while she teased his huge erection through his jeans. "Oh shit, Angel. You feel so good. Let me make you forget about everything, just for a little while."

She gasped when he bit down hard on the spot where her neck and shoulder met. A swipe of his tongue followed as he soothed the sting away. He knew her body wouldn't let her deny him, even if her brain wanted to. She needed what he offered—a brief period where her mind wasn't focused on the danger they all faced. "Yeeesssss."

The single word came out has a hiss as he increased the pressure on her clit and tweaked her nipple through her thin shirt and bra. He spun her around, wrapped his arms below her hips and lifted so she had no choice other than to hook her legs around his waist and her arms around his neck. The position put his rigid cock in contact with her mound, and she whimpered with need. She kissed him with all the passion and desperation inside her as he carried her into his bedroom, kicking the door shut behind them. After easing her down to the bed, Ian checked his phone to make sure the security system was armed and then put the device on the nightstand. His gun, which had been holstered at the small of his back, went right next to the phone.

Pulling her up into a sitting position, he yanked off her shirt followed by her sports bra. Her sweats and thong went next and soon his shirt and jeans were added to the growing pile on the floor. Kneeling next to the side of the bed, Ian put his hands under her ass and pulled her to the edge of the mattress. Placing his hand between her breasts, he urged her to lie down until she was flat on her back and then put her legs over his shoulders. The scent of her arousal hit his nose and his mouth watered. To hell with slow and easy. He parted her pussy lips with his thumbs and attacked her sex like a man who'd gone without for years. He licked her slit several times from bottom to top, moaning at the taste of her, and nibbled on both sides of her opening before stiffening his tongue and stabbing it into her. Angie's hips bounced off the bed as she screamed his name, begging for more. Her hands dove into his hair. While one hand held his head to her core, the other pulled on the short strands, making him growl as the sexual beast inside him was unleashed. He flicked her clit with his tongue while he plunged two fingers into her hot, wet pussy. Finding and rubbing the magic spot, he sent her flying, her shrill cry filling the room.

Not waiting for her to recover Ian stood, flipped her onto her stomach and grabbed the lubricant he'd found in Boomer's room and placed in the nightstand drawer along with the condoms he'd bought. He wouldn't need one of those this time. He'd been prepping her tight little asshole for over two weeks now and he couldn't wait any longer to take her there. With both of their health clearances signed and completed, he wanted to fuck her ass with nothing but skin between them. Popping open the lid of the bottle, he poured some lube down her crack while he took two fingers from his other hand and shoved them back into her still quivering pussy. She hadn't been expecting it and the sudden penetration sent another orgasm spiraling through her, her walls squeezing his digits together as he pumped them in and out of her channel. While she was still coming, he ran his free middle finger up the valley between her ass cheeks and coated it with the silky fluid before easing it into her back hole. She took it without a problem and it wasn't long before he added his index finger to join the other one.

"Oh God. Yes. Yeeesss. Yeeeeesssss. Oh God!" Her lungs heaved and she pushed her hips backward, trying to get him as far into her body as he could go. "Please, Sir. Don't make me wait. Take me now. Fuck my ass and come inside me. Pleeeaaasseee!"

Any other time Ian would've made her wait and drawn out the sweet torture, reminding her he was in charge and not allowing her to top from the bottom. But now he needed her as much as she needed him. While he made a scissor motion with the two fingers in her ass, stretching her more, he grabbed the bottle of lube again and poured some on his aching shaft. After tossing the recapped bottle aside, he pulled his fingers from her puckered rosette and grabbed her hips, tugging until her feet touched the floor and her torso was bent over the bed. Using one hand to spread her cheeks, he used the other to guide the tip of his cock to where it was begging to be. Slowly, he pushed forward and watched as her body yielded to his invasion.

"*Aaahhhh*. More. Oh fuck, Sir, give me more. It burns, but feels so good. Don't stop. Oh, please don't stop."

Her pleading spurred him on and once he was sure he wasn't going to hurt her, he thrust his hips forward until he filled her, making her gasp then beg him to do it again. When she tried to get him to move, he growled, holding back the desperate urge to take her like a rutting animal. "Fuck, Angel. You feel like heaven. I'm not going to last long."

He began to pump his hips at a slow pace, loving the drag of her tight rim along the length of him. Need whipped through him and he couldn't refuse his body's urgent desire to mark her as his in the most primal way possible. He sped up his thrusts until they were both grunting and groaning, reaching for the utmost pinnacle where they would take flight together. A tingling started in Ian's lower spine and spread to his heavy balls which were slapping against her pussy with every inward thrust. Reaching around her hip, he worked his hand between Angie's body and the bed and found her little pearl. Just before his own release ripped through him, he pinched her clit and sent her tumbling over before him. As the waves of her orgasm hit her, the muscles of her empty vagina and her full ass clenched in unison and she milked the seed from his body.

Ian wasn't sure how long he stood behind her, his cock still buried deep, while he covered her upper body with his. Most of his weight was placed on his forearms on either side of her shoulders and he kissed her on the head. His heaving lungs sated their desperate need for oxygen and his breathing slowed to a more normal rate. "Are you okay, Angel?"

"Mmm-hmm."

He chuckled at her exhausted response. His now flaccid dick slid from her well-used hole and they both groaned at the loss of contact. Pushing off the bed, Ian placed a hand on her buttocks until he was sure he was steady on his feet. Giving her right fleshy globe a squeeze, he told her to stay where she was while he retrieved a wet washcloth to clean her. As he finished wiping away the evidence of their wicked and wild make up sex, his phone chimed a text, followed by an alert that a vehicle had breached the security sensor on the road leading to the safe-house.

Grabbing his phone, he checked the text and saw it was from Carter, advising Ian he'd be pulling into the safe-house driveway in less than five minutes. *Fuck!* For once, the black-ops spy had shitty timing . . . and how the hell did he know they were here in the first place?

# CHAPTER 16

*R*eluctantly, Ian took a two-minute shower while Angie dozed under the covers he'd tucked around her after picking her up and putting her to bed properly. He wished he could join her in blissful slumber just to wake her in an hour or so and do everything again. Instead, he got dressed in his jeans and T-shirt again then left the bedroom in bare feet, shutting the door behind him. He found Carter helping himself to a cup of coffee, a banana, and two chocolate chip muffins.

While his friend stuffed his face for a few minutes, Ian grabbed a bottle of water from the fridge and gulped the entire contents down. Sex with Angie always left him parched, not that he was complaining. Tossing the empty bottle in the recycling bin under the sink, he grabbed another one and sat down at the kitchen island next to Carter. "Should I bother to ask how you knew we were here? And don't tell me you're here just for the food, ass-hat."

The spy showing up 'just for the food' was a long-standing flat joke between him and Ian's team, and was usually brought up when they ran into each other on a mission. If the spy said that's why he was there, it meant his operation was classified and he couldn't discuss it with anyone, not even the former SEALs with government clearance who he considered to be his closest friends. For a man in his deadly business, having six friends he could count on in life and death situations was a lot, and he never took them for granted.

Carter grinned as he chewed the last bite of his muffins then swallowed. He took a swig of his coffee knowing full well Ian was impatient for an answer. "Nope. This time the food is a bonus, and thanks, I was starving. As for why I'm here . . . I got a message from Athos saying he was in trouble and he couldn't trust anyone in his agency. Said he was heading to Spartanburg, South Carolina and I assumed this was his final destination. Have you heard from him yet?" Without waiting for an answer, he added, "I take it your new girlfriend is in your bedroom catching up on some much needed sleep."

Ian rolled his eyes as the other man waggled his eyebrows, à la Groucho Marx. "You can be a real asshole sometimes. You know that, don't you?"

"Of course. It's what I do best."

Letting out a snort, Ian shook his head at Carter's matter-of-fact statement. "Yeah, Angie's sleeping. We heard from Athos over an hour ago. Reverend and Egghead went to pick him up. Devon's holding down the fort, and CC is on his way to Tampa to bring back Boomer, Polo, and Tiny. I figured the big guy might come in handy if I need an extra body to watch over her. Once we get the full update from Athos, we'll decide what to do next."

Carter nodded, apparently satisfied there was nothing which needed his immediate attention. "Good. Since I have close to two and a half hours before they get back, I'm going to sack out for a bit."

As the other man got up and placed his now empty cup in the dishwasher and his garbage in the trash, Ian told him, "Take Jenn's room. I'll give Athos the spare room my folks use." His parents didn't visit Maggie Valley often, but when they did, the master suite on the main floor was theirs.

Without another word, Carter gave him a small salute, grabbed his military green duffel bag from where he'd left it next to the front door and headed upstairs for a quick shower and some shut-eye. Since his friend was now taken care of, Ian returned to his bedroom and locked the door. Stripping his shirt off once again, but leaving his jeans on, he climbed into bed, pulled Angie's sleeping form into his arms and closed his eyes.

AN HOUR AND A HALF LATER, Ian was sitting on the wide porch stairs, staring at the lake while Angie finished drying her hair after their shared shower, which took longer than necessary, as usual. He'd gotten a text a short while ago from Jake saying they would be back at the house in about forty minutes or so and Ian was getting antsy. The faster Athos got here, the faster they could figure out how to end the threat against Angie. His cell phone alerted him to another text and Ian checked the screen. Devon was letting him know Marco, Boomer and Tiny were heading out to the small airport to meet CC, and they would be in the air within the hour.

The door behind him opened and he didn't need to turn around to know it was his angel. The fresh scent of her shampoo and body soap hit him and he felt a stirring in his groin. Damn, the woman made it hard for him to think about anything but sex when she was near him. She walked down two steps, and plopped her sweet ass on the top stair next to him. "It's beautiful up here."

Ian put his arm around her and tucked her close to his body with her head resting on his shoulder. "It certainly is. I wish I could get up here more often for pleasure instead of business. If you hadn't noticed, the compound is kind of lacking in its landscaping within the fence lines."

She giggled. "I did kinda notice. Will you retire up here someday?"

"Maybe," he mused with a shrug of his unoccupied shoulder. "Or maybe I'll buy a small island in the Caribbean . . . my little oasis in the middle of nowhere. Wherever I end up, there has to be water somewhere, whether it's a lake or the ocean."

They sat in silence for a few minutes before the door behind them opened again and Carter walked out then down the steps to the gravel below, turning so he could face the couple. He'd changed out of his cargo pants and now wore a faded pair of jeans, a clean T-shirt and his combat boots. Ian gave Angie a squeeze. "Angie, Carter. Carter, Angie.

The spy held out his hand to her. "He speaks so eloquently sometimes, doesn't he?"

———

Angie laughed and shook the man's hand. "Yes, he does, but I don't mind. It's nice to meet you."

"It's nice to meet you too, sweetheart, but I wish it was under better circumstances." Ian had told her about Carter's presence in the house and why the man was here while he'd washed her hair in the shower. "Sorry I didn't have a chance to meet you at the club the other night, but I found myself . . . occupied . . . longer than I expected. I would've liked to have watched your first public scene because I heard it was fantastic and had a happy ending."

Angie dipped her head and blushed while both men laughed. She didn't know why she turned so red now when being spanked and brought to an intense orgasm in front of audience hadn't really embarrassed her at all at the time. Carter gave her a wink, and she shook her head, smiling at his teasing. She didn't have to ask what had kept him occupied at the time because Kristen had filled her in. Carter had joined the engaged couple for a repeat threesome, and for her second introduction to the good-looking Dom, Kristen hadn't been wearing a blindfold. There also hadn't been any time constraints which they'd had during their first tryst, so the three of them had been in one of the private playrooms for a few hours. Her friend didn't give her many details, but having read romances with ménages before, Angie didn't need a picture painted for her.

While she wasn't interested in experiencing a threesome for herself, she had no problem with anyone else having one. She barely survived the intense orgasms Ian gave her on a regular basis these days, and there was no way she could handle two men at once. Ian had been happy to see ménages were on her hard limit list she'd given him. He'd told her he'd been a third once, in his early days of being a Dom. And while it had been a great experience, he found he didn't like sharing his women, unlike his brother and some of their friends.

Angie got to her feet. "I was going to make myself a sandwich. Is anyone else hungry?" When both men said, "yes, please," she looked at Carter. "I know what he wants, but what would you like to eat?"

With a broad grin, he wiggled his eyebrows, and she laughed at his playfulness while Ian growled. "All right, since Ian's going to deck me if I say anything sexual, I'll take whatever you're making for him, but no mayo, please. I hate the stuff."

"No mayo, no problem." She ran her hand through Ian's short hair as she climbed the two steps back onto the porch then went inside to make them lunch.

---

IAN GROWLED AGAIN as Carter's blatant gaze stayed glued to Angie's ass until she disappeared into the house. "Really, asshole?"

The spy shrugged his shoulders then sat down next to Ian. "What? Like you've said many times in the past, 'just because I can't touch, doesn't mean I can't look.' Too bad you're not into threesomes because that is one beautiful backside, my friend, and I'd have to be six feet under not to appreciate it." He glanced sideways at the man who was still glaring at him and let out a snort. "So, she's the one, huh?"

Ian's eyes narrowed even further. Before he could respond, his phone chimed with an alert. A vehicle had activated a sensor when it turned up the road leading to the house. A second later, he received a text from Jake letting him know it was them coming up the hill. He glared at Carter again. "The one . . . what?"

"The one who's going to make you forget you ever had a bitch of a fiancée who fucked you over. It's about fucking time."

"Fuck you, asshole," Ian scoffed. "You know I'm never going down that road again."

"Ha! You keep telling yourself that, dude, but from where I stand, you're not only heading down a road, but you're heading down the *right* road. And here I thought you were going to wallow in sorrow for the rest of your life because the woman you weren't *supposed* to spend it with walked out on you. Did you ever think the reason it happened is making your lunch right now, and has a very nice ass?"

Before Ian could tell Carter to fuck off again, the team's SUV pulled into the driveway with Brody at the wheel and Jake in the front passenger seat. The vehicle parked and when the front doors opened, so did the rear passenger door and a clean-shaven, but tired looking Athos climbed out of the vehicle. The two men on the steps stood and approached the trio. As Carter shook hands with the DEA agent, commenting on his de-whiskered face, Ian eyed his teammates. "How'd everything go?"

"Good," Brody told him. "No trackers, no worries."

Ian nodded at the geek, who headed toward the house. As he reached the top of the porch stairs, Angie burst out the door and ran down the steps toward the car . . . toward her best friend and jumped into his waiting arms. Ian's heart squeezed and fists clenched as he watched his woman hug another man as tight as she could. Grinding his teeth, he forced himself not to beat his chest and yank her out of Athos' embrace, like the caveman in him wanted to do.

Next to him, Carter said in a low, amused voice which no one else could hear, "Uh-huh. Keep telling yourself she's not the one, Boss-man. Maybe someday you can convince yourself, but I doubt it."

---

TEN MINUTES LATER, Angie handed a plate with a heaping sandwich on rye bread to Ian and another one to Carter then got busy making sandwiches for Jimmy and herself. Jake stood on the opposite side of the kitchen island throwing together a similar lunch for himself and Brody. Egghead was upstairs in the den tracking down some information they needed concerning several agents from the DEA's Atlanta office, including Agents Jackson and Holstein. Athos confirmed their identities from the surveillance photos Brody had printed out.

When they were done making the sandwiches, Jake ran Brody's lunch up to the war-room before joining Angie and the rest of them at the large dining table. Angie noticed as she sat down that Ian hadn't touched his sandwich yet. She smiled to herself when she saw he didn't pick it up until after he watched her take a bite of her own. He'd waited until he was sure she was going to eat as well. Since she realized he was always putting her welfare before his own, she noticed a lot more of the little things he did and loved how they made her feel. The man may not be a romantic in the traditional sense, but he was a romantic in his own way.

While they all ate, Athos filled Ian and Carter in with what he'd told the others on the way back to the house. "Things seemed fine the first two weeks. I was using contacts I'd made a few years ago to work my way under. I got lucky. Met up with a guy who only knew my cover and he vouched for me. A local cop on the take ran me for the boss, found my established arrest record and I was in. Did some small time runs right off the bat. They had a few run-ins with the cops and local gangs recently so they were down a few guys, otherwise I don't think I would've gotten in so fast. Yesterday morning, I was doing some snooping around and overheard a big shipment was coming in next Monday through the Gulf of Mexico from Colombia's Diaz cartel—"

"Ah, shit, man," Carter interrupted, dropping his half-eaten sandwich back on his plate. He glanced knowingly at Ian, who was pissed as all hell the Diaz cartel was involved in this mess. "Emmanuel is behind all this? Damn, when you step in it, you really step in it, A-man."

Athos dragged a hand down his face in frustration. "Don't I know it. Aaron, the agent who I replaced, suspected that's where the trail ended, but I don't think Diaz was behind the hit on him and his family. I think it came from lower down the food chain with inside help from the DEA." He looked at the government spy. "You know there's dirt in every agency and mine has its fair share."

"How'd you find out you were blown?" Ian was trying to think past the cartel's involvement and his fear for Angie. His SEAL Team Four had been involved in investigating and eventually killing Emmanuel's brother, Ernesto, several years earlier. Not only was the cartel involved in drugs, they also, at the time, had a thriving sex trade and arms trade which Emmanuel was working hard to reestablish after his brother's death.

"Same conversation. After I overheard the details, the head honcho of New Orleans' drug trade, Manny Melendez, got a phone call from someone. Next thing I knew, he was ordering the hit on me and telling whoever was on the phone to find out my weaknesses. I got out of there as fast as I could and called you." Angie was sitting silently between him and Ian, and he reached over and took her hand. His eyes filled with deep regret. "I'm so sorry, baby. You know I'd never do anything which would result in you getting hurt. I've always taken precautions to keep you safe."

Ian didn't know who was surprised more, him or Athos, when Angie tore her hand free from her best friend's grip and stood while glaring at him. "Really, Jimmy? If that was true then I wouldn't have had two crooked DEA agents knocking on my door wanting to kidnap me and probably kill me. I wouldn't be running for my life and the lives of these men," she gestured around the table, "wouldn't be in danger because they were protecting me."

Athos got up from his seat and so did Ian, but neither man could get a word in because the woman was on a roll now, yelling and pointing her finger at her friend's nose. "I wouldn't be hiding out up here and worrying you might be dead somewhere. And don't think I forgot about you telling them to bug my house and put cameras in." She huffed and crossed her arms. "I don't even know how this whole mess is going to end. Am I going to be running for the rest of my life until one of those bastards catch up to me? Will I ever be able go home again? Will I—"

"Ang, stop yelling. Calm down and sit down."

As soon as the growled orders were out of Athos' mouth, Ian knew things were going to get worse from the look on Angie's face. He was just glad her ire had another target this time. She snarled at her friend, her hands clenched in rage. "Don't tell me what to do, and you don't get to pull that dominant crap on me because I get more than enough from Ian."

She turned on her heel and stormed out the front door while Athos glared at Ian who gave it right back to him in spades. "Is she fucking kidding me? I told you to watch over her and keep her safe, not fuck her and get her involved in your god-damned kink. And yeah, I know all about your fucking sex club, asshole, and you're not fucking taking her there."

While Ian tried to keep himself from punching the guy, the other two men stood from the table and started walking out the door after the very pissed off-woman. Jake glanced over his shoulder. "We'll go and keep an eye on Angie. Just don't kill each other until after we take care of the main objective, all right?"

Neither man answered him because it'd been a rhetorical question. Instead, they stared each other down and Ian was astounded when Athos broke eye contact first, sighing in frustration and running his fingers through his hair. "Fuck. Sorry. You can kick my ass later. I have no say about who she dates or what you two do. I just want her to be happy and safe. If you're the man to do that then . . ."

Athos left the rest of the sentence go unsaid and Ian could see the defeat in his expression. He crossed his arms over his chest and leaned against the dining table where the remnants of everyone's lunch still sat. He studied the other man for a minute. "Does she know?"

Athos looked at him in confusion. "Does she know . . . what?"

"That you're in love with her?"

The question was obviously the last thing Athos expected him to ask. Mirroring Ian's stance, he leaned against the back of the couch and stared at something over Ian's shoulder. "To love someone the way she deserves, you have to have not only a heart, but a soul as well. I lost both of those a long time ago. I've been trying to get even for my mother's and sister's deaths for so long . . ." He shook his head sadly. "I have nothing left to give her, which is why I stay away from her as much as I can, yet still hold on because she's all I've got."

He paused and regarded Ian a moment. "So, right back at you, Sawyer. Does she know you're in love with her? Because I'm not blind either, man."

Before Ian could respond, although he wasn't sure what his answer would've been, Brody came barreling down the stairs from the den with his laptop in hand. He placed it on the dining table so both men could see the screen. "We've got big trouble."

## CHAPTER 17

*I*an and Athos closed in on the table to read the news brief from Atlanta's CBS website and both started cursing. Athos' handler, Arthur Giles, Special Agent in Charge of the Atlanta DEA office, had been killed in a drive-by shooting. He had been gunned down as he got out of his car at his home on the outskirts of the city, at a quarter after seven last night. There were no reported suspects, but the police and feds were looking at a local gang of drug runners.

"Fuck! God-damn it!" Athos plunged both hands through his hair again and spun around looking for something to vent his anger on. Not finding anything other than a wall, he punched it and the pain didn't even register as his knuckles began to swell. "His daughter had his first grandchild a month ago. And now he's dead because of my fucking need to get even with those bastards."

"You don't know that for sure." Ian didn't believe his own words, but he needed to calm the man down. Athos rounded on him, getting in his face, but Ian didn't back down.

"Don't I? Come on, Sawyer, don't fucking patronize me. You know how this fucking goes. They're cleaning house after the cartel found two DEA agents from the same office had infiltrated them. Someone found out who our fucking handler was and put a stop to any more interference from him. No one from Atlanta was supposed to know where Artie sent us. Fuck, no one in Atlanta was even supposed to know who the hell Aaron was."

Ian didn't say anything more because they both knew the likelihood of Athos being wrong was very slim. There were very few coincidences in their line of work, and he doubted this was one of them. Carter had heard the commotion and came back inside to see what was wrong. Ian pointed to the still open laptop, and the operative walked over to read it, adding his own curses to the ones they'd spouted out earlier. He pinned the DEA agent with an understanding stare, having overheard his last rant. "Don't beat yourself up, A-man. If you didn't volunteer, Artie would've sent in someone else and the result would've been the same. Put the blame where it belongs—on the dirty agents and the cartel." He paused and let his words sink in to the man's brain. "Artie was the only one who knew you went under, wasn't he?"

The agitated man nodded. It meant he had no one left he could trust in his own department. They knew two of his fellow agents were dirty and had no idea who else at the Atlanta office was on the take. He couldn't risk contacting anyone until he knew for sure it was safe. For now, Carter and the Trident team were his only backup.

Ian arched an eyebrow at Carter. "Where's Angie?"

"She took a walk with Jake. She's still pissed off, and I wasn't stupid enough to stay in the line of fire. That woman is a firecracker."

Brody had been quiet since he first came down and now took a deep breath. "Okay, so where do we go from here? Athos has no backup from his agency. His handler is dead. We can't take out the whole New Orleans cartel without starting an all-out war or getting ourselves life in prison or worse. Angie's still in danger. Did I miss anything?"

"Nope, and thanks for stating the obvious, Egghead."

"No problem, Carter. Glad I could help keep you in the loop." Turning his sarcasm off, he asked, "Now does someone have a plan?"

While they all remained silent, trying to think of a way out of this horror story they'd found themselves in, Ian's phone rang.

Glancing at the screen, he saw it was the backup phone his brother kept in his car. "Hey, Dev, what's up?"

"Jenn's been kidnapped!"

Ian stiffened in shock, not believing what Devon had just blurted out. Panic assaulted him. "What do you mean, Jenn's been kidnapped?"

The other three men froze in place as well, wide eyes searching Ian's pale face as if it held all the answers to their questions. He punched the speaker button and set the phone down on the table so they could all gather around. His brother's frantic voice came through loud and clear. "Henderson called. I put him and his partner on Jenn, just in case. They were pulled over by an unmarked car while driving her to the college. From the description he gave me before I lost him, it sounds like it was the two agents who tried to get Angie. Henderson took a bullet to the chest and his partner was shot in the head. I think Henderson passed out, but the line is still open—it's why I'm on the backup. I'm on the way to the scene now and just heard the cops and paramedics arrive."

"Was Jenn hurt?"

"I don't know, Ian. All I know is she's gone. I'm about five minutes away. I'll call you back as soon as I know anything. Marco called about twenty minutes ago and said they landed and are on the road."

"I'll call them and have them turn around then make sure CC's ready to take off again. Keep me posted." Ian disconnected the phone.

"Don't turn them around." They all looked at Brody who was rushing up the stairs to get his gear from the den. He raised his voice so he could be heard without stopping. "If they're already on the road, we can have CC do a quick hop to the airport in Ashville. It's about halfway between us. We can meet them there and it'll save us some time."

"Good. Call him and get him in the air." Ian jerked his chin at Carter. "Can you go get Jake and Angie? We're out of here in five."

Without an answer, the man jogged out the door. Once he was

out of sight, Ian grabbed Athos by the shirt and shoved him up against the wall. The agent grabbed his wrists, but wisely didn't resist. Ian let out a low growl. "If anything happens to my goddaughter because of you, you won't have to fucking worry about the cartel. You hear me?"

Regret filled Athos' eyes. "I hear you, and I wouldn't expect anything less from you. For what it's worth, I'm sorry."

"I don't give a shit about your fucking apology. Just help us get Jenn back, then we finish this and guarantee Angie's safety."

Without waiting for a response, Ian released him and moved toward his bedroom. "Let's grab what we need and get the hell out of here. I'll call Marco from the road."

A FEW MINUTES after they were all in the air, Brody held out his hand to Boomer. "Did you bring my new toy?"

The man reached into his pocket of his jeans and handed the geek the piece of jewelry he'd asked him to grab from the war-room. Walking from the couch area to where Angie was sitting alone in the same seat she'd occupied on their first flight, Brody sat down beside her and asked her to hold out her left arm for him. She was still pissed about everything, and now terrified that Jenn had been kidnapped and possibly hurt, or worse. When he finished attaching the gold bracelet to her wrist, she stared at it in confusion. "Um, Brody, I don't have any allergies and I'm not a diabetic or anything, so what's with the medical alert bracelet?

"It just says you're allergic to bees, sweetheart. Nothing serious. In the meantime, if something happens, which we're going to avoid at all costs, I can track you with the GPS in there. If I'm close enough, there's also a one-way hidden microphone so I can listen in on what's going on around you through a receiver in my laptop. It's short range, but the GPS is long range. If I need to, I can always," he coughed the word "hack" before continuing, "into a satellite to track you. No one wears ID bracelets anymore and I needed the room inside, so I figured a fake medical alert was the best thing to use. It's a prototype and you're my guinea pig . . . sorry, figure of speech."

Still holding her hand, he hesitated a moment, as if struggling with what he wanted to say next. "Are you and I okay? I know you're still pissed over us bugging your house, but, sweetheart, my friendship with you was . . . *is* the real thing."

She nodded and saw his tense body relax. Her voice was forgiving, but tired. "I know, Brody. It's just everything hit me at once, you know? I've been independent for so long and I hate being left out of things which concern me. I'll get over it, but you better get your ass over to my house as soon as this is all over and take out every single one of those cameras and bugs." She gave him a glare to let him know she meant business. "Understand?"

"Yes, ma'am!" He grinned at her with his famous flirtatious expression. "You know, if I didn't know better, I'd think you were a Domme at times. That's called a switch, by the way. But don't tell Ian I told you. He'll shoot me for putting ideas in your head."

"Hmm. Maybe I can have Jake train me to be a Whip Master."

He looked at her in feigned horror and they both laughed, glad they had a chance to clear the last bit of friction still between them. When he stood to go back to the rest of the group, she got up and followed, then took the seat at the end of the couch between Boomer and Ian's recliner which was in its upright position. Ian smiled at her, but it didn't reach his eyes which were filled with worry. Angie leaned over and linked her right fingers with his left and set their joined hands on the armrest of the couch. His other hand was holding the jet's phone to his ear as he got the update from Devon. "Okay. Do what you can, call in whoever you need and keep me updated." Disconnecting the call, he looked up and told them what he knew, which wasn't much. "There's been no word from the kidnappers yet, or agents, or whatever you want to call those assholes. No leads either. An APB was put out on the agency vehicle. Dev called in a few favors with the locals, and so far, they've agreed to keep the DEA out of loop despite the connection. He also put a call into Keon just in case we need to override the local law enforcement." Their contact in the FBI, Larry Keon, was the Deputy Director, otherwise known as the number two man in the agency, and would help them with whatever they needed. "Henderson is alive, but still unconscious. He lost a lot of blood and they took him into surgery. His partner didn't make it. Dev's pulling in everyone he can and using our local contacts and snitches. Nothing so far."

"Why did they take her? I mean Jimmy has never even met Jenn."

Angie wasn't seeing the big picture, but the men were. Ian squeezed her hand. "Angel, they obviously don't know you well enough yet, otherwise they would've gone after one of your friends. It would've taken them a while to figure out who you would run to save. You have no other family except for Athos and vice versa. The only connection they could figure out fast is Brody since he helped you. Brody's trail led them to Trident. Their best chance to get you, and ultimately Athos, was to take either Kristen or Jenn. Kristen hasn't left the compound, so Jenn was taken. We'll get her back, but for now, we wait until they contact us."

Her bottom lip trembled, but she didn't break down. "They want you to trade me for Jenn, don't they?"

Ian tugged on her hand until she stood and he pulled her down on his lap. Wrapping one arm around her hips and holding her to him, he cupped her chin with his other hand and made sure she was looking into his eyes. "That's not going to happen, Angel. I'm scared to death for Jenn's safety, but I'll throw myself on the gates of Hell before I trade your life for hers. Once we find out where they're holding her, we're going to get her back . . . alive. It's what we do, sweetheart. Dev's called in some former team members who can get to Tampa fast. Boomer's dad is already on his way to help along with a few others. These bastards are going to rue the day they ever messed with Jennifer Mullins, I can guarantee you that."

Tiny chimed in. "Don't worry, Miss Angie. We got this covered."

Angie's gaze moved to each of the brave men's faces and she saw their determination. She nodded, but knew it was evident she was still terrified for Jenn's safety. Climbing off Ian's lap, she headed to the jet's bathroom, which was twice the size of regular airplane facilities, and shut the door. It wasn't until she was alone, did she allow her tears to fall. She didn't want them to know how upset she was because they had enough to deal with without her breaking down in front of them. It was a few minutes before she got herself back under control and began to splash some water on her face. There was a knock at the door, and she did a pat-dry of her hands and face before tossing the paper towel into the trash. When she opened the door, she was surprised to see Jimmy, and instead of standing aside to let her out, he stepped into the small space with her and closed the door behind him. "What are you doing?"

He took her hands in his. "I wanted a moment alone with you and this was the only option. I'm sorry, Ang. You have no idea how sorry I am that you and Ian's niece are in jeopardy because of me. I'm sorry I put my need to avenge Mom's and Ruthie's deaths before my relationship with you." He stared at their joined hands. Swallowing hard, he struggled to find the right words. "Before I got called into my CO's office and was told they'd been murdered, I was planning on finishing out my tour and then getting out. I was going to come home and ask you out on a real date." Angie gaped at her best friend while he lifted his sad eyes and shrugged his shoulder. "I know, crazy, right? But being away from you, so far away, I realized how much you meant to me. Somewhere in the middle of our letters, phone calls and my rotations home, I fell in love with my best friend. Hell, I'd been in love with you long before that, but refused to admit it to myself."

"Oh, Jimmy. Why didn't you ever say anything?"

"In the beginning, before . . . I was just plain scared. Here I was in Special Ops, and a cute, sassy, little blonde, who means the world to me, had me scared shitless, thinking she wouldn't say yes to a date. Besides, I wanted to tell you face to face. I didn't want to give you time to over-think things. Then my world fell apart, and I was so bent on revenge. When Artie approached me with a way to get even with the dirt bags who sold drugs to my sister and millions of other kids like her, I took it. And I didn't like who I'd become afterward. I couldn't expect you to fall for a man who'd become so blood-thirsty, he was willing to throw away the best thing that ever happened to him. You. You have been my world since the day I met you in ninth grade English and picked up the book you'd knocked off your desk and gave it back to you."

She gave him a sad smile. "I felt that way too, but I thought you didn't want to ruin our friendship for something which might not work out."

"I didn't. I thought if it didn't work out, I'd lose you altogether. And when I was finally ready to face my fear . . ." He took a deep breath and let it out again. "Sawyer is good for you. I watch him watch you. You come before everything else for him. I can't say the same, and you have no idea how sorry I am for that. At one point in my life I thought we were soulmates, you know? Now I think, while you may have been mine, I was never yours. But if he ever hurts you, there's going to be hell to pay." She started to say something, but he shook his head, stopping her. "I want you to be happy, baby, and despite everything going on, I see the way you look at him, too. I know you're in love with him and I'm okay with it. Well, maybe not at the moment, but I'll get there. Maybe when this is all over, I'll start looking for my true soulmate, if she's out there. But honestly, Ang, you're going to be a tough act to follow."

By the time Athos finished talking, Angie was crying again. He pulled her into his arms and held her until the tears stopped a second time. Then he let her go, but not before he placed a lingering kiss on her forehead. "I love you, Ang. I always will."

"I love you, too, Jimmy Andrews. You'll always be my best friend."

When the two of them stepped out of the bathroom together, Ian saw her swollen, red eyes, and she could sense the anger blasting through him as his stare shifted to the man who'd made her cry. Before he could say or do anything, Angie hurried over to him, climbed back into his lap and wrapped her arms around him, needing to soothe him along with herself. She felt his body relax when she whispered in his ear, "It's okay, Ian. He had some things he wanted to tell me, but it's you I want to be with. He'll always be my friend, but it's you I'm in love with."

Ian tugged her hair, pulling her head back until he could look into her eyes. He had to see the truth there—she *was* in love with him. Her heart belonged to him and only him. He leaned down so his mouth was next to her ear and spoke so no one else would hear. "And I'm in love with you, my sweet angel."

# CHAPTER 18

*W*hen they arrived back at the compound they were met with an almost full parking area outside of the Trident building. There were several government-issued vehicles and marked Tampa P.D. cars as well as personal vehicles belonging to whomever Devon had managed to get in touch with. Jenn had about forty surrogate uncles from SEAL Team Four, all of whom would drop everything for Baby-girl, but only a few of them were close enough to Tampa to get there within a short time frame. Even Beau knew he was 'on-duty' and had attached himself to Angie's side, as if knowing she was the human who needed him the most. Boomer's father, Rick Michaelson, and Devon approached Marco and Ian's vehicles, which they had driven home from the small airstrip.

As Boomer greeted his dad, who was also a former SEAL, Devon got down to business and filled them all in. "Still no word from the kidnappers and we can't figure out why because it's been over three hours. They've gotta still be in Tampa somewhere because Angie's their objective. In addition to Rick, we've got Bannerman, Rad and Urkel inside the conference room doing what they can to coordinate everything and try to figure out where they may have her. We also called Chase and asked him to spare whoever he had on hand, which was only five guys with the experience we need." When necessary, Trident contracted additional manpower from Chase Dixon, who owned Blackhawk Security. It was his two men who'd been assigned to protect Jenn. "But he'll have more tomorrow if it goes that long. He's at the hospital with Henderson who's still in surgery. His folks are on their way from Jacksonville. I told Chase to book them a room at the Hilton up the street from the hospital and bill it to me. He told me to fuck off, he's got it covered.

"We're keeping the DEA out of the loop until we know who we can trust. Instead, I called Keon. He's stuck in D.C., but contacted the local office and told them to help us out in any way they could. Unfortunately, it means Frank Stonewall is here and he's not happy about it."

The local FBI Special Agent in Charge had been far from thrilled with his supervisor, Trident, and Carter after he was shut out of the investigation when Carter killed the hit-man targeting the team several months ago. While the rest of the team groaned at Devon's announcement, Carter smirked. Last time he and Stonewall met, the SAC almost crapped his pants when the pissed-off operative lit into him. It would be interesting to see the fed's reaction to seeing him again.

"Angie!" All heads turned as Kristen came running from the residence building straight into the other woman's arms and held her tight. The two of them tried hard not to crumble, but they couldn't stop the few tears which fell down both their faces.

Ian walked over and stood next to them, rubbing his hands up and down their backs in comfort. "Kristen, why don't you take Angie up to your apartment for now, *hmmm*? There are too many people inside the offices and you'll just be in the way. Take Beau with you and we'll let you know when we hear something." Turning his head toward Angie, he added, "We're doing everything we can. We'll find her and bring her home. I promise."

The two women nodded, neither one trusting themselves to speak at the moment. Ian kissed both women on the head, lingering longer on Angie's. Then he watched as they staggered back to the apartments, their arms around each other in mutual support as Beau trotted beside them. Taking a deep breath, he turned back toward his now extended team and gestured for them to head into the offices. It was time to make good on his promise.

Inside, Colleen was sitting at her reception desk, calling in an order for pizzas and two cases of bottled water for the men who were now occupying the conference room. Devon's office, as well as two vacant desks in a small bullpen area behind her, were also in use. The young secretary's eyes were red and it was obvious she'd been crying earlier. As they walked by her, she gave them a watery smile filled with trust, as if she had no doubt the Doms would do everything they could to save Jenn's life.

Brody went straight to his war-room, unlocked it and started booting up the different computers he would need. Curt Bannerman, who'd been their backup computer specialist on Team Four, joined him, taking a spare chair and rolling it over to assist his fellow geek. Neil 'Rad' Radovsky and Steve 'Urkel' Romanelli gave Ian and the rest of the team lazy salutes while staying on their respective phones with their contacts, trying to find where Jenn might be being held.

Inside Devon's office, the five men borrowed from Chase were checking their weapons and waiting to be called to duty. One was on the phone, and from the sound of it he was talking to his boss and checking on Henderson. Ian would have to find out about the slain bodyguard later to see what they could do to help the man's family deal with their loss. Earlier on the plane, Ian had told Devon, who agreed, they would take care of all costs for the funeral and burial. If he had wife and children, they would make sure they were well taken care of. It was the least they could do for a man who had given his life trying to protect Jenn.

The conference room was filled with three FBI agents, including a scowling Stonewall, two uniformed policemen and two plainclothes detectives from the local P.D. If the situation wasn't so serious, Ian might have laughed when Stonewall paled at the sight of Carter walking into the room. As it was, he heard Boomer chuckle behind him when the kid noticed the same thing. Carter in turn gave the SAC his best Dom glare, then ignored the fed and got to work, calling his own contacts.

Also present in the room were Colleen's Dom, Reggie Helm, and Ian's cousin, Mitch Sawyer, both of whom shook Ian's hand and offered whatever help they could give them. Mitch asked,

"What should we do about the club? Do you want me to shut it down for the night?"

Ian looked at the clock on the wall and sighed. They still had about three hours before the club opened at nineteen-thirty hours. "Yeah, the less people here at the compound the better. We don't know how long this is going to last. Whatever you do, don't let the members know about Jenn, otherwise every Dom will be showing up to help and while I'd appreciate it, they'd be in the way. We have enough personnel here as is."

Mitch nodded. "I'll send out the mass text from my office." He turned to Tiny. "Do you mind helping me call the staff? I want to make sure everyone knows not to show and the phones will probably start ringing off the hook when the members find out we're closed, wanting to see what the problem is."

Ian spoke in a low tone to Reggie so he couldn't be overheard, "I'd appreciate it if you took Colleen home with you. She doesn't need to be here for this and the less you know the better. We may need you after this is all over."

Reggie was one of Trident's lawyers, and this was Ian's way of keeping the man out of the loop for when the shit hit the fan. If Reggie needed to defend them in court for any reason, like for a murder charge, it gave him plausible deniability. When lawyers spoke to their clients accused of crimes they rarely asked them outright if they were guilty or not. They didn't need to know in order to defend their clients, and usually didn't want to know.

Right after the two Doms and Tiny left with Colleen in tow, the company phone rang and Ian picked up the line on one of the conference room phones sitting on the table. As soon as he heard the computer-altered voice, he began rapidly waving his other hand and snapping his fingers to alert everyone in the room that the kidnappers were making contact. Everyone stopped in mid-sentence and remained silent. Marco ran out the door toward the war-room to tell Brody to start tracing the call as Ian hit the speaker button so they could all hear.

". . . see her again. Tomorrow morning at eight o'clock, you'll receive a text. Have Agent Andrews bring Angelina Beckett to the address you're given, and we'll release your pretty niece, although she may not be too pretty anymore if you don't do as you're told."

The hair on the back of Ian's neck tingled as his fear and anger intensified. Leaning his two hands on the conference table, he growled at the person on the other end of the phone. "Listen you fucking bastard, if you hurt one fucking hair on that girl's head, there won't be anywhere on this fucking earth where you can hide that I won't find you. And when I'm done with you, you'll be fucking begging me to kill you to end your suffering! You hear me you piece of shit!"

He'd been in such a blind rage and was yelling by the end of his rant that he didn't realize the caller had disconnected until Devon put his hand on his bicep. "Ian, he hung up."

Devon's voice was low, trying to calm his brother down, but it didn't work. Ian grabbed the office phone, ripped out the cord, and threw it against the wall where it shattered.

No one was hurt by the flying debris although several of the men were hit. Not a word was spoken as the usually unflappable man stormed out of the room and made his way to his office, passing a stone-faced Marco on the way. He slammed the door behind him, and they heard a roar of frustration and anguish. The men all knew the call time was far too short for a trace. They were equally frustrated because, despite all the missions and cases they'd been on over the years, this time it was personal. Devon looked at everyone else. "Give him a few minutes. In the meantime, get back to harassing your contacts."

---

ANGIE WAS in Ian's bedroom after telling Kristen she'd be up in a few minutes. Brody had programmed her hand print for the lock-scanners at Ian's request earlier in the week so she'd been able to let herself in as Beau followed Kristen upstairs to her and Devon's apartment. This was the first time Angie had a moment to herself since Jimmy had shown up, her brief time in the plane's bathroom notwithstanding. She needed some time to come to terms with a few things. In addition to her worry about Jenn, she was still reeling from Jimmy's confession and then the fact that she'd told Ian she was in love with him. She hadn't expected him to say the words back to her, and although she knew he meant them, she couldn't help but think he was still holding himself back from her. His ex-fiancée must have done a number on him and she was glad the woman didn't live anywhere nearby because she might have gone looking for her and pounded on her for hurting him.

Entering the bathroom, she washed her face again then brushed her teeth with the spare toothbrush Ian had given her to use after her first overnight stay. When she came back out, she started pulling the pieces of her disassembled cell phone out of the sweatshirt Ian had given her to wear when she started shaking at the news of the kidnapping. She'd retrieved the phone parts from the backseat of his SUV where he'd tossed it yesterday, and shoved them in her pockets. God, was it only yesterday afternoon when she and Brody had been running for their lives? So much had changed in less than thirty-six hours.

Putting the SIM card in, followed by the battery, she closed the cover and powered the phone up. At once, it began alerting her to missed texts and calls. Checking the call log first, she saw four voice mails from her friend Mandy, Shelby from the club, Red Rose Books and one other client. Then she checked her texts and saw more of the same, but one *Unknown* message caught her eye. When she opened it, Angie was horrified to see a photo of Jenn and felt her blood run cold. The girl had been bound, gagged and blindfolded. The message with the photo told her to contact the sender immediately without telling the cops or Trident team, or they were going to kill Jenn. Checking the time stamp, she saw the message had only been received twenty minutes ago. She sent a return text as fast as she could.

**I'm here. Tell me what I should do.**

Less than fifteen seconds later the phone rang in her hand and she'd been so startled, she almost dropped it. The screen read

*Unknown Caller.* After punching the connect button, she brought the phone to her ear. "H-hello?"

A computer disguised voice came over the line and Angie's hands began to tremble. "Come alone to the address I'm going to text you. If I see your boyfriend, the cops or anyone else, I'll kill her. You have fifteen minutes."

Before she could respond, the call was disconnected. She stared at the phone until a text message alert sounded.

### 1795 Route 301 . . . Alone!

Frantic, she ran out to the living room and began to search for her purse and car keys before remembering her car wasn't here. It was still in the driveway at her house. She spotted Ian's spare set of keys sitting on a shelf of his entertainment center. Snatching them, she ran out the front door and jumped into his Audi, pushing the keyless start button as she grabbed the seat belt. She couldn't risk telling Kristen where she was going, or anyone else for that matter. But she wasn't stupid though. When she reached the destination, she would send Ian a text letting him know where she and Jenn were.

Relieved to see no one was outside except two security guards, who she barely knew, she put the car in drive and accelerated as fast as she dared without alerting them something was wrong. The gates had been left open to allow the police and feds to come and go as needed, and Angie drove out of the compound, heading for the main road. Ian and Jimmy were going to kill her if the drug dealers didn't do it for them, but she knew they wouldn't exchange her life for Jenn's and she refused to be responsible for the girl's death. It didn't take her long to get to Route 301, but when she reached it she didn't know if she needed to go north or south. She programmed her phone's GPS with the address and turned north when the annoyingly cheerful woman's voice told her to. A few minutes later the same voice spoke again. "You're approaching your destination on the right."

Pulling to the shoulder, Angie viewed at the structure set back from the road. It was similar to Ian's compound, but had fewer trees, no fence, and only two warehouse buildings which were the only ones in sight on the unpopulated strip of highway. From where she sat she could only see two vehicles—a black SUV and a plain, four-door sedan which she assumed belonged to the DEA agents who had been at her house. Grabbing her phone, she typed a text to Ian.

**Kidnappers called. They're at 1795 Route 301. I'm trading myself for Jenn. Hurry.**

After pressing the send button, Angie tossed the phone on the passenger seat. She put the car back in drive and eased forward, turning onto the long driveway leading to the buildings. She parked next to the SUV and got out of the car, leaving the engine running with the key-fob in the center console so Jenn could escape. Angie looked back and forth between the two buildings trying to figure out which one she was supposed to go into when the door to the one on the left opened. Agent Jackson was standing inside the door jamb pointing his gun at her. "Inside. Now!"

With trembling knees and heavy feet, Angie began to trudge toward him, praying Ian got there before it was too late.

# CHAPTER 19

*D*evon was about to knock on the still closed door when it swung open and he took in Ian's wild expression. He knew immediately what he saw in the blue eyes so similar to his own —terror . . . sheer terror. "What's wrong?"

Instead of telling him, his brother shoved his phone in Devon's face, so he could read the text Ian had received seconds earlier.

**Kidnappers called my cell. They're at 1795 Route 301. I'm trading myself for Jenn. Hurry.**

"Ah, fuck!"

Ian ran to the reception area. "We gotta move! Now!"

The team, former SEALs, Chase's men, Carter, Athos, the feds and cops all came running and followed the Sawyer brothers out into the parking lot. "We've got an address. Not only do they have Jenn," Ian paused and looked directly at Athos, "but they contacted Angie on her cell and she decided to play Wonder Woman. She's on her way to trade herself for Jenn."

Athos' eyes mirrored the same fear which was in Ian's. Around them were a chorus of curses and frustrated groans. The men knew there was no way the kidnappers were going to let Jenn go, even if they had Angie. Not meaning to, Ian's little angel had made their job twice as hard and when he got a hold of her, she wasn't going to be able to sit for a month. He'd make sure of it, but first they had to rescue the two women he loved.

"Where are they?"

The question came from Stonewall and Ian looked at Carter who gave him a slight shake of the head. Ian agreed. They were doing this without the local law enforcement's involvement. This is what his team did best. If they let the cops and feds show up at the scene, it was going to become a cluster-fuck in the first degree, with Jenn and Angie's lives on the line. The FBI and Tampa P.D. had protocols which, by law, they had to follow. Trident didn't have those restraints, and it was better to apologize later than have to ask permission before they acted. Carter pulled out his cell phone, one of his many throwaways, and dialed a number from memory while stepping away from the group.

Stonewall saw Ian's hesitation and started yelling, turning bright red in the process. "Oh no, Sawyer! Not again! You're keeping us in the loop on this or I'll arrest all of you, right here, right now!"

As much as Ian wanted to race to save the two women, he knew if he took off, the feds and locals would be right on his tail. He probably assumed Carter was calling Keon and forced himself to wait a moment.

While the SAC continued to rant, his two subordinates and the local police didn't look too happy at the prospect of trying to arrest seventeen hyped-up men. Men who'd killed plenty of terrorists and criminals while in the military and were currently out for blood. Most of the specially-trained operatives were ignoring the irate agent and had gathered around Marco's vehicle. The communications specialist was handing out headsets so they could all talk with each other without needing their hands. Weapons were being double checked and Jake was loading up his favorite sniper rifle, along with his backup MK11 which he would loan to Carter if needed.

Amid the commotion, Kristen came running down from the residences with Beau on her heels. She ran straight to Devon and blurted out that Angie was missing. He explained what had happened and a look of shock came over her face. He grabbed her chin for her attention. "I need to know you're safe. Tiny and Mitch are in the club office. You're to go directly there and do everything they tell you, Pet. I can't do my job if I'm worried about you. If you give them any trouble, you'll get a public spanking you'll never forget. Understand?"

She knew he was serious when he'd said the word 'public' because, while she loved to watch other subs be disciplined in front of everyone at the club, she wasn't thrilled when it was her ass on display. "Yes, Sir. I love you. Be safe."

He kissed her on the lips. "I love you too. Now go. Beau is coming with us. I'll call you as soon as we have them safe."

As his fiancée headed straight for the building which housed the club, Devon ordered Beau to heel. The dog's rear end spun around and he attached himself to Devon's right leg, not looking happy to see his previous protection detail walk away without him. His human reached down and scratched behind his furry ear. "It's all right, boy. She's fine. We need to rescue Jenn and Angie, and maybe even give you someone to sink your teeth into."

While Dev knew the dog should understand very little of what was being said to him, the canine seemed to know exactly what he meant. Beau let out an excited bark at the prospect of biting someone who deserved it.

In the meantime, Carter had stopped talking on his cell and approached Stonewall. With a glare which had made some men tremble in their boots, Carter handed him the phone. The fed blanched and looked confused, but took the device. Trying to salvage his authority, he barked into the speaker. "This is FBI Special Agent in Charge Stonewall, who the hell is this?" Ian, Devon and Athos watched as the last of the man's blood drained from his face. "Yes, Director Moran, sir . . . I understand, sir . . . no problem, sir . . ."

Without waiting for the SAC to finish getting his ass handed to him by his boss, the men, minus the law enforcement, scrambled for their vehicles and flew out of the compound single file behind Ian's SUV. Carter and Athos sat in the back, behind the Sawyer brothers, with Beau between them. The dog seemed to be thrilled with the action as his tongue hung from his panting mouth.

Ian drove while Devon sat in the passenger seat bringing up the

GPS coordinates. After that was done, he dialed his cell phone and waited for Tiny to pick up. When the head security guard did, he told him, "I need you to take Kristen and lock her down in the panic room until further notice. Tell Mitch to stay locked inside the club if he doesn't want to go with you, but make sure he's armed. Shut down the gates whether the cops leave or not."

When the big man confirmed the orders, Devon disconnected the phone and looked over his shoulder at Carter. "Did you really use one of your get-out-of-jail-free calls to Mr. Big? Why didn't you just call Keon?"

The spy shrugged, but his face remained expressionless. He rarely contacted Director Moran unless it was necessary, preferring to deal with the deputy director instead. Fewer politics. "Actually, I tried calling Larry, but he didn't pick up, so I went up the ladder. The director was already in a foul mood and all too happy to threaten the jackass with a transfer. I think he might've mentioned some town in Alaska with a population of two."

Devon let out a sharp bark of laughter and shook his head in disbelief before Brody's voice came over everyone's headsets. On his laptop was a live stream from one of the many satellites orbiting the Earth and it was zoomed in on their destination. "Don't ask whose SAT I'm using, because you don't want to know." A few chuckles came through the headsets. "Ian, when you get to 301, you're going to go north. Four point three miles up there's a dirt road on your right. Take it about a hundred yards in and approach from the south on foot with a two-minute ETA. The address has two warehouses on it running west to east. There are three vehicles—it looks like your Audi is one of them and I think another is the DEA sedan from yesterday, but without seeing the plates, I can't be positive. The other vehicle is a dark SUV. From their parking jobs, I can't tell which building they're in, so we need to check both. A second team can drive past without suspicion and pull off about a half mile up the road and come in from the north."

Ian acknowledged the information and asked for a breakdown of who was in which vehicle. When he had the info, he broke them down into three teams. Marco would lead Team Two while Ian took

Team One. Marco had Jake, Brody, Rick, Bannerman and Rad with him. Ian's team consisted of the three men in his vehicle along with Boomer, Urkel, and one of Chase's men, Tanner. And, of course, Beau. The remaining four contract agents would take position across the highway and storm the driveway after the entry teams made their way inside whichever building held the hostages, and intercept anyone trying to make a run for it.

Less than ten minutes, later the vehicles were in position and the men poured out of them. While waiting for information back at the compound, Dev had instructed Chase's men to load up the vehicles with equipment they would all need to stage a rescue. The men had worked with Trident on several missions and knew what was needed. Now all three teams were suiting up with bullet-proof vests, KA-BAR knives, sidearms and flash bang grenades. Either Colt M4 Carbines or HK MP5's would be used, depending on each man's preference for their assault rifles. Jake and Carter would carry their sniper rifles. Individuals grabbed other equipment which the team needed, but wasn't necessary for each member to carry. Beau was outfitted with a harness and specially designed canine bullet-proof vest. The dog's ears and tail twitched with excitement while his paws did an eager dance, but he remained silent. There would be no need to worry about him barking and alerting any one to their presence since he'd been trained well and the team practiced different drills with him often. Beau would do his job as precise as his human counterparts did theirs.

"Team Two, Team Three, ready?" Ian spoke into the headset attached to his right ear, as he handed Beau's short lead to Boomer. When the responses came back affirmative, he told them to move out. He didn't have to worry about the men who weren't part of Trident's core six. They all had Special Ops experience, including Athos, so they knew the basics of how each man and team would work in unison. Team One approached, bounding as two sections, which meant while half the team moved forward to the next tree or object to hide behind, the others covered them, ready to fire their weapons if needed.

In silence, they reached the southern-most building and Ian

signaled for Urkel and Tanner to approach the structure. While Tanner covered him, Urkel scanned the exterior wall with a heat-seeking hand-held device and came up negative for warm-bodied occupants other than a few rodents along the floor line. With hand signals, he gestured all clear to Team One and the rest of them joined the two operatives, using the building as cover. Brody's whisper broke through the intercoms. "Teams, hold position. I have audio coming through from Angie's bracelet. Hot damn, it works. Stand-by."

Ian tamped down his urge to rush into the other building and gun down everyone inside who wasn't a female in his life.

---

ANGIE TRIED her best to speak in a calm voice. She didn't want to upset Jenn any more than she already was. While Jenn could hear everything, the gag and blindfold were still in place. But apparently, the dirty DEA agents and three other men, who looked like gang members, didn't bring a second set, so Angie could still see and talk. She was sitting on a chair in the middle of the cavernous warehouse which was half-full with boxes and crates. Her wrists were handcuffed behind her, and it had taken her a while to remember the GPS bracelet Brody had given her also had a microphone in it. Grateful for the thing, she ignored the fact it was hurting her since it was under the metal handcuff and digging into her flesh. She prayed the tech geek was listening as she began to ask questions of the men holding them hostage. "I'm who you want. Why won't you let Jenn go?"

One of the dirt-bag gang-bangers with a knife scar on his face looked up from the three-man poker game and sneered. "Because I like the hot little mama. She and I are going to have some fun after that pig shows up and we get paid."

"Shut up, asshole," Agent Holstein snarled at Scarface who shrugged and made a vulgar gesture toward Jenn. Angie was grateful the younger woman wasn't able to see it as she was trembling enough already.

"So, it takes five of you to kidnap two women and handcuff them to chairs in the middle of a warehouse? We're helpless and not going anywhere, so can you please put away your handguns?" *Please Brody, be out there somewhere with Ian.* Not wanting the kidnappers to catch on she was hopefully giving Trident information, she changed subjects. "How did you find out about Jimmy and me, anyway?"

While the pacing Holstein didn't want any of the gang-bangers to answer her questions, the same didn't seem to apply to his partner. Agent Jackson was sitting on a crate about fifteen feet in front of her. "Saw the prick talking on one of those burner phones he used a lot and figured there was a good reason behind them. When I tried to get closer to hear what he was saying, he hung up. Tossed it in his drawer when an 'agent down' came in, courtesy of an anonymous call, of course. After he tore out of there with the rest of the squad, I picked the lock on his desk, checked the phone and copied your number. Figured it would come in handy someday. Andrews, or Athos, or fucking asshole, take your pick, was never the type of guy who could stay away from U/C. I knew he'd go back under again someday, and I was right. Traced the number and found you. When our connections from New Orleans called to see if we knew the new guy who was making them nervous and sent me a picture of him . . . well, let's just say I wasn't surprised to see your boyfriend."

"So, you're the one who told the drug dealers who he was, and the other agent who was murdered, too?" The man shrugged without a verbal response, but the cruel expression on his face confirmed what she'd asked. "So now what happens?"

"Now we wait a little while and when we're ready, you're going to call your boyfriend and tell him where to meet us. If he comes alone, you both die. If he doesn't, then you die, he dies and whoever he brings dies. Then we collect the money owed to us for this fucked up operation . . . simple enough?"

She didn't answer him.

"By the way, which one is really your boyfriend? Andrews or the hick who you escaped with?" He leered at her. "Or are you banging them both?"

She realized he still thought Brody was her boyfriend and knew nothing about her relationship with Ian. He jumped off the crate, stepped toward her and squatted in front of her chair. "Maybe I'll see what has all these assholes beating a path to your door, *hmm?* You that good in bed, darlin'?"

He imitated the Texas drawl Brody had used on him. When he dragged a finger down her face and neck to her chest, she shuddered. Instinctively kicking out her leg, she missed connecting her shin with his balls by mere inches. He shifted in time then backhanded her across the face, sending her and her chair toppling over. "You fucking bitch!"

Seconds after she hit the ground, the metal doors on both ends of the warehouse were kicked in, followed by flashes of blinding light and loud booms. Gunfire and pandemonium broke out and Angie pushed her legs against the cement floor, forcing her upper body toward where Jenn sat, frantically straining against her restraints while muffled screams emerged from around her gag. Unlike Angie, she was tied to the chair and couldn't get out of the line of fire. As the shooting continued, Angie managed to get to her knees and, using her upper body, knocked Jenn sideways, chair and all, to the ground then covered the helpless woman's body with her own the best she could.

---

"SIT-REP," Ian demanded.

They were still in a holding pattern. Brody was listening with one ear to a headset plugged into his portable tablet, which ran the same program as his laptop, while his com-set was in his other ear. Angie's voice was coming in loud and clear with the occasional scratching noise and he could just make out the male voices in the distance. He hit the record icon when he heard Angie start to ask the questions the team needed answers to. "Way to go, sweetheart. Teams, standby, our girl is giving us info . . . five tangos . . . principles are handcuffed to chairs in the middle of structure . . . handguns at ready. No hints at any other weapons . . . she's off topic. Your call, Boss-man."

"Team One, taking west end. Team Two, take the east end. Get me heat confirmation, Two." Ian signaled for his men to circumvent the empty warehouse they were still behind toward what was the front entrances to both buildings. The other team would work their way toward the back. He also indicated for Carter to find a way to the roof to see if he could get eyes into the northern building. If the buildings were the same, high windows would run along the south side of the other structure. "Reverend, south sniper looking for position, do the same on north if you can." His teammate acknowledged him. "Heat signatures?"

Rad's voice came through as a low whisper since he needed to be standing close to the target building. "Affirm. Looks like three sitting at a small table. Two others in chairs about twenty feet to my left, possibly our principles. One pacing east to west, looks like he's southeast of principles. One more sitting between duo and trio, maybe on a crate or something."

"Windows, doors?"

The men in the best positions to answer did so, starting with Rad at the north side and going clockwise. "Second story windows on North, no entry."

Marco's voice came next. "East, one kick-in door, no windows."

"South, windows, no doors," stated Devon, who was first in line along the front of the unoccupied building and could see the last two sides from where he stood. "West, one kick-in, one overhead, no windows."

Carter reported in. "Sniper position on top of south structure. Partial line of sight. Best I can do. Can get head shots on everyone but pacer—he's too close to my side. Lots of hiding spots, boys. There's a bunch of wooden crates and boxes in there. Princess A, sitting in chair, hands behind back. Princess J, five feet east, hands same, also blindfolded and gagged."

"I've got pacer in sight from north position in tree." Jake was straddling a limb in the tall tree he'd managed to climb about fifteen yards away from the target building. It wasn't the greatest spot because he couldn't rest his sniper rifle against anything, so it would have to be a holding shot without a spotter. As long as the branch didn't break under his weight, he'd be okay.

Ian acknowledged all transmissions. "Team One, breach west, Team Two, breach east. Team Three, standby for intercepts. On my go."

Marco took the remainder of his team and rounded the building to the back door and stated they were in position while Ian's team took the front. Before Ian gave the word for Devon to use the mobile ram to breach the front door and Bannerman to do the same at the back, Carter spoke into his headset from his elevated roost. "Crate tango hopped down, walking toward Principle A. Right in front of her, no weapon threat, lost head shot . . . smacked her, she's on the floor."

"Breach!"

Simultaneously the east and west doors were knocked open and two flash-bang grenades were tossed through each, far enough for them to cause the most confusion among the buildings occupants. Explosions, screams, yelled orders, Beau's barking and sounds of gunfire filled the air as the members of both teams made their entries—some going left, others going right—and took cover. Jake's calm voice penetrated the headsets. "Pacer down, head shot.

The trio from the poker table and Agent Jackson scrambled for cover while firing their weapons in the direction of the doorways. One of the gang members went down with a hole in his head, thanks to Carter.

Devon and Tanner had gone left after entry while Boomer and Urkel went with Ian to the right. They worked their way around a maze of crates and boxes as the two remaining gang-bangers tried to make a run for the front door using whatever they could find as cover. Boomer released Beau with an order to attack and the dog lunged for the nearest bad guy, clamping his jaw down on the man's arm. The suspect screamed in pain and tried to throw the dog loose, but only succeeded in falling to the ground with the angry beast on top of him. He brought his gun up to shoot, but Boomer was there, kicking the weapon from his hand and shoving his own gun in the dirt-bag's face. "Don't fucking move, asshole."

Ian and Urkel worked their way in further as the other team approached from other side of the long warehouse. A final gunshot sounded as Devon took out the last gang member who'd still been firing his weapon while heading for the door. All was silent except for heavy breathing heard through the headsets and Beau's barking as the teams searched for the missing tango, Agent Jackson. From Ian's spot behind a crate he could see Angie's prone body lying on Jenn's. His niece was thrashing against her restraints and he couldn't tell if Angie was moving because she was also struggling or if Jenn's actions were causing the body on top of her to move. Seeing no sign of the last suspect, and with Urkel covering his six, he ran low toward the women and knelt beside them, relieved when his angel turned her head to face him. "Ian!"

He put his assault rifle on the ground at his feet and reached to help her off Jenn. But the sound of near simultaneous shots had him drawing his sidearm and spinning toward where they came from on the other side of several large crates. Both teams converged on the spot and Ian heard curses and Tanner, their medic, telling someone to call for an ambulance. From where he was still covering the women, he could only see some of the team members and wasn't sure who'd been hit. Marco gave the "all clear, suspects all accounted for" then Brody appeared at Ian's side and handed him a handcuff key before turning to Jenn to begin setting her free. Ian released Angie's wrists and she threw her arms around his neck, hugging him as hard as she could. "Thank God, you're here."

"It's over, sweetheart. I've got you, but you've got one hell of a punishment coming to you, Angel." Returning her embrace, he watched his teammate remove Jenn's blindfold and gag then cut through the ropes which bound her to the chair. Like Angie, she was crying and shaking, but appeared to be unharmed aside from a few bruises. Adrenaline, fueled by Ian's anger, fear and relief, had him trembling as he held Angie tight, but he stiffened as his brother's voice came through the earpiece.

Angie cried out and scrambled to stand after she heard Devon say, "Come on, Athos. Stay with us." Her ear had been pressed against Ian's as the lowly spoken words had come over his headset. Ian helped her up and wrapped his arm around her shoulders as they hurried to the other side of the crates. Marco was standing over Agent Jackson's dead body while Tanner and Devon worked on slowing the blood which was pouring out of the side of Athos' chest.

The dirty agent had rounded the tall shipping crates and come upon the other agent's blindside. Jackson had fired a millisecond before Rick Michaelson spotted him and could get his own shot off, hitting the bastard in the head. But the damage had been done. The bullet had entered Athos' chest from the left side, in the thin area under his arm which wasn't covered by the bullet-proof material. It was one of the worst places to get hit while wearing a vest. Ian could see the regret in Boomer's dad's face that he hadn't seen the suspect two seconds earlier. 'What if' was something they'd all learned to deal with since their first moments in combat, but it never made it any easier. Jake and Carter appeared and cursed when they saw what had happened.

Angie rushed forward, falling to her knees as Devon made room for her at Athos' head. She grabbed her best friend's right hand while Dev leaned over his chest and continued to hold pressure on the wound. Tanner was quickly starting an IV in the injured man's left arm. Athos' eyes fluttered open at the sound of Angie's voice begging him to look at her. Struggling to breathe, his voice came out as a hoarse whisper. "Ang, you okay?"

"I'm fine. You are too, Jimmy. They're going to fix you up good as new." She wiped the sweat from his brow and the blood seeping out of the corners of his mouth, but it kept coming. His face was pale and his lips, blue. Tanner looked up at Ian who was standing behind Angie and gave him a small shake of his head. It wasn't good and unless a miracle happened within the next five minutes, the man was going to bleed to death and there was nothing any of them could do. The bullet had caused too much internal damage, probably nicking the heart or aorta before lodging somewhere in the lungs.

"Promise me something, baby." The wounded agent was fading

fast. His labored breathing was increasing and the blood filling his lungs was making him cough. "Promise me you'll be happy and remember I love you."

"I love you too, and you're not going anywhere, damn it! You stay here with me. That's what will make me happy! Stay with me!" The tears were pouring down her cheeks and her lips were trembling as she pleaded with him.

Athos' eyes shifted and met Ian's. "Take her. Take her out . . ." The rest of his words were lost to a coughing fit. He used the last of his strength to lift the hand which Angie was holding and gestured to the man he was entrusting her life to. Ian understood. Athos knew he only had a few minutes of life left in him, maybe even less, and he didn't want his best friend, the woman they both loved, to see his final moments.

Ian nodded and took hold of Angie's shoulders, pulling her up to her feet. She began to fight him, struggling to stay where she was, but her friend whispered, "Love you, baby. Go."

"No . . . no, Jimmy!" Angie became hysterical and Ian had no choice but to force her from the scene. "Let go, Ian! Put me down! I have to save him! Save him, please!"

Ian picked her up in his arms and cradled her to his chest as she continued to struggle and scream. He tried to offer words of comfort, but she wasn't listening to him. As much as it hurt her to be forced to leave, she might even think he was being cruel, he knew it would be worse if she stayed. As death neared, Athos would begin to cough up a lot more blood and it wasn't a sight she needed to see. She also didn't need to hear the death rattle as the man took his last few breaths. Ian could hear the sounds of the approaching sirens as he carried her to the door. Urkel and Boomer had the one remaining suspect, whom Beau had caught, in handcuffs. The others were all confirmed dead.

He brought her outside to where the paramedics, police, and a very pissed-off Agent Stonewall had just arrived. Carter had informed him, after the gunfight was over, he'd contacted Keon again. The deputy director would make sure the scene was cleaned up and no one, other than the one surviving gang-banger, would be in any trouble over the incident. Chase's men had secured the area and began to talk to the agents and officers in an attempt to give Ian and his team some breathing room.

Brody had taken Jenn outside as well, putting her into the front seat of Ian's still running Audi. One EMT ran over to check on her and Angie while the others rushed into the warehouse where they were needed the most. Angie finally stopped fighting him and he set her down on her feet, but refused to let her go, embracing her as she sobbed and mumbled into his chest. "He's going to die, isn't he?"

The painful acceptance in her voice caused a lump in his throat so instead of responding, he just held her tighter. A few minutes later, they both raised their heads when Carter approached. Placing a hand on Angie's neck, he leaned in and kissed the top of her head, whispering, "I'm sorry, little one. He's gone."

Her wail of grief was heard by all.

# CHAPTER 20

*I*an sat in the passenger seat of Jake's Chevy Suburban as his friend drove Angie and him home to the compound from the airport, and he was less at ease now than he'd been before they left. It was three months since they'd buried her best friend next to his mother and sister in upstate New York. Brody's recording of Agent Jackson's bragging had ensured James Andrews was put to rest following a full federal-government and military ceremony. A U.S. Marines honor guard had carried his coffin in and out of the Lake George church where he'd been baptized as a baby and made his First Communion and Confirmation. DEA agents and other members of law enforcement, fellow Marines, high school friends, and the Trident Security extended family had filled the church pews to capacity for the hometown hero's funeral. Flower arrangements covered the altar, and later again, the grave site. Some of the colorful memorial displays were from Will Anders, Roxy and Kayla London, Tiny and The Covenant staff, Shelby Whitman, several of Angie's friends from Florida, and one from Red Rose Books. Kristen must've let her editor know about their new graphic designer's loss.

Ian had spotted Carter, with dark sunglasses on, standing at the back of the church, and again, off to the side at the cemetery. The spy never approached them and disappeared after catching his and Angie's eyes, giving them a single somber nod of his head. At the grave site, three volleys of seven rifles were fired in salute, and Ian held a weeping Angie as Taps was played. A sharply dressed Marine

Corp captain knelt and handed her the U.S. flag which had been draped over the coffin, then folded with expert precision. He softly told her the President of the United States, the United States Marines, and the United States Drug Enforcement Administration were grateful for her loved one's honorable and faithful service to his nation.

With Jimmy's death, what was left of the drug cartel in New Orleans had no reason to come after Angie. Beside the fact she could no longer be used as leverage for anything, they were too busy trying to keep themselves from getting life-without-parole prison sentences. The investigations which followed had led to Manny Melendez being killed during a raid and subsequent shoot-out with the feds and local police. Three of his minions were killed as well. There had also been a city-wide round-up of suspects, including two DEA agents from the New Orleans office and three local cops, in addition to thirty-seven other people. For now, the Diaz connections in New Orleans were either in jail, on the run, or dead. The large incoming shipment of drugs had been seized from the transport cargo ship in a joint operation between the DEA, FBI, and Coast Guard.

Henderson had survived the bullet wound to his chest, but was out of commission for a few months while he recovered. Ian and Devon had kept their vow and paid for his partner's funeral, along with Chase Dixon. The team, Angie, Kristen, and Jenn had attended that burial as well, before flying to New York for Jimmy's funeral later in the same week. Jenn's bruises had healed and with the help of her psychologist, who'd counseled her following her parents' murders, she was getting past the memories of the kidnapping. Now she had to convince her uncles to ease up on their over-protectiveness which had increased ten-fold since the incident. They were back to arguing with her about running background checks on her prospective boyfriends among other ridiculous precautions.

Angie still had moments when her grief would hit her. Ian did everything he could to help her through those rough times and decided to take her away for a while. It took longer than he'd expected, but they'd both managed to clear their schedules and workloads a little over two weeks ago. They flew to the Philippines to meet his folks for ten days, followed by four days as guests of King Rajeemh, who was the ruler of the small North African country of Timasur near Mali. The king owned a home on Clearwater Beach near Tampa, and used Trident Security to offset his own protective detail whenever he and his family were visiting. He'd been inviting Ian and the team to his country for the past two years and this was the first time any of them had a chance to take His Highness up on his generous offer.

Introducing Angie to his parents had been a breeze. As he'd expected, they fell in love with her instantly. His mother had taken them on a tour of the facility where she'd been performing surgery and even had a chance to show Angie first-hand examples of before and after surgery on two of her patients. His angel had been in complete awe of the work his mother was doing and told her so, much to the older woman's embarrassment. His mom was proud of the work she did, however, she didn't do it for the accolades, but for the smiles of the children she helped.

Any reservations Angie may have had about meeting his billionaire father were quickly forgotten after the man had given her one of his big bear hugs. He'd worked side by side with them as they helped build a new school on one of the many Philippine islands while Marie Sawyer was busy at the local hospital. Within the first twenty-four hours of their visit, his parents had both voiced their approval of Ian and Angie's relationship. Ian just wished he felt as certain about it as they did.

He wasn't worried about the connection he felt with Angie because the woman was one-hundred and ten percent perfect for him in every way. She loved him, he was sure of it, and they were a good fit. She liked trying all sorts of new things with him—in and out of the bedroom—and she obviously enjoyed the sex as she was very vocal about it. And like him, she couldn't get enough of it. What worried Ian was, could he continue to make her happy for the rest of their lives? Was he good enough for her? Because the woman deserved the very best and then some. Yes, he had plenty of money for them to be financially comfortable, and yes, he made her smile . . . laugh . . . and come, over and over. He would give her the moon if he could, but what if sometime down the road, she got tired of him? What if one day she woke up and decided she didn't want to be with him anymore, took off his collar and walked out the door? Ian knew in his heart he would never recover from the loss, never love another woman the way he loved his angel. His fear of losing her was why he was so scared to ask her to move in with him and eventually marry him.

When they'd been in Timasur, they'd been guests of the king at the main palace—a beautiful eighty-room castle on twenty-five acres of manicured lawns and maze-like gardens where they were always getting lost. After the first day, Ian began to joke he needed to save some breadcrumbs from each of their meals to lay down a trail. That way they could get back to their opulent suite without wandering around for an hour looking for it.

The country was beautiful and they had spent their days with a guide who took them to many of the small nation's historical and natural sights. Kael had been full of history and wit, making them laugh often while showing them the wonders of his little corner of the world. Each night, Ian and Angie had been exhausted, falling asleep in each other's arms after a round or two of amazing love-making. He would never tire of this woman, but would she eventually tire of him like Kaliope had? Granted, he wasn't disappearing for months like he had been during his time in the Navy, but still his thoughts kept nagging at him. He couldn't get himself past his distrust of "forever" relationships.

Early the morning of their last day in Timasur, Ian had taken advantage of the complete gym located in the east wing of the palace while Angie slept in. By seven o'clock he'd been on the treadmill for over forty minutes, pacing himself at a comfortable ten-minute mile on his way to a seven-mile goal. His running workouts had been limited while on their trip, so that morning he'd pushed himself a little more. As he was in the middle of his fifth mile, Princess Tahira had walked in and jumped on the treadmill next to him. The twenty-three year old tended to drive the Trident team crazy on her visits to Florida where they were contracted to be her security detail. While the king, queen and Prince Raj were very laid back people who treated their employees with respect and gratitude, the princess came across as a spoiled brat—plain and simple. She also had a thing for American men, especially her physically fit bodyguards who she was always finding ways to touch. While none of them had taken her up on her numerous offers of afternoon delights, it hadn't stopped her from trying. And when they still didn't give in, she would find a way to torture them for denying her what she wanted. Her usual form of revenge involved a credit card, a mall, and five or six hours of trying on everything in sight, particularly shoes.

Ian had been a little surprised how different Her Highness had been acting during their visit to her homeland. She'd been polite, pleasant to be around, and very nice to Angie and him. And never once on their visit had she put the moves on him, which was so out of character for her. He spent most of his time in her presence waiting for the affable façade to drop and the real princess to emerge. After five minutes of silence while he ran and she walked on their respective treadmills, he couldn't take it anymore and slammed his hand on the stop button. When his feet came to a halt, he grabbed his towel from the machine's handle and wiped the sweat from his face before turning his body toward her. "All right, Princess, what gives?"

She didn't stop or slow down her pace as she glanced over at him with a confused expression on her face. She looked innocent, and he wasn't buying it for a minute.

"What do you mean, Ian Sawyer?"

He'd gotten used to the way she called most Americans by their first and last names. "Well, since Angie and I have gotten here, you've gone out of your way to be pleasant and cordial. You haven't come on to me once, which isn't like you, so what are you up to?"

She hit the red button on her treadmill and slowed to a full stop before turning to face him with a wry grin. "In spite of what you think about me, what you think you know about me, the one thing I don't do, Ian Sawyer, is . . . what is the word you Americans use? Oh, yes, I don't . . . poach . . . on another woman's man, no matter how attractive I find him."

After her last words, he'd expected her to place her hand on his bare chest, despite his sweat, but she didn't and it surprised him. He thought back to the times she'd been in Florida and realized the only men who hadn't complained about her constant advances were the few contract guards who wore wedding rings.

"I envy you, Ian Sawyer. You and Angelina Beckett have found something I have only dreamed about."

He tilted his head and stared at the gorgeous young woman as if he'd never seen her before. "What's that, Princess?"

She grinned at him. "I'm a firm believer in soulmates. But I also believe not everyone is lucky enough to find theirs. You two have—in each other. You have something between the two of you I have never had the privilege to see before up close."

Ian shrugged and took a drink of water. "Your parents have been happily married for a very long time, haven't they?"

She paused long enough to take a sip out of her own water bottle. "Not always, no."

At his raised eyebrow, she chuckled. As long as Ian had known the royals, they had been an affectionate couple with each other, and if they did argue about anything, it was never in view of others. "Yes, my parents are very happy now, but it wasn't always the way. As with my grandparents and great-grandparents, my mother and father were the result of an arranged marriage when they were eighteen, and neither one was happy about it at first. The way my mother tells it, although they thought each other was attractive, they . . . what is it you say . . . scrubbed each other the wrong way?"

He smiled at her flubbed cliché. "It's rubbed each other the wrong way, but I understood what you meant. I had no idea your parent's marriage was arranged. Wow, I can't imagine what it was like to have your spouse picked out for you with no input."

"Thankfully, my parents decided long ago to not force the same tradition on my brother and me. We are free to marry whomever we choose." She started her treadmill up again and began walking. "As I said earlier, I envy what you and Angelina Beckett have. You have found your one true love, the person you were destined to spend the rest of your life with. I'm worried I will not find mine, but if it is written in the stars, I will have to wait. In the meantime, I'm going to enjoy myself." She glanced at him before facing forward again. "I'm also jealous of the babies you will have. You are very handsome and she is a stunning woman. I'm sure your babies will be beautiful."

He couldn't help the panic which had settled in his chest. Him? A father? Could he be a good one? Could he be a good husband? He knew in his heart the answer was yes, but he still couldn't help but feel that one day it would all disappear when Angie walked out the door on him.

Tahira seemed to be done talking to him, so foregoing the rest of his workout, he started for the door to return to his suite, but then spun around and strode back to her treadmill. When she continued to walk, but looked at him inquisitively, he told her, "I hope someday you find who you're looking for, Princess. Your soulmate. You deserve it as much as everyone else does."

"Thank you, Ian Sawyer. I hope he is as handsome as you."

---

IAN DIDN'T REALIZE they'd pulled up to the compound's outer gate and stopped before Angie leaned forward from the back seat and placed her hand on his shoulder. He looked at her and then at a grinning Jake, neither of who said anything as the man handed Angie something. Darting back and forth between the two, his eyes narrowed. It was obvious they were up to something. "What?"

Jake remained silent as Angie held up what he'd given her. A blindfold. "Put this on."

"Uh, not without a good reason, Angel."

She sighed dramatically, and his mouth curved upward. "Please? It's a surprise for your birthday."

His chuckle and expression were filled with lewdness which made her blush. "You gave me my present on my birthday a week ago."

And what a present it'd been. For once, he'd let her completely take over the blowjob she'd given him while she was dressed in a frilly bra and panties. She'd also worn a garter, sheer hose and his favorite pair of fuck-me heels, which she'd packed without his knowledge. He hadn't been allowed to touch her with his hands and she wouldn't let him orgasm until she said so. It was an hour of the sweetest torture he'd ever been subjected to and he thought his heart would stop when she finally allowed him to blast his cum down her throat. Thank God he had been lying on a bed because it'd taken him a good fifteen minutes before his legs stopped quivering afterward.

She held out the blindfold. "Please, Sir, for me?"

How could he resist her? The answer was easy—he couldn't. Taking the blindfold with its elastic band, he slid it over his head and eyes then sighed. "This better be quick because I feel ridiculous."

She giggled as Jake put the SUV in drive again and accelerated. "Now you know how I feel sometimes." He knew she was kidding. His little angel loved being tied up and blindfolded while he had his wicked way with her, sometimes in public and sometimes in private.

Ian felt the car slow a bit as they approached the second gate, and when they didn't stop for Jake to have his hand scanned, he knew someone else had opened it for them. When the vehicle stopped, he estimated they were somewhere near the residential building. He heard the two of them exit the vehicle and shut their doors before his door was opened. Angie took his hand in hers and guided him carefully out of the car. She told him to take three steps forward and stop. When he did, she grabbed his shoulders and turned him a little to the right before releasing him again. "Okay, on the count of three you can take it off. One . . . two . . . three!"

A chorus of "happy birthday!" greeted him.

*Holy shit!* Ian's mouth fell open, and he couldn't believe his eyes. *What the hell have they done?* It was beautiful . . beyond beautiful. He took a step toward the large space between the third and fourth buildings and tried to take in everything at once. The area was wide enough to have three tractor trailers side by side and long enough for two of them to be bumper to bumper, so it was the size of a residential backyard . . . and now, it looked like one. Since he and Angie had left over two weeks ago, someone had transformed the paved, ugly unused space into a garden of sorts. It was complete with grass, trees, shrubs, flowers, sitting areas, a fire-pit, and even . . . was that a waterfall spilling into a small pond at the far end?

For the first time he could ever remember, Ian was speechless. He had a knot in his throat and, *crap* . . . tears filled his eyes and he wasn't ashamed of a single one of them. He took a few more steps, not knowing where to look and seeing something new with each pass. There was a bar and outdoor kitchen, which somehow blended well with the landscaping, along with a huge barbecue and a weather-proof flat-screen TV. Beau was rolling around on his back in the grass a few feet away, looking like he was in heaven. *I'm right there with you, dog,* Ian thought to himself. A small wooden sign two feet inside the grass line caught his eye. *Ian's Oasis.*

Okay, now he had to wipe away the few tears which had started to fall. He stared at Angie standing next to him with her hands clasped together at her chest, waiting anxiously for him to say something. His gaze then turned toward his team, Mitch, Jenn, Kristen, and Tiny, who were all sitting around the oblong fire pit. "Who . . . how?" He cleared his choked-up throat. "Shit, I can't talk."

They all laughed, and Angie clapped her hands in obvious glee. His brother stood and stepped toward him, grinning like a fool. He shook Ian's hand and tilted his head toward Angie. "Happy birthday, bro. This was your lady's idea, and she designed it all on paper for us. While you were away, we dug up the asphalt and had some people bring in the sod and landscaping and install the kitchen and koi pond. We all helped out as much as we could because we wanted you to know this came from our hearts. Angie picked out everything, and while you were away, Jenn and Ninja-girl took the list and went on shopping sprees for the furniture, barbecue, TV, and kitchen stuff. They did some major damage to the Trident credit card by the way."

Ian laughed and wiped away a few more tears, which insisted on falling, before looking at his beautiful angel. "This was what you three were doing a few weeks ago?" One day he left the office to join her for lunch. When he didn't find her in his apartment as they had planned, he went upstairs looking for her, knowing she was most likely chatting with Kristen. He'd interrupted a pow-wow between the two of them along with Jenn, and they'd clammed up when they saw him, while Angie tried to hide the sketch book she'd been holding. When he had attempted to find out what the little brats were up to, despite his best efforts, they all remained mum and broke up their little meeting. He'd forgotten all about it until now.

Angie nodded. "I wanted to do something special for your birthday, and I remembered what you said up at the safe-house about wanting your own little oasis in the middle of nowhere. This isn't exactly in the middle of nowhere, but it's close enough until you're old enough to retire. I was going to suggest we go up to Maggie Valley for the week, so they could get this done without you knowing, and then you suggested we go visit your folks. We couldn't believe we were able to keep it a secret from you. You, Sir, are a very good interrogator."

"Ha! Apparently not good enough."

Everyone else stood and there was a round of hugs from the women followed by handshakes and back-slapping from the men. After he finished with the reception line, he pulled Angie into his arms and kissed her senseless. When the whistles and cat-calls faded away, he ended the kiss which left them both breathless. She placed her hands on his cheeks and looked at him with all the love in her heart. "I love you, Ian. I love you now, and I will love you when you're old and gray. I will never walk away from you, even if you push me, without trying everything in world to stay by your side. And if you leave this world before me, I will look forward to the day I join you in the afterlife, because you're it for me. You're my heart, my friend, my Dom, my lover, and my soulmate, and I will love you forever."

Ian stared into the eyes of this incredible woman and, like a light bulb going on, everything clicked into place for him. She wasn't Kaliope or any other woman he'd been with over the years. She was the woman his heart had been searching for, and if any of those other relationships had worked out, he wouldn't be standing here next to his destiny. A line from one of his brother's country songs came to mind—something about God blessing a broken road leading him to this point and to her—and he knew it would be his mantra to her for the rest of his life. He took her hands from his face and kissed her knuckles once, but didn't release them. With a deep breath, he took a leap of faith. "Marry me."

"W-what?" Angie was stunned. Surely, she hadn't heard him right.

Ian barely heard the other women squeal, and the men chuckle and groan over the beating of his heart. "I'm not perfect. I'm not even a romantic. I'm not a flowers and perfume kind of guy. I don't spout poems out of my mouth or break out into song. Hell, I don't even have a ring for you . . yet. I will probably drive you crazy with my demands. We'll argue, we'll fight, but then we'll make up and that's what I'm looking forward to the most. But the one thing I know is . . I love you, Angel, and I will love you long after the day I die. You are my soulmate. Marry me. Have beautiful babies with me. Please."

He waited a heartbeat, and then a few more—hell, he'd wait forever—for her answer before her mouth turned up in a sexy grin. "Who says you're not a romantic? Because you most definitely are one, and yes, Sir, I will marry you."

Overjoyed, Ian picked her up by the waist and swung her around before capturing her mouth with his and kissing her like crazy again. From the group surrounding them came a chorus of cheers and clapping, but for him, his angel was the only person there.

Check out the Best Reading Order of the Trident Security series
and its spinoffs on my website!

Want to know what the Trident Security compound looks like?
Check out the map under the "Extras" tab on my website.
**www.samanthacoleauthor.com**

# WAITING
# FOR HIM

Book 3

# SAMANTHA A. COLE

Suspenseful Seduction Publishing

*Waiting For Him*

*Waiting For Him* is a work of fiction. Names, characters, businesses, organizations, places, events, and incidents either are the product of the author's imagination or are used fictitiously. Any resemblance to actual persons, living or dead, events, or locales is entirely coincidental.

Editing by Eve Arroyo

*For my Family*

# CHAPTER 1

*B*oomer sat at his office desk, his eyes narrowing as he studied the paper before him. The answers should be easy, but for the life of him, he couldn't come up with the solution. He glanced at his cell phone to check the time and noted it was eighteen-twenty hours. The six-thirty appointment Colleen had scheduled for him was later than normal, but she'd told him the new client had requested the evening hour, so here he was trying to kill a few more minutes.

Mondays and Tuesdays were the only evenings it wasn't a problem for Trident clients to come to the compound where their offices were. The rest of the week, Ian and Devon Sawyer's other venture, The Covenant, was open, and Trident clients might be a little shocked to see the BDSM club's members in varying stages of undress walking through the parking lot.

The fenced-in compound consisted of four warehouses and was off the beaten path on the outskirts of Tampa, Florida. The first building after the guarded gate was home to the club. Beyond that was another gate leading to the remaining three buildings. Trident's offices, bunk rooms, firing range, training areas, gym and a vehicle garage occupied the next two structures, and the final one had been renovated into two large apartments. The bottom one belonged to Ian and his fiancée, Angie, while Devon and his fiancée, Kristen, lived on the second floor. The rest of the building was empty space, and plans were being drawn up to construct two more apartments. One would be home to Ian's god-daughter, Jennifer Mullins, when she wasn't at college. The men of Trident were her surrogate uncles, having served under her father in the teams. Ian had taken over her guardianship after her parents were killed in a home-invasion the year before. The last unit would be offered to the youngest Sawyer brother, Nick, whenever he decided to opt out of the Navy. He'd made it through BUD/s, the SEALs' intensive training three years ago and was now with Team Three in Coronado, California, so the twenty-five-year-old wouldn't be joining them anytime soon.

As Boomer tapped his pen on the desk, he looked over the hints available to him and became more frustrated because he still couldn't figure it out. He glanced up as Ian walked in and sat in one of the two guest chairs on the other side of the desk. "What's a nine-letter word for vague? Starts with an 'A' and fifth letter is a 'G.'"

"Ambiguous." Ian rolled his eyes. "And if you're going to keep asking me for help with the daily crossword puzzles then I'm getting you a fucking thesaurus for Christmas this year instead of your bonus."

Boomer gave his boss a smirk as he filled in the blank spaces of the puzzle. "You do, Boss-man, and I'm signing you up for an anchovy-of-the-month club."

Even though he knew his friend and employee was joking, Ian got a queasy look on his face. Boomer always found it funny how, out of six retired SEALs, he was the only one who liked the oily yet salty fish, considering how much time they'd spent in and on the ocean while in the Navy. Well, maybe that *was* the reason.

"Not funny, Baby Boomer." Ian picked up the stress squeeze ball the other man kept on his desk and tossed it back and forth between both hands. "So, did you find out any information on this new client?"

Boomer threw the pen down on the newspaper and leaned back in his chair. "Nope. Colleen said the woman, a Kate Zimmerman, needed to hire Trident, but she wouldn't deal with anyone except me. I've racked my brain and can't recall ever meeting anyone by that name. I tried calling the phone number she'd left, but got the standard computerized voice telling me to leave a message. It comes back to a throwaway cell."

"One-night-stand?"

He snorted but didn't take offense since all the guys on the team had participated in more one-night-stands over the years than any of them cared to admit. Their time in the military and then the security business hadn't given them many opportunities for long term relationships. Even if it did, Boomer wasn't interested. "I'd be lying if I said I remembered the first and last name of every woman I've ever slept with or scened with. But I'd like to think it would ring some sort of bell. Maybe she's a friend of a friend or something."

"Could be." They both knew a lot of their business was gained by word of mouth. "Guess we'll know in a few minutes. If she has no objections, and even if she does, I'll be sitting in on the meeting until we find out what she needs from us. If it's a bullshit my-husband's-cheating-on-me thing, I'll leave you to it."

"Fine with me. Are we the only two left in the office?"

Both men's phones chimed a text. The guard at the front gate was alerting them to their new client's arrival. Murray would buzz her through the second gate and instruct her where to park. They stood, and Boomer grabbed a legal-sized yellow pad and his pen, while Ian headed for the door. "Yeah. Colleen left. Polo and Egghead are on their way to New York to escort a shipment of diamonds from a dealer to the buyer here in Tampa. Jake is trying to track down one of his informants who he's worried about—hasn't seen the guy in about two months, which he says is unusual. And my lucky brother is wedding venue shopping with Kristen and picking out pink tablecloths with matching napkins as we speak."

"Ha!" Boomer barked and shook his head. "I wouldn't fuck with him, Boss-man. You're right behind him, and karma's a bitch. Angie's going to be dragging your ass through the same tablecloths and napkins someday soon."

"Don't I know it. I'm trying to talk her into eloping, but I'm not having much success." The pained look on his face was mostly false since Boomer knew he'd give his woman the world if she asked for it. Well, if he didn't have to help pick out matching flowers, cummerbunds and bridesmaids' dresses, he would. "I'll go get your client and meet you in the conference room."

"K. Just going to hit the head really quick."

---

WHILE BOOMER HEADED in one direction for the bathroom, Ian walked in the other toward the reception area. The front door could only be opened from the inside by a lock release behind Colleen's desk, or by a hand-scanner which unlocked the door for only those whose prints had been programmed into the system. He pulled the door open and found himself looking at a brown-haired beauty who seemed to be about Boomer's age of thirty. Wearing a pair of jeans and a short-sleeved, navy blouse, she stood about five-foot-five in her flat, off-white shoes which matched the belt at her slim waist. Her slender build made the shirt and pants look a little big on her, as if she'd recently lost some weight, but had yet to find clothes to fit her new frame. In Ian's opinion, she looked too thin. She took off her sunglasses and peered up at him, with big chestnut-colored eyes. "Hi, my name's Kate Zimmerman. I'm looking for Ben Michaelson. I have an appointment with him, and the guard told me he was in this building."

When she glanced over her shoulder to where Murray was keeping watch at the front gate, Ian's eyes didn't follow hers. Instead, he looked with interest at Beau who was sitting near the driver's door of Ms. Zimmerman's Ford Focus. The goofy-faced dog was panting, but something about his posture and the fact that he seemed to be in a "stay" position had Ian eyeballing the woman in front of him. She saw where his gaze had been, and the corners of her mouth curved upward a tad as he raised a curious eyebrow at her. Her smile didn't quite meet her anxious eyes and when he got no answer to his unasked question, he opened the door wider. "Please come in, Ms. Zimmerman. I'm Ben's boss, Ian Sawyer. It's nice to meet you. If you don't mind, I'll be sitting in on your appointment."

Her smile faltered a little before she recovered. "Um, no. I mean, it's fine. I don't mind. It might be better that way."

Ian's curiosity was now further piqued, but he wasn't getting any bad vibes from her, other than her nervousness, so he let her last comment slide for the moment. He glanced back at Beau who was still sitting there with his tongue hanging out of his mouth and seemed to be waiting for a command. Ian tapped his leg. "Beau, *heir*." The dog rushed over to his master, stopped, and when he received a slight hand signal, trotted past him on the way to the darkened conference room. Ian had discovered the dog when it was a young puppy. Its dying mother had dug under the compound's perimeter fence to find a human who would take care of the little guy. When Beau was old enough, Ian took him to a friend who trained dogs for police departments and private security firms. Now, the silly looking mutt was trained as an aggressive tracking dog as well as a guard dog. All his commands were given in German since it wasn't a common language in the states.

"He's beautiful. Lab and Staffordshire Terrier, correct?"

"We think so. I found him as a pup . . . well, actually, he found me." He shut the door and gestured her toward the conference room. "The vet thinks there may be something else mixed in there, maybe Great Dane, because his legs are a little longer than normal for the two breeds." He turned on the overhead lights to the room as they entered. "Please have a seat. Boomer will be here in a moment.

"Boomer?" she queried as she placed her large purse on a chair while he pulled out the one next to it for her to sit in.

Ian took the seat across from her, leaving his usual chair on the end empty. Although this was his company, he trusted his employee to take the lead in the unknown case. The client had requested him specifically, and Ian was willing to cede his authority for the moment, therefore giving Boomer the "head" seat at the table. He studied the woman for a few seconds before answering her. "Sorry, I meant Ben. Boomer is his call sign from the Navy. No one uses his first name around here, but it's out of habit." He heard the man in question come down the hallway and saw him enter the room a second later. Ms. Zimmerman's back was to the door, but Ian knew the moment she realized Boomer was there without having seen him. Her body stiffened.

"Sorry to keep you waiting, Ms. Zimmerman. I . . ." Boomer walked over, peered down at the woman's face, and froze. Confusion in his eyes turned to pure shock, and Ian watched as the blood drained from his teammate's face. His normally strong voice dropped to a hoarse whisper. "Katerina?"

And with that, Benjamin Thomas "Boomer" Michaelson did something he'd never done before in his life. He fainted.

---

*Yes, Benny, I will. I promise I'll wait for you, forever . . . forever . . . forever.*

"Boomer. Boomer! Wake up, frog, that's an order!"

The words and a knuckle digging painfully into his chest finally penetrated Boomer's fog-filled mind, and his eyes blinked open. Ian was kneeling next to him with a look of concern on his face, while on his other side, Beau sat regarding him with a curious tilt of his furry head. And since Ian was kneeling and Boomer was flat on his back, it meant he was on the floor for some stupid reason. Rubbing his sore sternum, he asked, "W-what happened?"

"You okay? You fainted."

Snorting, the younger man stared at his boss as if he had two heads. "Yeah, right. I've never fainted in my life. Not even when I saw the bone sticking out of my leg after the RPG attack." It'd been a little over two years ago since the incident in Afghanistan and the resulting injuries had almost cost him his leg. As it was, he'd needed a knee replacement after several surgeries to repair the other damage to his shinbone. After he'd recovered, his tour was just about up, so he opted out of the Navy and rejoined his former teammates here at Trident.

Ian shifted back a little as his friend sat up. "What's the last thing you remember?"

Boomer's eyes narrowed as his head finally stopped spinning. "I was dreaming . . ." Shock came over his face again, and he dragged a hand through his hair. "Ah, fuck. It wasn't a dream, was it?"

Standing, Ian offered a hand to help him up. "No. It wasn't."

"Where is she?" He looked around the room as if Katerina would suddenly reappear.

"Sitting out by Colleen's desk. I asked her to step outside so I could wake your ass up and find out what the fuck is going on. Now start talking, Ben. Who is she?"

Boomer knew his boss was not only worried, but pissed, because the man never used his given name unless he was in trouble, but at the moment he didn't give a shit. "In a minute." Striding out the door of the conference room, he went in search of a ghost.

# CHAPTER 2

*Twelve Years Earlier . . .*

*B*en waved goodbye to the last of his friends heading to their cars parked a short distance away from the James River beach where they'd all gathered. An almost full moon was high in the sky on the warm summer night, and his going-away party had dwindled down a little after one in the morning. It was the Friday night, actually Saturday morning, before he left for basic training the following weekend. He was joining the Navy and would hopefully make his way into the elite SEALs like his father before him.

Much to his wife's relief, Rick Michaelson had done his twenty years with only a few non-life threatening injuries before getting out for good. He was now working for a friend who ran a private investigation company while also teaching history classes at the local community college. But since their only child had graduated high school and was leaving the nest, Ben's folks were talking about selling their home in Norfolk, Virginia, and moving to somewhere in Florida—maybe near his aunt in Sarasota.

He glanced around and saw Katerina sitting on a large rock near the shoreline. He'd told his best friend, Alex Maier, he'd make sure his sister got home safely. That way Alex could hook up with Daniella Silverman, who'd been flirting with him all evening. Ben didn't mind driving Kat home since all three of them had grown up together these past seven years. Alex was six months older than Ben, who was six months older than Kat. But despite their closeness, she was a year younger than them in school because of her early December birthday.

Grabbing two colas from his cooler, he climbed up on the rock and sat down next to her before handing her one of the cans. This close to his goal of a military career, he wasn't taking any chances with drinking and driving, and had stopped the beer after nursing three of them in four hours. Katerina smiled at him, and he tried to ignore the twitch in his crotch which had been happening often around her for the past few weeks, ever since she'd been his date for the prom. He couldn't figure out why, out of the blue, he was seeing her as less of a buddy and more as the beautiful woman she was becoming. But there was no way he was putting the moves on his best friend's sister, no matter how attracted he was to her. The attraction would pass after he started meeting all the uniform bunnies who wanted to hook up with any man in the military. He just had to keep reminding himself of that.

"Thanks, Benny."

He rolled his eyes at her, and she giggled. She was the only person who still called him by the juvenile nickname. Everyone else had been calling him Ben, at his request, since the start of high school. "So, what're you going to do without Alex and me being around all the time to bug you and chase your boyfriends away?"

She shrugged and let out a tiny snort. "I'll be fine. It's only one more year until I get to go away to college, too. And I still have Alex for most of the summer until he leaves for Villanova." Her smile faded and her voice dropped to a whisper. "I'm going to miss you."

Throwing his arm over her shoulder, he pulled her in for a sideways hug. "I'm going to miss you too, Kitten. But maybe I can get an assignment out of Little Creek, and then we'll be able to see each other all the time again."

They sat that way for a while, looking out over the water, with her head resting on his collarbone. When she placed her hand on his bent knee and her thumb began to rub the bare skin his shorts didn't cover, his dick decided to betray him, taking notice of how good her touch felt. He tried to subtly adjust himself by shifting his hips. Without pulling her head away she tilted it up to look at him with those soft chestnut eyes of hers. "Are you uncomfortable? I can move."

"No, you're fine." And boy, was she. The sudden intimacy between them was making him forget all the reasons why he shouldn't be thinking of kissing her. The urge to claim her got worse when her eyelids lowered and she stared at his mouth. He felt the soft puffs of her breath on his neck and smelled the mint gum she'd been chewing earlier, in addition to the shampoo she'd used to wash her hair. He was now painfully aware of her lush right breast crushed against his ribcage, and he thought he could feel her hardened nipple through the cotton tank she wore over her bikini top.

He tried to distract himself by counting down from one-hundred in Spanish in his head, but it failed when her little pink tongue peeked out to moisten her tender lips. He stifled a groan, but when he attempted to pull away and put some distance between them, the hand on his knee tightened. Looking back down at her sweet face, he was surprised to see desire in her eyes, and it hit him —she was as attracted to him as he was to her. The knowledge sent every other thought from his brain, and he slowly lowered his head. When their lips were just shy of touching, he paused, wanting her to close the final gap between them. He wanted to make sure they were both on the same page, the one which would change their relationship forever. His brain tried to override his body, but it was too late. She moved the scant inch and fireworks filled his mind as they kissed.

*Fuck!* She felt so incredible, tasted so incredible, he thought he'd died and gone to heaven. He shifted and eased her back until she was lying atop the flat rock with him on his side next to her. All the while, he continued to kiss her, moving his lips over hers in a sensual caress. Cautiously, he began to lick the seam of her mouth, encouraging her to open and let him in. He almost thought she wasn't going to when, all of a sudden, her lips parted and granted him entry.

Her tongue dueled shyly with his, and it made him even harder, which he hadn't thought was possible. Ben knew she wasn't experienced because he'd overheard a conversation she'd had with her two best friends a few weeks ago. Kat and Melanie were both shocked when their other friend, Tina, told them she'd lost her virginity to her boyfriend after the prom. When Tina had asked when they were planning on giving up their cherries, Katerina replied she was waiting for the right guy to come along and she wasn't in any hurry. Ben had been happy with her answer, but the way she'd said it made him think she had some guy in mind and it annoyed the hell out of him. Then when he realized he was annoyed, it pissed him off because he wasn't supposed to be jealous of any guy she dated. He was supposed to help Alex warn the jerks off by threatening to kick their asses if they tried anything with her. He was supposed to act like her brother, wasn't he? At least he'd thought so . . . until tonight.

He was leaning on one arm while his other hand rested at her waist. He began to move it up and down, closer and closer to her left breast. When she didn't stop him, he cupped it in his hand, squeezing it a few times before rubbing his thumb over her taut nipple. Her moan of pleasure spurred him on as she arched her back slightly, pushing the delectable orb further into his touch. He was desperate to rip her shirt and bikini off so he could find out if her naked body was as beautiful as he'd imagined. The other morning, he'd been shocked to wake up with his hand around his morning wood while an image of her lips around his cock faded like the fantasy it had been. He hadn't been able to look her in the eye for several days afterward for fear his cheeks would heat in embarrassment, and she would know he'd jerked off in the shower after the incredible dream.

Continuing his tender assault on her mouth, he brought his hand down to the hem of her shirt, tucked his fingers under it, and began to inch his way upward again. The second his hand touched the skin of her abdomen, he groaned. It was softer than anything he'd ever felt. Not being able to stand the torture anymore, he lifted his head and was pleased to see her swollen, red lips and heavy-lidded eyes. "Take off your shirt, Kat. I want to see you."

Her eyes widened as she bit her lower lip anxiously, and he thought he'd pushed her too far. Even though he was aware of her virginity, he didn't know how far she had gone with the few boyfriends she'd had. Had any of them ever seen her naked? Had she let one of them lick and nibble on her breasts? Had any guy ever gotten his hand down her underwear and touched the place which Ben was beginning to think belonged to him. All of her belonged to him, and God help him, Alex was going to kick his ass.

He was about to tell her it was okay if she wasn't ready to take the next step, but his cock leapt for joy when she reached down and grabbed the hem. It was the sexiest thing he'd ever seen when she lifted her shoulders and head off the rock and removed the tank top. He'd seen her in her bikini earlier in the day, but seeing her now in the skimpy top and her jean short-shorts, coupled with a mix of passion and uncertainty in her eyes, she blew him away. "You're so beautiful, Kitten."

Her shy blush thrilled him in a way he hadn't thought possible. She looked away from his intense stare. "You don't have to say that. I know it's not true."

Shocked, he cupped her chin and forced her to look at him. "Are you crazy? What makes you think it's not true?" Katerina shrugged her shoulders and tried to break eye contact, but he wouldn't let her. "Answer me, Kitten, because in my opinion, you're the most beautiful girl I've ever known."

"Oh, please." Her sarcasm was punctuated by an eye roll. "You and Alex have dated every gorgeous girl in your class and mine. I can't even begin to compare myself to most of them. My chest is too flat, my ass is too big, my legs are too skinny, and my eyes are too far apart."

When she finished rattling off what she thought were her worst attributes, Ben wasn't sure if she was kidding or if she really thought those things about herself. It only took a few seconds before he realized she was serious and his eyes narrowed in anger. "Kitten, there is nothing about you I would change. Your eyes are so expressive, sometimes I can't stop looking at them, especially when you laugh. Your chest . . ." his hand closed around her left breast again and squeezed just enough to make sure he had her attention, ". . . is the perfect size—not too small or too big—it's just right." He moved his hand down to her denim covered hip and squeezed again. "Your ass . . . jeez, do you have any idea how many guys check out your ass when you walk by? Especially in these sexy shorts of yours. And your legs are a mile long. Baby, men drool over legs like yours and most women would kill for them. If I ever hear you put yourself down again, I'm going to spank your sweet ass. Do you hear me?"

It was obvious she thought he was joking about smacking her backside because she giggled, and he relaxed a little. Wanting to prove how desirable she was to him, he leaned down and took possession of her mouth again. This time he wasn't as gentle as before, but was still cautious. He knew he had to walk a fine line here—the one between scaring her by moving too fast, and making her see how good they could be together. Her hands began pushing his T-shirt up and he reached back, grabbed a handful of blue cotton and stopped kissing her just long enough to yank it over his head and toss it aside. Her hand scorched his chest when she timidly touched him. As his lips found hers again, his fingers started a new exploration of her breasts through her bikini, but he knew he couldn't go much further. He wanted her first time to be special— not out here on a huge rock where anyone could drive up and interrupt them. She deserved better.

Ben was about to pull away from her mouth, when his fear happened. He heard the car a moment before a bright flood light hit them and they both jumped up into sitting positions. Damn. A cop had to pick this moment to check out the popular party spot. At least they were both still decent. Instead of getting out of his patrol car, the lazy cop blared his air horn once. In other words—*get in your truck and drive away, jackass, because you're not getting laid here tonight.*

As they scrambled for and threw on their shirts, he gave the officer a quick wave of his hand, letting him know the message was received and understood. Taking Kat's hand, he helped her down from the rock, and they headed for his dad's pick-up, grabbing his cooler on the way. He opened the passenger door for her and lifted her up into the high seat, then emptied the cooler of its leftover melted ice before stowing it in the truck's bed. Hopping in the driver's seat, he started the engine and grinned when she broke out in a fit of giggles. "What's so funny?"

"Your shirt is on backward and inside out." She looked so cute covering her mouth as if she'd accidentally spilled the beans about something.

He looked down, saw she was right and laughed along with her. Before putting the truck in drive, he pulled off his shirt, flipped it around then put it on correctly. The last thing he needed was for her dad or brother to see that and put two and two together. He would need to eventually tell Alex he planned on dating Katerina, but not yet. As he drove down the dirt road which led out to the highway, he reached across the center console and took her hand in his. He gave it a squeeze then set their joined hands on the armrest between them. Driving her home was the last thing he wanted to do, but if he kept her out any later, her parents, Ivan and Sylvia, were going to be ticked off. At seventeen, Kat still had a curfew. The only reasons she'd been allowed out until two a.m. was because school was over and she was with Alex and Ben. That, and it was a special occasion since it would be a while before Ben would get a chance to come back home to visit.

Aside from the low music on the radio, a silence had fallen over the inside of the cab and at the last second, he pulled into the elementary school lot just up the road from her house. Putting the truck in park, he turned to look at her. "I . . . I'm sorry we were interrupted back there. It took me by surprise. I never thought . . ."

She pulled her hand from his and stared out the side window. "It's okay Benny. We'll pretend it never happened. I mean, it's not like we actually did anything."

Taking hold of her chin, he turned her head until she was facing him, but her eyes remained downcast. "Kitten, look at me." He waited a moment, but she still didn't look up. "Kat, please, look at me."

His heart almost broke when he saw the unshed tears in her eyes. *Crap.* She misunderstood him and now she was on the verge of crying. He did his best to embrace her despite the center console between them and kissed her on the top of her head. A shudder passed through her and he hugged her tighter. "Shhh, baby, you didn't let me finish. Just because I never thought you and I would . . . you know, get together . . . doesn't mean I'm not happy we did. I've been thinking about you and me ever since the prom when we danced those slow dances together. For the first time, I realized you're more than my friend. You're also a very beautiful woman who I suddenly found myself attracted to. I was just surprised you felt that way about me too." He froze for a second. "You do feel that way, don't you? I mean, it wasn't just an experiment for you, right?"

She pulled away so she could look up at him again. "I've felt that way for a lot longer than you have. I was so happy when you asked me to the prom even though I knew it was only because you and Mary Jo Dwyer just broke up and everyone else was already paired up for the most part."

He at least had the decency not to deny it. That *was* the reason why he'd asked her, but he wouldn't have done it at all if he hadn't thought they'd have a good time together—which they had.

Taking a deep breath, she blurted out, "I didn't want to stop tonight."

Her face turned beet red as the implications of what she said sank into his brain. Was she telling him she would have given him her virginity tonight if the cop hadn't interrupted them? *Holy shit!* What was he supposed to say to her? Any other girl, he would have been all over her without a second thought. He knew he could be a dog sometimes. He'd lost his own virginity two months before he turned fifteen. And like every other normal, red-blooded American male, he rarely said no when a girl offered him a roll in the sack or in the bed of his truck. But he needed *her* to be sure this was what she wanted and it wasn't a spur of the moment thing because he was leaving. He couldn't . . . wouldn't do that to her. Kissing her had already changed the dynamics of their relationship, but having sex with her would put them in another orbit. And he knew it wouldn't be just sex. With Katerina, it would be making love. "Baby, do you know what you're saying?"

She nodded and then began to babble nervously. "I wanted you to be my first . . . you know. I still do. I mean, I know you've been having . . . you know, sex, for a long time now. I mean, everyone at school talks about who's doing who, but I haven't . . . you know . . ."

"You're still a virgin." He'd meant to say it as a question, not wanting her to know he'd overheard the conversation with her friends, but she didn't seem to notice.

"I know it's silly, but . . ."

He cupped her cheek with his hand. "It's not silly, Kat. Not at all. But as much as I want to say yes to you . . . to us, I think it would be better if we waited until I finish basic training and find out where I'm being stationed. I don't want to have one or two nights with you and then end up on a base on the opposite side of the country. It's not fair to you." He covered her mouth with his fingers when she tried to interrupt him. "But I'll make you a deal, baby. If this is what you want . . . if you're sure, then I'm willing to tell every woman I run into from here on out that I have someone special waiting for me back home and she's the only one I want. Will you wait for me, Kitten? Will you be my girlfriend and wait until the time is right for us?"

"Yes, Benny, I will," she whispered. "I promise. I'll wait for you . . . forever."

Alex was going to kill him.

---

RICK MICHAELSON STOOD between his wife and child at the cemetery and kept his hand on his grieving son's shoulder. His boy was on the verge of entering the military and becoming a man, but in the blink of an eye, his life had been turned upside down. They watched as the funeral director's crew unloaded scores of colorful arrangements from four matching hearses and placed them beside the caskets. The area around the grave sites was filling up with close to two hundred people who'd known one, two, or all members of the Maier family and come to pay their respects.

A somber priest made his way to the head of the graves in order to give the deceased their final blessing. Ivan and Sylvia would be buried side by side, just as their children, Alex and Katerina, would be in the plot next to them. The Sunday after Ben's going-away party, the family had taken off on an hour-long afternoon drive to visit Ivan's mother and sister, but they never arrived. A fiery crash on a lonely stretch of highway snuffed out the lives of four people, and left many others, like Ben, struggling to find a reason behind the terrible tragedy. Rick knew, although his son's overwhelming grief would one day become bearable, the loss of his best friend, and the boy's family, would forever change Ben's life. He just hoped when his son emerged from his grief, he came out on the right side.

# CHAPTER 3

*Present Day . . .*

*K*ate had known Benny was going to be shocked when he first saw her, but she hadn't expected him to pass out. As far as he knew, she was dead and buried in a cemetery in Norfolk, Virginia, and not living and breathing at his place of business. His boss, Ian, had asked her to have a seat out here in the reception area, but she couldn't sit. Instead, she was pacing back and forth, trying to keep her feet from running out the door and taking the rest of her body with them. Benny would've been better off if she'd never come looking for him, but it was too late to change her mind now. The last thing she ever wanted to do was to cause him any more pain, but her life was in danger, and there was no one in the world she trusted more than him. It was sad he wasn't going to be able to trust her in return. Not after what she'd put him through, even though none of it had been her fault. Her father was to blame for everything . . . her recently-deceased father. And for the first time in Kate's life, she was all alone.

The sound of footsteps caused her pacing to cease, and she turned to see Benny stalking toward her followed by his boss and the lab mix. The look on the man's face, the man who'd once been the boy she'd fallen in love with, was now hard. Shock was giving away to anger, and it was evident by the raging inferno in his beautiful amber eyes. Eyes which still haunted her dreams after all these years.

He stopped in front of her and crossed his arms. The Navy had taken his gangly, teenage physique and made it broad, strong, and sinewy. She longed to have him pull her into his powerful arms and hold her while telling her everything would be okay. Instead, he glared at her from several feet away. "Do you want to explain how a woman I watched being buried twelve years ago, is standing in front of me? Because as far as I know, reincarnation is still a myth."

"I—I'm sorry, Benny. I'm so sorry. But if we can go sit down, I'll explain everything. I promise."

Benny's clenched jaw ticked at her use of his childhood nickname and again at her vow. The last time she promised him something, she'd said she would wait for him forever. As far as he knew, that hadn't happened. When he didn't say anything, Ian took a step around him and extended his open hand to her. "Ms. Zimmerman, please come back to the conference room, and we'll talk this out."

A growl from deep in Benny's throat escaped his mouth, and he ignored the warning look Ian sent him. "Her name is Maier, Katerina Maier, and you're damn right we're going to talk." While the two of them walked back to the room, she heard him take several deep breaths before turning around and following them.

Upon reentering the room they had moments ago vacated, Ian took the seat he'd earlier planned on giving Boomer. The meeting had taken a dramatic turn before it even began, and he needed to take control of the situation before it blew up in their faces. Boomer sat in the seat across from Kate with his arms crossed, and glowered at her. Sighing, Ian rolled his chair back a few feet to a small refrigerator in the corner and grabbed three bottles of water and put them on the table. They were going to be here for a while. "Boom? Why don't you tell me how you two know each other, and we'll go from there."

Benny waited a moment before his harsh words came out, his eyes never leaving hers as if she would disappear again if they did. "Boss, this is Katerina Maier. She was my best friend's sister. She's also supposed to be six feet under along with her parents and brother in a cemetery in Norfolk, so I don't have the slightest fucking idea what she's doing here. They were *allegedly* killed in a car accident a week before I left for basic training. Tell me, Kat—are all four caskets empty or just yours?"

She winced at his accusatory tone. It also hadn't escaped her notice when he referred to her only as his best friend's sister and not his friend as well. She heard the pain under the anger in his voice, but knew he'd never admit to it. Her own voice came out a little louder than a whisper as she stared at the table top in front of her. "Mom and Alex are there. The accident was real, but it wasn't an accident. We were forced off the road and rolled down a hill. My dad and I barely managed to get Alex out before the car exploded, but my mom had been killed on impact. Alex died in my arms a few minutes later. Dad and I went into hiding afterward."

She hadn't realized she was crying until Ian put a box of Kleenex in front of her, and she grabbed two tissues. When a sympathetic warm nose poked her arm, she gave Beau a scratch behind his ear as his master spoke. "I get the feeling this is leading to Witness Protection."

Kate nodded at the man's gentle and understanding statement. "Yes. It's exactly where it leads to." Not being able to look at Benny, she instead turned her gaze to the man who didn't currently hate her. "My dad is . . . was a CPA with some questionable clients at the time. Mom, Alex, and I had no idea some of the people he dealt with weren't on the up-and-up, but he drew the line at certain . . . crimes, I guess you can say. He said the money was too good to pass up, especially when he'd been starting his own accounting business, but his conscience wouldn't allow him to let some things slide by. He tried to know as little as possible about who he was working for because he figured the less he knew the better off he would be. It worked for him for over ten years."

"What happened?"

She drew in a trembling breath, reached for one of the water bottles, and took a few sips to quench her sudden thirst. "He found out he was doing the books for a member of a Russian organized crime family. Dad wasn't the only one. They used several accountants and gave each the books to only a few businesses, so if one turned on them, he didn't have access to all the accounts. There was one man in particular Dad was dealing with. He owned a few bars in Norfolk, Newport News, and Virginia Beach among other businesses, both legal and illegal."

Ian raised an eyebrow. "Do you know the man's name?"

Nervously nibbling on her bottom lip, she nodded. "Mm-hm. Sergei Volkov.

"Are you fucking kidding me! Sergei 'The Wolf' Volkov?" Kate flinched at Benny's sudden outburst as he jumped up and sent his chair flying back into the wall. He started pacing the room, ignoring Ian's angry glare. "Even I knew that bastard should be avoided at all fucking costs, and I was a fucking teenager!"

She looked at him with eyes that begged him to understand something she, herself, had never been able to. When her father tried to explain it to her in the days after the crash, she'd been in shock and nothing would sink into her brain and stay there. After the U.S. Marshals gave them new identities, and they began their new lives in hiding, her father never wanted to talk about it again. He didn't want to be reminded how his stupidity and greed had cost him his wife and son, in addition to the life he and his daughter had known. "Dad swore he didn't know who Volkov was until it was too late, and he was in too deep. So, he did what he was paid to do and tried to stay out of trouble. But then he accidentally found out they were selling teenage girls into white slavery. The summer and spring breaks in Virginia, the Carolinas, and Florida were the perfect times for them to kidnap a girl and make her disappear.

"Dad got a bunch of receipts and stuff he was supposed to add to the books, and he found an envelope with a list of . . . God . . . he said it was like a shopping list with the type of girls they were looking for. Specific hair color and eyes, fair skin, a certain build, that sort of stuff." She shook her head at the thought of any girl being taken because of what they looked like. "There were also a couple of photos of girls tied up. Dad recognized one of them from the newspaper. Her parents were rich and were making a lot of noise about her disappearance. He found out later most of the girls who'd been taken were the type no one would be surprised about if they took off on their own. Mostly they were teenage hookers or runaways. He said when he realized what he had in his hand, he thought about how he would feel if one of those girls had been me. So, he called the phone number in the paper, and the FBI came to talk to him. They wanted him to wear a wire and get them more information, but dad refused. He was too scared for our safety. He told them that if he started asking any questions, Volkov would immediately know something was wrong because my dad only talked about the accounting when he met with him or his right-hand man."

"But they found out about the information he gave the feds, didn't they?" Boomer gritted his teeth as he sat down again and grabbed one of the bottle waters.

She nodded. "Yes, right before the accident. Apparently, the FBI thought my dad knew more than he was telling them, or he might lead them to Volkov. They were following us to my grandmother's that day. It was her sixty-fifth birthday, and we were going to take her and my aunt out to dinner to celebrate. The agents were using a tracking device, so they could stay further back, and weren't close enough to stop a car that came out of nowhere and forced us off the road."

A shudder went through her at the memory. "All I remember is everyone yelling and screaming as the car rolled over and over down the embankment, and then silence. Dad and I got our seatbelts off and crawled out of the car. It was upside down. We managed to get Alex out through the window with the help of the two agents who'd been following us. They saw the dust and smoke and realized what happened. After we got him out and far enough away from the car, they went to get my mom. I remember wondering why they came back without her, shaking their heads, and then the car exploded. I tried to run back to get my mom, but they stopped me. I was screaming and hitting them, but they wouldn't let me near it. I found out later she'd died instantly from a broken neck.

"A few minutes before the ambulance and police got there, Alex took his last breath." She swallowed hard, trying to clear the thick lump in her throat, while wiping away the flood of tears rolling down her face. "I—I don't remember much of what happened over the next few days. I guess I was numb. Dad and I ended up being moved from one safe-house to another until the FBI decided we could never return to Norfolk and put us in the Marshals' Witness Protection Program. We changed identities and locations three times before we settled in Portland, Oregon. We've been Joe and Kate Zimmerman for the past eight years."

At some point toward the end of telling her tragic story, Kate had closed her eyes, but her tears were still falling. Her voice had become little more than a hoarse whisper, and she swallowed again, trying to regain her composure. Slowly she raised her lids and was relieved to see some sympathy in Ben's hardened gaze. At least he knew she was telling the truth. "I wanted so badly to talk to you, to explain what happened, but they wouldn't let me. When they came to give us new identities, I told them the only way I would agree to go was if our handler kept tabs on you and let me know how you were doing. He followed your career for me as best he could since a lot of it was classified. When I heard you were in the Naval Medical Center in Maryland with a bad leg injury, the only thing that kept me from flying to see you was my father had just been diagnosed with liver cancer. It wasn't long before it spread and . . ."

Her words trailed off, and it didn't take a rocket scientist to figure out what had gone unspoken. She was surprised when Benny spoke in a gentle, sympathetic tone. "He's gone, isn't he?"

"Almost two months ago. The chemo and radiation did a number on him, but he lasted longer than the doctors expected."

There was silence in the room for a few moments as what she'd been through over the past twelve years hung in the air. Finally, Ian cleared his throat and spoke. "You told our secretary you needed to hire us. Was it just a ruse to see Boomer or do you need our help? There's obviously a lot more to your story we're not aware of, but I would hope with your father's death, it would be safe for you to come out of hiding."

"I thought it would all be over after my father passed away," she told them with a shake of her head. "But then I noticed I was being followed, and my condo was broken into and trashed."

Benny had been looking down, but at her words his head jerked back up. "What? When the hell was this?"

Looking back and forth between the two men, she told them the details. "All last week, I was getting the feeling I was being watched. Then Friday afternoon, I got home from work and found my condo in shambles. The police said whoever it was had picked the lock. A few things, like my laptop, camera, and jewelry were missing, so they assumed it was just a random burglary, but I didn't think it was. Saturday, I tried to contact my handler at the Marshals, but was told he was killed in a car accident two days earlier. A new handler had taken over and wanted to meet with me, but with everything that happened, I wasn't sure I could trust anyone there. So, I grabbed a few clothes and money, and came to the one person I knew I could trust to help me."

Anger returned to Benny's face as his gaze flickered toward his boss. "Someone was looking for something."

Ian nodded and rubbed his chin with his index finger. "But what? Why now and how did they find her after all these years?"

She cringed, and whatever Benny had been about to say was lost as his eyes narrowed, focusing on her face. "How did they find you, Kat?"

"It was an accident." She sighed, knowing she had to explain a few more things. "Dad couldn't work as a CPA anymore when they changed our identity. In the beginning, we both worked odd jobs because we never knew when we'd have to change cities and names again. But after we settled down in Portland, and two years went by without any trouble, our handler helped dad get his teaching license, and he taught high school math. When he got sick, the teachers and students held fundraisers and stuff to help me pay for whatever his insurance didn't cover. They were a big help to me. His students were always stopping by and visiting him."

A small smile appeared on her face as she recalled how his students were always able to lift her father's spirits. "They loved him. Anyway, when he died, I had him cremated and told everyone he was going to be buried back east with my mom and brother, but didn't give them any details. I told everyone it was my dad's wish to not have a funeral, and I didn't put an obituary in the paper, even though it would be in his new name. But the students arranged a memorial at the school for him. At first it was just supposed to be his students and fellow teachers at an assembly during school hours, but then it grew and they posted it on Facebook. A local reporter saw it and ran a story about the death of a well-liked teacher. It included a picture of dad taken at a school basketball game last year before he got too sick. I think one of his students took it not knowing my dad avoided having his picture taken because the Marshals told us to. By the time I saw it, it was too late. It was in the print edition as well as online and on Facebook."

"Shit. Any facial recognition program could have found it." Boomer rolled his eyes and ran a frustrated hand through his hair. Sometimes technological advances could be a bitch.

Nodding his agreement, Ian leaned forward and rested his elbows on the table. "But the question remains—what are they looking for?" His gaze went to Kate's face. "Any ideas? Did your father keep something as evidence in case he needed leverage down the road?"

She shrugged and shook her head. "Not that I know of, but he gave me this . . ." she pulled a key out of a small inside pocket of her purse, ". . . just before he died. He was kind of out of it at the end. Hospice had him on morphine, so half of what he was telling me didn't make sense. When he gave me this key, he told me to go home again. I asked him what he meant, and he just kept saying it was 'the key to the wells.' I couldn't get him to explain it."

Ian took the key from her and inspected it. "It looks like a safety-deposit-box key. Did he have one at his bank?"

"I checked, but they had no record of it. Maybe I should have checked another branch or another bank. But there's so many banks in Portland, it would take days to check them all. Should I start calling them? Would they give me the information over the phone?"

"No, you don't need to call them. It's not in Portland." Ian and Kate both looked at Boomer in confusion. He grabbed the conference room laptop, pulled it toward him and booted it up. "It's in Norfolk. Your dad said, 'go home again,' so that had to be what he meant. I remember your family used Bank of America, like mine did, but . . ." He paused as he tapped a few keys. "Here it is. Not far from your house is a Wells Fargo Bank. 'The key to the wells.' That's where we start looking."

"Your house," he'd said, but the colonial was no longer hers. Some other family was living in it now. A strange girl or boy was sleeping in what was once her bedroom and some other parents were joking with their children at the dinner table. Did they change the color of the walls? Her mother had painstakingly picked out just the right hues to go with the furniture. Was some other teenager reenacting the scene from *Risky Business*, when Tom Cruise slid across the wood floor lip-syncing to Bob Seeger's "Old Time Rock and Roll"? Alex always made her laugh when he did it.

She shook off the bittersweet memories. "So, what should I do? Just walk into the bank and ask if my dad has a box there? Will they let me open it?"

Ian tapped his fingers on the table. "Not yet. They won't let you near it without proper ID and a death certificate in your father's name . . . his real name. And even then, it might take a court order if your name isn't attached to the box's account." He eyed Boomer. "I'll give Larry Keon a call and get what we need. The court order might take longer to get, but we'll worry about that if it turns out we need it. I'll also have him get me everything the FBI has on this Sergei Volkov." Having the deputy director, the number two man of the FBI, on speed dial came in handy at times, and this was one of them. "In the meantime, we have to keep Kate . . . I'm sorry, but I have to ask . . . do you prefer I call you Kate or Katerina? After this is over, if it's possible, are you planning on going back to your real name?"

She gave him a wistful smile. "I hadn't given it a lot of thought. I never believed . . . I'd like to be me again, Katerina Maier. I miss her and the life she was supposed to have." A life which was supposed to include Benny Michaelson. "But you can call me Kat, if you'd like. It was the one habit my father was never able to break. I was always his Kitty Kat."

He returned her smile with an optimistic one. "Then Kat it is, and we'll do everything we can to try to get your life back. But for now, we need to keep you out of the public eye. Are you sure you weren't followed from Portland?"

"Actually, I was." When she saw their surprised expressions, she quickly added, "But I got rid of them. About an hour out of the city, I started thinking about all the movies I've seen about people being followed by the bad guys or cops. And then I remembered about the agents who had a tracking device on our car, and I got a little paranoid. So, I pulled into a truck stop and convinced a couple of truck drivers that I was afraid my 'abusive ex-boyfriend,'" she made finger quotes in the air with both hands, "may be using a device to stalk me. They looked under my car for me and found one by the trunk. One of the drivers was nice enough to take it with him, and it's somewhere in Southern California now."

"Smart girl." Ian dipped his head in approval of her survival instincts. "Good. Then until we get you the paperwork you need for the bank, we have to keep you hidden for now. There are bunkrooms and bathrooms upstairs here, and the compound is secure."

"She'll stay with me at my condo." The look on Boomer's face told them not to argue with him.

The corners of Ian's mouth twitched, and Kat realized he'd figured out there was more between Benny and her than just the memory of a teenage boy and his friend's sister. "Fine. But to be on the safe side, I'm calling Tiny and having him sit outside your place."

Benny nodded his head. "Works for me." At her confused look, he added, "Tiny is one of the bodyguards we use when we need one. He'll watch our six . . . our backs." He turned back to Ian. "I'll double check her car for trackers then leave it here in the garage so it's out of sight."

"I can get a motel room," Kat told them. "I don't want to put anyone out."

Benny growled at her while Ian shook his head and stood. "You're not putting anyone out, Kat. The safest place for you to be is either here or with Boomer. His place is secure, and we'll have someone monitoring his condo. We're not taking any chances someone might've figured out you came to him for help." He glanced back at his teammate. "After I call Tiny, I'll call Keon and see what he can do for us. Jake or Dev will relieve Tiny in the morning, and I'll call you with a rendezvous time so we can plan our next steps."

Nodding his agreement, Boomer stood. "Let me have your keys, Kat. You can wait here while I take care of your car."

She handed him her keychain and then both men left her alone in the room. Well, not exactly alone. Beau was sitting next to her with a curious tilt to his head. She reached out to pet his velvety ears. "*Braver hund.*" Good dog.

## CHAPTER 4

*K*at washed her face in the bathroom of Benny's condo. After he'd taken care of her vehicle and retrieved the three duffel bags which were full of her clothes and necessities, they had driven in silence to his place. She felt so drained after telling the two men about the horror story which her life had become, and she couldn't find any more words to say to Benny. But it bothered her that he was just as quiet. It shouldn't since the poor man had had the shock of his life tonight, having an old girlfriend . . . no, an old friend . . . come back from the grave. She couldn't actually classify what they were back then as boyfriend/girlfriend, since they'd only kissed that one night, and he'd asked her to be his girlfriend barely thirty-six hours before she "died." The way he'd reacted upon seeing her again, she wasn't sure if he would want to be friends with her ever again. But one step at a time. First, they needed to find out who was following her and why. Then, and only then, could she think about Katerina and Benny. For now, they were Kat and Boomer, and there were twelve years of each other's lives they knew nothing about.

She heard the doorbell ring and suddenly wondered if Benny had a girlfriend. He wasn't married, her handler would have told her, and his condo was definitely a bachelor pad, but it didn't mean he wasn't dating anyone special. When she opened the bathroom door, she heard another male voice along with Benny's, and her shoulders relaxed in relief. If he was dating someone, she couldn't handle meeting the other woman just yet.

Walking out to the living room, she was surprised to see a man who made Benny look small, which was no easy feat considering he was six-foot-one and about two hundred and fifteen pounds of solid muscle. Benny only came to the man's shoulders and was outweighed by about sixty pounds. He had soft-looking, café-au-lait skin and was shaved bald. With his mustache and goatee, he reminded her of some actor from an old TV show, but she couldn't remember who. She was wary about the man's intimidating size until he spotted her and smiled a smile which probably had women falling at his feet.

Turning, Benny gestured for her to join him. "Kat, this is my friend, Tiny. He's going to be watching the condo overnight from across the street. Tiny, this is Katerina."

The bear of a man extended one large paw toward her. "It's a pleasure to meet you, Miss Katerina."

"It's nice to meet you too, Tiny." She smiled at the diminutive nickname for such a huge man, and shook his hand. "Please call me Kat. I appreciate you looking out for me."

He gave her an "aw-shucks" look and waved his mitt of a hand as if batting away a fly. "Don't worry about it, ma'am, it's what I do. I'll keep an eye on things so you can get a good night's sleep. No offense intended, but you look like you could use it." Tiny gave her a wink and Boomer a fist bump then headed out the door to start his watch.

Boomer locked the door behind the bodyguard and set the security system. He then turned and eyed her speculatively. "When was the last time you ate or slept?" The way she took a moment to remember wasn't lost on him. "Forget it. Come with me."

Kat followed him into his kitchen and took a seat at the table after he'd gestured to it. She watched as he began to take bacon, eggs, spinach, and cheese out of the refrigerator. "You don't have to cook for me. I can make something for myself."

He ignored her comments and continued to pull out a large frying pan, followed by the utensils he would need. Placing the pan on the stove, he turned on the gas and a *poof* sounded as the burner lit. He then peeled off half the slices of bacon from the package and lined them up neatly in the pan. After throwing the remaining bacon back into the fridge, he pulled out a bowl and started cracking the eggs. She assumed he was making enough for both of them when the sixth and final egg made its way into the bowl. His shoulders and arms moved with fluidity as he beat the eggs into submission. Her eyes crossed over his sinewy back from one shoulder to the other and then downward. There wasn't an ounce of fat on him as his waist narrowed. She couldn't help herself when her gaze went to his khaki-covered ass, and her mouth watered. He was a perfect specimen of the male body. Even if he didn't have a girlfriend, she was certain he was propositioned all the time. In high school, Alex and he had been on almost every girl's "I want to kiss" list, and most of the "I want to fuck" lists, too. Neither one of them had ever lacked in the female companionship department, and she doubted things had changed for Benny.

The silence between them was becoming unbearable. "How are your folks? The last I heard from Chris, our handler, they were living in Sarasota."

He didn't stop making their meal, but at least he answered her. "They're fine."

Okay, the two flat words were technically an answer, but she'd hoped he would open up a little more. This reunion was just as hard on her as it was on him. Not knowing what to say next, she let the silence return.

A few minutes later he brought two heaping plates to the table and set one in front of her and the other in front of the chair across from her. While he turned to retrieve knives and forks for them, she stared in astonishment at the full plate. Five slices of bacon, a huge three-egg omelet with spinach and provolone cheese, and two slices of multi-grain toast with butter, which she hadn't noticed him make. "There's no way I can eat all this."

He put a set of utensils next to her plate then took one of her slices of bacon, throwing it on his own plate as if it made a huge difference in the amount of food he'd given her. "Yes, you can, and you will. Your clothes are hanging off you. Either you're wearing someone else's stuff or you've lost weight. Now eat."

She tried to glare at him for ordering her around, but he disregarded her and pulled two glasses out of a cabinet. After filling them with orange juice from the fridge, he brought both to the table and sat down across from her. He pointed at her plate. "Eat, Katerina."

If her stomach hadn't picked that moment to growl and let him know it did indeed want to be fed, she would have tossed the food in the garbage just because of his attitude. But she admitted to herself she was starving, having realized she hadn't eaten in over twelve hours. She'd grabbed two cereal bars and a coffee from a truck stop where she'd pulled in for gas and had nothing else since. Picking up her fork, she dug into the omelet, and a moan of ecstasy escaped her mouth when the flavors hit her taste buds. "Oh, my God, this is delicious. When did you learn how to cook?"

Clearly satisfied she was going to eat, he picked up his own fork. "Don't be too impressed. Omelets are pretty much the extent of my culinary expertise, unless it's meat on a grill. Bachelorhood forces a guy to learn how to do things like cooking, cleaning, and doing your own laundry."

His voice lacked any emotion, and she wished she could think of a response which might make him at least smile, but nothing came to mind. She watched him take a bite of his eggs, and was shocked when a question blurted from her mouth. "You never married?"

"No." The answer was short and an indication for her to drop the subject. He kept his gaze on his plate and continued to eat in silence. His demeanor had her food turning bland as she quickly lost her appetite.

He finished his meal faster than she did. "Eat it all." Ignoring her annoyed expression, he stood and began cleaning up the kitchen. After every item he'd used was either washed, dried and put away, or in the dishwasher, he turned around, eyeing the two pieces of bacon, a piece of toast, and a third of the omelet left on her plate. She stared at him defiantly and he raised an eyebrow at her while crossing his arms. His eyes filled with something she couldn't name, but a shiver went through her as he lowered his voice. "I said all of it."

"Too bad, because I'm full." She wasn't the child he once knew, and she refused to let him treat her like one, although she almost gave in to his sexy, deep voice. She got up from her seat and tried to push him out of the way so she could dump the leftovers in the trash, but the solid wall of muscle wouldn't budge. "Please move."

Benny continued to stand in her way for a few seconds, and she expected him to start arguing with her. His eyes scanned her face, and he must have seen the exhaustion which was taking over her body because he relaxed his stance and took the plate from her hands. The commanding tone was replaced by a softer one. "I put your bags in the spare bedroom. Why don't you get some sleep? Ian should have some information for us in the morning."

Her first attempt at a response disappeared with a huge yawn, and she covered her mouth. "Sorry. I hope so." She began to pivot toward the doorway but stopped and looked up at him, her eyes filling with tears which didn't fall. "I know me showing up out of the blue has shocked you, but thanks for helping me. I don't have anyone else to turn to."

Benny's gaze turned into something from their youth, which she never expected, but only for a split second before becoming indifferent once more. "No problem. It's what I do," he mumbled before turning away to take care of her plate which was still in his hand. She hesitated, hoping he would say something more, but after a few moments she sighed and left him alone.

---

KATERINA HAD GONE to bed over four hours ago, but Boomer was still tossing and turning in his king-sized bed. As much as his body needed the sleep, his brain wasn't cooperating. Throwing off the covers, he got up for the eighth or ninth time and walked on stealth-like feet to the bedroom door across the hall from his. He had left the light on in the guest bathroom in the hallway in case she needed it in the middle of the night. Easing the bedroom door open, he was able to observe her in the dark room without the light shining directly on her. She was sound asleep facing him.

He studied her for the first time with a critical eye. Tiny had been right. She did look exhausted. And thin. Too thin. Her light brown hair had highlights he hadn't noticed before, and he wished he could see her dark brown eyes once more. Those eyes had haunted him for years. Her pouty pink lips made him yearn to kiss her awake, like Prince Charming and Snow White. He shook the ridiculous thought from his brain. Time and the military had changed him, and he was no longer worthy of the young woman she once was. He doubted he was worthy of the woman she'd become either—whoever she was.

*Damn.* She was more beautiful than he remembered, which was saying a lot. Although they were coming less and less frequently over the years, he still had dreams about her. About the one night she'd belonged to him, and how incredible it had felt to kiss and touch her. Many times, he'd debated the adage—was it better to have loved and lost or to never have loved at all? It was an argument he'd never settled in his mind.

Closing her door again, he headed out to his kitchen. Using the soft blue glow from his digital microwave clock to see, he located a bottle of Jameson Irish Whiskey on the bottom shelf of his pantry. He thought about taking a swig straight from the bottle, but one would lead to another, and then another. Despite Tiny watching his six, he knew he had to keep his wits about him in case someone figured out where Kat was. So instead, he grabbed a rocks glass from a cabinet, poured two ounces into it, and returned the bottle to its perch.

He sat in the seat he'd been in when she'd asked, "You never married?" He'd kept his eyes on his meal, but through his eyelashes, he'd watched her try to analyze his one-word response. No way was he going to explain to her why he would never get married. There'd been a thirty-six-hour timespan, twelve years ago, when she was the only woman he'd wanted to spend his life with. After she'd "died," no other woman had ever captured his heart the way she had. No other woman could hold a candle to his Kitten.

*Damn it!* He wasn't going there with his personal pet name for her. She was "Kat" or Katerina, which was as familiar as he wanted to get with her again. He understood she had no say in the matter about leaving him, thinking she was dead, but the anger and heartbreak had long ago been embedded into his psyche. There had been many a night he'd cursed her for leaving him, the universe for taking her, himself for loving her.

The team would figure out who was after her and why, and when she was safe, Boomer would send her on her way to wherever she wanted to go. Because there was no way he was putting his heart on the line again. He wouldn't survive it this time when she realized the man he'd become.

He brought the glass to his lips and drank the brown liquor before he had more than a split second to compare the color to Kat's eyes. The alcohol burned its way to his stomach, and he forced himself to put the glass in the dishwasher and head back to his bed. He had no idea how long he lay there until sleep finally overtook him, and he dreamed of her—his Kitten.

# CHAPTER 5

*B*oomer awoke to the smell of coffee, and he glanced at the alarm clock next to his bed. Oh-eight-thirty. He sat up before the events of the prior evening assaulted him and he groaned. It hadn't been a dream. Kat was out in his kitchen, at this very moment, making coffee. Tossing his covers off, he got up, headed to the master bath, and took care of business. Then he grabbed a clean T-shirt and sweatpants from his dresser and put them on over the boxer-briefs he'd slept in.

As he walked down the hallway, he noticed her bedroom door was shut, but it didn't register in his mind before he entered the kitchen and stopped short. *Fuck!* How the hell could he have forgotten he had plans this morning? Easily. The excuse must still be asleep down the hall. Well, at least it was only his father standing in his kitchen. He had driven up from Sarasota to go four-wheeling with Boomer today. Whoever was now keeping watch outside the condo, Jake or Devon, wouldn't have stopped Rick Michaelson from entering. The man had the same training as their entire team with a few more years of experience and was one of the few people outside of Trident Security he could trust with Katerina's life. "Hi, Pop."

His dad turned and stepped out of the way, allowing Boomer to shuffle forward and make his own cup of coffee. "Hey, you slept in late today. I take it we're not going four-wheeling. Want to tell me what's going on and why Reverend is watching your place?"

"Noticed him, huh?"

"Almost missed, if you're worried about it. Just happened to recognize his truck. Now, why is he there?"

He wasn't worried that his father spotted Jake on surveillance. Like the rest of Boomer's team, there was little his father missed. Being vigilant had been drilled into him and the others during their time as Navy SEALs. The younger Michaelson shrugged as he grabbed a mug from the cabinet above his Keurig and prepped the machine before hitting start. He turned around and leaned against the counter while crossing his arms and ankles. "Something happened, Pop, and I have no idea how to sugarcoat it, so I'm just going to say it." Rick's eyes narrowed, but he waited for his son, who'd paused and seemed to be weighing his words, to continue. "I had an appointment with a new client scheduled for last night at the office. Boss-man was with me. Pop . . . Katerina Maier walked in the door."

As Rick paled, his eyes grew wide, and he sat down in the closest chair, almost missing it and ending up on the floor. "Holy shit. How?"

Boomer grabbed his now brewed mug of coffee and took the seat opposite the older man. "Two words—Witness Protection."

He proceeded to fill his dad in on the story she'd told them. He'd just finished when the lady in question came into the kitchen and stopped when she spotted the familiar face she hadn't seen in twelve years. Rick stood with his mouth open for a moment before he recovered. "Katerina . . . wow, it really is you. I mean, I knew Ben was telling me the truth, but it's like seeing a ghost."

Boomer watched as his dad did what he, himself, had yet to do. The older man opened his arms, and Kat walked right into them, letting him hug her. He couldn't hear what Rick was saying to her in a low soothing voice, but he saw her nod her head a few times in silence. She was wearing a T-shirt and pajama pants and both were too big on her. He would have to make sure she put back on some of the weight she must have recently lost. With everything going on, it didn't surprise him, but one of the things a good Dom did was take care of his submissive's safety and well-being.

*Fuck!* He had to stop thinking like a Dom and just be the

operative and former SEAL he'd trained to be. She wasn't his submissive. She was a woman from his past who needed his help. Nothing more. *Yeah, jackass. Keep telling yourself that.*

The embrace between the two lasted about a minute before they both took a step back. Kat blushed as she looked over at Boomer and then back to his dad. "Hi, Mr. Michaelson. You . . . uh, look great."

Obviously knowing the woman wasn't sure what to say to him after all these years, Rick pulled out a chair for her. "I think you're old enough to call me Rick, if you want. And you're a sight for sore eyes, too. Let me get you a cup of coffee."

She nodded and took the seat he offered. "Thanks, Mr. Mi—I mean, Rick. With a little milk, if Benny has some, please."

He backed up, not taking his eyes off her until his butt hit the counter, and Boomer knew how he felt. It was as if they looked away, she would disappear. Finally, he turned to the coffee machine and began to prepare a mug for her. "So, where do we go from here. How do we keep Kat safe?"

Boomer took a deep breath and let it out. "Well, Ian called Keon to get us ID for her along with a death certificate." The ID they could've gotten from one of their contacts who was a master forger, but the certificate was a little harder because of the raised stamp authenticating it. Besides, they were better off having documents officially forged by the FBI. "He's also getting us the file on Volkov. We should be able to head to Norfolk tonight and be at the bank early tomorrow morning." He shrugged. "Where we go from there depends on what's in the box."

Handing Katerina her coffee with milk, Rick nodded his agreement. "I'll go with you."

"No, you won't."

Boomer's dad narrowed his eyes at him. "What do you mean 'no'? You can't do this alone. You need backup."

"And I'll have it, Pop. But I don't know how long we're going to be, and your birthday is Friday. Mom would kill both of us if you missed it." Boomer wasn't going to tell his dad that his mom had made special plans for his birthday. She'd gotten tickets for an intimate concert starring Rick's favorite singer, Billy Joel. There were only one hundred tickets available, and she'd won hers through a local radio station two months ago. Since the date of the event was the same as his birthday, she'd decided to make it a surprise.

"Ian will probably send Jake with me. We've got it covered." Not wanting his dad to think he didn't need or trust him to help out, he added, "After Friday, if this isn't settled, you can cover my six if you want, but don't get mom pissed at me again. She's still mad that I won't go out with her friend's niece."

Rick harrumphed, but then smiled. "You made the right choice there, son. I've met Diane's niece, and she gives new meaning to the word . . . uh, never mind. You're just better off and leave it at that." Boomer and Kat chuckled. It was evident Rick had forgotten she was in the room for a moment. "As for not going with you, fine. As long as someone from the team has your six. And promise me, if you need me, you'll call no matter what."

"Of course. There's no one else I'd rather have covering my ass." Boomer's cell phone rang, so he stood and grabbed it from the counter. Glancing at the screen, he hit the call button. "Hey, Boss-man . . . uh-huh . . . okay. See you in thirty."

He hung up, looking at Rick and then Kat. "Ian's got info for us, so we're heading to Trident. You have about fifteen minutes for a quick shower, if you want, and we'll grab some breakfast on the way."

Rick finished the last of his coffee and set the cup in the sink as Kat left the room to go shower. He gave Boomer a pat on the back before walking toward the front door. "I'll run to the bagel place you all like and grab breakfast for everyone. This way you don't have to stop. I'll meet you at the compound."

As he headed toward his own shower, Boomer glanced over his shoulder. "Thanks, Pop. Grab a few extra because I'm not sure how many of us will be there. See you in a few."

———

As KAT LATHERED the shampoo into her hair, she replayed the conversation she'd had with Benny the night before. After she'd thanked him for helping her, his response had been, "No problem. It's what I do." It was close to what Tiny had said when she'd thanked the big man earlier.

Well, what did she expect Benny to say after all this time? She'd been "dead" to him for longer than the seven years she'd been in his life. He had gone on to live without her. Now, she was just a girl he used to know, who needed to hire him to keep her safe and help her get out of the mess she was in. Nothing more.

Rinsing her hair, she thought about how good he looked this morning after she'd recovered from the shock of seeing his dad again. He must have rolled out of bed a few minutes before she did. His dark brown hair was a little shaggy and sticking up in several places. His eyes were tired-looking, yet still the sexiest ones she'd ever seen. Her dreams of him over the years hadn't done the man he was now justice. He was handsome as hell, with a body which would make a nun have dirty thoughts. She may still be a virgin, but it didn't mean she was naïve about sex. In this day and age, it wasn't possible. Sex was all over the TV and Internet. It was in the movies she saw, and in the books and newspapers she read on a daily basis.

The thought of Benny and sex had her aroused, and she mentally calculated how much time she had before they left the condo. Taking her bottle of body gel, she squirted a small amount into the washcloth she'd found under the bathroom sink, along with a few guest towels. She washed her entire body before sliding the lathered material between her legs. She gasped as it rasped over her clit and sent waves of desire through her. Dropping the cloth, she replaced it with her fingers and began to rub in earnest. She imagined her fingers were Benny's and how he would arouse her further before replacing them with his lips and tongue. The daydream sent her over the edge faster than she expected, and she bit her bottom lip to keep from yelling out her pleasure.

After she recovered, she picked up the washcloth again and wiped away the evidence of her masturbation. She pushed her wants and needs for Benny back into the furthest corner of her mind, shutting and locking the metaphorical door behind them. Now was not the time to think about him . . . about them . . . about how good she knew they would be together. Her life was in danger, and by him helping her, so was his. Sex and fantasies were out . . . logic and reality were in.

Damn.

When they walked out the condo front door a short while later, it was within the allotted time he'd given her. Waiting outside the door was a good-looking man who Ben introduced as Jake Donovan, a.k.a. Reverend, one of his teammates at Trident and in the SEALs. He was a few inches taller, and older than Benny, but otherwise he had a similar physique—broad, hard and sinewy. His hair color was a shade somewhere between her own light brown and Benny's dark brown, and his eyes were covered by sunglasses which only enhanced his Hollywood good looks.

He smiled and shook her outstretched hand before turning around and leading the way to the parking lot with Benny taking the position behind her. She realized they'd placed themselves to protect her like bodyguards would. *Well, that's what they are, you idiot. That's why you came here—for protection and nothing more. At least not yet.*

Benny drove her back to the Trident compound with Jake following him in his own vehicle. As she sat in the passenger seat of his Dodge Charger in silence, her stomach growled, and her cheeks burned red when he chuckled at her.

"My dad's getting us breakfast, so we can go straight to Trident."

"Okay." She turned a bit in her seat so she could look at him without straining her neck. "If Ian has what we need, are we going to Norfolk?"

He checked his side and rearview mirrors then changed lanes before answering her. "Most likely. I wish I could leave you here and run up there myself, but I'm not sure what safeguards your father might have left. I may not be able to do it without you since you're his next of kin."

His words impaled her like a sword. "I wish I could leave you here . . ." Whatever he'd said after that was a jumbled mess. She knew she'd been hoping for the impossible. He didn't want to be near her. He'd rather do what needed to be done and kick her out of town when it was all over. When she didn't say anything more, he glanced over. She kept her eyes downcast and took a ragged breath.

"Kat, what's wrong?" She didn't answer. "Damn it, Kat, look at me. What's wrong?" A few seconds ticked by before he cursed. "Fuck!" She flinched, but refused to look at him. He slowed then stopped for a red traffic light. Reaching over, he tilted her chin up until her gaze met his. "Kat, I didn't mean whatever you think I meant. When I said I wanted to go up there alone, it was from a tactical standpoint. It would be safer for you to stay at the compound. I don't know what'll be waiting for us in Norfolk and the last thing I want is you in a position of danger. That's all."

The driver behind Jake honked his horn, and they both looked to see the light had turned green again. Taking his foot off the brake, Benny accelerated and split his attention between her and the road. "Do you understand me?"

She nodded her head and adjusted her body so she was facing forward again. There was no way she was going to tell him his words had her thinking he wanted to get as far away from her as possible. She'd lost so many loved ones in her life, and she'd just reconnected with the only man she'd ever been in love with. Kat couldn't give him up again. Not yet, and hopefully, not ever.

She'd made a few friends in Portland, but she never knew if she and her dad would need to move again, so it was easier to keep those friendships to a minimum. Her closest friends were her boss of over seven years and his wife. Jeremy and Eva Pierce owned the canine training facility where Kat had found a career she was good at, which also afforded her some protection. Kat's handler, Chris, and Jeremy had served in the army together and the latter now trained dogs for the law enforcement and private firms along with his retired police officer wife. When Kat had been greeted by Ian's dog yesterday, she'd immediately recognized the dog's training. While Beau hadn't been one of J&E International K9's dogs, the training was similar for the specialized dogs world-wide, and most of the U.S. dogs were trained in the German language.

Chris had never broken his non-disclosure oath about his safeguarding Kat and her father in the Witness Protection Program, but Jeremy wasn't stupid. He knew who his friend worked for, the U.S. Marshals, and could figure things out from there. But the afternoon Jeremy had agreed to see if the young woman had it in her to be a canine trainer, he knew she had the right stuff. While she was shy around people, when it came to dogs she showed her alpha side, and the animals respected her as one of their pack leaders. At least when this was all over, she had a life to go back to if things didn't work out with Benny.

---

THEY ARRIVED BACK at the compound without saying another word to each other. Boomer got out of the car after he parked and went around to open Kat's door for her. But he was too late. She was standing outside the vehicle and closing her door. His eyes narrowed, but he left it alone. *Remember ass-hat, she's not your submissive.* His dick would like to rectify that, but his head told him "no."

At least she let him hold the door to the office open for her, and he followed her inside along with Jake. He introduced her to Colleen, their secretary, who'd just started her work day. The two women shook hands before he led her into the conference room where his life had changed a little more than fifteen hours ago. Ian and Devon were waiting for them and neither one looked happy.

Boomer held out a seat for Kat. "Katerina, this is Ian's brother, Devon. He's the co-owner of Trident. Dev, this is Katerina."

She held out her hand to shake Devon's before taking the offered seat. "It's nice to meet you. Please call me Kat."

Devon took the seat across from her with Jake sitting in the one next to him. "Kat it is. And it's nice to meet you, too." He glanced at Boomer. "Everything all right last night?"

Boomer sighed as he dropped into the seat next to Kat. "Yeah. Just forgot about Pop coming by this morning. He was as shocked as I was. He's stopping for breakfast for everyone and should be here in

a few minutes." His gaze flicked between the Sawyer brothers.
"What's the scoop?"

Ian tossed him a few papers he'd printed from an email. Some
were text, others were photos. "These are from Keon. Sergei 'The
Wolf' Volkov was found murdered in an empty warehouse three
weeks ago. Double tap and clean." Meaning he'd taken one bullet to
the head and another to the heart. No bullet casings were found.
"No suspects, but the guy had lots of enemies, so it could have been
anybody. But tell me what you think."

Rick walked in as Boomer was studying the pictures of the
crime scene photos. He looked at them over his son's shoulder after
handing a bag of egg sandwiches to Jake to distribute. Boomer
suddenly zeroed in on what Ian wanted him to see. "It was someone
he knew, someone close to him. The warehouse is empty. If he was
killed there, and it looks like he was, he was meeting someone. He
wouldn't have gone there without at least one of his bodyguards."

Ian nodded. "Exactly what I was thinking. Keon, too. The FBI
has the case because he's been on their watch list for years.
Everyone they've interviewed in his inner circle has denied knowing
what he was doing there. So, the questions keep mounting, but the
big one is . . . if Volkov is dead, who the hell is after Kat? And
why?"

As Rick took the seat next to Boomer, the five men turned their
attention to the bewildered woman. "I have no idea. All I know is
what I've told you. My father was dying and high on morphine, so
all I have is his mumblings and hearsay from twelve years ago."

Boomer's mind was spinning with details, none of which added
up. "What did Keon say about Mr. Maier's involvement from back
then?"

Ian shook his head as he accepted the wrapped sandwich sliding
across the table at him. He left it unopened. "Not much more than
what Kat told us. Maier got himself in too deep to cut and run, and
he ended up with information he should have never seen.
Information which resulted in a price on his head."

"So, we head to the bank in Norfolk." Boomer couldn't think of
anything else which would help them at this point.

"Yup. Jake, I want you to go with them and keep us updated every four hours. CC will be at the hanger at eleven-hundred to fly you all up there." Conrad Chapman, otherwise known as CC, was a retired Air Force pilot Trident contracted to fly their jet wherever they needed to go. The small private airport they used was about twenty minutes from the compound. Ian directed his next statement to Boomer and Kat. "Keon will arrange for someone to meet you with ID and the death certificate. Kat is to stay hidden as much as possible. I don't want the chance of someone from her past recognizing her."

She frowned. "I doubt anyone would recognize me from twelve years ago, but you never know. I can get a wig or dye my hair if you want."

Before Ian answered her, Boomer spoke up. "I can grab a wig from the club."

He mentally kicked himself for mentioning The Covenant. The first building in the compound gave no indication it was a BDSM club. There was a small store on the top floor, and it specialized in fetish wear and toys. Blonde wigs were popular, and they had several in stock, but he'd have to run over there without Kat. There was no way he was letting her inside the club. He'd never been ashamed of his lifestyle, but at this moment, he couldn't bring himself to tell her about it. He thought back to the shy, little virgin she'd been twelve years ago and figured she would run to the hills if she knew about his kinks. Thankfully, she didn't seem to notice his flub, and Jake sensed his predicament.

"I'll grab one before we go."

Boomer nodded his thanks, then said to the room in general, "Anything else?"

Ian and Devon looked at each other for confirmation and both shook their heads. Ian stood and picked up his egg sandwich. "At the moment, no. Brody and Marco are due back this afternoon. I'll get Egghead on his computers to search for everything he can find on all the players in this." Brody "Egghead" Evans was their computer and tech specialist, and a world class hacker of the first degree. And Marco "Polo" DeAngelis was their communications specialist and backup helicopter pilot. He was also Brody's occasional ménage partner. "When you get to Norfolk, let me know where you're staying, so I can have Keon's man meet you with the paperwork."

After Boomer acknowledged his order, Ian left the room as the others stood. Jake pointed to Rick. "Do you mind following them back to Boomer's condo? I need to swing by my place to grab my go-to bag. It's usually in my truck, but I was cleaning it out yesterday and didn't have a chance to put it back together."

"No problem at all," the older man answered.

They all picked up their unopened egg sandwiches and headed for the door. They could eat on the way to grab their gear. As they passed Colleen's desk, the secretary handed Boomer a piece of pink paper. She had taken a phone message for him while they were in their meeting. He glanced at the message before folding the paper twice and sticking it in his back pocket. He'd take care of it later.

As they headed back to his condo, with his father following him this time, Boomer turned his head toward Kat when he noticed she was rubbing her temples. "You all right?"

She winced. "It's a headache. I've been getting them about twice a month for the last few years. I take over-the-counter migraine meds and they help, but I ran out of them. Can we stop at a pharmacy really quick?"

"Yeah. There's one up ahead." He grabbed his phone and dialed his father's cell. Using the car's Blue-tooth feature, he told Rick their plan to stop.

Pulling into a Walgreens, he waited for his dad to park next to him, get out, and approach the Dodge's passenger door, before exiting the car. Rick opened Kat's door and extended his hand to assist her from the vehicle. When the two of them met Boomer on the walkway between the car and building, Kat swayed. Boomer grabbed her around the waist before she could fall, and eyed her in alarm. "Kat? You all right? Are you going to pass out?"

Kat rested her arms on his broad shoulders and steadied. Boomer's body reacted immediately to her close proximity, and he inwardly cursed, fighting the urge to pull her flush against him.

"Uh, no, I'm okay. Just got a little light-headed. It happens when I get a migraine."

After making sure she had her balance again, he forced himself to step back, but kept one hand at the small of her back as he escorted her into the store. Rick remained three steps behind them, his head swiveling from side to side, always on the lookout for danger. It was highly unlikely the people after Kat were lying in wait at a Florida Walgreens on the off chance she'd stop there, but one never knew.

They headed down the OTC medicine aisle, and Kat quickly found the brand she used for her headaches. Before they had a chance to reverse their direction, a pretty brunette came around the far corner of the aisle, and her face lit up as she spotted Boomer.

"Hi, M—Ben."

Boomer winced at the woman's cheerful voice and near slip of his title of Master. "Hi, Cassandra."

She approached and stopped a little too close for comfort. Normally, Boomer wouldn't have minded running into the petite submissive he'd topped a few times, but with Kat at his side, he was a little uncomfortable.

"We missed you at the club last weekend."

He scratched the top of his head. "Uh, yeah. I was working the whole weekend."

Cassandra's eyes flashed to Kat who had taken a step closer to him and looked as if she was waiting for Boomer to introduce them. "Hi. I'm Cassandra."

Kat shook the woman's outstretched hand. "I'm Kat."

"Nice to meet you." Her eyes went back to Boomer's face. "Will you be there tomorrow night?"

Boomer gently grabbed Kat's arm and shook his head. Cassandra was a sweet submissive who waitressed at The Covenant, and he knew she wouldn't step on another woman's toes intentionally. She also wouldn't publicize what kind of club The Covenant was. "Uh, no, I don't think so. Maybe over the weekend, but I'm not sure."

Cassandra's gaze flicked to the possessive hand on the other woman's arm, and she took a step back, her eyes full of apology to Boomer. She must've realized she'd almost said too much. "Okay. If not, I'll see you some other time. Kat, it was nice to meet you. Have a nice day." Without waiting for a response from either of them, she spun around and waved goodbye over her shoulder.

Boomer's hand gripped Kat's arm a little tighter as he turned her in the direction of the cashiers. His father had been a few steps behind them and gave him a "you're so fucked" smile before leading the way. Boomer wasn't sure what that was all about. Cassandra and he were friends. Friends who occasionally fucked during a scene at a private BDSM club. What was wrong with that? He glanced at Kat who had a curious expression on her face. He knew she wanted to ask him about Cassandra. Yup, his father was right—he was so fucked.

# CHAPTER 6

They had about another half hour before they landed in a small airport outside of Norfolk, Virginia. Boomer hadn't been up this way in over a year, but his last trip had been a long weekend of catching up with people he hadn't seen in a while. Another one of his old high school friends had taken the plunge and gotten married. They were dropping like flies these past few years. His mind drifted to Alex, and he wondered, if his friend had still been alive, would he have found some woman and put a ring on her finger. He doubted it. Alex had been worse than he'd been back in the day. His friend had a new hook up almost every weekend, going through girls as if trying to win a new Guinness world record At least Boomer had dated several girls for a few weeks before moving on.

But all that changed after his Kitten had "died." He'd only fallen in love once in his life and look how it'd ended. She was gone less than thirty-six hours after he professed his love. Yeah, it hadn't been her fault, but it still hurt like hell.

He glanced over to where she was curled up on the plane's couch reading a book since her migraine had faded. Damn, she was still the prettiest woman he'd ever met despite her recent weight loss. She'd passed on the egg sandwich, letting him have it instead, because she couldn't eat with the headache. He had Jake stop for a turkey and cheese sandwich for her to eat on the plane and had been happy to see her finishing it off about fifteen minutes ago.

In the recliner next to him, Jake was taking a power nap. His teammate had been up half the night trying to find his missing informant. He'd finally found the little punk in a local crack house, and Jake was pissed. The kid had been clean for six months before this set-back. Jake dragged his ass out of there, and into a hospital. The next stop was an agreed upon rehab facility. Boomer had never met the informant, but if the former SEAL was putting this much work into trying to save him from the life of a homeless junkie, then there had to be something there which impressed him. Boomer hoped the kid was worth the effort.

He got up and sat down on the couch next to Kat. Against his better judgment, he grabbed her ankles and pulled her feet into his lap. She'd removed her slip-on flats earlier, and without conscious thought, he began to rub the arch of her right foot. As he dug his thumbs deep into the tissue, she closed her eyes and groaned. The sound went straight to his groin.

"God, that feels so good. Please don't stop."

His mouth twitched, and he wished he was doing other things to her which gave him the same response. "So, tell me about Portland."

Her eyes opened just enough for her to see him through the slits. "What do you want to know?"

"I don't know. Everything? Anything? Do you have a job there? Friends?" *Boyfriends?* He was torn between wanting and not wanting to know the answer to that.

She shrugged. "Only a few close friends, but I have a great job which I love. When we first ended up there, our handler, Chris, sent me to see an old army buddy of his. Jeremy Pierce and his wife Eva own a canine training facility for protection and law enforcement. We clicked right away, and he taught me how to train the dogs. I've been working for him ever since. I train them in drug and explosives detection, as well as passive and aggressive tracking, depending on the dog and the agency. Passive tracking is for missing persons, and aggressive is for suspects."

"What differs?"

Groaning, she bit her lip when he dug into a particular spot in her arch. "Passive tracking, the dog will lead its handler right up to the person. When you're tracking a possibly armed suspect, you want some warning before he's suddenly right in front of you. There's a funny story about one of our graduates. His dog was a passive tracker and drug detector, but a few months ago, they had a suspect disappear into the woods, and they didn't have an aggressive tracker available. So, what they did was put two officers, with their guns at the ready, on either side of the team because the handler's eyes had to be on the dog, looking for tells. This way if the suspect suddenly appeared, they were covered. Anyway, they were tracking for about ten minutes when the dog suddenly sat down in the middle of nowhere. The handler was trying to get him back on track, but the dog wouldn't budge. It took a few moments, but they realized the dog was sitting on a pile of leaves, and one of them spotted the heel of a sneaker. The suspect had buried himself under a pile of leaves, hoping they'd walk right by him, and the darn dog was sitting on his back." They both started laughing. "The handler kicks the guy's leg and says, 'Don't move.' The suspect answers, 'Wasn't planning on it.'"

Laughing harder, Boomer couldn't help but be impressed. It was obvious she loved her job. "Wow. That's awesome. Beau went through a training place like that in Florida. He was about six-weeks old when Ian found him at the compound. His mother was a stray who'd just died, so Ian took him in."

"I noticed his training," she told him while nodding.

"Do they know where you are? Your bosses? I mean, do you still have a job after we find who's after you?" Part of him wanted her to say no, but they would both be better off if she said yes.

She glanced out the window of the plane. "Yes. Sort of. I told them I had a family emergency." At his raised eyebrow, she shrugged. "It was all I could think of at the time. Anyway, even though no one ever came out and told Jeremy I was in witness protection, he's very astute, and I'm sure he figured it out. He just told me to keep in touch and to call him if I needed anything. I should call him later to let him know I'm still alive."

"Good idea. Use your pre-paid phone, since they're very hard to trace. Then we'll throw it away and get a new one. Ask him if anyone suspicious has been snooping around asking about you."

Kat nodded and tapped his hand with her left foot. It was a blatant hint to give it the same treatment he was giving her other one. He chuckled and swapped them. "Better?"

"Yes, much." She groaned as he worked his thumbs deeper. "I can't remember the last time I had a foot massage. I used to get them all the time when I treated myself to pedicures, but it's been a while."

He was glad it was a professional service where she had gotten the massages, and not from a boyfriend. A pang of jealousy at her dating some guy hit him in the gut, and he forced himself not to question her about other men. Who she dated was none of his business.

Glancing down at her lap, he eyed the book she'd been reading, and . . . *oh, fuck* . . . it was *Leather & Lace*, by Kristen Anders, soon-to-be Kristen Sawyer, Devon's wife. While Boomer hadn't read the whole thing, he'd flipped through and read the steamy sex scenes after Devon mentioned how hot they were. It was fucking hot porn in written format, plain and simple. It also involved BDSM, and he was shocked Kat was reading it. Did she just like reading about the lifestyle or was she into it? And if she wasn't, would she be interested in trying it? Did she fantasize about a man doing to her the things Master Xavier did to his submissive in the book?

He shifted uncomfortably and shoved his thoughts back where they belonged—in the gutter. She was a job and an old friend, nothing more. *You might as well give up trying to convince yourself buddy, because it's not working.*

"Prepare for landing." CC's voice came over the intercom and Jake's eyes flew open. That was the thing about being in special ops —you got used to catnaps and waking up completely refreshed.

Boomer swung Kat's feet to the ground so she could sit up and put her seatbelt on. He then strapped his own around his waist. They would be on the ground and in their waiting car within fifteen minutes. After he had the plane refueled, CC would get a room at the closest motel for the night, so he would be nearby if they needed him. Meanwhile, Boomer, Kat, and Jake would head into the Norfolk residential area where the two childhood friends used to live. There was a Best Western near the bank they needed. From what Boomer had been able to access online it was the ideal motel for them. There were plenty of escape routes if things went south.

Next to him, Kat visibly shuddered.

"You okay?"

She gave him a tiny smile. "Yeah, I think so. It just hit me. I haven't been here since I was seventeen with a bright and happy future ahead of me."

Boomer reached over and squeezed her hand because he couldn't think of anything to say which didn't sound cliché. He just hoped, when this was all over, she did have a happy life in her future, even if it wasn't with him.

---

As JAKE LET himself into the adjoining room to the left, Kat followed Boomer into their motel room. He tossed his duffel bag on the bed closest to the door and gestured for her to take the other one. It wasn't even one in the afternoon yet, and she wanted nothing more than to crawl under the covers and take a nap.

He saw the look of longing on her face before he turned to unlock the go-between door connecting the two rooms. "Take a nap if you want. Jake and I will be next door working on a few things for tomorrow."

"Okay." Kat pulled off the blonde wig she'd donned before getting off the plane and scratched her itchy scalp. Reaching to pull the bedspread down, she kicked off her shoes at the same time. "Don't let me sleep past three, please. Otherwise I'll be up all night."

"Sure." Boomer watched as she climbed into the bed fully clothed. She shifted a few times trying to find a comfortable position and finally settled on her side facing away from him. Her long brown tresses fanned across the pillow and his hands ached to run his fingers through the soft strands. The longer he was around her, the more his old feelings for her pounded in his chest. But there were new feelings there too. Feelings he didn't know what the fuck he was going to do about.

Sighing, he walked into the other room and left the door ajar in case she needed him. Jake was exiting his bathroom and drying his hands on a towel. He raised an eyebrow at seeing Boomer alone.

"She's lying down for a while."

"Ah." They both sat down at the table for two, and Jake opened a folder with all the pertinent information they had so far. "So . . . you want to talk about work or what it's like to have an old girlfriend come back from the dead?"

Boomer knew his friend was being sympathetic despite how his words sounded. He ran a hand through his hair and glanced at the partially opened door behind him before turning his attention back to Jake. "How do you know she was a girlfriend?"

"Ian keeps me around for my sniper skills and powers of observation. If she wasn't your girlfriend, there was a time you wished she was."

He leaned forward, resting his elbows on the table and keeping his voice low so she wouldn't hear him. It'd been a long time since he'd told anyone about his Kitten. "She was my best friend's sister and a year behind us in school. I never thought of her as anything more than a good friend until I took her to my senior prom. One minute she was my friend, the next minute I wanted something more. Hit me from out of the blue, you know?"

Jake nodded, but didn't say a word.

"The night of my going-away party, a week before basic training, I found out she felt the same way. I asked her to be my girl and to wait for me. She agreed and two days later . . . her entire family was gone."

"From what Ian told me, she didn't have a choice."

Boomer leapt from his chair in frustration and began pacing, but kept his voice low. "Damn it, I know it wasn't her fault. But too much time has gone by. We don't even fucking know each other anymore. I'm not the same eighteen-year-old kid without a care in the world. I've seen and done shit she could never imagine. I've changed, and I doubt she'll like the guy I've become."

Crossing his arms, Jake narrowed his eyes at his teammate. "Close the door."

"What?"

"Close the damn door and sit the fuck down for a minute." After Boomer eased the door shut and plopped back down in his seat, the harshness ebbed from his friend's voice. "I'm a little confused here, Baby Boomer. Are you talking about the Navy and the shit we've done, or are you talking about the club and the lifestyle?

"Both, I guess," he mumbled, staring at the floor.

"Well, the SEAL shit is easy. You've served your country proud and followed orders like the good frog you are. Yes, you've killed more people than anyone will ever know about, but what it boils down to is you killed because you had to. You're not a murderer. You saved lives—civilians', your teammates', and your own. There's nothing wrong with anything you've done in the name of Uncle Sam and apple pie. I don't think your girl in there would have any problem with that, especially since you can't tell her most of it."

Boomer shrugged and kept his eyes downcast.

"Now, about the lifestyle. You're not the first Dom to question himself, and you won't be the last. The point is . . . which is more important to you? Can you love her without topping her? Or do you need it like the air you breathe? You said before, you don't know each other anymore . . . maybe this is your chance to get to know her again. Maybe she's changed, too. Maybe she wants to be topped, did you ever think about that?" He paused a moment to let the idea sink into the other man's head. "Now, stop being an ass, and let's get your girl out of trouble, all right? Think about fucking her after this is all over."

Boomer snorted then grinned. "You're a prick, Reverend."

"Hey, I tell it like it is. You want sensitive, call Polo."

# CHAPTER 7

*A*s he slipped back into his shared room, Boomer quietly shut the door behind him, but kept it unlocked. Kat was still sleeping and he didn't need to wake her yet. Jake and he had spent about thirty minutes going over what they knew and what they needed to find out. They'd called Ian to let him know where they were staying, so he could forward the information to Keon. The paperwork they needed for the bank would arrive sometime after eighteen hundred this evening. Jake was heading out in a few minutes to scout the area around the motel, and also the bank, which was three blocks away. In the meantime, Boomer was left alone to watch over Kat. He double checked the front door locks and peeked out the window through the thin gap of the closed curtains. Nothing seemed out of the ordinary.

Spinning around one of the straight back chairs at the table, he straddled it and sat. Kat was now laying on her other side, facing him, and his eyes roamed over her features. Her cheeks, pert nose, and soft, full lips helped form a face which could grace a magazine cover, when combined with the beautiful eyes he would recognize anywhere. The sheet had shifted down to her waist leaving her upper torso exposed. His mouth watered as he stared at the lush cleavage peeking out of her V-neck shirt. Damn, he wanted her more now than he had as a teenager. Maybe Jake was right. Maybe the universe had sent her back to him for a reason.

Being a Dom was a major part of his life. He'd found the lifestyle he loved before he was assigned to Team Four and met Ian and the rest of his current teammates. One of his buddies from basic training had brought him to his first club after they'd been stationed together in San Diego. He spent two years there until he was accepted into the SEALs Bud/s training program. After graduating with his trident, he was assigned to Team Four, which was his father's old team in Virginia. He'd been happy to learn several of his new teammates also participated in the lifestyle and joined the club they all frequented.

Kat stirred and moaned, but stayed asleep. The sounds coming from her mouth had him growing hard, and he adjusted himself in his jeans. What would she do if he woke her by nuzzling her ear . . . her neck . . . her breasts? Would she push his hand away as he cupped her mound and flexed his fingertips into her core through her pants? Would she allow him to undress, restrain, eat, and fuck her? Would she scream when she came for him? Would she beg for more? Would she . . .

Fuck, he needed a cold shower. But that would leave her vulnerable. He'd have to find another way to tame his raging hard-on until Jake returned to keep watch. Grabbing a *Men's Fitness* magazine from his duffel, he moved to his bed and sat with a pillow between his back and the wall while crossing his ankles. He covered his erection with another pillow and flipped through the pages until he found an interesting article to read.

A few minutes later, he caught movement out of the corner of his eye and turned his head to find Kat staring at him. Her sleepy expression made him smile. "Feel better?"

She stretched her arms and back and he bit his tongue as the actions thrust her chest toward him. "Yeah, I needed that."

Snorting, he tore his eyes away from her breasts and focused on the magazine in front of him. But he couldn't concentrate on any words at the moment "I'm sure you did. Jake went to check a few things out. Are you hungry? I'll have him pick up a pizza or something on his way back."

Throwing the sheets off her hips and legs, she stood and walked toward the bathroom. "I don't know what it is about being around you guys, but I'm hungrier now than I've been in months. Pizza sounds good, and maybe a salad?"

". . . I'm hungrier now than I've been in months." *Baby, you have no idea . . . I haven't been this hungry in years. And I'm not hungry for food.* "Yeah, sure, I'll let him know."

"I'm going to grab a quick shower to wake up."

"Mm-hmm. 'Kay."

The door closed behind her and Boomer clutched the pillow in his lap, pumping his hips a few times in frustration. It'd taken everything in him not to reach out, pull her down on top of him, and ravage her. Now all he had to do was not think about her getting undressed and lathering her naked body. *Fuck—easier said than done.* When Jake got back and took over the watch, he'd jump into the shower and give himself some relief. Picking up his phone, he typed off a quick text to his teammate and tossed it on back on the nightstand.

The bathroom door opened a few inches, and Kat stuck her head out. "Benny, I should've brought my bag in with me. Can you hand it to me, please?"

*Shit, was she kidding?* If he walked over to her, there would be no way she would miss his rigid shaft bulging through his jeans. And why couldn't she come out and get it herself? A light bulb went off in his head . . . she'd started getting undressed. *Ah, hell.* Now he was hard and throbbing.

She was patiently staring at him. *Fuck!* He didn't have much choice. Biting his lip, he threw caution to the wind, along with the pillow, and stood. He grabbed her bag and strode over to the bathroom door, hoping she wouldn't look at his crotch. And of course, the moment he had the thought, her eyes flickered downward and her cheeks bloomed as she spotted his package.

Boomer's eyes traveled up her bare arm as she reached out for the bag. There was nothing but pure ivory skin on her shoulder, and he caught a peek of the white towel she was using to cover herself. Before he could say or do anything, she shyly looked away and closed the door with a muttered thanks. Bracing his arms on the door jamb, he let his head drop forward. A few seconds went by before he realized he hadn't heard the lock engage. *Was that an invitation?*

He reached for the doorknob and hesitated. If he was wrong, he'd screw up everything. He still didn't know if she had a boyfriend back in Portland, and that was the first thing he needed to address. Sighing, he left the doorknob alone and ran his hand through his hair instead. *First things first, ass-hat. Get her out of danger, then you can start thinking with your dick again.*

Plopping back down on his bed, he grabbed his phone again when a text message chimed. It was from Georgia Branneth.

**Hi, Master Ben. I was hoping we could negotiate a scene tonight. Please let me know. g.**

Boomer stared at the message. He'd hooked up with the submissive several times over the past few months, but had made it clear what they had together stayed at the club, and she was good with it. The short, raven-haired cutie was a recently divorced high-school teacher and had no desire to jump into another relationship. She was sweet, fun, and an incredible fuck. In addition to teaching, she was also a gymnastics coach, and was extremely limber, which made for interesting sexual acrobatics. And less than twenty-four hours ago, he would've been fantasizing about some new positions. But now, in his brain, Kat had replaced the women in every one of his fantasies. Shit, he was a goner. And now he had to find a way back into her heart because he didn't think either one of them would settle for anything less.

**Sorry g. Out of town.**

**:( K. Next time.**

Boomer sighed. There might not be a next time, but he wouldn't tell the sub that in a text. And he definitely wouldn't say anything until he was sure Kat was single and on the same page as him. The room was silent, and all he could hear was the shower running.

*Damn it.* He was never going to get rid of his erection if he kept thinking about Kat lathering herself under the spray of warm water. Grabbing the TV remote, he hit the power and then volume buttons.

By the time Kat opened the door and exited the bathroom, he had his cock back under control, and he willed it to stay that way. She'd changed into a pair of gray sweat pants and black T-shirt with the logo for *J&E International K9* over her left breast. Her feet were bare and he wondered if she would be opposed to another foot massage. His cock twitched, and he shoved the thought from his brain. If Jake didn't get here soon, Boomer was going to have a serious case of blue balls. For fuck's sake, he couldn't even look at her feet without getting aroused. How screwed up was that?

He heard two then three knocks on Jake's door, before it swung open, and his teammate walked into the other room. Striding through the go-between door, he carried in a large pizza box and several bags. *Thank God.* Boomer jumped up, grabbed his duffel, and headed to the bathroom. He passed a curious looking Kat. "Start without me. I'm taking a quick shower."

"Okay. But you better hurry, otherwise I might eat yours."

Boomer shut the door a little harder than he should have.

"Okay . . . I might eat yours." His mind was racing. Jesus H. Christ, ass-hat. Get your fucking mind out of the gutter. Not everything out of her mouth is an innuendo. Get in the shower, fire off your rifle, and keep it under control.

He turned on the shower and took a deep breath. *Fuck!* The room smelled of her body soap. This was getting so out of hand. Stripping fast, he climbed into the tub and grabbed the courtesy bar of soap. Tearing the paper off, he got it wet and lathered up. One hand against the wall, the other around his aching cock, he closed his eyes and groaned softly. He dragged his fist down to the root and back up to the head. Up and over, down and back up again. His hips began to pump as Boomer imagined Kat on her knees, sucking and licking him. Her lips would be soft and plump, her mouth warm and inviting. He'd grasp her hair and guide her in taking him deeper and deeper until he hit the back of her throat. *Take it, Kitten.*

*Lick me like I'm a bowl of cream.* He tightened his fist and picked up the pace. *Yeah, baby, suck it hard. I'm going to come down your throat, and you're going to swallow every drop. Are you ready, Kitten?*

"Ah, fuck," he hissed as he shot his jizz into the shower spray, then yanked on his cock until there was nothing left. Light-headed, he leaned heavily on his other hand against the wall, and tried to catch his breath.

Yup, he and Kat were going to have to have a talk, because he wanted her more than ever.

---

KAT FLIPPED BACK and forth from one side to the other, sleep eluding her for several reasons. She was in a strange room and bed, and the walls were paper-thin, so she heard every noise outside their room in the parking lot. But Benny sleeping on the other bed, and her body hyper-aware of the fact, were the main reasons she was wide awake at two a.m.

She flopped back over to her left side and stared at the beautiful man lying a few feet away. She could see him thanks to the light from the motel sign breaching the curtains' edges. Sometime in the last hour, he'd kicked his covers off. While he was wearing a pair of sweatpants, his torso was bared for her viewing pleasure. And what a pleasure it was. His shoulders, chest, and abs were sculpted perfection and she longed to touch each valley and peak. With her hands. With her tongue.

Moisture pooled between her legs, and she squeezed her thighs together. Over the years, she'd only had a few dates. She tried to have a normal life, but the whole time she always kept one eye looking over her shoulder, ready to run at a moment's notice. And most of those dates had never panned out. The closest she'd ever come to having a boyfriend was about two years ago.

Tim Hartman was a local police officer who'd gotten a new canine partner. He'd flirted with Kat during his training time at the facility where she worked, and she was flattered. He was a good-looking man, two years older than her, and he made her laugh, which wasn't something she did often. She had too much sorrow in her life, too much stress. They had dated six weeks, but every time she tried to relax during intimate moments, she couldn't. He'd been understanding at first, but after several weeks of not advancing past kissing and petting, he'd gotten frustrated and then lost interest.

On the other bed, Benny took a gasping breath and began to twitch and moan. Flailing his limbs, his breathing increased, as Kat sat up. What was he dreaming of? Whatever it was, it wasn't good. When he let out a pain-filled cry, she threw off her covers and leapt to his side. If she didn't wake him soon, Jake would hear him and think they were in trouble.

Kat sat down on the thin space between him and the edge of the bed, shaking his shoulders. "Benny. Ben, wake up." He groaned louder and thrashed his legs. She tried harder. "Benny, please wake up."

---

BOOMER LUNGED into a sitting position and grabbed his left leg. The sudden movement almost sent Kat flying onto the floor, and she clutched his arm to prevent it. He was panting and disoriented for a moment, before the present came rushing back to him. His arm went around her waist to keep her from falling. "Holy shit, Kat, are you okay? What happened? I didn't hurt you, did I?"

"N-No, you didn't, no. Are you okay? You were moaning and stuff."

Running his other hand through his hair, he felt the dampness on his forehead. He was sweating like a pig--*damn it*. The frequency of his nightmares had been easing off these past few months, but every once in a while, they reared their ugly heads. He could still hear the roar of the RPG as it hit the truck he'd just jumped out of, the screams of the injured, the ringing in his ears which had taken days to disappear. The image of his shin bone sticking out of his leg still made him nauseous to think about. But he was alive . . . and still had all his limbs attached. Some of the other SEALs and Marines, who'd been there when they'd come under attack, hadn't been as lucky. As he concentrated on getting his breathing back to normal, he downplayed the nightmare to Kat, trying to ease the worried expression in her face. "Yeah. Just some flashbacks to when I got hurt. I guess it's a good thing they only come when I'm sleeping. Some guys I served with get them while they're awake."

"Stay here a sec." She jumped up and disappeared into the bathroom. Boomer heard water running and then she returned with a wet washcloth. He was shocked when she sat beside him again and began to wipe the sweat from his face, neck, and shoulders. His muscles froze, and as cool as the cloth felt against his sizzling skin, he wished there was nothing between her hand and his flesh. Goosebumps popped up everywhere, and his dick twitched. Swallowing hard, he watched her face as her gaze followed the cloth gliding down his arms. He couldn't stand it anymore. He had to touch her. Kiss her. Own her. He'd deal with the fallout later.

Reaching up, he cupped her chin and she started, her eyes flashing up to his in surprise. He was in awe of her, and his voice came out as a raspy whisper. "You're still the most beautiful woman I've ever known, Kitten."

Her jaw dropped at his statement, and he took advantage of it. Rubbing his thumb across her bottom lip, he inched his head forward. He gave her time to back away. But when a small gasp escaped her and her breathing increased, all the reasons why this was a bad idea flew from his mind. Drawing her closer, he tilted his head and replaced his thumb with his mouth. *Oh, dear God in heaven!* He'd dreamed of this moment, a moment he'd been certain would never happen again. She tasted of wine, roses, and sunshine, and everything else poets compared women to.

Boomer leaned back and pulled her with him until she was draped across his bare torso. Holding her head in place, he plunged his tongue into her mouth, tasting and savoring. His other hand skimmed down the T-shirt she'd worn to bed and clutched her ass cheek through her cotton shorts. He shifted and grinded his hard shaft against her mound, causing her to moan and shiver. Mouths melded, teeth clashed, and tongues dueled as she buried her hands in his hair.

Flipping her on her back, Boomer followed, never taking his mouth from hers. His hands were everywhere at once. Her hair, breasts, waist, and hips. Skin, he needed to feel skin. Grabbing the hem of her shirt, he began to tug it upward and felt her stiffen. What the fuck? She wanted him to stop? Fuck, she did have a boyfriend, didn't she?

He ripped his mouth from hers and sat up. Trying to get his breathing and cock under control, he stood and paced the room while running his fingers through his tousled hair. "Shit, Kat. I'm sorry. I shouldn't have . . . I mean . . . you must have a boyfriend, right?"

"No."

Boomer screeched to a halt and gaped at her. "No?"

Swallowing hard, Kat shook her head. "No. I don't have a boyfriend."

No? Then why did she freeze when he tried to take things further? *Because you haven't seen each other in twelve years, you ass-hat. You've only known she was still alive for about thirty-six hours and you're ready to rip her clothes off. She deserves better than that.*

"Oh." He ran a hand down his face. "Well, I'm still sorry. I shouldn't have jumped you like that. We should . . ." He cleared his suddenly dry throat. "We should get back to sleep. We've got to get up in a few hours, because I want to be at the bank when they open."

---

KAT BIT her lip and nodded before moving back to her own bed. She watched as Ben made a quick run to the bathroom, then lay back down. His eyes were avoiding her, and he shifted onto his left side, facing away from her. She sighed inwardly.

Her heart was still pounding, her blood still boiling with arousal. The dampness and tingling between her legs was proof she hadn't wanted him to stop. She should have told him she'd never . . . but she hadn't been able to. He'd felt and tasted so good. His body, his touch, was what her own had craved for the past twelve years. A few more minutes. She'd wanted a few more minutes in his arms. For the first time since she'd kissed him as a teenager, she wanted more. She wanted him. All of him. A few more . . .

He was right, they needed sleep, not . . . not what they were just doing. But damn, she hadn't wanted to stop. Maybe when this was all over, if she was still alive, they could pick up where they left off. Turning on her side, she closed her eyes, but it was a long time before sleep overtook her once more.

# CHAPTER 8

"You see anything, Reverend?" Boomer spoke into his cell phone. It was ten after eight in the morning and Jake had been across the street for the past hour, scouting the area.

"Nothing out of the ordinary. No one lingering except a bum in the alley over this way. I checked, and he's sleeping off a bender. You're good to go."

"'Kay. I'm putting my phone on vibrate if you need me." He disconnected the call and scanned the bank's parking lot one more time before getting out of the rental they were using. On full alert, his head swiveled as he walked around to the passenger door and opened it for Kat. He hurried her across the lot and into the large brick building which housed the Wells Fargo Bank. There were a few occupants, but no one paid them any attention as they strode past the tellers and approached the only desk of three which didn't have a rep already assisting a customer.

The man stood and gestured for them to take the seats across the desk from him. "Good morning, my name is Brad. How may I help you today?"

"My friend's father passed away, and we found out afterward he had a deposit box here," Boomer told him as they all sat down. It was a small lie, since they weren't positive this was where Mr. Maier had opened the account. "The number on the key is 522, and we have his death certificate."

"Okay, I'll need a proper form of ID and then I'll look up the account to see if there are any restrictions on it."

Kat handed the man the certificate and Florida ID which an FBI agent had dropped off last night. It was the first time in twelve years she'd had a driver's license in her birth name. The picture was one Ian had snapped two nights ago at the office and then emailed to his contact in the federal agency. Since she hadn't been wearing her wig in the photo, they'd left it in the car. Boomer had been nervous about it, but they didn't want to make anyone in the bank suspicious.

Her knee began to bounce as the banker studied the document, then began tapping away on his computer. Boomer reached over and placed his hand on her thigh, stilling her nervous movement. The contact sent tingles and heat up his arm, and a quick glance at her face told him she also felt the electricity between them. Giving his brain a mental shake, he focused on Brad across the desk from them.

The banker stopped typing and frowned. Kat's muscles clenched under his hand as Boomer asked, "Is there a problem?"

"Uh, no, sir. I was just surprised to see the box hasn't been accessed in over twelve years. But it was paid in full for twenty, so there's no problem. The joint box-holders included Ms. Maier here, as well as an Alexei Maier and Sylvia Maier."

Kat eyes filled up. "Alex was my brother and Sylvia was my mom. They're both deceased as well."

An expression of sympathy crossed the man's face. "I'm sorry for your loss, Ms. Maier."

"Thank you."

He stood and skirted the desk. "If you give me a moment, I have to retrieve the bank's access key from my superior."

"Sure," Boomer replied. "No problem." He watched as the banker walked toward a closed door labeled "Branch Manager" and knocked.

"So, we lucked out, right?"

He couldn't see into the now open door from this angle, but kept it in his peripheral as he turned back to Kat. "Huh?"

"No court order needed."

"Right." He gave her a tentative smile, scanning the faces of the bank occupants as the two of them waited. The hair on the back of his neck raised in caution. His inner alert system was telling him something was wrong, but he couldn't see anyone or anything out of place. Pulling out his phone, he shot off a brief text to Jake, however, the "all clear" response did nothing to ease his sudden anxiety.

About two minutes later, Brad returned with a large keyring. "Sorry for the wait. If you'll follow me, it's right this way. We'll retrieve the box and you can examine the contents in private."

Leading them into the security box vault, the banker quickly located the long-ignored box, number 522, and placed his key in one of the two slots. He then stepped back to allow Kat to do the same. After it was unlocked, he slid it from the wall and handed it to her. "You can use the room on the right outside the vault. I'll wait here until you're done."

"Thank you." Despite her calm outward demeanor, Boomer knew Kat's insides must be a bowl of Jell-O. Whatever her father had hidden here in the bank, it was something people wanted to kill for. He followed her into the room and shut the door behind them. The space was the size of a closet and there was nothing in it except a shelf and an overhead light. Her hands shook as she set the box down.

The tension rolling off her was doing nothing to calm his thoughts that something wasn't right. "Do you want me to open it?"

Kat bit her bottom lip and shook her head. "No. I've got it." After taking a deep breath, she lifted the lid and stared at the contents in confusion and disappointment.

"That's it?" he asked over her shoulder. It couldn't be it.

"I don't understand. My father had a security box all these years for a . . . a picture?" She picked up the old, three-by-five color photo and studied it. "This is my dad when he was a kid. He's what, about four or five years old here?"

Boomer checked the box for anything more and found it completely empty. He took the photo from Kat and turned it over, but the back was blank. No name, date or message. Strange. Flipping it back over, he examined it. "Looks like it. Any idea where it was taken? Is that his childhood home he's standing in front of?"

"I'm not sure. If I remember correctly, they moved twice before settling in Murfreesboro, North Carolina, when my dad was eleven or twelve. But I don't know where they lived before that." Her eyes flashed to Boomer's face as a thought must have occurred to her. "My aunt would know. Last I heard she was still alive. Chris told me that about . . . I don't remember. A year ago, I think."

"Where does she live?" he asked as he replaced the lid and picked up the box.

She tucked the photo into her purse. "In Murfreesboro. She still lives in my grandparent's old house. It's just over an hour from here. It's where we were going when . . ."

Not needing her to finish her statement about the tragic day so long ago, he took her hand and headed for the door. "Let's get out of here."

---

"It's Glen Patterson, from Wells Fargo? You told me to call when anyone accessed the Maier deposit box . . . A guy and a girl . . . I don't know his name, but her ID says she's Katrina, uh, I mean, Katerina Maier . . . They're in there now, but I'm sure they won't be for long . . . A license plate? Yeah, I can probably get it . . . My office window faces the parking lot . . . After this, we're through, right? I don't owe you anything anymore . . . Good . . . I'll text you the plate and car info."

The bank manager disconnected the call, relieved the last of an old debt was paid off. He'd sworn off gambling several years ago after his wife threatened to leave him and take the kids. It'd taken a while, but he'd finally repaid all his monetary debts. This last "information" debt was the only thing he still owed. Now all he needed to do was one more thing . . . he parted the window blinds and waited for the couple he'd seen follow Brad into the vault.

## CHAPTER 9

*F*ifteen minutes later, they were back in their motel rooms and packing their things. The plan was to head to Murfreesboro to talk to Kat's aunt, and wasn't that going to be a jaw-dropper for the older woman. As far as she knew, her brother and niece had died twelve years ago, and she had no other family left. Kat's grandfather had died when she was seven, and her grandmother passed away four years ago, never knowing the true fate of her son and his daughter.

While Jake was next door, collecting his stuff and the FBI files, Kat came out of the bathroom with her toiletries. Boomer winced at her pale, pinched face framed by the wig she was once again wearing. "You okay?"

She tossed her things into her duffel and sighed. "Yeah. I'm just wondering where this is all going. I mean, what if we don't figure it out? And on top of everything, I'm about to shock the shit out of my Aunt Irina. What am I supposed to do, knock on her door and yell 'surprise'? Look how well it turned out when I did it to you. You fainted, so the poor woman will probably have a heart attack."

Her rant was stopped when Boomer grasped her arm and pulled her into a comforting embrace. "Shhh. It'll be fine. She'll be shocked, but then I think she'll be ecstatic to know you're alive. Yes, I fainted . . ." He grabbed her chin and forced her gaze upward. On his face was a teasing frown. "And don't ever repeat that to anyone else. Ian is already blackmailing me with shit assignments for the next year." She smiled as he intended. "But now I'm past my shock, and I'm thrilled you're alive, Kitten."

It hadn't been his intention when he first pulled her into his arms, but he couldn't resist her. Bending forward, his lips caught hers and his cock sprung to life. He teased the seam of her mouth with his tongue and rejoiced when she opened, granting him access. Last night, he'd been spouting poetry at the taste of her, but now, she must've just brushed her teeth again because she was minty fresh and delicious. Poetry was the last thing on his mind.

One of his hands went to the nape of her neck, and his fingers spread out to hold her head in place. His other hand clutched her hip, pulling her flush against him and his bulging erection. They moaned almost simultaneously when he shifted his head and the new angle allowed him to plunge his tongue deeper. Her tongue tangled with his as her hands slid up his shoulders and into his hair.

"Ah, shit. Sorry, but we need to get on the road."

They jumped apart. Kat's face turned red before she spun around and began throwing the last of her stuff into her bag. Shit, Boomer thought. What the hell was he doing? If it wasn't for Jake's interruption, he would have forgotten the danger Kat was in and thrown her on the bed for a hard, fast, and sweaty rutting.

Adjusting himself, he acknowledged his teammate over his shoulder. "Yeah. Give us a minute. We'll be right out."

"No prob."

A few seconds later he heard the door to Jake's room open and close again. He'd be getting the car started for their trip and Boomer hurried to grab the last of his stuff. He glanced around the room, making sure they weren't forgetting anything before taking Kat's bags for her. Pinning her with an intense stare, he told her, "We're not done, Kitten. Not by a long shot. Just wanted to let you know. Once you're out of danger, we're picking up where we left off, and there will be no interruptions. Understood?"

She bit her lip and nodded, but her gaze lowered from his face to his chest. Convinced she knew he meant to have her in his bed soon, naked and sated, he turned and headed for the door. Because his hands were filled with their bags, Kat hurried around him and opened the door.

"I can carry my stuff if you want."

"Not," he snorted. She may be used to doing things on her own after all these years, but that was about to change. It went beyond wanting to be her Dom. His parents had raised him to be a gentleman, and Kat deserved to be treated like a lady.

Jake was standing by the open trunk while the sedan was running. "Radio says there's an accident on the highway and traffic is backed up for miles. We'll have to GPS around it."

"'Kay." As Boomer tossed the bags into the trunk, an SUV came squealing into the lot and both men's heads turned.

Drawing their weapons, they backed up to use their rental car as cover and stood in front of Kat, protecting her. Four large men climbed out of the Escalade and each had a semi-automatic in hand, but didn't point them at the trio. It was the only reason Boomer and Jake didn't open fire.

"Give us girl and you can valk avay."

*What the fuck?* From the accent, it was obvious the Russians had found Kat, but how the hell had they known where she was? Jake would have spotted anyone casing the bank, so the info had to have come from someone inside. Brad, maybe? It really didn't matter how they'd been found, the point being it was four guns against two, with one unarmed woman. And since the guns weren't blazing, Boomer knew they wanted Kat alive . . . for now.

He eyed the man who'd spoken. The cocky bastard was the smallest of the group, but that wasn't saying much since he was about six-three and built like a brick wall.

"Not going to happen. Why don't you take me instead?" Boomer heard Kat's surprised gasp behind him but ignored her. His mind was too busy assessing the threat and trying to figure out how to eliminate it without getting Kat, Jake, or himself killed in the process. Both of their motel room doors were now closed and locked, and even if they weren't, the three of them would've been trapped inside with a small window as their only hope for escape. Their rooms had been at the far end of the motel, so around the side of the building was their closest large cover. An unoccupied minivan parked next to their rental would also provide an obstacle to hide behind. They had to avoid a public shootout unless it was absolutely necessary. Boomer didn't want to risk a hail of bullets flying around the motel possibly hitting an innocent bystander, although at the moment, they were the only seven people in sight. He reached back and grabbed Kat's arm, never taking his eyes off the foursome. They would only get one shot at this, and he needed to be ready.

The lead Russian narrowed his eyes at them. "Vhy don't I shoot you dead like dog, and take vhat I vant?"

It was time to bluff. "Because if you shoot me, you'll never get what you're looking for."

"Vhat you mean?"

Boomer took a small step to his left, keeping Kat behind him and the rental car between the threat and them. He was confident Jake knew his intentions and would be right behind them. But first, he needed to get the focus off Kat. "It means, Ivan left a series of clues, and I'm the only one who knows what he was talking about. I'm the only one who knows how to find the treasure."

At the mention of "treasure," recognition gleamed in the Russian's face. *Bingo!* If they thought Kat was of no use to them, it would be easier to protect her.

"Then you and girl come vith us and ve let friend live."

*Shit!* Boomer opened his mouth to respond, but sirens sounded nearby and the Russians' attention flashed to the parking lot entrance. The cops might be on their way, however, they were still too far to help. But it was the break Boomer had been waiting for. Without a moment's hesitation, he took off to his left, pushing Kat in front of him, knowing Jake had his six. Shouts, followed by gunfire, filled the air. He blocked Kat's body from the threat of flying bullets as best he could as they rounded the building at full speed.

As they cleared the corner, Jake was on their heels and returning fire. "Fuck! Goddamn it!"

Boomer didn't slow, but checked over his shoulder. The sirens were getting closer and the gunfire came to an abrupt halt. Shouts in Russian reached his ears, but he had no idea what was being said. "What?"

"Nothing, keep going!"

Skirting the back of the motel, Kat stumbled. If Boomer's hand hadn't been around her arm, she would've face-planted. A screech of tires came from the front of the building as he plastered her between his body and the rear wall. Jake stopped next to them, breathing heavily, and peered around the corner. "Sounds like they're taking off. I think we're good."

There was something in the other man's voice which caught Boomer's attention. When he glanced over, what he saw had his heart rate surging again. Blood was pouring from a wound on the left side of Jake's pale face. "What the fuck!"

He watched in horror as Jake slid to the ground and Kat's scream pierced the air.

# CHAPTER 10

*B*oomer stepped outside the emergency room with Kat and scanned the area for any danger. Keeping her hidden in an alcove, he pulled out his phone and called Ian. When his boss picked up, he gave him the rundown of what had happened.

"So, Reverend's going to be okay?"

A car drove by, and Boomer eyed it before answering. "Yeah. A bullet hit the wall as he was coming around the corner, and it kicked out a nice-sized chunk of brick. Struck him near the eye and scratched the cornea, but the doc says it's not as bad as it looks. He's got some stitches for a laceration right above the eye. The fucker bled like a bitch and scared the crap out of us. He needs an eye patch and some eyedrops for a week or so. Then he's got to follow up with an ophthalmologist. They had to give him something for pain. The fact that he took it, tells you he's hurting."

Ian snorted, clearly relieved the injury wasn't worse. "Yup. The fucker even hates taking Tylenol. So, what's the plan from here?"

"I'm going to call CC, have him come pick up Jake when he's released and fly him home. We told the cops it was an attempted carjacking. Whether they believed us or not is another story. One of the detectives is an old friend of my dad's, so I think he gave us some leeway. It also helps the only witness was the motel clerk who hid behind his desk while calling 9-1-1. I'm just glad we still have carry permits in Virginia, otherwise we'd still be in interrogation." His eyes met Kat's. "We're heading to Murfreesboro in North Carolina. It's about an hour or so from here, and Kat's aunt lives there. We're hoping she can tell us about the photo from the safety deposit box."

"All right. But watch your six. When CC lands with Jake, I'll send Dev and Marco up to meet you. Depending on how much sleep CC's had, they may not be there before tomorrow morning. I want you to check in every two hours until your backup gets there. And I've activated your tracker so don't lose your phone."

"Anything else, Mom?"

"Cut the sarcasm, frog. I don't like knowing these guys are gunning for Kat, and you're in their way. From what you told me, they want her alive, which means you and anyone else can end up as collateral damage. Watch your ass and call me the second you see trouble. Worse comes to worse, I'll call Little Creek and send some of Team Four to help you. They're training stateside at the moment."

"Yeah, I doubt Uncle Sam would like that, Boss-man, but I hear you. I'll be careful and keep you posted."

"Every two hours or I start calling people."

Before Boomer could respond, his boss disconnected the call. Beside him, Kat was still pale, but at least she'd stopped shaking. She'd been great at the scene, administering first aid to Jake while Boomer had made sure their assailants had indeed taken off moments before the cops arrived. It wasn't until after the EMTs took over that the shock of being shot at had finally hit her. Now, he pulled her in for a hug. "You okay?"

In his arms, she began to shake again. "I'm so sorry, this is all my fault. Jake or you could've been killed. What if he loses his sight in that eye?"

He hugged her tighter and ran his hands over her back. "Shhh. Calm down. None of this is your fault. And you heard the doc, Jake is going to be fine. Please, for a Navy SEAL, this is the equivalent of a hangnail."

Kat huffed. "How can you joke about this?"

Pulling back so she could see him, he cupped her chin. "It's one thing you learn in the military, Kitten. Joking is a way of dealing with things. The alternative is going nuts. And I'm serious. Jake and

I have been in far worse situations than today. I was only freaking about you being in the middle of it all. If something happened to you, I don't know what I would've done. I just got you back, and I'll be damned if I lose you again."

He dipped his head, and her breath hitched a split second before he claimed her mouth. This wasn't the time or place for a make-out session, but he needed to give her something else to think about. And since he was constantly thinking about the two of them having sex, why should he be the only one? He kissed her hard and fast, plunging his tongue into her mouth and taking a quick taste of her. When he ended the brief kiss, he was pleased to see she was flushed, glassy-eyed, and out of breath. Soon. He had to make her his soon. But first he had to keep her safe and find out what the fuck was going on.

"Come on, let me fill Jake in, and then we're getting on the road. I want to put as much distance as I can between us and the bad guys."

It was now after four p.m. Between the police interviews and waiting for an eye specialist, the rest of the morning and afternoon flew by. With rush-hour traffic, it would be closer to six by the time they hit Murfreesboro, if not later.

———

As it turned out, with an unplanned stop and the traffic worse than they expected, it was twenty-five after seven when they pulled into Irina Maier's empty driveway. They both climbed out of the car, and Boomer looked around. He'd been confident they hadn't been followed.

Before they left Jake, he'd told them to go back to the car rental place and switch cars, just in case one of the goons had tagged it. Boomer could've kicked himself for not thinking of it first. They'd even gone one better and returned the car to one rental place before walking across the street to get a new car from another one. And this time, he used an alias credit card and ID, which he was pissed he hadn't done with the first rental. They hadn't thought the Russians would know they were in Virginia less than twenty-four hours after they'd arrived. It was too late to change things now, so he had to pray the goons hadn't memorized their license plate and traced it.

After driving a mile down the road, he'd pulled over and disabled the GPS tracker most agencies used nowadays to track their vehicles. Once he was sure they didn't have a tail, he'd gotten on the freeway heading south-west. While sitting in traffic, they'd taken advantage of a truck stop and grabbed dinner to go. It wasn't great, but had been some much needed nourishment since they'd missed lunch.

Ivan Maier's childhood home was a one-story ranch on approximately two acres of land. Trees dotted the property, and it was obvious Irina Maier liked to garden, or at least hired someone to do it. Fall flowers were in bloom, and their beds were strategically placed around the property so wherever one looked, there was an array of color—pinks, reds, yellows, and blues. The brick home was well taken care of and it looked as if the white shutters had recently received a fresh coat of paint.

Taking Kat's hand, Boomer approached the front door and rang the bell. He could hear the chime go off, but there was no other sound from within. Knocking was met with the same result. Peering in the front window, he saw nothing amiss, but just to make sure, they circled the house.

"Maybe she's out to dinner with friends."

Boomer hoped Kat was right and there wasn't a more nefarious reason for her aunt not being home. They had no idea if Volkov's people would come here looking for answers to whatever questions they had for Kat. "Come on. Let's go find a room for the night. We can come back in a little while and see if she's home."

She sighed. "Okay. I guess we don't have a choice."

He opened the passenger door for her and closed it after she swung her legs inside. Skirting the hood, he glanced toward the end of the driveway and noticed a man in his late sixties getting mail at a row of boxes. Holding up a finger to Kat for her to wait a minute, he jogged down the drive. "Excuse me? Sir?"

The man was eyeing him suspiciously, so he stopped several feet away and lifted his palms to indicate he was no threat. "I'm sorry, sir. My girlfriend is a . . . a distant relative of Ms. Maier. We were passing through and thought we'd stop in and say hi. You don't happen to know where she might be, do you?" He didn't know what Irina's neighbors knew about her brother's family, so he didn't want to mention Kat was her niece.

The man's eyes shifted to beyond Boomer, so he glanced back and saw Kat was out of the car and walking toward them.

"Damn!"

Boomer's head whipped around again to face the old man. "What's wrong?"

The neighbor seemed to realize he'd alarmed him. "Oh, nothing to worry about, boy. Any thoughts I had about you snowballing me with your bullshit story went out the window when I saw your girlfriend there. She looks exactly like Irina . . . well, younger of course. What did you say your name was?"

"I didn't, sir, but it's Ben Michaelson. And this is Kate Zimmerman." Again, he didn't want to tip the man off about Kat's lineage. He held out his hand, and the man shook it.

"Name's Harry Bernhard. I live across the street. What branch of the military are you, son?"

Boomer's eyebrows raised in surprise. "Navy, Sir. Retired SEAL to be exact. How'd you know?"

"Retired from the Marines about twenty years ago. Major. Can always spot someone who has seen combat. It's the way they carry themselves. Iraq? No, don't answer. Sometimes I forget you black-ops boys can't answer that question."

Boomer's mouth ticked upwards. "No, sir, I can't. Let's just say I've been around the block a few times."

"I hear you. Now, about Irina. She expecting you?"

From his side, Kat answered before Boomer had a chance. "No, she's not. As a matter of fact, she's going to be very surprised to see me. I—I haven't seen her in a very long time." Boomer gave her a subtle look. Realizing she'd said too much, she tried to cover her ass.

"I've been living on the West coast for over ten years and just moved back East. I was hoping to surprise her."

"Well, I hope you're not in a hurry, because she and a few members of her women's group took an overnight road trip to Roanoke Rapids. They go every other month to see a show and play some slot machines at the Royal Palace out there." At Kat's look of dismay, Harry added, "Don't fret, missy. She'll be back tomorrow by noon."

Smiling, Boomer put his arm around Kat's shoulders and squeezed. She got the picture and put on a happy face while he spoke. "That'd be fine, sir. We just got into town and came straight here, so can you recommend a motel nearby?"

Harry scratched his head. "Well, you're a little out of luck there because Murfreesboro doesn't have any motels. Nearest one is about twenty miles away in Franklin. But we do have a nice bed and breakfast in town. Always clean and not too expensive. And it's right across the street from a good place to eat."

"That'd be great. What's the name of the B&B?"

"Carmichael's. Drive straight back into town, and it's on your left after the first traffic light. Can't miss it."

Extending his hand again, Boomer thanked the man. "And I'd appreciate it, sir, if you see Irina before we do, please don't spoil the surprise."

"No problem, son. And call me Harry. I might see you both tomorrow anyway. Irina always brings me back a blueberry pie from this great bakery they have out there. Good night, now."

"Good night."

As they made their way back to the car, Boomer peeked over his shoulder and caught the old man doing the same. He might be friendly toward them, but he was protective of Irina and it showed. "I think your aunt has a boyfriend."

"Huh? What are you talking about?"

He jerked his thumb toward the end of the drive. "Harry. I wouldn't be surprised if he's got a thing for her."

Kat glanced over her shoulder at the older man before climbing into the car. "Really? Well, good for them. She's a sweet woman and I always wondered why she never married."

After shutting her door again, Boomer rounded the car and got into the driver's seat. "Maybe she never met the right guy until now."

"Maybe."

---

KAT WAS quiet as Benny drove back into town. Now that the stress from this morning was leaving her body, her mind was filled with everything that had happened in the past twenty-four hours. Unfortunately, one irrelevant thing kept popping up. It was what she'd found on the bathroom floor this morning. The pink piece of paper from a memo pad must've fallen out of Benny's pocket by accident. She knew it was his because it said "Ben" in his secretary's neat handwriting. Apparently, Kat wasn't the only one who didn't use his nickname. The message scrawled on the paper was what was bothering her as she replayed the words in her mind.

> ***Tanya would like to play with you at club tonight. Please call. 813-555-9438.***

Kat had never asked him if he had a girlfriend, and she hadn't heard anyone mention one, but it didn't mean he wasn't dating. And what did Tanya mean by "play with you"? Play what? Darts? Pool? And what club? Night club? Country club? There were too many variables, but her mind kept flashing to the book she was currently reading—*Leather & Lace*. It was a romance novel, but the sex was not "vanilla," which was a term used by book websites when the sex in the story was tame. By comparison, Leather & Lace was what they called erotica, and the sex involved BDSM—Bondage, Discipline, Sadism, and Masochism. Kat loved to read, and while she didn't fully understand "the lifestyle" as it was called, the fictional books about the subject were fun. And hot. Holy shit, were they hot. Her vibrator tended to go through quite a few batteries when she was reading one of those novels.

It was the word "play" which was bugging her. It was used a lot in BDSM books and those stories were usually set in clubs. Sex clubs. Didn't the woman they'd met at the pharmacy yesterday mention a club? Could Benny be into something like that? And how did she feel about it? Kat didn't know what to feel or think at this point. And she was too embarrassed to ask him about it. What if she was wrong? Oh God, what if she was right?

"Kat."

She jumped at the sound of his deep sexy voice. "Wh-What?"

Pointing at the large house they were parked next to, he said, "We're here. You okay?"

"Um, yeah. Sorry." She blushed. "My mind was elsewhere."

"Yeah, it's been a long day. Come on. Let's get a room and climb into bed."

*Oh boy.*

# CHAPTER 11

*W*hile Benny was in the bathroom, Kat stood in their bedroom and stared at the king-sized bed. Due to some local couple getting married over the weekend, there was only one room available at the B&B. It was a large room with a sitting area as well, and Benny had offered to sleep on the couch. But by the look in his eye when he said it, Kat knew the couch was not where he wanted to be. He wanted to be in the big bed . . . with her. Together. Naked. And if she was honest with herself, she wanted all that and more.

She thought back to the kiss they'd shared in the motel before Jake had interrupted them. Kat hadn't known which end was up, or whether she had been coming or going. All she knew was, she'd been lost and didn't want to be found. Lost in Ben's arms was where she always wanted to be, and, Lord help her, she wanted more. She'd longed to rip off his shirt and explore the hard chest her breasts had been crushed against. His cock had been stiff against her abdomen, and she'd wanted to climb his body and wrap her legs around her hips, so he'd have been lined up with her pussy.

Recalling the delicious moment had her wet with desire. She might be inexperienced, but there were things the human body knew instinctively. And her body wanted to mate. Here. Now. With the one man she'd been waiting for all these years.

The toilet flushed, and she jumped. Hurrying, she pulled the covers back and climbed into the bed. She'd only brought one of her duffel bags with them, so she was wearing the T-shirt and shorts she'd worn to bed last night. They weren't exactly sexy, but hopefully she wouldn't be wearing them long. Losing her virginity while people were trying to kidnap her was not the way she wanted it to happen. But she did want it to happen with this man. The man she'd been waiting for since she was seventeen.

Taking a deep breath, Kat pulled back the covers on the other side of the bed in a blatant invitation for Benny to join her. And waited. God, she was so nervous. What if he turned her down? What if she did something wrong? He would know instantly she wasn't experienced, wouldn't he? Would it turn him off?

The bathroom door swung open, and Kat's eyes flashed to Benny's as he walked into the room. She knew the moment the pulled back covers registered in his brain because he froze and raised his eyebrow at her. She gushed, "There's no, uh . . . no reason for you to sleep on the couch . . . I mean, we're adults, right? And, I . . ."

Her words trailed off, and Benny smiled at her nervousness. She was sitting on the side of the bed closest to him, and he stalked over then sat down beside her, crowding her a little. Her heart began to pound in her chest as her eyes dropped from his intense stare. "If I share this bed with you, Kitten, sleep will be the last thing on my mind. I want you. I want to be on top of you, under you, behind you, and *in* you. If it's not what you want, too, then say the word and I'll sleep on the couch." He glanced over at the offensive piece of furniture. "No matter how much it pains me to do so."

Wetness coated Kat's panties, and she was close to coming from his sexy voice alone. Her hands twisted together in her lap. "I want . . . I want you to sleep with me . . . I mean, not sleep-sleep, but . . ."

---

BOOMER CHUCKLED and covered her trembling lips with his fingers. "I know what you meant, Kitten. Damn, you're beautiful when you blush. Just like back in high school." He moved his hand to cup her cheek, yet continued to brush her lips with his thumb. He'd thought she'd be too tired and stressed for intimacy tonight, but sex was a great stress reliever. His dick had hardened when he saw all the signs of her arousal—rapid pulse, increased breathing, swallowing hard, and nipples pebbling under her thin shirt. When her eyes had dropped to her lap, the natural reaction of a submissive excited him.

Fuck, her plump bottom lip was made for him to nibble on. He couldn't wait any longer and leaned forward, replacing his thumb with his lips, teeth, and tongue. Groaning at the taste of her, he plunged his hand into her hair and held her in place while his mouth and tongue did wicked things to hers. His other hand found her breast and massaged the lush flesh.

When her hands went around his neck, he pulled away, and she whimpered at the loss of contact. "Wh-what's wrong? Did I do something wrong?"

A rumble came from his chest. "Are you kidding? No, you didn't do anything wrong. It's just . . ." He sighed heavily. There were things he had to tell her. "Kitten, when it comes to sex, I've changed, and I'm not sure what your response is going to be." His cock was yelling at him to shut the fuck up and get on with it, but his brain and heart were telling him this was important. He couldn't go any further without telling her about his wants and needs. Her submitting to him was something he craved, and he didn't think he could live without it.

"What is it?"

The wariness in her voice was killing him. "When I'm with a woman . . . in bed . . . I need to be in charge . . . of everything. I like to . . . shit, this is the first time I've ever been nervous about telling a woman this. I'm a Dominant, Kat. Do you know what that means?"

Her eyes widened in surprise, but for some reason she didn't seem as shocked as he'd expected her to be. "Um, it means you're into . . . um . . . tying women up and spanking and stuff. The opposite of 'vanilla' sex, right?"

He wasn't sure why he was stunned with her answer. After all, she'd been reading Kristen's book about BDSM. "Yeah. That's part of it, but it's so much more. It's about a power exchange. While a Dom may seem to be in charge of the scene, it's the submissive who has all the power."

Kat's eyes narrowed in confusion. "I don't understand. I mean, I've read books on the subject, but it's hard to separate fact from fiction sometimes."

"Yeah, well, a lot of books out there give false impressions of the lifestyle. You see, when a Dom and sub are scening, or playing as it's also referred to, then a sub sets all the limits and boundaries. There are lists we use at the club and they cover every form of play—what a sub enjoys, wants to try, or absolutely will not do under any circumstances. A good Dom will honor that list. He'll push the sub's limits, but if the sub says her safeword, all play stops. So, you see? A sub has all the power."

She was biting her bottom lip again, and he used his thumb to rescue the abused piece of flesh. "What are you thinking about, Kitten?"

"I guess I don't understand what people get out of it. I mean, if a sub has all the power, like you said, then what does a Dom get out of it?"

Getting uncomfortable in his current position, Boomer stood and circled the bed. He lay on his side facing her and propped his head up with his hand then rested his other hand atop hers over her abdomen. His thumb rubbed her wrist in small, sensual motions as little goose bumps appeared on her skin. "A Dom gets satisfaction in knowing he has his submissive's trust that he'll take care of her. Her submissiveness is his greatest pleasure, and in return, his greatest desire is to give *her* pleasure beyond her wildest dreams. Her mind, body, and orgasms belong to him, and he treats each as if they are the most precious gift in the world, because they are."

Kat's pulse sped up again as he spoke. He could see she was struggling with something, but waited it out. He couldn't rush this—it was too important.

"Can I ask you something?"

From her tone, he wasn't sure it was something he wanted to hear. "Of course, baby. You can ask me anything you want."

"You . . . um . . . you dropped a note in the bathroom this morning. From Tanya."

*Shit.* He didn't even realize his secretary's call-back note was missing. He'd forgotten all about it. "And you want to know about her and the club." She nodded, and he sighed. "Yes, I belong to a private club. Ian and Devon own The Covenant, and it's in the first building at the Trident compound, but you'd never know it from the outside. Tanya is a friend, nothing more. We've played in the past, but there is nothing between us relationship-wise. I don't have a girlfriend, if you're worried about that. I would never cheat on a woman I was in a relationship with."

"I didn't think you would."

He interlocked their fingers and squeezed. "Well, honesty is a big part of my lifestyle, so I just wanted it on the record. And the lifestyle is a big part of my life." He took a deep breath and forged ahead. "I want you to be part of my life too. We can start off slow. I'm not going to handcuff you and do wicked things to you . . . well, at least not yet. But I'd like to introduce you to my lifestyle and show you how good things can be between us. Can you give me . . . us a chance?"

Her hesitation was killing him. He prayed her answer wasn't no. Holding his tongue, he noticed Kat shift nervously. "There's, um . . . something I need to tell you. Something important."

Oh, God help him. This was over before it'd begun. His wariness crept into his voice. "Okay. You can tell me anything, Kitten. Whatever it is, we'll deal with it."

"I, um . . . I mean, I've never . . . shit, this was easier in my head . . . I've never had sex before." The last five words came out in a rush, and she stared at their twined hands, not daring to look at him.

Boomer froze. *Huh? What the fuck!* Was Kat saying she was still a virgin? She was twenty-nine years old! How the fuck had she made it to twenty-nine and never had . . . never done . . . *holy shit!*

Clearing his throat, he tried to remain calm and not freak her out. "Uh, wow, um . . . damn, didn't see that coming. How . . . I mean, why . . . shit, help me out here, Kat. I'm not mad or disappointed . . . just shocked you never . . . that you're still a virgin." *Yeah, well, that all could've been said a lot better.* He reached up and touched her chin, turning her head so she was looking at him.

She was embarrassed, that was evident. But she had nothing to be embarrassed about. In fact, he was thrilled no other man had ever taken her. "Don't be embarrassed. Talk to me, baby. You said earlier you wanted to have sex with me. If you want to do this, we need some communication here. I need to know things in order to make it good for you. The first time can be uncomfortable if I don't do things right."

"If you're talking about breaking my . . . you know . . . I did it years ago with . . ."

His eyes narrowed, and he growled. "With who? You just said you were a virgin."

"I am! But just because I've never been with a man, doesn't mean I didn't have urges and needs. So, I took care of it myself, with—"

"A vibrator," he finished for her.

Kat nodded, her cheeks getting redder by the second.

"Damn, that's hot. The thought of you . . . shit!" Boomer hadn't thought he could get any harder than he already was, but the images bombarding his brain were sending his hormones into overdrive. He was wishing he'd changed into a pair of sweatpants because he was going to have zipper marks on his cock from his jeans. He needed to keep his inner beast in check or he'd scare the shit out of her. "I have to ask, baby, why haven't you ever had sex before? Don't tell me there was never an opportunity. You're gorgeous and must be beating them off with a baseball bat. I know you were in hiding and all, but after starting a new life in Portland, there had to have been guys who tried to get you into their beds. Otherwise, it doesn't say much for the male population in Oregon."

She snorted. "Please, I know I'm not ugly, but I'm far from gorgeous. I'm a plain-Jane, nothing special."

Was she kidding him? Growling again, Boomer snatched her hip and tugged until she was on her side, then sent a stinging slap to her left butt cheek.

"Ow! What was that for?" Her eyes were wide with shock . . . and something else . . . arousal.

"Rule number one of my world, Kitten, is you never . . . *ever* . . .

put yourself down. It's one of the fastest ways for you to earn a punishment. There is no way you're a 'plain-Jane.' I still remember the night of my party, and I told you how beautiful you were to me. But it doesn't even come close to how beautiful you are today. You're the woman who walks into a room and men instantly want you in their beds. But then you speak, and they want to fall down on their knees and worship you. You're sexy as sin, both inside and out, and I want to prove it to you. But you still haven't answered my question. Why haven't you had sex before now?" He knew it was ridiculous to hope she'd been waiting for him. Waiting for a time when she could be with him again. But that's what he was dying to hear from her lips.

"I don't know. I mean, I dated a few guys, but it never felt right. It felt like something was missing. And now, I think I know what it was."

Boomer held his breath.

"It was you, Benny. None of those other guys were you. My heart and my body always knew they wanted you and no one else."

His heart felt like it was going to burst from his ribcage. Hauling her against his hard chest, he grasped her hair. "Jesus, that's the sexiest thing I've ever heard."

Rolling on his back, he pulled her with him and claimed her mouth again. Tasting . . . savoring . . . marking her as his. His other hand slid down her back until it reached her ass, and he gripped her cheek. A thought popped into his frazzled brain and he tugged on her hair to break their lip-lock. Breathless, he said, "Kitten, I need you to tell me this is what you want. I'll make it good for you, I promise. We'll keep things 'vanilla' for now, but I'm going to give you a safeword anyway. If I do anything that scares or hurts you, say the word 'red.' I'll stop immediately, and we'll talk about what's wrong, okay?"

Kat tried to nod, but his hand was still holding her hair. "Yes. This is what I want. And if anything doesn't feel right, I'll say 'red.'"

"It's important, baby. I'm not a mind-reader. You have to tell me if you don't like something or it hurts. Don't let me keep doing something because you think it's what I want. The only thing I want is to give you pleasure, and a hell of a lot of orgasms." Her eyes widened. "Oh, yes, Kitten. I'm going to give you plenty of those. Now sit up for a second and take your shirt off."

He really wanted to rip it off her, along with her shorts, but he had to take baby steps for her first time. And a few harmless orders would get her used to him issuing them. As he watched her intently, Kat pushed off his chest and knelt next to him. Blushing, she reached for the hem of her T-shirt and lowered her eyes.

"Uh-uh, Kitten. Eyes on mine. You'll be able to see how beautiful I think you are."

---

KAT LIFTED her eyes at the same time she lifted her shirt. Her vision was blocked for a moment while she pulled it over her head, but when her gaze met his again she saw heat. Desire swirled in the amber irises and made her think of molten lava. She felt a rush of juices between her legs and bit her lip.

"You're going to leave teeth marks in your bottom lip, and I'd prefer any marks to be made by me." His gaze swept her body as she blushed. "You're gorgeous, Kitten, and don't even think of correcting me. I love what I see, but I want more. I want to watch you play with your tits like you do when you're alone and no one is watching."

"Holy shit!" Kat clasped her hand over her mouth, mortified the words had escaped her. "I mean . . . you want me to do that in front of you? It's embarrassing."

Boomer chuckled. "Oh, this is going to be so much fun. Your innocence is the biggest fucking turn-on I've ever had. And there's nothing to be embarrassed about, sweetheart. Things are going to get a lot more intimate than this. I'm not asking you to do anything billions of women haven't done for thousands of years." He sat up and pulled his own T-shirt over his head. "But I'll tell you what . . ." To her amazement, he grasped the garment in two hands, ripping off a long strip of the fabric. "Let's make this more about feeling, instead of seeing."

Kneeling in front of her, he put the strip over her eyes and tied it behind her head. When it was secure, she felt him lay back down. "Okay, let's try this again. Lift your hands up and cover your tits, Kitten." Her hands moved slowly, unsure, but she followed his commands. "Mmm, good girl. Now squeeze and massage them. Push them up and in . . . damn, that's hot."

Kat couldn't believe she was doing this. But Benny's voice was low and commanding, and she couldn't help but want to do his bidding. As she followed his orders, she felt herself relaxing into the moment. She pushed down her embarrassment and nervousness, and let his voice rumble through her veins.

"Take your thumbs and index fingers and pinch your nipples for me, baby. Roll them and pull them."

She felt the bed shift again, but couldn't see what he was doing, and the unknown made her shudder in anticipation. Playing with her nipples, she moaned at the sensations which raced through them and straight to her pussy. Her thighs clenched involuntarily as her clit throbbed with need.

"Cup your breasts again, Kitten. Up and in."

She brought her hands down a little then lifted. The bed dipped once more, and she cried out as his mouth closed around one nipple. Her clit went into overdrive as he sucked, licked and—*holy crap*—nibbled on the taut peak.

"Oh, oh, Benny! Oh my God!"

He didn't say a word. Instead, he switched to the other nipple and gave it the same attention. Her thighs began to quiver, and just when she thought they'd give out on her, he wrapped his arms around her and eased her down to the mattress. His mouth never left her breasts as he continued to ravage them. Every hum, slurp, and pop seemed to echo throughout the room. Part of her wanted to watch him, but another part wanted the suspense of not knowing what he would do next. She could feel he was straddling her hips, and the bed shifted back and forth as he moved downward. Soft kisses rained on her ribs and abdomen until he reached the top of her shorts. Grasping the sides, he slid them down and kissed every newly-exposed inch of skin.

Kat gasped as his tongue licked the crease between her hip and thigh, and more moisture seeped from her core. Before she knew it, she was completely naked and wondering what he was thinking as he stared down at her. She wasn't sure how she knew what he was doing, but she could sense it. His hands slid up and down her outer thighs, from her hips to her knees, and she wished he would do the same to the inside.

"I've dreamed about this since my senior prom, Kitten. Even when I thought you were gone, you invaded my dreams. For the longest time, I prayed it'd all been a nightmare that never happened, but then I'd wake up and . . . I'd grieve again. And the worst part was, while I grieved for the loss of my best friend, I grieved more for the loss of the woman I loved. I've never loved another woman and never will. To have you in my arms and in my bed is a miracle I'll never take for granted."

During his speech, he'd kissed his way back up her body until he claimed her mouth once more. Her heart filled with love for this man, and she wrapped her arms around him. She was drowning in his passion and moaned when his bare hips came in contact with hers. His hard erection pressed into her lower abdomen, and she had a fleeting thought—when had he removed his jeans? Oh, who the fuck cares? She was just glad he did. As he nuzzled her neck, she panted, "I want . . . I want to see you."

"Hmm, you will, baby. But for now, I want you to use your other senses—feel, hear, smell, and . . ." He licked her lips. "Taste. Well, I'll be the one tasting for a little while. Spread your legs for me, Kitten. Wide."

The bed dipped back and forth until she felt him settle between her thighs. His hands spread her a little wider, and she had a sudden urge to beg him . . . for what she didn't know. She felt a puff of air a second before his tongue licked the length of her slit and her hips surged upwards. "Oh my God! Holy shit!"

GRINNING AT HER RESPONSE, Boomer licked her again, but this time he held her hips in place. He groaned as the flavor of her juices saturated his taste buds. It was the sweetest cream he'd ever tasted, and he lapped at her relentlessly. She was trimmed, not bare, but it was fine with him. All he cared about was he finally had her in his bed, and he was going to make this a night neither one of them would ever forget. He wanted to ruin her for any other man. His Kitten would know him, and only him. She squirmed, moaned, cried out, and begged as he took her higher and higher. Her hands clutched the sheets . . . his hair . . . her own hair . . . everything within reach, as if looking for a lifeline to hold on to. His thumb strummed her clit like a guitar string as he impaled her with his stiff tongue.

He replaced his thumb with his mouth, sucking on her little pearl. Two fingers plunged into her quivering pussy which was soaked for him. Damn, she was on fire for him, her heat scorching his fingers as he thrust them in and out of her tight channel. He shoved them all the way in and searched . . . she gasped . . . there it was, the spot he was looking for. As he rubbed it, her pleas became frantic. "Come for me, Kitten. Let go and come." He sucked her clit hard.

Kat threw her arm over her mouth to muffle her screams of release as she came in waves of ecstasy. But Boomer didn't stop, and as one orgasm ebbed, another built right behind it. As pleasure crashed over her again, he licked and stroked, prolonging it as long as he could. When she came down from the second one, he eased up. Pulling his fingers from her pussy, he gave her clit and slit a few last licks.

Sated, she lay there panting, her skin glowing with a sheen of perspiration. Reaching up, he removed her partially dislodged blindfold and waited for her eyes to meet his. When they did, he slowly licked the last of her juices from his fingers. Her eyes widened slightly, but they got as big as saucers when her gaze slid down his body to his rigid shaft standing impressively proud.

"It's all for you, Kitten. And don't worry, it'll fit."

Nodding, she reached out tentatively and his hips jerked forward when her fingertips brushed against him. Taking her hand, he wrapped it around his cock. "Tighter, baby." He showed her how to give him a hand-job, from root to tip. His head tipped back on his shoulders, his eyes closing as he groaned loudly. "That's it. Cup my balls, but be gentle. Not too hard with the family jewels."

He grinned when he heard her giggle. "Yeah, right like that. Roll them in your hand."

Her touch was the sweetest of tortures, but he wanted to give her the opportunity to explore a little. When the bed shifted, he opened his eyes just enough for him to see what she was doing. Kat was on her elbows and knees, and he realized what she was up to a second before her mouth closed around him. "Fuck!"

She recoiled, releasing him. "Sorry!"

Grabbing her hair, he guided her down again. "Don't be sorry, Kitten. It felt incredible, and I want you to do it again. Just watch the teeth and you'll do fine. Taste me, baby. Lick me."

He hissed when she did as she was told. Her mouth was pure sin. Hot, wet, and wild. She was shy at first, but started to get into it quick. Her tongue swirled around his shaft as her head bobbed up and down. Boomer held back the urge to thrust his hips forward until his cock hit the back of her throat. Soon, but not tonight. He had other plans for tonight and there was only one place his cock wanted to be right now . . . deep in her pussy.

Tightening the grip on her hair, he pulled her off him. "That felt amazing, but lay back down. Tonight isn't about me."

As she scurried into position, he reached across the bed and grabbed his wallet from the nightstand. Finding the condom he had in there, he swiftly opened it and rolled it onto his aching cock. Spreading her legs wide, he used two fingers to make sure she was still wet enough . . . well, that was an understatement, because she was drenched. She watched as he lined himself up with her entrance. "You're tight, baby, so I'll take this slow. It may feel a little uncomfortable until you stretch more, but it shouldn't hurt, okay?"

"Please, I want you. I know you'll make it good."

Her faith in him tugged at his heartstrings and humbled him. She was panting again, the anticipation showing in her gaze. He eased the tip in and her hips tilted for more. He slowly pumped in and out, using short strokes and going deeper each time. "Fuck, you're so tight. Am I hurting you?"

"N-no, more, ooohhhh, pppleassse mmmmmore. Oh God, it feels so good, so good. Benny, pleasssssse!"

His fingers found her clit and rubbed it in circles as her body greedily took him inside. When he was finally all the way in, her hips began to undulate. Her legs wrapped around his hips and her feet dug into his ass. He couldn't hold back anymore. Rising above her on his elbows, he started to fuck her faster and harder, urged on by her erotic cries for more. The feel of her tight walls around him was heaven. Dipping his head down, he sucked on one nipple and toyed with the other. She was getting close, and he fought to hold his own release back until she came again. Shifting to his knees, he grabbed her hip with one hand and pinched her clit with the other. As she began to fly off the cliff, he clutched both her hips hard, probably leaving fingerprints, but he'd worry about that later. All that mattered now was his need to come, to be one with her. His balls drew up tight, and after three or four more thrusts, he followed her into the deep chasm, grunting as he came inside her. Black spots appeared before his eyes, and he knew right then, he'd found his forever home.

Collapsing, he used his arms to keep most of his weight off her. His lungs heaving, he buried his face in the crook of her neck. "Are you okay, Kitten?"

"Better than okay."

He chuckled at her mumbled response. Groaning, he reached down to secure the condom and pulled out of her. He kissed her nose. "Don't move. I'll be right back."

"Mm-hmm."

Boomer hurried into the bathroom as fast as his shaking legs could carry him. He disposed of the condom and grabbed two washcloths, wetting them both. Walking back to the bed, he quickly swiped one over his deflated cock and balls then dropped it on the floor atop his torn shirt. When he placed the other warm cloth between her legs, Kat's eyes flew open and her thighs clenched together. Well, as much as they could with his hand and arm sandwiched between them.

"W-what are you doing?" Her startled words came out as a squeak.

"Taking care of you. Now, open up, so I can clean you."

"I can do it."

He grabbed the hand she was reaching down with and pinned it to the bed. Growling softly, he said, "It's my job to take care of you, baby. This is one of those things a Dom does, and it brings me pleasure. Now, open your legs for me."

---

SHYLY, Kat eased her legs wider and closed her eyes as Benny washed away the evidence of their lovemaking. None of the orgasms she'd ever given herself had been so intense, and she savored the last of the sensations coursing through her body. Part of her was embarrassed by what he was doing, but the other part felt . . . adored and . . . loved? He'd said earlier, he'd loved her . . . past tense. But how did he feel about her now? She opened her eyes until she could just see through the slits and watched him as he bathed her. When he was done, he dipped his head down and kissed her hip, making her smile.

He saw her amusement and shrugged. "Couldn't resist."

Standing, he tugged the covers out from underneath her and placed them on top of her. He then shut off the light and climbed in behind her. Spooning her, his arms held her tight. "Sleep, Kitten."

And she did.

# CHAPTER 12

$S$itting across from Kat in the little coffee shop, Boomer was happy to see her digging into her breakfast. She'd told him after their morning round of love-making that she was starving from burning off all those calories. If that was all it took to get her to eat and put some meat back on her thin bones, then who was he to complain?

He popped the last of his toast in his mouth, chewed, and washed it down with a sip of strong coffee. "You ready to see your aunt again?"

She swallowed a mouthful of French toast and syrup. "Yes, but I'm not as nervous as I was last night. I'm excited now. I only hope she doesn't faint."

Her eyes glistened, and he knew she was teasing him. Shit, he was never going to live that down. "Keep it up, Kitten, and next time I get you naked, I'll give you so many orgasms, *you'll* be the one fainting."

He chuckled at her blush. Damn, she was adorable. He eyed her plate and saw she was almost done, so he signaled the waitress for their check. Glancing up at the wall clock by the exit, he noted it was just after 11:30. They'd slept in since Harry had said Kat's aunt would be home around noon.

Boomer had checked in with Ian before breakfast and learned Jake was back at the compound, irritable, but resting. The Trident women—Kristen, Angie, and Jenn—were fussing over him and driving him bat-shit crazy. CC was flying Marco and Devon to an airport about thirty minutes from Murfreesboro, and they would rendezvous with them around thirteen-hundred hours. Hopefully, by then, they would know where they were headed next.

Tossing enough money on the table to cover the check and tip, he stood and helped her out of the booth. He didn't let go of her hand, but instead, linked their fingers together, smiling to himself on how right it felt. This morning while he'd been lying in bed watching her sleep, he realized he was in love with her. Some might call him insane, since she'd only walked back into his life less than three days ago, but the truth was, he'd never stopped loving her. And now they had a chance at the future they'd been denied so long ago.

He held the car door open for her, scanning the little town for any threats, but nothing seemed out of the ordinary. Yeah, there were a few people eyeing them, but this was a town where everyone knew everyone, and the two of them were strangers. He smiled and said hello to an older couple on his way around to the driver's side, then climbed in and started the engine. There wasn't much else to do but hope Irina and friends had made it back early, so he did a U-turn and steered the car toward her house.

Glancing at Kat, he noticed she was getting nervous again and squeezed her hand. "Everything will be fine, Kitten."

"Oh, I know everything will be okay with my aunt, but I'm scared she won't know anything that will help us find out why those men are after me."

"If she doesn't, then we'll find some other way to figure it out. Brody is still hitting the computer, trying to find what we're missing. Maybe by the time Marco and Dev get here we'll have some more info."

Pulling into the driveway, they saw a tan Toyota Camry, and Boomer sighed in relief. He knew, despite what she'd said at breakfast, Kat was stressing over the first few minutes of this upcoming reunion, and he was grateful she didn't have to wait any longer. Parking the car behind the other vehicle, he got out and walked around to her door. As he helped her out, the front door to the house opened, and Boomer wasn't too surprised to see Harry walk out.

The older man met them halfway. "I kept my word and haven't said anything to her, but I thought it'd be best for me to be here. It's not every day a woman's niece comes back from the dead."

His words startled them, but Boomer was the first to recover. "How'd you know?"

Harry grinned. "I ain't stupid, son. I've known what happened to Irina's brother and family for years, or at least I thought I did. Their pictures are all over the place in there. It wasn't hard to put two and two together. Although, I'm sure I'm missing a few pieces of the puzzle, along with Irina. So, how do you want to do this? She's in the kitchen making coffee and heating up my pie."

Boomer looked at Kat, who shrugged, then back at Harry. "You know her better than we do at this point, so I'm willing to follow your lead."

The other man nodded. "Okay. Why don't you wait out here then, and give me a few minutes?"

The couple agreed and watched as Harry disappeared back into the house. It was four, maybe five minutes before the door flew open, and a shorter, older version of Kat came barreling out to the front yard. She gasped and cried out but never slowed down, running straight to her niece with open arms. Tears fell from both women as they embraced. Irina kept pulling back, staring at Kat, and then hugging her fiercely again. "Katerina, Katerina! Oh, my Lord! I don't understand, but I've never been so happy in my life. My Katerina is back!"

Boomer joined Harry on the front steps and gave the two women a few minutes alone.

"I take it this is going to be a long story, isn't it, son?"

"Yes, sir."

Harry raised an eyebrow at him. "If you'd like, I can come back later. I just wanted to make sure Irina didn't need me."

He thought about it a moment and decided Harry might come in handy. Once they left, they'd need someone to keep an eye on Irina just in case anyone came here looking for them. He'd also call

Ian and see if Trident had some contacts they could use to protect the older woman. Kat would be devastated if anything happened to her aunt. "If it's all right with you, sir, I think it would be better if you heard everything."

Harry tilted his head in acknowledgement and continued to watch the tearful reunion.

Twenty minutes later the four of them were sitting around Irina's dining room table, sipping coffee. The pie in front of each of them went untouched, except for Harry's. While listening to Kat tell the older couple what had happened twelve years ago all the way to the present, Boomer regarded the quaint little home. There were pictures of Katerina, Alex, and their parents strategically placed throughout the rooms, and it was obvious how much Irina had loved and missed her family. Sadness filled his chest as he spotted the picture from Alex and Boomer's graduation ceremony. He remembered the photo of the Maier family well, because he'd been the one to take it with Kat's camera at her request. The four of them looked so happy, their futures bright with promise. But all the happiness had been destroyed by greed and evil. He shook his head to clear the anger which was building up inside him, and came back to the present.

Kat's story was interrupted by the occasional "oh, dear" and "you poor child" from Irina. She hadn't let go of her niece's hand since they'd come into the house, and Boomer knew the feeling of needing to be connected to the long-lost woman.

When Kat took a breath after telling them how she ended up at Trident, Boomer took over. "We're doing everything we can to keep Kat safe, Irina, but we need your help. Ivan gave her a key to a safety deposit box in Norfolk. There was only a photograph inside it, and we were hoping you could tell us where it was taken."

As Kat took the picture out of her purse and handed it to Irina, Boomer gave the retired Major a military hand signal to indicate more had happened in Norfolk and he'd fill the man in later. Kat had agreed with him when he'd suggested they not tell her aunt about the attempted kidnapping the day before. It would only worry her.

"Oh my, this brings back memories. This is your dad when he was about five or six years old. So, I was about seven then. That's my mother's prized rose bush at the corner of the house. It was beautiful. This is the house we lived in first, before we moved to Durham. We moved to Murfreesboro when I was twelve, almost thirteen. That's when Daddy took over the pharmacy here. Before then, he worked for other pharmacists."

Normally, Boomer wouldn't have minded the woman reminiscing the past, but she'd skipped over some important information. "Irina, do you remember the name of the town the first house was in, the one in the picture?"

"Oh, of course. That's what you needed to know, wasn't it? This was our house in Mint Hill, about a half hour east of Charlotte."

Boomer nodded. "I've heard of it. My bosses grew up in Charlotte and their folks still live there. You wouldn't happen to remember the address in Mint Hill, would you?"

"Of course, dear. It was 58 Sycamore Road, but it's not there anymore."

Everyone stared at the woman in confusion as Kat asked, "What do you mean, Aunt Irina?"

"Didn't your father ever tell you? Well, obviously, he didn't. Our home in Mint Hill burned down, there's nothing left."

"What? How come I never heard of this?" While Kat was shocked, Boomer held back a groan. He'd thought for sure it's where they had to go next, but now he wasn't so certain.

Irina patted Kat's hand. "It was no secret, Katerina. I guess you just don't remember ever hearing the story. The house was struck by lightning one night and went up in flames. Luckily, we all got out unharmed, but the house was a total loss. The only things left were a pile of rubble and the chimney. That's when my father took a job at a pharmacy in Durham. The pay was better there and my grandmother had just passed away, so we were able to stay in her house for a while."

Irina stood, went to the bookshelf, and retrieved an old photo album which looked like it was from the 1970s. She brought it back to the table and handed it to Kat. "This has all our pictures from back then. The only reason we still have them is because my mother had brought them to her sister's house one day and accidentally left them there."

Kat fingered the flower covered album. "I remember this. Mom kept it with all our other albums."

"I have them all, Katerina." She pointed to the shelf, and Kat's eyes followed. They filled up when she saw the stack of albums her mother had kept in the family room. "When I had to sell your house after . . . after the accident, I kept everything with sentimental value. Some of it's up in the attic, but I liked flipping through these at night when I was missing you all so terribly. I always wondered what would happen to everything after I was gone, but now . . . now it all belongs to you, my beautiful Katerina."

Kat stood and hugged her aunt, and the flood of tears started again. Harry caught Boomer's eye and jerked his thumb toward the front door. Happy to get away from the crying—he never knew what to do or say around women in tears—Boomer followed the older man out to the front steps. Harry gave a fake, exaggerated shudder and shook his head. "Damn, I hate when women cry. Gives me the fucking willies."

Boomer barked out a laugh. "Same goes for me."

"Glad they waited until I was done with my pie. Now, why don't you tell me what you don't want Irina to know."

He filled the man in on the abduction attempt. "I'm going to call my boss before we leave and have him send someone to keep an eye on Irina, just in case."

Pulling out his cell phone, Harry replied, "No need. We may be a small town, but our sheriff is former special ops himself. Makes sure his deputies aren't slackers. He also happens to be my younger brother. If it's all right with you, I can have him come by and you can fill him in. If you hadn't noticed, strangers kind of stick out around here, especially city-slickers."

Boomer knew the man was right, but would reserve judgment of the locals' ability to protect Irina until he met the sheriff. "Okay. Why don't you give him a call while I check on the status of my team? My backup should've landed by now."

As if summoning them, Boomer's phone rang and Marco's nickname of "Polo" appeared on the screen. Answering it, he gave his teammate an update and Irina's address for their GPS. Confirming they were about thirty minutes away, he hung up and waited for Harry to finish his own call. With everything under control at the moment, the only thing bugging him was they had no idea where to go from here.

When the two men reentered the house, they were relieved to see the waterworks had been turned off again. The women were sitting at the table going through the old photo album as the men sat down again. Kat flipped a page, and Boomer immediately noticed something . . . actually several somethings. "Kat, let me have the album a second, please."

At his excited tone, she glanced at him and shrugged. "Sure, what's wrong?"

He quickly scanned the pages before and after the one she'd been on. There were six photos on each page and every one had been neatly lined up with the others. But on the left side of the current page, there was one picture missing, probably the one from the deposit box. And the picture next to the empty space was turned upside down. Boomer gently peeled back the plastic sheet protecting the photos and removed the inverted one. It was another picture of Ivan standing at the corner of the old house, but Irina was also in this one. The seven-year-old was grinning and showing off her missing front tooth. Boomer flipped it over and found what he hoped was their next clue.

"That's my dad's handwriting."

Kat hadn't needed to tell him. After all these years, he still recognized Ivan Maier's precise penmanship.

"What's it say, son?" Harry asked.

He read off what was appeared to be some sort of code. "NW-X-17D-24A."

"Anyone know what it means?"

They all looked at each other with confused faces. Kat asked what they were all thinking, "Now what?"

Boomer sighed. "I'll call Brody. Maybe he can figure out what your father was trying to tell us. Kat, while I'm doing that, can you check the backs of all the other pictures in there. Irina, is it okay if we take this album along with the others? There might be something else in them we're missing."

"Of course, Benny. They belong to Katerina anyway."

Boomer tried to hide his wince at her calling him "Benny." She obviously picked it up fast from Kat's use of it. He strode to the front door and took out his phone again. By the time he was done filling in Egghead, a patrol car was pulling up to the mailboxes next to the road. Harry must've heard it because he came outside at the same time the sheriff exited the vehicle.

Harry introduced the two men, and they shook hands. "Pleased to meet you, Sheriff Bernhard."

"Same here, Ben. But call me Marty. Harry tells me we might have a problem here."

"I hope not, Marty." Boomer filled the other man in, and just as he was wrapping things up, a rental sedan pulled into the drive. "Here's my backup."

More introductions were done as Devon and Marco joined the group. Devon clapped his teammate on the back. "So, what's up next, Baby Boomer?"

Boomer growled, but didn't take the teasing bait. The guys only added the "Baby" to his nickname when they wanted to get a rise out of him or ease tensions. Instead of getting snarky, he told them about the note on the back of the photo. "I think our next stop is Mint Hill. There's gotta be some reason why Ivan used those two pictures as clues."

"I agree. It'll take about four and a half hours to get there, which means it'll be too late to take a look around tonight. We can stay at my folks' place. They're out in San Diego visiting my brother while his team's INCONUS." The youngest of the Sawyer family, Nick, had followed in his brothers' footsteps and was a Navy SEAL on Team Three. It'd been a few months since he'd been on U.S. soil.

Boomer looked at his boss in confusion. "Why can't we make a puddle jump in the jet? We can be there in under an hour."

"CC's daughter went into labor about two hours ago with his

first grandchild. He was refueling and heading right back down to Tampa. I'll call Ian and have him get a hold of Chase. He can send one of his jets to Charlotte for us." Chase Dixon owned Blackhawk Security and supplied Trident and other companies with additional trained personnel or transports if needed.

"All right. Then we better get on the road. Let me get Kat." He rolled his eyes. "Get ready for more tears as she and her aunt say goodbye."

Almost as one, the other men all shuddered.

# CHAPTER 13

*I*t was just after six p.m. when they all walked into a pub not too far from the Sawyer family home. Kat couldn't help but notice the drooling stares from most of the women toward the three handsome men who surrounded her. The guys were impressive by height and physiques alone, but add in their good-looking faces, and she could just imagine how many of the women wished they were her at the moment. She was sure they might change their minds when they found out people were trying to kidnap and possibly kill her.

After they sat at a table, a pretty waitress with fake tits openly flirted with Benny, Devon, and Marco, but only the latter flirted back. From what Kat had been told, Devon was happily engaged while Marco was currently single. As for Benny, he only seemed to have eyes for her, and it made her body tingle when she saw the heat in his gaze. She hoped it meant he wanted her as much as she wanted him. Not knowing how many bedrooms there were in Devon's parents' house, she didn't know the sleeping arrangements for the night. Kat prayed Benny and she would be sharing a room.

"So, Kat, what was Baby Boomer like as a kid?"

She looked at Devon in amusement. "I know his nickname is Boomer because he's trained in explosives, but why do you call him Baby Boomer?"

"Two reasons. One, because he's the youngest guy on the team. And two, because he hates it."

Kat giggled as Benny rolled his eyes. "So, of course, the more he hates it, the more everyone uses it."

A grin spread across Devon's face. "Pretty much, yeah. A lot of call signs received in the military are not ones we would've picked for ourselves. Mine's 'Devil Dog,' and while it's a long story, let's just say it involved my foot locker and a month's supply of Drake's Devil Dogs."

She laughed. "I love those! Mom always used to stock up on those and Yodels." She looked at Benny's other teammate. "So, Marco, what's your nickname, or don't you have one."

"I got lucky with mine, no embarrassing story behind it. They gave me 'Polo' as in Marco Polo."

"Oh, how cute!"

The other men chuckled, and Marco pretended to be insulted. "First time someone's called my name cute."

The waitress returned with their drinks, and Kat thought the woman was going to melt when Marco winked at her. But as soon as the giggling blonde walked away, he turned his attention back to Kat. "So, tell us about when Baby Boomer was a juvenile delinquent. Give us some good dirt we can use against him."

They spent the next hour eating and telling tales. She told them about Benny, Alex, and her antics back in high school, and they told her what they could from their military and Trident days. She quickly found out teasing and practical jokes were a large part of the teammates' relationships. When they'd finished with dinner, she realized she felt more relaxed than she had in years.

From the pub, it didn't take them long to reach the Sawyer home. As Benny followed the other rental car up the long driveway, Kat couldn't help but gawk at the . . . estate, she guessed she could call it. "Holy cow! This is where Devon and Ian grew up?"

The large home sat on several acres of land, but despite its size, it wasn't ostentatious. The lawn was beautifully manicured, and trees, shrubs, and flower beds dotted the landscape, similar to her aunt's place, but on a grander scale. Four columns were spaced evenly across the front of the brick and stucco house, and both vehicles parked in the circular drive which surrounded a water fountain.

"Actually, no. Mr. and Doc Sawyer bought this the year after Dev enlisted. I'm not sure if you've ever heard of their dad out on the west coast. His name is Charles, but those close to him call him Chuck. He made a fortune in real estate when his boys were younger, and now they've got houses all over the place. Doc Sawyer is a plastic surgeon, and they both do a lot of charity work, so they travel a lot."

"Wow. The name doesn't sound familiar, but I'm not big on reading about people I don't personally know."

"They visit Tampa a few times a year, and we visit them when we can. They've kind of adopted the rest of the team as their own. You'll get along with them great. Nicest people in the world. Laid-back. Despite the nice houses and cars, you'd never know they were loaded. They remember what it's like to be a struggling middle-class family."

Benny grabbed their duffel bags before they followed Devon and Marco into the house. After shutting the door, Devon reactivated the security system. "Polo, you can crash in Ian's room. Boomer, you and Kat can take the two guest rooms at the end of the upstairs' hallway."

"We only need one room."

Devon raised an eyebrow, but didn't question the statement. "Okay. Why don't you show her to a room and I'll check in with the office? I'll see if Egghead made any sense of those letters and numbers."

Kat followed him up the elegant staircase and down the hall to one of the guest rooms. He shut the door behind them, dropped their bags, then drew her into his arms, kissing her senseless. She lost track of time before he pulled away then stared at her with lust-filled eyes. "I've wanted to do that all day."

Giggling, she admitted, "I've wanted you to do that all day. Well, and a few other things."

He pinched her ass, and she squeaked. "Little tease. I have to go back down and find out if Brody has any information for us.

Why don't you relax or take a shower, and I'll be back up in a bit?"

Placing a swift kiss on his lips, she turned and sashayed to the bathroom, swinging her hips seductively. "Don't be long."

WHILE KAT WAS TAKING a shower and getting ready for bed, Boomer joined his teammates in the entertainment room, but not before taming the hard-on she'd given him. A glass of Jack Daniels was waiting for him, and he thanked Devon for his foresight. "Anything from Egghead?"

"No, but he's running the sequence through every code-breaking program he has. And a few you don't even want to know he has access to." The geek was one of the most talented hackers in the business, and if the FBI, CIA, and NSA couldn't have him as one of their own, they were just grateful he was on their side of the law.

Marco was occupying one of the recliners and had the TV tuned to a baseball game with the volume on low. As the other two took seats on both couches, Boomer's phone rang. He pulled it from his pocket and checked the screen.

**Caller Unknown**

That wasn't unusual. "Michaelson."

"Boom-Boom. What's going on?"

"Hey, Carter, what's up?" Boomer was a little surprised to hear from the black-ops agent. It'd been over two months since he'd seen him at The Covenant, enjoying an evening of play. T. Carter had become close friends with the men of Trident after running into them on numerous missions over the years. Each one of them owed him for being in the right place at the right time on several occasions. If it hadn't been for him, one or more of the team could've been killed by a sniper at the Trident compound almost a year earlier. Boomer had no idea which one of the U.S. alphabet agencies the man actually worked for, but from experience and the stories he'd heard over the years, he was glad Carter was on their side. You could sum the man up in one word: deadly.

"Spoke to Ian then Keon this morning, and they told me what you've been up to the past few days. I did some digging and found some intel for you."

"Shit—you're the best. Hang on. Polo and Dev are with me. Let me put you on speaker." He punched the correct button and sat the phone on the coffee table, so they could all hear the information. "All right, go."

The man's deep voice rumbled from the speaker. "Rumor has it Sergei Volkov's own people put a hit out on him. It was suspected he was making deals under the table and not telling those above him on the food chain. He was getting greedy, and it was pissing some people off. Again, rumor has it, his second-in-command did the dirty deed and then replaced him. Name's Viktor "The Bull" Dryagin, a mean mother-fucker. Not a guy you want to be fucking with. Word is he immediately began looking for buried treasure."

"'Buried treasure'... what the fuck does that mean?"

"Apparently, many years ago, an accountant of theirs was killed along with his family in a car accident... sound familiar?"

"Yeah," Boomer replied cautiously. He didn't like where this was going.

"Yeah, well, three days *after* this accountant was allegedly killed, a large sum of money disappeared from several accounts this guy had access to. Transferred off-shore and then to parts unknown."

"Fuck!" he spat out. "How much money are we talking about here, Carter?"

"Fifteen mil."

"What? Holy shit!" Boomer shoved his hands into his hair and almost pulled a few chunks out in frustration and disbelief. "Aw, fuck me. Ivan stole fifteen million dollars from the Russian mafia. Was he fucking crazy?"

"My guess... it was his form of revenge, Boom."

Marco nodded in agreement while Devon spoke. "Sounds like it. From what I understand, Ivan was a simple, family man. Looks like he extracted his revenge where he could hurt them the most—in the purse strings."

Still trying to wrap his head around this new development, Boomer stared up at the ceiling. "I don't get it. From what Kat's told us, they both worked and lived middle-class lives. Nothing to indicate that kind of money. So, what the hell did he do with it?"

"That's the big question. Carter, any ideas?" Devon asked.

"Sorry, Devil Dog. All I know is Volkov had been looking for the money for years, even though the higher ups wrote it off as a loss. If I get wind of anything else, I'll give you a buzz."

"Thanks, man."

The call disconnected and after going over a few more things with his teammates, Boomer headed upstairs to the bedroom he was sharing with Kat. He wasn't sure if he should hit her with this news tonight or wait until morning. He had to tell her soon because there were questions he needed answers to. Opening the door, he froze at the sight before him. Damn, she was so fucking beautiful, she took his breath away.

Kat was sitting on the queen-sized bed in nothing, but a soft, green towel. Her bare arms and legs glistened with newly applied lotion, and the tropical scent of coconuts hung in the air. It must be from Doc Sawyer's guest stash because it was different than what Kat had used earlier at the bed and breakfast. She was running a brush through her towel-dried hair, struggling to get a few knots out. Boomer shut the door and strode purposely toward her, holding out his hand. "Let me do it for you."

Surprise popped up in her eyes, but she handed over the brush, then turned so her back was to him. Sitting behind her, he took a section of her long locks and glided the bristles through them. When he hit a snag, he made sure he wasn't hurting her as he began to work the light brown strands free. Wordlessly, he continued, section by section, until the brush flowed easily with each pass.

"There. All done."

When she peered at him over her shoulder, there was no mistaking the heat in her gaze. Her voice was low and husky when she asked, "How did you do that?"

His eyes narrowed in confusion. "Do what?"

"You turned something I do every day into an erotic gesture. I thought only guys in romance novels did things like that."

Boomer smirked and leaned forward to lick her ear. "You ain't seen nothing yet, Kitten."

Encouraged by the shiver which coursed through her, he moved her damp hair to the side, and she tilted her head to give him better access to her neck. He kissed, licked, and nibbled the sensitive skin there as he reached around and tugged the towel free from her body. Bringing one hand to her breast, he plucked and rolled the hard little peak until she was squirming and begging him for more.

"Do you trust me, Kitten?" he whispered in her ear while his hands continued to push her arousal higher and higher.

She was panting as her back arched in pleasure. "Oh, God, yes. Yes, I trust you."

He growled and kissed her bare shoulder. Scanning the room, Boomer spotted what he needed. He hurried over to the French doors leading to a small balcony and removed one of the tasseled ropes holding the heavy curtains back. It was perfect for what he wanted to do to her.

Returning to her, he chuckled at the doe-eyed expression on her face. "I promise you, baby, you're going to love this. Put your hands behind your back." He was pleased when she only hesitated a split second before doing as he requested. With practiced ease, he secured her wrists together, then checked to make sure the rope wasn't too tight. The material used to create the crimson braid was soft and silky, so he didn't have to worry about it chafing her tender skin.

He caressed her cheek. "Your safeword is 'red.' If you get scared, or something doesn't feel right, just say 'red' and I'll untie you right away. Okay?" He kept it simple for now, like an on-off switch. As things progressed between them, he would introduce the "yellow" safeword which she would use to slow things down before continuing.

"Okay."

"Mmm. That was rule number two. Rule number one was no

putting yourself down. Now, rule number three is, when we are playing like this, I want you to call me Sir or Master. Can you do that for me, Kitten?"

"Yes. Yes, Master."

He leaned down and brushed his lips to hers. "Damn, it sounds so nice coming from your mouth. Say it again."

Her tongue peeked out to moisten her lips. "Yes, Master."

Boomer snarled like a beast that'd just sensed its mate was in heat. He crushed his mouth to hers, holding her in place by grasping her hair. Lips melded, teeth clashed, and tongues dueled as he reveled in the taste of her. His cock was thick and hard in his jeans, but he wasn't ready to take her . . . yet. He had some dirty, delicious plans for her first.

Abruptly, he broke them apart. There was another set of lips he wanted to claim. Pulling his wallet from his back pocket, he placed it along with his gun on the nightstand. It was then he spotted the box of condoms they'd grabbed earlier while gassing up at a truck stop. Snagging one, he grinned when he realized she'd opened the box for him. *Such a naughty girl.*

Stripping quickly, he laid across the bed, picked her up and positioned her so she was sitting on his face. Her legs were next to his ears and her core, just inches above his mouth. Her scent was driving him crazy, but before he began his feast, he told her, "Rule number four, Kitten, is no coming without permission. Concentrate hard and you'll be able to do it. The longer you hold out, the more pleased I'll be. And the more pleased you make me, the harder you'll come when I let you."

Kat whimpered with need, and her pussy wept with it. "Y-Yes, Master."

"You can make some noise if you need to. The guys are on the other side of the house." He chuckled and rubbed his chin stubble against her inner thigh. "Just don't scream too loud, otherwise they may think we're in trouble down here."

"O-Okay. Please."

"Mmmm. I like that word. Please what, baby? Tell me what you want, and maybe I'll be nice and give it to you."

Her entire body blushed, and her thighs quivered in anticipation. "Oh, God. Please . . . um . . . please lick me."

"Lick you where?" he teased.

"T-There. Between my legs."

"Uh-uh, Kitten. You can do better than that. We need to work on your dirty bedroom talk. Ask me to eat your sweet pussy." His hands moved from her hips to her ass cheeks, and he squeezed and massaged them. "Think about all those naughty books you read. Tell your Master what he wants to hear."

She closed her eyes and swallowed hard, but he wouldn't make another move without her verbal request. "Please, Benny . . . I mean, Master. Please eat my . . . my sweet pussy."

"With pleasure, baby. With pleasure."

———

BENNY TUGGED HER DOWN, and she cried out the moment she felt his mouth kiss her pussy lips. Alternating, he suckled on each one, then licked and nibbled them. His tongue lapped at her slit, while his nose bumped against her clit. Kat suddenly realized why he'd restrained her hands. She was at his mercy and could only, literally, sit there and take it. He teased, tantalized, and tortured her. His strong hands held her in place as she tried to squirm and grind her mound into his mouth.

"More, oh please, more. Don't stop, please don't stop." Her own words sounded incoherent to her, and she hoped she was making sense to him. Behind her, her hands found the skin of his chest and scratched it. Sensations bombarded her as years of sexual frustration boiled to the surface. His tongue did more for her than her vibrator had ever done. If it wasn't for his hands holding her, she would've fallen flat on her face, into the mattress. Higher and higher he took her. Oh God, she was so close!

His tongue impaled her, and she shattered into a million pieces. Her body shook with the impact. Up was down, down was up. Nothing made sense as wave after wave tumbled over her. White lights and black dots filled her vision and she thought she was going to pass out. She soared to the heavens and back again. How had she lived her entire life without knowing what it was like to fly?

*Oh, shit! That wasn't supposed to happen, was it?* He'd told her not to come without permission. "I'm s-sorry," she sobbed and heaved, her body still reeling.

Boomer shifted her until she was sitting on his chest. His mouth and chin were coated with her juices, and he licked off what he could reach. "Shh. It's okay, baby. We can work on it." He chuckled. "After all, practice makes perfect. And I plan on practicing with you over and over again. But next time, Kitten, you will be punished if you disobey me. And your punishments will consist of my hand spanking your bare ass until you beg me to fuck you."

His words almost made her come again. The thought of him draping her over his lap was something she'd been thinking of ever since he'd slapped her ass the night before. She saw him grab the condom he'd tossed on the bed, and her sex quivered. Never had she known such lust and desire. He reached around her and covered himself before his hands grasped her hips and positioned her over his hard shaft. Kat rose up on her knees to give him room and moaned as he rubbed the tip along her slit. Her body yielded to him as he inched his way into her tight channel. The drag of his cock against her walls was pure heaven.

Benny lowered her slowly until she was fully seated on him, then held her there. "Oh, fuck, woman! You're burning me alive. I'm not going to be able to take this slow for long, sweetheart."

Every nerve inside Kat was alive. Each slide and twitch of his cock was sweet torture. Her walls clenched, and she loved how it made him moan. "Don't want slow," she panted. "Fast . . . please . . . fast."

"Thank fuck!"

Tightening the grip on her hips, he began to raise and lower her in time to his thrusts. This position felt so different from last night, and she quickly felt her orgasm building. With her hands still behind her, her chest was shoved forward and her tits bounced with every movement. He pulled her down across his torso and took one of the orbs into his mouth. The dual assault on her pussy and nipple had her begging. "Oh, shit! Oh, Benny . . . Master . . . more, please. Oh my God, I'm going to . . . oh, please . . . I need . . . oh, help me . . . I need . . . please . . ."

She felt one of his hands slide between them and as his fingers found her clit, he stopped sucking on her nipple only long enough to command, "Come, Kitten. Come for me."

He pinched her clit at the same time his teeth bit down on her taut peak, and she began to fall. "Oh . . . oh . . . oh, shhhhhiiiiiittttt!"

BOOMER WATCHED as she spiraled down into oblivion while he continued to pound into her from underneath. Her pussy was his home, and there was nowhere else he wanted to be. His balls drew up tight as his lower spine tingled. A few more thrusts, and he was there.

"Fuck, baby, yeah . . . oh, fucking yeah . . . *aaaaahhhhhhhh*, shit!" His body went rigid as his seed filled the thin barrier between them. Her walls were milking every last drop from him, and she melted on top of him. He slowed their rhythm to a stop, gasping for breath. Sweating, panting, tingling, quivering—he swore it would take hours to recover.

Boomer reached around and untied her wrists. His hands massaged her arms all the way up to her shoulders, making sure her circulation hadn't been cut off. "You okay, baby?"

"Mm-hmm."

Chuckling, he reached between them and squeezed the rim of the condom before pulling out of her. She moaned in protest as he rolled her off him onto her side. Leaning toward her, he kissed her pert little nose. "I'll be right back."

"Mm-hmm."

He was back moments later with a washcloth. "Spread your legs for me, Kitten."

"Mm-hmm."

Snorting his amusement, he began to clean her. "Mm-hmm? Is that all you can say?"

"Mmm," she mumbled. "You knocked the dictionary out of my head. Can't think."

He grinned and tossed the cloth back into the bathroom where it landed on the tiled floor. Pulling back the covers, he picked her up and settled her sated body on her side of the bed and nestled in behind her. Her ass cheeks cradled his softened cock as he squeezed her hip. Once this craziness was behind them, he planned on preparing her ass to be taken. He hoped like hell it wouldn't be on her hard-limit list.

*Shit!* How the hell were they supposed to make plans for the future with a fifteen-million-dollar price tag hanging over her head? Not wanting to spoil her contentment, he decided to wait until the morning to tell her about the money. Although, she hadn't given him much of a choice as he realized her breathing had turned shallow and she was asleep. Holding her close, he cupped one breast and closed his eyes.

# CHAPTER 14

*K*at awoke in a sweat, and it took her a moment to comprehend it was Benny's body heat which had her ripping off her covers. When he didn't move or say anything, she realized he was still asleep as he spooned her from behind, his arm anchored around her waist. The morning sun was peeking through the sheers covering the French door's clear panes, and she had the sudden need to use the toilet. When she tried to ease out of the bed, his arm tightened around her and his hand found her breast and squeezed. She bit her lip and tried again. This time when she shifted, the hand went south to her pelvis and his hips thrust forward. His morning wood was now nestled between her lower cheeks and he pumped a few more times, groaning, but still in slumber.

*Shit!* It felt so good, so naughty, but if she didn't get up soon her bladder was going to stage a protest. "Benny?" She shook his arm. Of course, all that did was make him grind his erection into her flesh again. She raised her voice a little louder and tried again. "Benny, I have to get up."

"Why?" he mumbled.

"I have to use the bathroom."

Slowly, he released her, and she crawled out of the bed. She was halfway to the door when he asked, "What time is it?"

Kat glanced at the bedside clock. "Seven-fifteen," she told him before entering the bathroom.

GROANING, Boomer shifted onto his back and watched her ass disappear into the bathroom. He grabbed his stiff cock and gave it a few rubs, then scratched his balls. Behind the now closed door, the toilet flushed and then he heard the sound of the shower coming on. He laid there for a minute, letting the morning fog clear from his brain when a thought occurred to him. This time he didn't have to worry about what she would think if he joined her. Throwing the covers off, he strode across the room and was happy to find the door unlocked. Deciding to have a little fun, he used his stealth training and slowly cracked open the door. Steam had filled the room, but through the mirror he could still make out her naked form stepping into the shower. It was an open walk-in stall behind thick glass blocks with no door or curtain to shut.

Kat's back was to him, as he slipped into the room and shut the door behind him. Silently, he eased over to the shower opening, stepped inside, and leaned against the tiled wall. He watched as she tilted her head back, and with closed eyes let the water sluice down her face, neck, shoulders, and lower. His eyes followed the writhing streams of liquid as her hands pushed her wet hair off her forehead. A rivulet flowed down her spine and disappeared into the crack of her ass. And still her back remained toward him.

Boomer's pulse raced as his eyelids and balls grew heavy. Gripping his hard, thick cock, he slowly stroked it while he watched her grab a pink loofah and a bottle of body wash. The scent of coconuts filled the air and it made him even harder, reminding him of how good she smelled last night. The loofah was now lathered and soap bubbles began to coat her skin. He tugged on his cock, and pre-cum oozed as his gaze followed the pink bundle as it passed over every inch of her skin. She spread her legs and moaned loudly as she soaped up her pussy. Boomer bit his lip trying to stay silent.

"Are you going to stand there all day, watching me, and playing with yourself?"

A grin spread across his face. "How did you know I was here, you little tease?"

Turning, she gave him a saucy smile. "I felt the cooler air when the door opened. And I also have great peripheral vision." She continued to run the loofah over body as she watched his hand pump up and down.

"Are you sore this morning? Be honest, because you rode me pretty hard last night."

A blush spread over her cheeks as she nodded.

"It's okay, Kitten. I can just take care of this," his chin dipped toward his groin, "while you finish showering over there."

Kat bit her bottom lip, then her tongue caressed her upper one. "Or, I could . . . you know . . ."

Boomer snorted in amusement. "We're going to have to work on your naughty vocabulary. Does 'you know' mean you're offering to blow me?"

Her eyes stayed on his hand as it continued to slowly work his cock—up, over, back, and down in a mesmerizing rhythm. "Last night was the first time I ever did . . . you know, but I've read lots of books, so I was just doing what they said."

"Well, you did a fine job. I loved fucking your mouth, but this time I want to come down your throat. Do you think you can handle it?"

"I—I don't know, but I want to try . . . Master."

Boomer growled. "Fuck, I love hearing that from your lips. Sit down on the bench, baby, and let me rinse off really quick. Then, I'm going to fuck your sweet mouth."

The built-in tiled bench was in two separate sections, one higher than the other. The lower one would be the perfect height for her to sit on while she gave him a blow-job. He took the pink loofah from her hand and lathered up his body, taking extra time to clean his cock and balls for her. After rinsing the suds off, he stepped toward her. She licked her lips, and he groaned as he guided his aching cock to her waiting mouth. "Lick it, baby. Like a lollipop."

---

KAT'S TONGUE glided up the thick vein on the underside, and Benny hissed. "Oh, yeah. Do it again."

Encouraged, Kat began licking in earnest. Gripping him by the root and cupping his sac, she remembered how he told her he liked it the night before. A drop of pre-cum appeared at the tip, and she ran her tongue over it. It was salty, but that's all that registered to her taste buds.

His hand grasped her wet hair and pulled her closer to his groin. "Open wide. Take me in as far as you can."

Her mouth formed an "O" and she wrapped her lips around his hard flesh. Being careful not to hurt him with her teeth, she sucked him like he was a straw in a thick milkshake.

Groaning, he started to thrust his hips, forcing her to take a little more of him each time. He was so wide she wasn't sure if she could get all of him in her mouth, but she wanted to try. Swirling her tongue around him made him tighten his grip on her hair, and the pain from her scalp went straight to her clit, making it throb with need. She didn't care if she was sore and brought one hand to her mound.

"Uh-uh, Kitten. I didn't say you could play with yourself. You save that for me. I'll take care of you after I come in your mouth."

She whimpered around his cock. She needed to touch herself, but she wanted to please him more. Her mind had become focused on her clit, and she lost track of what she was doing. Kat gagged and coughed when his tip hit the back of her throat. Reflexively, her jaw closed a little, and he jerked his hips. "Shit, baby, watch those teeth!"

Releasing him, her eyes filled with apology. "Sorry! I didn't mean . . ."

"Shhh. It's ok. This is something you have to practice. I'll hold back a little, so you don't choke. Okay?"

Kat nodded and tried again. This time she kept her mind on what she was doing because she didn't want to bite him. His hand guided her, and she followed his lead. Slow at first, his thrusts gradually became faster and shorter.

"I'm going to come, baby. Swallow what you can."

"Mm-hm."

———

BOOMER'S BALLS drew up tight and black spots appeared before his eyes. "Oh, fuck! Damn, you feel so good. Swallow, baby."

Boomer shot his load into her mouth, and almost immediately Kat began to choke.

"Shit!" He quickly pulled out, and the rest of his cum hit her in the face and neck. What had made it into her mouth came right back out as she spit on the shower floor. Coughing and hacking, she looked at him in horror as he knelt before her. He used his hands to wipe her face clean, using water still flowing from the showerhead. "Shhhhh. Baby, it's okay. Shhh. Breathe, Kitten, breathe through your nose."

"I . . ." Her voice was barely audible as she tried to catch her breath. Watery, red eyes tried to focus on him and failed. She coughed a few more times and then finally cleared her throat. "I'm s-sorry."

Boomer pulled her into his arms and rested her head on his shoulder. His hands rubbed up and down her back. "There's no reason to be sorry, baby. No reason at all. Most women do the same thing their first time. I should have warned you. Sex gets sloppy sometimes . . . most times. And swallowing cum isn't for everyone. But I'm proud of you for trying. Are you okay?"

She took a ragged breath. "I-I think so?"

Pulling back, he looked at her and grinned. "I gather it wasn't what you expected."

"Not at all." She giggled and wiped the last of her tears away. "I'm sorry, but in the books, they always write how sweet and delicious it is, and it's not." She winced. "Sorry, I didn't mean to insult you."

Boomer stood and helped her up as well. "C'mere. Let's get you cleaned up again. And I'm not insulted. That's one thing about those romance books . . . everything is perfect in them. In reality, some people find cum bitter and salty, while others enjoy the taste."

As they washed each other, Kat's embarrassment over the incident seemed to ebb from her body. Wanting to return the pleasure he'd received, he put his hand between her legs, but she hissed and grabbed his wrist. "No. Don't."

"Sore?"

"Yeah, sorry."

His hand gripped her chin, and he made sure her eyes were on him. "Stop saying you're sorry, Kitten. Everything you're feeling is normal. Stop living in those fantasy worlds for a minute. Sex is dirty, messy and, yes, sometimes a little painful. But I'm looking forward to showing you how the pain can be turned into pleasure. I know you're reading Kristen's book, and from what I've read, she does a pretty good job of getting her sex scenes true to reality. If you have questions when we get home, she'll be a good person to talk to."

"Kristen? You mean, you know Kristen Anders? You've read her books?"

He almost smirked at the hint of jealousy in her voice. "I've only skimmed through the sex scenes, and yeah, I do know her. Except she'll be Kristen Sawyer soon. She's Devon's fiancée and submissive."

Wide-eyes stared back at him. "Oh, my God! I didn't know that. Why didn't you tell me?" She playfully smacked his chest then shut off the water. They'd be prunes if they stayed in any longer.

Boomer took one of the guest towels from the rack outside the stall and wrapped it around her before taking another for himself. "Sorry, I kind of had other things on my mind."

"Like people shooting at us and stuff." Her voice had grown quieter, as if the reality of the past few days had come back to her in a rush.

Grimacing, he followed her into the bedroom to get dressed. "Yeah, stuff like that."

Ten minutes later, they joined Devon and Marco in the large, eat-in kitchen. The two of them eyed Boomer and he shook his head—no, he hadn't told her yet. When they were settled with coffee and bagels at the table, he squeezed her hand. "Kat, we found out some information last night and have a few questions for you."

Warily, she put down the coffee cup she'd just picked up. "Okay. Shoot."

"What happened in the few days following the accident?"

The color seeped from her face, and he squeezed her hand again. Taking a deep breath, she took a moment to think back to that terrible time. "Um . . . the FBI brought us to a hospital for treatment, then arranged for us to be pronounced . . ." She swallowed hard. "Um . . . pronounced dead. They snuck us out of there and took us to a safe house. We changed safe houses after twenty-four and forty-eight hours. I was so numb and upset, I don't even know where we were."

"It's okay, baby. Do you remember if your dad had access to a computer?"

She shook her head. "I don't . . . I don't remember. I'm sorry. I remember they took our cell phones, and we had TV, but no, I don't think we had a computer. One of the agents may have had one though. It was so long ago, I honestly don't remember. Why? What did my father do?"

The tears in her eyes were killing him. "We think your dad stole money from the accounts he was in charge of for the Russians, a few days after the accident. Did he give you any indication he'd come into a large sum of money over the years?"

---

"OH. MY. GOD. NO . . . NO . . . NO!" Anger boiled within Kat as she shook her head. How could her father have done this to her? It had to be why those men were after her. "We had a joint account at the bank. The only money there was what the marshals' had given us to start over with, and our paychecks were direct deposited. As far as I know, it was the only account he had. How much . . . how much money did he take?"

When Benny didn't answer her immediately, she looked at Marco and then Devon. "How. Much?"

"Fifteen million dollars," Devon told her quietly.

Whatever color had returned to her face, drained again. She jumped from her seat and began to pace the kitchen, her hands raised in disbelief. "Fifteen . . . fifteen million. Holy shit! Holy! Fucking! Shit! Daddy, what the fuck did you do? Fifteen million dollars! Where . . . where . . ."

Devon interrupted her rant with his soothing voice. "It's what we have to figure out, Kat. From what our contact told us, Sergei Volkov was killed by his own people. A man name Viktor Dryagin has taken over, and we think he's the one who wants to find you and the money."

"But I don't know where it is!"

Benny stood and embraced her. His strong arms and body heat instantly calming her. "They don't know that, Kat. But your dad left us clues which will hopefully tell us where the money is."

"And if we don't find it, what then?" she cried into his shoulder.

"One step at a time, baby. We'll find a way out of this. One step at a time."

# CHAPTER 15

"*V*iktor? It's Ruslan."

"Vhat you have for me?"

"Ve traced rental to business in Tampa. Trident Security. Former military. Place vell-guarded. Paranoid group."

"*Blyat!* Any sign of girl?"

"Nyet."

"Keep looking. I vant that money. Kill anyone who gets in vay."

"*Horosho.*"

Viktor the Bull hung up the phone and tossed it on his desk. He was this close to getting the money the fucking accountant had stolen from Sergei the Wolf years ago. The higher-ups had written it off long ago, despite it being a lot of money, because they had plenty to burn. But thanks to a talented computer geek, fifteen million dollars was finally within Viktor's reach. When he'd gotten the okay to off Volkov, he'd renewed his efforts to find Ivan Maier. With a little money thrown in the right direction twelve years ago, they'd learned the accountant and his daughter had survived the "accident." Unfortunately, the trail went cold after a few sightings. Now with a facial-recognition program, he was on the hunt again. And this time, he would succeed.

---

THE TWO RENTAL vehicles pulled up to the forgotten piece of land. It, along with surrounding properties, had been abandoned long ago. A few dilapidated barns and houses, built over seven decades in the past, dotted the area. Brody was able to hack into the local government computers and get the coordinates of Ivan Maier's childhood home, or what was left of it. Irina had been right. All that remained from the old home was the foundation, charred pieces of wood, and a brick chimney. The weeds and a few animals in the area had made their home in the ruins.

All four of them exited the vehicles and stared in dismay at the sight before them. A breeze blew Kat's hair in several directions and she quickly put it up into a pony-tail with a band she pulled from her pocket. "So, now what? What are we looking for?"

Boomer held out his hand to her. "Watch your step. There's lots of old debris around, and you can't see it well with these damn weeds."

As Boomer led her closer to the foundation, Marco jumped down into what had been the basement. It looked like the area was a hangout for juveniles with nothing better to do. Empty beer bottles, soda cans, garbage, and the occasional used condom littered the area. Devon circled the area around the foundation and inspected the chimney before joining his teammate in the hole. Instead of jumping, he pushed aside a useless metal door and took a set of cement stairs which once lead to the backyard.

From the former front steps, Boomer and Kat scanned the area below. "Anything?"

"Aside from all this crap, Boom, I'm not seeing anything out of place," Marco told him while kicking some rubbish out of the way. "It's either long gone or well-hidden. Did Kat's aunt say anything about an underground shelter or well on the property?"

Kat pulled out her cell phone. "No, she didn't, but I can call her."

Boomer nodded his agreement. "It's a possibility, but there were other pictures from this property in the album. He picked the ones in front of the house for a reason."

They spent the next twenty minutes searching above and below ground, and Kat made several calls to her aunt whenever they had questions. Frustrated, but unwilling to give up, Boomer jumped into the basement.

Devon walked over to where his teammate landed and held out his hand. "Let me see the photo again."

"Here." He gave his boss the picture, and they examined it together. Young Ivan was standing at the corner of the house, where the front and chimney sides met. Nothing stood out, and Devon turned it over to the writing on the back.

"Fuck." Boomer threw his hands up in irritation and spun around in a circle. "Ivan couldn't fucking say 'X' marks the spot?"

The others mumbled in agreement as he stood facing what was left of the fireplace on the first floor. There had to be something they were missing. He tilted his head back and stared at the sky as if it held the answers. The morning sun was still over his right shoulder. *Son of a bitch!* He quickly checked the compass on his military watch and then stared up at the chimney again.

"Holy shit! I think I've got it." Praying his epiphany was right, he scrambled up the stairs to the backyard and jogged around the foundation to the right.

"What?" Devon was on his heels with Marco not much further behind. "What is it?"

The three of them stopped and gazed at the partially damaged brickwork, but only Boomer understood what he was looking at. "This side of the house is facing northwest." He took the photo back from Devon. "It says 'NW dash X'. Northwest. And look at the upper left corner before the chimney narrows . . . there's an 'X' on that brick. It's like a crossword puzzle, I think. I remember Ivan doing them all the time . . . in ink! '17D dash 24A' Seventeen down and twenty-four across."

As Marco stepped up to the bricks and began counting down and across, Devon smacked Boomer on the back. "I'll tell Ian not to bother with the crossword dictionary as your Christmas present."

He snorted, then yelled for Kat to join them. She was skirting the foundation when Marco pulled out his Leatherman knife. With her phone to her ear, she gaped at the trio clustered close to the brick wall. "Aunt Irina, I'll call you back." She disconnected the call. "What is it? Did you find something?"

"Nice code-breaking, Baby Boomer, the brick here is loose." Marco slid the blade into the mortar cracks and wiggled it a few times. When the brick was out far enough, he used his fingers to pry it the rest of the way and stepped aside. "You solved it, you get to put your hand in there."

The opening went further than the brick had and Boomer shivered as he thought about all of the creepy-crawlers which might be in the dark crevice—spiders were not one of his favorite things. Peering into the small space, he announced, "I think there's something in there." Reaching in, his hand found a small shelf inside and sitting on it was a long, round piece of plastic. He pulled the object out and glanced at the others. An old Pepsi bottle with a piece of paper rolled up and tucked inside was apparently their next clue. "Why do I suddenly get the urge to sing 'Message In A Bottle' by The Police?"

Kat took it from him and with a turn, unscrewed the cap. Using her pinkie, she was able to slide the note out, and then unrolled it with Boomer watching from over her shoulder. Ivan Maier's handwriting appeared. "Is he kidding me? Really, dad? Another bunch of numbers? God, even in death the man can be infuriating! He's lucky I still love him."

Taking the paper from her, Boomer handed it to Marco and said, "Looks like routing and account numbers. Think Egghead can find it?"

"Is whiskey wet?" the man retorted, as he pulled his phone from his pocket and brought up the number he needed.

"Don't tell him I asked, he'll go on an hour-long tangent."

"Try a five-hour tangent. Egghead? Got a job for you."

---

TWENTY MINUTES LATER, they were all headed back to Charlotte with Devon driving the lead car. In Benny's passenger seat, Kat stared out the window, still in a state of disbelief. Brody, whoever he was, had been able to trace the numbers to a bank and an account in the Cayman Islands without any trouble. From what he was able to figure out, Ivan Maier had opened the secret account three years before the hit was put out on he and his family. The initial deposit had been a mere one thousand dollars with no other activity until the day fifteen million dollars was transferred in from a bank in Switzerland. Since then, the money had just sat there collecting interest, to a grand total of twenty-three million dollars and change.

It was obvious her father had planned his revenge ahead of time, in case he ever needed to go through with it. While he never touched a cent of the money, two years after he and Kat had settled in Portland, he'd contacted the bank and named her as a joint account holder. Kat was a millionaire on paper, but the money was tainted with the blood of her mother, brother, and anyone else those bastards had killed or hurt in the name of greed. And she wanted no part of it.

"Now what do we do? I mean, I don't want to hand the money back over to criminals, but I'll do it if it means I get my life back."

"First things first. We'll head back to the Sawyers' and get the rest of the team on a conference call with our FBI contact. We'll figure this out, I promise you, baby." He brought her hand, which he'd been holding to his mouth, and kissed her knuckles. "I promise. Then you and I are going to get to know each other all over again." Leering at her, he licked her fingers. "Over and over and over again."

Kat groaned, then giggled. "We have people trying to kidnap me, with probably no qualms about killing you and your team if you stand in their way. I have over twenty-three million dollars in ill-gotten gains in a bank in the Cayman Islands, and you're thinking of sex."

"Kitten, when it comes to you, I'm always thinking of sex." Benny froze, then moaned and smacked the back of his head on the seat's headrest. "Shit!"

"What's wrong?"

"I forgot my dad's birthday was yesterday. I never called him. Shit."

She squeezed his hand. "I'm sure he'll understand. Weren't they going to the Billy Joel special last night?"

"Yeah. We're almost at the Sawyers'. I'll call him when we get there."

"Will you tell him happy birthday from me, too?"

Benny glanced at her before his eyes returned to the road. "Of course, baby. But I'm sure he'd love to hear it directly from you. My folks have always loved you." And she had always loved them. After returning to Sarasota Wednesday evening, Rick had told his wife about Kat's miraculous return, and she'd called Benny's cell phone right after their pizza dinner in the motel. Kat and Eileen Michaelson had laughed and cried over the phone for about twenty minutes before promising to see each other as soon as possible.

Kat's smile grew wider as he pulled into the long drive, waiting behind Devon for the electronic gate to open. They had reached their temporary home. "I've always loved them, too. I still remember the barbeques at your house when your dad's team returned home from wherever they'd been. Those are some of my favorite memories from back then."

Snorting, he put the car in park. "You were just hot for the guys on my dad's team. So were my cousins, Jessica and Vicki."

"Oh, my God, I forgot all about them. How're they doing?"

"Jess is in California working for some big-shot Hollywood producer, and Vicki is married to a cop in New York and is a pediatric nurse."

"Wow." They climbed out of the car at the same time. "That's great. I'm happy for them. Do you see them at all?"

He shrugged and pulled out his phone. "Not as much as we'd like. The last time we were all together was about a year and a half ago at Vicki's wedding."

Before making the call, Benny escorted Kat inside. While there was a fence surrounding the entire property, she knew he felt better if she was out of sight. Following her up to their bedroom to pack up once more, he hit the speed-dial for his dad's cell. "Hey, Pop. Happy belated birthday. Sorry, I didn't get a chance to call you."

RICK MICHAELSON's deep voice came over the line. "No problem, son. How is everything going? You all right?"

Boomer filled him in on what had happened since they last spoke two days ago, and assured him, despite Jake being injured, everything else seemed to be falling into place. Now they had to figure out what to do with the money and how to get the Russians' target off Kat's back for good.

"You need me?"

Sighing, he sat on the bed while Kat began to gather her things from the bathroom. "Not up here, Pop. We have one of Chase's pilots heading up to Charlotte to bring us home. We'll be having a team pow-wow in the morning if you want to take a ride up, but it's up to you."

"Margaret wants to take us out for breakfast for my birthday in the morning, so I'll head up after we eat. Figure I'll get to you around fourteen hundred. Sound good?"

"That's cool. Tell Aunt Margaret I said hello. Ian is getting in touch with Keon, and Carter has been hitting up his contacts, so maybe we'll have a plan by then." Kat walked back into the room looking lost and confused over everything that had transpired. A thought occurred to Boomer. "Why don't you bring mom with you, so she can see Kat? They can visit with Angie, Jenn, and Kristen."

Her mouth turned upward, and she nodded enthusiastically while his father agreed it was an excellent idea. He let Kat say a quick "happy birthday" before she handed the phone back to him and began to fold her clothes into her duffel bag. After Rick said his goodbyes, Boomer hung up and hooked his finger into a belt loop on her jeans. Pulling her in between his legs, his eyes met hers. "You okay? You know I'm not going to let anything happen to you, right?"

This time when she nodded, it wasn't in delight. Her gaze shifted to the side, and he knew something was bothering her. "Kitten, listen to me." He waited until she was looking at him again. "I know with everything going on, the last thing you want to hear from me is a bunch of D/s rules. But one thing I'm going to insist on from this point on is honesty. I need you to be honest and tell me what you're thinking and feeling."

"About what?"

He shrugged then pulled her closer. "About anything and everything. I want to know when and why you're happy, sad, scared, excited . . . horny." She giggled while he smirked and waggled his eyebrows at her. "There's the smile I was looking for. But I mean it, baby, talk to me. Tell me what's going on in your pretty little head."

Biting her bottom lip, she pushed on his shoulders until he was laying down on the bed with his feet still on the floor. She climbed on top of him and straddled his hips with her knees. Boomer sensed, despite their position, she needed to say something important, and he rested his hands on her waist.

"I'm scared."

The words came out on a whisper, and he almost didn't hear them. "About what, baby? I told you, the boys and I are not letting those bastards anywhere near you. I'd die first."

Kat's eyes widened and filled with tears. He could have kicked himself in the ass at that very moment.

"Shit, Kitten. That's not what I meant. I mean, it is what I meant, but nothing is going to happen to me. I promise. Ian, Devon, and the rest of the team, we're damn good at what we do. We're not going to let anything happen to you." He rubbed his knuckles up and down her sides. "I just got you back, and I'll be damned if someone comes between us ever again." *Tell her,* his mind yelled at him, *tell her you love her!* But he couldn't. Not yet. She wasn't ready for that yet. But soon. Soon she was going to know she belonged to him. And he belonged to her. She was the only woman who would ever hold his heart in the palms of her hands.

She was staring at her hands where they touched his chest. "I'm just scared someone else will get hurt because of me. Jake could have lost his eye."

"And he could've been killed a thousand times over on one of our missions. He could be hit by a bus walking across a street tomorrow. It's the way life is, baby, you should know it better than anyone. But we will protect you, and whether you agree with it or not, your life comes before the team's. Every one of them will tell you that. It's who we are, and who we trained to be. And when this is all over, you and I . . . I want a future with you, Kat. The future I never thought I'd have."

"I want that, too, but I can't bear the thought of losing you. So, if you get hurt," she clenched her fists, taking his T-shirt with them, "I'm going to kick your ass, you hear me?"

"Damn, you're fucking sexy as sin."

She rolled her eyes. "I'm serious, Benny."

Before she realized what was happening, he sat up and pushed her down to the side so she was halfway across his lap and face first into the comforter. Lifting his palm, he let it slap down on her ass cheek. Not too hard, but enough to make it sting.

"Ouch! That hurt!" She reached back with her hands to cover her backside. Since this was new to her, and they weren't actually playing at the moment, he let her. But when she looked over her shoulder at him, he saw heat in her gaze, and his cock stirred.

"It was supposed to hurt, Kitten. The next rule is . . . no rolling your eyes at your Dom. That and sarcasm are the fastest ways to get a spanking." He helped her to stand. "And the only thing saving you from a proper spanking is we have to head to the airport soon, so finish packing while I grab my stuff." He got to his feet as well, and patted her ass. "But real soon, my hand and your butt are going to get very well acquainted, and you'll be begging me to let you come. Trust me."

Ignoring her gaping mouth, he began to gather his things, chuckling to himself. Oh yeah, teaching her was going to be fun.

# CHAPTER 16

*K*at was trying to concentrate on reading *Leather & Lace*, but was finding it very hard to not replace Master Xavier with Benny in her mind. Master X was paddling Rebecca for lying by omission. She hadn't told him she'd been getting death threats, and he'd found out when someone tried to run her off the road. Kat imagined she was the book's female lead, draped over a spanking bench, and tied down with her bare ass in the air. Master X/Benny paused after several strikes to caress her red-hot cheeks. The fictional heat and pain were going straight to Kat's pussy and making it throb. Oh, she knew Rebecca was crying and not enjoying her punishment, but Kat was remembering how the sting of Benny's quick smacks had startled her both times. And then they had made her wet. Wet and wanting more.

She squirmed a little in her first-class-style seat on the private jet taking them back to Tampa. They'd had some time to kill before the plane landed in Charlotte to retrieve them, so Devon had taken them to one of his favorite places for lunch. It was a sports bar, which she hadn't minded, having grown up watching almost every sports game her brother and Benny had played in high school. In the fall, it'd been football, followed by hockey in the winter. Then springtime came and Alex had pitched while Benny played third base. Kat had always been on the sidelines, cheering and giggling with her girlfriends over how hot the guys all looked in their uniforms. But unlike some of her friends, Kat had paid attention to the games and learned enough to be able to hold her own when it came to men talking about sports.

Devon had introduced her to the main reason he'd pick that particular restaurant—the hamburgers. Kat almost ordered a house salad, but the men had all insisted she get a burger, telling her they were the best ones she would ever have in her life. When she gave in, Benny had smiled and squeezed her knee under the table. She knew he was worried about her weight loss, which was still noticeable, but she had to admit, it felt nice knowing he wanted to take care of her.

Devon and Marco had filled her in on some more funny stories about Benny while he'd rolled his eyes and tried to put a different spin on things. It'd been obvious he was very close to these men, respected them, and valued their friendship. A pang of loss hit her again, and she wondered if Alex and Benny would've still been best friends if things had turned out differently for everyone. She liked to think so, and then wondered how the boyfriend/girlfriend thing would have worked out between her and Benny.

"What are you thinking so hard about, Kitten? You almost have steam coming out your ears."

Benny sat beside her and took her hand in his. She shrugged, then remembered what he'd said about honesty. "Just a bunch of what-ifs. I was wondering, if my father had never gotten mixed up with Volkov, how our lives would have turned out. Yours, mine, and Alex's. Would you and I still have been together?"

His thumb rubbed the back of her hand in soothing circles. A sad smile appeared on his handsome face. "I want to say 'yes,' but honestly I don't know. I'd like to think so, but we've both changed so much in twelve years, it's hard to tell. My parents' marriage was in the minority when it comes to SEAL team members. Many of them don't make it." Kat turned in her seat to face him better, and he lifted her legs so her calves crossed his lap. "Don't get me wrong, there were times my mother wanted to throw him out on his ass. He'd come back from a mission, like most of the guys, and be in a deep funk for a while until his mind caught up to the fact that his body was back in the States. Sometimes, the things we've seen and done are hard to shake. And since SEALs aren't allowed to discuss most of our missions outside of the team, it put a strain on my parents' relationship. I'm just grateful they were able to stay together through the rough spots. My mother is a strong woman, stronger than most." His smile changed and now lit up his handsome face. "And now that I think of it, so are you. So, yeah, I think we'd still be together."

"I'd like to think that, too. Do you think we'd have kids? As close as we used to be, there are so many things I don't know about you now. I don't even know if you want kids."

He grabbed her around the waist and pulled her into his lap. "Kids with you? Hell, yeah." He nuzzled her neck. She was glad his teammates couldn't see them from where they sat toward the back of the plane, as he cupped her breast, squeezing and massaging it. "As many as we can have. Don't think of me as a caveman . . . well, in some ways I can be . . . but the thought of you 'barefoot and pregnant' with my children is a big, fucking turn-on. And just think of all the fun we'd have trying."

His hand left her breast and worked its way between her thighs. He rubbed her sex through her sweatpants, and she knew he could feel the heat and moisture emanating from her. Kat moaned lowly and separated her legs to give him a little more room to work with. She completely forgot they weren't exactly alone. All she knew was the pleasure he was giving her. She squirmed on his lap trying to get closer to him and felt his rigid cock against her hip.

Benny lowered the tone of his voice. "Sit still, Kitten. Put your arms around me and your face in my neck. Try to stay quiet."

Desire flooded her. She did as she was told as he loosened the tie to her sweatpants and put his hand inside them. His fingers brushed over her clit and went lower to her wet pussy. Her breathing increased as her lips touched his neck. Putting one finger inside her, he stroked her gently at first. "You like this, don't you, Kitten? You like how I'm playing with you, knowing Marco or Dev could walk up here at any moment and see my hand down your pants. They could see how flushed and aroused you are." He added a second finger, maintaining the same slow, torturous pace. "Answer me, Kitten. Do you like this, knowing you could get caught being so naughty? Do you want to come?"

"Yes," she moaned into his neck. "Please. More. Faster."

She let out a low, disappointed cry. Instead of doing as she wanted him to, he removed his hand from her pants, and brought it to his mouth. Pulling back to watch him, her eyes widened as he licked her juices from his fingers.

"Mmm. So sweet and delicious." His hand went back down her pants, and this time he began to play with her clit. His eyes were on her face, watching her reactions. "I wish I could throw you on one of the couches and bury my face between your legs. I could eat you for hours, making you come over and over again until I've had my fill. And then I'd put you on your hands and knees, and take you from behind. Fucking you. Claiming you. Owning you. You're mine, Kitten. Mine."

His last word had come out on a growl, and she moaned with need and want. He'd spoken the truth. She was his. She always had been and always would be. He owned her heart, mind, and soul. No other man could make her feel the way Benny did. She loved him. Still. Now. Forever.

Her heart rate and breathing increased as her eyes closed. With his other hand, he grabbed her hair and pulled her mouth to his. She instantly opened her lips and let his tongue in to duel with hers. He increased the pace and pressure of his fingers against her clit, but it wasn't enough to send her over. And, holy shit, she wanted to. She wanted to fall into an orgasmic abyss.

His teeth came out to nibble on her bottom lip and then along her jaw. Lowering his hand, he put two fingers back inside her as his thumb took over the assault on her clit. Sucking on her neck, he marked her as his fingers pumped harder and faster. "Come for me, baby. Fly for me."

Her orgasm hit her hard. Pussy walls squeezed and throbbed around his fingers as a rush of fluid escaped her. He'd taken her mouth again, muffling her sounds of release, and waves of pleasure assailed her. His fingers slowed while she floated back to him. He smiled at her flushed face and sated expression. "Liked that, didn't you?" Pulling his hand out of her pants, he licked his fingers as she cuddled closer.

"Mmm-hmm." Her cheeks flushed, but this time it wasn't from arousal. "Do you think they heard?"

Chuckling, he gave her a quick kiss. "If they did, it's nothing they haven't heard before in the club." He lifted her and placed her back in the seat next to him. "Stay here a second while I get a towel to clean you up."

A few moments later he was back with two paper towels, one damp, and the other dry. "This was all they had on board." She sat blushing while he quickly cleaned between her legs, and retied the strings of her sweatpants. He left her briefly again to dispose of the paper towels then adjusted himself before sitting beside her. "Next time, we'll have to officially induct you into the mile-high club with my cock deep inside you."

She giggled and snuggled against his chest as he wrapped his arm around her shoulders. "You're incorrigible."

***

Boomer loved the feel of her in his arms. She fit like she'd been created just for him. And if he had his way, he'd never let her go. His fingers brushed against the mark he'd left on her neck. He needed the world to see he'd staked his claim until he could get a collar around her throat. Shifting slightly, he adjusted himself again. He was harder than granite, but would have to wait until later to take care of it. This had been all about Kat. About pleasing her and showing her she belonged to him. "What's the first thing you want to do when this is all over? I can get some time off, and we can travel a bit. Maybe go down to the Caribbean for a few days. Find ourselves a deserted island where we can walk around naked and fuck like rabbits."

"Is sex all you think about?" she teased.

"When it comes to you, yup. I have a very long list of wicked things I want to do to you, and all of them end with my cock deep inside your body. But I'm sure we can find some time to do other things, like eat and sleep."

As she shook her head in amusement, her hand settled on his cotton-covered six-pack. He squelched the urge to push it lower, not wanting to start something they couldn't finish. "You know what I want to do the most?"

He placed a chaste kiss on her forehead. "Name it and we'll do it."

"I want to go bowling."

"Ha! What?" Boomer couldn't stop the bubbly laughter which escaped him if he'd tried. "Bowling? Are you serious? I'm offering you a trip to the Caribbean, filled with incredible monkey-sex, and you want to go bowling?"

A wide grin and playful eyes lit up her face. "Yes. Bowling. And stop laughing at me."

"I can't help it, Kitten. You say the funniest things. You've always been able to make me laugh." She pinched his side, and he grabbed her wrist to stop her. "Okay. Okay. I'm not laughing *at* you. But why bowling?"

Her head went back to rest on his strong upper body. "Because we always had the best times when we were bowling. You, me, and Alex. Especially on the Retro Disco Nights we used to go to." She lifted a shoulder and let it drop again. "I don't know, it just seemed like that's when we all let loose and didn't care about anything but enjoying ourselves. I remember our last Halloween, when the two of you had everyone lined up in the alleys dancing 'The Hustle.' You were dressed like John Travolta in *Saturday Night Fever*, and Alex was the *Grease* version of Travolta. I don't think I've ever laughed so hard in my entire life."

Boomer roared at the memory. "Oh, my God! I forgot all about that. My mom taught us the steps. It took Alex two weeks to get it right because he had no sense of direction. He'd go left while everyone else was going right. So we ended up having him face everyone, like a dance instructor, and it worked out."

"It was the best night ever, and it's why I want to go bowling." Her laughter died, and she picked at an invisible piece of lint on his shirt. "I haven't bowled since . . . since my world fell apart."

Tightening his hold on her, he lifted her chin with his other hand. "I can't change the past, baby. But I'm going to do everything I can to make sure you spend the rest of your life laughing and living life to the fullest." His lips met hers. It wasn't a seductive kiss, but one filled with promise. "I love you, Kitten."

Kat froze then pulled back so she could see his entire face and stared at him in disbelief.

"Do you want me to say it again?" She nodded slowly, and he grinned. "I. Love. You. Katerina. Maier. I've loved you for a very long time. And I plan on spending the rest of my life showing you how much you mean to me. You're the only woman I will ever say those words to."

Her eyes filled with tears at his declaration. His pounding heart tried to escape its confinement as Kat's words came out on a whisper. "I love you, too. Always. And I'll never say those words to another man."

"Good. Now that we've gotten the mushy stuff out of the way, kiss me."

And she did.

---

"THEY JUST ARRIVED AT COMPOUND. Girl, three men. Too many people. Vill have to vait until alone."

Listening to his minion report in, Viktor the Bull paced back and forth in the bar's office. It had once belonged to Volkov, but Viktor had taken ownership within days of killing the greedy bastard. The main difference between the two men was Volkov had been stupid and sloppy, whereas Viktor had common sense. He knew to make sure anyone who was privy to his secrets was eliminated as soon as they outgrew their usefulness. Sometimes even before then.

Growing up an orphan in the USSR, Viktor had come to rely on no one but himself. Making his first kill at fourteen had been a blessing in disguise. The perverted bastard had tried to molest him in an alleyway after catching the teen stealing food from a sidewalk vendor. While struggling on the ground, Viktor had managed to grab hold of a broken bottle and shoved it into the creep's neck, slicing the artery. Instead of running, he stood there and watched the man's life end in a puddle of blood. What he hadn't known was someone else had been standing in the shadows as the whole incident unfolded. A man known only as Dmitry *Sishnik*—the Scavenger.

The trained assassin had taken Viktor under his guidance and taught him everything he knew. At first, the teenager thought Dmitry was another deviant, using his offer of food, shelter, protection, and education as a way to extract sexual favors. But he soon learned that wasn't the case. The older man had merely wanted a protégé to pass his craft on to. He'd been trained by one of the best in the same manner, and it had been his way of paying it forward and passing on his legacy.

After learning everything he could from his mentor, Viktor's final act before leaving his birth country was to kill him, quickly and painlessly. It was the least he could do for the man who had changed his life for the better, and was dying of cancer. As a frail Dmitry was struggling to get out of bed one morning, Viktor could see the pain and humiliation in his eyes. He couldn't stand to see his suffering anymore, and without a word, he swiftly broke the man's neck. Viktor knew the Scavenger was grateful to his apprentice, for he would've never been able to bring himself to commit suicide, and a slow agonizing death would have been worse.

Since coming to America, Viktor had been working for a Russian network of criminals as an enforcer/assassin. But he was getting older and wanted to start enjoying the good life like his bosses were. Now, there was only one thing standing in his way. It pissed him off the Maier woman was being well protected, but he'd be damned if they couldn't find a way around it. He wanted the money, and she was the last known connection to it. He'd figured out how to hide the funds from his bosses, funneling it into his recently acquired businesses. It would also help him advance further in the association. Knowing he couldn't take the chance of his men screwing up, he made a decision. "I'll be on next flight to Tampa. Find way to get girl, but do nothing until I get there."

# CHAPTER 17

*W*hile Jenn, Angie, and Kristen entertained Eileen Michaelson and Kat near the koi pond, Boomer, his dad, and five teammates sat around the unlit fire pit. A few months earlier, for Ian's birthday, everyone had helped Angie surprise him by transforming the area between the last two buildings in the compound into *Ian's Oasis*. They'd ripped up the asphalt and laid down sod before adding things like an outdoor kitchen, a TV, seating areas, and shrubbery. The backyard, as it was often referred to, had quickly become a place to hang out and relax. At the moment, country music played in the background, and a misting system was keeping the area cool despite the elevated Floridian temperatures.

Ian handed Boomer and Rick their new beers then sat back down and opened his own. He continued to fill the older man in on what they'd talked about earlier with the Assistant Director of the FBI. "So Keon will be discussing things with his boss and the head of the task force who's been leading the investigations into the Russian mob in Norfolk. Obviously, they have no desire to hand the money back over to them. But as it stands now, even though the money is a part of a criminal investigation, he thinks any statutes governing it may have expired. So, it means the money might belong to Kat, whether she wants it or not. I have Reggie checking into things on his end." Reggie Helm was one of Trident's lawyers as well as a Dom at the club. They consulted with him and his three partners on everything from criminal to civil to contract laws.

Boomer popped the cap off his beer and took a swig. "Kat said she wants nothing to do with it. As far as she's concerned, it's tainted money. I wouldn't be surprised if she donated all of it when this is over, but we'll deal with that once she's out of danger."

Rick nodded at his son and then turned back toward Ian. "Has Carter turned up anything new?"

"Of course I have. I'm not a fucking slouch like this bunch of pansies."

The men looked up in surprise as the black-ops agent strolled onto the grass from the parking lot. Usually, at least one of them was alerted when someone entered the compound unannounced, but the guards were under orders to allow Carter entry at any time. The team hadn't known he was in town, but that was nothing new. The man was a ghost, coming and going as he pleased. From where he'd been sleeping by the women, Beau ran to greet the man who took a moment to roughhouse with the dog before grabbing a beer from the outdoor refrigerator. He downed half of it then shook hands or fist bumped each of the men with a few more insults mixed in. Taking a seat next to Jake, he smirked. "Finally got a scar on that Hollywood face of yours, huh? The whole pirate thing you've got going on is pretty fucking hot. You know, blow the man down . . . or up . . . or whatever you're into. Too bad you're not my type."

While the others roared with laughter, Jake snorted and gave his friend the finger. "Fuck you, jackass. This fucking patch is driving me crazy, but not as much as the women are." He hitched a thumb toward the far end of the backyard. "You'd think I was paralyzed from my eyebrows down the way they're trying to do everything for me. I'm just glad the mother hens have Kat to fuss over now."

The men agreed. With the exception of Boomer's dad, they were all Doms and preferred to take care of their subs, not the other way around. And in Jake's case, a gay man with no sisters, having a bunch of women worrying over him was a little unsettling. He loved the Trident women dearly, but wasn't used to all the attention.

"So, Boom-Boom. You going to introduce me to the pretty brunette over there?" Carter did his best imitation of Groucho

Marx's eye wiggle while eyeing the group of women. The man loved the ladies, all types, and could be the biggest flirt at times.

Boomer growled. "Hands off, jackass. Don't even think about it."

"Oh well, a man can dream, can't he? She's a sexy little thing, you know, in case you're ever looking for a third." Ignoring his friend's scowl, he took another drink and sighed while settling into the Adirondack chair. "Damn, that tastes good. Anyway, back to the current problem. I've done a little research on Viktor Dryagin. He's been in the U.S. for about twenty years, but before that, he trained under one of the best assassins in the USSR at the time."

"Shit." Boomer dragged his hand down his face in frustration. A trained assassin was not someone he wanted anywhere in the same hemisphere as Kat.

"Yeah, I know. But it seems he's been backing off on his enforcer role in the mob and using Volkov's death as a way to move up in the organization. From what I hear, the higher ups wrote the money off years ago. So, my best guess is, Dryagin will be hiding it from his bosses if he ever gets his hands on it."

Leaning forward, Ian scratched Beau's ears after the goofy-faced dog sat at his feet. "So, there's a good chance very few people know Kat has access to the money. And if she does give it away, then we can eliminate the threat altogether."

Boomer shook his head. "I don't like it. What if he doesn't believe she gave it away? And, we have to wait on the legalities to make sure she *can* give it away. This guy wants the money, and Kat is the only link."

"Which is why I want you two to stay here at the compound. Lord knows it won't be the first time we've been under attack, and I'm sure it won't be the last. I'll call Chase and post a few more guards."

"What about the club?" Devon asked his brother. "Tomorrow and Tuesday we're closed, but what do you want to do about tonight?"

Ian thought about it for a few moments. "I don't think we have to close at this point. With a few extra guards at the gate and in the compound, we should be good. And with Egghead's increased perimeter security system, no one will be getting anywhere close to the compound without being noticed. You and I will sit down with Tiny and Mitch tonight and go over all the precautions." Devon nodded his acknowledgement. In addition to being a bodyguard, Tiny was head of the club's security, and Mitch Sawyer was their cousin and The Covenant's manager. While Ian and Devon had gone into the Navy, Mitch had gone to college and gotten his MBA. As a result, he'd been the obvious choice to run the club the three of them co-owned.

Brody stood and smacked Boomer on the shoulder. "I'll grab one of those medical alert bracelets I used on Angie. Kat can wear it until she's out of danger, so we can track her if we need to."

"Thanks, that'd be great." Boomer and the others knew firsthand how well the geek's little toy worked. Angie and Jenn had been taken hostage a few months ago, and while organizing the rescue, the team had been able to gain vital information via a one-way microphone hidden in the GPS bracelet. As his buddy jogged to the office to get the device, Boomer glanced over and saw Kat walking toward him, her pale face bothering him. He reached up, took her hand, and pulled her into his lap. "You doing okay, Kitten?"

She cuddled against his chest. "Yeah, just getting a little tired, and I think I might be getting a migraine, so I want to take my meds as a precaution. Is there a place I can lay down for a bit?"

"Sure. We have some bunk rooms above the offices. We'll be staying there tonight anyway." He helped her to her feet and then stood as well. "I'll grab our bags and take you up there."

"I can read you a bedtime story if you want. Women tell me I'm quite entertaining in bed."

---

KAT GAPED at the stranger grinning at her, amusement swirling in his dark blue eyes. He'd been talking to Jake when she first walked over, but now that his attention was on her, she wondered how she hadn't notice what a hunk he was. His dark blond hair must fall right below his shoulders because he had it tied back in a small ponytail. A snug T-shirt covered his upper torso, and his jean-clad legs were long and lean. From how he had them stretched out in front of him, she guessed he was a few inches taller than Benny. And like the men of Trident, he had the physique of a warrior, sculpted from hard work and training. No health club or steroid needle could produce such a perfect male specimen. Holy crap, the man was gorgeous in a dangerous, bad-boy sort of way. "Um . . ."

"Stop being an asshole, man." Benny snarled, putting his arm around her and drawing her into his side. It was a blatantly possessive gesture and made her shiver in delight.

The hunk feigned being insulted, his large hand spread across his broad chest. "Who me? I'm a jackass. Egghead's the asshole."

"I heard that!"

As Brody plopped back down in his chair, the other man chuckled. "You were supposed to hear it, asshole." He turned his attention back to Kat and his gaze softened. "Sorry, little one. The name is Carter, and your boyfriend here should know by now that I'm just joking, although his obvious jealousy tells me you're something special to him. If he treats you wrong, you just let me know, and I'll kick his scrawny ass for you. Okay?"

When he winked at her playfully, Kat couldn't help the smile spreading across her face. It was hard not to like the man instantly. "Nice to meet you, Carter. I'm Kat. And thanks for the offer, but he treats me just fine. He knows I swing a mean baseball bat if he doesn't."

"Ha! You've got claws. I like you already, Miss Kitty-Kat. It's my absolute pleasure to meet you." Her heart clenched at the nickname her father used for her, as Carter's eyes flickered toward Benny. "She's a keeper, man. Don't let her get away."

"Yes, she is." Lowering his head, he gave her a quick kiss. "And I don't plan on losing her again."

A FEW MINUTES LATER, Kat was stripped down to her underwear and Boomer was pulling the covers up to her chin. Some of the six spare bedrooms had bunks, but this was one of two which had a queen-sized bed. An attached bath meant she didn't have to go out into the hallway for any reason. He placed the bracelet Brody had given him around her left wrist. "This has a tracking device in it, Kitten. If something happens to you, which we're going to do everything we can to avoid, it will help us find you. It's just a precaution." He brushed her hair away from her cheek. "Are you sure you don't want me to stay with you?"

She nodded, her eyelids growing heavy. "I'm good. Your parents aren't staying much longer, so go sit with them. I'll be asleep in no time."

Kissing her on the forehead, he saw she was right. By the time he shut off the light and opened the door, she was already going under. When he returned to the backyard, he noticed a few people had left. Jenn had gone into work, having switched shifts with another waitress at the pub owned by Jake's brother. Marco and Brody were also gone, and Devon mentioned they were in the office working on an embezzlement case. Kristen and Angie were over by the outdoor kitchen, getting a dinner of grilled chicken, salads, corn, and potatoes ready while Ian turned on the huge gas grill.

Boomer sat down next to his mom, who'd joined his dad by the fire pit. Eileen smiled at him. "I'm still having a hard time wrapping my mind around the fact she's back, but I have to say, I haven't seen you this happy since high school. And I'm thrilled for you, too. For both of you. Back then, I could see how good you two were together, even if you didn't."

Blushing wasn't something he did often, but he never talked about women with his mom. He knew she wanted grandchildren one day, but wasn't one of those mothers who nagged their sons to get married. "She's the one, Mom. She always was, and I've said it several times within the past few days, I'm never letting her go."

Eileen reached over and squeezed his hand. "I know you won't, Ben. Just keep both of you safe."

"I will."

"Fuck!" Boomer's dad leapt from his chair, holding his shoulder. "God-fucking damn it! I just got stung by a fucking bee. Leaned back on the fucker."

His wife and son jumped up and began pulling on Rick's shirt, trying to get a look at the site. The last time he'd gotten stung, his foot had blown up like a balloon, and they knew if a bee got him again, the reaction could be worse. Eileen now carried an Epi-pen and Benadryl capsules in her purse just in case.

Boomer saw the large welt forming at the back of his shoulder. "The stinger's out. Any trouble breathing, Pop?"

"No. But look, I'm already getting fucking hives. Eil, just give me the Benadryl. I'll take the pills first, and if it gets worse I can use the pen."

She dug them out of her purse as Kristen stepped forward with a bottle of water. Rick quickly popped the pills into his mouth and washed them down with the cool liquid. "Fuck. How the hell could something so damn tiny hurt like such a bitch? 'Scuse my language, ladies."

The women all chuckled at him, having heard a lot worse from the men. Angie had made an impromptu icepack with a zip-lock baggie and handed it to Boomer. After ordering his father to sit back down, he stuck it between the affected shoulder and chair. "Mom will have to drive home. The last time you got stung, the Benadryl knocked you on your ass, old-man."

Rick grumbled and cursed the dead bee some more.

"You don't have to drive home tonight," Kristen informed them. "You know you can always crash in one of our spare bedrooms."

Smiling at the younger woman, Eileen shook her head. "Thanks for the offer, Kristen. But I have an early dentist appointment in the morning. It'll be better if we go home. I just want to wait awhile to make sure Rick's reaction doesn't get worse."

About a half hour later, Rick's hives were gone, but he was having a hard time keeping his eyes open and was barely touching his dinner. Boomer helped him to their car while the women packed up some food for Eileen to take with them. Opening the driver's door for his mother, Boomer gave her a kiss on the cheek before she climbed in. "Text or call me when you get home, so I know everything is okay."

"We'll be fine, but I'll text you anyway." She glanced at her husband who was trying to stay awake, but failing. "He'll be asleep before we hit the highway. Love you, Ben. And tell Katerina we said goodbye. Try and come visit us next weekend, please."

"If this is all over, we will, Mom."

He shut her door and watched his parents drive away. For the first time since he was a teenager, Boomer saw his future and loved it. He was going to make Kat his wife, and they were going to give his parents grandchildren to spoil rotten. Maybe he could convince them to move closer than Sarasota. Smiling, he went to fix Kat a dinner plate, looking forward to feeding her in bed . . . among other things.

---

"FOLLOWING CAR with same last name as boyfriend. Must be parents."

Viktor smiled as he walked down the hallway leading to his plane. His men had taken down the license plates of vehicles driving toward the Trident compound. It was the only property off that road, so it was easy to assume someone using it could be a possible target. Thanks to his contacts in law enforcement, they'd been able to run the plates and find out who they belonged to. If they couldn't get into the compound to get the girl, they'd have to make the girl come to them.

"Don't lose them. I'm on vay." Disconnecting the call, he winked at the pretty stewardess as he boarded the plane. Things were looking up.

# CHAPTER 18

*K*at tried to pull the short skirt lower, but it wouldn't go any further. After taking a nap and eating the dinner Benny had, literally, fed her in bed, she felt confident she'd nipped her migraine in the bud. She'd been surprised and then excited when he'd asked if she wanted a tour of The Covenant. Sunday nights tended to be their slowest nights, he'd told her, but it didn't mean there wouldn't be plenty to see. He'd provided privacy papers she had to sign, as well as a limit list and protocols she needed to adhere to. Most of them were easy enough to remember, and Benny had assured her everyone would help her if she accidentally did something wrong. She hadn't been cleared to play since she needed a mandatory background check and blood work, so he told her they would fill out the limit list together at another time. Tonight, she was only allowed to observe and learn what BDSM was all about.

When Angie and Kristen discovered she would be joining them, they'd been thrilled and offered to lend her something to wear. They'd taken her over to the huge apartment Ian and Angie shared on the first floor of the compound's last building. Kristen and Devon had the unit above theirs, and it was just as spacious. Since her stress-induced weight loss, Kat had dropped to a size six from her normal size ten, but Angie had a few items they'd been able to adjust to her smaller frame.

The black skirt she now wore was a wrap-around which tied at the back of her narrow waist. It had a slight A-line cut and covered her ass as long as she didn't spin around, making it flare outward.

On top, she sported a teal-blue camisole with lace trim. While her assets were covered, barely, she was still self-conscious of the fact she had no underwear on. Benny had insisted, and she had to admit, doing so made her feel naughty and sensual. But that didn't mean she wanted to be flashing anyone other than him.

Glancing at Kristen and Angie as the three of them walked across the compound to the club, she realized she was the least scantily dressed. Angie wore a snug pink teddy which stopped at the middle of her thighs. The stretchy lace material was just sheer enough to see through, but the woman acted as if it was no big deal her nipples could be seen. Kat could also see she was wearing a matching thong, and she was almost jealous of the woman's toned yet curvaceous body. Angie had told her Ian had a thing for lingerie. He loved to browse through some of the nicest and naughtiest intimate catalogs looking for new things for her to wear.

Kristen's outfit fell somewhere between the other two. She had on a matching black bra and panty set with a sheer black overlay. While it was sexy, it wasn't any less than what some women wore poolside or at the beach.

As they walked through the gate separating the club from the rest of the Trident compound, flip-flops slapped against their heels, almost in sync. The girls had told her the floors of the club were carpeted, with the exception of inside the scene areas, so most of the submissives went barefoot. No glass was allowed in what they referred to as "the pit," so they didn't have to worry about anything which might cut their feet. The scene areas were polished wood and constantly being wiped clean by the staff to eliminate any "ick" factors.

Walking up the stairs to the second-floor entrance, the butterflies in Kat's stomach took full flight. Her nervousness must have shown on her face because Angie gave her an encouraging smile while holding the door open for her. "Relax. You'll be fine. Boomer is going to give you a collar to wear, so no one else will be allowed to touch you. If you have any questions, just ask one of us. We've all been in your shoes before . . . well, actually, your flip-flops."

Kat walked through the door and her eyes immediately found

Benny's. He was waiting for her in the club's lobby along with Devon and Ian. And holy hell, did they all look like they just stepped out of a *Playgirl* magazine photo-shoot. Ian and Devon both wore leather pants, but the styles were slightly different. Ian's had a zippered front, and he paired the black pants with a snug grey T-shirt. Devon's crotch was laced up, and he wore a matching black leather vest sans shirt. But it was Benny who she thought was the sexiest, and she hoped she wasn't drooling. Under his open brown leather vest, he was shirtless with his rock-hard chest and abs showcased in skin bronzed by the sun. His faded jeans fit like a glove, and the bulge behind his zipper made her mouth water. A brown leather belt went through the loops at his waist, and was a close match to the well-worn boots on his feet.

He held his hand out to her, grinning broadly as she took it. "Damn, baby. Just when I think you can't get any sexier, you prove me wrong. I think I'm going to start calling you my little sex-kitten."

Pulling out a simple, black leather collar, he indicated for her to turn around and lift her hair. His fingers brushed against her skin as he placed it around her neck and connected the hook and eye clasp in the back. Fingering the thin strand, she faced him again. "Okay?"

"For now. I'm going to have to start thinking about a permanent one for you, like Angie and Kristen have. I want to design it myself."

Kat was thrilled he wanted to show everyone she belonged to him. She'd noticed the other women's collars earlier. Kristen's was a platinum choker with evenly spaced diamonds along its entire length. She'd shown Kat the removable sapphire pendant which she occasionally wore with it. The custom-designed collar matched the engagement ring Devon had also given her, which had tiny blue stones surrounding the large teardrop diamond. Angie was wearing one of two collars Ian had gotten for her. Her everyday one was a yellow-gold, Byzantine-styled chain with a padlock pendant which she'd been wearing earlier. The one she had on now was a two-inch wide, white-gold necklace with a diamond heart in the center. It was stunning and must have cost a fortune. But Kat didn't care what collar she wore, as long as it was Benny's.

He reached for her hand again and placed a yellow "no-play" band on her wrist. "Are you ready to go in?"

A nervous giggle escaped her, and she took a deep breath. "Oh, what the hell. You only live once, or, in my case, twice. Let's do this before I lose my courage."

The group laughed with her as she followed Benny to the large wooden doors leading into the main club. Tiny was standing guard and pulled open one of the doors for them. It didn't escape Kat's notice he was wearing a holstered gun on his hip. She'd been told they'd increased security at the compound until she was out of danger. The huge man smiled at all three women as they were escorted past him. "Hello, Miss Katerina. Hello, ladies. Looking beautiful as always. Have a nice evening."

Kat thanked him as she crossed over the threshold on Benny's arm. Her jaw dropped as the sights, sounds, and smells of the club assailed her senses. She tried to look everywhere at once, but it was physically impossible, so she took in one section at a time. The second floor was basically a horseshoe which overlooked the floor below. To their left at the base of the "U" was a curved, dark-wood bar with intricate carvings. A shirtless bartender was serving drinks to the members. His red bowtie and black pants were what she'd been told was the submissive male employee's uniform. A female server was waiting for her round of drinks, dressed in a short black skirt, red bra, and bowtie.

But it was the patrons who had her agape. While some were dressed in clothing which would be suitable for any club in the city, others were practically, if not completely, naked. Chatting at the bar were two women dressed in fashionable outfits, but kneeling at their feet was a guy wearing only a thong and black collar attached to a leash. Other people were walking around in various stages of dress, and Kat was grateful for what little she was wearing. At least her tits and ass were covered.

Scanning the area, Kat loved how the grey carpet and burgundy walls gave the club a warm atmosphere. Lighting consisted of wrought iron chandeliers and sconces, and there were numerous seating areas with couches, chaise lounges, winged-back chairs, and dark, wood tables. Across from the bar was a grand staircase to the floor below. Brass railings ran down the side of the steps and around the balcony. More seating, in the form of pub tables and stools, allowed members to sit and observe the activities in the pit from above.

Two men, one of whom looked eerily similar to Ian and Devon, approached the group, and she guessed this was their cousin Mitch. He was a little shorter than the brothers and his blue eyes weren't as striking, but his hair and facial features were definitely from Sawyer DNA. Dressed in a pair of black dress pants and a snug black T-shirt, he carried himself with confidence. The other man was slender and, with his salt and pepper hair and goatee, she assumed he was in his fifties. With his black leather pants and dress shirt, an image of Dracula popped into her mind. All he was missing was a cape and some fangs. The way he looked her up and down made her shiver and step closer to Benny. Studying the two men, the first word which came to mind was dominant, and Kat realized she was able to categorize the club patrons by their dress and/or manner.

Next to her, Benny put his arm around her shoulders and gestured to the two new-comers. "Kat, this is Master Mitch, co-owner and manager of the club. And this is Master Carl, who better be nice if he wants to remain standing."

Master Carl ignored Benny's warning as he took Kat's hand and kissed her knuckles. "So, this is the little kitten Master Carter was talking about. He didn't lie when he said you were one mighty fine-looking feline. Me-ow. You're welcome to use my scratching post anytime you want, my little pussy . . . cat."

While Benny growled and plucked her hand from the other man's grasp, Kat blushed awkwardly. The group laughed, and Ian tugged on Master Carl's arm forcing him to step back out of her personal space. "You'll have to forgive Master Carl, Kat. We've been trying to housetrain him for a while now. One of these days he's going to piss in the wrong sandbox. Aside from being a sadist, he's harmless."

"Um . . . okay." Kat wasn't sure what else to say to that.

Kristen put her hand on Kat's arm. "Don't worry. He comes off as a shark, but he's actually a big teddy-bear. But if he offers to show you his bullwhip, run in the other direction."

Master Carl tried to frown, but wasn't successful. "Everyone ruins all my fun. However, it is a pleasure to meet you, little one, and I welcome you to our club."

Before anyone could say more, Tiny rushed over and addressed Ian. "The front gate has three unknown males in a vehicle demanding entry to the club. The guards have them at gunpoint."

As Tiny and Devon took off for the door, Ian turned to his cousin. "The women don't leave your sight, and no one goes out to the parking lot until we clear this."

"Got it. I'll post extra security at the doors." Mitch waved over two men in red, button-down shirts and began to bark out orders.

Meanwhile, Benny pointed at the manager, but his eyes were on Kat. "You stay with Mitch, no matter what, and do exactly what he says. I'll be right back."

Kat felt the blood drain from her face, but she managed to nod. "O-Okay. But be careful."

She wasn't sure if he'd heard her because he and Ian were already running out the double doors to the lobby. Angie put her arm around Kat's shoulder as Kristen stepped in front of her, drawing her attention. "It's going to be fine, Kat. This is what they do, and they're the best trained men out there."

Neither one wanted to tell her how they both knew that first hand. Last year, Kristen had almost been collateral damage when a hit-man was after Devon, Ian, Jake, and Brody. And five months ago, Angie and Jenn had been held hostage by dirty DEA agents after Angie's best friend's undercover operation was blown. Unfortunately, her friend, Jimmy, had been killed during the successful rescue of the women, and Angie was still grieving and having nightmares over the incident.

Mitch rejoined them and suggested they take Kat to one of the empty seating areas. "She's very pale, and I don't want her to faint." As the women sat, he signaled one of the waitresses to bring over some bottles of water. Taking one, he opened it and placed it in Kat's hand. "Drink, Kat."

She had no memory of how the water bottle had gotten into her hand—she'd been concentrating on the doors leading to the lobby. At Mitch's words, she glanced at her hand, then up at the pretty brunette waitress who was smiling at her.

"Hi, do you remember me? We met at the store the other day. I'm Cassandra. It's nice to see you again."

Recognition dawned. Now Kat had two things running through her mind. One, was Benny okay outside? And two, had he had sex with the petite woman standing in front her? She tried to be polite despite the waves of jealousy coursing through her. "Oh, yes. Hello. It's nice to see you too."

Cassandra handed water bottles to Kristen and Angie, who thanked her. She turned back to Kat. "I had a feeling I'd see you here soon. It looks like Master Ben is off the market, and I'm happy for you both. He's a great guy and deserves someone special. Anyway, if you need anything else, just let me know."

Watching the friendly waitress walk away, Kat felt Angie's hand on her arm. "I know what you're thinking, Kat. You have to get past the fact that Boomer had a life while he thought you were gone. The point is, he's with you now, and I can tell by the way he looks at you, he doesn't want anyone else."

Kat nodded then took a sip of water, knowing the other woman was right. Sitting near the koi pond earlier in the day, the subject of her walking back into Benny's life and right into his arms was the main topic of conversation. Angie and Kristen hadn't talked much about the club in front of Jenn and Eileen Michaelson, but they had while finding something for Kat to wear. They explained how some of BDSM interactions were just physical, without the emotional entanglements and drama which came with traditional relationships. And whether she liked it or not, there were women at the club who Benny had played with. She knew they were trying to put her mind at ease. It wasn't as if she'd expected him to be a celibate monk for twelve years when he thought she was dead. But the few men she had dated over the years had never given her a reason to be jealous, so it was a new emotion for her. One she would have to get past if she wanted this to work between them—and she wanted that more than anything else in the world.

It was a good ten minutes before the men came back into the club, and Mitch visibly relaxed. Kat could tell by the way they were joking and laughing nothing serious had happened. The three women began to stand as their men approached, and Ian waved for them to sit back down. "Nothing to worry about. Just a few, barely-legal, drunken jackasses looking for some slap and tickle. Somehow, they heard about the club and thought it was a combination strip-show and whorehouse. Idiotic driver pulled out a knife when the guards wouldn't let them in, then wet his pants when faced with a full arsenal. The cops arrived and are taking care of them."

The group broke out into chuckles and comments about stupidity as Benny took Kat's hand and pulled her up into his arms. "You okay? I'm sorry we had to scare you."

She melted into him. "It wasn't your fault. I'm just glad no one got hurt. I wouldn't be able to live with myself if they did."

"Hey." His hand went under her chin and tilted her head back so she could see his face. "I keep telling you, none of this is your fault, Kitten. I know it's hard for you to believe, but the bad guys and your dad are to blame. Although I doubt he realized he was putting you in danger by taking the money, but he should have." Leaning down, he lowered his voice, his lips touching her ear. "Now, since the excitement is over, how about I give you a tour and get you excited in another way? A way that will get you wet and begging me to do wicked things to you."

Blushing at his suggestion, Kat shivered and let him lead her to the grand staircase. He handed a club card to one of the security guards who scanned it through a hand-held computer. It showed Benny had two or less alcoholic beverages served to him, and they were allowed to enter the pit. Kat's yellow wristband indicated she wasn't allowed to play at all as a guest so they didn't need to know if she'd had anything to drink.

Descending into the pit, Kat's butterflies were back, and she shuddered. Benny must've felt her reaction because he stopped and pulled her to the side of the stairs, out of the way of traffic. "Are you okay? Are you sure you want to do this? If you don't, we can leave now, Kitten. This is a part of my life, but I want you in my life more than anything. I can give it up if I have to."

She knew he meant it by the look in his eyes. He loved her and wouldn't let anything stand in the way of them being together. Not even something he'd enjoyed for years without her. "No, I don't want to leave yet. I don't know if this is something I can do, but we won't know until I try, right? Can we just take it slow?"

With a tender touch which melted her heart, Benny cupped her cheek. "Absolutely. I'll tell you what—we'll walk around for a bit and observe a few scenes that are relatively tame. Then we'll go back to our room and discuss what you liked and didn't like, okay? We can't play here tonight anyway. If something bothers you, tell me, and we'll move on. You mean more to me than the lifestyle, Kitten, and every good relationship has a compromise between both parties. We just have to find ours."

---

TAKING THE LEAD, and her hand again, Boomer weaved his way through the crowd. He bypassed Mistress China whipping a male submissive, a wax-play scene, and another where the female sub's nipples and clit were in clamps. They came upon a spanking bench where a submissive named Shelby was strapped down and getting her ass reddened by Carter. The real-life blonde was known for wearing different colored wigs to match her skimpy outfits, and tonight was no exception. Her straight purple hair complimented her polka-dotted bra and mini-skirt which was currently pulled up around her waist. Boomer glanced at Kat and smiled at her shocked, yet interested expression. She wasn't looking away, and he took it as a good sign. Stepping behind her, he grabbed her hips and let her feel his erection against her ass. He was pleased when she gave him a little wiggle in acknowledgement.

The position Shelby was in let everyone see her bare ass and shaved sex. Her cheeks were red with Carter's handprints, and her pussy wept. The Dom stood to the side of the bench and leaned down to say something to the sub while his hand squeezed her tender flesh. Whatever was said had her nodding her purple-coifed head. Grinning, he took two steps toward a black duffel bag sitting on a side table and began to rummage through it. Boomer felt Kat hold her breath while waiting to see what Carter would pull out of his toy bag. The Dom selected a small, new package and broke the seal. A black item fell into his hand and before turning back to his sub, he also retrieved a tube of lubricant.

Boomer moved Kat's hair off her shoulder so he could whisper in her ear. "This is what I want to do to you someday soon. He's going to plug Shelby's ass, and it'll stimulate all the nerves until she begs him to let her come."

KAT COULDN'T TAKE her eyes off the scene in front of her. It was the most erotic thing she'd ever seen in her life, and even though a part of her was embarrassed for watching, she found it arousing and couldn't shy away. While Benny's words tickled her ear, Kat eyed the handsome Dom who was definitely enjoying himself. His cock was bulging behind the zipper of his brown, leather pants and she couldn't help but think, good Lord, he was huge. A snug, short-sleeved Henley showed off his sculpted torso, and she would have to be dead not to appreciate his physique. At the V-neck, she could see a hint of his bare chest, and his chin had a dusting of evening stubble. As her eyes traveled further upward, she realized he'd caught her staring at him. Kat blushed when he gave her a playful wink before returning his attention to his restrained submissive.

She couldn't take her eyes off Carter's hands as he prepped the anal plug then used his lubed fingers to prepare Shelby to take it. Music filled the air, and, to the beat, he pumped one, then two fingers in and out of her back hole. The submissive obviously loved it because she was begging for more. "Faster. Harder. Please, Sir." But the Dom just chuckled and took his time stretching her, getting her ready to take the large plug.

Kat was shocked to realize her pussy was clenching to the beat as well. Benny rubbed his erection between her ass cheeks, and she moaned and tilted her hips, wanting him to do it again. And he didn't disappoint her. From behind, he reached between her legs, and she gasped when he plunged a finger into her own dripping pussy. She clenched her legs together. Glancing down then around, she made sure her skirt was still covering her in the front and no one was looking at them. No one was, and Benny began stroking her at a sensual pace, following Carter's tempo.

His sultry voice whispered in her ear. "My Kitten is nice and wet. I hope Carter makes this scene quick, otherwise I'm going to say to hell with the rules. I'll bend you over the back of a couch and fuck you right here in front of everyone."

One of his other fingers brushed across her clit, and Kat's legs started to shake as more moisture flowed from her pussy. The desire running through her body had her embarrassment quickly taking a back seat to her need for more pleasure. "I—I thought we could . . . couldn't play."

She almost cried in disappointment when his fingers retreated and he lowered the back of her skirt down again. Turning her head toward him, she watched in awe as he licked her juices from his finger.

"You're right. But I couldn't help myself. I'll be good, I promise. Very, very good."

The wicked amusement in his voice told her he was speaking innuendos, and she wished they were allowed to play. She wanted nothing more than to bend over and feel him deep inside her, pounding into her from behind. Raw need flooded her. She licked her lips as she stared at his. "Would you be disappointed if I said I wanted to go back to our room right now and play?"

A satisfied smirk crossed his face, and Kat knew the one thing he didn't feel was disappointment.

# CHAPTER 19

*E*ileen Michaelson rolled over and studied her fifty-eight-year-old, but still handsome husband. It was two-thirty in the morning and she couldn't sleep while Rick snored off the remaining effects of the Benadryl. He hadn't needed the Epi-pen, thank God, but he'd dozed the entire ride home, then had barely made it through the evening news before climbing into bed. An over-the-counter medication did what many terrorists and bad guys had tried, but failed to do over the years—knock her big, bad Navy SEAL on his cute ass.

At times, she couldn't believe they'd been married for almost thirty-five years. Their anniversary was six months away, and she loved Rick more than ever. They had a rough first few years with him being out of the country for weeks or months at a time, and phone calls had been sporadic depending on the team's mission. But it was moments like this when she was grateful she'd weathered the storms and stuck by him.

When they'd been married five years, after two miscarriages, she had been losing hope of giving Rick the child she knew they both wanted so desperately. Then one day while he was deployed God-knew-where on the other side of the world, she brought home a pregnancy test after missing her period for the second time in as many months. She'd been terrified to hope it was positive and that she could carry the baby to term if she was.

It had been another three weeks before she was able to tell Rick he was going to be a father. She had just passed into her second trimester and the only two people who knew were her mother and his. The two grandmothers-in-waiting had noticed the subtle changes in Eileen's body and had been sworn to secrecy until Rick could be told. He'd been on cloud nine after she'd given him the news over the phone, but five more weeks went by before they were in each other's arms again. And, somehow, he'd been stateside several months later when she'd given birth to their son.

Over the years, they'd had their ups and downs, but managed to keep their marriage afloat despite Rick's long absences for missions he couldn't tell her about. Now they were enjoying their semi-retirements in Florida. She worked as a part-time tutor for children with learning disabilities, and volunteered at a local animal shelter. Rick picked up an occasional assignment for Trident or filled in when a fishing buddy needed an extra mate for his charter business. But despite their happiness, something was missing. Eileen hoped Katerina's return meant their son was going to settle down and give them the grandchildren they were looking forward to. If any two people deserved a happily-ever-after, it was Kat and Ben.

Lightening flashed outside their bedroom window and a crack of thunder followed. Fast storms were normal in Florida, and it would probably clear within thirty minutes or so. Unable to go back to sleep, Eileen decided to go make herself a little tea and maybe read for a while. Using a hint of the light coming through the blinds from the street lamp out front, she grabbed her light-weight bathrobe and crept out into the hallway, closing the bedroom door behind her. She flipped the light switch, but nothing happened. Trying again, she assumed the storm had knocked out the power and used her hands along the wall as a guide. It wasn't until she stepped into the kitchen that a thought occurred to her. The street lamp wouldn't have been lit if the neighborhood had lost power. She realized she wasn't alone a second before a strong hand covered her mouth blocking her scream.

"Be quiet or I vill cut throat."

BOOMER'S ARM was around Kat's naked waist, and his hand found her breast. He knew he should let her sleep after the sexual gymnastics they'd performed earlier, but his cock was hard and he wanted her again. He'd seen the exchange between Kat and Carter earlier, and while a part of him was jealous, another part wondered if she would be interested in letting the other Dom join them someday. It was all about pleasing her in every way possible. He'd taken part of several ménages over the years and a few were with the black-ops agent. Carter would never poach another man's woman, but the guy loved the female population, and any way he could please them sexually was fine with him.

Massaging the lush breast, Boomer kissed Kat's bare shoulder and ground his erection against her ass. She stirred in his arms and rolled toward him letting him replace his hand with his mouth. He teased the nipple, sucking and licking until her back arched. A moan escaped her, and his eyes lifted to see she was fully awake. And there was just enough moonlight coming through the blinds for him to see she was very much aroused.

Giving the taut nipple another swipe of his tongue, he grinned at her. "Sorry, I woke you."

She shoved her hands into his hair and tugged downward until his mouth closed around her breast again. "No, you're not, and neither am I. Don't stop, it feels so good."

Legs, hips, shoulders, and arms shifted, and soon his torso was cradled between her thighs. One hand plucked her other nipple as he continued to suck on the first. Her sighs and gasps were making him harder. "Hands above your head, Kitten. Hold onto the headboard and don't let go. I heard Carter crash next door about ten minutes ago, so you might want to keep those sounds of yours on the low side. Although I doubt he'd mind hearing you."

Her hips bucked against him, and he pinched her nipple making her cry out. "Oh, oh, shit!"

Boomer swapped tits, latching his mouth onto the one he'd just pinched. He sucked the stiff peak into his mouth and shifted his body to the side so his hand could slide down to her pussy. With one finger, he circled her clit once, then twice before going lower to her engorged lips. She was ready for him, but he wasn't ready to take her yet. He wanted to tease her until she begged him like she'd done earlier when he'd eaten her through three powerful orgasms.

He cautiously eased a finger into her hot channel, hoping she wasn't sore. When she opened her legs wider, giving him better access, he added another finger and began to flick her clit with his thumb. One of her hands left the headboard and grasped his hair. He let her breast go with a pop. "Uh-uh, Kitten. What did I tell you? I've been waiting for an excuse to spank you tonight, and you just earned it."

Kat squeaked. "W-what? Are you serious? I'm ready to come, and you want to spank me?"

"Damn straight. C'mere." Sitting up, he grabbed her hips and flipped her onto her stomach, ignoring her gasp and squeal. He lifted and then settled her across his lap. Her naked ass taunted him, and he caressed the pale cheeks as she squirmed. Another idea came to mind and he reached over to the nightstand where he'd placed a new tube of lubricant earlier. He couldn't take her virgin hole yet, but he could give her a little taste of what was to come.

Boomer parted her ass cheeks, and Kat instinctively reached back with her hands to cover herself. "What are you doing?"

He grabbed her wrists with one hand and held them at the small of her back. "Shh. Easy, Kitten. I'm not going to do anything I don't think you'll enjoy. Give it a chance, that's all I'm asking. Okay?

Her tense body relaxed a little, and he let go of her wrists. Caressing her back, ass, and legs, he felt her melt into him even more. His thoughts strayed to what he'd been thinking of before she woke. Figuring he would never know unless he asked her, he decided to go for it. "What do you think of Carter?"

"What do you mean? He seems like a nice guy."

"Are you attracted to him?"

Kat looked at him over her shoulder, her brows furrowed in confusion. "I think most women would say he's good-looking." She didn't add, "as long as they weren't dead," but he was sure the words were on the tip of her wet little tongue.

"That's not what I was asking, Kitten, and you know it." He

squeezed her ass, then slid his fingers to her wet pussy, teasing her as she wriggled in his lap. "Now that you're no longer a virgin, if you and I weren't together, and Carter hit on you, would you sleep with him?"

She gaped at him. "Are you mad at me? There's nothing for you to be jealous about. I'm with you, not Carter. Just because I think another guy is good-looking doesn't mean I want to sleep with him."

He flicked her clit and smiled when she shifted her hips, trying to get closer and top from the bottom. Raising his other hand, he slapped her ass hard and then plunged his finger back inside her, stroking her higher, but not high enough.

"Ow! Ohhhhh, shit!"

"Like that, hmm? Put your hands under your cheek and keep them there. Pain can be very pleasurable, Kitten. I plan to show you just how much." He slowed his teasing pace. "Now, back to my question. I'll admit I had a moment of jealousy earlier, but I know Carter well enough that it's not an issue. What I'm trying to find out is, how you would feel if I asked him to join us . . . in here . . . right now."

Kat tried to flip over to stare at him, but he held her firm. "You—You mean like a ménage? A threesome? Seriously?"

"Seriously. And if you say no, then it's fine. We haven't gone through your limit list yet, so I figured I'd ask."

Pushing up on her hands, she twisted her upper torso. "Can you stop so I can turn over a sec, please? So we can talk about this first. I can't think when you're doing that. I'm not saying no, but I'm not saying yes either."

Pulling his finger out of her pussy, he turned her over and sat her on his lap, his rigid cock pressed against her hip. Whether her answer was yes or no, he was still going to give her a few orgasms before finding his own release. He'd been involved in a few first-time ménages, but this was Kat, and *all* of this was new to her. Reaching over, he turned on the bedside lamp so they could see each other better. "Let me explain a few things first before you answer me. One of the things about a ménage is trust. You have to trust me to make sure the third, whether it's Carter or someone else, doesn't do anything you don't like or anything that would hurt you. Everything he does will have to be cleared by me first, and I won't allow anything you're not comfortable with. The third in a scene is there to enhance the woman's pleasure. Imagine I have four hands instead of two, touching you and pleasing you. Maybe while my mouth is eating your pussy, his will be sucking these luscious tits of yours." He closed his hand around one and began to tease her. Moaning, she wiggled in his lap and thrust her chest out, inviting him to do more. "While I'm fucking your sweet cunt, he'll be fucking your mouth. But don't worry, he won't come in your mouth . . . he'll come all over your chest at the last second. Then I'll make you come before I do. So, tell me, Kitten. Do you want to experience two men doing nothing but pleasing you, making you shatter into a million pieces over and over again?"

"Yesssss." Her answer came out as a hiss, all but begging him to do whatever he wanted.

He stopped his sensual assault on her breast and grabbed her hair, holding her so she was looking directly at him. "Say it again, Kitten. I need to know you won't have any reservations after we start. Is this what you want? You, me, and Carter?"

Her hand came up to cup his jaw, his stubble rough against her soft palm. "Yes, as long as you're the one in control, then yes, I want this. I want to try new things with you, but only if you want them too."

"I love you, Kitten. I promise this will be good. If something scares you or doesn't feel right, use your 'red' safeword, okay?" Leaning down, he took possession of her mouth, tasting, teasing, and savoring before pulling away again. "Okay?

"Okay. And I love you, too."

"One other thing. While we're playing, don't forget I want to hear 'Master' from your pretty mouth, and call Carter 'Sir.'"

She licked her lips. "Yes, Master."

Raising his hand above the headboard, Boomer knocked on the wall between their room and Carter's. He wasn't too surprised when the door opened a second later and the man walked in wearing only a pair of sweatpants. The grey cotton was doing nothing to hide his prominent hard-on. His hair was still damp from a shower and slicked back, down from its earlier ponytail.

"Jeez, it took you fucking long enough. I thought I was going to have to start whacking off in there." At Kat's astonished expression, he added, "Hello, little one. Yes, the walls in here are thin enough to hear through. We need to have Ian fix that. But if you'd said 'no,' I wouldn't have let you know I heard anything because I wouldn't want to embarrass you." He stopped next to the queen-sized bed, regarding her appreciatively. "Damn, you're even prettier naked."

---

KAT HAD BEEN SO shocked at his sudden appearance, then his bare torso had snagged her attention, and she'd forgotten she was nude. She was about to raise her hands to cover herself, but Benny stopped her.

"Uh-uh, Kitten. There's no need to hide. Let him look at how beautiful you are." He turned her in his lap so her legs fell to either side of his and his erection nestled against her ass and lower back. Taking her wrists, he brought her hands up behind his neck while her head rested against his shoulder.

She shuddered at the heat she saw in Carter's eyes as they traveled over her body, lingering on her breasts and exposed pussy. His intense gaze made her wetter, and she blushed more deeply.

While Benny's hands closed around her breasts, Carter cupped her cheek. "I love seeing women blush, little one, but don't be embarrassed. You have a gorgeous body, and it's a privilege to see it. But I need to hear you say you want me here one more time. I'm not going to do anything Boomer doesn't approve of. He knows what you like and what you don't. Do you want me to be a third in your bed, fucking you, and pleasing you? I need a verbal answer, sweetheart."

Kat was so turned on by his words and by how Benny had been playing with her nipples that she didn't hesitate. "Yes . . . Sir. I do." Kat still couldn't believe that she'd agree to this, but she didn't want to take it back. She'd read many books with ménage relationships in them and had several fantasies about it happening to her. But only if Benny was with her.

"Thank you, and I'm truly honored. I promise you'll enjoy every minute of it, starting now. Boom, I do believe you mentioned a spanking, hmm?"

Kat's eyes went wide and a little squeak escaped her. "What? I'm supposed to enjoy that? Seriously?"

"Ha!" Benny barked and chuckled. "As I told you before, Kitten, yes, seriously. I've been itching to spank your sweet ass and, yes, done right, you'll enjoy it. Now, would you like to continue or say your safeword?"

Both men patiently waited as Kat worked her way through this in her mind. She couldn't deny the idea of being spanked turned her on, but would it hurt too much? He'd said they wouldn't hurt her, and there was some pain which was gratifying. She also had her safeword which she knew without a doubt would be heeded if she said it. The few spanks Benny had given her so far had aroused her, but she was still nervous. "Is this a punishment spanking or a pleasure spanking, Master?"

"Since you used my title so nicely, it will be a pleasure spanking, Kitten. Let us show you how a little bit of pain can take you higher than you've ever been."

Without saying a word, Carter held out his hand to her. Making her decision, she took it and let him help her stand. Smiling down at her, he addressed Benny. "Why don't we up the heat factor for her? She can sit on my face while you redden her ass.

Kat's mouth dropped open as Benny climbed off the bed, apparently not embarrassed he was naked in front of the other man. "Excellent idea, my friend. Before I forget, when Kat blows you later, she's not a fan of swallowing yet, so that's a hard limit for her right now."

Her entire body blushed in embarrassment, but neither man seemed fazed by it.

"Understood." Carter laid down on the bed with his head at the edge closest to them. "Climb on up, Kitty-Kat, and let me taste your sweet pussy."

Kat's legs shook as Benny helped her back onto the bed so she was straddling the other man's head, facing his bare feet at the opposite side. Carter pulled her knees a little wider apart, so she was closer to his mouth, but didn't start tasting her yet. When she was positioned right, Benny pushed on her back until she lowered her upper body onto Carter's, her head resting on his rock-hard abs. Rolling her eyes upward, she could see his stiff cock bulging in his sweats and wondered what he looked like. Would he be bigger or smaller than Benny? Would they taste similar or completely different? She didn't know, but was curious to find out. Feeling Carter's breath against her wet sex, she shivered in anticipation. *What was he waiting for?*

"Are you comfortable, Kitten?" Benny caressed her back and ass as goose bumps popped up all over her porcelain skin.

"Yes, Master."

"Good. Go for it, man."

Carter wasted no more time before feasting on her. His tongue and mouth attacked her, and she cried out how good it felt. He licked her entire slit from end to end then back again, over and over, like she was an ice cream cone, as his fingers found her clit. The pressure on her little nub was light, only enough to tease, but nothing more . . . and she wanted more. Oh fuck, how she wanted more! He nibbled on her pussy lips, and she felt her juices flow. Moaning, she ran her tongue along the right side of the muscular "V" which disappeared into his sweats. His hips flinched, and his dick twitched in response. Kat smiled wickedly, feeling empowered she could evoke a response like that from a noticeably experienced man.

Just as he impaled her with his stiffened tongue, a hand landed hard on her right ass cheek, and she jumped, but Carter held her hips so she didn't get far. Pain, then heat, then pure desire shot through her. Another slap sounded a split second before she felt the same on her other cheek, and the pain barely registered in her mind. All she could concentrate on was the euphoric high she was climbing. This time Benny massaged the flesh he'd struck, and the sensations he evoked made her juices flow into Carter's mouth. The man groaned and lapped up every drop. Kat didn't know what to react to, or how. The dual assault on her buttocks and pussy had her head spinning, and all she could do was moan, pant, and enjoy. Her hands clenched Carter's thighs through his sweatpants as she tried to grind her pelvis into his face. He speared her with his tongue again. "Oh, shit. Holy fucking shit, it feels so good. Oh, God!"

---

BOOMER'S COCK grew harder at the words and sounds coming from Kat, and he spanked her ass a few more times, spacing them out until his handprints covered her cheeks and the sit-spots at the top of her thighs. The mix of white, pink, and red was so enticing. Pressing his hands against her flesh, he held the heat in and let the pleasure-pain mix with whatever Carter was doing to her. Boomer knew it wouldn't take much more for her to go over the edge. Earlier in the night, she'd been able to hold off and orgasm twice on command, so he decided to give her a break this time. "Come whenever you need to, Kitten."

"Y-Yes, M-Master. Thank you. Oh, shit! Don't stop, S-Sir, please! Holy hell . . ."

Carter must have done something she really liked, because her words became mumbled amid her keening as she buried her face into his abdomen. Boomer found the tube of lubricant near the pillows and grabbed it. Squirting it on his fingers, he instructed his friend, "Spread her cheeks for me, man. It's time to introduce her to a little anal."

Not stopping his assault on her pussy, Carter reached back and squeezed her tender ass cheeks, separating them. Her puckered virgin hole winked at Boomer, and he coated it with lube. Gasping, she clenched, and he heard Carter's muffled chuckle.

"Whatever you just did, do it again. It made her gush. Damn, she's fucking delicious."

"And I didn't even push in yet, but that's next. Relax your ass, Kitten. You're going to feel some pressure, but I'm only using my finger, so it won't be too uncomfortable. Once you relax, you'll feel it in your pussy.

"Y-yes, Master. I'll t-try."

"Good girl." Boomer rimmed her entrance, making sure there was plenty of lube, then eased his index finger into the center. Using an in-and-out motion, he advanced a little further with each pass. "Relax, Kitten. Let me in, and I swear you're going to come hard when I get there."

---

"Oh fuck! I'm ready to come now. Just a little more, please . . . more!" She had no idea what "more" she was begging for, and it didn't matter as long as they continued what they were doing. Between their four hands, Kat couldn't move her pelvis. She was at their mercy, and there was no place else she wanted to be at the moment. Without realizing it at first, she dug her nails into Carter's thighs until his hard muscles tightened further. Her fingers flew open. "S-Sorry."

His mouth left her pussy long enough for him to say, "Don't be sorry, Kitty-Kat. I like being clawed. Just don't draw blood and we're good."

"Oh shit!" Kat cried out. Benny had used her distraction to plunge past her sphincter, and the nerves in her ass lit up like the Fourth of July. He'd been right—all the nerves seem to be directly connected to her clit, which was pulsating relentlessly. If only someone would . . . "Pleeeassseeee . . . I need to . . . Oh, fuck . . ."

Carter sucked on her clit and that was all it took for her to come, her orgasm sending her spiraling into an abyss. She was flying and falling at the same time, not knowing which way was up. Her body shook as wave after wave of ecstasy rippled through her. Screams of pleasure assailed her ears, and it took her a moment to realize they were coming from her. Twisting the sheets in her hands, she bucked her hips, trying to get away . . . trying to get closer. Carter's mouth and tongue continued their onslaught as Benny fucked her ass with his finger, and the combination had her on a steep climb once again. "No . . . yes . . . oh shit, yesssss . . ."

A slap landed on her right butt cheek then her left. It was all too much, and she went over again, quivering and shouting. Spots appeared before her eyes as she spun out of control. Never in her life could she have imagined an orgasm this good . . . this intense. She'd always thought women claiming they'd had one like this had been exaggerating. Now she knew they did exist and she was capable of having them . . . more than once.

The men eased off, then stopped as Kat collapsed on Carter's body. Her lungs heaved for oxygen, and Benny picked her up and laid her on the bed. "Okay, Kitten?"

While she nodded, trying to catch her breath, Carter stood, wiped his glistening face with his hand, and then removed his sweatpants. Holy shit, the man was perfection. His impressive cock was standing proud as he gave it a few strokes. The two men stared down at her as she eyed them both. Damn, they were hot. She thought of all the women who'd pay a million dollars to be in her position, or any other position Benny and Carter wanted to put her in. *Tough cookies, ladies, I'm not trading places with anyone. I'm playing catch up with the rest of the female population.*

"Ready for more, Kitty-Kat?" Carter knelt on the bed while Benny grabbed a condom from the box on the nightstand. He was going to have to get more if they kept going at this rate. It was the third one he'd used tonight.

"Hell, yeah!" She covered her mouth as they chuckled at her. Her brain-to-mouth filter had to be broken when it came to sex. "I mean . . . oh, whatever . . . hell, yeah!"

"Boomer's going to fuck your sweet pussy while you suck my cock. Don't worry, I'll pull out and come all over those pretty tits of yours instead of in your mouth. Okay?"

She nodded in agreement.

Carter grabbed her chin. "Uh-uh, Kitty. The answer is 'yes, Sir.' Before was all about you. But now, you be a good girl, do as we say, and we'll let you come again before we do."

He'd transformed before her eyes. His face was stern, and he'd dropped the tone of his voice. Gone was the teasing playmate and in his place was a commanding Dominant—sexy and sinful. She glanced at Benny and saw the same intense expression. Holy hell, she'd do or say whatever they wanted her to, as long as they kept looking at her like she was the sexiest thing they'd ever seen. Her pussy clenched as she turned back to Carter. "Yes, Sir."

"Boom, how do you want to do this?"

---

CLIMBING ON THE BED, Boomer grabbed Kat's hips. "On all fours, Kitten. I'm going to fuck you from behind while you suck him off. When he's ready, I'll pull you upright so he can come on you."

Following orders, Kat got on her hands and knees facing the foot of the bed. Carter knelt in front of her as Boomer settled in behind her. He quickly donned the condom and lined his aching cock with her slit. Watching his friend guide Kat to take him into her mouth was so fucking hot, he wasn't sure he'd last long. But they'd make it good for her again before that happened. Carter hissed as her mouth closed around him, and he firmly grasped her hair, showing her the pace he wanted. Boomer rubbed his tip along her pussy lips and found she was still soaking wet. Clutching her hips, he thrust forward and was rewarded with a sexy moan from her as he buried himself inside her to the hilt.

Carter cursed. "Shit, her mouth is a fucking deadly sin. Make her moan again."

"No problem." He was gliding in and out of her channel, reveling in the feel of her tight walls. He dreamed of the day he could take her with no barriers between them. Flesh on flesh. Reaching around, his fingers found her clit and soon she was moaning repeatedly.

On either end, both men set the same pace. In and out. Slow, at first. Each staring down where their cocks were disappearing into her body, filling her. Hisses, moans, groans, slurps, and slaps filled the air as all three took their pleasure and gave it back in return. Carter reached down and moved her hair which had fallen around her face again. "Can you take me a little deeper? Breathe through your nose."

"She's got a strong gag reflex." Boomer's hands rubbed her bare back, sides, and hips as he continued to pump into her tight, hot pussy.

Carter wrapped his fingers around his thick shaft about three-quarters of the way down. "I won't go too far, Kitty. Just a little further."

Without releasing him, Kat nodded and took a deep breath through her nose. Carter's hand pulled not-so-gently on her hair, while his other one found one of her tits and rolled the perky nipple between his fingers. Simultaneously, Benny reached around her hip and pinched her clit. Her muffled scream of pleasure made both men smirk, knowing it wouldn't take much more for her to explode. Her moaning, breathing, and heart rate increased as both cocks fucking her picked up their pace. All the signs pointed to her impending orgasm, and Carter addressed his friend. "She's getting close, man, and so am I. Get ready to lift her up."

Clutching her hips, Boomer adjusted his knees. He then leaned forward, put his arms under her armpits and grabbed her shoulders. The new position allowed him to impale her harder and faster on his cock, driving deeper. He felt her inner walls begin to pulsate around him, but waited for the other man to tell him it was time to pull her up.

Carter's grip on her hair intensified as he murmured words of how good she was. A growl escaped him. "Now!"

Boomer drew her upright, and she had no choice but to release the cock from her mouth. The new position made her sink further onto the shaft in her pussy. Carter's fingers pinched her nipple and sent her over the edge as he squirted his hot cum on her breasts and abdomen. Dual cries and curses of release were joined by a third as Boomer shot his own load deep inside her.

No words were spoken for a few moments as all three regained their breath. Kat let out a groan as Boomer eased from her body and turned her onto her back. He quickly disposed of his condom in a nearby garbage pail. Carter stood on shaky legs and went to the bathroom to retrieve damp and dry towels. He handed both to Boomer, who began cleaning her, and then leaned down to kiss Kat's forehead. "Thank you, Kitty-Kat. You were amazing. I'm going to leave you in your Dom's care. Sleep well."

"You, too," she murmured, fading fast into slumber.

Carter chuckled as he grabbed his sweatpants and pulled them on. "Thanks, man. Like I said before, she's a keeper."

Finishing with Kat's torso, Boomer found a clean section of the damp towel and started wiping between her legs. "I know. You going to be around in the morning?"

Opening the door, Carter looked back at his friend. "Unless I get called away on something, I figured I'd stick around, just in case you need me for anything until she's safe. You guys . . ." He jutted his chin toward Kat. ". . . and your ladies, are the closest thing I have to family, and I'll do anything I can to keep you all around. Later."

Boomer's hand slowed to a stop as he stared at the now closed door. The black-ops spy had been there many times when they'd needed him, but he wasn't known for sticking around long. And saying the team and their women were family to the loner was something Boomer had never expected to hear. They knew very little about their friend's life, even less about his past, and he was sure they knew him better than most. Hell, Carter had always been a nice guy, patient with the submissives, and certainly loyal, but how could a man with hands so deadly hide such a loving heart?

Turning his attention back to Kat, who was almost asleep, Boomer picked her up and put her head on the pillow. He tossed the towels on the floor and reached over to shut off the light. Lying down next to her, he drew the sheet over their bodies and soon fell victim to gratified exhaustion.

# CHAPTER 20

*K*at woke up wrapped in Benny's arms, and hotter than a pig on a spit. She wasn't used to sleeping with someone, and while she loved being near him all night, at times she wished his body temperature was twenty degrees lower. Easing away from him, she threw the sheet off and sat up. According to the bedside clock it was a little after ten, and she didn't know why she was surprised she'd slept so late. After all, she'd been up half the night having incredibly naughty sex, and loving every minute of it. Stretching, she stood and headed toward the bathroom. A humming reached her ears and she realized it was coming from the pile of clothes they'd practically ripped off each other the night before. Searching through the shirts, skirt, and pants, she found his cell phone, still on vibrate from being in the club. Noting the name and number, she decided to let him know he had a call.

"Benny?" No answer. Kat walked back to the bed and shook his shoulder. "Benny? Wake up. Your mom's calling."

"*Mmm,*" he mumbled into his pillow. "Ooo's ih?"

"Your mom."

"-All -ack -ater."

Kat grinned as he went right back to sleep like a little kid. Placing his phone on the nightstand, she once again headed for the bathroom.

Fifteen minutes later, after a nice relaxing shower, she ambled out to common area of the second floor where the kitchenette and living area were. Her wet hair, combed back, dampened her clean

T-shirt. She'd been staring down, past her baggy sweatpants to her bare toes, noticing they were in desperate need of a pedicure, when she realized someone else was in the room. Blushing at Carter's presence, she made her way over to the coffee machine.

He grinned as she brushed past him, then took a seat at the table. Never taking his amused eyes off her, he took a sip of his coffee. "Good morning, Kitty-Kat."

"Um, good morning." Concentrating on the Keurig as if it was the most complicated piece of machinery she'd ever used, Kat busied herself. She wasn't sure what to say to the man who'd been a third in her and Benny's sexual escapades. Was she supposed to thank him? That might be weird. Maybe she should just act like nothing happened. While she was embarrassed seeing him this morning, she didn't regret what they'd done. She may have only recently lost her virginity, but like most women, she'd had her fantasies—although she'd never dreamed that particular fantasy would happen to her. And, oh boy, had the reality been a hundred times better than anything she'd ever thought up. Running out of things to do at the counter, she hoped he would leave the room, saving her from making a fool of herself. However, after her coffee was ready, she had no choice but to turn around and face him.

Using his foot, he pushed out the chair across from him and indicated with his chiseled chin for her to sit. It would be more awkward if she refused, so she sat with her coffee in hand, her eyes downcast. She startled after a moment when he let out an exaggerated sigh and stood. Kat watched as he began to pull out a Cheerios box, a bowl, and milk from the cabinets and refrigerator and then set them down in front of her. He grabbed a knife and spoon from a drawer, and a banana from the counter, adding them to the other items. A napkin was the last thing he placed in front of her. Sitting back down, he pointed to her and then the food. "Eat, little one. Your clothes are hanging off you. It's obvious you've lost weight recently, and I doubt it was intentional."

Kat snorted, but started pouring the cereal into the bowl. "Are all Doms this bossy? You all keep ordering me to eat."

"Yes, when it comes to a submissive's health and safety, we're very bossy." He regarded her for a moment as she prepared her breakfast, adding milk and sliced banana, until he seemed satisfied with how much food she'd filled the bowl with. "Now, while you're eating, there are a few other things we need to talk about." When her hand stopped the loaded spoon halfway to her mouth as she gaped at him, he reached over with his fingers and got it started again. "I said 'while you're eating.'" She put the spoon into her mouth, then pulled it out empty. "Good girl. Now, what happened last night, or early this morning as it were, is between you, Boomer, and me. No one else. If you choose to have some girl talk with the others, that's one thing, but I will not be letting anyone know what happened between us. I don't kiss and tell about things that happen behind closed doors. Understood?"

Kat nodded and swallowed. "I mean, yes, Sir."

"You can drop the 'Sir' this morning, Kat. Only when we're playing or in the club is the formality necessary. Now, I don't want you reading too much into what happened and being all embarrassed around me. There's no need for it. Boomer is a good friend and, as I said before, it was an honor to play with you. If it was a one-time thing, that's fine." He shrugged. "If it happens again, that's fine, too. But think of it as . . . I don't know . . . as we all went out bowling and had a fun time. Nothing embarrassing about bowling, right?"

Surprised he'd used the same activity she'd been talking to Benny about on the plane, Kat laughed, the tension she'd felt disappearing. "Um, no I guess not. Unless it's naked bowling."

"Now there's a sport that won't be on TV anytime soon." He sat forward and took another sip of his coffee. "You're a beautiful, sensual woman, Kat. Never be embarrassed about that. Just because you enjoyed something outside the norms of society, doesn't mean it was wrong. You were just brave enough to try something millions of women want but don't have the courage to experience for themselves."

"I never thought of it that way."

"And that's what's wrong with society nowadays." Evidently having overheard some of their conversation, Benny walked into the room, fresh from his own shower. He stopped next to the table, eyeing her breakfast, apparently satisfied with what he saw. "Everyone is too scared to try something they've only dreamed about. And it's nice to see you eating. You two okay?"

The question was addressed to them both, but it was apparent the only person he was worried about was Kat. She glanced at Carter, who nodded at her, then grinned back at Benny. "Yup. We're good." After tossing his cell phone on the table, Benny kissed the top of her head then made a beeline to the coffee machine. "Did you call your mom back?"

"Not yet. Need caffeine first. She's probably already planning for us to go visit for a few days. But before we do that, we have to figure out how to get the target off your back."

Kat looked down at the phone which had landed next to her. For some reason the screen had lit up, and what she saw had her brow furrowing. "Um, Benny. It says you have twenty-seven missed calls."

———

SPINNING AROUND, Boomer snatched it from the table and stared at the screen. "What the fuck? Shit, they're all from my mom. Fuck, something must have happened to Pop." He hit the speed dial for his mother's phone, pacing impatiently until she picked up. An evil chill ran down his spine. When it connected, his words rushed out. "Mom? It's me. What's wrong? My phone was off."

"B-Ben? Y-You have to come h-home quickly, and bring K-Katerina. T-They're going to k-kill your father if you don't."

He froze at the terror he heard in his mother's voice. "What? Who? Mom, are you there? Who's going to kill Pop?"

An astute Carter immediately pulled out his phone and called Ian. "If you're not already in the office, get there. They've got Boom's parents." He hung up on the other man's loud curses.

"Mom! Fuck! Hello?" At first Boomer thought they'd been disconnected, but then he heard his mother cry out in the background as someone else took the phone. "Who the fuck is this?"

"This is man who vill kill parents if you don't bring vhat ve vant. You have two hours or I start playing vith knife. I vill kill if see police. Bring girl and money."

"You son of a fucking bitch! I'm going to kill you if you hurt one hair on them! You hear me you piece of shit! Hello? Hello? Fuck!" He threw the phone across the room and didn't even care it broke into a million pieces. They had plenty of back up phones downstairs, and Brody could switch Boomer's phone number over to one.

"The team's alerted. Ian will be downstairs in a minute." Carter was almost to the hallway when he turned around. "I'm grabbing my stuff. We'll get them, Boom. We'll get your folks out of this, and Kat too."

Boomer nodded his thanks and looked at Kat who was crying, her mouth opening and closing without any sound. Pulling her out of her seat and into his arms, he hugged her tight. "It's all right, baby. He's right . . . we'll get my folks out of this."

"H-How? You have to take me with you, and—and the money too. T-Trade me for your parents."

"No! Fucking! Way!" He grabbed her shoulders and gave her two short shakes until he was sure he had her attention. His angry eyes flared at her. "No fucking way am I doing that, Kitten. Not happening. This is what we do. We rescue people. These assholes have messed with the wrong team. And there's no fucking way I'm trading you for my parents, much less bringing you with us. You're staying right here in the compound."

"You can't leave me here! What if . . . what if they see I'm not there and kill your parents, Benny? I can't let that happen! You have to take me with you! We'll give them the money! Please!"

She was becoming hysterical, and there was no time for it. He shook her shoulders again, talking over her rambling, putting his best Dominant tone into his voice. "No, Kat. No! Listen to me, dammit! You're not going anywhere near these fuckers. You're staying right here, and unless you don't want to sit for the next year, you'll do exactly what I say. Your safety is my number one priority, and I can't do my job if I'm worrying about you *and* my folks. Now, we don't have time to argue, so are you going to obey me, or am I going to have to tie you to a fucking chair?"

Carter jogged past them, heading for the stairs with his gear. "Time's a-wasting, dude."

"Kat? Answer me!"

She was shaking and sobbing, but somehow his words penetrated her scrambled brain. "Um, o-okay."

"Good girl." Snatching her hand, he led her toward the stairs. Now that he didn't have to worry about her, his mind was free to worry about his folks.

---

KAT WATCHED as the command van sped out of the compound followed by two black SUVs. Beside her, Jake put his arm around her shoulders. "Everything is going to be fine, Kat. Come on. Let's go inside. It'll be an hour or so before they get there, and we'll hear everything when they do."

She'd been adamant about listening in on the rescue along with Jake. It'd been decided he would stay behind to watch Kat, along with Murray, the compound's daytime guard, and one of Chase Dixon's men. The other two contract agents had gone with the rest of the Trident team and Carter. Since Jake's dominant eye was still covered by the patch, the black-ops spy was taking his place as team sniper. Jake wasn't very happy about missing the rescue, but he knew he might be a hindrance, and Kat needed guarding, too.

Thankfully, Kristen, Angie, and Jenn were on their way to a book promotion at a Barnes & Noble in Spring Hill, about an hour north of Tampa. Since Angie had designed the book cover for *Leather & Lace*, Kristen's publisher had thought it would be great idea for her to appear with the author. They'd invited Jenn to be their paid gofer for the day, and she'd switched shifts at the pub so she could join them. The three women had left an hour before Boomer had gotten the call from his mother, so they had no idea what was going down. Ian and Devon preferred it that way. No point in worrying them if it wasn't necessary. Hopefully the excitement would all be over before they returned later in the afternoon.

Beau trotted after Kat as she followed Jake into the offices. The team had opted to leave the trained canine behind as extra security for Kat. The only other person in the compound, besides the two guards, was Trident's secretary, Colleen, who looked up as the other two approached her desk. "Don't worry, Kat. These guys know their stuff, and they're the best."

"I know." She gave the younger woman a small smile. "I just won't be able to relax until I hear from Benny that everyone's okay."

"Can I get you something? Tea, maybe?"

Kat shook her head. "No, thanks. My stomach's a mess, and that'll just make it worse."

"Why don't you go upstairs and lay down for a bit?" Jake asked her. "You're pale, and I don't want you getting sick on me." She was about to object, but he held up his hand, stopping her. "I promise, I'll come get you when they get there. There's nothing any of us can do until then. Please, Kat? Don't make me get my bullwhip."

While Kat gaped at him, Colleen snorted, which earned her a stern look from the Dom. She just grinned at him, knowing he'd been teasing the other woman. "He's just messing with you, Kat. Just threaten to mother him until his patch is removed and he'll run in the other direction. Women scare him."

"Keep it up, little one, and I'll be on the phone to your Dom. Reggie will be more than happy to tan your hide tonight."

The secretary giggled. They both knew she loved to get spanked by her Master. "Yes, Sir."

Turning back to Kat, Jake pointed to the stairs. "All kidding aside, please go lay down for a bit, Kat. Take Beau with you. As soon as I hear them nearing the house, I'll come get you."

She grumbled, but headed for the staircase, her eyes feeling heavy from the stress. "Bossy Doms. *Hier*, Beau."

As the canine followed Kat, Jake turned to Colleen. "Did you get a hold of Tiny yet? I want him here as an extra precaution."

"I spoke to him, and he said he'd be here as soon as he can, but it'll be about two hours. He had to take his mom for an MRI of her knee to see if she needs surgery. As soon as he drops her off, he'll be on his way." The phone rang, but she continued as she reached for it. "And don't forget I'm leaving in about a half hour. I have to go take the firearms training course Ian scheduled me for, but I can cancel if you need me to." Not waiting for an answer, she brought the phone to her ear. "Hello, Trident Security. How can I help you?"

Happy it would leave him with one less person at the compound to worry about, Jake gave her a quick wave indicating she should leave for her course, and then headed for the war-room. He'd promised Brody he wouldn't touch anything except the camera feeds and communications equipment. The geek was very anal about who was allowed in his technological lair. There was also a spare company laptop which Brody had set up for him, refusing to give him access to the mainframe computer, or as Egghead called it, his baby.

Gripping the desk chair, Jake made sure it was under him before sitting. His perception was off because of the eye patch, but he'd gotten used to it after the first two days. Still, when he went to grab things, he didn't always get it on the first try. Waking the laptop from sleep mode, he checked the time. About fifty more minutes before they got there. Nothing to do, but wait . . .

# CHAPTER 21

"*C*an't you drive any fucking faster?"

"Relax, Boomer." Ian waited for an oncoming car to pass, then drove around the little old lady behind the wheel of her seven-year-old Ford Taurus, cruising at ten miles under the speed limit. The communications van driven by Marco followed suit, as well as Devon in the other SUV. "We're loaded to the gills with weapons and ammo, so I have no desire to get pulled over. They said two hours, and we only used an hour and ten of it. Five more minutes and we're there. Now chill, or I'm leaving you in the com-van."

"Like fucking hell!"

Ignoring his youngest employee, Ian continued to the Michaelson's house in a quiet neighborhood on the outskirts of the city. He parked a few hundred feet down from the driveway, out of view of anyone looking out the windows. The other vehicles pulled up behind him and the occupants got out, scanning the area. In this part of Sarasota, the property lots were larger, so houses were more spread out. Rick and Eileen Michaelson had fallen in love with their semi-retirement home after house-hunting for days with a realtor eleven years ago. It was secluded enough for quiet and privacy, yet close enough to others, so they could become friends with their neighbors. A six-minute drive was all it took to reach the more populated residential and commercial areas.

While it sucked their neighbors had been too far away to hear screams for help, if there'd been any, it was to the team's advantage.

Once they blended into the tree-line, they wouldn't have to worry much about someone calling the police regarding a small army of men with guns running around. While Boomer got out, joining the rest of the team, Ian tapped on the microphone of his headset. "Reverend, you there?"

A burst of static came through then cleared. "Yeah, Boss-man. What's your status?"

"Just pulled up. How are things there?"

"Five by five." The military code meant all is well. "Just going to go get Kat. Stay safe, brothers."

"Amen." Ian exited the vehicle and met the rest of the team by the side of the comm van where weapons and equipment were being double-checked and strapped on. The men were dressed in camouflage and armed to the teeth. "Carter, find yourself a sniper position. My guess is they're in the family room. It's the largest and has the most windows to see if anyone is coming. Rear of the house, northwest corner. Scan the front and side windows for tangos on your way." Without a word, the spy disappeared into the trees with his trusted MK-11 sniper rifle. "Polo, Dev, take one of the SUVs, drive past the house and park up the road. Approach by foot from that direction. Work your way around and stand-by to breach the kitchen door. Check the windows on your way, too. Egghead, I want to know where the heat signatures are and how many, then use the side door to the garage. Wait a count of three after we breach—I don't want you getting in the way of any crossfire." He turned to Chase's two men. "Burke, Dusty, you're with the geek."

Brody reached into the van and pulled out the handheld heat-detecting device, then took off after his two temporary teammates with all of them using the tree-line as cover.

"Boom, you're with me at the front door." Ian waited for a reply, but Boomer was staring in the direction of his parent's home. "Boomer!" He got in the younger man's face. "This is just like every other mission, frog. I need your head in the game."

Knowing his boss was right, Boomer took a deep breath and went into battle mode. Anything else could result in one of his teammates getting hurt or killed, and he'd be damned if he was the cause of that happening. "I'm good. Let's just do this."

Ian waited a moment until he was clearly satisfied his friend was in the right mindset. Then readying his assault rifle, he took point, leading the way to the edge of the property. The house sat back from the road, and, thankfully, Boomer's mom loved to landscape with trees, shrubs and flowers. There wasn't too much to use as cover, but enough, so it was better than nothing.

Going about twenty feet into the trees parallel to the property, they stopped and waited for the team to check in with intel. Carter was first. "Blinds are all pulled shut. No signs of movement."

"Fuck!"

Ian glared at Boomer, but didn't say anything about his low-volume outburst. He'd do the same if the situation was reversed. "Heat signatures?"

It was a few moments before Brody's reply came over the airwaves. "Nothing at the front end of the house. Going around the east side. Blinds are shut here, too."

The waiting was killing Boomer, but he knew it was necessary. The more intel, the better chance they had at ending this without getting his parents killed—if they weren't dead already. Pushing the ugly thought from his head, he listened for his teammate's next report.

"No heat, east side."

"Take it around back," Ian replied before taking off for the front door. Staying low and watching for anything out of place, Boomer followed him. After using two trees to stop and scan the area, they reached the porch and silently flanked both sides of the front door, waiting for another update. Devon and Marco alerted they were ready for the breach command at the rear kitchen door.

"Two positives, full heat, ninety-nine and ninety-eight degrees. Both on the floor of the family room."

"Just two? What the fuck? Take it around the west side, Egg. Make sure there are no surprises. Dev, Burke, make sure there's no booby-traps on your entrances . . . I don't like this."

Boomer didn't either as he began to inspect the door frame. The only good thing was, if it was his parents lying on the floor, they were still alive, otherwise their heat signatures would be cooler. Unless they'd been killed and the tangos left only moments before the team arrived. But why would they have done that without Kat and the money?

On Ian's side, there was a thin row of paned windows down the length of the door. He took a quick peek then shook his head. "Nothing that I can see."

Brody rounded the house, jogging up to them. "No one else in the house, Boss-man."

Grimacing, Ian acknowledged him with a nod. Something was wrong . . . seriously wrong. But the only way to find out, was to enter the house . . . very carefully. "Burke, Egghead's with us, so it's just you two. Since you can't see inside, I don't want to take a chance the door is rigged, so wait for us to let you in. Dev, how's the back look?"

"Clean."

"All right. Pick the lock, instead of knocking it down. Let me know when you're ready."

Boomer was working on the dead bolt and once it clicked he turned his attention to the lock on the knob. In less than two minutes, they were ready to go. Ian got the "ready" from Devon as Boomer stood with his hand on the doorknob, waiting for the signal.

"On three. One . . . Two . . . Three."

The front and back doors opened simultaneously, and the five teammates stormed in. Since he didn't have a shot from the trees, Carter had shouldered his rifle and hoofed it to the back door, two steps behind Marco, with his Sig Sauer pistol in hand. Weapons at ready position, they moved systematically through the house, clearing each room, closet, and hiding place along their way to the family room. Brody stopped at the door leading to the garage, and after checking for booby-traps, opened it for the others.

Nothing could have prepared Boomer for what waited for them in his parent's family room. His mother was frantically trying to get out of the duct tape which was wrapped around her bare legs from ankles to knees. Her arms were also taped behind her in similar fashion. The bastards had even put it over her eyes and mouth. All the poor woman could do was squirm futilely.

But it was his dad who held Boomer's shocked attention. Lying in a pool of blood, the man was ashen. Like his wife, Rick had been trussed up, but it appeared the Russians didn't see a need to cover his face as well. Boomer's feet were nailed to the ground as the others pushed past him, cursing and dropping to their knees to help the couple.

Next to him, Ian was barking into the phone, demanding 9-1-1 send an ambulance to their location for a home invasion gunshot victim. That broke Boomer from his shock, and he dove to help Devon and Brody free his father. Now that he was closer, he began assessing Rick's injuries. In addition to a gunshot wound to the abdomen, he'd been beaten . . . viciously. His face and torso showed bruises, swelling, and split skin which had to have occurred over several hours. Brody began handing them items from an emergency medical pack, ripping open the packages as he went. Pressure dressings were applied as Devon worked to start an IV. Rick's breathing was labored, but, thank fuck, he was alive.

Behind Boomer, Marco and Carter cut through Eileen's bindings, and began to peel the tape from her face, very slowly. They'd wait until they got her to the hospital and let the doctors use an anti-adhesive to pull the rest off. Duct tape could be like glue against the skin and was more painful to remove the longer it was on. As it was, they couldn't help but peel off a layer of skin from her lips and parts of her eyebrows. But it didn't seem to bother her, because when they freed her mouth, she started screaming for her husband, desperately trying to get to his side as they held her back. Knowing he needed to calm his mother, Boomer switched places with Marco, who took over holding the pressure bandage to staunch the flow of blood from Rick's abdomen.

"He's alive, Mom. Pop's a fighter. We got this. We're gonna get him to the hospital and he's going to be all right." Sitting on the floor, Boomer had his arms wrapped around his crying mother, rocking and assuring her everything was going to be okay. He released her only for a moment when Burke and Dusty began collecting everyone's weapons to hide them in a concealed compartment in the van before the cops showed up. Since none of them had been fired, the guns weren't needed as evidence and would only cause trouble with the locals. The camouflage clothing could be explained by saying they'd been on their way to play paintball, or something stupid like that.

Ian squatted down next to Boomer and his mom. Taking her hand, he squeezed until he got her attention. "Eileen, we're doing everything we can for Rick, but I need you to tell us what happened before the cops get here."

When she didn't answer right away, Boomer knew her adrenaline was wearing off and shock was setting in. He gave her a shake and tugged her chin so she was facing him. "Mom, help us out. You gotta tell us what happened. Where'd they go? When did they leave? How many of them were here?"

"I . . . uh . . . oh God, Ben!" Her body began to shake.

"It's going to be all right, Mom. But we need to know. When did they leave? How long ago?"

Eileen shook her head, trying to clear her mind. She'd no concept of how long she'd laid there, struggling to free herself or reach Rick after she'd heard the gunshot. "It was . . . it was a few minutes after you called. They . . . there were three of them . . . they said that was all they needed us for, then they covered my eyes and mouth. They were being . . . being rough with me, and Rick yelled for them to leave me alone. That's when I heard the gunshot. They had beaten him a few times while . . . while we were trying to get a hold of you."

Boomer swallowed the guilt swarming through him. He'd been getting laid while his parents were being brutalized.

"I don't know how long it's been. They left right after that. Rick was able to talk for a while, but then he started fading. When he stopped talking, I thought he was . . ." She choked on the last words.

"He's not, Mom. Pop's alive, and he's going to stay that way." When she began crying harder again, he pulled her back into his arms and looked up at Ian, who now stood next to Carter. "They're going after Kat. This was all a ruse to get most of us away from her."

The two men nodded in grim agreement. Boomer reached for his headset only to find it'd fallen from his ear in the confusion of the room. "Tell Reverend to get her to the panic room."

Ian looked at Carter and jutted his chin toward Eileen. The spy knelt and took her from Boomer so he could stand to talk with his boss. Ian grabbed his arm and pulled him into the kitchen. It was far enough away for Eileen not to overhear them, yet Boomer could still see what was going on in the other room. "We can't get a hold of him. He's not answering the com or his cell. There's also no answer at the office or front gate."

"Fuck!" His words were hissed low, but urgent and desperate. "They're already there! We've got . . . shit!" He looked at his watch. "If they left right after the call . . . an hour drive . . . fuck, they would've gotten there almost thirty minutes ago. How are we going to get back there? It's probably too late! Shit!"

At the beginning of Boomer's panicked rant, Ian had hit a speed dial number on his cell. He held up a hand to shut him up as the connection was made. The younger man glared at him, then turned to watch his teammates work on his dad. Fear like he'd never known punched him in his gut—fear for his father, and fear for the woman he loved more than life itself. Sirens penetrated his brain. Help was on the way, and it was getting closer by the second. Help for his father, but what about Kat . . . and Jake and the others?

---

PLACING his hand on his teammate's shoulder in sympathy and solidarity, Ian waited impatiently for his call to be answered.

"Can this wait, Ian? I'm walking into a meeting with POTUS."

He didn't give a crap that the deputy director of the FBI was entering the Oval Office. Not when Kat, Jake, and the others were in danger. "No, it can't."

Larry Keon sighed heavily over the phone then said something to someone else before coming back on the line. "You've got two minutes."

After filling the man in, Ian told him what they needed. "How fast can you get me a chopper back to the compound? And as much as I hate to ask, can you send Stonewall's SWAT? Things may go to shit by the time we get there, if they haven't already." The Tampa FBI Special Agent in Charge, Frank Stonewall, and the men of Trident weren't the best of friends after a few past incidents. The man hated Carter even more, with the feeling being mutual. The order coming from the SAC's superior would ensure there were no arguments or delays in the SWAT team's response.

"I'll call you back in a minute. Text me the coordinates of their house. And tell Carter to stay out of trouble. I'm going to need him by the time my meeting is over, and I don't want to have to bail him out."

"Will do." He hung up just as a slew of police officers and paramedics filled the house. Burke and Dusty had met the cops outside and told them the suspects were long gone, so no weapons were drawn. Brody, Marco, and Devon moved out of the way for the emergency personnel to take over, but stayed close to assist if needed. Carter stood by Eileen, holding her hand as a female EMT began to assess her for injuries.

Next to Ian, Boomer's brow was scrunched in confusion. "Why didn't they kill both of them? I mean, I'm thanking the good Lord they didn't . . . but why? These guys don't give me the impression they have any ethics, so why let them live?"

Ian gestured to the organized chaos with his hand. "For this. This is to hold us up even further. It's giving them more time to get to Kat and force her to give them the money. If we walked in, and there was nothing more we could do here, we would've already been on our way back to the compound." He was about to say more, but his phone rang. "Keon, what've you got?"

"State Police chopper will be landing in the schoolyard up the street from the Michaelsons' within the next ten minutes. SWAT is on the way to the compound. Give me the officer in charge at the scene, and I'll clear you out of there." Waving over a sergeant, Ian explained who the other man on the line was then handed him the phone, ignoring the supervisor's astonished expression.

---

BOOMER WAS BEING TORN in half. He wanted to stay with his folks, but Kat needed him. As the paramedics placed his father on a gurney, he approached his mother who was sitting on the couch with Carter. Boomer knelt in front of her, taking her attention away from Rick. The pale complexion of her face served to make the tape's sting glaringly obvious, and he winced, knowing it had to be painful. "Mom . . ."

Eileen cut him off. "Katerina's in danger, isn't she?"

"Yeah, she is. We have a chopper coming to take us back to the compound. I want to stay with you and Pop, but I—"

"No. You go get her and bring her back with you. Your dad will be okay and I'm fine." She cupped his cheek and he leaned into her touch. "She's your future, Benjamin. Go save her."

Boomer swallowed the thick lump in his throat. Standing, he helped her up and hugged her tight. "I'll be back soon. With Kat. Call my cell . . . shit . . . I broke mine and didn't have time to replace it. My calls are being forwarded to Ian's. I'll call Aunt Margaret to meet you at the hospital. Okay?"

"I'll call Margaret. You just do what you have to. I love you. Stay safe and bring her home."

"I will. Love you, too, Mom."

With the help of the female EMT, Boomer escorted his mother to the waiting ambulance. The medics told him his father was stabilized, but he was still unconscious. As they loaded his parents into the back of the rig, in the distance he heard the *thump, thump, thump* of the approaching helicopter.

Ian sidled up next to him. "Our ride is almost here. Keon cleared us to take off, and file the police reports later. Burke and Dusty are taking one of the SUVs and following your folks to the E.R. I want them guarded until this is over."

The ambulance doors slammed shut and the vehicle started down the driveway. "Thanks, Boss-man. I appreciate it."

Ian clapped his teammate on the back as they started jogging toward his SUV. It was faster to drive the quarter mile to where the helicopter was landing on an empty baseball field. The rest of the team was already on their way in the communications van. "It's what family does, Baby Boomer. Now, let's go get your girl."

# CHAPTER 22

For about fifteen minutes, Kat tried to get comfortable on the couch in the recreation room above the offices, but her mind wouldn't settle down to let her. This was all her fault. If she hadn't brought her problems to Benny, then his parents would have been safe. Now, she had to pray the team got to them in time to save them. The wait was killing her. Finally giving up on getting some rest, she stood and headed for the stairs with Beau at her heels.

Instead of going toward the offices, she went out the front door to get some air. She smiled when Beau made a beeline for a hard rubber ball and came back to drop it at her feet.

"So, you want to play, huh?" The goofy-faced dog seemed to grin at her before answering her with a low woof. "Fine, we'll play fetch for a few minutes. Maybe it'll make the time go faster."

Beau gave her another woof and then took off after the ball she threw across the compound. As she waited for the dog to return, she glanced to her left and saw Murray standing guard at the front gate. In the opposite direction, the man from Blackhawk Security, who had been introduced to her as Jason Tanner, was walking toward the back of the compound, keeping watch for anything out of the ordinary. Both men were armed and Kat felt safer knowing they were there. Beau ran up to her and dropped the ball which was now covered in dog drool, but she didn't mind since she was often slobbered on by the dogs she trained. Throwing the ball again, she heard the office door open behind her and turned to see Colleen walk out, carrying her purse. "Are you leaving?"

The younger blonde woman stopped next to her. "Yes. The team has been training me to shoot, but I still have to take a course to obtain my firearms permit before I can carry a gun. Ian and Reggie want me to get it because of all the guns on the premises. With the bad guys they deal with here, they wanted to be sure I could use one if I had to. I have to admit though, it makes me feel like some bad-ass chick when they take me shooting."

Kat laughed as Colleen giggled and posed like one of stars of a popular TV show from the 1970s with her fingers forming a pretend weapon. "Oh, that's awesome. I love the *Charlie's Angels* reruns. Maybe Kristen, Angie, and I should join you. I think the original three were two brunettes and one blonde, and then another blonde replaced the first, so we'd be perfect. And I love those retro clothes."

"Oh! Maybe we can talk the Doms into having a seventies theme night at the club. That would be so funky."

Laughing harder, Kat reached back and grabbed her ass cheeks. "A spanking to disco music? Now that sounds really kinky."

"Shelby would love it! She loves theme nights. I'll run it by her and see what she thinks." Checking her watch, Colleen added, "Shit. I'm going to be late if I don't leave. I'll see you later. Jake promised to text me and let me know everything is okay with Ben's parents."

Kat waved goodbye as the secretary ran to her Toyota Prius and drove away. Checking her cell phone, she saw she still had a least another fifteen minutes or so before the team reached Sarasota. Not ready to go back inside, she began to wander around the compound while continuing to play fetch with Beau. Finding herself in the club parking area, she ambled over to the guard gate to see if Murray needed water or anything. She was just about to speak when the guard's head turned toward the road at the sound of an approaching vehicle. A black Cadillac Escalade with tinted windows pulled up to the closed gate and stopped. The guard eyed the vehicle warily and placed his hand on his sidearm, ready to draw the 9mm handgun if necessary.

Everything seemed to move in slow motion as Kat watched the driver's window roll down and Murray pull his weapon from the holster at his hip. But it was too late as the driver fired his own silenced pistol, and she gaped in horror as the burly guard's body jerked with the impact of the bullet hitting his upper right chest. Stunned, Kat was frozen in place, staring at the man as he fell to the ground, blood starting to saturate his shirt, and the weapon dropping from his hand.

Three doors to the SUV opened, and two large men exited from the front, both armed with black handguns. The driver was a little taller and leaner than his counterpart who Kat thought resembled a pig with his flat nose and pock-marked skin. Another man climbed out of the backseat and she gasped. It was one of the Russians who'd tried to kidnap her from the motel in Norfolk, dragging a terrified Colleen out of the vehicle, holding a gun to her head. Next to Kat, Beau growled and barked, sensing his humans were in danger, but unable to get through the closed gate.

"Call off dog and toss cell phone on ground. Come vith us or I kill friends. Now!"

Keeping her eyes on the wide-eyed secretary who was trying to hold it together, Kat placed a shaky hand on the security scanner until the gate began to slide open. "Beau, *platz*." The canine continued to growl with the hair on his back raised, but laid down as ordered. "Let her go, and I'll come with you. If you hurt her, I'll never tell you how to get the money."

The big man smirked, and Kat shivered, knowing he would gladly torture her for the information. Pig-face from the front passenger seat had his gun trained on her while the driver had his aimed at Murray who was, thankfully, still alive. The injured guard looked more pissed than anything, but with his gun lying near his feet and being outnumbered, there wasn't much he could do. Pulling her phone out of her pocket, Kat placed it on the ground and stepped forward, her hands in the air. The sunlight hit the gold medical alert bracelet on her wrist, and she remembered Benny telling her about the GPS unit in it. If she went with these men, he still had a way to track her. She had to do it, refusing to let anyone else get hurt because of her. "Please, let them go. I won't fight you. I'll show you where the money is."

The man holding Colleen's arm was obviously in charge as neither of the other men spoke. Shoving the woman viciously to the ground next to the guard, who struggled to put his body in front of hers for protection, the Russian indicated for Kat to get into the vehicle. "Come. Now. Or vc kill them."

Kat hurried over to the rear driver's side door as the man stepped back and let her scramble into the vehicle. He slid in next to her, forcing her to move to the other side. Before he shut his door, he instructed his driver, "Kill them."

Horrified, Kat dove for the door handle next to her, but the bastard grabbed her hair, preventing her escape. Pain shot through her scalp. "*Packen,*" she shouted past the open driver's door and was relieved to see Beau respond to the command, lunging toward the man aiming his weapon at the two people on the ground. The driver brought his arm up to block the vicious attack, and his gun went off into the air, the slug striking a nearby tree. Twisting wildly, the man screamed in pain as the dog's razor-sharp teeth tore through his flesh, down to the bones in his forearm.

The chaos gave Murray the chance he needed to snatch and fire his own weapon, dropping the driver with a bullet to the head. With what should have been an easy kill from across the hood, a distant shout caused Pig-face to turn his head and botch his own shot, missing Murray by inches when he rolled to protect Colleen. Through the windshield, Kat saw Jake and Tanner running toward the front gate, weapons in hand. The combination of reinforcements arriving, and Beau releasing the driver and turning his attention to the second threat, had Pig-face diving into the front seat and slamming the door shut. He climbed over the console, threw the vehicle in reverse and floored the accelerator as Beau made a futile attempt to find access on the passenger side. None of Kat's would-be rescuers could risk taking a shot with her in the line of fire. A quick turn of the steering wheel spun the car around and they took off toward the highway at a high rate of speed. At the end of the road, before they turned left to take the northbound lanes,

Kat spotted Colleen's vehicle on the shoulder with its driver's door wide open. The Russians must have ambushed her and forced her from the car.

"Where are we going?"

Neither man answered her. She urged herself to remain calm and look for a way to escape, but she couldn't stop trembling. Not knowing what else to do, Kat prayed.

---

LEAVING the head and walking back toward the war-room, Jake continued to listen to the banter of his team members on the overhead speakers he'd turned on, and cursed because he was missing the action. He knew Carter was the perfect person to take his place, but it was still irritating he was out of commission until his eye healed.

Just as he entered the room, Ian's voice came over the air. "Reverend, you there?"

Stepping up to the microphone, Jake pressed the transmit button. "Yeah, Boss-man. What's your status?"

"Just pulled up. How are things there?"

"Five by five," he answered. "Just going to go get Kat. Stay safe, brothers."

"Amen."

Turning around, Jake headed out past the reception area to the stairs, taking them two at a time. He hoped Kat had gotten some rest because she needed it. When this was all over, he wouldn't be surprised if Boomer planned on taking her somewhere quiet to recuperate. The kid could use a vacation after this, as well.

Striding into the rec room, he glanced around and found it empty. Figuring she was in the bedroom she and Boomer had used last night, he made his way down the hallway and knocked on the only closed door. Not receiving an answer, he knocked again and instead of waiting, turned the knob and opened the door. Empty. "Kat?" Still no answer. He raised his voice. "Kat? You up here?"

A quick check of the rest of the rooms told Jake she wasn't on this floor. He hurried back down the stairs and into the war-room again to scan the live camera feeds and figure out where she was. As he'd headed to the bathroom earlier, Colleen had been collecting her purse to leave for her class. Now, on one monitor he could see her car was gone and Tanner was on the north side of property, walking the perimeter behind the buildings. His gaze shifted to the other feeds, looking for Kat. His blood ran cold when he saw the view of the front gate. A black SUV was idling at the entrance, Murray was on the ground, three men were holding weapons with one pointed at Colleen's head and Kat was opening the gate.

"Fuck!" Pressing the button for the frequency Tanner and Murray's headsets were on, Jake barked into the microphone, "Tangos front gate, man down, man down!"

Seeing on the monitor Tanner had heard him and was running from the far end of the property toward the gate, Jake unholstered his Sig Sauer P226 and took off like the hounds of Hell were on his heels. He hit the front door running just as Tanner rounded the building at full speed. Tearing across the compound, they heard Kat scream the German command for Beau to attack one of the men, before Murray retrieved his weapon and fired a shot. The driver was dead by the time he hit the ground. But the gorilla on the other side of the SUV aimed his gun at Murray, and Jake brought his own sidearm up, yelling at the top of his lungs, "Drop your weapon!"

He was still too far away to make an accurate shot, and he couldn't take the risk of hitting either of the women or Murray. His command had the bastard missing his kill shot, thank God, but unfortunately the guy dove through the passenger door and threw the car in reverse. Beau took off after the retreating vehicle, barking ferociously.

"Fucking-A! Get your truck, Tanner!"

As the operative reversed directions, Jake ran to the gate where Colleen was ripping open Murray's shirt to expose his wound. The guard groaned and turned his head toward Jake. "They've got Kat. Two tangos left. Both with 9mms, didn't see any other weapons."

Hearing Tanner revving his Ford F-150's engine, Jake glanced at

Murray's shoulder wound which was now visible. "How bad? Can you get to the war-room? I need someone on the radio."

"Yeah, it's a through and through. I'll live. Help me up."

The phone in the guard shack rang, but everyone ignored it. With Jake and Colleen's assistance, the guard stood while letting out a roar of pain. "Fuck, that fucking hurts. 'Scuse my language, Colleen."

Holding his good arm, the still pale secretary rallied and took charge of the situation, aiming the big man toward the Trident building. If the situation wasn't so serious, Jake would've smiled at how far the once timid secretary had come out of her shell these last few weeks. Their training her on how to respond to different emergency scenarios was paying off. "Like I haven't heard Ian curse fifty times a day. Let's get you inside. Jake, I'll call 9-1-1, but what else do you need?"

Tanner screeched to a halt next to them, and Jake threw open the passenger door. As he jumped in, he ordered, "Murray knows the tracking system. Bring up Kat's GPS location. Give it to us on the compound's frequency. Then get on the team's frequency and let them know what's going down."

He slammed the door, confident the secretary and guard, a retired Army sergeant, would do what needed to be done. Tanner floored the accelerator and swerved around the dead body outside the gate.

As they approached the intersection to the highway, Tanner demanded, "Which way?"

The vehicle slowed, and Jake frantically searched in both directions. "Left! Holy shit, I owe that fucking dog a steak. Slow down, so I can grab him."

Beau was about fifty yards north of the intersection, running on the shoulder of the road, still trying to chase after the long-gone vehicle, but at least he pointed them the right direction. As Tanner slowed the truck, Jake opened his door. "Beau! *Hier!*"

The lab-mix ran back to the truck and took a flying leap up onto Jake's lap. He pushed the dog into the back seat and slammed the door. Punching the accelerator again as soon as Beau cleared the doorway, Tanner was already speeding back up. Jake reached up to tap his headset before remembering he never had one on—he'd been listening in through the speakers in the war-room.

"Let me have your headset." The operative ripped the device from his ear and tossed it to Jake who hooked it to his own ear. "Murray, you there?"

Static came over the earpiece and then the guard's pain filled voice. "Yeah, I'm here. Bringing up the GPS. Give me a sec. Colleen's on the phone with 9-1-1. What direction are you heading?"

"North. Beau was heading that way, but we haven't caught up to them yet. Have you gotten a hold of Ian yet?"

"I will as soon as I get Kat's location for you. Here it is. Looks like they're still on the highway in front of you. I'm bringing up the GPS in your phone . . . they're about a mile ahead of you. I'll let you know if they change direction."

Motioning with his hand, Jake confirmed they were heading in the right direction, and Tanner sped up even more as they both scanned the vehicles in front of them. "Good enough. As soon as we spot them I'll try to get a plate for you. Black Escalade, right?"

"Affirm."

Tanner glanced at Jake. "What do you want to do? Follow to see where they are going until we get backup and a road block?"

Lifting his hand to adjust his eye patch, Jake had to agree. They couldn't risk Kat's life by running them off the road. "Yeah. Get them in sight and hold back."

Just as they spotted the Cadillac up ahead, Murray's voice came over the headset. "Hey, Jake? I've got Ian on the other channel. Get this. They're just boarding a state police chopper en-route back to the compound. And they have FBI SWAT responding here. They figured out it was a ruse to get most of them out of here."

"A little late to the party, but better than nothing. The team is still too far out." He pulled his cell phone from the side pocket of his cargo pants. "Get me a phone number for someone on SWAT, instead of playing telephone tag with you."

"Stand-by."

Trying to formulate a plan, Jake prayed Boomer wasn't going to lose his woman again . . . and permanently this time.

---

BOOMER COULDN'T BELIEVE what Murray had just told them over their headsets . . . ah, fuck, yes, he could. They'd all fallen for the deceptive ploy and it'd worked. While he knew they would've still rescued his parents, in hindsight, they should've put Kat and the others into the compound's panic room until they had more information about what was going on. But it was too late for that. Now, Kat was in the hands of men who had no trouble killing anyone who got in their way, and once they had their money, she was expendable. Damn it, he couldn't lose her again—he wouldn't survive the loss this time.

The helicopter's rotors were thumping in time to his pounding heart rate. The only chatter at the moment was from the pilot and co-pilot. The team and Carter were waiting for updates from Murray about what was going on. The pilots were pushing the bird as fast as they could, but Boomer was afraid they weren't going to get there in time to save Kat. Even at full throttle, it would still take them about twenty minutes from Sarasota to Tampa. He'd have to trust Jake and Tanner to do what they could until their backup arrived. It was just frustrating to sit and wait for info without being able to do anything.

From what Murray had said, one of the tangos was dead next to the compound's gate. That meant there were only two more they were aware of. With Egghead's medical alert tracking bracelet, they would at least know where Kat was. The FBI's SWAT team was now in direct contact with Jake and rerouting to intercept the getaway vehicle. There were too many variables, and Boomer didn't like the odds.

Brody shifted in his seat. "You know, Ian, this is why we need our own fucking bird."

Nodding, their boss crossed his arms. "Not that it helps us now, but it's being delivered in two weeks. We're storing it at the airport with the jet until the helipad is built. That starts next week, by the way, along with the obstacle course Devil Dog planned out."

As his teammates and Carter added some more mindless chatter through the chopper's headsets, the ground below them was coming and going at a fast clip. Boomer just hoped it was fast enough. He glanced at his dive watch—seven minutes down, about thirteen minutes to go. "Fuck."

# CHAPTER 23

*S*hivering, Kat tried to sit as far away from the man who she now recognized as Viktor "The Bull" Dryagin, Volkov's right-hand man and self-appointed heir to the dead man's criminal empire. Ian had shown her pictures of the man who Benny and Jake had confirmed was the leader of the group who'd tried to kidnap her from the motel in Norfolk. Dryagin and Pig-face hadn't said a word to her since they'd fled the compound about ten minutes ago, speaking to each other in Russian, which only enhanced her fear and anxiety. What were they planning on doing to her to get the money? She'd gladly give it to them if she could only be certain she would still be alive once they had it in their greedy little hands. The only thing she wanted was the chance to have the life she craved . . . the life she deserved with Benny. She didn't even know if Rick and Eileen were alive and doubted the Russians would tell her. All she could do was pray Jake and Tanner were tracking her and coming up with a rescue plan. Benny had assured her that was what his team specialized in, and she trusted them to get her out of this damn mess.

"*Blyat!*"

Kat didn't know what Pig-face had said in Russian, but by the way he spat it out, she guessed it was a curse word. A split second after he said it, he slammed on the brakes, sending her flying forward, her head smashing against the headrest of the seat in front of her. Black spots and white stars filled her vision as a myriad of sounds assaulted her ears. Loud screeching, yelling, whaps, pops, and the rush of air escaping surrounded her. It took her a moment to realize both her head and the car were spinning as Pig-face tried to control it on four shredded tires. The bare rims were grinding against the asphalt as the vehicle rapidly slowed. What the hell was happening?

Somehow, he managed to keep them from flipping over, and the vehicle finally came to an abrupt halt in the middle of the highway. Before Kat had a chance to think about escaping, Dryagin snatched her by the hair and hauled her to his side, his weapon pressed against her temple. Tears filled her eyes as she tried to ease the pressure on her scalp. Outside the SUV, smoke from the blown tires began to settle, and all was quiet except the three occupants' heavy breathing and Pig-face's cursing in both languages.

"*Yobaniyi ment!* Fucking cops blew tires. Vhat now?"

Hope flared in Kat's chest as she heard sirens approaching. She just prayed these two men didn't do anything stupid that would get them all killed. The sirens switched off one-by-one as several vehicles came to a screeching halt, surrounding them at a distance. Kat tried to glimpse what was going on, but the only direction Dryagin's grasp allowed her to see was through the window next to him. She realized they were now turned sideways on the highway, facing the southbound lanes. Further past the line of idling patrol cars with their flashing lights, and unmarked SUVs, she saw the signs of traffic beginning to build past the road block which had been quickly put in place. There were police officers—some in uniform, others dressed in all black—using their vehicles as cover and pointing handguns, shotguns, and rifles at the get-away vehicle. If Kat thought she was scared earlier, she was now beyond terrified. *Please, God, don't let them decide to go down in a hail of bullets.*

Several minutes went by before two men behind one of the police cars caught Kat's attention, and she gasped when she focused on Jake. His arms gesturing wildly, Boomer's teammate was arguing with a red-faced man in an ill-fitting suit. It was obvious the man wanted Jake away from the scene, but he wouldn't budge.

A sudden voice over a loudspeaker interrupted the Russians'

rapid conversation in their native language. "Throw out your weapons and come out with your hands in the air."

Pig-face rolled his window down halfway and yelled, "Fuck you."

*Okay*, Kat thought, *that command didn't go over well. Now what?* "Please let me go. We're surrounded. If you cooperate, I'm sure the judge will go easier on you." Actually, she wasn't sure of it at all, but it sounded good, right?

"Shut up." Dryagin's head swiveled as he eyed what was going on around them. "Ruslan, demand new car or ve kill girl."

Well, shit, that didn't sound comforting, but at least the bastard had let go of his grip on her hair, and she was able to sit up a little better. Before she could move away from him, the big man grabbed her upper arm, pulled her across his lap, and switched their positions in the backseat, putting her between him and the majority of the police officers. He held her close, still pointing the deadly end of his pistol at her head. She listened as Ruslan, aka Pig-face, shouted their demand out the window, and the hostage negotiator on the megaphone responded. Kat got the feeling she was in for a very long and stressful afternoon.

---

STANDING ABOUT twenty-five yards away from the disabled Escalade, Jake gritted his teeth as SAC Frank Stonewall got in his face, demanding he and Tanner leave the area. "You're fucking civilians, and this situation is now under the jurisdiction of the FBI. Get back in your fucking truck, and get the hell out of here, so we can do our jobs."

Keeping his voice low and threatening, Jake towered over the shorter man and leaned in, so he wasn't overheard by anyone else. "Listen, you fucktard. The only reason you were called in was because we were short-handed and Ian couldn't get a hold of us. You know damn fucking well Keon will ream you a new asshole with one quick phone call. Now, we're willing to step back and let the SWAT commander take over, but I'll be fucking damned if I let that woman out of my sight again, so take your attitude and shove it up your ass."

The SAC looked ready to explode, but held his tongue when a tall, dark-haired man, dressed all in black and carrying a megaphone, approached them. "Jake? I hear this mess started at Trident. Fill me in, so I know what we're dealing with. You'll have to tell me what's up with the eye patch later."

Jake shook Calvin Watts's extended hand. The agent was the lead negotiator in charge of the Tampa area FBI SWAT team. Having mutual friends, they played basketball against each other almost every Tuesday night at the local YMCA, and Jake was relieved the man was here. He'd seen Watts's team in action before and was confident they could get Kat out of this in one piece. "Hey, Cal. I appreciate the fast response. Thank God Ian had you en-route, and TPD had cars nearby with the spike strips available. The tangos kidnapped Boomer's woman from the compound. They shot our guard in the shoulder, but he was able to drop the original driver, so now it's just two of them in there, plus Kat. Tangos are Russian mobsters from Virginia. Kat's father appropriated a large sum of money from their boss about twelve years ago, and they want it back."

Ignoring the SAC who stood by, still seething, Watts, who was officially in charge of the incident, gestured then started walking toward the newly arrived SWAT command van, and Jake followed. "Okay, how much money are we talking about here? I doubt they'd be taking such a big risk for a few thousand."

"Try fifteen million, plus twelve years' interest, sitting in the Cayman Islands." Cal whistled his amazement as he opened the back door of the large truck and climbed in after Jake. "Yeah, I know, far from chump change. From what I understand, Kat's dad was an accountant for the mob, but didn't realize who he was really dealing with until he was too far in. After keeping his nose clean for a few years, he discovered evidence of white slavery, and gave it to the FBI. A few days later, Kat's family was run off the road. The crash killed her mother and brother, and sent her and her dad into the Witness Protection Program. Kat didn't know it until her father died recently, but the old man transferred money out of the mob's accounts a few days after the accident and sent it to a dummy account. Revenge, I guess. A string of unrelated events put these bastards back on her trail leading us here."

Watts shook his head. "Damn, you boys don't like anything simple, do you? All right, let's get this rescue underway. They're demanding another car and a free pass or they'll kill her. The usual shit these idiots think we'll cave for. Any idea what their names are, so we can start developing a profile?"

A tech typing away on a nearby computer keyboard looked up at Jake, waiting for his answer. "No ID on the driver, but the guy in the back seat with Kat is Viktor Dryagin, a trained assassin who took his boss's place in the organization after he got the okay to off the guy. From what I hear, he's not going to go down easy."

"Guys like him never do. Anyone else here from Trident?"

"One of our contract guys, Tanner, is over by his truck, staying out of the way and keeping our dog from staging his own rescue. The rest are on their way. When Brody gets here, he'll be able to listen in on a microphone Kat's wearing. It's one of his toys we've used before."

Picking up two headsets, Watts tossed one to Jake. "Okay. Stick around and stay out of Stonewall's face. I'm not in the mood for his fucking blubbering. And ears only. Keep your microphone off— you're here out of professional courtesy, and I trust your input, but I won't have you interfering with the negotiations."

Understanding the man was making a huge concession allowing him to stay, Jake replaced the Trident headset over his left ear with the new one, pocketing the former which was only on the compound's frequency. Murray was now in an ambulance on his way to the hospital with Colleen in tow, so there wasn't anyone back at the war-room for him to talk to. "Thanks, and no worries. I trust you to do your thing."

"Sir?" Both men looked at the second tech who was monitoring several radio frequencies among other things. "We've got a State PD chopper requesting permission to land nearby. Says they have the rest of the Trident team with them."

Cal raised an eyebrow at Jake who shrugged. "Friends in high places, what can I say?"

The negotiator barked out a laugh. "Yeah, okay, Smitty. Since the highway is shut down in both directions, tell TPD on the ground to clear a landing zone in the southbound lanes, south of us, and ask the state boys to stick around. We might be able to use them."

"Yes, sir."

"Hey, Cal?" The agent followed when Jake took a few steps backward, away from the techs, acknowledging whatever Jake was going to tell him was for his ears only. "We've got an extra man with the team. Black-ops with federal clearances up the ass, and don't ask for any other information because I can't tell you. Just know he's got Moran, Keon, and POTUS on speed dial, and the same in reverse." The agent's surprise was evident at the mention of the director and assistant director of the FBI, along with the President of the United States, but he let Jake finish. "The man is one of the best snipers I know, and he's got my spare rifle on board the bird. Not stepping on your toes here, just know I trust him with my own mother's life."

"That's saying a lot coming from a SEAL sniper." Jake waited while Cal mulled things over, knowing he would have to accept his response either way. "All right, I hope we don't need him, but here's what we'll do."

---

UNDER THE WATCHFUL eyes of his teammates, Boomer paced back and forth behind the line of law enforcement vehicles and personnel. The only reason he was back there and not leading a full out assault on the Cadillac Escalade in the middle of the highway, some forty yards away, was Ian threatened to handcuff him to Tanner's truck. "This is taking too fucking long."

Since they all knew how this had to play out, no one answered him, letting him vent his frustrations verbally. Hostage negotiations were a psychological game for the lead negotiator. There were five steps to the technique of communicating with the hostage takers—active listening, empathy, rapport, influence, and behavioral change.

An ideal situation would have the bad guys releasing the hostage and surrendering without any escalation of events. Unfortunately, very few hostage situations were ideal.

For a trained team of former Navy SEALs, such as Trident, it was difficult to sit back and let another team take over. But they all knew Calvin Watts's SWAT was one of the best nationwide, with a long history of successful missions to their credit. If they had to relinquish the rescue to a law enforcement agency, they were lucky it was his team.

It'd been over an hour since the police spike strip had been thrown on the highway, blowing all four tires on the Russians' SUV. Kat must be going out of her mind with fear, and Boomer knew exactly what it felt like. At least the team had an inside man. Jake was still in the communications van and using Marco's borrowed earpiece to pass on information to them. Occasionally he would ask a question, in order to give the hostage negotiator some intel, which Ian or Boomer hopefully had the answer to. Also in the comm van was Egghead, who was using a program on his tablet to listen in on the conversation taking place between the two Russians, thanks to the microphone in Kat's GPS bracelet. The men were speaking mostly in their native language, but the geek had a TPD officer also plugged in and translating for him. Unfortunately, they weren't learning anything from the exchange which could help them end the incident peacefully.

"Ian?" Jake's voice came over the team's earpieces.

"Go."

"These guys are getting antsy. They're insisting on taking the State PD chopper or they'll start cutting her up with a knife. With Dryagin's background, Cal thinks we're running out of time." Boomer's eyes widened in horror, but a glare from his boss had him keeping his mouth shut. There had to be a reason why Jake was telling them this, knowing he was listening in. "We have an idea, but we need your input to see if it'll work. Cal wants you and Boomer in the comm van."

Both men headed to the FBI command center after being waved under the yellow Do-Not-Cross tape spanning the width of the highway. They ignored a dirty look from SAC Stonewall as they passed him and a few other agents along the way. Now wasn't the time for a pissing match with the Special Ass-hat in Charge.

Ian opened the door and allowed Boomer to climb in ahead of him. Both men shook hands with Cal Watts before the negotiator laid out the plan Jake and he had come up with. Ian stated he thought it was a good strategy since they were down to the wire with Dryagin's threats, but Boomer was terrified something would go wrong. "What if she doesn't get it or even fucking see it? She's probably petrified. What if she doesn't understand what we want her to do?"

Crossing his arms, Ian addressed Jake. "You've seen Kat in action twice now. Once at the motel and again at the compound. Do you think she'll be able to focus on what we're telling her? If she doesn't, this shit is going to get ugly real fast because we can't let the chopper take off with her in it."

Even though it seemed Boomer was playing the pessimist, that's what the team did—examined a situation from every angle before giving it a go. Jake took a deep breath and let it out. "At the motel, she didn't hesitate, and from what I heard afterward, she jumped in to make sure I was okay. The injury didn't bother her. Same goes for what just happened at the gate. Yeah, she was probably scared shitless, but both she and Colleen made us proud. Kat was able to think fast enough to give Beau the command to attack. And from what I saw really quick on the monitor, she also didn't hesitate to open the gate and do what she had to do to save the others. I'm positive, as long as we get her attention on the way to the chopper, this will work."

All eyes turned to Boomer. They were out of options, and he knew it. "It's gotta be me. Out of all the voices, it'll be mine she'll be listening for and focus in on."

Cal nodded. "Agreed. But just in case, I want Ian with you, and you'll be flanked by two of my men." He pointed his finger at Boomer. "You know how this goes, man. Don't do anything stupid out there and fuck up my operation."

A lesser man would have been insulted, but Boomer knew the

negotiator was right. The SWAT team trained day in and day out with each other, knew exactly what each other was thinking, how they would react. Bringing in an unknown, such as himself, no matter how well trained, could throw someone's timing off, and that's when things became a cluster-fuck. "Let's do this."

---

KAT COULDN'T HAVE HEARD right. The man on the megaphone said the Russians could take the police chopper wherever they wanted to go if they released her. When the response was she was going with them, the jackass agreed. *What the fuck?* Maybe they were going to continue to track her through her GPS and stage a rescue somewhere else. Or maybe they had something up their sleeve. *A trick. That had to be it. Right?* God, she hoped she was right. At least Dryagin had put away the sharp knife he was threatening to cut off her fingers with. But then again, the gun was pointed at her head once more, so she was still in deep shit.

Down the road, the helicopter's rotors sped up, and they all watched as the craft hovered a few feet off the ground, moving north in the southbound lanes until it was directly across the median from the disabled Escalade. The pilot positioned the chopper so the tail was facing them, but turned slightly so they could see the open door on the left side, then set it back down on the ground. From what she could see there was no one inside except for the solo pilot.

Kat decided to try one last futile attempt at getting the Russians to leave her behind. "Please, let me go. You have the helicopter to escape in, and I'll write down the account number and password for the bank account the money is in. Please."

"Shut up!" Dryagin tightened his grip on her arm and eyed the activity surrounding them. "Open door and get out. Be stupid and you regret it."

"I have a feeling I'll regret it either way," she mumbled, pulling on the handle and easing the door open. She climbed out slowly, still in his tight grasp as he got out behind her. Once she was blocking the officers' line of fire, Pig-face also exited the vehicle, his own gun pointed toward her as well. As a unit, they started making their way over the grassy median with Kat held close to both of them.

"Kitten!"

Her head swiveled at the sound of Benny's voice as Dryagin forced her down a slight incline toward a low guardrail. It took her a moment to spot him in the southbound lanes standing next to Ian and two men dressed in black holding very large weapons. Kat's eyes filled with tears as she climbed over the thigh-high railing. Would this be the last time she ever saw him?

"Kitten, I love you! Remember, a sub always listens to her Dom!"

*What?* Was he fucking kidding her? Okay, the "I love you" was great, but why bring up subs and Doms?

Behind her, Dryagin growled, "Faster. Move." He urged her up the small incline.

"Kitten! Remember!"

Kat focused on Benny again. He and Ian were waving at her. *No! Wait!* They weren't waving. They were signaling her. One. Two. Three fingers. And then their right arms, palms down, making the sweep out in front of them from their waists up over their heads— the K9 sign language for "down." Holy shit, on the count of three, they wanted her to hit the dirt and stay down!

She copied the silent command, hoping the Russians thought she was waving. "I love you, too!"

Keeping her eyes on Benny and the chopper in her peripheral vision, she waited for the signal and prayed she understood them correctly. Two steps before she would need to duck for the slow-moving rotor, he raised his hand in a fist and one-by-one, uncurled his fingers.

*One.*

*Two.*

*Three.*

Kat let her knees buckle, and she dropped to the ground so fast that Dryagin had no chance of stopping her. She felt his hand release her arm, unable to hold onto her sudden dead weight. The man shouted something foreign in surprise, then roared his anger.

As she covered her head, two simultaneous shots sounded, followed by shouts and running feet. She didn't dare look up until she heard Benny's voice again. This time he was right next to her. "Kat, are you okay? Please, tell me you're okay!"

His words came out rushed as his hands quickly roamed her body. She rolled onto her side, thrilled to see his handsome face. "I'm okay, I'm okay. What happened?"

He hauled her to her feet and wrapped his strong arms around her, coming close to crushing her. "Oh, thank God, you're all right! I was so fucking scared. Are you sure you're okay?"

Leaning back, he searched her face for confirmation. She nodded as her body began to tremble in the aftermath of the crisis. Glancing over her shoulder, she saw both Russians dead on the ground a few feet away, surrounded by men in black. Dryagin was missing half of his head, while Pig-face had been shot in the chest, leaving a bloody gaping wound. Kat quickly turned back around, her stomach threatening to revolt. Benny wisely moved them several yards away from the dead bodies.

Ian approached and ran a hand down the back of her head as if reassuring himself she was indeed okay. "Well, Kat, I'm sorry this happened, but you can add yourself to a growing list of people who owe Master Carter their lives."

It was then she noticed Carter and a man dressed in black on the far side of the southbound lanes, handing their rifles to another man. "What happened?"

"Carter and another sniper were in the woods over there and as soon as you dropped, the Russians aimed their guns at the cops. The snipers took them out. These two weren't going to let themselves be taken alive."

Kat shuddered, knowing it was true and she could have been dead as well.

Jake appeared next to Ian, shaking his head and jerking a thumb toward the spy and two feds. "Damn, I know they have to take my rifle for a while until the required investigation is complete, but I'm getting tired of going through all the paperwork to get them back. This is the second time in less than five months." He gently pulled

Kat from Benny's grasp and into his own embrace. "You are one kick-ass lady, you know that? Giving Beau the attack command was quick thinking. You kept your head together and helped save not only your own life, but Murray's and Colleen's, as well."

Her eyes widened when she realized she'd forgotten about them. "Oh my God! How are they? Murray was shot. Is Colleen okay?"

Releasing her back into Benny's arms, Jake nodded. "Murray's as tough as leather—he'll be back to work in no time. The bullet went straight through and didn't hit anything vital. It's also not the first time he's taken one, although it's the first time with us. Colleen only has a few scrapes, but she's fine, and Ian told her to take a few days off. Reggie is with them at the hospital. Once we're done here, I'll go check on them. Then I'm getting Beau the biggest fucking steak I can find. Thanks to him we were able to figure out what direction they took you in and catch up pretty quick."

"In that case, I owe him a steak, too. And you, too. All of you." Jake just grinned and waved her off. Facing Benny again, she saw the worry still in his eyes. "Are your parents okay?"

He paled and her heart clenched. "Mom will be okay, but Pop was shot in the stomach." She gasped and brought her hand to her mouth. "He's in surgery, and we have to get back down there. I want the paramedics to look at you really quick while I see if we can hitch a ride back down on the chopper."

Kat shook her head. "I'm fine. Let's just go. We have to be there for your mom."

Ian stepped aside to let a female medic into their little group. "I'll get us clearance, but I'm sure we have a few minutes before we can take off anyway, so let this nice lady check you over."

Although she was just as anxious as Benny to get going, she knew it would be pointless to argue with a group of Doms. She was quickly learning that when it came to someone under their care they were extremely protective. A few minutes later, she was medically cleared. Aside from a hematoma on her forehead, where she'd hit the headrest, and bruising on her arm from Dryagin's grip, the only other thing which hurt was her scalp from having her hair pulled.

After thanking the medic for the quick examination, Kat turned toward where Benny was talking to Ian, Carter, and Marco. The rest of the team had split up with Devon and Brody heading to the hospital to check on Murray and Colleen. Jake was on his way back to the compound with Tanner and Beau, followed by several federal agents. There was still a dead body there which needed to be hauled to the morgue, and a crime scene to be processed. She walked over to the group of four men and straight up to Carter, throwing her arms around him. "Thank you for not missing."

The black-op spy barked out a little laugh and hugged her back. "You're welcome, Kitty-Kat. And there was no way I was missing. I've grown quite fond of you. Besides, Boom-Boom would've never forgiven me if I let anything happen to you."

He kissed the top of her head then released her. Kat stepped back, and Benny extended his hand toward Carter. "Thanks again, man. My list of IOUs keeps growing. I hope someday I'll be able to repay you."

Taking the younger man's hand, Carter pulled him in for a man-hug and slapped him on the back. "No offense, but I hope I never need you to repay me. I'm going to catch a ride back to the compound, and then I have to head out. Duty calls. But I'll be in touch to check on Rick. Give your mom a kiss for me."

"Will do."

As their friend walked off to hitch a ride with one of the many officers and agents still on the scene, Benny took Kat's elbow and steered her toward the helicopter behind Ian and Marco. It was time for her to start praying for one more miracle.

# CHAPTER 24

$\mathcal{K}$at held her breath as the helicopter began to descend to land at a heliport near Sarasota Memorial Hospital were Rick had been transported to. Benny had contacted his mom before they lifted off from the Tampa highway and had been told his father was still in surgery. Ian and Marco planned on waiting with Kat, Benny, and Eileen until Rick was out of surgery. The two teammates would then retrieve the other two vehicles still parked near the Michaelson house, driving the comm van back to Tampa and leaving the SUV for them. The rest of the team would take care of the cleanup at the compound, the reports which needed to be filed with both the FBI and local law enforcement, and anything else that needed to be done.

From information Ian received from the FBI, it seemed as though Dryagin had not shared the knowledge that he'd found Kat to the rest of the Russian mob. They had no idea she was the only living link to the money, so the feds and Trident didn't think anyone else would come looking for her. She planned on giving the money to charity, so hopefully soon it wouldn't matter if anyone else made the connection. But it would have to wait for now.

A Florida State Police car was waiting for them at the heliport to drive them to the hospital. As soon as they landed, and it was safe to do so, they disembarked and piled into the vehicle with Ian taking the front passenger seat. Kat was sandwiched between the other two men in the backseat, and Benny hadn't said a word to her since he told her to let the medic examine her. She understood he was worried about his dad, so she remained quiet as well and took his hand in hers in silent reassurance that she was there for him. He gave her hand a quick squeeze and an even quicker smile, which didn't quite reach his eyes, before turning back to stare out the window.

When they reached the hospital, the four of them stopped at the reception desk to find out what floor the surgery waiting room was on, then took the elevators up to the third floor. Dusty and Burke were standing guard in the hallway, and Ian told them the threat was over, allowing the contract agents to head back to Tampa. Eileen and Rick's sister, Margaret, were sitting in the warmly decorated room with other patients' family members as they waited for word on their loved ones. Eileen stood as soon as she spotted Benny, and he went right to her, hugging her tightly. When he let her go and greeted his aunt, Eileen embraced Kat. "Thank God, you're okay. I was so worried until Ben called me to say you were safe."

The stress of the day finally hit Kat as a huge sob escaped her. "I'm so sorry. This is all my fault."

"Hush, now." Benny's mom pulled away just enough so they could see each other's faces. The worry was evident in both women's eyes, but sympathy also showed in the Eileen's gaze. "This is not your fault, Kat. And Rick will be fine, I know it. He's a fighter, and I know he'll come through this. We just have to pray until it happens."

Despite everyone telling her it wasn't her fault, Kat couldn't convince herself it was true. Stepping back, she gave Ian and Marco a chance to give their words of comfort to the older woman. Kat had no idea how Eileen was able to stay so calm. Her face and arms still showed the redness where the duct tape had been removed by the emergency room staff. A pair of scrubs they'd given her to wear covered the same marks on her legs. If their roles were reversed, Kat was certain she'd be hysterical by now. As it was, she was close to it. Not wanting to upset anyone, she took a deep breath and sat in one of the empty chairs, trying to get comfortable for what was most likely going to be a long wait.

BOOMER PACED the hallway outside the waiting room, needing to move instead of just sit. Three and a half hours had passed since his father had been wheeled into the surgery suite, and they still had no word on how he was. From what his mom knew from the ER doctors, Rick had needed a transfusion to replace the blood he'd lost, and he didn't regain consciousness while they worked on him. What if his dad died? His mother was a strong woman, but losing her husband of almost thirty-five years would devastate her. And what about Kat? He knew she was blaming herself for everything that happened, no matter how many times they'd all told her it wasn't her fault. If his dad didn't make it, how would they convince her that sometimes bad shit happened to good people, and there was no use playing the "what if" game?

At the end of the hall, a set of automatic doors swung open and a grey-haired man wearing blue scrubs appeared, walking toward the waiting room. Hoping this was the news they'd been waiting for, Boomer hurried back in time to hear the doctor ask for Rick Michaelson's family. The group of six huddled around as Dr. Finkelstein explained what happened. "The bullet nicked the large intestines, but we were able to repair it. The bullet also bounced around and damaged some blood vessels before ending up in the spleen, which we had to remove to stop the bleeding. He was very lucky to have gotten here when he did. Another half hour and he wouldn't have had a chance which, as it stands now, is fifty-fifty. I wish I could say it was better odds, but you need to prepare yourselves for the possibility. He's heading to the recovery room now, and we're giving him another transfusion to get his blood volume back up. We also have him in a medically-induced coma for now. Once his blood results stabilize, we'll see about easing him out of it."

"When will we know if he's going to make it?" Boomer couldn't help the grief and worry in his raspy voice. Even though he'd thought about it earlier, it wasn't until the doctor verbalized that

Rick could die, did Boomer truly believe his mother may become a widow.

"It'll be at least ten to twelve hours before I expect to see any significant improvement to the point he's out of danger."

"Can my mom and I see him, please?"

Dr. Finkelstein nodded his head. "Sure. I'll have one of the nurses come out once they have him settled in Recovery. You'll only be able to see him for a few minutes. He's got a lot of tubes going in and out, plus he's intubated and on a respirator while we have him in the coma, so just prepare yourself for that. I'll be back in about an hour or so to check on him and send him up to the ICU."

Boomer shook the man's hand. "Thanks, Doc."

Five minutes later, a heavy-set female nurse, with a gentle smile, escorted his mother and him into the Recovery Room. The usual hospital antiseptic smell was even stronger in here as they approached the gurney where Rick was resting on his back. The doctor was right; there were tubes everywhere—an intubation tube in his mouth, IVs in both arms, transfusion tubing, and wires from a monitor hooked up to the middle finger of his left hand. A bloody drainage bag and a urine bag hung low on one side of the stretcher. The *beep-beep-beep* indicating his heartbeat did little to reassure Boomer his father was going to make it. In Afghanistan, he'd lost two friends who he'd been certain would survive their combat injuries, only to have their hearts stop beating due to excessive internal bleeding.

He touched his father's arm as his mother kissed Rick's brow, murmuring words of love and encouragement. The man was so pale, he almost blended in with the white bedsheets. Glancing at the monitor above the stretcher, Boomer noticed the blood pressure reading—82/40. It was way too low. Hopefully, the blood being forced into his veins would bring the numbers up soon.

Leaning down, he kissed his father's cheek, then straightened and wiped the tears which began to spill from his watery eyes. "Love you, Pop. You keep fighting, you hear me? We still have a lot of fishing and shit to do. I plan on giving you some grandkids one day, and you better be here to spoil them rotten."

They stayed there in silence, willing Rick to heal and come back to them, until the nurse kindly told them they had to leave. She would let them know when he was transferred to the ICU. As they left Recovery, Boomer noticed his mother trembling. He took hold of her elbow in support while anger began to overtake his worry. Anger at himself and the team for not foreseeing the possibility of his parents being in danger. Anger at Kat's father for starting this whole mess. Anger at the Russians who dared to hurt the people Boomer loved. And on top of it all was the frustration of not knowing if his father was going to live or die. His jaw clenched, and he could feel the vein in his temple ticking away with every beat of his heart. His free hand was balled into a fist, and he forced himself not to punch the nearby wall.

With a white hospital blanket wrapped around her upper body, Kat was standing with Ian in the hallway outside the family waiting room. Unable to control his emotions at the moment, he held up his hand to stop her from approaching him. He needed a few minutes to himself to settle down, otherwise he was going to start throwing things, and he didn't think the hospital staff would appreciate it. Handing his mother off to Ian in silence, Boomer kept walking to the end of the hallway and slammed the down button for the elevator. A brisk walk around the outside of the huge hospital would help him clear his mind. There had to be a deli nearby where he could get everyone something to eat. He didn't want to leave the hospital until his dad was awake, and he doubted his mother did either. Some sandwiches would hold them over for a few hours.

The last thing he saw as he boarded the elevator and the door closed was his beautiful Kitten watching him. At least he knew she was safe and back in his arms for good.

---

KAT STOOD with Ian in the hallway, her gaze fixed on the double doors which Benny and Eileen had disappeared through a few minutes ago. She shivered, wondering why it always seemed so cold in hospitals. Her T-shirt and Bermuda shorts, which had felt stifling during her time with the Russians, now seemed inadequate to keep her warm. Every time her father had gone for treatment, or had been admitted for one reason or another during his illness, Kat always made sure she brought an extra sweater with her, even in the summer.

Ian must have noticed her shiver because he walked over to a door marked "Linens" and returned a moment later with a knit blanket he'd taken from one of the shelves. Wrapping it around her shoulders, he stated, "It's always seems cold in hospitals, plus your adrenaline from earlier has worn off and post-shock has kicked in. This will keep you warm for now. Marco and I are going to retrieve my truck and the comm van after Boomer and Eileen come back. I'll grab a sweatshirt I keep in the trunk for you."

She gave him a weak smile. "Thanks. I think you're right. I'm suddenly very tired. Once they move him to ICU, I'll try to take a nap in a chair for a bit."

As he nodded his agreement, the doors to the Recovery Room swung opened and Benny and his mother walked toward them. Eileen was paler than before as she wiped her eyes and nose with tissues. But it was the look on Benny's face which had Kat's stomach clenching. He looked so livid she half expected him to start yelling and punching things. She'd never in her life seen him so angry, and it scared her.

She stepped forward to hug him, to comfort him, but he held up his hand, stopping her in her tracks. Her heart squeezed as tight as her stomach had, and she held back a sob of grief. He blamed her. He blamed her for everything. She should never have brought this to his doorstep. She should have found a way to get out of the mess herself, and then, if she was still alive, she could've come to him without danger dogging her heels.

Benny didn't say a word to anyone as he gave his mother's arm to Ian, and then continued down the hallway to the elevator. She watched him punch the down button harder than necessary. When the car arrived, he stepped inside, and her happy future disappeared behind the closing doors.

# CHAPTER 25

"*H*ey, Kat. Wait up."

*Damn it! Twenty feet away from avoiding the obnoxious asshole!* She'd thought she could slip away without being hit on for the eighth or ninth time in four days, but apparently, she wasn't that lucky. If she could get rid of him now, she wouldn't have to see him again until Tuesday. The Friday training ended at twelve-thirty today, so the officers with long commutes heading home for the Fourth of July weekend could beat rush hour traffic.

Pasting a not-too-friendly smile on her face, she turned around to face Officer Rob DaSilva of the Eugene Police Department, as he stopped in front of her. He was just under six-feet tall and good-looking, but he also thought he was God's gift to women and was sexist. The worst part was the man couldn't seem to take "no, thank you" for an answer. "Yes, Officer DaSilva. Did you have a question about today's training?"

"Uh, no. Look, I know you playing hard-to-get is just an act in front of the other guys, so now that we're alone, do us both a favor and agree to go out with me."

His leering grin and the way he talked to her chest had her temperature at a near boil. The only reason she wasn't telling him where to shove his egotistical attitude was she tried very hard to be seen as a professional, aggressive-K9 trainer in a predominantly male-oriented career. But it didn't mean he was allowed to harass her.

He must have placed his German Sheperd in his department-issued, air-conditioned vehicle, since the beautiful animal was nowhere to be seen. She felt sorry for the dog, being partnered with an arrogant ass. Glancing around, she saw the rest of the trainers and trainees had either left, were still out on the practice field, or heading toward the kennels. At least fifty yards away, no one was close enough to be used as a diversion. She'd been heading toward her little cabin on the large ranch, which was a mere twenty feet away. After returning to Portland two weeks ago, she'd sat down with her bosses and explained everything to them. They had been wonderful and offered her the use of the empty cabin instead of returning to her apartment where she no longer felt safe. Jeremy had also hooked her up with his attorney who was starting the process for her to be "Katerina 'Kat' Maier" again, now that she no longer had to hide from anyone. She'd been shocked when the deputy director of the FBI had called her, at Ian's request, to tell her the money in the Cayman Islands was hers to do with as she pleased. Any statutes which may have covered the money had expired, and since there was no one left alive who would fight her for it in a court of law, she was now a reluctant millionaire. Kat wanted no part of it. After she got over the shock and her name changed, she would look into charities which could benefit from the ill-gotten gains.

"Look, Officer DaSilva—"

"Rob."

God, she hated his smirk. Gritting her teeth, she crossed her arms, making sure they covered her breasts, instead of thrusting them upward. He didn't need any more encouragement, just the opposite in fact. What he did need was a two-by-four cracked over his thick skull. "Officer DaSilva, I'm here to train you, not date you. I'd prefer if you would please keep things on a professional level."

Taking a step toward her, it was obvious he wasn't deterred. "C'mon, babe. I'll show you a really good time." She saw something click in his eyes, like a light bulb went off in his dense brain, and he tilted his head. "Oh, wait a minute . . . I get it. I saw you chatting it up before with the dike from Salem P.D. You play for the other team, don't you? Well, it's all right. With one good fuck, I can fix that. Why don't you let me show you what a real man can do for you that other chicks can't?"

"Oh, don't worry. She knows what a real man can do. Don't you, Kitty-Kat?"

At first, she'd been gaping at Officer Obnoxious, but now she was staring opened-mouthed at Carter sauntering toward them. *Where the hell had he come from?* His look was deadly, matching the tone of his voice, and she was so glad it wasn't boring into her. Instead, it was aimed at the cop who suddenly didn't look too sure of himself. Carter had a good four or five inches on the other man and was twice as broad in the shoulders. He looked like he could take DaSilva down with *both* hands tied behind his back and not even break a sweat. Wearing faded jeans, which fit like a glove, black leather boots, and a snug grey T-shirt from Jenn's University of Tampa, the man was sex on two long legs. Add in his surfer-boy good-looks, hair pulled back into a small ponytail, and chiseled body, she was certain he left soaking wet panties, broken hearts, and satisfied women everywhere he went.

The hunky spy walked up to her, pulled her into his arms and . . . *holy shit* . . . dipped her! His lips locked on hers as he kissed the ever-living-shit out of her. Kat was so stunned, all she could do was hold on for dear life. Ending the kiss, he winked at her before setting her upright as she stared at him in utter shock. The corners of his mouth ticked upwards, as if he was trying to hold back his laughter, while his gaze never left hers. "Now, if you'll excuse us, we have better things to do. Come along, beautiful." He took her arm and turned her toward the cabin, before glancing back at DaSilva. Like a coiled deadly cobra, Carter glared at the other man as if he were prey. "Oh, and by the way, if I ever hear you disrespect a woman the way you just did, especially this one, they'll never find your body. Understood?"

Kat's blood chilled at the unveiled threat, but apparently Officer Obnoxious was too stupid to know not to poke the viper who was more than ready to strike. DaSilva blustered, his face flushed blood red in his attempt at bravado. "You can't threaten me! I'm a cop! I can have your ass arrested so fucking fast you won't know what hit you."

Releasing her arm, Carter pivoted toward the other man. He took two deliberate steps forward and, faster than she could blink, grabbed DaSilva by the throat, leaning in so only the cop could hear him. She longed to know what Carter had whispered because the formerly arrogant man flinched and paled before being freed and taking a step backward. Without another word, he turned tail and scurried away like the weasel she thought he was.

"Let's go inside, Kitty-Kat. We have things to talk about." Carter gestured toward the door, waiting for her to lead the way.

As her shock faded, Kat's pissed-off attitude returned. She crossed her arms again and stomped her foot, glaring at him. "What the fuck was that all about? I had it under control. What did you say to him? And who do you think you are, walking up and kissing me like that?"

A smirk appeared on his handsome face, and she couldn't help but think it looked so much better on him than it did on Officer Obnoxious. The cocky bastard mirrored her stance but left out the foot stomp. "Like what? I didn't give you any tongue . . . well, not a lot of tongue. Just pretend we're bowling partners again . . . who just happen to kiss when we want to get rid of pricks like him. The other option was to beat the shit out of him, but I doubt your boss would've appreciated it. And I know you had control, but mine was better." He lifted a shoulder and let it drop again. "It's a Dom thing, so you might as well get used to it. As for what I said to him, sorry Kitty-Kat, you're better off not knowing—gives you plausible deniability if I ever have to follow through with it. And before you ask, Boomer doesn't know I'm here. Now, we can have this conversation out here, or we can go inside and eat the lunch I've been keeping warm in your oven. Hope you like Italian, I was in the mood for pasta."

Kat was blinking, twitching, and gaping at the man who strolled past her and held open her door. Furious, she didn't even know where to begin. "You were in my cabin? How did you get in there?

Wait . . . how the hell did you find me in the first place? And what do you mean, 'it's a Dom thing . . . get used to it'?"

An exaggerated sigh escaped him as he rolled his eyes. "So many questions. Uh, let's see." He ticked off the fingers of one hand. "The answers are—yes, I was; I picked the lock; and please, finding you was like finding a cat in a fishbowl—pun intended. We'll discuss the 'Dom thing' after we eat. Now, either get your pretty ass inside or I'm going to spank it out here where anyone can see."

Her eyes narrowed, and she scoffed in disbelief. "You wouldn't dare."

He mimicked her stare, and she shivered as a chill went up her spine, knowing his was more lethal looking than hers. "Oh, yes, I would, little Kitty. One thing I don't do is issue idle threats. Would you like me to prove it to you? I can guarantee you'll regret it."

*Holy shit!* He really would do it. Refusing to lower her gaze, like the good submissives she'd been reading about, she held her head high and stomped into her cabin. The aroma of garlic, tomatoes, and oregano assailed her sense of smell as the door closed behind her. Her mouth watered, but she swallowed, not wanting him to know it smelled delicious. Brushing past her, Carter strode into her kitchen as if he belonged there. Plates, utensils, glasses, and napkins for two were set on her dinette table. She stared daggers into his back as he busied himself at the oven. Using her mitts which she kept in the bottom drawer, he removed several aluminum containers and a foil-wrapped loaf of bread.

"Make yourself at home, why don't you?"

Transferring the food to the table, he gave her an impish grin which caught her off guard. "Thanks, but I already did. You can help by getting us something to drink. I brought beer and soda, since I didn't know what you preferred or had already."

Kat snorted and headed to the refrigerator. "What? That wasn't in your investigation of how to find me and break into my home?"

"Watch your tone, Kitty-Kat. You're in enough trouble with me at the moment, but again, we'll discuss that after we eat. I'll take a beer, please. Then sit, because I'm starving, and I'm sure you are too. You've had a long day."

"How do you know?"

He shrugged his shoulders and then tossed the mitts on the counter. "Because I've been watching you all morning. The last thing you ate was a granola bar at six-thirty, unless you snuck something in while I ran for our meal, which I doubt. You still haven't regained the weight you lost, and from what I can tell you've lost more. You can't go that long without fueling your body, little one. And despite what advertising executives believe, most men like some meat on their women—gives us something soft to hold on to. Now, sit . . . please."

Gaping at him again, she put two beers on the table and sat in the chair he was holding out for her. She was so confused about why he was here as she watched him fill her plate and then his own. Once he seemed satisfied all was in order, he took the seat across from her.

"Dig in."

Like she'd noticed Benny had done every time they ate together, he waited until she picked up her fork and took the first bite of her lasagna. Her eyes rolled back into her head as the flavors hit her taste buds. "Oh my God, this is heaven. Where did you get this?" She didn't wait for his answer before shoving another forkful in her mouth.

Carter chuckled then started on his own meal. "Glad you like it. I found a little Italian deli about five miles from here called The Red Pepper."

"Wait a minute. I've eaten there before, and it's never been this good." Putting down her fork, she reached for a piece of garlic bread, offering him one, which he thanked her for.

"The sign said, 'Under New Management,' so maybe they have a new chef."

They ate in comfortable silence for a few minutes until Kat started feeling full and her curiosity started getting the best of her. "Okay, so tell me why you're here."

Picking up his napkin, he wiped his mouth then took a sip of his beer. "That was going to be my question to you. What the fuck are you doing here, Kat, when the love of your life is moping around Tampa, driving everyone bat-shit crazy?"

Her gaze fell to the table. "I'm not the love of his life. Benny hates me. I almost got his parents killed. And Jake and Colleen and Murray and . . . and . . ."

She didn't realize she was crying until he reached over and brushed away the tears on her cheek. Leaving the last of his meal, he stood and pushed her chair back from the table. Before she knew what he was doing, he'd picked her up in his arms and carried her to the couch. Sitting again, he settled her on his lap and gently guided her head to rest on his shoulder. The tender Dom held her while she sobbed, until she slowly got herself back under control. "He doesn't hate you, little one, and I don't know why you would think that. I've known Boomer for many years, and this is the first time I've ever seen him depressed. He wasn't this bad when he was laid up in the hospital and they weren't sure if he'd lose his leg or not. Now, why are you here instead of with him? I know it's not because you don't love him. Anyone can see how much he means to you. So, talk to Master Carter, and we'll see what we can do to fix this. And Rick is fine, by the way. He was discharged from the hospital the other day."

"I know. I called the hospital every day. Before I left, I told the desk clerk I was his niece so I could check on him." She took a shuddering breath. "I can't face him and Eileen. And I sure as hell can't face Benny. This was all my fault. I should never have gone to him for help."

He let out a low growl. "It was not your fault. You weren't the one working for the Russian mob and stealing money from them. And you sure as hell didn't tell those bastards to go after Boomer's folks. So, try again. *Why* are you here when you're still wearing his collar?"

Her hand flew to her throat. She hadn't been able to remove the simple collar Benny had placed around her neck. No matter what, her heart knew she would never love any man as much as she loved him. The collar was her last connection to him. Instead of throwing out another lame explanation, she concentrated on Carter's question this time, trying to find the real answer. "I guess . . . he was so angry at the hospital, I was afraid he'd tell me to leave. So, instead of giving him the chance, I left. Deep down, I was hoping he would come after me, but . . . but he didn't."

"Oh, Kitty-Kat. I am so going to make sure he spanks your ass for that. Do you know the reason why he didn't come after you? The reason he's been getting drunk almost every night at the club? Or why he's turned down every sub who's offered to help him forget you?" Feeling more miserable by the second, her gaze fell to her lap and she shook her head. "Because the first time you left him, it wasn't your choice or your fault. But this time, Kat, you *chose* to leave. You walked out on him when he needed you the most. He wasn't angry with you . . . he was frustrated at the situation. And I'm sorry you misinterpreted his frustration as anger. He loves you. But he's hurting, thinking you don't love him enough to stay with him."

Her tears started again, and she tried to wipe them away as fast as they rolled down her cheek. "Oh God, w-what've I done? I do l-love him, and I'd never hurt him on purpose. I was j-just scared. Everyone I've ever loved is gone and . . . and the one person who's still here, I pushed away. C-Carter, w-what am I going to do?"

Holding her head in his big, calloused hands, he forced her to look him in the eye. "What you're going to do is go dry your eyes while I clean up, and then we have a plane to board in . . ." He glanced at his black military watch. "In a little over an hour."

Her mind spun in five different directions. "What! What are you talking about? I can't just get on a plane and leave. I have to work and . . . and . . ."

He lifted her from his lap until she was standing on her own two feet, and then rose from the couch. Grabbing her shoulders, he turned her toward her bedroom. "I spoke to your boss. I told him you were leaving and to consider this your resignation."

Kat put on the brakes so quickly, he almost tripped over her. "When was this? And, holy shit, you can't just tell my boss I quit. What if I didn't want to go with you?"

"Oh, you're going with me, Kitty-Kat. It was never a question. I explained the situation to Jeremy and Eva, and they're happy for you. They also said if it doesn't work out, you will always have a job here. But the choice is yours. You either go check the bags I packed for you to see if I missed anything important, or I tan your hide and carry you out of here. I suggest you don't take option number two, because it's a long flight, and you'll want to be comfortable. Now, go wash up."

He gave her a gentle shove toward the door, ignoring her sputtering and shock. She tried to glare at him over her shoulder, but he was already on his way to her kitchen. Her mind racing, she hurried to her bedroom and, sure enough, there were her three duffel bags all packed. Undoing the zippers, she searched through them and found he'd pretty much thought of everything she would need for now, including her migraine medication. One bag had all her toiletries, while another was full of shirts, pants, shorts, and two pairs of her favorite shoes. The last bag . . . *oh, fuck a duck* . . . had her intimates—panties, bras, pajamas . . . and, *what the heck?* Pulling out the lacy garment, she blushed while holding it up.

"I figured you would need something for the club tonight, so I found a little boutique near the deli. The cute, blonde salesclerk was all too happy to help me pick something out."

His appearance in her doorway had startled her for a moment before she recovered and gave him an unladylike snort. "I'll just bet she was. She probably offered to model it for you, too." As he leaned against the doorjamb, the corners of his mouth ticked upward. Kat examined the black lacy teddy which left nothing to the imagination. "Um . . . where's the rest of it? I can't walk around in just this."

"Why not?" Kat gaped at him while he grinned like the devil himself. "Don't panic, love, the bra and panties that go with it are in there too. That's just the coverup."

Snorting again, she shoved the lingerie back into the bag. "You and I have different definitions of a coverup."

Carter stepped over to the bed and grabbed all three bags by their handles. "Did I forget anything? I cleaned out your fridge earlier, so nothing would spoil, and I just took out the garbage. I told your boss you'd be back in a week or so to say goodbye and pack up the rest of your stuff."

She ran to the bathroom, wet a washcloth and wiped her face as fast as she could. Finding him waiting at her front door, she glanced around for anything else she needed. Her purse and the book she was currently reading were on her coffee table, and she snatched them up. A quick check assured her that her phone was still on her hip. "I think we have everything I need for now. You're so sure Benny and I are going to work this all out, aren't you? What if the damage is done and he doesn't forgive me?"

"Then I kick his ass and keep you for myself."

He held open the door for her and she turned the lock on the inside knob before passing him. With one hand, he gestured for her to walk around to the back of her cabin where a rental car sat. After opening the passenger door for her, he popped the trunk for her bags and then climbed into the driver's seat.

"I think we'd kill each other if you kept me for yourself, not that I'd let myself be kept. You're quite infuriating at times, you know?"

"Ha! I've been told that a time or two, Kitty-Kat." He started the car and put it in drive. "Shit. I keep forgetting to ask. I was talking to Eileen, when I was checking on Rick, and I called you 'Kitty-Kat' to her. She said it was your father's nickname for you. I didn't know, Kat, and if it bothers you, I can stop. Does it?"

Kat shook her head and turned to face him after putting her seatbelt on. "No, it doesn't. The first time you said it, it threw me a little. But then I realized how much I missed hearing it. Just like when Benny calls me Kitten—no one else but him ever called me that. As long as it's said with the affection I know you mean, then I like it, and you can keep using it. It makes me feel special."

"Then I'm honored." He pulled out of the long driveway onto the road leading to the highway. "You are special, little one, and don't you ever forget it. Now, let's go get you and your Dom back together, shall we? Before Ian finally breaks down and kicks his ass."

## CHAPTER 26

*A* little after midnight, Boomer handed over his car keys before Tiny would open the club door for him. How sad was it the big bouncer knew he was here to get drunk . . . again? Aside from Monday and Tuesday, when The Covenant was closed and he'd gone to Donovan's, he'd been here every night since his dad had been released from the hospital. He'd offered to stay at his parents' house until Rick was more mobile, but his mother had insisted she could handle things, and he should go after Kat. Instead, Boomer returned to Tampa and began drowning his sorrows.

The other Doms had taken pity on him and put up with his morose drinking, making sure someone drove him home every night. Then, after popping Tylenol for his resulting hangovers, he'd take a taxi back to work the next day or catch a ride with one of his teammates. Ian had wanted him to crash in one of the rooms above the offices, but it would only bring back painful memories of the night he and Kat slept there—well, after they had done other things, of course. At least at his condo, she'd only slept in the guest room. And damn, her scent was still there—he knew, because he went in there all the time just to sniff her pillow like a heartbroken ass.

There was no way he was chasing after Kat. She'd ripped his heart out and stomped on it on her way out of the hospital to return to Oregon. When he'd returned, much calmer, with a sack of sandwiches and sodas, he'd discovered Kat missing. Ian and Marco had left to retrieve the vehicles. Leaving the food with his mother and aunt, he searched the entire hospital, starting with the cafeteria, thinking she might have gone for coffee. After not finding her in any of the public places in the building, he'd asked the security guard at the main entrance and found out Kat had left, taking a cab to God knew where. He couldn't call her to find out where she was going because her phone was still back at the compound, and she had given the medical alert bracelet back to Brody, so the GPS was out as well. An hour of worrying later, Jake called to say Kat had arrived at the compound and packed her duffel bags in her car which had still been parked in the garage behind the offices. After speaking to SAC Stonewall she drove away. Jake hadn't been able to stop her, since, in all the confusion, he hadn't known she was there until it was too late. He had to check the security videos to see what she'd done.

Boomer had told her he loved her, and although she'd said the words back to him, she'd obviously not meant them. Or maybe she had, but his job and the violence involved in it was too much for her to handle. While he hadn't been the one to kill any of the Russians, a fact which still pissed him off, Kat had seen up close and personal how dangerous his job was. Maybe she couldn't deal with it. Either way, the ball was in her court. He'd be damned if he would beg her to come back to him.

He said hello to a few people on the way to the bar and almost winced when he saw the bartender, Master Dennis, grab a bottle of Jack Daniels to start making his drink. Had he become so predictable in less than two weeks? Maybe he should fuck with the guy and switch to Southern Comfort. The thought left his brain as fast as it'd come. He wasn't in the mood to joke around. Instead, he sat his sad-sack ass on an empty stool and nodded his thanks when the drink, mixed with a dash of Coke, was placed in front of him on a cocktail napkin.

He'd spent most of the day and half the night following some fucktard around who was cheating on his wife of six years. The guy was in deep shit because his suspicious spouse was the one with the purse strings and their prenup was clear—cheat and he doesn't get a cent. And Boomer had the pictures which were going to make the bastard drop to his knees and cry buckets. Mulling over his boring yet successful day in solitude, it wasn't long before clinking ice was the only thing remaining in the glass, and he caught the bartender's eye for another one.

"Scratch that, Dennis. Master Ben will be playing tonight."

Boomer glared at Carter as the Dom smacked him on the shoulder then leaned against the bar with an annoying grin on his face. "I'm not fucking playing tonight, Dennis. Fill it up."

Picking up the empty glass, Carter handed it to the amused bartender, while shaking his head. "Nope. You're playing, so no more booze. Two waters please, Den." Turning back to Boomer, he ignored the dirty, pissed-off stare he was getting. "I've got a lovely new submissive who wants a little action, and I think she's just what you need to get out of this fucking funk you're in. Your other option is the one Ian and Devil Dog came up with, but I think you'll choose door number one after you hear what's behind door number two."

His eyes narrowed. He wasn't in the mood for this shit, but apparently, everyone was done with his pity-party except him. "What's their option?"

"A session with Mistress China, who I must say is head-over-her-pretty-ass about the idea. You know how much she loves to whip pathetic guys back into shape." Carter paused to take a drink from one of the water bottles which had been placed in front of them. "So, what's it going to be, Boom-Boom? Some hot sex with an even hotter sub, or China's bullwhip?"

Astonished, Boomer grunted. "You've got to be fucking kidding me?"

"No, he's not."

He sighed heavily and spun around on the barstool to face Boss-man and found the rest of his team in attendance. *Shit.* Just what he fucking needed—an intervention. All five of them had their best Dom faces on, daring him to give them shit. Add in the super-spy and there was no way he was getting out of this. His choices were clear—a lashing from the sadistic Whip Mistress, or fucking a willing submissive who might let him forget about Kat for a little while. The problem was . . . he didn't want to forget about her. He wanted her by his side and in his bed for the rest of his life. Fucking another woman would never change that. Instead, it would make him feel like he was cheating on the only woman who would ever own his heart. And that right there was his answer. "If I lay off the booze and get my head on straight, can I pick door number three?"

Ian's cocked one eyebrow. "Door number three?"

"I need some time off. I've got to go after her . . . to Portland." He swallowed hard, refusing to break down in front of the men who were brothers to him. "She's my life. I don't care if I have to get on my knees and beg, or tie her ass up and kidnap her, but damn it, I'm not letting her get away this time. I love her, and I've got to get her back."

"Thank fuck! Now we can put an end to this fucking pity-party of yours. I was about to start watering down the Jack." Ian took a step toward him. "But she's not in Oregon, Boom."

His eyes narrowed as he slid off the stool and stood. Panic assailed him. If she wasn't in Portland, where the hell was she? "What do you mean? She's somewhere else? Where? Her aunt's?"

He might have asked Ian the questions, but it was Carter who answered. "Downstairs in room four, waiting patiently and presenting herself for her Dom. Don't fuck it up. And don't freak out when she tells you I kissed her."

Running toward the grand staircase, he barely heard the other Dom's last words and the chorus of snorts and chuckles from his teammates. All he could think about was Kat was waiting for him on the other side of the building. Ian or Devon must have waved at the bouncer at the top of the stairs because he let Boomer pass without checking his membership card for alcohol consumption. Tamping down the urge to push people out of his way, he made his way through the crowd as fast as possible, dodging bodies, and cursing along the way. On the other side of the cavernous room, there were two sets of hallways which led to twelve private rooms, six off each. An on-duty Dungeon Master, stationed between the entrances to both hallways, nodded at him as he ran past. Grinding to a halt outside room four, he paused to catch his breath and calm himself down. Carter had said she was presenting herself for her

Dom, so her Dom is what he needed to be when he walked into the room.

He didn't know who had taught her how to present, but he had a strong feeling it was Angie and Kristen. Since their Masters knew about Kat being here, it was pretty much a given for them to know as well. And he was positive those two match-makers couldn't pass up an opportunity to help create a happy-ever-after.

*Wait . . . what the fuck?* Did the fucking spy say something about kissing Kat? Damn, he'd kick the guy's ass later if he didn't have a fucking good excuse for it—and maybe even if he did.

Inhaling deeply, he turned the knob and opened the door. His breath caught at the sight of her and got stuck in his chest. She was kneeling on a red satin pillow in the center of the room, knees shoulder-width apart, back straight, head bowed, and her upturned hands resting on her thighs—presenting perfectly. Dressed in a black bra and panties with a sheer lace teddy over them, she was the most beautiful thing his eyes had ever seen in his life, and his cock agreed. He noticed a shiver go through her body, and it thrilled him. When he remembered to breathe again, he entered the room, closed the door behind him, and stepped over to stand in front of her.

For a few moments he remained silent, letting her anticipation build while he took in her beauty. His hands were shaking, itching to touch her. He was about to speak when he noticed papers spread out on the bed behind her. Skirting around her, he picked them up and was surprised to see her completed limit list and a note from one of the doctors on staff clearing her for play after an earlier examination. There was also a note from Ian saying Kat's background check had been done by Brody. *Holy shit.* Obviously, several people had a hand in expediting her clearance for the club. He'd have to remember to thank everyone.

Scanning her limit list really quick, he grinned when he saw a check mark in the green column of several activities he wanted to do with her tonight. Stepping back in front of her, he spread his legs and crossed his arms while wiping the smile from his face. She had some punishments coming to her before they talked and then had some fun. He lowered his voice. "Stand, Kitten, and strip for me. As pretty as your outfit is, I want to see you naked."

He was pleased when she didn't hesitate, and impressed at her gracefulness as she rose up on her feet in one fluid movement. One by one, she removed the three garments and handed them to him, all the while keeping her gaze on his feet. Damn, she was gorgeous. Her hair was pulled back into a simple ponytail, and he couldn't wait to wrap the silky strands around his wrist. Tiny goose bumps popped up on her soft skin, and he knew it was from desire and anticipation instead of cold. The rooms were kept at a comfortable seventy degrees for that reason. A blush spread across her chest, but it wasn't as pink as her nipples which were already puckered and distended, waiting for him to feast on them. His gaze traveled south and when it reached the junction of her hips and legs, his cock hardened painfully and his knees almost buckled. She was waxed bare, and since the skin wasn't red he knew she had to have done it before today. Tossing the lingerie on the bed behind her, he asked, "What's your safeword?"

She spoke for the first time since he entered the room. "Red, Sir." Her voice was husky and seductive, and he held back a reactive groan.

"Good girl. Look at me, Kitten." When her head tilted up, he was floored by the different emotions he saw flash through her eyes —anticipation, fear, and hope. He prayed the fear was only because she was worried he was mad at her. Well, part of him still was, but it was fast being pushed aside by relief over her being here. For now, a little fear in her was good. A jolt of awareness passed through him when he noticed his collar around her slender neck. *Holy fuck*! He was about to throw out his man-card and break down crying in front of her from the sheer pleasure of seeing the leather band still in place. He swallowed the lump in his throat. "When did you wax your pretty pussy and why?" When her eyes shifted away from his in evident embarrassment, he added, "Uh-uh, Kitten. Eyes on mine. If you look away again before I permit it, you'll just add to your punishments."

Her gaze met his again, but this time her eyes were wide in

surprise . . . and there it was—unadulterated lust. God, he loved her. "Yes, baby. You have some punishments headed your way, but I'll explain that in a minute. Answer my question. When and why did you wax? I'm not complaining . . . quite the opposite really."

"The other day, Master." His pounding heartbeat sped up further, threatening to burst from his chest at her use of his title, but he stayed quiet, letting her finish. "I was reading everything I could about the lifestyle, and there were a lot of mentions of how both Doms and subs liked it because it made a woman more sensitive."

Boomer hadn't thought he could be more stunned or pleased than he already was. Her punishment would have to wait—they definitely needed to talk first. "You've been researching BDSM? Why?"

Her cheeks turned tomato red, but to her credit, her eyes remained focused on his. "Because it means so much to you, and I . . . I hoped . . ."

"You hoped what?" This time her gaze fell, and he used his fingers to tilt her head back up, waiting for her to meet his stare again. His heart squeezed when her eyes filled with tears, but he didn't let them sway him. She couldn't be allowed to top from the bottom, whether it was intended or not. He needed to be firm with her if this was going to work between them. "That's five more spanks on top of the ones you already deserve. Now, you hoped what, Kitten?"

Kat swallowed hard. "I hoped you would change your mind and come after me. I wanted to please you by learning as much as I could about being your submissive. I know I haven't learned everything yet, but I was hoping you'd teach me the rest."

A bullet to the gut wouldn't have hurt as much as her first statement did. His brow furrowed in confusion. "What do you mean you hoped I would change my mind, baby? I never wanted you to leave in the first place. I came back to the waiting room, and you were gone. I figured you were just going to clear your head, get a cup of coffee, or something. Next thing I know, Jake's calling to say you showed up at the compound in a taxi. You collected your things and drove away in your car. Stonewall said you went to the office, gave your statement, and left." Much to his embarrassment, his voice cracked with emotion. "I needed you, and you were gone. But this time you chose to leave. I was never more hurt in my life, Kat."

Her tears were now streaking down her face, but neither one of them moved to wipe them away. "I—I know I hurt you . . . I mean. I know now. Carter t-told me when he showed up in Portland to bring me back. I never meant . . . meant to hurt you. But you were so angry at the hospital and didn't want to talk to me, s-so I thought you were blaming me for your dad being shot. And . . . and for your mom, Jake, and the others being hurt and almost killed. I thought you hated me for putting everyone in danger. I've lost everyone I ever loved and d-didn't want to wait around for you to push me away. I'm so sorry."

She finally stopped talking and took a deep ragged breath. Boomer couldn't handle it anymore and pulled her into his arms, holding her tightly while stroking her hair and bare back. "Shh . . . it's okay, Kitten. I wasn't mad at you. I was just mad in general, over things I couldn't control. I was mad at myself for not thinking my parents might be targeted, and then I was pissed we fell for the ruse and you could've been killed because not enough people stayed behind. At the hospital, my adrenaline crash, combined with the doctors telling me it would be hours before we knew if my dad was going to make it, sent me into a tailspin. I walked away from you because I didn't want to inadvertently take it out on you. You didn't deserve it, and I was afraid I'd hurt you. Not physically, of course, but I just needed a few minutes to get myself back under control."

He loosened his embrace so he could see her face. "I love you, baby. I would never push you away. But I thought you didn't want to be part of my life because of the potential for violence. My job can be dangerous at times. I thought you realized that and didn't want to be a part of it."

"And I thought you were mad at me. Guess I should have asked you."

A wry smile appeared on her red, wet face. Cupping her chin with both hands, he used his thumbs and then his lips to wipe away her salty tears. "Yes, you should have, but I'm as much to blame as you. I should have explained why I was walking away from you. We're going to have to work on our communication, but we have the rest of our lives to do that. Right now, I want to pick a few things off your limit list and have some fun. Because of our mutual misunderstandings, I'm going to clear the slate for everything up until I walked into this room, which means you'll only be getting those five spanks you've earned. I can't very well punish you for something that was also my fault. After that, we're going to start fresh. Okay?"

"Okay, Sir."

His thumb brushed over her plump, pink lips and he imagined how they were going to look circled around his aching cock. But first things first. "I liked it better before when you called me 'Master.'"

For the first time since he walked in the door, Kat truly smiled at him, and it was as if the sun had come out. It brightened the room as much as his heart. He hadn't lost her, and as soon as he could get a permanent collar designed for her, they were going to have a ceremony so everyone would know who she belonged to. "Yes, Master."

Glancing around the room, he quickly categorized which one they were in. Each of the private rooms were designed differently and some of the play equipment varied. Several of the rooms were like this one, with a few pieces of equipment and assorted chains, hooks, and restraints hanging from the walls and ceiling. Other rooms were theme rooms, such as an office, classroom, doctor's examination room, police station lock-up/interrogation room, and a harem/stripper pole room. Due to the popularity of the rooms, Devon, Ian, and Mitch were talking about putting an addition on this end of the warehouse for more rooms. This room, however, was perfect for the scene he had in his mind. Taking Kat's hand, he led her over to a spanking bench sitting in one corner. "Hop on up, Kitten. Let's get your punishment over with so we can get to the fun stuff. We'll talk some more later, but I'm so fucking hard for you, I can't wait much longer." It was the truth—his cock felt like it had an impression of his zipper on it.

Boomer was thrilled when she didn't hesitate to kneel on the bench and place her torso on the upper flat portion. It was then he got his first look at her bare ass, and what he saw had him dropping to his knees behind her. *Holy fuck!* She had an anal plug in her! Caressing her soft butt cheeks reverently, he couldn't resist the urge to lean forward and lick her exposed, dripping pussy. Her moan shot straight to his dick, and he had to open the button and zipper of his pants to relieve the painful pressure. "When . . . holy shit, Kat . . . when did you start using an anal plug? Damn, that's a beautiful sight."

Without waiting for an answer, his tongue attacked her hairless pussy again. Her honey was the sweetest thing, and he ate her like a man who had been without for eons—licking, nibbling, and suckling on the swollen lips between her legs. The more juices he lapped up, the more her body produced for him. Shit, he could do this all fucking night.

"Oh, oh, Benny! Oh my God, please don't stop!"

Her breathy demand told him she was getting close, and, unfortunately for her, he did stop. Punishment before pleasure. Squeezing her cheeks a few times to get the blood flowing to them, he rose to his feet again. "Answer my question, Kitten. Tell me about this plug in your ass. And I hope you did it on your own, otherwise I may have to kill someone."

In between gulps of air, she responded, "Y-Yes, I did it myself. L-Last week, I found a shop in Portland that sells them. The woman there helped me pick out a beginner's progressive set. I loved when you . . . you fucked my ass with your finger, and I wanted to be ready for you, if you came after me."

Damn, she just kept the surprises coming. He ground his thick erection against the flat head of the plug, grinning as she moaned and cursed. "Your dirty language is improving, Kitten, and I love it. I also love the fact that, despite being on the other side of the country, you still felt compelled to please me. After your spanks, you will definitely be rewarded. What size plug is this, baby?"

"The largest one, Sir . . . Master."

She was going to be the death of him tonight. With practiced ease, he attached the restraints to her wrists, ankles, and waist, making sure none of them were too tight. Eyeing the assortment of implements hanging from hooks on the wall, he spotted one he liked. Retrieving the leather-covered, oblong paddle, he rubbed it against her ass. "Just so you know, little kitten—before I found out you were in here waiting for me, I was ready to hop a plane to Oregon to beg you to come back to me. But now that you're here, I think you'll be the one begging tonight. Count for me, Kitten." He drew the paddle back and let the first strike land hard on her right cheek. *Smack.*

"Ow!!! Holy shit! Holy . . . oh, fuck! W-What's happening?"

He was lucky she was facing forward and didn't see his evil smile. He knew exactly what was happening as he held his hand against the red mark left from the paddle. The pain was turning to heat and then to pleasure. Tilting his head, he saw she was indeed feeling gratification as more moisture coated her sweet pussy. "Pain then pleasure, baby. That's what's happening. Now count for me, or I might forget I gave you one."

"One!"

Not able to hold back his chuckle at her rushed response, he aimed the paddle again. *Smack.* This strike landed on her left cheek.

"Shit! Two! Holy shit!"

"Baby, I love how your ass looks all nice and red." As much as he wanted to warm her ass slowly, he wanted to fuck it even more. The next two spanks were on her sit spots and the final one he placed over both cheeks just below the plug.

"Fuck! Five!"

Tossing the paddle to the side, he massaged her tender flesh, tapping the flat end of the plug causing it to vibrate against the nerves inside her. Her moaning and panting was driving him crazy. He slid one hand between her legs, reveling in the amount of moisture he found there. Two fingers probed her swollen flesh, then eased into her, urging her arousal higher. Using his other hand, he pushed his jeans down to his ankles, wanting to be ready as soon as he made her come. He continued to fuck her with his fingers as he reached over to a drawer in a nearby cabinet and felt around for one of the tubes of lubricant he knew was there. Finding one, he put it on the bench between her legs and sped up his thrusts. Her moans, curses, begging, and breathing all increased for him. "Come for me, Kitten. Scream so everyone in the place hears you take your pleasure."

He found her G-spot and stroked it rapidly with his fingertips while tugging on her anal plug with his other hand. The combination of dueling sensations sent her flying over the edge, and he wouldn't be surprised if at least half the club heard her cry out. Her walls rippled against his fingers as he extended her orgasm as long as he could, flicking her clit with his thumb. Kat's screams faded to groans and then whimpers as he slid his fingers from her pussy and the plug from her ass. "Damn, Kitten. I have to take your ass now before I explode. Can you stay like that or do I need to take you over to the bed?"

As he spoke he grabbed the lubricant tube, popped the top, and covered the tip of his cock with the clear liquid. Fuck, it was cold! Of course, the lube warmer was across the room out of reach. Well, it wouldn't be cold for long. "Answer me, because I'm ready to take you right now."

"Yes! Fuck! Now! Please!"

If he wasn't so desperate to get inside her, he would have laughed at her one word sentences, but he was sure he'd be in the same frame of mind in under a minute. Her asshole was still slick from the lube she'd used for the plug and he lined his cock up with it. Pushing forward, he was relieved when she didn't instinctively clench. She was still open from the plug, and he slid past her sphincter with ease. "Holy fuck! Damn, woman, you feel incredible."

He was thicker than the plug, but by pumping in and out, he continued to gain inches until he was in far enough to give them both pleasure, but not too far to hurt her. She was panting and gasping, but hadn't complained at all. Still, he needed to make sure she was all right because as soon as he started fucking her hard, he wasn't going to be able to stop. "Give me a color, Kat. Green is good, yellow is wait a minute, and red is stop." He wanted to add "please, don't say red," but he wouldn't want her to lie to him just because this is what he wanted.

"Green, Master. If you don't start moving, I'm going to go insane. Please!"

It was all the encouragement Boomer needed. Grasping her hips, he dragged his cock out to the tip and then shoved it back in, making her yelp then moan. She was so tight, the friction had him seeing black and white spots before his eyes. Again and again, he repeated the slow-fast routine until she begged and cursed for more. Unable to deny either of them what they wanted any longer, he began fucking her faster and faster.

"Yes! Benny! Oh, God, yes! Please! Hurry!"

She was close, and so was he. Tingling shot from his lower spine to his balls, and he knew he had to send her over again before he came. Reaching around, his fingers searched and found her clit. The second he flicked it, she went off like a rocket and her ass clenched with her orgasm as she shrieked her release. The pressure increased around his cock and sent him flying with her as his cum filled her ass. Bright lights appeared behind his closed eyelids as he forced his legs to keep him upright. His energy drained when the last of his orgasm faded, and he almost collapsed on top of her. As much as he wanted to rest, he knew he had to release her from the restraints and carry her over to the bed where they would both be more comfortable. He tilted his hips back and reluctantly slid from her body. After undoing the waist strap, he reached down to release her ankles. "Kat, baby? You okay?"

"Wonderful," she murmured, her voice raspy from screaming earlier.

Boomer chuckled as he freed her wrists. "Glad to hear it. Lift up for me so I can carry you to bed."

"I can walk."

Despite her protest, her limbs quivered like a bowl of Jell-O. Picking her up in his arms, he grinned when her head fell heavy against his shoulder. "That may be, but this is one of those things your Dom wants to do, and you shouldn't argue with him unless you want another spanking."

Exhausted, she cuddled closer. "'Kay. Love you."

"I love you, too, my little Kitten. I always will."

He placed her in the middle of the big bed, before retrieving two moist washcloths from a warmer in the corner of the room. After cleaning Kat, he took care of himself, then tossed the used cloths in a hamper and joined her on the bed. She was almost asleep as he turned her on her side, his heart bursting with love for this beautiful woman. Spooning behind her, he finally gave in to the afterglow of the scene and closed his eyes.

# EPILOGUE

*A*s the organ music started, Boomer stood tall in his Navy dress whites and watched Kat glide elegantly down the center aisle of the quaint little church. Damn, she looked stunning . . . and she was all his. It was three months since he first saw her in the Trident offices and fainted at the sight. He was still getting razzed for that, but he would gladly suffer through it to have her back in his life . . . for good. A ring on her finger and a permanent collar around her neck told the world she was spoken for.

The day after finding her in the club, they'd spent hours in his bed, having kinky sex, making sweet love, and talking about their future. They'd only showered and gotten dressed that evening to attend an impromptu barbecue at the compound because his mom had driven up to get his dad's bored ass out of the house for a while. His folks had also wanted to see Kat for themselves and reassure her they didn't blame her for things which had been beyond her control.

Instead of attempting to beat the crap out of Carter for kissing Kat, Boomer kicked his ass on the compound's basketball court in the parking lot outside the training building. He wasn't stupid enough to challenge a lethal black-op assassin to a sparring match, so he took the bastard down on the court. Of course, there were some scuffles, along with plenty of elbow jabs to the jaw, ribs, and gut, which were returned just as hard. By the end of the game of one-on-one, both men had been sore, bleeding, and laughing, much to the women's horror. The female gender just didn't understand how men enjoyed beating each other up out of friendship and gratitude. Boomer was just thankful Carter had taken the initiative to get Kat back to Tampa, and he would owe the man his life . . . again.

With Reggie Helms' legal help and Dr. Marie Sawyer's contacts, Kat was setting up multiple large donations to a wide assortment of charities which would best benefit from the millions of dollars in the Cayman account. She was making all the donations in memory of her parents and brother, finally happy something good had come from their tragic deaths.

After they packed her things and shipped them by freight, then said goodbye to her friends in Portland, Boomer had taken the time off Ian had offered him. He flew Kat to the island of St. Lucia where they'd fucked like rabbits for a week straight, in between sunbathing on the beach and acting like tourists. Their last night on the scenic Caribbean island, they'd taken a moonlit stroll. Shaking with a mixture of fear and anticipation, he'd gotten down on one knee and proposed to her with his grandmother's antique engagement ring. His mother had surprised him and given it to him the night of the barbecue with her and Rick's blessing.

Gentle waves had lapped at the shoreline as a full moon hung high in the star-filled sky. Taking Kat's left hand, he'd gazed into her chestnut brown eyes as they welled up with stunned but happy tears. "Kitten, I love you with all my heart. You're my sunshine, my moonlight, my past, and my future. My life was beautiful with you in it the first time, and it's beautiful again, now that you're back in my arms. I had a dream last night about Alex. I know it sounds weird, but he gave me his blessing and made me promise to take care of you forever. Whether real or imagined, it's a promise I intend to keep. Marry me, sweetheart. Grow old with me and make the rest of my life beautiful too."

He'd barely uttered those last few words before she shouted, "Yes!" As he'd slid the ring on her trembling finger, a round of applause and whistles came from a small crowd of tourists who'd stopped to watch the romantic proposal. Ignoring them, Boomer had stood and scooped Kat up into his arms, kissing her with all the love in his heart.

"Benny?"

He shook the perfect memory from his mind and looked down at the petite woman standing next to him, holding his arm. Kat's Aunt Irina looked stunning in her simple, lace wedding gown. It was then he noticed the music had changed and the guests were waiting for him to escort the bride down the aisle. The corners of her warm brown eyes crinkled in amusement, and she grinned at him as if sensing where his mind had gone. "It's time."

"Right. Are you sure about this? You know I have a getaway car right outside if you're not," he teased her.

She squeezed his arm, then gazed toward the other end of the aisle where Ret. Major Harry Bernhard stood proudly, waiting for his wife-to-be. On the opposite side of the altar was Kat, the maid of honor, smiling back at Boomer and her aunt. "Oh, I'm very sure. Like the story of you and my little Katerina, I've been waiting for him all my life."

---

**Keep reading for the first chapter of**
**Not Negotiable:**
**Trident Security Book 4 (A novella)**

# NOT NEGOTIABLE: A TRIDENT SECURITY NOVELLA

PREVIEW: CHAPTER 1

Mentally rolling his eyes, Parker Christiansen listened as his older brother droned on about life in Boston—a life Parker felt he never fit into and had left behind years ago. Dave was just like their parents—stuck-up, arrogant, and rich. He'd even followed in their father's footsteps and became a successful corporate attorney. Meanwhile, Parker had taken his love for using his hands to build things and become an architect/builder/contractor. And no matter how successful he'd made his company, New Horizons, his father always managed to put him down. Nothing he ever did was good enough for the old man. Their family came from wealth and privilege, and Judge Alan and Janet Christiansen couldn't accept that their youngest son liked getting his hands dirty. They also didn't like that Parker was a Dom in the BDSM lifestyle—a fact Alan had found out by accident several years ago—and he never let his son forget it.

But his brother had always been curious about the lifestyle—not in front of their parents, of course. Dave had called him a few weeks ago, saying he was going to be in Florida on business this weekend and he wanted Parker to bring him as a guest to the club he belonged to. The Covenant was a private and elite BDSM club in Tampa and Parker had been a member since the doors opened over four years ago. His company had done some of the work on the club, as well as the other three warehouses in the gated compound. He had converted one of the buildings into two apartments for the club's owners, Ian and Devon Sawyer, and was in the process of adding two more apartments in the currently unused half of the building. From what he was told, Ian's goddaughter, Jenn, was getting one, while their younger brother would be given the keys to the last unit for when he retired from the Navy. One of the other buildings was home to the Sawyers' company, Trident Security. The ex-Navy SEALs had a thriving business in both ventures, but their cousin Mitch Sawyer was the third co-owner and manager of the club. The club Parker and Dave were en-route to.

Parker had given Mitch his brother's name to get him cleared to be a guest. The Covenant was extremely strict with running background checks on potential members and visitors. Legally-binding privacy contracts had to be signed to ensure what happened at the club, stayed at the club.

"Why do you want to check out the club again? I thought Carol was against the lifestyle."

Dave shrugged. "She agreed our marriage needs a little spicing up. I'm thinking about joining a club outside Boston, but wanted to check one out first with you, so you can fill me in on the lifestyle a little more."

Pulling off the highway, Parker drove down the private road leading to the compound. "Take your license out. You need to show it to the guard."

"There's a guard?"

"Yeah. The Sawyers take the security here seriously." He took the ID his brother handed him, rolled down the window, and gave it to the guard. "Hey, Murray. What are you doing here? Thought you only worked days."

The burly, armed guard swiped the license through his hand-held computer, compared the picture and name to the approved list, then handed the card back to Parker. "Just grabbing a little overtime. One of the guys called in sick. You're all cleared. Have a good night."

"Thanks. You, too."

Parker found a spot for his truck and killed the ignition. "Give me your cell phone."

"Why?" Despite his question, Dave handed him the device.

"They aren't allowed on the floor of the club." Well, they were if they remained in a pocket or purse. Any texting or talking on phones had to be done in the lobby or parking lot. But Parker didn't want his brother to be tempted to use it inside. He tossed the phone, along with his own, into the glove compartment. "All right. Remember. I'm responsible for you in here. At the front desk, you'll get a yellow wristband that indicates you're a guest and not available for play. You don't do anything without checking with me first. When I introduce you to anyone, you ask permission of the Doms or Dommes to speak to their submissives. There's a two-drink limit for guests and anyone who is going to play. Don't ask for more than that because they keep track."

Waving him off, Dave climbed out of the Chevy Tahoe. "I got it. I read all the stuff you sent in the email. No worries."

Despite his brother's assurance, Parker still couldn't help but think this was a big mistake.

---

Shelby Whitman walked out into the main room of the club and let the pulsating music flow through her body. Ian's new submissive seemed nice. When they'd met a few minutes ago in the women's locker room, Angie appeared nervous, but that was expected for a sub's first time in a BDSM club. Shelby hoped she'd eased the woman's anxiety with her little pep talk.

Taking a quick glance down her body, Shelby grinned at her new outfit. Tonight's color was electric blue. Her bra, mini-skirt, which flared out when she turned, and wig with straight hair to her shoulders, all matched perfectly. What had started as a way to hide her thinning hair from radiation treatments years ago, had become a fashion statement which had remained long after her treatments for ovarian cancer were completed. Now, cancer-free for six years, she still wore a different colored wig to match her outfit every time she came to the club.

Glancing around, she tried to tell herself she wasn't looking for *him*, but her gaze still searched for those gentle brown eyes and blond crew-cut. There were plenty of single, hot Doms at The Covenant, but something about Parker Christiansen always drew her in, making her libido wake up and take notice. Totally drool-worthy, he was continually tan from working outside. She knew he owned his building company, however, he wasn't the type of guy to sit behind a desk and let others do the dirty work. Parker got right down in the trenches with his employees.

But the Dom wasn't for her. He needed more than a submissive . . . he needed a wife. Parker was the type of guy who should grow old with the woman he loved, spoiling lots of children and grandchildren. Something Shelby could never give him. It was part of the reason why she liked the lifestyle—well, besides the awesome orgasms she tended to receive on a regular basis from any of the other single Doms who wanted to play. She could hook up with anyone who wasn't looking for long-term . . . anyone who only wanted a relationship here at the club and not out in the "real" world.

Before her cancer, she had wanted a long-term relationship with a Dom/husband, two-point-six kids, a dog, and a house with a white picket fence. But that was before fate had been cruel. Now she had nothing to offer a man except sex and friendship. So, she came here, put on her best smile and the bouncy personality everyone loved, before going home . . . alone.

Taking a deep breath, she pushed Master Parker from her mind and headed over to the submissives' waiting area. Maybe Masters Brody and Marco would be here and willing to indulge her in one of their ménages. The two of them always left her sated and well-cared for without emotional attachments. And that was just fine with her.

An hour after they arrived, Parker was dying to get out of there. It wasn't that he didn't want to be at the club, he just didn't want to be there with his brother. He knew this had been a mistake. While Dave had been asking a whole bunch of questions, it was obvious he still had no clue about the lifestyle and didn't belong in it. It was also pissing the Dom off that his brother was leering at every scantily dressed sub that walked by as if she were a piece of meat. Having him here was a recipe for disaster.

In addition to his brother issues, he didn't want to watch Shelby scene with the Masters of Ménage. Brody Evans and Marco DeAngelis were the popular tag-team duo for the female submissives, and a few minutes ago, he'd watched from afar as Shelby and the two Doms negotiated a scene. Well, mostly Brody did the negotiating with the blonde sub. Marco was on Dungeon Master duty at the moment and had kept one ear on the other two and his eyes on everything else going on around him. The DMs were all experienced Doms or Dommes who took shifts to ensure no harm came to any submissive, whether intentional or not. And Parker was one of them.

Forcing himself to stop mooning over Shelby, who was chatting with a few other people in a sitting area designated for submissives, he bit the inside of his lip in frustration. She was probably waiting for Marco to get off his scheduled shift. Parker glanced at his watch. The DM would be free in about fifteen minutes. "Hey, Dave. Since you can't play and I can't leave you alone, why don't we go somewhere else and have a few drinks."

His brother tilted his head. "I'm fine here, but if you want, we can sit upstairs, have a few drinks, and watch from one of the balcony tables."

Not the response he wanted, but at least they'd be out of the "pit" as the members called the huge, downstairs playroom. The entrance was on the second floor where the bar was. The U-shaped balcony had numerous seating areas, with some along the railing so members could observe the scenes from above. He could pick the side over the spanking benches, so he wouldn't have to watch Shelby's threesome and dream she was his submissive—and his alone. He'd tried to negotiate with her twice in the past and she'd turned him down both times. It was a single submissive's prerogative to play or not play with whomever they wanted, and a Dom had to accept it. He only wished he knew why she wanted nothing to do with him.

Parker stood. "Yeah, that's fine. Let's take a walk through the locker rooms. I need to hit the john."

Their table was not far from the submissives' waiting area, halfway between the grand staircase and the St. Andrew's cross on a small stage in the middle of the room. Usually the stage was reserved for highlighted scenes or commitment ceremonies. Devon and his sub/fiancée, Kristen Anders, had their ceremony on it a few months ago, and Parker was glad his friend had finally found someone to love. He only hoped someday he could be so lucky.

Still eyeing the activity around them, his brother remained seated. "I'll wait here for you. No rush."

"I'm not supposed to leave you unattended."

Dave rolled his eyes. "Come on, Park. I'm a grown man and don't need a babysitter. I promise to wait right here."

Hesitating, Parker was about to say no way, but Dave gave him that stare that always made him feel like the idiot of the family. That fucking holier-than-thou look that said I'm better than you'll ever be. "All right, fine. But stay here and don't talk to anyone unless they approach you first. I'll be back in a minute."

He headed to the locker room, glancing over his shoulder once at his brother. The cocky bastard gave him one of those condescending waves like he was shooing away an annoying gnat. Parker winced and disappeared into the men's lounge. In here the sounds of flesh, or leather, smacking flesh, and orgasms being reached, faded away while the thumping music was muffled enough so he could hear himself think. Why he agreed to come here tonight, he had no idea. It wasn't like Dave and he were the closest of brothers . . . hell, if it wasn't for the blood relation, Parker wouldn't even consider him a friend. Four years younger than

Dave's age of thirty-five, he had always lived in the guy's shadow. That was one of the reasons he'd moved to Florida . . . to get away from his family.

Brody stepped up to the urinal next to Parker. "Hey, man. How you doing?"

"Good. You?"

"Not bad at all. Especially since little Miss Shelby negotiated a scene with Marco and I for later. Damn, I love that little firecracker."

Parker clenched his teeth. He knew Brody didn't have anything but respect for the submissive, however, it irked him that the big bastard knew her in a way Parker had never experienced. The computer geek of Trident Security was a former Navy SEAL, as was each of his co-workers. He also had a heart of gold and seemed to be well-liked by everyone who met him. Brody treated every female submissive as they should be treated . . . like they were the most precious women in the world.

Zipping up his pants, Parker turned toward the sinks and tried to pretend it didn't bother him who Shelby hooked up with. "Well, then, have a good time."

"Hey, before I forget . . . can I call you during the week? I want to overhaul the master bath in my new place. Pink tile and I don't exactly go together and the shower is way too fucking small." He finished at the urinals and stepped over to where Parker was washing his hands.

"Yeah, sure. Monday's usually a busy day, but I should have time Tuesday afternoon to swing by and take a look." Shaking the excess water from his hands, Parker reached over and grabbed a paper towel. He glanced back to see the other man was nodding.

"That should work. I'll call you Tuesday morning to confirm. Thanks. I appreciate it."

Slapping Brody on the shoulder as he walked by, he told him, "No problem. See you later."

Wanting to get out of the club now more than ever, Parker strode back out to the pit, where two things hit him at once. One— his brother wasn't where he left him—and two—there was a large, loud crowd near the submissives' area and it didn't appear to be for anything good. *Fuck!*

Shoving his way through the group, he wasn't expecting what he saw, although he wasn't too surprised. Dave was on the floor, being held face-down by a furious Marco, with one arm hitched high behind his back. His brother was no match for the security operative who worked out on almost a daily basis.

Parker had a sinking feeling in his stomach when he saw three women also on the floor a few feet away. Mistress China and a woman he didn't recognize had their arms around . . . *shit* . . . a crying Shelby. Wide-eyed, she was holding a trembling hand against her cheek, while the Domme looked ready to spit nails.

With his fists clenched, he turned his attention back to the two men and barked, "What the fuck, Dave? What the hell did you do?"

"I didn't do anything. Now get this fucking gorilla off me. I'm going to sue if he doesn't get off me."

The whiny, pain-filled order didn't gain any sympathy from Parker. His gaze went to Marco, who growled and returned the questioning look with a pissed-off glower. "This asshole backhanded Shelby. I had people in my way and couldn't get here fast enough to stop him."

*What? The bastard hit Shelby? My Shelby? A woman who wouldn't hurt a fly.* Parker was livid. Glancing back toward the crying submissive, his blood hit the boiling point. Through gritted teeth, he addressed the other Dom. "He's my brother. Let him up, Marco."

Marco's eyes flickered to Ian who was standing next to Parker. Travis "Tiny" Daultry, the head of club security, and several other guards had pushed the crowd back to give the Doms some room. Ian crossed his arms and studied Parker's face. Parker knew his fury was showing, and he silently begged the owner to let him take care of this. Ian didn't say a word, but nodded at Marco, who let go of the bastard and stood.

As Dave got to his feet, Parker couldn't believe he was stupid enough to say, "What's the big deal? Everyone is slapping women around here, and I get in trouble for what you all are doing."

Parker took a step closer to him, his voice low and barely controlled. "You okay?"

Obviously not realizing how pissed his brother was, the idiot grinned. "Yeah, Park, I'm fine."

"Good." Without missing a beat, he reared back and punched Dave in the face, knocking him unconscious. He ignored the round of cheers from the crowd and hurried over to Shelby, crouching down in front of her. "I'm so sorry, Shelby. It's my fault. I shouldn't have left him alone."

He helped her stand, but Mistress China and the other woman stayed by her side for support. Parker gently pulled Shelby's hand from her cheek and growled, "I'm going to kill him," when he saw the red and swollen area which was starting to bruise. He'd known bringing the stupid prick here was a mistake, but the fact that harm had come to Shelby, of all people, had him wanting to wake his brother up, so he could knock him out again.

She grabbed his forearm, her eyes pleading. "No, don't, Sir. I should have grabbed Master Marco or one of the other DMs. He was trying to negotiate with me. I saw his guest wristband and knew he wasn't allowed to play, but he wouldn't take no for an answer. When I tried to walk away, he hit me."

Parker drew her into his arms and held her for a moment while everyone else looked on. He saw Ian cock his head at Tiny, who began breaking up the crowd with the other guards. The Head Dom then spoke quietly to Parker. "Let's take this to the office. What do you want us to do with him?"

Parker didn't answer him right away—he had a sub to take care of first. She may not be his, but, for now, he was responsible for her. He could hardly hold back the anger and guilt in his voice. "Go to the ladies' lounge and put some ice on your cheek. When I'm done with Ian and my asshole brother, I'll take you home."

"You—You don't have to do that, I can drive myself." Shelby's face flushed and her eyes avoided him. Even though her trembling seemed to ease while in his arms, it appeared she didn't want to be there.

"I need to do this, Shelby, please. I need to make sure you're okay and get home safe. This is not negotiable." He tipped her chin up with his fingers until she looked at him. "Please?"

She bit her lip, but nodded her consent. Mistress China wrapped her arm around the sub's shoulder and eased her from Parker's arms. Despite being a bit of a sadist, the Domme tended to be a mother hen to the submissives. "I'll take care of her. We'll be in the lounge when you're ready."

He murmured his thanks to her while Ian spoke to the other woman with them. Parker figured she was the owner's new submissive whom he'd heard someone mention earlier. "I'm sorry, but I have to take care of this. Please go with them and wait for me in the lounge. I'll be a few minutes."

"Yes, Sir."

The two women walked Shelby toward the locker room, and before he joined them, Marco gave Parker a heated glare which he knew he deserved. He'd broken one of the rules of the club—never leave a guest unattended—and the results had been devastating.

Ian asked one of the nearby waitresses to bring an ice-pack to Shelby, before turning to Parker, who still wanted to commit familial homicide. Handing his keys to Tiny, Parker asked, "Can you do me a favor? Toss him into my truck. And don't bother being gentle about it. He deserves every fucking bruise he gets."

The six-foot-eight, two hundred and seventy-five-pound, part-time bodyguard grinned. "My pleasure. We'll take care of him . . . you just make sure Miss Shelby is okay."

"I will." Parker then turned to Ian, his face filled with embarrassment, anger, and regret. "Let's get this over with."

---

## Not Negotiable: Trident Security Book 4

Shelby Whitman has had a huge crush on the one man who deserves more than she can give him, so it's best to keep him at arm's length.

Dominant Parker Christiansen has been craving the perky, petite submissive ever since he laid his eyes on her, but she's turned down his every attempt to negotiate with her.

When Parker finds out Shelby's hiding a devastating secret from her friends, he steps in to help, and this time he won't take no for an answer. Can he convince her he's fallen in love with her, and if they only have this time together, they should make the best of it?

# Other Books by samantha a. cole

## THE TRIDENT SECURITY SERIES

*Leather & Lace*

*His Angel*

*Waiting For Him*

*Not Negotiable: A Novella*

*Topping The Alpha*

*Watching From the Shadows*

*Whiskey Tribute: A Novella*

*Tickle His Fancy*

*No Way in Hell: A Steel Corp/Trident Security Crossover: Books 1 & 2*

*Absolving His Sins*

*Option Number Three: A Novella*

*Salvaging His Soul*

*Trident Security Field Manual*

*Torn In Half: A Novella*

## THE DEIMOS SERIES

*Handling Haven: Special Forces: Operation Alpha*

*Cheating the Devil: Special Forces: Operation Alpha*

## THE TRIDENT SECURITY OMEGA TEAM SERIES

*Mountain of Evil*

*A Dead Man's Pulse*

*Forty Days & One Knight*

## THE DOMS OF THE COVENANT SERIES

*Double Down & Dirty*

*Entertaining Distraction*

*Knot a Chance*

### THE MALONE BROTHERS SERIES

*Take the Money and Run*

*The Devil's Spare Change*

### THE BLACKHAWK SECURITY SERIES

*Tuff Enough*

*Blood Bound*

### HAZARD FALLS SERIES

*Don't Fight It*

*Don't Shoot the Messenger*

### MASTER KEY SERIES

*Master Key Resort*

### LARGO RIDGE SERIES

*Cold Feet*

### AWARD-WINNING STANDALONE BOOKS

*The Road to Solace*

*Scattered Moments in Time: A Collection of Short Stories & More*

### THE BID ON LOVE SERIES (WITH 7 OTHER AUTHORS!)

*Going , Going, Gone: Book 2*

### THE COLLECTIVE: SEASON TWO (WITH 7 OTHER AUTHORS!)

*Angst: Book 7*

### SPECIAL PROJECTS

*First Chapters: Foreplay Volume One*

*First Chapters: Foreplay Volume Two*

*First Chapters: Foreplay Volume Three*

*Word Search For Warriors: Authors For a Cause*

*Word Search For Warriors: Volume II*

*Trident Security Coloring Book*

*Shaded with Love Volume 5: Coloring Book for a Cause*

*Cooking with Love: Shaded with Love Volume 6*

# About *samantha a. cole*

USA Today Bestselling Author and Award-Winning Author Samantha A. Cole is a retired policewoman and former paramedic. Using her life experiences and training, she strives to find the perfect mix of suspense and romance for her readers to enjoy.

Her standalone collection of short stories, *Scattered Moments in Time*, won the gold medal in the 2020 Readers' Favorite Awards in the Fiction Anthology genre. Her standalone novel, *The Road to Solace* (formerly *The Friar*), won the silver medal in the 2017 Readers' Favorite Awards in the Contemporary Romance genre.

Samantha has over thirty books published throughout several different series as well has a few standalone novels. A full list can be found on her website listed below.

Sexy Six-Pack's Sirens Group on Facebook
www.samanthacoleauthor.com
Subscribe to my newsletter: eepurl.com/b2hNQj
www.samanthacole.allauthor.com

facebook.com/SamanthaColeAuthor

twitter.com/SamanthaCole222

instagram.com/samanthacoleauthor

pinterest.com/samanthacoleaut

CPSIA information can be obtained
at www.ICGtesting.com
Printed in the USA
LVHW092129311021
702078LV00011B/54/J